DAWN OF
SWORDS

ALSO BY DAVID DALGLISH

The Shadowdance Series
A Dance of Cloaks
A Dance of Blades
A Dance of Mirrors
A Dance of Shadows
A Dance of Ghosts
A Dance of Chaos

The Half-Orcs
The Weight of Blood
The Cost of Betrayal
The Death of Promises
The Shadows of Grace
A Sliver of Redemption
The Prison of Angels

The Paladins
Night of Wolves
Clash of Faiths
The Old Ways
The Broken Pieces

Others
A Land of Ash (Compilation)

ALSO BY ROBERT J. DUPERRE

The Rift
Book I: The Fall & Dead of Winter
Book II: Death Springs Eternal & The Summer Son

Others
Silas
The Gate: 13 Dark and Odd Tales (Compilation)
The Gate 2: 13 Tales of Isolation and Despair (Compilation)

DAWN OF
SWORDS

David Dalglish

Robert J. Duperre

47NORTH

Printed in the United States of America.
No part of this book may be reproduced, or stored in a retrieval system, or transmitted in any form or by any means, electronic, mechanical, photocopying, recording, or otherwise, without express written permission of the publisher.

Published by 47North
P.O. Box 400818
Las Vegas, NV 89140

ISBN-13: 9781477809792
ISBN-10: 1477809791
Library of Congress Catalog Number: 2013940227

Cover design by Mark Winters
Map design by Paula Robbins & The Mapping Specialists

To Sam and Jessie, for putting up with our obscenely long phone calls.

ASHHUR'S PARADISE

NELDAR

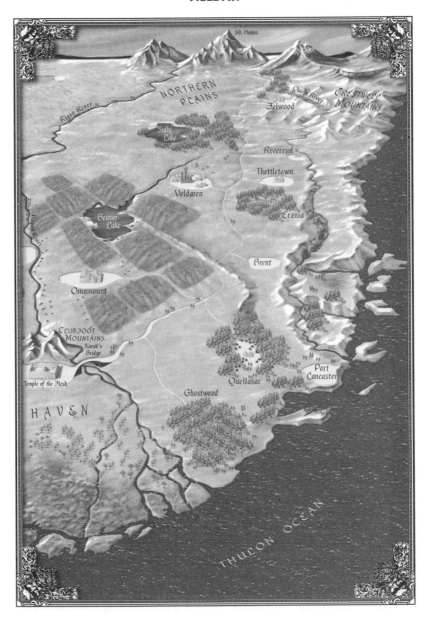

CAST OF CHARACTERS

ASHHUR'S PARADISE

SAFEWAY

THE SANCTUARY

ASHHUR, God of Justice, creator of ASHHUR'S PARADISE

—JACOB EVENINGSTAR, child of two gods, First Man of DEZREL, sworn servant of ASHHUR

—BENJAMIN MARYLL, his student, a boy 14 years old

—ROLAND NORSMAN, his steward

—AHAESARUS, a Warden of the west

—GERIS FELHORN, his student, a boy 13 years old

—JUDARIUS, a Warden of the west

—MARTIN HARROW, his student, a boy 14 years old

—CLEGMAN TREADWELL, master steward of ASHHUR

—AZARIAH, a Warden of the west, brother of JUDARIUS

MORDEINA

HOUSE DUTAUREAU

ISABEL, DUTAUREAU first child of ASHHUR

—RICHARD, her created husband

—ABIGAIL ESCHETON, their first daughter, 70 years old

—TUROCK ESCHETON, her husband, 38 years old

—their children:

LAURIA DAGEESH, daughter, 23 years old, wife of UULON

CETHLYNN, daughter, 21 years old

DOREK, son, 18 years old

BYRON, son, 17 years old

JARAK, son, 15 years old

PENDET, son, 7 years old

—PATRICK, their only son, 65 years old

—BRIGID FRONIN, their second daughter, 62 years old, wife of BAYEN

—CARA, their third daughter, 61 years old

—KEELA NEFRAM, their fourth daughter, 58 years old, wife of DANIEL

—NESSA, their fifth daughter, 31 years old

—HOWARD PHILIP BAEDAN, master steward of the house

KER

HOUSE GOROGOROS

BESSUS GOROGOROS, second child of ASHHUR

—DAMASPIA, his created wife

—BARDIYA, their only son, 87 years old

—GORDO HEMPSMAN, a man of KER

—TULANI, his wife

—KEISHA, their daughter, 7 years old

NELDAR

KARAK, God of Order, Divinity of the East, creator of NELDAR

HOUSE CRESTWELL

CLOVIS CRESTWELL, first child of KARAK

—LANIKE, his created wife

—AVILA, their first daughter, 72 years old

—JOSEPH, their first son, 68 years old

—THESSALY, their second daughter, 62 years old

—MOIRA ELREN, their exiled third daughter, 52 years old

—UTHER, their second son, 41 years old

—CRIAN, their third son, 38 years old

HOUSE MORI

SOLEH MORI, second child of KARAK

—IBIS, her created husband

—VULFRAM, their first son, 67 years old

—YENGE, his wife, 33 years old

—their children:

ALEXANDER, son, 18 years old

LYANA, daughter, 16 years old

CALEIGH, daughter, 12 years old

—ORIS, their second son, 66 years old

  —EBBE, his wife, 26 years old

    —their children:

    CONATA, daughter, 9 years old

    ZEPPA, daughter, 7 years old

—ADELINE PALING, their first daughter, 63 years old,
  widow of CATSKILL

—ULRIC, their third son, 59 years old

  —DIMONA, his wife, 41 years old

    —their children:

    TITON, son, 20 years old

    APHREDES, son, 19 years old

    JULIAN, son, 16 years old

—RACHIDA GEMCROFT, wife of PEYTR, 51 years old

VELDAREN

—KING ELDRICH VAELOR THE FIRST, second king of NELDAR

  —KARL DOGON, the king's bodyguard

—MALCOLM GREGORIAN, captain of the Palace Guard

  —PULO JENATT, personal guard of SOLEH MORI

  —JONN TREMMEN, personal guard of SOLEH MORI

  —RODDALIN HARLAN, personal guard of SOLEH MORI

—ROMEO CONNINGTON, high merchant of RIVERRUN

—THEO CONNINGTON, high merchant of RIVERRUN

—MATTHEW BRENNAN, high merchant of PORT LANCASTER

ERZNIA

—BROWARD RENSON, rancher, widower of KATHERINE

—BRACKEN, his son, 33 years old, husband of PENELOPE

  —KRISTOF, son, 15 years old

—MUREN WENTNER, magister of KARAK

HAVEN

—DEACON COLDMINE, Lord of HAVEN

—APRODIA SUNNETT, priestess of the TEMPLE OF THE FLESH

—CORTON ENDER, mercenary

—PEYTR GEMCROFT, high merchant of HAVEN,
  husband of RACHIDA

THE ELVES

THE DEZREN

STONEWOOD

—CLEOTIS MELN, Lord of STONEWOOD

—AUDRIANNA, his wife

—their children:

CARSKEL, son, 181 years old

AUBRIENNA, daughter, 103 years old, lover of JACOB
EVENINGSTAR

AULLIENNA, daughter, 12 years old, betrothed to KINDREN
THYNE

—LUCIOUS ANDERS, guardian

—KARA ANDERS, guardian

—NONI CLANSHAW, nursemaid of AULLIENNA

—DETRICK MELN, brother of CLEOTIS

—ETHIR AYERS, confidante of DETRICK

—DAVISHON HINSBREW, confidante of DETRICK

DEZEREA

—ORDEN THYNE, Lord of DEZEREA

—PHYRRA, his wife

—KINDREN, son, 16 years old, betrothed to AULLIENNA
MELN

THE QUELLAN

—RUVEN SINISTEL, Neyvar (King) of QUELLASAR

—JEADRA, his wife

—CEREDON, their son, 95 years old

—IOLAS SINISTEL, cousin of RUVEN, member of the TRIAD

—CONALL SINISTEL, cousin of RUVEN, member of the TRIAD

—AESON SINISTEL, cousin of RUVEN, member of the TRIAD

—AERLAND SHEN, chief of the EKREISSAR

Dawn of
SWORDS

PROLOGUE

Today, thought Clovis, *is a perfect day for bloodshed.*

The air was hot, the wind dead, and the tall grass still. The flags his bannermen carried hung limp on their shanks. To Clovis Crestwell's right was a vast open plain, empty of settlements for miles. To his left were the tightly packed trees that formed the edge of the Ghostwood. The soft, insect-like whispers that oozed from the haunted forest carried without any apparent need for wind. The whispers caused a collective shudder to work through the battalion that marched on the Gods' Road, intermixing with the sound of marching feet.

Clovis sat tall in his saddle, his shoulders pulled back and his long silver hair swept from his face. While on the outside he exuded calm indifference, his insides shuddered with anticipation. It was on this day—this bright and windless day—that his years of planning would finally be set in motion. Today was the day he paved the way for his god to rule the world.

The man riding astride the lead stallion, Lord Commander Vulfram Mori, raised his hand. Immediately, the progression halted. The fighting men removed their helms and unhitched the waterskins from their belts, taking long gulps and wiping sweat from their brows. They'd marched all the way from Veldaren, the capital of the eastern land of Neldar, and the long journey had left them exhausted. Their leader, though, showed not the slightest sign of wear from the trip. Vulfram looked barbaric; naked from the waist up, his muscular physique was an intimidating sight that dwarfed the greatsword strapped to his back. His head was shaved bald, though a lengthy auburn beard speckled with gray fell from his chin to the middle of his breastbone. But the Lord Commander's deep brown eyes contained a wisdom that betrayed the impression of barbarism. Vulfram was forthright, cautious, and loyal, and he did not question his superiors. His choice in appearance was purposeful; he demonstrated his boldness by donning no protective armor, inspiring his armored charges to be as fearless as he was. He was a suitable man to lead the army of Karak, the God of Order made flesh, Divinity of the East.

Though deep down, Clovis knew *he* should have been granted those duties, not Vulfram.

"How much farther?" he asked.

The Lord Commander swiveled in his saddle.

"We should be on the bridge in forty minutes, Highest," he replied, bowing low in his saddle. Clovis allowed himself to smile at this gesture of respect, his jealousy lessening. Forty-two years before, Karak himself had bestowed Clovis with the title *Highest*. It had happened on the very day that the First Families, House Mori and House Crestwell, crowned the first king of the eastern realms. *Highest* meant that none were more trusted in the eyes of their god, granting Clovis sovereignty as the king's advisor. Humanity was in its infancy, Karak had told him, and they needed strong men like him to show the way.

Vulfram gazed west, to where the Gods' Road wound off into the distance.

"Are you certain we must show force, Highest?" he asked. "Would a warning not suffice?"

"It is not your place to question the will of our god," Clovis said. "It is your duty to obey."

"Yes, Highest," said Vulfram, bowing low once more.

Kicking his horse, the Lord Commander galloped around the resting troops, shouting for them to make ready for the onward march. The men groaned but offered no complaint, sacking away their waterskins, and putting on their helms. They formed two lines and advanced once more, their chainmail glimmering with the water that had dripped from their chins. Clovis noticed that many were red-faced from the heat, even though they'd been fitted with light filament shirts and breeches instead of sterner steel. He grunted, thought of delaying. It would not do to have the men passing out on the Gods' Road before fulfilling their duty to their god and realm. His impatience won out, and he joined Vulfram in urging them onward.

The dusty road passed with numbing steadiness, and Clovis allowed his mind to wander. He had not seen his god in decades. Shortly after the naming of Neldar's king, Karak had left the realm and not been spotted by living eyes since. Clovis's only interaction with his deity had been through a series of recent dreams and visions, which had instilled in him a desire to teach a wayward faction of his people the price of blasphemy. Yet Clovis had been hesitant, as dreams were unreliable. He pulled out the pendant he wore around his neck, which had mysteriously appeared at his bedside one morning, its crystal forged by the breath of the last dragon of the land. Were it not for the Whisperer, a being of shadow that contacted him through the pendant, he would never have acted. At first he had thought the Whisperer to be Karak himself, come to offer him guidance from wherever the god had isolated himself, but even when he learned that was not the case, Clovis could not deny that the Whisperer's desires mirrored his own—a longing for a land ruled by a single, divine presence. Those most blessed by Karak, such as Clovis and the rest of his immortal House

Crestwell, perhaps even the mysterious Whisperer, would hold stations of divine power in this new realm. This vision of holy unity began with one simple act, confirmed to him in the dreams sent by Karak—a show of force against the people of Haven, the township nestled within the delta that sprouted from the southern tip of the Rigon River, the body of water that split the land of Dezrel into two equal halves.

The trees of the Ghostwood soon gave way to the eastern spine of the delta that lay before them, and the rocky soil was replaced with marsh grasses. The Gods' Road flattened out, and at the Lord Commander's urging, the men picked up their pace to a brisk jog.

"Who do we fight for?" Vulfram yelled, and the soldiers answered, *"For Karak!"*

They came upon Karak's Bridge minutes later, a sturdy overpass of wood, granite, and black marble fifty feet across. On the other side of the river was the stumpy rise of the Clubfoot Mountains. To the south, obscured behind a thick line of evergreens, was a series of crude huts. They were the beginnings of a new extension of the Haven Township. And at the base of the nearest mountain, rising into the sky like a stone guardian, was the end result of the peoples' blasphemy. This was it, the reason they had come, the edifice whose destruction the Whisperer had preordained since the first day of its construction.

The Temple of the Flesh.

Vulfram held up a single fist, and the soldiers halted their advance.

"Ready arrows!" he shouted, and his men pulled the bows from their backs. They nocked arrows and lifted them skyward, one hundred taut strings awaiting the call.

The Lord Commander turned and directed a questioning look at Clovis, who gestured at the monstrosity before them with an open palm. For a brief moment he saw worry, perhaps even a glimmer of defiance, and then Vulfram shook his head and galloped to the rear of the convoy. He did not give the order, which disappointed Clovis. So be it. Such a weighty responsibility should be his anyway.

There'd be no warning. No message beyond what was delivered with steel barbs. No chance for the men, women, and children to seek shelter within their blasphemous temple.

"For Karak!" he shouted, and the soldiers loosed their arrows. With a smile, Clovis watched the shafts sail into the afternoon sky.

CHAPTER

1

W hen the first arrow impaled Martin Harrow's chest, the sun was at its highest point in the sky. Thirteen-year-old Geris Felhorn stared at his friend as blood poured from the wound, flowing around the shaft in a puddle of crimson. Martin's hands came up to touch the end of the shaft, his eyes bulging in pain and disbelief. He teetered to the side. Geris stepped forward, reaching tentatively for his injured friend, but he was too late. Martin collapsed onto the hay-covered ground, shuddering, his life's fluid spreading around him in a lake. Geris dropped to his knees, his mind a whirl of bewilderment. He touched Martin's leg, and the shuddering stopped.

That's when the screams began.

The first came from Ben Maryll, Geris and Martin's friend. Ben hovered over Martin's body, his blue eyes wide and filled with tears. He tugged on the fallen boy's auburn hair, looking like he would rip it out of his head. Geris wanted to cry out to him, to ask his friend what was happening, but his voice stuck in his throat. The screams grew louder, and something whistled past his ear, followed by a soft *thud*. People rushed by, shouting in panicked, shrill voices.

Geris sat motionless, watching as the Guardmaster of the Haven township—a tall, stout man named Torgen—was impaled in the throat by an arrow. Blood spurted as he gasped and fell just inches from Geris's feet.

Still the pointed shafts rained from the sky.

A group of five huntsmen, clad in leather skirts and sashes, ran past him, hunting bows on their backs. They climbed the ladders propped against the high wall of the newly completed Temple of the Flesh. When they reached the top, looking at what lay outside the wall, they nocked their own arrows and began firing blindly.

Geris watched it all with disbelieving eyes. He wanted to move—*tried* to move—but his body betrayed him. His heart raced and his throat tightened. Glancing back at the wagon, he spotted Ben staring at him from beneath it, his expression the same as when he awoke from a nightmare. He must have managed to drag himself under it without Geris noticing. Geris felt his bladder threaten to release. He could not name the emotions he was experiencing—only knew he had never felt them before. It was all so unreal. He shouldn't even be here.

He, Ben, and Martin were kinglings from the west, brought here from the Sanctuary to learn. He wished Ahaesarus, his mentor from home, were with him now, wished that he had the man's wise council. Perhaps the Warden would know what to say to make his legs work, to banish the terrible shaking of his hands and the tears streaming down his face.

"Ben! Geris!"

At the sound of his name, Geris swiveled his head. It was Jacob Eveningstar, the kinglings' chaperone and mentor for this journey. Jacob sprinted down the hay-strewn corridor between the temple's central hub and its outer wall. His long, dark hair streamed out behind him as he ran like a man possessed. Geris raised his hand in greeting, as if this were a normal day and he were eating a lunch of apples and salted beef in the golden fields surrounding the Sanctuary.

Taking note of Jacob's clenched jaw, squinting eyes, and the reams of sweat soaking the front of his shirt banished Geris's momentary relief, instead magnifying his already overwhelming fear.

Jacob swept him up in his strong arms as another arrow sailed overhead, and then swung him around and threw him across the alleyway, where the arrows couldn't reach. Geris struck the wall and slid down, letting out a cry of pain. Meanwhile Jacob pulled Ben from beneath the carriage and dragged him across the slender pathway too. Ben collapsed beside Geris, who sought out his friend's hand. Their fingers intertwined, and they stared at each other, matching tears dribbling down their cheeks. Jacob hovered over them, shielding the two potential kings from the death that came from the sky.

Balanced on the ladders that lined the wall, the huntsmen were but shadows beneath the blazing sun. At regular intervals they poked their heads over, and whenever the pace of the attack slowed, they slipped arrows from their quivers and launched them into the air. Bringing his gaze down to the streets, Geris realized that they were covered with blood. He watched as a woman was skewered through her stomach. Her bare breasts flopped as she doubled over, the bells adorning her silver girdle tinkling as she fell. She struggled forward, clawing at the dirt, until another arrow pierced the back of her skull. Geris squeezed his eyes shut for a long moment, desperate not to see any more. Ben trembled beside him. Jacob was standing over the two of them, his sturdy hand clutching Geris's shoulder. He could feel the man's hair brush against his cheek as he scanned one side of the path and then the other.

Before long, all the people who were still alive had their backs pressed against the wall. Jacob ceased his protective hovering and sat down beside his two remaining charges. The arrows still came, but they were slower now, harmlessly pelting the ground and piercing already deceased bodies. Geris shivered, watching as the spilled blood formed tributaries in the open space. He spotted

Martin beside the carriage, six shafts sticking out of his body. His eyes were open and unblinking, his face pale and bloodless. An irrational desire filled Geris, a yearning to see his friend shake off the arrows as if they were props from a game. Martin, so long the favorite for the kingship, would laugh and roll his eyes as if it were nothing. But Martin didn't move, didn't breathe. Geris's eyes filled with tears. Jacob grasped Geris's chin and turned his gaze away from the scene.

Then, just as quickly as it began, the barrage of arrows ceased. All was silent but for the cawing of the birds and the moans of the dying. It stretched on for a long moment before it was broken by an unnaturally loud voice from the other side of the wall.

"Citizens of Haven!" it shouted. "There is no need to hide any longer. Show yourselves, or risk our renewed wrath!"

The huntsmen on the ladders glanced at those gathered below them. The people who were huddled at the base of the wall stepped back into the alleyway, weaving through the arrows and corpses, their faces masks of shock and incomprehension. One among them, a brawny man wearing a long, silken robe, stepped forward. His broad chest heaved as he ran his fingers through his beard. His name was Deacon Coldmine, and he was the appointed lord and leader of the fledgling city. Deacon gestured to the man beside him, who darted down the alley and disappeared through a doorway cut into the side of the rounded temple. A few minutes later a woman emerged. Geris's gaze lingered on her. Her name was Aprodia. She was the temple's priestess and was beautiful beyond words. Her hair was long and black, and her flesh was a tantalizing bronze. A tattoo of an eagle with spread wings adorned the space between her ample breasts. Only yesterday, the three boys had snuck a look through a peephole in the temple wall, watching in wonder as the woman danced like a dervish among the gathered worshippers. Feeling sad and strangely shamed, Geris turned his eyes away from her bare body.

Together, Deacon, Aprodia, and a large gathering of other citizens exited through the gates in the wall, vanishing from sight.

Jacob snapped his fingers before Geris's face, commanding his attention. Geris looked up at him, surprised to see a hard gleam in the man's eye.

"We are here to learn," Jacob said. "And even in moments of death and horror we may still find wisdom."

He slid three ladders together along the wall.

"Come see what is happening," he said. "I trust you are wise enough to understand and endure."

Now that the arrows had ceased their flow, Geris felt his paralyzing fear slowly start to ebb. With his back to the dead, he put a hand on the rung. Jacob's trust in him sparked a bit of pride, giving him the will to climb the ladder. Geris was only thirteen, and although Jacob looked no more than a decade his senior, the man was older than time itself. Still, Jacob treated Geris more like a younger brother than a kingling who needed to be shielded from the world. He didn't fawn over him like his mother did, or act stern and distant like his father. Jacob even treated him better than Ahaesarus did, as the Warden was often annoyed by Geris's flights of fancy. Granted, perhaps this was because it was Ahaesarus's responsibility to teach him, whereas Jacob was only in charge of Ben's training.

Jacob scaled the middle ladder, gesturing for the two boys to follow.

"Let's go," Geris said to Ben, but the other boy was still shaking, his head between his knees. Geris waited, and when it became obvious that Ben would not be moving, he left him there and climbed the rest of the way up.

Once he reached the top, he peered over the edge, as his chaperone was doing. He gazed on the fields of yellow poppies and marsh grasses that grew along the banks of the eastern spine of the Rigon River delta. Just beyond those grasses was Karak's Bridge, at the end of a dirt roadway less than a mile away, its black marble trusses shimmering in the sunlight. Geris's breath caught in his throat. Beside him, Jacob whistled.

Over a hundred men stood on the Haven side of the bridge. They wore light bronze chainmail over simple tunics, with red paint splattered across their chests. Most of the men were equipped with bows and swords. Two men held aloft silver banners adorned with the black outline of a roaring lion, the sigil of the eastern god Karak. In front of them all was a lone man with flowing white hair, whose horse shifted side to side, as if impatient. The delegation from Haven approached him, stopping not far from the safety of the wall. As they neared, another soldier rode from the back of the army to join the man with the white hair. He had a shaved head and a long beard peppered with white, and was naked from the waist up. The largest sword Geris had ever seen hung from the man's back by a thick leather strap.

Geris turned to Jacob and tugged on his sleeve. Jacob's head swiveled around, revealing his soft blue eyes and furrowed brow. It was always strangely difficult to read his expression, but he seemed worried.

"What's going on?" asked Geris.

Jacob shook his head.

"I'm not sure."

Geris had never seen Jacob uncertain before. It frightened him. He closed his eyes and prayed to Ashhur that everything would be all right.

Vulfram Mori sat motionless in his saddle, stroking his beard. His heart pounded with anticipation, his stomach churned from indecision. Despite the distance, he could still hear people sobbing from the other side of the wall. He had never liked bringing pain to anyone, even the wrongdoers he'd been obligated to punish in his days as Captain of the City Watch back in Veldaren.

Beside him, Highest Crestwell cleared his throat.

"You have their attention," Clovis said, his voice reedy and grumbling like a whistle blown beneath the water. "Why do you delay in giving them Karak's orders?"

Vulfram straightened on his horse, and he met Clovis's piercing blue eyes. Though Clovis was older than him by more than two decades, he had not aged a day since the first moment Vulfram laid eyes on him. Agelessness was a gift bestowed upon the forbearers and children of the First Families, a gift Vulfram had renounced the moment he dedicated his whole heart to his wife, Yenge.

"In due time, Highest," said Vulfram. "Our display of force has frightened them beyond measure. I wish to let them regain a sense of order."

Clovis's mouth twisted into something resembling a smile.

"Karak would be most proud," he said, urging his horse backward.

Vulfram let out a deep sigh. He tried to guard his thoughts at all times, just in case his god could see into his very soul, but it proved a difficult task. He had not been confident in the decision to march on the temple. The residents here had fled the east long ago, their chaotic souls unable to adhere to the order of Karak. This isolated land in the delta had gone unclaimed by the religions of the east and west for the last ninety years, and it was only when they began worshipping themselves that Karak had even seemed to notice. Although Karak had not been seen by mortal eyes in over two score years, Clovis assured the people of Neldar that he still held the god's counsel. Vulfram remembered when Karak's orders had been read to him, Clovis's voice crystalline clear in his mind.

This temple is an act of chaos. They are citizens of an unlawful land, denying worship to their creator to instead worship the very forms

*I crafted. It is defiance; it is disorder; and they must be taught a lesson.
They must choose a better way or succumb to the cleansing fire.*

Deep down, Vulfram did not agree. He saw no harm in these
people constructing a meeting place to celebrate their earthly bodies. He and Yenge celebrated their own bodies in a similar fashion
each night back at his childhood home of Erznia. To be honest, the
thought of having an entire edifice dedicated to the carnal pleasures
intrigued him.

Yet never once had he voiced these doubts, for he knew it would
be akin to sacrilege. Karak was divine; Karak was the wisest of the
wise; Karak was the creator of life. If Vulfram had a problem with
the verdict, it was a problem for him to solve within himself. Fulfilling the order of his deity was what mattered, not the dead inside
the temple or the two of his men who had perished from return
volleys launched back from the temple walls. Those two men were
in Afram now, the afterlife, free from pain as they waited for their
loved ones to join them. Vulfram would meet them again one day,
and then they would drink and cavort and fill the afterlife with
good cheer.

Vulfram shook his head. The decision had been made, and as
Lord Commander of the newly formed Army of Karak, it was his
duty to see it through. He had no use for uncertainty, for Karak
waited for no man.

"Citizens of Haven," he said, while fingering the rune-carved
onyx stones in his left hand, using their magic to amplify his voice
so that it carried across the expanse. "We come in the name of
Karak, God of Order, Divinity of the Eastern Realm of Neldar.
This structure you have built, this Temple of the Flesh, is a blasphemy of the greatest offense. By the authority given to me by the
Council of Twelve and our beloved King, I order you to tear down
the walls of this atrocity. Turn your eyes away from one another
and set them on Karak, the true god of this land. If not, this is only
the beginning. We will return on the night of the third full moon,

with the Divinity himself by our side. If you have not repented to the supreme law, you will be judged, and judged harshly. Three months' time. Do not tarry."

He loosened his grip on the stones, cleared his throat, and then squeezed them again.

"Please, I beg of you, do not force Karak's hand in this matter. Unlike we faithful, he shall not leave you with a second chance."

With those words, Vulfram lifted the giant sword Darkfall from his back, raised it into the sky, and roared. He then resheathed the sword and pulled back on his horse's reins. The stallion whinnied and circled around the throng, clomping back onto the bridge, its hooves clacking on the smooth stone. The men bearing the banners of the lion kept formation, mimicking the horse's strides with their human feet, breathing heavily, never looking back. Vulfram followed their example, keeping his eyes fixed straight ahead. He did not want to reveal any of his skepticism. Uncertainty was weakness, and weakness was unbecoming of a Lord Commander.

Once they reached the other side of the bridge, Clovis took his place again at Vulfram's right. On his left appeared another horse, a marvelous black mare whose rider was a lithe woman of ghostly pallor and long silver hair. She fixed him with a bitter and curious glare.

"What is it, Avila?" Vulfram asked.

Avila was Clovis's daughter through and through. She shared his complexion, his coldness, and his unwavering faith in Karak. Her youth remained as eternal as her father's, and she served as Shepherd of Southern Neldar, doling out punishment to wrongdoers in the growing provinces of Omn and Revere.

"Do you think they heard you?" Avila asked, her voice just as grating as her father's.

"Aye," replied Vulfram. "They heard, and they will obey."

"And you are certain Karak will be with us when we return?"

Vulfram gestured behind him. "Ask your father. They were his words I spoke."

Avila grinned, an expression that contained all the joy of a block of granite. Vulfram shivered and urged his stallion onward without another word. The horse settled into a mild canter as it maneuvered down the well-worn path through the sparse grasslands, pulling ahead of his vanguard. He wished he were home, back in bed with Yenge, touching her, tasting her, loving her. It had been eight years since he had been given the mantle of Captain of the City Watch, and his home visits were limited to once every six months. Each time he returned home, he wished to stay longer than he was allowed. He missed the simplicity of life *before*.

"Is that so wrong?" he whispered into the dead wind.

His only replies were the phantom memories of the screams from behind the wall, coupled with the marching feet of his army. He put them all out of his mind and rode in silence as the sun began its journey toward the other side of the world.

CHAPTER

2

T he road was narrow, cutting a jagged swath through the rocky, desert terrain. Jacob bounced in his saddle, the pain from the cuts and bruises on his thighs beginning to work its way up his spine. The sound of his horse's thumping hooves filled his ears. He glanced to his left, where one of the Rigon's snaking tributaries flowed in the distance, and then to his right, gazing down on the cracked red clay speckled with sparse brown grasses. The heat in the south was so insufferable that the river's nourishment died only a few feet from its banks.

He wiped a bead of sweat from his brow, yanked on the collar of his tunic, and then ran a clammy hand through his hair. Yes, the heat was oppressive, but it would have been so much more tolerable had he been able to walk. Whereas Jacob hated riding, he loved walking; it was a pastime he had indulged in for over one hundred years. But it had taken days to reach this far on horseback, and he wished to return to the Sanctuary in haste, which meant that traveling by foot was out of the question.

Besides, he would not make the kinglings walk such a distance.

Someone sniffled behind him, and Jacob cast a glance over his shoulder. There he saw Ben and Geris following on their tethered donkeys. Ben's posture was slumped, and each time his donkey took an odd step, the boy swung far to the side, coming close to falling off. It was up to Geris to reach over and assist his fellow kingling, straightening the boy in his saddle and patting him on the back. For his part, Geris seemed to be handling the whole situation rather well. Whereas Ben's eyes were constantly downcast, Geris would periodically steal a look at the third donkey trailing behind them. On its back Jacob had tied the body of Martin Harrow, draped in a cloth etched with the symbol of the golden mountain. Geris appeared solemn whenever he looked back, but there was an acceptance about him, a stalwartness that Ben, even though he was almost two years the boy's elder, simply didn't have. Geris was a born freeman, an independent soul with a quick wit and even quicker hands; his memory was short in regard to failure or, in this case, grief.

In other words, he would make a noble king.

"How much longer?" asked Geris, his voice soft and distant.

Jacob peered behind once more. "Shouldn't be long now. Are you well?"

The boy shrugged. "Yes," he replied. "Just getting tired."

"This nightmare is behind us, and in time it will fade from you like a half-remembered dream."

Geris nodded, not quite looking like he believed him. Jacob faced forward again and let out a sigh. The Lordship, which included himself and the Wardens, Ahaesarus and Judarius, had been formed four years earlier with the purpose of finding the three human children they believed best suited to take up the mantle of leadership under the watchful eyes of Ashhur, the loving god of the lands west of the Rigon. All three boys had come from strong and loyal families spread throughout Paradise—Martin from Mordeina, Ben from Conch, and Geris from Ashhur's home city of Safeway—and had been chosen after a lengthy process during which the three mentors watched and observed a great many youths, testing their skill and intelligence, for a span of eighteen months. The newly appointed kinglings were then sent to Safeway, along with their families, to continue their training in the shadow of Ashhur's Sanctuary. Of the three, Martin Harrow had demonstrated the greatest potential. Martin had been a hardened youth possessed of high intellect, a sense of empathy for his fellow man, and the desire to learn all his instructors had to offer. But now Martin's body was rotting atop a donkey. Jacob shook his head; the boy's mentor, Judarius, would be greatly upset by the news.

That left Ben Maryll and Geris Felhorn as the two in line to become king of the western lands of Paradise. Jacob knew that Geris would easily best Ben in any physical competition or game of wits. However, in deciding whom to crown ruler, the most essential qualities were faithfulness and charisma. Geris was a private child, happier when climbing the red cliffs around the Sanctuary than taking part in his lessons. But Ben drew people in. When he was comfortable, his sense of humor and timing were impeccable. He was certainly not a risk-taker, but he came across as cautious rather than fearful. As Ben's mentor, Jacob nurtured that aspect of the boy's personality, while seeking to instill a sense of fairness. Although Geris would be a stronger king, potentially leading the realm to greatness if Ashhur ever granted his subjects true self-rule, Jacob felt that, with the relative naïveté of the human race in Paradise, the people deserved a leader more like the one Ben would become.

Again Jacob caught Geris stealing a glance at the third donkey.

"Martin is in Afram now," Jacob said, hoping to ease the boy's lingering distress. "He is descending through the peaceful void, reaching out for Ashhur's golden mountain. Cry if you must, but do not let it overwhelm you."

Geris nodded again, the resolve in his eyes increasing Jacob's respect for him.

What had been intended as a teaching opportunity for the kinglings had suddenly become a nightmare. After Ashhur had expressed concern about the goings-on in Haven a few weeks back, Jacob had suggested taking the three kinglings with him to preach Ashhur's word at the Temple of the Flesh. He had been adamant that his words would reach the people of Haven, that the voice of Jacob Eveningstar, the First Man of Dezrel and Ashhur's most trusted servant, would carry weight among the heathens.

And yet it hadn't. The people did not wish to hear his sermons. All they wanted was to enter their temple, watch Priestess Aprodia dance erotically, and then fill the rest of their days with copulation and brandied wine. They truly were a lost people, so lost that a part of Jacob felt they deserved what had happened to them.

But there were other whispers that concerned him, tales told to him by Peytr, a merchant of precious gems from the delta, who had recently returned from the northern Tinderlands on his raft. He said there were signs of civilization in those dead plains, the remnants of fire pits and haphazardly created shelters. The bones of chickens and pigs had been scattered about the area, as well as the imprints of what could have been countless marching feet. At first Jacob had given no thought to the man's discovery. Sinners had often fled to the vast emptiness of the Tinderlands, a place unclaimed by either Paradise or Neldar, to escape Karak's judgment. But now that Jacob had seen a fraction of the forces led by Vulfram Mori, a new theory had begun to grow in his head.

What if Peytr had seen the first signs of an army making its way toward Paradise?

He licked his dry lips and glanced around.

"Are you thirsty, Ben?" he asked, trying to calm his nerves. He turned enough to see the boy nod.

There was a small watering hole close to the river, mostly hidden by a thatch of tall, swaying grasses. He steered his horse over, dismounted, and patted the mare on the nose. The horse whinnied in reply. He then assisted Ben and Geris in stepping down off their donkeys, and the three of them knelt beside the pool and filled their skins with cloudy water. The pool was located in a slight divot in the earth, likely created by runoff after one of the South's rare cloudbursts. It was drying up, mostly gone after they'd filled their cups, but there were wolf and antelope tracks surrounding its muddy embankment. Jacob tapped the curved skinning knife tucked into his belt as his stomach grumbled. He wished the wildlife still lurked nearby, for he would certainly appreciate some meat, even if was the coarse and gristly canine variety.

He left Ben and Geris sitting beside the pool and wandered toward the riverbank. The river branch was relatively thin, only twenty feet across, but the measureless swampland forest on the other side, with twisted mothertrees and slanting undergrowth—so different from the arid land where he stood—gave it a deep, immense feel, as though it were a spiritual divide between two separate worlds. With the rushing of the water came a light breeze, and Jacob closed his eyes and tilted his head back, allowing it to play with his long hair. Then he gazed south, watching the river wind into the distance until it melded with the horizon. They were nearing the Sanctuary now, which meant they were close to the shores of the Thulon Ocean. The winds would be stronger there, and the rocky coast would tempt one to sit and take in the splendor of the sea.

Jacob lived by that sea, but not once had he relaxed in front of it since he'd dedicated his services to Ashhur seventeen years before. He had been free before that, for Jacob was the first—and only—human created by the hands of both brother gods. He was indelibly perfect, but that status carried a responsibility all its own. The rest of mankind had been made by either Karak or Ashhur, and with the River Rigon as a divider, they had split the world to make their nations. Jacob, as the First Man, was to be the link between the four First Families, two for each deity, who served as young humanity's guiding light. It was only after he had spent time with the followers of both gods over the past ninety-three years that he'd decided his presence was most needed among the people of Ashhur. The eastern society of Neldar was much further along, having cast out the Wardens and replaced them with industry and towns and a ruling class and caste system. In the west the Wardens were all but necessary, and those that had been ousted from Neldar were welcomed into Paradise with open arms, for mankind hadn't even decided on a king yet, and many in Paradise still debated over whether they should even have one.

He took another sip from his skin before kicking at a loose stone, which bounced down the steep riverbank, crossing from reddened clay to brown mud. The stone plunged into the water, and Jacob watched the ripples it created expand in an ever-widening circle.

Jacob had been formed from the magma at the center of the planet, birthed beneath the light of Celestia's star as a fully grown man with the intelligence of the ages. His very first act had been to bow before his creators, the brother gods made flesh. His next was to bear silent witness with his two fathers as Celestia, the goddess who'd originally created this world and populated it with beings of her own design, stood before her two elven races, the Dezren and the Quellan, and asked them to act as wardens to a new race of beings that would soon be created by the brother gods. The leaders of both races declined, pleading with her that their numbers were still depleted from the great war many years before, and that if any beings required assistance, it was they. The goddess turned her children away, disappointment painting her glimmering, otherworldly features. With or without the elves' help, she said, the decision had been made.

Jacob stood by in awe when, a day later, Celestia forged this very river to split the land for the brother gods to share. He watched as a fissure formed in the center of the world, slowly widening like the maw of a great serpent, separating the land into east and west.

The sound of splitting crust had been deafening, the echo of the boulders tumbling into the new crevasse like the constant beating of a drum. And when the gap was broad enough to please the goddess, water rushed into it from the snow-capped mountains in the far north. The rushing tide resonated with the deafening hiss of a massive windstorm, and with it the ecology of the land changed in an instant. The northern expanse, which had once been Kal'droth, the lush green homeland of the elves who had populated the world in the two thousand years since its creation, was particularly altered. The new twin rivers, the Rigon and Gihon, dried the Formian Lake and sucked the nutrients from the fertile soil, depositing them farther south along the new rivers' banks. The trees shriveled and died in the elven homeland; the grasses browned and rotted; and the wildlife fled to the Northface Mountains, where vegetation still grew. With little choice, the Dezren and Quellan elves moved south, along the banks of the new rivers. Kal'droth became known as the Tinderlands—a wasteland of rocky soil nestled above the northern wedge of the conjoined rivers—where crops refused to grow, and neither god bothered to lay a claim.

That had happened on the third day of his existence. On the fourth he embarked on a ten-year-long journey, one that took him from one corner of Dezrel to another, crisscrossing the landscape by foot. He was privy to wondrous sights: the southeastern coast, where the surf dashed against the shore, chiseling giant cliffs into wide beaches of fine sand; the Knothills and Craghills of the northwest and the giant grayhorns that grazed between them, beasts of thick gray hides, horned noses, and docile temperaments; the Kiln mountains on the outskirts of the far eastern Queln River, where flocks of multicolored brine geese migrated, forming living rainbows in the sky during the summer; the desert that would become Ker and the infinite prairies that surrounded it, oceans of flowing golden wheat that stretched far as the eye could see; the Pebble Islands off the southern coast, brimming with tropical flora and fauna and surrounded by crystal-blue waters; the snow-capped mountains of the northeast, offering frigid temperatures and deep caves in which Jacob often explored, discovering more than a few strange creatures that existed in almost pure darkness.

He observed the cycle of life, watching as creatures struggled to survive, fighting each other for food and then huddling together for warmth once night fell. He witnessed the act of birth for the first time, one of the few miracles that he, as a forged man, had been denied. On a boulder outside the Ghostwood, he'd sat and looked on the last of the great dragons, a winged creature fifty feet long with glinting copper scales and fire dripping from its jaws. It had been swallowed whole by a glowing blue portal, ripped away from its home and sent to another reality by Celestia as she finished preparing the world for the coming of humankind.

Finally, the gods summoned him back. It had taken Ashhur and Karak the full duration of his journey to gather the power and materials necessary for the spell that would bring forth life as well as form the Gods' Road between the two nations and prepare the amenities that would allow their newly created children to thrive. Clay vessels were laid out on either side of the Rigon, with Jacob sitting in an anchored raft between them. First he looked on as the originators of the First Families took form—Clovis Crestwell, Isabel DuTaureau, Soleh Mori, and Bessus Gorgoros—four beings molded of the earth from the corners of Dezrel that would become their homes, coming into life just as Jacob had, as adults filled with knowledge, able to choose their own names from the ancient language that would become the world's common tongue. Next he saw the new Wardens arrive, refugees from a different world, chosen after the elves dismissed Celestia's offer. A thousand of them, males all, stepped into Dezrel as if passing through an invisible doorway. Half went to Ashhur, half to Karak. The tall, beautiful, elegant beings began filling the clay ewers with the same materials that had been used to create the First Four: silt from the

Great Lake of the northwest, red sand from the south, chunks of quartz from the frigid northern mountains, and blue clay from the eastern coastal cliffs.

Then the brother gods chanted, and Celestia's star doubled in brightness overhead. The ewers glowed and shook, and their shapes changed. The light was so vivid that Jacob was blinded to what came next. When it was all over and his vision cleared, he saw that the ewers were gone; in their stead were two thousand fully developed young men and women, a thousand on each side of the river. They were new beings, infused with preternatural knowledge by the gods yet still frightened and confused, and the Wardens called them into their arms and quelled their fear. Ashhur and Karak then shared a silent nod, brother deities acknowledging their mutual respect for one another, and led their children away, deep into their separate lands.

Thus went the birth of humankind.

"We're ready now," said a timid voice, tearing Jacob from his memories.

Jacob turned to find Ben standing there, hands tucked inside his cotton breeches, cheeks flushed and eyes watery. He placed a hand on the boy's back. Geris was off wandering the road, looking beneath rocks in search of centipedes and scorpions. It seemed some things never changed.

Just as dusk began to settle over the world of Dezrel, Jacob and his charges finally entered Safeway, the growing community surrounding the Sanctuary. The land shifted—where once there had been reddish, cracked earth, now there were green, cultivated fields. Much of Safeway looked just like this—miles upon miles of flatland, two days across by foot, bordered by the river to the east and the Kerrian desert to the west, the clay cliffs to the north and the shores of the Thulon Ocean to the south. The whole area was peppered with small tent- and hut-dwelling communities for as far as the eye could see. Near ten thousand men, women, and children called it home, just as they all in turn called Ashhur their kind and loving god.

Bareatus—one of the Wardens Ashhur and Celestia had brought over from some different reality—stood off to the side of the dirt road, hand raised in greeting. Just like the rest of the Wardens, he was tall, almost seven feet, and sublimely graceful. Jacob always thought the Wardens looked eerily similar to elves, only with rounded ears and hair like spun silk. Though all were male, their smooth ivory features held certain feminine qualities, which made them seem approachable despite their size. Bareatus glanced at the trailing donkey and the wrapped lump atop it, and his smile of greeting wavered. His hand fell to his side, and he stood still as a stone, his eyes narrowed to mere slits framed by a mane of straight, golden locks.

"Are Ahaesarus and Judarius about?" asked Jacob.

Bareatus shook his head, his gaze still trained on Martin's covered body.

"They are in Ang, holding court with Bessus and Damaspia."

Of course, thought Jacob. The masters of House Gorgoros were always requesting spiritual guidance.

"And our Lord? Is he here?"

Bareatus nodded.

"He is."

"Good. I will meet with him at once. Please send word to my fellow mentors that their presence is required back at the Sanctuary."

"Very well, Jacob. I will send a crow bearing that message. In regards to our Lord, please be forewarned that Ashhur is spending time with the children. 'At once' may not be as quick as you wish."

Jacob gestured for the youths to follow him and kicked his mare, leaving Bareatus alone on the road. He heard the massive Warden's long strides as he loped away, heading for the tents that were just visible at the tip of a distant rise.

The road rose and fell, rose and fell, and as the sun slowly descended, casting the sky with a deep burgundy pallor, people came into view all around him. There was a group of men in the meadow to his right, dressed in dirty rags and hacking away at the soil, seemingly vacant smiles plastered on their faces. To his left were seven children, running and laughing through a field of short corn, ducking below the stalks and daring others to find them. Beyond the children was a mixed group of men and women, twenty of them at least, on their knees facing the setting sun, their eyes closed and chins held high. Farther ahead, a group of women sat around a small fire. A young mother, no older than fourteen, held a babe in her arms, and she put it to her breast as they passed. One of the other women, much older and more wizened looking, tended the small garden before her. She sprinkled dust onto the carpet of dirt, chanted a few choice words, and from the ground sprouted three buds. The buds grew and grew, and in a matter of moments the three sprouts joined to became a full strawberry bush. The woman plucked a ripe fruit from the vine and fed it to the young mother, whose child continued to suckle at her breast.

That was life in Safeway: praying, farming, breeding, and playing, all under the watchful eye of Ashhur, their god made flesh.

"They're back!" shouted the voice of a young boy. "Jacob and the kinglings!"

A crowd gathered, running alongside their mounts as they made their way down the uneven road. The people called out to them, cheering for each of the kinglings in turn. Jacob glanced at them, taking in the hope on their faces. Geris waved, and even Ben's spirits seemed to lift, if only a little. Someone shouted out Martin Harrow's name, but none of those who gathered let their gaze linger on the sack draped over the rear donkey.

"Where is he?" asked a woman's voice. "Where is Kingling Harrow?"

Jacob peered over his shoulder to see that there was still a smile on the querying woman's face. She did not understand. None of them did. Around here, with Ashhur, the Wardens, and the healers tending to the wounds and ailments of the populace, unnatural death was unheard of. In western Dezrel, over the span of ninety-three years, no one had perished before his or her time.

Jacob had a feeling that was about to change.

The crowd gradually thinned as the land sloped downward, and Jacob and the kinglings entered the Cavern of Solitude, a tapered passage cut through the middle of a foreboding hillock. Jagged spires of stone protruded from the sides of the cliff, narrowing the road. Jacob was grateful that it was still daylight, as the passage could prove treacherous when traversed in the dark. The cavern was guarded by the great statue of Ashhur, a twenty-foot behemoth carved into the side of the red clay cliff. The deity's statue stared down at them as they passed beneath it, his left hand holding an olive branch to the heavens, his right hand crossed over his immortal heart. Jacob heard Ben whistle a quiet lullaby as the statue disappeared behind them—the very same lullaby the god himself had sung to the kinglings on the night they were anointed.

When they exited the Cavern of Solitude, the horizon stretched out before them. Clay huts and lean-tos constructed of desiccated animal hides peppered the land. From these abodes more people emerged, forming an assembly in front of the colossal building at the center of it all—the Sanctuary itself, forty feet high and circular, built with smoothed stone from the northwest coast. It was the only building in Safeway, and the tallest in all of western Dezrel. On its sloped crest, above the solarium, was etched the Golden Mountain of legend, the final, peaceful resting spot of the spirits of the dead in Afram. Below that were etched Ashhur's two guiding principles, both of them concepts to revere and commands to obey: *Love* and *Forgive*.

Jacob saw the Marylls and Felhorns emerge from their crude domiciles, making their way toward the passageway that was cut into the short wall bordering the Sanctuary. He searched for the unmistakable bald pate of Stoke Harrow, Martin's father, and eventually found the burly man in the crowd. He was wearing a burlap robe and pulling his wife Tori along. Soon the families of all three kinglings stood front and center, waiting with wringing hands and expressions overwrought with excitement.

At the edge of the gathering, Jacob veered his mare off to the side and dismounted. He tapped the horse's flank, and it began to saunter away obediently. He then helped Ben and Geris down from their donkeys. The two boys immediately found their families, who were waiting with open arms, and ran to them.

The Harrows stood confused, their gazes shifting from the other two kinglings to Jacob and then to the wrapped carcass atop the third donkey. Hesitantly, Jacob approached it, gesturing for Stoke Harrow to come forward. The large man did as he was bidden, that perplexed expression still smeared across his face. Tori followed meekly, hands clenched over her mouth. Jacob lifted one end of the bulk, untied the rope, and pulled back a flap of fabric. The pale face of Martin Harrow emerged, mouth slightly agape, eyes sewn shut. His cheeks were sunken, and his red hair had lost its luster. The scent of rot wafted off the dead child, the result of three days riding in the sweltering southern heat. Jacob cringed and pinched his nose shut while Stoke's face twisted into a manifestation of stupefaction.

Tori shoved past her husband, and Jacob backed away, letting her grab hold of the dead boy's shoulders.

"Martin?" she whispered, lifting the child's head. She shook him, hard, and his body flopped like a dead fish on the saddle. Her eyes brimmed with tears as she took in the reality of the situation. Her husband was behind her the next instant, his strong hands on her back, holding her up. Tori spun around and buried her face in his chest. Stoke wailed in disbelief as his wife's tears saturated his burlap robe. The cry she released was shrill in its anguish, threatening to shatter the hearts of all who heard it.

The Marylls and Felhorns gathered around the weeping parents, embracing them, consoling them in the only way they knew how, while the rest of the throng stood in shocked silence. Suddenly, Stoke Harrow's head shot upward, and he fixed Jacob with a murderous stare. The anguished father stepped away from the other grievers, his meaty hands balled into fists. The tears that ran from his eyes created ravines on his muddy cheeks.

"You were supposed to protect him!"

Jacob stood his ground as the larger man stormed across the narrow space between them. He never flinched, not even when Stoke's arm cocked back, the rage in his eyes burning as hot as the sun.

"Stop!" said a voice like booming thunder.

Stoke's arm fell mid-swing. The man's shoulders hunched as he turned around. Jacob glanced up at the Sanctuary. The great door was open, and now children were streaming out of it, filing down the cobbled path and into the milling crowd. A giant figure ducked beneath the doorframe, stepping out of the darkness and into the light. He was as tall as two men standing atop each other. His broad shoulders looked capable of carrying the world upon them, and yet all they held up was a gown made of glimmering white silk. On the front of the gown was stenciled a mountain surrounded by a field of red roses. His beard was trimmed but pronounced, and his blond hair, cut shoulder length, swooped back from his skull like a wave receding into the ocean. His eyes, golden as sunlight, seemed to see everything at once.

Jacob stepped away from Stoke, bowed on one knee, and placed his right fist over his heart.

"My Lord Ashhur, I beg your pardon," he said. The rest of those gathered, save the children who had exited the Sanctuary, fell to their knees.

The god-made-flesh offered Jacob a nod as he stepped with a single stride over the low wall surrounding the Sanctuary. The crowd parted before him, shuffling sideways on their knees, as their god approached the still-weeping couple. Ashhur placed his index finger gently on the forehead of their dead son, and then lowered himself and wrapped both arms around the grieving parents. Stoke began sobbing anew, until his mood shifted back from sorrow to fury.

"Why did you let this happen?" he kept repeating, driving his fists into Ashhur's enormous knee. The god touched the man's chin with his palm—the sheer size of his hand swallowed Stoke's entire skull—and the outburst ceased.

"Let us speak in the Sanctuary," he said, his voice still booming across the countryside.

The god led the Harrows into the tall edifice, and the donkey carrying Martin's body was ushered in after them. When they were gone, the crowd looked to Jacob for instruction. He waved them away as kindly as he could, and they dispersed. Geris Felhorn was the last to leave, staring at him for a while before relenting and finally joining his parents on the short walk back to their domicile.

Jacob breathed heavily out his mouth, making his way in the opposite direction. He followed the dirt path along the west side of the Sanctuary wall, where the path broke away from the structure and passed through a field of wildflowers. Unlike the roads into and out of Safeway, this path was smooth, flattened by the constant foot traffic. Not many people left, after all. The land—along with Ashhur himself—supplied them with all they needed. There was a reason that the west had been named Paradise by the people who lived there.

He trotted down a gulch, and the sound of crashing waves reached his ears. The sun dipped low on the horizon, and the sky lit up in a brilliant shade of purple. A cabin of rough-hewn stone came into view, the straw of its roof bristling with the gentle sea breeze. Jacob had purposefully built his home far away from the Sanctuary to allow himself respite from the prayers that rang out seemingly without end. He was rarely visited, and when he was, it was usually by the Sanctuary stewards coming to tell him that Ashhur required his presence.

As he approached, he noticed that a ladder was propped up against the side of the cabin. A figure was braced on the top rung, applying a layer of wet tar to the areas where the roof had grown thin. He was a handsome man of twenty years, stocky of build and good with his hands.

"Hello, Roland," Jacob said to his steward.

"Hello, Master Jacob," Roland replied. He never took his eyes off his work. "I wasn't expecting you back until next week. How were things in Haven?"

Jacob stopped once he reached the side of the ladder. "They were...not well."

Finally Roland gazed down.

"You wish to speak of it?" he asked, his piercing blue eyes glinting between strands of his sandy-brown hair.

"Not at the moment. How goes the labor?"

"Laboriously. I set out grain for the chickens, milked the cows, and helped Fela Felabosi construct a new shelter for his son Bronta. The boy is expecting a child soon and wanted to strike out on his own. I just started the household chores an hour ago."

"It's late, son. Your work is done for the day."

Roland gave him a queer look.

"Are you sure? There are three more weak spots on the roof, and I haven't begun mortaring the loose stone on the eastern wall...."

Jacob chuckled. Roland didn't like stopping before his work was complete, which was an honorable characteristic. Not many in the west shared the boy's work ethic, perhaps not even Jacob himself.

"It's fine. If it showers tonight, I will set out a bucket. Go home. Get some rest. I will see you on the morrow."

Roland hopped off the ladder and then lowered it to the grass. Despite his nonchalant attitude, Jacob could tell he was intensely curious about his master's trip to Haven.

"So, tomorrow we will speak of what happened, yes?"

"We will. I promise you."

The boy smiled, and just like everything else about him, it was beautiful.

"I bid you good night then, Master."

With that, Roland bowed before turning tail and sprinting up the path, heading back into Safeway. Again Jacob chuckled. Over the nine years the boy had served as Jacob's steward, he had headed for home in that exact same manner each evening. His energy was awe-inspiring.

It was energy Jacob could have used at the moment. Suddenly his arms felt too heavy, his knees too weak. He slumped his shoulders, turned around, and pulled open the door to his cabin. Stepping inside, he found the embers of a recent fire, glowing in the inglenook. Above it, resting on an iron rack, was a steaming pot. He dipped a finger inside. Roland had left a meal for him—rabbit from the smell of it. His stomach cramped as he licked his finger; then he grabbed a wooden bowl from the niche above the inglenook and ladled himself a helping.

The soup was warm and spiced with lemongrass and sage, which made it taste a tad sour. He gulped down mouthful after mouthful, feeling his hunger pangs decrease with each swallow. Making his way to the window, he pushed open the shutters with his free hand, allowing the breeze to tickle his flesh. The stifling heat from the embers was slowly whisked away.

When he finished eating, he went to his desk on the far side of the room. The desk had been a gift from Norman Astencroft, the lone carpenter to take up residence in Safeway. Norman wasn't particularly skilled, and the ash desk wasn't particularly well made, but it served its purpose. That was all Jacob could really ask for.

Setting aside his bowl, he reached beneath the desk and pulled out a leather-bound book. He placed it on the flat surface, wiped dust from the cover, and undid the iron clasp. The food might have settled his stomach, but it had done nothing to stifle his exhaustion from riding three days straight with little sleep. Nor did it calm the dissonant thoughts running through his mind. He had not yet decided what he would tell Ashhur about the events at the temple. His hand shook as he took out a folded piece of paper from the inner pocket of his tunic, flipped open the cover of the book, and turned until he reached a blank page.

He unfolded the paper and began inscribing the words written on it. With each letter he formed, he sensed his fatigue—and his anger—lessening. It was as if documenting his adventures and discoveries in his journal was setting his soul afire. Other than serving his god, *this* was what he lived for: unlocking the mysteries of the world, slowly assembling the building blocks of life in Dezrel, one word at a time.

His earliest entries had originally been written on the huge leaves of the barrow elms that grew atop Mount Ire in the northwest, using excretions from nightworms as his ink. It wasn't until his twenty-fourth year, when Ashhur showed his people how ink could be made by mixing iron salts with gallnut tannins, that Isabel DuTaureau, the matriarch of House DuTaureau of Mordeina, had had this particular tome created for him.

The journal was filled with oddities—descriptions of plants and animals beyond number. He chronicled humanity's progress, from their early days as youths under the watch of the Wardens to the time when those in the east began to earn their independence. The chronicles also served as a comparison of the burgeoning cultures in the east and west, both their similarities and their vast differences.

Though magic was sparse within Paradise, used only to heal the sick and urge crops to grow, the study of it was what interested Jacob the most. Page after page of his journal was scrawled with psalms, ingredients, runes, powerful words, and the laws of tribute. One could open the book to any random page and discover something wonderful: practical magic, such as how to conjure food from topaz or create a bubbling stream with onyx dust; earth magic, derived from the elves, about how to divine power from the molecules in the air itself to form balls of fire, shards of ice, or even cause plant life to obey commands; astral magic on how to bend time and space to travel between two points in an instant; psychic magic, explaining how to use the power of one's mind to manipulate physical objects on a whim or commune with others over great distances, using select totems, such as sea-worn copper or dragonglass. There were also vast sections on metallurgy, botany, chemistry, astrology, and what he had learned about the inner workings of the human mind. Rarest were the segments dealing with blood magic, an ancient form of conjuring that existed only in the legends told to him by the elves.

According to those legends, two millennia ago there were three demon kings—Darakken, the thunder lord; Velixar, the beast of a thousand faces; and Sluggoth, the slithering famine. When they ascended from the underworld, they brought terror to the elves. A war lasting a hundred years ensued, until Celestia, apparently upset that these hellbeasts were laying waste to her creations, sent the demons and their minions back to the underworld and locked it up tight. The demons were said to have possessed great mystical abilities. Through their words and strength of will they could control the dead, inflict insanity upon all who gazed on them, and rip apart a living body and reassemble it as they pleased. Their story fascinated Jacob. He wanted more than anything to discover the truths hidden within the legends, to inscribe the words of these beasts' ancient magic in the pages of his tome. Sadly, barring a few obscure carvings in the crypts of Dezerea, there was no hard evidence that the demon kings had been anything but bedtime stories. The section on them in his journal was maddeningly sparse.

His current work for the night dealt with medicinal herbs. Living in the west meant a life free from disease and physical maladies, so it intrigued him how those in the east—and in Haven—got through each day with all the potential dangers surrounding them. He had catalogued all the different herbs and their uses, both medicinal and recreational, from poppy to crimleaf to the silia fungus. During his visit to the Temple of the Flesh, he'd spoken with the priestess Aprodia, who had told him that by sucking the milk from the large seeds of nectarines, her people avoided the Wasting that inflicted many throughout the east. That information might not have much practical use in Ashhur's Paradise, but Jacob was nothing if not fastidious, so into the book it went.

He was in the middle of writing his last word of the evening when a board creaked behind him. The quill halted mid-stroke, and he cocked his head. All was quiet but for the whistling of the wind through the open window. Just then, something grabbed the back of his hair, forcing his head back. Sharp steel pressed against his throat. He reached for the skinning knife he kept tucked into his belt, but it was no longer there.

"Looking for something?" asked a low, mocking voice.

"It seems I have misplaced my knife," Jacob replied, calm as could be. "You wouldn't happen to have it, would you?"

"I might."

"Please be careful. The blade is quite sharp."

The voice snickered, and the knife was pulled away from his throat. The hand dropped from his forehead, silken fingers tracing a sinuous line down his cheek.

"So many apologies, kind sir," the voice said, now sounding high-pitched and childish. "I knew not."

Jacob stood from his chair and turned around slowly. The corners of his mouth rose into a sad grin when he saw the elf girl standing there.

"Brienna, one of these days you might actually hurt me. I may not age, but I'm not indestructible, you know."

"I wouldn't have broken the skin. Where's your sense of humor?"

He shook his head. "It seems to have abandoned me this night. Forgive my lack of charm. You took me by surprise, Bree. Shouldn't you be at the homestead, preparing for the engagement?"

"I reckon my sister could do without my company for a few nights. There are only so many flower arrangements a girl can make, and to be honest, I have no desire to spend time in Dezerea. Our cousins there are so…stuffy and staid." She clucked her tongue. "Now I ask, would I not be of more use to you here?"

Brienna gestured to the bedchamber, leaned her head forward, and gazed at him from under slanted eyelids. Her hair hung down to her waist in a straight sheet the color of sun-drenched summer wheat. Her skin was like fresh milk, pale and shimmering in the light of the dying coals in the inglenook. She was slender yet durable, muscular yet womanly. The green, satin-threaded petticoat she was wearing offered the faintest hint of her shapely body. She was Brienna Meln of the Stonewood Forest, daughter of Cleotis and Audrianna, Lord and Lady of the southern Dezren elves. At just over a century old, she was eleven years Jacob's elder, and they had been partners for twenty-two years. Jacob had been infatuated with her since the day they met, before the dawn of man, and had eventually wooed her by defeating her shamed older brother Carskel in a duel. He depended on her for many reasons, not least of which was her ability to make him laugh.

But now that laughter seemed so far away.

"What's wrong?" she asked, a look of concern crossing her normally mischievous face.

"The Temple was attacked. Martin Harrow died."

Jacob was becoming accustomed to the expression that crossed Brienna's face—blatant incredulity.

"Attacked?" she asked. "By whom?"

"A small battalion from the east, flying Karak's banners. They demanded that the people of Haven swear themselves once more to Karak or else face more violence."

"And Martin was caught in the middle?"

Jacob nodded. Brienna frowned, and he could tell that her sharp mind was already working through the problem.

"So Karak's followers have formed an army," she said.

"It seems so, though I cannot begin to guess at the size. The hundred men who attacked Haven may only be a fraction, or they may represent the entirety of their power. Either way, it means we now have a rather unfortunate problem. If Neldar is lashing out at those in Haven, who have done nothing wrong save exercise their freedom, how long until their soldiers cross the bridges and do the same to us?"

"You know that can't happen, Jacob. Ashhur won't let it, and neither would Karak. Nothing good can come from that way of thinking. Nothing at all."

He sighed, and even to his ears it sounded defeated.

"I know."

"So what are you going to do? What does your god say?"

Jacob shook his head. "Nothing as of yet. He is consoling Stoke and Tori Harrow as we speak. I assume he will send for me come morning."

"What will you do until then? Do you want to talk of it?"

He stepped forward and wrapped an arm around Brienna's slender waist. The downy feel of her petticoat helped ease his mind, and he suddenly felt tired once more.

"I'd rather not," he said.

"Is there anything I can do for you?"

He smiled at her.

"You know there is."

Brienna blew a strand of hair from her eyes, which sparkled with life.

"Indeed I do."

CHAPTER

3

It was still dark when a loud banging woke Jacob from a dreamless sleep. He slowly rose to his elbows on the feather mattress. Brienna lay on her back beside him, mouth slightly open. She was snoring. He reached over and pinched her small, pointed nose shut. She licked her lips and rolled over, forcing his fingers off her. When she settled in again, her snoring ceased. The banging, however, did not. Jacob grumbled as he slid out from beneath the thin, corded sheets, the rough material grabbing at the hairs on his legs. He walked out of the bedchamber, his body sore and his head groggy, not bothering to slip his bedclothes over his head. Moonlight poured in through the windows he'd forgotten to shutter earlier.

"Give me a moment," he muttered.

He opened the door to his cabin, naked as the day he was created. The brightness from the moon turned the man standing on his stoop into a squat blue toad. The man looked up into Jacob's face, his jowls shaking as he spoke.

"Master Eveningstar," said Clegman Treadwell, Ashhur's Grand Steward.

"Clegman," said Jacob. He let the name hang in the air for a moment, knowing that the short, fat man grew uncomfortable during long periods of silence. "Why are you here at this ungodly hour?"

Clegman cleared his throat.

"His Grace wishes an audience with you."

"Now?"

"Yes, yes, now."

Jacob leaned out of the cabin. He gazed east, where the horizon was still black, though the tiniest thread of crimson was working its way into the sky.

"Let me get dressed."

"Very well. I will wait here."

Jacob rolled his eyes. "You do that."

Throwing on his old breeches and a somewhat clean tunic, Jacob followed the portly man down the path. Though still annoyed by his interrupted slumber, he couldn't help but admire the way the change in lighting altered the feel of his surroundings. How amazing it was that a simple difference could completely transform a person's outlook. It was as if all of life existed in multiple worlds layered over one another.

They took the road up and out of the gulch, but instead of heading for the Sanctuary, Clegman led him toward the grassy hill overlooking the valley on Safeway's western border. Even from a distance, he could see the god sitting there on the crest, legs crossed and hands on his knees, facing the desert. The serenity of his posture caused Jacob to shiver.

"I bid your leave here, Master Jacob," said Clegman, bowing and backing away.

"Thanks," mumbled Jacob.

Ashhur did not move as he approached. The god's head was tilted back and his eyes were closed. Jacob sat on the ground before him, crossing his legs in the same manner. Even sitting, the god towered over him by more than two heads. There he waited without making a sound, until at last Ashhur's shimmering gold eyes fluttered open.

"Jacob," the god said, his voice low and soothing. It was the tone he usually took when meeting with his most ardent disciple.

"My Lord," said Jacob, pitching forward on his knees and bowing so low that his nose brushed a blade of grass.

"Sit up, my son," Ashhur said. "We must talk."

Jacob did as he was told, but kept quiet. In conversations with a god, it was best to let the deity speak first.

"The Harrows are very upset over the death of their son," Ashhur said.

"They should be."

Ashhur sighed. "Indeed."

Again there was silence. Jacob waited it out, rocking back and forth until his sides cramped. Ashhur was staring up at the twinkling stars above—one in particular. Jacob's irritation began to build, and he kneaded a fold in his leather pants, trying to calm his nerves. When he'd had enough, he blurted out, "My Lord, why did you drag me out here, if not to speak?"

Ashhur's eyes turned to him, those eyes that glowed with the wisdom of ages. But they also held something different this time—accusation.

"There will be no response," the god said.

Jacob's brow furrowed.

"What do you mean?"

"There will be no retaliation for the attack on Haven or for Martin's death. I forbid it."

Jacob held out his hands. "I beg your pardon, my Lord, but I had not once considered it."

"I see the truth in all things, Jacob Eveningstar. You are no fool, so why do you lie to me now?"

Jacob sighed. Ashhur could sense when men spoke falsehoods, so it would do no good to dance around the subject.

"Forgive me, Father. It is true, I had wondered if you might think countermeasures necessary. I assure you, I would never act on your behalf without consulting you first."

Ashhur nodded. "Yet I tell you now, and still you doubt."

"I do, my Lord."

"Are you questioning my wisdom?" the god asked, peering at him through squinting lids. Jacob shot upright, his spine straightening like an iron rod. A stone of concern dropped in his belly. He was treading on dangerous ground here, no matter how much his god adored him.

"My questions stem from my own confusion, my Lord. You are God of Justice. Do these events not require a just response?"

Ashhur leaned forward, and it seemed the earth beneath them shifted when he did. A great gust of breath left his mouth, and he began tracing runes in the dirt with his massive finger.

"Do you trust your god, Jacob?"

"Of course."

Ashhur's voice took on a somber, dreamlike quality. "Then listen closely, my son. We have existed for an eternity, my brother and I. We have watched humanity in all its forms, in many worlds that even now twinkle in our night sky. When given a paradise, mankind squanders it each and every time. I have watched brother kill brother over something so beautiful as the love of a woman. I have seen pointless death, felt the ravenous appetites that feed it. I have seen great metal birds drop flames from their bellies, laying waste to the land. And yet even with all this destruction, all this sorrow, there remains a light in the heart of every man, woman, and child, the potential to love and be loved, to care for kin and neighbor alike, nearly divine in their passion for preserving life. My brother saw it as well.

"When Celestia offered Karak and me this land, we both agreed that we would find out for ourselves what caused such madness. We crafted man by our own hands, this time vowing we would not let our children squander the wonderful gifts we have given them. Karak and I may not agree on methods, but that is part of why we have chosen to partake in this mutual act of creation; to at last discover the *right way* to avoid the death and destruction that always seems to follow. And so I choose to lead my children toward a path of civility and nonviolence. We have no weapons; we have no aggression toward one another or any outsider. That is the way it will be. That is the way you *chose*, my son, when you joined my side."

Jacob sighed. "You are right, and it all sounds as idyllic as the first time I heard you utter it. Yet the fact remains that the east has built an army, and your brother's people do not live in any such peace as you describe. No one has heard word or tale of Karak in decades, my Lord. For all anyone knows, he has left this realm altogether."

"He has not," Ashhur said, and there was no questioning him. "He is still here, watching from a distance. I can feel him. He would not allow a grave act to be made in his name if he did not condone it."

"So you're saying that Karak knew of the attack on the temple and permitted it?"

"You must understand something," said Ashhur, fixing Jacob with the stare of a father lecturing an indignant child. "Almost all who reside in the delta are his children. He created them, and he is free to punish them in whatever way he sees fit. That they fled to unclaimed land does not alter this fact. I may not agree with his methods, but I respect his decision…both as a brother and as a fellow deity."

"And what if this new army doesn't stop at the temple? What if Martin's death was not a fluke, but a planned event? Please, I fear your brother is deceiving you. Neldar has had a ruling class in place for over forty years, yet we bicker among ourselves as to whether we even *need* a king. Now our most capable candidate for kingship has been destroyed, and if not for my protection, the other two might have perished as well. The Temple of the Flesh has been fourteen years in the making. Does it not strike you as convenient that their warning against the blasphemers occurs *now*, while we were there? Or what if your brother, watching from afar, doesn't know all that his children plan?"

Ashhur cocked his giant head to the side. Arguing with a god was risky business, but Jacob trusted Ashhur to hear him out. He always had in the past and hopefully wouldn't stop now.

"If there is any truth to your concerns, then they are worrisome indeed," the god said. "However unlikely, I suppose it is possible that some of my brother's children are deceiving him. Who commands their forces?"

"Vulfram Mori."

Ashhur smiled. "Vulfram is a good man, honorable and fair. His family has guided the people of Neldar well since the beginning."

"He has, and I agree that he is honorable," said Jacob, resting his chin on his fist. "Yet the Crestwells were there as well, and I trust them far less. By my own eyes and ears I have witnessed their deeds, and I assure you, they do not hold the lives of humanity in high esteem."

"My brother has dubbed Clovis Crestwell as highest among his children, his most dedicated of followers. He would never betray Karak or Karak's children. Should he dare to do so, my brother would strike him down with a thought. Did you speak with Moira Crestwell while you were in the delta? I've heard she now lives in Haven."

"Moira no longer considers herself a Crestwell, not since her father exiled her. She holds no love for her family, and they hold none for her."

"I assure you, a father never loses his love for his child. If Clovis truly meant to destroy the entirety of Haven, he'd have made sure she left before it happened."

Jacob ran both hands through his hair in frustration. "Then why was she there when the first volley of arrows hit? Vulfram warned that if the people of Haven have not renounced their blasphemy in three months' time, he'll return with Karak at his side. He did not say it, but the punishment would be death for all of them, I have no doubt. How would that be so different from the war-torn worlds you've told me about? What will happen if Deacon Coldmine convinces the people there to refuse? Will we stand by and let them be slaughtered?"

Ashhur fixed him with a hard stare. "Yes."

"Even if they move on to us next?"

"They will not."

"Yet I have heard rumors of a force gathering in the Tinderlands. What if that is the rest of the eastern army? If it is, what are we to do?"

Ashhur pulled a chain out from beneath his robe. A circular bas-relief of a lion standing atop a mountain dangled from it, looking comically small in the god's huge hands. It was a pendant both he and Karak wore, a symbol of their cooperation.

"It is not. The pact between us is binding."

"Humor me."

Ashhur opened his mouth to answer, but the blackened pre-dawn sky lit up with a blinding radiance. From the heavens descended a white-hot comet, its tail spewing flames hotter than those from a dragon's maw. The falling star soared over their heads and struck the Sanctuary. The building glowed brightly for a moment in the distance, and then the light dimmed, coming to rest inside the solarium. Brightness shone through the cracks above and below the shuttered windows.

As the early morning sky darkened once more, the god's expression changed. For the first time in their entire meeting, Ashhur seemed to relax.

"I must go now," he said and turned his back on Jacob. With long steps he strode down the hillock, back toward the Sanctuary.

"And what of my worries?" Jacob called out after him.

Ashhur paused ever so slightly. Amazingly, he seemed hurried, perhaps even annoyed. It was the first time Jacob had seen him this way.

"If you have concerns, I grant you leave to explore them. But do not act rashly, Jacob, nor betray my trust. If anything, these troubles only show that my brother's way may not be the true path he believes it to be."

With that, Ashhur turned around and continued his descent. With the considerable length of his strides, he made it to the Sanctuary in a fraction of the time it would have taken a normal man. Jacob stood unmoving, watching from a distance as his god reached the entryway. A feminine figure, glowing with the light of the stars, greeted him when he opened the door. Ashhur stepped inside, falling into Celestia's embrace. The door closed, and Jacob saw no more.

Jacob pivoted away from the valley, gazing out at the endless expanse of eastern dunes. The desert sand shone cobalt under the moon's light. He wanted nothing more than to be back in his bed with Brienna by his side, but he had work to do. In the morning he would send out hawks bearing word to Isabel DuTaureau, requesting the aid of her son, Patrick, in keeping an eye on the happenings in the delta. Then he would gather Roland and one of the Wardens and head north for the Tinderlands.

As he walked down the path leading back to his cabin, Jacob Eveningstar began to hum. It was all he could do to keep from shaking.

CHAPTER

4

rowds packed the streets of the far-eastern city of Veldaren, swarming the walkways on either side of the cobbled streets filled with horses pulling carts of merchandise. Soleh Mori walked among the people, buildings of gray stone on either side of her. The entirety of the developed sections of the city looked the same to her—cold, gray, and lifeless. She felt out of place among the unwashed hordes as she made her way to the castle. She wore an elegant, lime-colored dress of woven cotton and silk. The bodice of the dress was embroidered with miniature Gemcroft pearls cultivated off the coast of the Pebble Islands, and the hemline was rounded with stylish lace. The rest of those around her were dressed in sullied leathers and burlap, their faces streaked with grime as they perused the markets. Many of them were common laborers on their midday break, drawn in by the catcalls of vendors selling fruit, vegetables, and freshly butchered or salted meats. On occasion, Soleh would spot a covered wagon and see the occupants through the netting that hid them from view. These were the lords and ladies of the city, the high merchants, dressed in their expensive silks and satins, fanning themselves as they sat atop feather-filled pillows.

Soleh wished she could join them in their luxury, but as Minister of Justice in the capital city of Neldar, she needed the people to see her face, to know that she walked among them. They had to believe she existed in the same world as they did, even if it wasn't true. Even if she felt dirty in their presence. So badly she wished to be back in Erznia, in her courtyard on the border of the forest, sitting beside the spring eating apples, drinking wine, and teaching her children the lessons of Karak. Only rarely had she gone back to visit over the forty years since she had been handed the mantle of Minister, and she missed it more than anything.

But this is my life now, as it has been for a long while, she thought. It had been Karak's will for her to sit in judgment of the crimes of the populace, and Soleh Mori never questioned the will of her god.

The afternoon crowd steadily thickened as more and more laborers—bricklayers, smiths, gardeners, tailors, caterers, and house servants—exited their places of employ and joined the torrent of human flesh in Veldaren's southern district. She knew she had to stay wary, for within the midst of the honest men and women were the liars and beggars and thieves. It was the price of a free economy. Though every man could readily earn himself a silver coin for a day's labor, there were just as many for whom the concept of *earning* was a five-fingered proposition. That was why the men of the City Watch were stationed on every street corner, standing rigid in their dull, mailed armor. Their spears held high and their shortswords sheathed at their waists, they held a constant vigil. It was because of them that Soleh declined protection on her journey to the castle each day. There was plenty of protection around already.

The City Watch had once been her son's responsibility. Thinking of Vulfram caused her heart to patter. She missed him terribly, missed his assuredness and sense of honor. Soleh fell into dreary bouts of loneliness far more often since her eldest boy had been granted the title of Lord Commander by King Vaelor five years ago and put in charge of the newly created military. She loved Vulfram entirely; none of her other four children came close, not even Rachida, her youngest, the legendary beauty who had fled Neldar at the age of eighteen. His visits were almost as rare as her journeys back to Erznia. And so Soleh's dreariness grew, and only by gazing upon the many statues of her beloved god could she hold her depression at bay.

She passed by one of those statues, a nine-foot-tall likeness of Karak wearing his plate armor, the sigil of a lion emblazoned on his chest, a great flaming sword held skyward in his hand. Her hands reached out, her fingers caressing the smooth marble foot perched atop the base. A fluttering filled her belly, flushing her cheeks. Her husband Ibis had carved this statue and many others situated around the city proper. His workmanship was exquisite; he was a man with gifted hands. She would do well to return to his workshop in the Tower Keep when her workday was finished, so he could prove once more just how gifted those hands were.

The crowd parted slightly and the presence of the City Watch became more pronounced as the gates to the Castle of the Lion came into view. It was a majestic creation, built by the hands of Karak in the year before he disappeared. The wall of the castle stood thirty feet high, and the three towers behind it stood higher than that. The first was Tower Honor, the residence of King Eldrich Vaelor I. Tower Servitude housed the large royal staff, and Tower Justice was where the High Court was held. The dungeons were tucked away beneath it. The wall itself was constructed from giant hunks of stone wrestled down from the Crestwell Mountains, polished to a crystalline sheen at the top and engraved with drawings by the greatest artists of the nation. The sight of it took Soleh's breath away, just as it did every time her eyes fell on it. The images of the unwashed masses fled her mind. Seeing the Castle of the Lion in all its glory only confirmed the heights humanity could reach when its passion for righteousness was strong. They had already accomplished so much in a scant ninety-three years, and for nearly half that time Karak, their guiding light in the darkness, had left them on their own. It only made their achievements all the more impressive.

Our *achievements*, Soleh corrected herself. *You may be timeless, but do not forget you are one of them.*

The portcullis was open, framed on either side by a pair of leaping lions carved from onyx. Their claws stretched out, their mouths frozen open in a primal roar. Civilians drifted in and out of the gate, some carrying goods for the king, some bringing food for the granaries. A few entered with heads held high, while others did so with the downcast gaze of the timorous. Still others exited the portcullis with tears streaming down their faces. Guards bordered either side of the entrance, ushering them all to move along.

Soleh approached the wide aperture, stroking the nose of the soaring lion on her left. The Palace Guard recognized her immediately, and the sound of plated boots clomping together rang out as they came to attention. She called out their names one by one, causing smiles to stretch across their faces. "Hoster, Jericho, Luddard, Smithson, Bardot, Crillson." The men appreciated it when members of the First Families remembered their names, though Soleh knew she was one of the few who did.

She crossed the courtyard, passing through the crowd of jugglers, poets, puppeteers, and salesmen who made every day a bazaar on the castle lawn. She greeted as many as she could, whether she knew them or not, offering them broad smiles and good tidings. For a moment she reconsidered her longing to be back in Erzia, but then she came on the ominous oak door of Tower Justice, where she would be spending the rest of her day, and realized that the smiles and good tidings ended there.

Pushing open the door—it was tall, quite heavy, and creaked on its iron hinges—she strode into the vestibule. The tower was immensely wide, and the lower chamber was round, with a short ceiling. A staircase wound up the northern curve of the wall leading to the main courthouse above. Guards stood at attention, safeguarding the sixteen doors that lined the interior. Each of those sixteen doors led to holding cells that held up to thirty prisoners. Those prisoners would be her responsibility for the day.

"Minister," said Malcolm Gregorian, Captain of the Palace Guard. He was a solidly built man dressed in a dyed black leather overcoat over a vest of chainmail. The golden half helm he wore was adorned with catlike ears at the top, whereas the rest of the guards' helms were plain silver and without decoration. His face was marred by four ugly scars that ran diagonally from his milky left eye, over his nose, and down to the lower right corner of his jaw. He stepped forward and handed Soleh a folded piece of parchment.

She unfolded it and read it line by line. It was the day's docket, and from the looks of it, the day would be a long one.

"My cloak please, Captain," she said.

Malcolm snapped his heels together, marched to the alcove on the far side of the circular room, and brought out a black woolen cloak emblazoned with a red lion. He draped it over her shoulders, fastening the silver buckles around her neck, taking care not to brush her breasts. It was considered sacrilege to touch the most sensitive areas of the Minister, even by accident—though Soleh never let anyone know that should it happen, she would not create a fuss. She grabbed the corners of the cloak, pulled the hood over her head, and wrapped the heavy material around herself.

With the cloak all but covering her extravagant green dress, she climbed the stairs. It was late summer, and the heat outside the castle walls was intense, but inside the tower was a permanent chill. She placed one foot over the other and ascended into the Hall of Judgment.

Two women were waiting for her in the antechamber The first was Thessaly Crestwell, possessed of gently flowing hair that tread the line between white and chrome. She looked regal in an elegantly woven suit of crushed velvet leggings and leather chemise. Beside her was Soleh's daughter, Adeline. Deep, gouge-like wrinkles surrounded her eyes, her hair was gray and thinning, and an ill-fitting dress wrapped around her slender frame. Each day Soleh witnessed the two of them standing side by side, and each day the sight caused her mood to plummet. Thessaly looked the same as she had in her youth, stately and smooth, whereas Adeline, born eight months before her, showed every day of her sixty-three years. Adeline had married the love of her life at twenty, whereas Thessaly, like all the Crestwells, had remained single. Soleh's sorrow grew, for she herself had not aged a day in ninety-three years, and each of her children was slowly withering away before her. In accordance with the law of the First Families, the first generation brought forth by the original four remained timeless until the day someone other than their god took primacy in their hearts, until they felt a love so completely that they might crumble without their beloved. Each of her children had fallen in love and started families, sealing their fates, and Soleh was plagued by the knowledge that they would perish while she would go on. It gave her no solace that their memories would be kept alive through her grandchildren and beyond, and she had no desire to continue bringing forth children.

An unbalanced grin stretched across Adeline's face, and she dropped to one knee.

"Mother," she said, her voice reedy and wavering. "Welcome, welcome! I've been told there will be many beheadings this fine day!"

Soleh sighed, placed a gentle hand on her daughter's forehead, and said, "Get up, child." Adeline did as she was told, a stifled cackle leaking from between her tightly clenched teeth. Adeline's husband had died of the Wasting eleven years prior. Every day since, her sanity had diminished, an agonizingly slow devolution that had left a crowing madwoman in place of a once beautiful and competent girl. Adeline had taken to wandering the streets, shouting at peasants and attacking the City Watch in fits of madness. Soleh had named her Mistress of Punishment, if for no other reason than to give the girl something to focus on, but in the end her appointment had been fruitless. Adeline suggested beheading for every offense, even for something as minor as stealing a loaf of bread. She only kept her title because of Soleh's insistence.

Thessaly bowed and stepped forward. She was Mistress of the Treasury, a necessary advisor when it came to crimes in gold and trade. "The court is ready for you, Minister," she said. "Shall we begin?"

"We shall," replied Soleh. She breezed past the two women and through the arched portal. The courthouse was immense, every bit as wide as the foyer below, but there was no ceiling. The area above rose up and up, the tip of the tower spire a mere pie plate from the vantage point of those standing in the Place of Judgment. The room was lit by hundreds of candelabras, coupled with the sunlight that streamed in through the slatted windows. It was a barren, depressing place, bereft of any furniture other than the three massive chairs sitting atop a rostrum opposite the antechamber. Soleh strode across the empty courthouse floor, climbed the short staircase on the raised platform, and sat in the Seat of the Minister. It was a tall-backed, white marble throne just as large as King Vaelor's throne in Tower Honor, though much less extravagant. Above the throne hung a tapestry. Written in elegant calligraphy on it were the Laws of Karak.

Do not kill without reason. Do not murder the unborn. Do not take what is not yours. Do not defile the temple of worship. Do not turn away from Karak.

Adeline sat below her to the left and Thessaly, to the right. Moments later, the sound of marching footfalls sheathed in steel echoed through the room, and Captain Gregorian appeared. He saluted his Minister with a fist over his heart and clomped into the center of the circular common floor.

"Court is in session," he bellowed.

One by one, guards led prisoners up the winding staircase to stand in judgment before the Minister. They were brought in order of the severity of their crimes, beginning with those accused of minor theft or uttering offensive language in a public place. For every accusation Captain Gregorian read off, Adeline would yell, "Take off their head!"—a proclamation Soleh politely ignored. Thessaly proved much more useful, doling out the charges and collecting fines from the convicted to be placed in the coffers and used for the betterment of the realm. The charges grew steeper as the day went on, each prisoner groveling at Soleh's feet, begging clemency. Sometimes she granted it; often she did not. The City Watch did not tend to detain the innocent, and their evidence was often ironclad.

It was past the high point of the day, after an hour break for lunch, when the most severe crimes were heard. Arsonists, rapists, murderers, organized thieves, and blasphemers all stood before her. This was when Adeline's constant calls for death might be acted upon. No man or woman guilty of such offenses was set free, in accordance to the Law of the Divinity. The guilty could either accept the sentence handed down—death or a lifetime of servitude in the Sisters of the Cloth for women of birthing age—or attempt to prove their repentance to Karak by standing before the Final Judges.

Soleh's head pounded as she sent yet another man to his grave. The day couldn't end soon enough. The final and most egregious of the offenders was hauled before the Seat of the Minister. He was a thick, brutish thug with a black beard filled with lice and a head of long, unkempt hair. Blood covered his face and clothes, and he panted out streams of red spittle while staring up at Soleh. His arms and legs were shackled, like those of all major offenders. Two members of the Palace Guard forced him to his knees with heavy knocks from hollow rods. Joining the accused in the room were Romeo and Cleo Connington, a pair of fat, bald brothers, dressed in elegant silk shifts, whose fingers were adorned with expensive jewels. Soleh couldn't have been less happy to see them. The Conningtons were high merchants specializing in luxurious textiles, but more recently they had branched out to supply armor and weapons to the City Watch. The family was close to King Vaelor and had been granted special amnesty by Clovis Crestwell himself. The brothers stood off to the side, smirks on their waxed and powdered faces. Their house guard surrounded them.

"Why are you here?" asked Soleh.

Romeo, the older, stepped forward. "This man, Gronk Hordan of Thettletown, stands accused of raping and murdering my brother's daughter, Pricilla. Her body now lies in the crypt below our holdfast in Riverrun. She had been defiled so grievously that we had to hide her from her mother."

"The man is scum," said Cleo. "We've come to ensure that retribution is swift and brutal, and that those who paid him to do it are equally punished."

Soleh was disgusted by the lack of emotion on Cleo Connington's rotund face and the amused expression on Romeo's, but she kept her feelings to herself.

"Paid? What do you mean by that?"

"If it would please the Minister," said Captain Gregorian, bowing low. "It is claimed by some that Matthew Brennan ordered the attack."

"And have you investigated the matter, Captain?"

"I have."

"What are your findings?"

"Inconsequential, as of the moment."

Soleh had suspected as much. The Brennans, who had built a shipping empire out of Port Lancaster, had long been at odds with the Conningtons. Matthew Brennan often violated palace trade regulations and willingly paid his fines on the rare occasions when the local magistrate came calling. Soleh knew that the Conningtons would do anything to dishonor their rivals. This was not the first time they had tried to connect Matthew with a heinous crime. The possibility of his involvement seemed remote at best.

He was a good man, despite his penchant for bending the rules in his favor.

"And you," said Soleh, turning her attention to the prisoner. "What do you have to say on the matter?"

Gronk Hordan fixed her with a brutal stare.

"I weren't paid by no man," he growled. "And I didn't attack no girl, either. Lies, all of it."

The denial meant nothing to Soleh. The accused always proclaimed their innocence, no matter how heavy the proof against them.

"Is that so?" she said.

"It is, Minister."

Soleh looked to Captain Gregorian. The soldier straightened up and said in his gravelly voice, "Milady, the bite marks on her abdomen match the dentition of the accused."

"Castration!" shouted Adeline, spittle flying from her lips. It was the only other punishment she ever demanded. "Cut off his cock and make him choke on it!"

"Shush, dear," Soleh whispered out the corner of her mouth. She regarded the men standing before her. "Masters Connington, Karak appreciates your concerns, and they are duly noted. Please exit the court at once."

"And what of my retribution?" asked Cleo, finally showing some emotion. "You're going to let that Matthew bastard get away with this forever?"

Soleh shuddered at the sight of the sickening man.

"Escort these men from the court," she told her guards, who immediately laid their hands on the brothers and pushed them into the antechamber. Their house guard followed, mindful not to oppose those in authority.

"Karak's justice is Karak's justice," Soleh called after them as they disappeared into the porthole. "It is not for you to demand retribution, but *him*."

"The prisoner awaits sentencing," announced Captain Gregorian once they were gone, his grip tight around Gronk's chains.

"Very well," replied Soleh. "By the power of this court, handed down by Karak, the Divinity of the East and father to us all, I hereby sentence you to death by beheading. Do you accept this judgment with an open heart, knowing that Afram awaits if you are repentant, or do you wish to prove your faithfulness before the Final Judges?"

"I done no wrong," muttered Gronk Hordan. "I'll prove my faithfulness."

"So be it," sighed Soleh. She wasn't surprised, as at least one prisoner a day thought himself or herself worthy of Karak's forgiveness. The existence of the Final Judges was no secret, but none seemed to understand what it meant to face them and how few lived to tell the tale. "Captain, escort the prisoner to the arena."

Adeline opened her mouth again, but Soleh silenced her daughter with a glare. She glanced down at Thessaly, who stood from her minor seat and curtsied before taking her leave. The silver-haired Crestwell grabbed Adeline's wrist, yanking the aged woman to a standing position before dragging her along the wall to the antechamber. As Mistresses, the two were not allowed to observe the decision of the Final Judges. Her daughter struggled and swayed on failing old knees, and Soleh was again pummeled with shame and guilt. It wasn't until both women were out of sight that she rose from her throne, lifted the corners of her cloak, and descended the staircase. She strode past the prisoner, who was snatched by two guards, and crossed the courthouse floor, stopping to rinse her dry face at the washbasin, before taking the winding stairwell down. Captain Gregorian followed behind her, the prisoner with his rough escorts after him.

They did not stop when they reached the vestibule, instead continuing down into the depths below the castle. With each step they took, the air grew colder and wetter, and the rough gray walls were slick with moisture. The clanking of plated feet on stone echoed throughout the chamber, the only sound other than the prisoner's labored breathing.

The stairwell finally came to an end, the path branching in two directions. The left led to the dungeons, and the right was a plain door lit by a single torch. *Here Awaits the Final Judgment* was carved into the old, moldy wood. Soleh gripped the door's brass ring and pulled. It slid open, emitting a waft of air that was pungent with refuse and rot. She had to hold her hand in front of her face to shield herself from the intense brightness on the other side.

The stairwell emptied out onto a raised platform overlooking a circular ring of tall boulders, with another set of stairs leading down to the arena's gate. The underground hollow was lit by a thousand torches that were never extinguished, the combined flames as bright as the sun on a brutal summer day. Soleh drew back her hood for the first time in hours, approached the barrier of smooth sandstone, and placed her hands on it. The surface was warm from the heat of the torches. After a tilt of her head, the guards shoved their prisoner down the second set of stairs, tossed him unceremoniously into the middle of the ring, and then beat a hasty retreat. They tossed a key at him before slamming and locking the tall iron gate behind them. Gronk stood, spit out a glob of blood and dirt, and jangled his manacles. He picked up the key, and a few turns later the chains on his wrists and ankles fell to the ground with a heavy *clank*.

"You have requested audience with the Final Judges," Soleh said. "We shall bear witness to their decision. If you live, you are a forgiven man. If you perish, you have been deemed unworthy, and your soul awaits eternal damnation."

She nodded to her Captain.

Gregorian pulled a lever, raising a pair of metal gates from the walls of the arena below. Gronk faced the now opened portals, rubbing his hands together, breathing heavily. A soft, staccato-like purr filled the air, followed by an ear-splitting roar. The prisoner's knees began to shake as he struggled to hide his fear.

The judges stalked out of their cages like deadly shadows, and Soleh watched a puddle of liquid leak from the cuff of Gronk's filthy pants.

The two lions, Kayne and Lilah, Karak's Final Judges, stepped fully into the lighted arena. They were massive beasts, almost the height of a man on their four legs. Their golden fur shone with streaks of white, and their pale yellow eyes glistened in the torchlight. Kayne opened his mouth, exposing his lethal fangs while letting out a low, guttural snarl. Lilah strode alongside him, her tongue flicking her nose.

The lions paced a circle around the whimpering prisoner, growing ever closer with each revolution. They were toying with the man, goading him into histrionics and madness. Finally, Gronk snapped. He shot to his feet, shouting obscenities as he attempted to dart through the gap between the two lions. Kayne seemed to tilt his head and smirk as Gronk leapt onto the smooth stone that served as the arena wall. The man's hands could find no purchase, and he slid back down until his feet touched ground.

That was when Lilah charged, letting loose a throaty bellow as her gigantic paws kicked up dirt and dust. It took mere seconds for her to close the gap and leap onto Gronk's back. Her claws raked down to the spine, opening four gaping maws that spat crimson blood. Then the lioness's jaws closed around the man's skull. She pulled him down, shook him twice, and then whipped her head to the side. Gronk Hordan tumbled through the air, landing in a heap, just inches from Kayne's enormous feet.

"You have been judged," whispered Soleh.

The man was not dead. He lifted his head as if lost in a dream. Blood poured from the incisions where Lilah's teeth had pierced his face and neck. He swayed and rocked, swayed and rocked, moaning, unable to get to his feet. Kayne watched him for a moment before lashing out. His right paw raked across the prisoner's chest, opening four gashes that mirrored the ones on his back. Gronk collapsed belly-up, his eyes staring at the ceiling. Lilah sauntered over to stand beside her brother, and the two lions exchanged a momentary glance before they began to feed. One of the guards standing on the platform doubled over as the prisoner's screams filled the air. Coils of intestines slithered out of the man like so many eels, spraying all over the dirt-covered ground. The lions devoured Gronk where he lay, and his shrieks and wails slowly ebbed until all that could be heard was the smacking of the judges' tongues as they lapped up every last ounce of blood.

"Leave me," Soleh told Captain Gregorian, who ushered his two guards up the stairwell and out of the arena.

Kayne and Lilah were the only lions in all of Dezrel—and perhaps the only two that had ever existed. They'd been discovered on the doorstep of the Mori homestead sixty-seven years ago, on the day Soleh's precious Vulfram was born. They were but cubs then, gifts from Karak, and Soleh's family raised them as their own kin. The lions ate the food Soleh prepared for her family, slept in Vulfram's room, and ran and played with him and the rest of the children, even when they grew so large that they dwarfed the girls. Soleh didn't consider them pets; to her, they were another son and daughter. Unlike her flesh-and-blood children, however, Kayne and Lilah did not age. They simply grew larger with each passing year. Sometimes she wondered if they would grow to the size of horses.

It was Karak himself who had informed Soleh of their true reason for existence. Kayne and Lilah could sense a person's faithfulness, could understand the depths of his or her beliefs and loyalty. When the Castle of the Lion was built, and the first king was named to assist in governing their burgeoning society, the lions were brought north to Veldaren to fulfill this purpose. If any accused wished to prove their loyalty to the one true god of the land, he or she could face the lions in the arena.

In all her years as Minister, of all the hundreds of men and women she had escorted down into the bowels of the castle, only one man had passed the test. He still bore the four wicked scars running across his face to prove it. That man was Malcolm Gregorian, who now served beside her as Captain of the Palace Guard. A man who, even when the lions bore down upon him, refused to show fear.

She stood there for a long while, listening to Kayne and Lilah finish their meal. When they were done and had returned to their lavish pens, she pushed back the lever. The two gates slowly lowered, the winches squealing as thick ropes rubbed against them.

"Do you not like watching your children fulfill their duties?" asked a commanding yet familiar voice from behind her.

Soleh whirled around, eyes frantically scanning the darkness behind the torches' powerful glare. Her heart began to beat excitedly, and she feared she might faint.

"Of course not," she replied, her voice high and innocent, like a child's. "But I do so because it is my duty, just as it is theirs to punish the guilty."

The torches before her extinguished—the first time they had gone dark in more than forty years—and a pair of glowing yellow eyes stared at her from the new darkness. The eyes came closer, and a colossal figure stepped into the light of the remaining torches on the far wall. He was a picture of beauty, with hair a deep shade of earthy brown, eyes rich with wisdom, and thick and powerful arms and legs. He towered over her, wearing an outfit of woven black and a silver breastplate embellished with his sigil, the roaring lion. Soleh dropped to her knees as he offered her his hand.

"Karak, my Divinity, my Lord, my Father," she whispered. She began to weep.

"Stand, child," said Karak, his voice as soothing as hot milk on a chilly evening. "Stand and do not cry."

Soleh rose to her feet, and with a racing heart, brushed aside the large hand before her and threw herself at him. She collided with her god's belly, just below his metal breastplate, and wrapped her arms as far around his waist as she could. She buried her face into his clothes. He had the smell of winter about him, of snow and pines and smoke.

"You have been gone for so long," she said into his clothing. "I feared you wouldn't return."

"Forty years is not long, child," her god replied. He brushed back her hair, his touch warm and comforting. "Not to those like us."

"It seemed like a long time to me."

Karak laughed, and the sound filled the arena. Kayne and Lilah bellowed in their cages.

"You were always such a sweet girl, Soleh. So beautiful and innocent, so pure." He slipped a huge knuckle beneath her chin and lifted her head. "And those eyes, still like a babe filled with wonderment. The most beautiful thing I have ever created. I could gaze into them forever."

"So why did you leave me, my Lord?" she asked.

"I did not leave you, child. I have been near. I have heard your prayers, uttered every night by your bedside. I have watched as you dutifully fulfilled your promise to help the people learn to serve their own justice. You have helped our society grow strong, yet it cannot stand on your shoulders alone. You make me proud. You are one of the few who do."

Soleh took a step back. Doubt began to infiltrate her pure thoughts.

"I don't understand, my Lord," she said. "If you have been watching, then you know of the ugliness that has been spreading across our lands. The sickness, the greed, the violence. Years ago we had riots over the price of wheat. You are the God of Order, my Lord, and yet all I see is chaos."

Karak shook his head and smiled softly.

"You do not understand, my child. There is order in all things, eventually. I stepped away because you, my children, needed to grow up. You needed to learn to exist on your own, without me lording over you day and night. My children need to make their own decisions, to build their own destinies, to maintain their *own* order. If that does not happen, you will never be free. You will be slaves, just as the children of my brother are. You deserve freedom. I have given all of you the framework for success, and I leave it up to you to carry those lessons forward, to improve, to *thrive.*"

Soleh gazed once more into those beautiful eyes, larger than life itself, and saw the kindness and honesty in them. She could not help but smile. She stepped back and bowed, sweeping her arms out wide so that her cloak flowed over her like the cascade of a waterfall.

"You have, my Lord, and we are trying."

"That is all I can ask of you, sweet Soleh," replied the god. "Now if it pleases you, I should like to visit my temple and rest. The journey home has been a long one."

"Of course, my Lord."

"Will you walk with me for a while?"

"I would never think to do otherwise."

Soleh led Karak up the stairwell and out of Tower Justice. The god-made-flesh needed to stoop beneath the doorframe, even though it stood over ten feet tall. It was early evening, the half-moon low on the horizon, and yet the castle courtyard was teeming with people. All activity stopped when Karak emerged, and in an instant the crowd was dropping to their knees and singing his praises. Karak waved to his children, most of whom had never before seen him, a smile still painted across his large, handsome face. He bestowed his graces on them before guiding Soleh out of the main portcullis, leaving the people groveling and praying on the castle lawn.

All across Veldaren the same scene repeated itself over and over again. The evening crowd parted, and guards and commoners and thieves alike all chanted the name of their god. There was no violence to be seen, only reverence, and amidst this sudden outpouring of peace and togetherness, Soleh dared question Karak's decision to be gone for so long.

But Karak talked to her and only her, as if the multitudes around them didn't exist, and she forgot all of her doubts. He spoke of the sunset over Mount Hailen, of projecting his form from his body and soaring through the heavens. He told her of touching the constellations that lit up the northern sky, of the worlds that existed within each burning star, of lives beginning and lives coming to a close. All of these words he spoke in a velvety and intimate voice, luring her closer with each step, wrapping her body in the comforting embrace of his voice, until they reached the hub of the southern end of the city, where four roads met at a roundabout. At its center was a great fountain, on which stood a statue of the god that was taller than he was in real life, a regal work of art, created by Soleh's husband, showing the divinity on one knee, handing a child a spear. Karak stopped there, staring at the effigy, and the heavy weight of his arm fell on Soleh's shoulders. She leaned her head into his side, feeling the rumblings in her belly, the excitement that caused her legs to quiver.

It was then Karak left her, kissing her lightly on the forehead before stepping into the darkness of the northern road, no doubt riding the shadows to his temple far across the city. Soleh whirled around when he disappeared, her feet light as feathers. She danced through the worshiping populace, down the boulevard and across the cobbled walk. Her soft-soled shoes barely touched ground. She didn't notice the people around her, exiting pubs and closing their shops for the evening. All recollection of the day's docket left her mind, as did the memory of Gronk Hordan and his ugly demise. She didn't care that she'd forgotten to remove her Minister's cloak. Only one thought circled in her mind, and she whispered it again and again while she danced.

He is back! My Lord is back! Karak has returned to me.

She danced all the way to the Tower Keep in the center of the city, the place she had called home for the last forty years. It was a solemn building, designed by Jacob Eveningstar, the First Man, before he took up residence on the western side of the Rigon River. The tower had originally been intended to serve as the inner sanctum of the palace of the king, but Karak had built only half of it before deciding it was not lavish enough to inspire awe and obedience in the populace. Its cold gray walls were unwelcoming; its height and angularity, strangely dour; and the spire that rose into the night sky was like a fist constantly shaking at the city in anger. But Soleh didn't care, for her Lord was back. Karak had returned to her.

She threw open the door to the keep and slipped inside, spinning and singing and stomping her feet. The sound of clanking reached her ears, and she knew immediately what it meant. When she stepped into her husband's studio, the candles were lit on the walls, and the space was filled with the smell of the oils and acids used for curing stone. She tiptoed around chunks of discarded rock and sediment, and dozens of statues of her god, exacting replicas carved from mica, onyx, and marble. A few of the statues showed Karak flanked by Kayne and Lilah. On the wall beyond the main workstation, resting on a slightly raised platform, hung a huge painting crafted with unmatched skill and detail. At the center of an elaborate landscape swirled a giant portal, a great fire burning within it. Standing before the portal were the brother gods, one blond and the other brown-haired. Perched on the clouds above was a woman with hair as black as coal and eyes that were empty orbs of shadow. The painting had been created by the brother gods as a way of commemorating their arrival on Dezrel. It showed them with Celestia in front of the gateway that had brought them into this world. The painting had hung on that very wall since Karak began building the Tower Keep decades ago. It was the only work in the entire studio that had not been created by the sculptor who resided there.

At the center of it all was that sculptor, hacking away at a tall block of jet with his hammer and chisel. Soleh tiptoed up behind Ibis and slid her hands around his waist.

"Soleh, darling, you're home," said her husband.

She stepped back, giving him room to turn around. His eyes, jaw, hair, and physique were all perfect imitations of the statues he carved and installed throughout the city. He was Karak's absolute likeness, albeit in a smaller body. In the days after Karak and Ashhur created humanity, they gave each of the First Four a clay ewer with which to forge their mate. It was the first and only time a human had been granted the power of a god. Soleh, who had loved her creator since the moment she opened her eyes and saw his face, chose to make Ibis in his image. In a way, she told herself, he was like Karak made flesh, made flesh yet again.

"I have a surprise for you," she said, coyly.

"What is it?" asked Ibis.

Soleh backed away, beckoning him with her finger.

"In time," she purred. "But first, you must catch me."

It was a game they'd played since the very beginning of their ninety-three years of marriage. She tore off her cloak, spun around, and darted up three flights of stairs, heading for their chambers. By the time she reached their bed, she was already naked and soaked with sweat. And when Ibis leapt atop her, she took him into her arms and held him close, smelling his sweat, feeling his strength, allowing herself to pretend that he was the god he'd been molded to resemble.

My Lord is back, she thought as he kissed lines across her neck. *Karak has returned to me.*

CHAPTER

5

The girl moaned and thrashed her head while she rode him, her hair a sweat-soaked mess that whipped from side to side. Her young, slender body glistened in the candlelight, and her breasts bounded with each seductive motion. She couldn't be more than sixteen. She kept her eyes closed the entire time, shouting his name as she traced the outline of his body with tense hands. That alone convinced Patrick DuTaureau she was faking it. He'd experienced sincere lovemaking a few times before, most recently with a blind woman during a fishing trip to the seaside town of Conch. Not that this girl's fakery mattered much to him. The illusion did its job, and he felt his gut tighten. He shot his seed deep inside her, grinding his teeth and groaning as the girl let out a wild screech and threw back her head.

When it was over, the girl slid off him and lay on her back, giggling into her fists. She began singing a quiet tune, one her mother had most likely sung to her when she was just a babe. The innocence in her voice was enough to remind Patrick of how youthful she really was, forty-nine years his junior. He rolled away from her, slipping his feet over the side of the bed. The elation of the lovemaking faded quickly, his constant physical torment seeping back into the hidden chambers of his body. He dropped his head into his hands, stroked the knobbiness of his eyebrows, and abruptly stood. His sudden ascent from the downy mattress brought a surprised yelp from the girl, but she went right on singing a moment later.

Patrick wandered across the room, eyes downcast and gait lurching, and poured himself a glass of wine. He reached for the water pitcher next and splashed some water over his face. It was warm and not at all refreshing. He wiped the water off his flesh with an old tunic that was draped over the side of the basin. His fingers brushed the lumps above his eyes, his wide jaw, and the nonexistent slope of his sunken chin. He closed his eyes and said a quick prayer to Ashhur before finally lifting his gaze to the silver mirror hanging above the basin.

He stared at his ugliness head-on, ignoring his misshapen face, the welts covering his mottled skin, and the hideous, fanglike appearance of the crooked teeth in his much-too-wide mouth. What mattered was atop his head, the thatch of blood-red hair that coiled at odd angles like the tentacles of a sea beast. He leaned in closer, observing every strand as he worked his fingers through the untidy mop.

"Come on," he muttered, turning his head from one side to the other, frantically searching for a single strand of gray. His younger sister Brigid had told him she'd found her first silver mere moments after lying with her husband for the first time. Patrick didn't know how many times he had lain with a woman, but it had to be over a hundred by now.

Perhaps you simply haven't met the perfect someone, a girl who will love you completely in return.

Brigid was fond of saying that each time he complained about his dilemma. Patrick glanced over his knotted shoulder, watching the young, naked girl roll back and forth on the bed, knees held to her chest. She was certainly beautiful, but Brigid was right. She wasn't the perfect one for him. *How long will I need to search?* he wondered. *How long will this go on?*

Forever was the answer that trickled into his head, for he knew no girl could truly love him, not with his twisted spine, hunched back, monstrous hands, uneven legs, and repulsive face. He was an immortal monster who wished for mortality, who loved his family and his god and wished to experience *life*, not the repetitive droll of agelessness that had beleaguered him ever since his eighteenth birthday, the day his body had stopped growing. The way he understood it, only the love of someone other than Ashhur could cure him of this plague called *forever*. He wanted to grow old, to grow wise, and eventually to die a natural death. It was all he dreamed about.

The girl on the bed continued her repetitive swaying, the song on her lips much louder now. Patrick turned away from the mirror and faced her, and the expanse of the stone floor between them seemed like a thousand miles.

"What *are* you doing?" he asked.

The girl stopped her rocking and sat up on the bed. She caught sight of him in the flickering light of the candelabra and grimaced for the briefest moment. It was a look she smoothed away as fast as she could, with a quick shake of her head. The smile that stretched across her face was genuine, but he sensed the repulsion hidden beneath it. She deliberately slid her legs downward, parting them somewhat, and arched back her shoulders.

"I was quickening the seed," she replied almost sheepishly, which sounded outlandish given her pose. "I'm going to have a child of a First Family." She stroked her stomach, which shimmered with moisture. "I can feel it working already. In here."

Patrick laughed, holding his deformed face in his hand.

"What you're feeling is most likely indigestion from the shrimp we ate earlier, or maybe a bit too much of wine. Either way, you aren't with child. Not mine, anyway."

The girl looked confused. "Why is that, sir?"

"My seed is as ruined as myself, I fear. I can have no children."

"How do you know?"

"I'm sixty-five years old. I have bedded many women, and none of them have quickened."

"Oh." The girl's lower lip quivered. She looked like someone who had just stepped in a pile of manure. "I didn't know."

Patrick limped toward her and hunched down, getting on one knee and taking her hand in his. She recoiled once more but did an admirable job of keeping her composure.

"Was that why you came here?" he asked. "To beget a child?"

The girl nodded.

He frowned. "You might have told me so. I would have been honest with you."

"But I thought," she said, her voice shaky, "I thought you'd be insulted, sir."

"Ha! Look at me, girl. Take a good look. I'd have bedded you even if you were only doing it to take revenge on a jilted lover. Trust me; in matters of sex, I'm not picky." He leaned back and held his arms out wide to prove his point. "I can't afford to be."

That elicited a laugh from the girl. She brought her fist to her mouth and sucked on her knuckle for a moment before saying, "I apologize for exploiting you, sir."

Patrick guffawed. "Really, there was nothing to exploit. I enjoyed myself. Did you?"

The girl shrugged. "I suppose so, sir."

Patrick rolled his eyes.

"Fantastic. Glad I could be of service, Bethany. And stop calling me *sir*. That is a knight's title, and in this world knights only exist in the Wardens' stories. Just one person here calls himself that, and if I'm being honest, that man is something of a prick."

"Um, my name's Brittany, sir...sorry...what do I call you?"

"Patrick is fine. It is my name, after all. And I apologize for forgetting yours."

"'Tis all right, sir. I mean Patrick."

Patrick rose unsteadily to his feet and grabbed the gray hemp shift the girl had been wearing off the floor. He tossed it to her. "You should get dressed. I'm sure your father is quite worried about you by now."

Brittany slipped the shift over her head, gradually covering up that wonderful body of hers. She seemed relieved to have an excuse to leave.

"You're right, I should be getting home. But don't worry about Father. He's most likely at temple praying. He and Mother do that every night. It's only just dark, and they don't usually get home until later in the evening."

"Of course they don't," said Patrick.

Hurriedly, Brittany gathered up her sandals, slinging them over her shoulder. She breezed past him, but Patrick seized her arm lightly, stopping her in her tracks.

"Do you think you could ever love someone like me?" he asked. He knew how pathetic the question sounded, but he needed to ask it.

Brittany lowered her eyes and shook her head.

"I thought not. Good night, Brittany."

"Good night, Patrick," she replied, and hastened for the exit. Her footfalls were already halfway down the hall when the door to his room slammed shut.

"By Ashhur," he muttered. "At least she was a good lay."

He immediately regretted his words and offered a silent apology to his god. A chill came over his naked body as he thought again of how the girl had called him *sir*. He was a good man—Ashhur insisted he was—but was he truly noble? *Could* he be noble? He had his doubts.

With this in mind he walked across the room and reached for the sword leaning against his bedpost—a long, gleaming, silver mammoth of a blade that had been given to him twelve years before, when he had escorted his sister Nessa through the southern marshlands on the other side of Ashhur's Bridge. She'd been nineteen at the time, the youngest DuTaureau by nearly three decades. Obsessed with wildlife, Nessa had wanted to look at the giant water lizards that congregated on the banks of the tributaries, warming their bellies beneath the intense southern sun.

It was during their journey home with a disappointed Nessa— the water lizards had been chased out of the area by the burgeoning township of Haven—that they stumbled upon a pack of bandits attacking a horse and carriage bearing the banners of Karak. The bandits were chopping at the wooden cart with their swords and daggers as someone shouted desperately from inside. Patrick left Nessa sitting astride her horse and rushed to the aid of the helpless occupant of the carriage, moving much more quickly than anyone would have believed him capable. Though he had no fighting experience other than wrestling Bardiya Gorgoros—the other freak of Ashhur's First Families—he'd been able to hold off the bandits until a beautiful and strong young man leapt from within the wagon, a huge sword in his hands. Together they fended off the thieves, leaving them to flee, bloodied and beaten, into the swamp. The tip of the young man's sword still dripped blood when Patrick approached him. The stranger introduced himself as Crian Crestwell, son of Clovis and Lanike of House Crestwell, one of Karak's First Families. Crian had dropped to his knees, thanked Patrick for his help, and handed him his sword as a token of appreciation. "The smith calls it Winterbone, as it was forged in the snows of the northern mountains that bear the name of my family," the young man had said. "It is a good blade. It will never dull." And with that young Crian Crestwell departed, leaving a kiss on the back of Nessa's hand as his final parting gift. The girl had blushed for weeks afterward.

Patrick cocked his head and stared at the weapon. From what he could tell, Winterbone was the only sword that existed in all of Ashhur's Paradise. There was simply no practical need for swords. But *Patrick* needed Winterbone. His possession of the massive blade impressed many of the ladies who would have normally offered him looks of disgust. They were drawn in by the long and slender cutting edge, the golden pommel cast to look like a femur, and the strange, reflective crystal that jutted from the base of the handle. Possession of the blade made him attractive when he was by all rights ugly, made him interesting when he was anything but.

He drew the sword from its scabbard and lifted it. Crian had been correct; the blade never dulled. It whistled through the air with even the gentlest of movements. At over four feet long, it was a heavy sword. Even with his oversized shoulders, Patrick had a difficult time keeping it steady. He braced his feet apart, unbalanced given the unevenness of his legs, and a familiar shooting pain charged up his mangled spine. He pushed himself through it, flinging his free arm out wide and gradually bringing his sword arm up, flexing his muscles to steady them both. He held Winterbone parallel to the ground, its tip aimed at the mirror that mocked him from across the room.

There was a knock at his bedroom door, and Patrick's first thought was that Brittany had forgotten something and returned.

"Come in," he shouted, keeping his pose even though his right arm began to tremble. Perhaps this show of strength, holding a two-handed broadsword out straight with one hand, might impress her.

"Patrick, put your clothes on."

His concentration broken, his sword arm faltered, sending agony into his forearm, and the blade came crashing down. He leapt out of the way on his too small feet just as the cutting edge swung close to his toes. Winterbone rattled against the stone floor. Shaking his hand, he turned toward the door. His sister Cara stood there, hands on her hips. A single streak of gray weaved its way through her strawberry-colored hair, taunting him.

"You're going to hurt yourself," she said.

"I'm fine."

"You almost cut off your toe."

Patrick grabbed a pair of pants from atop his bureau and sat down on the bed to pull them on. "I was *fine*," he mumbled.

Cara gestured to his bed and the mussed sheets atop it. "Your guest seemed nice," she said.

"She was."

"She left in a hurry."

"They always do."

"Oh. That's a shame."

Patrick slapped his knees and glared at his sister. "Do you have a reason for being here, Cara?"

His sister frowned. "Mother wants to see you in the atrium."

"Now?"

She nodded.

"Fantastic."

Cara slipped out the doorway without another word, leaving Patrick alone with his guilt. He knew his sister cared for him—all of his sisters did. But Patrick had long tired of their constant attention. They treated him like he was a child, despite the fact that he was the second oldest of their parents' children and a ripe old sixty-five. Despite their love, he knew only Nessa saw him as an equal. And if he was being honest with himself, he often believed himself inferior to the others as well.

He picked up Winterbone with care and slid the sword back into its scabbard, then stepped out into the candlelit hallway. The corridor of Manse DuTaureau, the bastion of House DuTaureau, was so long that when he was younger, he used to pretend it could stretch across the Rigon and into the land of Karak. Soft rugs sewn by the elder women from the first generation decorated the hall. They tickled the bottoms of his bare feet with their swooping lines and giant ovals colored red, green, and gold. He passed bedroom after empty bedroom before seeing soft flickering light from Nessa's billet. He stopped at her doorway, looking in on her. The youngest DuTaureau was huddled in the corner at her desk, her back to him, scribbling away on a piece of parchment. He thought about asking her to join him, but decided against it.

He threw open the double doors to the atrium and limped inside. His eyes widened when he took in the fact that the rest of his family was gathered inside. His mother sat in her large chair by the window, her eyes fixed on the scroll in her lap, as his father crouched on the floor in front of her, rubbing her feet. Cara stood behind her mother, directing an unsure glance in Patrick's direction, and Brigid and Keela, two of his younger sisters, played blocks with Patrick's nephews. Besides Nessa, the only sibling missing was Abigail, who lived with her husband, Turock Escheton, in a northern village where the western half of the Gods' Road reached its end.

The window behind his mother was open, and a hawk was perched before it. The bird's crest had been plucked of feathers and a red stripe had been painted on its pale flesh, identifying the creature as a herald from Safeway.

"Someone sent a bird," Patrick said, uncomfortable with the hushed gathering.

"Someone did," replied his mother.

Isabel and Richard DuTaureau turned their attention to him. His parents were shockingly similar in appearance, both of them possessing the same fiery red hair and willowy frame. They also shared high cheekbones, slender jaw lines, slightly upturned noses, and a spattering of starburst-like speckles on their faces. The braver commoners whispered that Isabel had fallen in love with her own image so that when Ashhur granted her the power to create her lifetime companion, she had made him look just like herself. There were even those in Mordeina who whispered that Isabel's act of vanity had been the cause of Patrick's deformity. Patrick wasn't sure if the story had any truth to it, but it seemed odd that he would be the one singled out and not his sisters, who were all near perfect replicas of their mother and father. Still, he had never explored the matter or asked Ashhur about it. Honestly, he didn't want to experience the pain that would come with knowing the truth, whatever that truth might be.

"I assume the message is for me?" he asked.

"It is," said Isabel.

Richard backed up a few paces, allowing his wife and matriarch the space to rise from her chair. She approached her son and handed him the bowed scroll. He took it in his knobby fingers and flattened it against the wall.

"It's from Jacob," he said, his eyes flashing over the tight scrawl of the First Man of Dezrel. "He's heading north, passing by Mordeina to go on a scouting mission to the Tinderlands. It seems—"

"I know what is in the letter," said Isabel abruptly.

"So you've read it? It is good to know my privacy means so much to you."

"This is no laughing matter, Patrick. An army of Karak attacked the township of Haven, killing Martin Harrow. You remember Martin, correct? The youth Judarius chose as a kingling? Jacob wants you to ride to the delta in the hopes that you can convince Deacon Coldmine to tear down his temple. Apparently, he sees more use in you than I do."

Patrick leaned his head back as far as it would go, so that it was resting against the bulge of his humped back. It was a gesture of frustration that he had perfected since childhood.

"Thank you for saving me the trouble of actually *reading* the note addressed to me."

His mother's expression didn't change. It rarely did. The only time that look of stern consternation dropped from her face was when she was staring at her husband. He thought again of the story of his parents' creation, and shuddered.

"This is important, Patrick. I am trying to make you understand that."

"I understood it when I read *This is important*, spelled out right here. Look."

"Don't mock me."

"No. Don't mock *me*."

Isabel fixed him with a venomous stare. His father averted his eyes, avoiding any involvement in the scene. Unlike Patrick's sisters, his mother had never doted on him. She'd acted like he was a burden for as long as he could remember. It struck him as humorous, in a very sad way, that a timeless woman who preached Ashhur's sermons of love and forgiveness should treat her own child with such coldness. But at least coldness was *something*. His father hadn't spoken to him in over a decade, even though they lived beneath the same roof. It was as if, in Richard's eyes, it would be better if Patrick didn't exist.

Without another word, Isabel returned to her position in the straight-backed chair. Her husband started rubbing her feet again, and she picked up her knitting from beneath the dais and began clicking away with her needles. Patrick rolled his eyes at them both. Apparently their business with him was done.

"What I want to know," he said, his voice dripping with irritation, "is why Jacob doesn't go there himself. It's only a three-day journey to the Tinderlands from here. If I write him and ask what he's seeking, I would be more than happy to look for it myself. As it is, we will likely pass each other on the way, which seems impractical."

"Jacob speaks for Ashhur," his mother said without lifting her head from her knitting. "Do not question the orders of your god."

"But, Mother, if—"

"Enough. The decision is made. Leave us."

"Fine."

Patrick wheeled around and stumbled out of the atrium. Brigid and Keela moved to follow him, their faces awash with pity, but he brushed away their consoling hands. He heard the sound of Cara weeping softly behind him, followed by his mother's scolding. Disgust roiled in his midsection, and it struck him that only a few minutes earlier there had been something much more pleasant churning down there. He wished Brittany were still around. Another roll with the young temptress would have done wonders for his morale.

He slammed the double doors of the atrium shut behind him. When he turned, he was startled to see Nessa, her hands clenched just below her mouth. She had been listening in at the door. Tears streamed down her cheeks, dripping into the collar of the heavy white nightdress she wore. Her strawberry hair was a tangled mess. Though she was over thirty, she still looked like the same innocent babe she'd been when she was but a teen. Even her stature, shortest of the DuTaureaus, hinted at incredible youth. It seemed as though Nessa's development had been irrevocably arrested in almost every way.

"I'm sorry, Patrick," she whispered, throwing herself into his arms.

Patrick huffed when she rammed her head into his chest. He embraced her, feeling her warmth. When he leaned her back and kissed her cheek, he could taste the salt of her tears.

"It's all right, Ness," he whispered. "I'm used to it by now."

"But why is Mother so *mean*?"

He shrugged. "Guess she doesn't like having a monster for a son."

She punched him in the shoulder. He was surprised by how much it hurt.

"You're not a monster."

Patrick laughed. "So you keep telling me, sister. You almost make me believe it."

He blew out the candles closest to the atrium door and, throwing one huge arm over his sister, escorted her down the hall.

"You know," he said, "we should run off together. You and I. You with your shortness, me with my freakishness—we could take the south by storm. Maybe in Karak's lands we could establish ourselves a career as performers. We could learn about money, and how quickly it vanishes. It could be fun!"

Nessa passed him a hopeful look. "Or we could simply go to the delta."

Patrick laughed. "And why would you choose to go with me? Didn't you visit there just last month?"

"Yes, but it's late summer, and the barking cranes are migrating. I've heard they gather in such great numbers that the marshlands look like they're covered with writhing maggots for miles."

"That's a pleasant image."

"They're not gross maggots. They're…feathery maggots. Please, Patrick, take me with you."

Patrick laughed.

"Very well. Just make sure you're the one who tells Mother you're coming. I don't think I have the stomach to speak to her for a few years, maybe even a decade."

"I imagine not," she replied with a tinkling laugh. "When will we be leaving?"

Patrick let out a grunt. "Let me get some sleep, and we'll go first thing tomorrow."

"That's good, actually," said Nessa. Her eyes brightened and she wiped the last vestiges of tears from her speckled, rosebud cheeks. "Make sure to wake me at dawn. I must go feed the birds."

She spun around and ran down the hall, her tiny feet making no impression on the thick rug.

"Feed the birds?" he shouted after her. "Now? But it's dark."

"I forgot earlier," he heard her reply as she disappeared around the bend in the hall. Patrick shrugged his shoulders.

"Strange little girl," he said and then chuckled. Who was he to talk?

He returned to his room and flopped down on his bed, which still smelled of Brittany. Pulling the covers up and nestling them beneath his nose, he let the smell of femininity carry him off into a very much needed and dreamless sleep.

CHAPTER

6

M*y love,*
It has been only forty-nine days since our last con-gregation, forty-nine days since my lips kissed yours, and I miss you so. Each passing day is like torture as I lie alone, dreaming of your face, the sweep of your hair, the smell of your skin. My family surrounds me, oftentimes oppressively so, and yet I have never felt so alone.

I wish to see you. I need to see you. Not a moment goes by that I don't wish to be in your bed once more. I long to hear your voice as you prattle of tariffs and trade laws and the courts. You have a way of brightening even the dreariest of subjects. I want to hear you speak of your battles with the Carstakian mobs, your hunts for the immense wolves of the northern hills. Life is dreadful here, all prayer circles and farming and preparing meals for the family. Surely we, as a people, were made for much more. And when I look at the life you live, it all seems so much more interesting, full of adventure and struggle, each day a new challenge. Yes, I know it's sometimes daunting, and the thought of thieves roaming the night sends a chill up my spine, but I know that if you were by my side, I would always be safe.

I know our love is forbidden. I know our two worlds were meant to be kept separate. But I cannot bear another day without you. I need to see you. Tomorrow I leave for the delta with my brother. I do not know how long we will stay, but from the way my brother speaks of things, the visit may last for many months. I beg that you bid leave of the city you call home and meet me here. Please, come quickly. It will be difficult to evade the eyes of my brother, but if we must, we can meet at your sister's cabin by the river bend as we did before. Perhaps this time we will make a son, and then neither of our families can deny our bond.

I love you entirely, my fearless warrior of the light.
Yours forever, in this world and the next,
   Nessa

Crian Crestwell's eyes traced back to the beginning of the note, taking in every looping letter written in Nessa DuTaureau's whimsical penmanship, every *i* dotted with a circle, every *g* swooping low to invade the line below. He folded the curled parchment in half, then leaned back in his chair. The hawk perched on the windowsill crowed, and he tossed a hood over its head to silence it. His mind drifted back to the three days he and Nessa had spent at his exiled sister Moira's secluded cabin by the river. It was then that they'd finally consummated their long-secret relationship, and now he could think of nothing but her. He felt a sort of lightness pervade his being.

Last month, his father had sent him to Brent, which bordered the Quellan forest, to assist his sister Avila in pushing back a group of brigands who had been poaching on elven lands. On his way back he'd tarried in Haven under the pretense of seeing Moira. It had been difficult to hide his meetings with Nessa then, and it would be even harder to see her now. As Left Hand of the Highest, it was his duty to keep Karak's peace in the townships beyond the northern borders, where the regime's authority was at its weakest. Both he and his brother Joseph, the Right Hand, served as de facto judge, jury, and executioner when outside the boundaries of Veldaren or Erznia. Only now, given Vulfram Mori's ascension to Lord Commander, Crian's responsibilities included acting as Captain of the City Watch in Veldaren. Finding a suitable excuse for traveling to the delta was a troublesome proposition. His place was in the city now, not trolling the outlying townships in search of poachers, bandits, blasphemers, and other such lawbreakers.

The other fly in the ointment was the volatile nature of Haven itself. When last he visited, the town had been an afterthought for both his father and his god. But the attack had changed everything, and Karak himself had just returned after four decades. Though he had never met the deity in person—Karak had left Neldar before his birth—he and his family were still beholden to the god above all else.

Yet Crian knew he would still try, for even with his duties to his god and his realm, Nessa DuTaureau was all he could think about. It had been that way since their first meeting, and those feelings had only grown over their twelve years of clandestine correspondence.

Crian sighed, and walked over to the fire that burned in his room's hearth. He placed a kiss on the folded parchment, and then dropped the letter atop the coals. He watched as it was burned away into nothing, ensuring that their secret was kept for one more day.

A commotion from the window summoned him over for a look. The heartless geometry of the cold, drab city beyond the castle walls simmered in a heat-wrought haze. Down below, inside those walls, a brigade of armored men marched through the portcullis and into the courtyard, followed by three figures on horseback. A fleet of supply wagons rolled in after them. Crian gasped as he recognized the polished dome of the Lord Commander and the shock of white atop the heads of his father and sister. He had not expected the party back for another two days at least.

Someone knocked on his door.

"Sir Crestwell," shouted the voice of Leonard, his squire, "your father has returned."

"I know," Crian replied, his heart racing in panic.

"Do you wish me to help you dress?" the squire asked through the door.

"No…yes…just prepare my armor in the sacristy. I'll be there in a moment."

He heard Leonard's steps quicken down the hall. Crian rushed to his mirror, a framed, foot-and-a-half square chunk of rare dragonglass, a gift from his father on his eighteenth birthday. It was his most prized possession, tangible proof that the man whose seed created him truly cared. Leaning forward, Crian examined his reflection. His jaw was rigid, his chin wide, his cheekbones sturdy. His eyes were hazel, imbued with emerald threads that shot from his pupils like starbursts. He was handsome and robust, resembling his mother more than his father. As the youngest of the Crestwell children, he had always looked upon his visage as a blessing, setting him apart from his brothers and sisters, who had all inherited their father's silver hair and smooth, regal features.

But now that blessing had turned into a curse. A single strand of white pierced his flowing brown hair. It stuck out like a wolf in the middle of a herd of sheep, and he plucked it from his scalp, letting it drop to his feet while he anxiously searched for more. Thankfully, he found none. In a panic he dropped to his knees and searched for the rogue hair, dashing to the hearth once he found it. Onto the coals it went, to burn like Nessa's letter. Then he went to his desk, jotted a quick note on a small scrap of parchment—*I will try. Love, C*—and fastened the message to the hawk's leg. Afterward he opened a hidden compartment in his desk, removing a tiny swath of fabric from within. He cut free the wisp of birch bark that was tied below the hawk's neck, replacing it with the fabric. Poking his head out the window to make sure his father and sister were no longer in the courtyard, he thrust his arm out the portal, the hawk perched atop his thick leather glove.

"Fly, Atria," he said after removing the bird's hood, and it took flight.

Atria was Nessa's bird, trained over the last ten years specifically to act as courier for the messages between them. Fasten birch bark to the bird's neck, and it would seek out Crian. Do the same with a small bit of cloth dashed with rosemary perfume, and it would seek out Nessa. The system had never failed them in the past. He prayed to Karak that it would remain that way.

"Leonard!" he shouted.

It took ten minutes for his squire to assist him in putting on his plate armor. It was a bothersome ensemble, cast from pounded iron dipped in liquid silver. The breastplate was ornamented with the sigil of House Crestwell, that of a snake wrapped around the torso of a seated lion, their noses touching. A forked tongue, painted red, flicked from the face guard. As a finishing touch, he slid Integrity, the jewel-encrusted, curved saber that had been forged for him when he accepted the title of Left Hand, into the scabbard at his waist. The entire suit was heavy and uncomfortable, but his father, the Highest, had a weakness for custom and required his Left and Right dress according to their station on entering Tower Honor.

Sometime later, he stepped through the arched portal and into the Tower Honor, sweat beading on his brow from descending seventeen floors while in full platemail. The Palace Guard formed a line on either side of the corridor, eyes trained distantly on nothing, expressions blank. Crian passed between them, his footsteps muted by the purple carpet that led the way to the huge doors of the throne room.

Crian's father stood before those doors, Avila beside him, both dressed in their black leather riding attire. They appeared to be deep in conversation. Lord Commander Vulfram was nowhere to be seen. At the sound of his rattling movements, his father and sister looked up. The Highest offered Crian a dismayed look.

"You're late," Clovis said. "Tardiness is not an admirable trait for the Left Hand. In an altercation, the left strikes first. If the left hand is slow, the right will not be able to land the finishing blow."

It was a phrase Crian had heard a thousand times before. Inwardly he rolled his eyes, but he kept his expression as firm as granite. His father was critical of all his children, expecting the absolute best of them at all times. In his own way, Crian guessed, it was how he showed he cared.

"I beg your pardon, Highest," Crian said, dropping to one knee, taking his father's hand, and kissing it. From the corner of his eye, he saw Avila smirk. "I was not expecting you back so soon."

After he stood back up, his father fixed him with a sideways glance.

"And what were you doing?" he asked.

"I was getting some rest, Father."

"But it is nearing noon. A little early to be tired, is it not? I have just ridden for a week, sleeping in a dingy tent each night, and I am as alert as ever."

Crian tried to hold back an irritated sigh, but a slight puff of air escaped his lips.

"There was a riot in the financial district last night, Highest. A faction of disgruntled laborers set fire to the Brennan Depository in response to a supposed lowering of wages. It took most of the night to get the blaze under control and arrest the guilty parties. I did not return to the castle until dawn."

His father shook his head. "Exhaustion is no excuse. You are a Crestwell, ageless and mighty. You have many years ahead of you in which to rest."

"I'm sorry," Crian said, bowing. "As always, you are right."

A hand fell onto his plated shoulder. "Stand up, son. We must make our audience now."

They opened the doors and stepped into the throne room. Inside was a madhouse. People were everywhere, commoners and high merchants alike, shouting at each other, seeking the ear of the king with some complaint or another. The Council of Twelve, a collection of eleven men and one woman from different points around the kingdom, chosen by their people as representatives, cowered against the walls at the back of the room. Interspersed throughout were members of the Sisters of the Cloth, wrapped head-to-toe in fabric so that only their eyes were revealed. The women were legal property of the merchants, and their job was to ensure that their owners were satisfied.

The noise was thick, the vitriol thicker. Ulric Mori, the Master at Arms, stood in the center of the mass, trying to adjudicate a heated argument between fat, bald Cleo Connington and the distinguished Matthew Brennan. Sentries from both houses were being held back by the Palace Guard. The atmosphere in the room was like dry kindling, needing only a single spark to set it ablaze.

Overseeing it all was a bored King Eldrich Vaelor the First. The king was a tall, willowy man of thirty-seven, his cheeks sunken and his hair sparse, with a beard that had grown in splotchy and incomplete. The crown resting atop his head was a plain gold band—*simplicity for a simple job*, as Eldrich's father, the first king, had said. He sat on an ornate throne made from grooved ivory and positioned on a raised platform on the other side of the room. Grayhorn tusks, brought from the west by the earliest traders, formed a halo of curved spikes that encircled the king's head and torso, exaggerating the carved lion that roared from the throne's peak. Another set of tusks formed the armrests, and the king's fingers tapped atop them, causing a barely perceptible *twang* to echo through the chamber. He had ascended to the throne eight years ago, after his father, Edwin, had died, succumbing to the red cough. Having been stationed outside the city for much of his life, Crian had rarely seen the king before assuming command of the City Watch. Since then, he had gotten to know the man quite well. The king's style of leadership was haphazard and inconsistent, and half the time he seemed drunk with his illusionary might. But his true calling lay in his ability to consolidate power. Unlike his father, most of the high merchants were completely dedicated to him, which kept gold flowing into the realm.

King Vaelor pointed at Cleo Connington and beckoned him forward. The Highest led his children out of the throng, and stepped in front of the fat rich man, cutting him off. Clovis bowed before the king and swept his arm wide.

"King Vaelor," he said, "we have returned from the delta, and are ready to disc—"

"What the *fuck*," the king bellowed, his voice unusually gruff for such a lithe man.

Clovis straightened, a look of shock on his face. Crian and Avila exchanged glances, just as stunned as their father was.

"How dare you interrupt me when my court is in session?" the king asked. He didn't look bored any longer, and his eyes burned with rage. "Highest of Karak or not, you are still a servant of the throne, Clovis. I *will not* be disrespected."

"Yes, my Lord," the Highest replied. His voice seethed with resentment, and if a look could kill, all of the king's insides would have liquefied in an instant.

King Vaelor waved dismissively. "Wait in the vestibule. I'll see you when I'm done."

Without another word, Clovis led his children around the raised throne and through the door behind it. When the door slammed shut, the ruckus in the throne room dulled to a muted hum.

The vestibule was mostly empty, and it felt like a gray, stony cave. The table where the Council debated sat squatly on the far side of the room, thirteen chairs surrounding it. Behind that was a large briarwood cabinet stocked with an assortment of liquors. Avila approached the cabinet and poured herself a mug of wormwood extract. Crian leaned against the wall, as far from his sister as he could get, his armor creaking and badly in need of oil. Clovis stood in the center of the room, his normally ashen complexion red as a beet. The man ran both hands through his long white hair, and in an instant his normal coloring returned. Not that Crian was surprised. Clovis Crestwell was an expert at controlling his emotions.

The air in the vestibule was tense, but Crian refused to speak first. Thoughts of Nessa danced in his head, and he feared he would betray those feelings should he open his mouth. His father spared him the indignity of silence by strolling up to him as if nothing were wrong and asking after his brother, Joseph.

"He's fine. Wonderful, as a matter of fact. He sent a bird four days ago; he says the Dezren elves are treating him nicely and feeding him wine by the bucket load while they await the tournament. I think his exact words were, *"I never thought being a diplomat would be so damn enjoyable."*

The Highest cocked his head. "You do not sound pleased for Joseph."

"No, I'm very pleased for him. He'll represent us well."

"But you wish you had been the one to go."

"Hardly. He's attending a betrothal. Not my idea of fun."

Avila wandered closer.

"But the tournament is," she said, her breath reeking of stale liquor.

Crian didn't answer because he knew his expression gave him away. He did not possess the Crestwell impassivity.

"Son," his father said, "there will be other tournaments."

Crian slapped his gloved hand against his thigh plate. "You're right, there will. But how many of them will *both* the Dezren and Quellan attend? I'm the best swordsman in all of Neldar—you know that, Father. Fencing is as natural to me as swimming is to a fish. It's not the same for Joseph. What chance does he have against those elves? Their best warriors have been wielding weapons for hundreds of years. He'll present himself well, but he won't win." He shook his head. "Not like I would have."

His father's expression didn't change. "Your brother is there to strengthen Karak's relationship with the elves. *Winning* is not the purpose. You are the son of the Highest. These things should be evident to you."

"I know, Father. And they are. I'm sorry."

"Jealousy is a shifty demon, Crian, and given your place as a son of a First Family, you must be increasingly wary against it. What are you, thirty-eight? And yet you think you can teach centuries-old elves how to wield a blade? You don't know how far from true beauty your skills really are. I do. I have witnessed Karak, our true Father, wield a blade. Now that…that was a sight to remember, a dance like none I have ever seen. His greatsword sheared trees and cattle with ease, and it seemed as though the very earth trembled beneath his feet. You are so much like him, yet so far from him at the same time. If only you had been born prior to his departure. You are a great warrior, Crian, but he could have made you *legendary*."

Crian felt his neck flush at the dressing down, but something tickled at the back of his mind through it all. With a sudden jolt, he realized it, and he stared at his father in surprise.

"You…you don't know?"

His father frowned.

"Know what?"

"Karak. He returned nine days ago."

Clovis crossed his arms, narrowed his eyes.

"Is that so?"

"It is. He visited Minister Mori and held audience in the streets for a time before retiring to his temple. He hasn't been seen since, but the Minister assures us he is still in Veldaren."

He watched as his father's expression subtly changed. He didn't look surprised, but his normally detached gaze shifted for a moment.

What was that expression? It looked almost like concern. This baffled Crian, for why would Karak's Highest not rejoice upon his return? He didn't dare ask. Such a question was far beyond his standing, even as Clovis's own son.

Finally, his father said, "Praise be to Karak."

"Praise be to Karak," answered Avila.

Crian just nodded his head.

The door to the vestibule crashed open, interrupting their talk. All three turned to see King Vaelor step into the room. The leader of his personal guard followed, a brutish thug dressed in thick leather armor. The king was all smiles now, though his cheerfulness seemed forced, and he struggled to hold aside his heavy wool cape to allow his legs freedom of movement. He had the look of a child who'd done wrong and hoped his parents wouldn't notice.

"Ah, Clovis," he said with false cheer. "Good to see you. I apologize for my words earlier—busy day and all. How were the travels? How was Haven? Did you shed plenty of blasphemers' blood—"

Without so much as a warning, Crian's father lunged forward with the grace of a stalking cat. His fist struck the side of King Vaelor's face, followed by a heavy *crack*. Vaelor's neck snapped back, and his flesh rippled as he teetered on his feet. A glob of blood shot from his lips, smattering the wall behind him. The king fell over, landing hard on his elbow. His guard, Karl Dogon, took a step forward, reaching for the pommel of his sword, but one look from Clovis froze him in his tracks.

"Go outside," said Crian's father. "Do not come back in until I call for you."

"Yes, Highest," replied the large man, and he backed his way out the door.

The king stared up at Karak's Highest with fear in his eyes. Clovis kicked the prone man, eliciting a womanly scream. Crian winced, knowing this would only goad his father into delivering a worse beating.

And beat the king his father did, mercilessly pummeling him with an endless barrage of kicks and punches. By the time he was finished, King Vaelor looked like a stuck pig ready for the spit. Blood ran down his frilly white shirt, dripped from his necklace of thick gold links, and stained the corners of his royal cape an even deeper black. The man whimpered and cried, tears falling from the creases in his now swollen eyes.

And never once, Crian realized, had his father uttered a word. When he was finished, Clovis removed his blood-soaked gloves and handed them to Avila.

"You will never disrespect me again, *your highness*," he said, venom leaking out of every syllable. "You are but a man, destined to live out your days and die, whereas I am forever. Your rule is a sham. Everything you have is because of me. It was I who poisoned your father's rival so that your father might win the Tourney of Rule. *I*—not Karak—named him king, just as I named you king after he died. And how do you repay me? By giving another the mantle of Lord Commander and treating me as a common beggar in front of the court. With but a word, I can take back all I have given you. Do you understand?"

The whimpering king nodded.

Clovis gave him one last kick in the ribs and called for his guard to reenter. "Get him cleaned up," he demanded. "And have the court whores apply powder to hide the bruises. We don't want anyone to know our king is a craven who cannot defend himself, now do we?"

"Of course not, Highest," Dogon replied.

The bodyguard helped the dazed king to his feet and led him out the side door of the vestibule. Beyond was a staircase leading to the royal bedroom and the stable of whores that Clovis had allowed the man to keep. The Highest straightened his shirt, cracked his neck, and turned to his children. If not for the faint stains of blood on his clothes, there was nary a sign of the beating that had just taken place.

"Crian, you are to leave with your sister. I want you both in Omnmount with a faction of the new army."

Thoughts of Nessa leapt to the forefront of Crian's mind. He couldn't believe his sudden good fortune. Omnmount was barely a few days ride from the delta. The timeliness of it, however, gave him pause.

"I will, Father, but may I ask why? And what of the City Watch?"

"There are dark days coming, son. Dark days for which we must prepare. You will command five hundred green soldiers and continue their training. Enlist the help of the township if you wish. You say you are the best at swordplay? Very well. Then let the best teach our men. Humanity is weak, from the east to the west. It is up to the children of gods, up to *us*, to guide them. We have seventy-eight days before Haven will get their reckoning, and I want our men to be prepared. As for the City Watch, I will have the king hand those duties over to Captain Gregorian. He is capable enough for a regular human."

"What of Vulfram? Will he not come with us?"

"Perhaps. For now, I have granted him leave, for being Soleh's child, he is weak and requires time with his loved ones. We are a blessed few, we Crestwells. The world is young, and only the strong, the dedicated, will inherent the fruit when the vine ripens. We must endure the weaknesses of those who are useful to us, but we must never envy and never indulge. We are the snakes that dine with the lion. Karak is always with us, no matter how far away he might be."

With that, Highest Crestwell pivoted on his heel and headed for the vestibule door. Crian watched him go, guilt stirring in his stomach. It was Avila who called out to their father before he exited the chamber.

"Highest, what will you do in our absence?" she asked.

He turned to his children, caught in the half-darkness between the covered doorway and the torchlight. The shadows slid over his face, concealing his upper half, making him look like a partially formed apparition.

"I will hold court with my god," he said, and walked out the door.

The banner flapped on its pole, puffed out for all to see by a strong late summer breeze. Vulfram knelt before it, gazing up at the leaping doe that served as the sigil of House Mori. It was a welcome reminder of the warmth of home in an otherwise cold city of stone. When he was young he'd watched whole herds wander through the plains outside the Erzn forest. Those days he had hunted with a bow and gutted with a knife, killing for the evening meal and always showing respect to the beasts he slew.

Those days were long gone indeed.

He rose to his feet and entered the Tower Keep, the tall, ugly building that served as his family's home away from home. There were only three of them living in the large structure: his mother, his father, and his sister, Adeline.

Entering the front gate, he trudged through the entrance hall, making sure to cut a wide swath between himself and the ingress to his father's studio. He could never explain why, but he always experienced a sort of vertigo that made him feel ill beyond belief whenever he so much as approached his father's workplace, the room originally meant to hold a throne, now adorned with the mystic painting of Karak, Ashhur, and Celestia.

His knees ached as he climbed the stairs. The walls were thick and rough, hewn from granite from the north, and he pressed his hand against them for support. Unlike the Castle of the Lion, which always felt cold, the Tower Keep seemed not only to retain heat, but also to magnify it. The huge sword on his back weighed him down, and the effort of his climb caused sweat to bead on his shaved head and gather in his thick eyebrows. His swaying beard left a crescent of moisture on his bare chest, and his horsehide breeches clung to his buttocks, chafing him between the legs. It was just past noon, but as far as he was concerned, the sun couldn't set soon enough.

On the third level, the muted sound of two women speaking reached his ears. This was odd, as it was midweek, which meant his mother should be in the Tower Justice courtroom, doling out punishments and keeping an eye on his crazy sister. Something catastrophic must have happened for her to be here now. He cautiously approached the closed door to her chambers and rapped it lightly with his knuckles.

"Mother?" he asked.

"Come in," replied his mother's voice, sounding strange and conflicted.

Pushing open the door to her large room, he saw the eminent Soleh Mori sitting on the bed, her dark, wavy hair hanging to the middle of her waist, her soulful brown eyes wide and attentive. Her hand drew to her mouth at the sight of him and she gasped. Beside her was Lanike Crestwell, wife of the Highest, a small, mousy woman whose petite features spoke more of cutesiness than outright beauty. They both looked like schoolgirls, what with their perfect complexions and youthful veneers.

It took him a moment to realize that *the lady of House Crestwell was in his mother's room*, and once that understanding hit him, he went to the corner of the bed, fell to one knee, and kissed each woman's hand in turn.

"Stand up, son," his mother said, sounding edgy even though she was obviously overjoyed to see him.

"Yes, Vulfram, stand," said Lanike kindly.

"I would prefer to sit, if you don't mind," he replied, looping Darkfall's scabbard over his head and setting it down before sitting cross-legged on a stone floor that seemed to pulse with warmth. His mother began to cry, happy tears now, and she couldn't keep her eyes off him.

"My son, my wonderful Vulfram, is home. Karak is good."

"That he is, Mother. But why are you not at the castle?"

His mother grinned and cast a cautious glance at Lanike.

"There has been…news, my son. Both for good and ill. Because of that, Lady Crestwell gave me leave today. But I do not wish to speak of such things now. Can I simply bask in the knowledge that you are *home?*"

"Bask all you want, Mother, but please tell me the news."

"Well," his mother said, clearing her throat, "for the good, Karak has returned to us. He visited me in the Arena nine days ago. He is as strong and wise as ever, and he insists his return is permanent. I have visited him four times over that span, but he will not take any other visitors for the time being. I believe that he is tired from his journey."

"I see," said Vulfram. So *that* explained the differences he had noticed as he walked north from the Castle of the Lion to the Tower Keep. People were out in abundance, as was usual in the city, but their demeanor was different somehow. Lighter. He had even seen one of his old charges from the Watch, a surly sort, grinning at passersby as he manned the corner in front of Graymare's Apothecary.

"You're right, Mother," he said. "This *is* a good thing."

Soleh's face soured, turning suddenly sad. "It is," she agreed.

He reached for her, but she moved before he could touch her.

"Mother, what is it? What ills you?"

"I…it is just…"

"A letter came this morning from your manor in Erznia," said Lanike Crestwell, taking Soleh's hand. Her high-pitched voice matched her mousy features. "It seems your daughter Lyana has found herself in a rather…compromising position."

Vulfram's heart skipped a beat. "Lyana? What has she done this time?"

Lyana Mori was his second child and a bit of a wild soul. She was always getting into spats with the local farmers, one time even earning a high merchant's ire by attempting to bed his thirteen-year-old son. She had been nine at the time. Now she was sixteen.

"The letter did not say," said Lanike. "It was an official epistle sent by Magister Wentner, requesting the presence of a high official to sit in judgment of your daughter. We've been given no word of the charges. With Joseph in Dezerea, I thought to send Crian to settle the matter."

"No other man will sit in judgment of my daughter," said Vulfram. "I am Lord Commander of Karak's Army. I will take care of this myself."

The idea of him leaving seemed to break his mother, and she turned her face to hide her tears. Lanike gave him a hard look and said, "You have your responsibilities to the realm and its forces to consider."

"Responsibilities from which your husband the Highest has granted me leave. I have a month to do as I please. This changes nothing, for I was already planning to return to my family. Come morning, I'll ride. If the weather holds, I can make it there in less than two days."

Lanike squeezed his hand, hard. "Remember, Lord Commander, that you are bound by Karak's laws. As much as you love your daughter, it is your creator to whom you owe loyalty."

He ripped his fingers away. "I realize this, Lady Crestwell. No one loves Karak more than I. And whatever Lyana has done, I will punish her as the law demands. Of that you have my word, not that you would need it. Now, if you will excuse me, I must gather my things from the castle and ready my horse."

His mother stopped weeping into her pillow and leapt off the bed. She barreled into him, wrapping him tightly in her arms, wetting his chest with her tears. It never ceased to amaze him how different his mother was outside of a public setting; in court she was steel, unflinching, whereas behind closed doors, among her husband and children, she was like a ball of yarn that couldn't keep itself together. It was something he admired about her, really. He wished he could be as open with his emotions as she was, even if only on occasion.

Soleh pulled him close, standing on her toes so that her lips might reach his ear.

"I love you, Vulfram, and I love my granddaughter," she whispered. "Please, no matter what she has done, be kind to her. She has not known a father's love for many years. Show her the mercy she deserves."

"I will, Mother," he whispered, and after placing a gentle kiss on her forehead, he exited her chamber. First the show of violence against Haven, followed by countless insufferable nights spent listening to Highest Crestwell's endless proselytizing, and now his Lyana in trouble. An endless stream of tension that had tightened his chest and turned the hairs in his beard even grayer than before. His heart beat out of control, stealing away his breath.

I don't want to be the first of my family to die, he thought, and went about preparing for the journey home. *But by the gods, don't let it be Lyana either.*

CHAPTER

7

Years ago, before Celestia altered the landscape of Dezrel to prepare for the coming of humanity, the city of Dezerea had been nothing but a wide swath of forest just outside the borders of Kal'droth, underneath which sat miles of tunnels and catacombs filled with statues and monuments dedicated to the fallen of both the Dezren and Quellan elves. It was a mutual place of honor and tribute, and had been for nearly two thousand years.

At least that was according to the stories her nursemaid told her. Aullienna Meln of Stonewood was twelve, so she had never experienced Dezrel before the coming of the humans.

As she took in her surroundings, Aullienna found it hard to believe that the city was less than a hundred years old. When they had first arrived two days ago, their convoy had passed through a forest of tall trees, many of which supported great wooden homes in their sturdy branches, only accessible by hanging rope ladders. In the immense clearing in the center of the wood, giant spires of crystal rose from the earth, buildings fashioned from the rock beneath her feet by the goddess. It was a city that glistened even when the sky was cloudy. Palace Thyne was the biggest and shiniest structure of them all, towering above her head in shimmering emerald. Unlike when they first arrived, when the palace was docile, now eager faces appeared in the windows, hands coming together in cheers. Their shouts added to those of the multitude surrounding her, a noise so loud her ears rang and her brain rattled in her skull.

Each step closer to the palace filled her with dread. Aullienna squeezed her mother's hand, and Audrianna Meln, Lady of Stonewood, knelt down before her. She was a blaze of splendor in her satin-spun red dress, contrasted with her yellow mantle garlanded with tiny rubies. Her golden hair flowed straight as a comet's tail beneath a silver diadem. She stroked her daughter's hair, so very similar to her own, and playfully flicked the point of her ear. It was something her mother did when Aullienna acted nervous, and it always succeeded in making her laugh.

"What's wrong, Aully?" her mother asked.

Aullienna bit her lip.

"I'm scared."

"There is nothing to be afraid of. These people are our friends."

"I know." Aullienna lowered her gaze and kicked at a stone that stood out in the middle of the grass.

Her mother's head cocked to the side. "Wait…are you scared of meeting *him?*"

At Aully's blush, her mother let out a soft laugh.

"Oh, child, come now. He's only a boy. You've stood your own with many a boy before."

"But none of them were supposed to be my husband."

At that, her mother's expression shifted. A furrowed brow created the tiniest of creases in the pearly white flesh of her forehead.

"I know how you feel," she said. "I felt the same way when your grandfather told me I was to marry your father. I refused to come out of my room for hours. But your grandmother pulled me out, kicking and screaming, and when I first laid eyes on the boy I was to marry, all that fear withered away."

"But what if that doesn't happen for me? What if he's mean?"

"It will happen, my sweet. The boy is from a strong bloodline. The joining of our families will only strengthen our standing among our peoples, and he knows this. He will treat you with the respect a young woman deserves."

Aully smiled at her mother, but she wasn't convinced. It had been two months since she'd been told of her betrothal to Kindren Thyne of Dezerea, a boy she had never met. They were to be wed in the shadow of Palace Thyne, in a city she had never visited. It had seemed unreal at first, just another story spun by her mother and her nursemaid, but now she was here in Dezerea, preparing for the celebration that would mark the announcement of their betrothal. It all seemed so forbidding, so *big*.

More than anything she wished her sister were with her. Brienna would know how to set her nerves at ease. Even though Brienna was more than ninety years her senior, the two of them had been close for as long as Aully could remember. It was Brienna who had taught her to fire a bow, swing a staff, and conjure little balls of fire and ice. It was also Brienna who had told her horror stories of her *own* betrothal, an arrangement that had ended when Brienna set the pants of her would-be husband on fire. According to Mother, the damage done to the family name might have been catastrophic had they not been the Lords of Stonewood.

Brienna was a free spirit, and that was just what Aully needed at the moment.

The Barker, an elder from Dezerea with hair as white as the fields in winter, shouted over the din of applause. The crowd quieted. Aully's mother guided her daughter through the throng of elves that formed a tunnel of smooth white flesh and extravagant clothing. At the end of the living channel stood Aully's father, Cleotis Meln of Stonewood, his face slender and his smile charming. He wore a pleated green doublet over his brown tunic. To his left were the Sovereigns of Dezerea, Orden and Phyrra Thyne.

Where Aully's family was fair, the Thynes were dark haired, and they were clothed as lavishly as the rest, wearing the blue and yellow colors of Dezerea.

When she reached them, her father bent down and kissed her lips, followed by Lady and Lord Thyne. Then they all parted, and Aully's mother gently nudged her into place. She walked between the two sets of royalty, feeling naked in the thin, white satin chemise that hung from her shoulders.

Then she saw the vision of an angel.

He was a tall youth, with a slender face and kind eyes. His long hair was the color of the leaves on the ground in autumn, tied back tightly against his scalp, revealing his strong cheeks and dimpled smile. The look of a child still hung on him, but he possessed the grace of a man when his body was set in motion.

Kindren knelt before her, took her hand in his. She was wearing a bronze ring that was set with the symbol of Stonewood—the star of Celestia shining above a single tree. With only a brief hesitation, he placed a single kiss upon its polished surface. Then he stood, still holding her hand, and their eyes met. He winked at her and proceeded to turn and face the gathered crowd, lifting her arm in the process. The shouts of approval rose to a near-deafening level, and Aully felt the last of her apprehension flutter away like so many butterflies. She held her head up proudly, accepting the cheers from the gathering of elves, her strength reinforced by the young man beside her.

Kindren glanced down at her, and she up at him, and they shared another quiet moment, alone despite the hundreds of onlookers. An odd tremble scuttled through her midsection, and she felt the rest of her body echo the sensation. Kinden squeezed her fingers tighter, though not in an aggressive way. Her mind went blank, and what she did next came seemingly by instinct: she rose up on her tiptoes and placed a kiss on his perfectly smooth cheek. The cheers quickly began anew. Aully could feel the beaming smiles of her parents behind her, and her chest filled with a sense of pride that evened out the quivering in her midsection.

A thought came to her, and the realization both baffled her and made her feel like a silly young elf. She was awestruck by the Thyne boy, infatuated after only a few short moments in his company... and he had not yet spoken a word.

The Barker stepped to the middle of the circle and held up his hands. The crowd quieted, and for the first time Aully noticed the strange appearance of many of those around her. Elves with copper skin and black hair were interspersed throughout the host. Though their clothing was earthy and rustic, the priceless jewelry they wore made them appear just as noble as her parents. *The Quellans*, she thought. Aully had never met a Quellan elf before, having never left Stonewood. They had a certain exotic beauty, but she had to admit there was something hard in their expressions that she found off-putting, a kind of intensity she only saw on her father's face when he was talking about how much Brienna had embarrassed the family.

"We are gathered here today," the Barker said, "to celebrate the joining of two great houses. Kindren Thyne and Aullienna Meln, you are to link your hands, and thereby your lives, in a union that is to last forever. Will you accept this duty set upon you, *ambar meleth*, before Celestia, the bringer of light and life?"

The Barker looked to Aully first, and she dipped her chin and said, "I will."

He looked at Kindren next, and the boy said in a voice just as handsome as his visage, "I will."

The Barker touched both of their hands, which were still clasped together, and his wrinkled finger traced the image of a six-sided star, three points on Aully's flesh, three points on Kindren's. "Faith, family, and land, that is what you now share with this betrothal," he murmured, his ancient eyes rolling back in his skull. "So shall it be done."

"So shall it be done," echoed the voices of every elf in attendance.

Aully and Kindren's respective fathers stepped forward, shaking hands with each other to seal the agreement, and then the Barker turned to the crowd.

"Let the games begin!" he shouted.

The applause was riotous.

The betrothed couple were led across the field to a series of raised platforms horseshoeing around a section of freshly tilled and packed soil, seats that had been designated for the royal families. Her parents took their seats behind her, along with Orden and Phyrra Thyne and the lords of the Quellan, Neyvar Ruven and his wife. To her right was Ceredon, son of the Neyvar, intense and regal, his smooth cocoa skin seeming to blend in with the russet ribbon he wore about his neck. Kindren sat to her left, his previous confidence seeming to have fled him now that the opening ceremonies were over. He appeared nervous, his skin slick with sweat when his fingers touched hers. She wondered what she had done wrong, but the boy would barely look at her, much less offer her an explanation. Feeling alone between an intimidating man of royalty and her unresponsive fiancée, the butterflies in Aullienna's stomach came swarming back to life.

The Tournament of Betrothal began with an archery competition. She watched elf after elf, male and female alike, step into the horseshoed arena, shooting their arrows with deadly accuracy at targets that were gradually moved farther and farther away. The air filled with the *whoosh* and *thunk* of bolts hitting their marks, and she felt her nerves slowly ebb. *This* was how she spent her days back in Stonewood—shooting game, playing at magic, climbing trees, and skipping stones across the surface of Rocky Neck Pond. She wished she could be down there with the rest of them.

The targets were brought back in after another set of contestants finished. The Barker shouted four names, including *Kindren Thyne*.

Aully glanced aside to see Kindren nervously stand. He circled toward the back of the dais, retrieved a bow handed to him by his father, and descended the stairs. Gently twanging the string of his bow, he entered the arena, joining the other competitors in line. Despite the aged gracefulness of his posture, there was awkwardness to his movements that revealed his youth. He turned to look at her, smiling sheepishly, and then nocked an arrow. The three other competitors readied themselves as well, and all four released their strings in unison. The two Quellan elves on the left hit just outside the center, and the Dezren on the far right hit a perfect bull's-eye. The arrow Kindren loosed missed the target entirely. It flew over the rounded, stuffed fabric by a good yard and embedded itself in the dirt. The crowd, perched on their raised platforms, uttered a collective moan of despair. He stepped away from the firing line with his head bowed low, even as the Barker said, "Disqualified."

The prince of Dezerea skulked out of view. Aully held her breath as she heard him climb back onto the platform. She listened as the boy's father offered a disgusted grunt, as if shamed by his son's failure, and his mother gave him a too sweet word of apology. From the corner of her eye, she saw Ceredon roll his eyes and shake his head.

Kindren sat down beside her and held his face in his hands. He was shaking. Knowing she had to do something, she touched his wrist gently. He peered at her through his fingers, and she shrugged.

"It happens," she said.

His dropped his hands and gave her an apologetic look.

"I'm sorry to have insulted you," he said.

She shrugged again. "No shame in missing. I miss every time a cute boy's staring at *me*." She jabbed her thumb over her shoulder and whispered into his ear. "And don't tell anyone, but the Neyvar's son was staring at you something fierce."

Kindren laughed so hard that a string of spittle flew from his lips and dribbled down his chin. For a moment he froze in horror, but when Aully only laughed harder, he relaxed and joined in. She was so lost in amusement that she barely noticed when Ceredon rose from his seat and stormed away, a disgusted look on his face. Afraid of how the mass of royalty behind them might be reacting to their inappropriate mirth, she kept her focus squarely on Kindren's gorgeous face.

"Thank you," Kindren said when their laughter finally died down, keeping his voice low. The competition in the arena was going on as scheduled, oblivious to them. "I didn't mean to ignore you earlier…I was nervous. I'm not the best archer, but father insisted that I take part in the tournament. I knew I would make a fool of myself."

She elbowed him. "At least you do it well."

"Very funny."

"But it is," she said with a smirk, channeling her sister's demon-may-care persona. "I wouldn't have it any other way."

"So you're not embarrassed to be my betrothed?" he asked, disbelief heavy in his voice.

Aully shook her head. "I'd be more embarrassed if you'd thrown a tantrum."

He grinned. "Good."

"Besides, if you really want to impress me, all you need to do is conjure up a fireball the size of a redwood."

"I might be able to do that. I'm *much* better with magic."

"Really?" she said, her heart leaping.

"Really," he answered with a wink.

Orden Thyne's head poked between theirs, making both young elves jump. His expression was rigid, with narrowed eyes and firm lips.

"Children, this tournament is being held in your honor. It is disrespectful of you to ignore the proceedings," he said.

Given his grave air and tone, they both shut their mouths and looked on. From that moment onward, though, they kept their fingers intertwined as often as possible.

The archery competition ended, won by Argo Stillen, the master of the Quellan archers' guild. At almost four hundred years old, he was the oldest of the entrants, and yet he scored a staggering forty-three consecutive perfect hits, the last eleven from two hundred and fifty yards. Aully stood in awe of him, and gave a rousing ovation when the last of his bolts found its mark.

Next came contests of speed and strength. While an elf from Stonewood won the dash, Kindren's cousin Mordikay won the high jump. The Dezren swept the speed competitions, which was not surprising given the taller and leaner physiques of Aullienna's people. The Quellan were more compact and powerful, and when the strength contests began, they emerged victorious each time. Even the grumpy Ceredon got involved in the victory laps after he won the pole toss by a wide margin. He smirked up at Aully and Kindren, trying to appear superior, but the two youngsters laughed him off. Aully felt as though the newfound bond she and her betrothed shared was indestructible, and she wasn't going to let some spoiled royal brat ruin it for her.

When the time came for the fencing competition, the sun had nearly disappeared behind the glittering spires of Palace Thyne. The contenders lined up to be introduced, dulled iron sabers hanging limp at their sides. With each name called, the participant removed his or her helm and offered a bow to the crowd. Aully cheered vigorously for each one. Fencing was a favorite pastime in Stonewood, and she recognized many of the competitors. There were J'obeth and Kara, Lucius and Demarti, Crabtree and Shomor. Ceredon again joined in, appearing just as obnoxiously confident as he had during the pole toss.

Halfway through the procession, her clapping stopped. She stared, dumbfounded, at the light-skinned human with white hair and dark, haunting eyes who had just removed his helm. He was introduced to a stunned crowd as Joseph Crestwell of Neldar. The human seemed unaffected by the lack of support. He took a step forward, like all the other combatants, and raised a lightly armored hand in salute. There had been tension between elves and humans for as long as humans had existed. The elves were sharing a land that had once been theirs and their alone, and after their rulers had refused Celestia's request for them to act as wardens to the new species, they had lost their homeland forever. It had neither been forgotten nor forgiven. But if this man were bothered by the silence, he didn't show it.

Aully hadn't met many humans over the short span of her life, and other than her sister's love, Jacob, those she *had* seen were the dark-skinned ones who were constantly pilfering from Stonewood Forest—including the giant Bardiya, who seemed nice enough the only time she had met him but whom her father disliked more than anyone. This Joseph was tall and thickly built, his skin as pale as her own, but there was something dangerous beneath his calm gaze. He was more a bull than a gazelle, and according to her nursemaid, bulls couldn't go anywhere without breaking a few things.

Before the competition could begin, Joseph Crestwell stepped away from the introduction line and marched straight for her platform. Both she and Kindren leaned over the rail to see him better. The human stood below them and bowed low in respect. When finished, he lifted his hand to her, which she hastily grasped in her confusion over proper etiquette.

"I come to fight in your honor," the man said, his voice kind despite his hardened appearance. "But I do not wish to cause a disturbance. If the prince and princess of Dezerea so desire, I will withdraw from the competition."

He kissed the back of her hand, and then shook Kindren's. Aully stood and curtseyed.

"If it pleases the kind sir to fight in our tournament, then it pleases me to watch," Aully said. "It is not my place to judge."

The crowd murmured.

"It is not *our* place to judge!" shouted Kindren, offering the man a bow. With those words, the crowd resumed their cheering, louder than before. A wide grin spread across Aully's face, growing even wider when a stolen glance behind her showed that all three of the imperial families were nodding their approval. Neyvar Ruven even stepped up to the rail and shook the human's hand. A shrewd look passed between the Neyvar and the human, one that made Aully wonder what was afoot.

Soon after, the Barker announced the first pairing, and the competition began. The sound of clanging steel echoed through the crowd as the opponents lunged and parried. It was a complex dance, feet tapping forward and back, shoulders held straight, sabers acting as extensions of the combatants' arms. One pair after another entered the packed dirt arena and fought until someone yielded. The early matches lasted less than five minutes, until the last pairing of the opening round was announced.

It was Ceredon, son of Ruven, squaring off against the human, Joseph Crestwell.

Aully's hand found Kindren's, and their fingers interlocked as they watched the two fighters circle each other. Ceredon was graceful, seemingly floating over the ground. His chin was high, and he held his saber out like a lance, twirling it in circles, baiting his opponent. His movements were confident, but Aully noticed a somewhat lackadaisical look in his eyes, as if the prince were bored.

Joseph Crestwell plodded on heavy feet. He appeared unsteady, and held his saber at an odd angle—diagonally upward and turned to the side, with his offhand set close to the pommel as if for balance. And yet there was a permanent grin on his face, seeping excitement, as if he knew something his opponent did not.

Ceredon grew impatient, his feet moving faster as he danced his circular dance. The Quellan made the first move, striding forward, thrusting his blade forward when the tip was at its lowest point, aiming for a gut shot.

Joseph's cocked arm plunged down in a stroke that smashed into Ceredon's blade. The tip jabbed past the human's padded surcoat. Ceredon stumbled to the side, off balance, dropping his sword hand to the dirt for support. Crestwell swung his arm in the other direction, looping the sword over his head so that he could clutch it with both hands. Down came the rounded blade in a powerful, two-handed blow. Ceredon barely got his own blade up in time to block the human's blow. Aully gasped as she watched, her fingers tightening around Kindren's. The human had aimed for Ceredon's head, which was generally frowned upon in open competition.

Ceredon must have realized it as well, for his eyes were wide as he scrambled to his feet.

The elf's movements were still nimble, but there was an urgency to them now, a nervous energy that made him slip more than once. Aully found his strategy odd: he was on the defensive, utilizing only a handful of well-known techniques, while the human steadily advanced on him each time they circled. Ceredon lunged, hoping for a lucky poke, but his jab was easily batted away. The young elf no longer seemed regal and overconfident. He was breathing heavily, his eyes darting side to side, and his expression mirrored Kindren's during the archery contest.

During one of the elf's rasping inhales, the human went on the offensive. His slogging footfalls brought him forward as he chopped sideways, again with both hands. Ceredon tried to parry, but his sword was knocked into the bridge of his helm by his adversary's more powerful assault. He performed a slight pirouette to keep from falling—an astonishing feat in and of itself—and jabbed his saber into the dirt again for balance.

Joseph swung low for the elf's leg, this time from the other side. For some reason his attack looked slow, almost overly patient. In a flash Ceredon leapt over the blade, barely avoiding having his knees smashed. Aully stood in awe of the power the human possessed, but she found it strange that his attacks were so sluggish. Suspicion crept into her breast. Was he holding back on purpose?

Ceredon twirled away from the next attack, a diagonal downward hew, and Aully saw panic in his eyes. He was rushing around like a chicken trying to evade the butcher's knife, and she could tell that he was beginning to tire. He went on the offensive over and over again, trying to outwit the human with his speed, but Joseph appeared to be ready for every hit. The slightest shifting of his feet, the subtlest twisting of his sword, and Ceredon's swings would parry to the side. The elf's feet dragged and his back arched. When the human resumed his assault, there was little Ceredon could do but offer a weak block, falling to his knees from the force of the blow.

The human stood over him, and for a brief moment Aullienna thought the fight was over. This was where Joseph should have waited for his opponent's surrender, but neither combatant appeared ready to yield. Joseph brought his saber to the side, then swung it for Ceredon's throat as if he were trying to lop off his head. It appeared that he was putting everything he had into the attack, though his movements were still oddly unhurried.

But tired as he was, Ceredon proved even slower.

His head lowered with a simple shrugging of the shoulders, and Aully almost leapt over the railing. Time slowed, as the blade screamed toward Ceredon's thin metal helm.

And then Joseph's blade lifted as if possessed of a mind of its own, sailing over the elf's head.

Ceredon looked surprised, but he reacted quickly. He slashed his saber in a single tight arc, catching the human under the chin with the flat of the blade. Joseph's head snapped back, a thin stream of blood shooting from his mouth. He stumbled on weak knees, then collapsed onto his rear.

"I yield, I yield," Joseph stammered, tossing his saber to the dirt.

His surrender resulted in a sudden surge of cheers. Aullienna watched Ceredon stand on unsteady legs and raise a half-hearted salute to the crowd. The elf glanced behind him at the still bleeding Joseph Crestwell and then threw his saber down.

"Why is he leaving?" asked Kindren as Ceredon limped out of the arena. "He won."

"Only because the human let him," Aully said. "And he knows it."

"What? No he didn't. Ceredon ducked the attack."

Aully shook her head. "That's what it was supposed to look like. Sir Crestwell lifted the blade on purpose. I've seen my cousin do the same thing countless times when we played swords back home."

"But…why would he do that? Why would he allow himself to get hurt?"

"Don't know," she said with a shrug.

As if to answer the question, Joseph Crestwell struggled to his feet and approached the side of their platform, blood still dripping from his chin. Aully saw that Neyvar Ruven had made his way down the stairs, and she shushed Kindren with a finger to her lips so that they could listen. They peered through the slat beneath the balustrade, watching as the elf and man shook hands.

"Thank you for that, Joseph," the Neyvar said. "I'm sure my son will remember never to disregard his lessons…or underestimate an opponent."

"A lesson learned in victory is the best lesson of all, especially for one so young. How old is the boy now?"

"Just turned ninety-five last season."

Joseph offered a laugh. "He looks much younger."

"A century isn't even a third of the way through our lives. Elves of his age are no longer children, and many feel that they are beyond further learning. Which as you have seen, given the way he fought today, is an attitude he can ill afford."

"For how lightly he has taken his studies," Joseph said, rubbing his chin, "he still packs a wallop. Gods forbid he ever apply himself. Then he will be truly mighty. Now if it would please you, Neyvar,

I need ice for my chin and brandy for the pain. I fear your son may have cracked my jaw."

"I'll have a servant bring what you need to your room. Take rest, for we have much to discuss tomorrow."

With that, the two men strode away from the platform and out of Aully's vision. She sat up, and smoothed out the front of her chemise. Kindren echoed her movement, resting his back against the side panel of the balustrade and giving Aully a queer look.

"What was that all about?" he asked, and the way he asked it, full of wonder and confusion, made him seem younger than his sixteen years.

"Don't know. Maybe that's just how the Neyvar teaches his children lessons?"

Looking up at his own parents, who were watching the finals in the arena, Kindren said, "I'm glad *my* parents aren't like that."

"Me too," said Aully.

They retook their seats and watched the rest of the night's contests. By the time the last bout ended, the sky was dark and twinkling with stars. Palace Thyne lit up as if flames burned within its green crystal walls, illuminating the arena. The crowds began to file away, and an exhausted Aully stretched her arms high above her head and yawned.

"Long night," said her betrothed.

"Sure was."

His lips brushed her cheek, soft and tentative. Aully closed her eyes and let the sensation wash away the day. The competitions, the clang of steel, the human throwing his match—all became afterthoughts.

She turned to Kindren and gazed into his eyes; lit up by the glare of the palace, they looked like the surface of the ocean. She felt her face go hot and noticed that Kindren's cheeks were red already. She placed her fingers on one of those cheeks, soaking in its warmth.

"I like you," he said, his hand closing over hers.

"I like you too."

"Thank Celestia, right? I thought I was going to hate you."

Aullienna couldn't help but laugh.

"Me too," she said.

"But we don't. And you're going to stick around for a while, right?"

"Tonight? But my mother's calling me for bed."

His grin was infectious. "No, silly, not tonight. Tomorrow and the day after."

Aully felt her nerves threaten to jangle, but she shoved the feeling down.

"I'll be spending a lot of time here," she said. "My parents are leaving in two months, but I don't think I'm joining them. I think Dezerea is my home now."

"It is," said Kindren. "For now and forever. Does that scare you?"

"A little."

"Don't let it. I'll be here. And there are some wonderful things in this city I can show you."

"Like the crypts?"

"Like the crypts," he said.

With that, Aully stepped on her tiptoes and planted a kiss on Kindren's lips. She ran away from him afterward, giggling, the sound of her mother calling her to her quarters ringing in her ears.

CHAPTER

8

The grass was soft against Bardiya Gorgoros's rear end as he sat cross-legged beneath the shade of a cypress tree. His eyes faced north, locked on the slender Gods' Road and the small cloud of dust that had formed in the distance. The Gods' Road stretched the entirety of Ashhur's Paradise, running diagonally down from the northwestern township of Drake until it crossed the Corinth River, cut through the grasslands of Ker, and reached Ashhur's Bridge over the western spine of the Rigon Delta. From there it continued east, maintained by Karak's people instead of Ashhur's. The road was rarely traveled, and Bardiya knew this because he sat in that same spot beneath the soul tree almost every day, surrounded by mile upon mile of high plains grasses, to say his afternoon prayers to Ashhur. Only when an envoy from Mordeina or Safeway came calling was there any traffic at all. It was not that the two factions of Ashhur's children did not get along or that they considered themselves separate. In truth, the lack of travel and cohabitation stemmed from one simple fact: almost everyone in Paradise lived perfect lives, and no one had no real desire to go anywhere other than where he or she had been raised.

Bardiya leaned back against the trunk of the soul tree, and his head struck a branch. He muttered and rubbed the spot. Glancing behind him, he looked at the many notches carved into the tree, the highest groove added only a month ago. Bardiya sighed.

He'd grown again.

Over his eighty-seven years of life, Bardiya had never stopped growing. Each year had meant another inch or two of height, ever since the day he was pulled from his mother's womb, the first human child born in all of Dezrel. He now stood almost ten feet tall, towering over everyone. A few of the Kerrians thought his constant growth was a defect, but to the populace at large, the reasons for his gigantism were obvious: it was a sign of his undying belief in the teachings of his deity. Many whispered that Bardiya was Ashhur's most devout follower, an assumption that Bardiya himself doubted. He could never explain to them the deep ache he felt in his bones from such constant growth. At times, he just wished the pain would end.

Yet he could not deny how much he loved his deity. He felt genuine peace only when he was by his god's side, learning the virtues of forgiveness, family, honor, poise, and spiritual strength. He worshipped Ashhur completely, dedicating his life to his god's service, eschewing even something so simple as the love of a woman. He had become a beacon for his people, showing them how to live at peace with the land, teaching them how to respect the nature of *all* gods and their creations, not just those of Ashhur. Bardiya lectured to his fellow worshippers that the antelopes, wolves, bovines, and horses that Celestia had created were just as important as their own friends and families. He even expressed a vast respect for Karak, the deity of the east. *He and Ashhur are brothers,* he was fond of saying, *and as such, they are both divine.*

A thudding reached his ears, and he turned his gaze to the expanse of brown grass behind him. A large antelope, its antlers curved and regal, bounded through the swaying grasses. Chasing it were a group of people clothed in simple cured skins, their hair braided and their dark skin beaded with sweat. They used their spears as walking sticks. It was a hunting party, led by Bardiya's mother and father. The long pole for the day's kill hung empty, but given the antelope's exhaustion, it would not remain that way for long.

Hands rose in greeting, and Bardiya raised his own massive hand in return. The party knew better than to interrupt his prayers. His mother smiled up at him, her broad cheeks spread as wide as possible, and his father offered a gentle nod. Their ageless beauty, and the potency of their smiles, reflected the simple affection they held for their son. Bessus and Damaspia Gorgoros were dedicated to advancing their culture under the loving gaze of their god, so much so that they'd only had one child, eager as they were to devote their lives to leading their nation along the path of Ashhur.

Up ahead, the antelope slowed its frantic gallop, trudging through the field but keeping up a determined forward momentum. Bardiya watched as his father, Bessus, gestured for a young lady near the back of the party to come forward. The young girl approached them, the spear she held dwarfing her tiny frame. Bessus pointed to the antelope and mimicked a throwing motion. The girl followed his lead, her eyes focusing as she reared back, trying to stay upright while holding the much-too-long spear aloft. Two hopping steps, a thrust, and out soared the spear, wobbling as it flew.

The girl had been too slow, and the spear came in low, burying into the animal's rear thigh with a faint squirt of red. The hunting party cheered, but their merriment was short lived. The spear was not embedded deeply enough, and when the antelope jolted, the weapon bobbed and fell into the deep grass. The animal began to buck, picking up speed as it raced through the meadow toward the Gods' Road. Bardiya's mother shouted for the party to give chase, and they did, but human legs could not match those of a wounded beast. By the time it reached Bardiya and his tree, it had put a lengthy distance between it and the hunting party.

Bardiya cracked his back and slowly rose to his full height. Changing positions was murder on his joints, but he gritted his teeth and pushed through the pain. The section of the Stonewood Forest that rested on the southern bank of the Corinth River was visible on the horizon. He knew that if the injured antelope made it to the cover of trees, a much less dignified death awaited it, be it an agonizingly slow demise from blood loss or the slow horror of being devoured alive by the wolves and hyenas that prowled come nightfall.

Cupping his enormous palms around his mouth, he let out a low, vibrating hum, working his jaw up and down and circling his tongue, a trick taught to him by one of the Dezren elves before relations between the Kerrians and the elves had deteriorated even further than their original standoffish state. The sound shimmered in the air, causing everything in the path of his voice to appear hazy as a desert oasis. The antelope stopped in its tracks and turned to him, its head tilted at a curious angle. The beast seemed to forget the chase, seemed to forget about its injuries, and slowly approached the giant human, drawn in by the seductive sound.

The hunting party ceased their running, not daring to approach while he performed the *seducing whisper*. Bardiya raised his eyebrows in acknowledgment but didn't stop his humming until the animal was near. The creature's antlers were huge and deadly, and would have dwarfed a regular man, but they barely reached Bardiya's chest. It was certainly a healthy beast, strong and meaty. It would feed the village of Ang for at least a night, perhaps the children for two. He reached down and gently rubbed the back of the antelope's head, letting calming energy seep from his core, putting the creature at ease.

Bardiya gradually lowered himself back to the ground—he needed to stand to issue the *seducing whisper*, as the act stretched his lungs to their limit—and continued massaging the antelope's head. It nuzzled against him, wide antlers scraping past his cheek.

He examined its wounded thigh, which was still seeping blood. The leg beneath quivered with weakness.

He grabbed the animal beneath its narrow snout and lifted its head so he could gaze into its huge brown eyes.

"You are precious," he said while massaging the creature's jowls. "You are important. I give you Ashhur's grace and wish you happiness when you are once more in Celestia's arms."

He grabbed the immense antlers where they began at the top of the skull and jerked his arms in a circular motion. The antelope's expression didn't have time to change as its head was twisted around, snapping the bones in its neck and severing its spine. It collapsed to the ground, offering a final, gaseous moan before the light faded from its eyes. Bardiya placed his hand over its snout, leaned over, and gave it a final kiss.

"I am sorry," he said. In all honesty, he wished he had healed the majestic creature instead.

With the deed done, Bardiya's mother urged the hunting party to approach the scene. They drew near one by one, each offering him a bow or curtsey of appreciation. Then they began the process of roping the dead antelope to the carrying pole. They had to saw off its majestic antlers, which would have dragged along the ground.

His parents approached him last, while the rest of the hunting party began the trek back to the village. Bessus sat down across from him while Damaspia gently massaged the shoulders of her giant and tender son. He leaned his head back and gazed into his mother's eyes. They were sea blue, contrasting wonderfully with her skin tone, which neared black. Damaspia Gorgoros was at least five shades darker than her husband. Bessus claimed it was because he had created her using stones from the heart of the Black Spire, a mount that rose in the center of the desert and was considered a sacred monument by their people.

Bessus himself exuded dignity. He was understated, hardworking, fiercely loyal, and always questing to further his knowledge, the ideal figurehead for an infant species. He looked up at Bardiya and rested his hand on a knee that was wide as the trunk of the tree. Bardiya knew from the conflicted expression on his father's face, one black eyebrow raised higher than the other, that he wasn't pleased with how the morning had gone.

"Thank you, son," he said, his voice wavering from reverence to irritation. "Though I wish Taniya had stronger arms and better aim. The girl is eleven, and it is long past time for her to learn the art of the hunt."

"She will grow stronger, Father. And more capable."

"I know. I simply wish you had given us the chance to follow the beast."

"The antelope was beyond your hunting party and would have escaped into the Stonewood. It would have died a horrible death had I not intervened."

"Your mercy knows no bounds, my son. However, you must remember that every action our people make is a potential lesson to be taught. We must allow them to fail, even if that failure is embarrassing."

Bardiya shook his head. "We may use the creatures around us for clothing, shelter, and food, but it is still our duty to *preserve* the life that surrounds us, showing it dignity even in the face of death."

His father's expression began to grow angry, his dark cheeks turning a deep crimson as they often did during these sorts of conversations. Unlike the general populace, his father did not buy into Bardiya's impartial view of the gods. To Bessus Gorgoros, there was Ashhur and only Ashhur, and he would never see things differently.

"You are an overly sensitive fool," Bessus said in a hoarse whisper.

"Bessus!" exclaimed Damaspia. "Don't speak that way to your son."

Bessus turned on his wife.

"I will talk to him as I please. He disobeys my edicts, teaches sacrilege to our children, and usurps my authority at every turn, as if *he* were the patriarch." He pointed a slender finger into Bardiya's face. To the giant, it seemed small as a twig. "You forget that *I* was forged by Ashhur's hands, not you. *I* was given the ability to create an everlasting life to join with my own so we could lead our people into the golden forever. All you have done, Bardiya, is grow."

"Bessus, enough," scowled Damaspia.

Bardiya placed a hand on his mother's shoulder, stilling her rage. He refused to raise his voice under any circumstance, and decades of meditation and prayer had taught him to never lose his temper.

"Father, you are turning red," he said. "I have angered you. I apologize."

"Do *not* patronize me."

"I'm not. I truly am sorry."

He was, and his father knew it. He watched as the ageless patriarch's anger deflated ever so slightly. Bessus was a smart man, the most capable of all their people. He knew when a battle wasn't worth fighting. He dropped his head, frowned, and grunted.

"You disappoint me, Bardiya," he said, sadness in his tone. "You make the job your mother and I have undertaken much harder than it should be. Do not return to Ang for a week. Think about what you have done, and the lesson you have denied Taniya. Stay out here with your tree and sleep beneath the stars. However, do *not* offer your mercy to the wild things of Stonewood, and do not step foot within the elven lands. Should you bring Cleotis Meln's wrath down on our people again, I may have to send you away for good."

Bardiya sighed. *As if I need to be told that.*

Though he and his father had always clashed about faith, it was only recently that Bessus had taken to verbal outbursts or the occasional punishment. And it was Bardiya's own fault.

Two years ago, as he'd waded in the section of the Corinth River that flowed through Stonewood Forest, a flock of kobo had wandered into the water nearby. Bardiya had sensed a shift in the air, the scent of putrefaction filling his nostrils, choking him to tears. He'd stumbled toward the kobo, arms outstretched, his vision shaky from the horrific smell. A single touch on the beak of the majestic birds was enough to tell him that the entire flock had been stricken with the hacking, an uncommon disease that doomed its victims to cough up blood until their lungs finally ruptured. The worst part was that the hacking was seemingly immune to Ashhur's healing grace, at least when administered through Bardiya's hands. An entire generation of brine geese had been obliterated in his youth, and half the population of desert foxes not ten years after that.

So he gave the sick birds his mercy. One by one he dispatched them, right on the banks of the river, and then built a large fire to burn their remains. He sang songs of Ashhur's blessings as the flames crackled and hissed. It was there the elves had found him, on their land, filling the forest with smoke and destroying its creatures. The elves did not believe his story, as the hacking had never shown its ugliness in Stonewood before. Bardiya was thrown out, threatened with staffs; the elves had even fired arrows on him as he fled. Since that day, humans were no longer welcome in the heart of Stonewood Forest. Arguments over boundaries and ownership of land had followed ever since. Bardiya's simple act of mercy had driven a wedge between their two peoples, creating a chain of bad will that was yet to be broken.

"I apologize again, Father," he said.

"I know that you are sorry," his father replied, looking disappointed. "I simply wish you could see things from my perspective at times. It is no easy task, leading a whole society into maturity. You do not seem to respect that, or my wisdom, and you act as if my head is filled with nothing but air."

"There is something to be said for a head filled with air," proclaimed a familiar voice. "If not for women like that, I might still be a virgin."

Bessus whirled around, as did Damaspia. Bardiya lifted his head slowly, gazing down the slight rise to the edge of the Gods' Road. The dust cloud in the distance was gone, replaced by two gray horses that stood twenty feet away. How they had arrived without him noticing the sound of clomping hooves was baffling.

On one horse sat the youngest DuTaureau child, Nessa, her face youthful and naïve as she picked dirt from beneath her fingernails. Patrick DuTaureau sat on the other. Bardiya hadn't laid eyes on his oldest friend in nearly five years, but Patrick's unusual appearance couldn't allow his being mistaken for anyone else. Back hunched, sprays of wild orange curls dancing like sprigs on his head, and legs, too short for his large upper body and dangling like limp noodles over each side of his mare. The massive sword he always carried hung from his saddle, and an impish grin stretched his misshapen features.

"So," said Patrick, "how is my favorite dysfunctional family? Righteously fucked or fucking righteously?"

"Patrick!" exclaimed Damaspia, throwing a hand over her mouth.

Bessus rolled his eyes, but held back a biting comment and simply bowed. In that instant Bardiya appreciated, and even admired, his father's restraint. They might occasionally not be on the greatest of terms, but he could not deny how much he loved and respected the man whose seed had produced him.

"It has been a long time, Master DuTaureau," Bessus said. "But I ask that you refrain from profanity while visiting our lands."

"Not visiting," said Patrick. "Just passing through."

A bird cawed overhead, and Nessa lifted her pretty head to stare skyward. Bessus brushed dirt from his elbows, hefted his spear, and slipped his free arm around Damaspia. Bardiya noticed that his mother, while acting courteous, refused to lift her gaze to Patrick's deformities. But then again, most people didn't. That was something that Bardiya could not understand. Patrick might look different, and he was certainly crude and derisive at times, but in his heart he was a good man, as good as anyone else in Ashhur's Paradise.

"We will be going now," said his father, turning toward the trail that led back to Ang. "Have a good journey, Patrick, wherever it is you go. Bardiya…I love you, even if you anger me."

Bardiya leaned back, saddened. His head struck the same branch he'd hit earlier that morning. Bringing up a giant hand, he rubbed the sore spot and groaned.

Patrick whispered something to his sister and clumsily dismounted his mare. He waddled over to where Bardiya was leaning against the cypress tree, and cupped his eyes against the glare of the sun so that he could look east, to where the grasslands ended and the desert began.

"You and the old man are still fighting, I see," Patrick said.

"We are."

"Sounded a bit more…emotional than before."

"It was. It has been. A lot has happened since we last met."

Patrick raised an eyebrow.

"Care to elaborate?"

"Not particularly. Our people squabble with the elves. Let us leave it at that."

"There've always been squabbles with elves, from the day we first stepped out from the clay. What does that have to do with you and your father?"

Bardiya let out a long sigh.

"I might have made it significantly worse."

Patrick turned to his sister, who was still sitting on her horse and staring at the sky.

"Ness," he yelled. "I think I know why those Dezren acted like we didn't exist when we crossed the Corinth. Big bones over here made them *angry*."

"Big bones?" asked Bardiya.

"Eh, it's the best I can come up with at the moment. It's so hot I see three of everything. By Karak's fiery cock, I think I'd be more comfortable in mother's bed, and I haven't slid beneath *those* covers in sixty years."

Bardiya chuckled. Five years had passed since they'd last met, and Patrick was still Patrick.

"It's fine, my friend," Bardiya said. "I can handle fights with father. I don't need to be coddled any longer."

"You positive?"

"Yes."

"Good, because I'm tired of coddling you. You're *way* too big to be a baby."

Bardiya rose up on his knees, leaned forward, and wrapped his friend in a tight embrace, his size nearly swallowing the much smaller Patrick.

"I missed you, old friend," he said.

"Missed you too," replied Patrick. "But don't suffocate me."

"My apologies."

Patrick pushed away from him, swiping at his breeches to flatten the folds. "You're always so damn sorry," he said. "It doesn't have to be that way, you know."

"I know. It's my nature."

Patrick grinned his snaggle-toothed grin. "Well stop it already. It isn't becoming of the great Bardiya of Ker to be apologetic all hours of the day."

"I'll keep that in mind."

Using his right hand for support, Bardiya lifted his body off the ground. His knees popped once more.

"Oh shit," said Patrick, "you grew again."

"I did."

"I figured it would have stopped by now."

"I wish it had."

"Well I'll be," said Patrick, slapping him on the lower back, which was as high as the hunchback could reach. A wave of concern washed over Bardiya when Patrick's hand touched his flesh, a sensation that trickled into his mind from the ether. He silenced his old friend's banter with a single raised finger.

"Patrick, why are you here? Where is it you're going?"

Patrick shook his head. "Some obtuse garbage. I guess Karak finally tired of the folks in the delta not bowing down to him, so he sent some soldiers to teach them a lesson the really hard way. Don't know the whole story, really. Jacob wasn't very forthcoming in his letter—just said I need to go to Haven and convince them to tear down that temple they built."

"The Temple of the Flesh?"

"That's it."

"And Eveningstar sent you on this mission?"

"The one and only."

Bardiya frowned. He'd heard whispers from his people that the temple had come under fire, but he'd passed them off as wild fireside stories. Many Kerrians tried to outdo each other with tall tales of war and great battles, things none of his people, nor anyone in the west, knew about. It made for interesting mealtime conversations and nothing more…or so he'd thought. If Jacob, Ashhur's most trusted, was involved, then the situation was far more serious than a fireside tale. He breathed a silent prayer of thanks to his god that none of his people had been harmed.

"And what are you to do if they don't do as you tell them?" he asked Patrick, who shrugged.

"I guess I charm them into submission."

"Seriously?"

"Bardy, I don't know. I'm no diplomat. I'm walking as blind as a goat at the bottom of the ocean. But if you're so worried, why don't you come with me? The delta's still a few days' journey from here, and I'm sure you could use a nice escape from your father."

Patrick's easy smile vanished from his face.

"Please. I could use your help."

Bardiya wanted to go and hated that he couldn't.

"I apologize, my friend," he said, trying to ignore the guilt in his stomach. "My place is here in Ker, whether my father wants me or not. I'm bound to this land as its protector, its guiding light."

"You're sure?"

"I am."

"Patrick, come *on*," shouted Nessa from behind them, impatiently tapping her foot against her horse's flank. "This saddle is chaffing my thighs; we're running low on water; and I need a bath. Can we please go now?"

Patrick laughed and said, "She's an impatient one, isn't she? We've only been traveling for less than a week, and already she's complaining. Spoiled brat. With how much she whines, you'd think she was only ten years old."

"If she's spoiled, you know it's your fault."

"Don't remind me, please." His warped face softened as he gazed at the petite girl. "But it's tough to say no to her. She's so innocent and naïve. She looks at this world with Ashhur's love in her eyes. She doesn't know pain or suffering—can't even understand that they might exist. She's also one of the few who doesn't mind my appearance, which I much appreciate," he said with a laugh. "Other than yourself, of course."

"Patrick, *please!*"

"All right, Ness!" Patrick shouted back. He glanced up at Bardiya, shook his head, and extended his hand. "I guess I should be moving along," he said. "I *am* itching to get out of these riding pants and slip into something more comfortable. Besides, I shouldn't keep the princess waiting any longer, should I?"

"Not if you want to stay sane," laughed Bardiya. "Take care of yourself, Patrick."

His deformed friend slowly departed, shuffling sideways so he could still look at Bardiya despite the painful twist in his back.

"I'll do that," he said. "Always have. And you take care of yourself too, my friend. I know how difficult a distant father can be, and I'd hate it to get you down. Perhaps when I'm done in Haven, I'll come back for a spell. We can sit around the campfire, bitching about the bastards and how they lessened our lots in life. It'll be just like old times."

"That would be nice."

A pang of sorrow struck Bardiya's heart. As the only two male offspring of Ashhur's First Families, he and Patrick had always shared a special bond, one their mutual oddness only reinforced. But Patrick had it wrong. Bardiya's father was not distant, nor had he hurt him in any way that mattered. Richard DuTaureau, on the other hand, had damaged his son more than Patrick would ever know. Ashhur's forgiveness of that man was truly remarkable considering what he had done....

Bardiya shook the ugly thought from his mind.

"Stay safe, and stop growing already!" Patrick shouted, after awkwardly mounting his mare. He and his sister held hands as the horses broke into a slow trot. It was a sublime and beautiful moment, one that demonstrated just how pure Patrick DuTaureau was despite his flaws. Bardiya smiled and waved his giant hand, understanding that no matter how physically twisted he was, his friend was as perfect a creation as Ashhur had ever made. *I only give to my children the trials they are capable of overcoming*, the god was fond of saying. It seemed as though Patrick were capable of conquering anything. Bardiya decided that Jacob had chosen wisely when he'd selected Patrick to do whatever it was he'd been sent to do.

Bardiya watched brother and sister depart into the east, the dry dust kicking up behind them. When they disappeared from sight, he sat back down beneath the tree, crossed his legs, and closed his eyes. His stomach cramped from hunger, but he ignored it. Leaning his head back, this time twisting his neck to avoid the branch, he prayed to Ashhur to keep his friend safe, no matter what trials he might encounter along the way.

CHAPTER

9

Vulfram's heart beat a mile a minute as he guided his horse through the massive oaken gates surrounding the inner sanctum of Erznia, deep within the forest. The giant pines that served to shield the township from the outside world gave way to vast courtyards, humble wooden cottages, and lush gardens. The leaping doe was everywhere he looked, painted on the gates and on flags and banners that fluttered in the early afternoon breeze. Dread pulsed in Vulfram's veins, the opposite of what he should have felt upon entering his childhood home. He had seen his family so little over the past eight years that their reunions always ended up feeling more sad than joyous. His children and his wife needed him, but the realm needed him more.

He urged his tired horse down the dirt path that ran through the center of the township. Erznia had been the lovechild of his mother and father, built in the months after the creation of humanity and twenty-six years before his birth. They had chosen the location because of its isolation, natural beauty, and proximity to the Queln River. Erznia had originally housed all five hundred youths created to be the wards of House Mori, youth who would soon mature and have families. Over the inevitable march of the years, many in the first and subsequent generations had ventured out of the enchanted forest to build inland townships along the southern edge of the Gods' Road and the eastern coastline. Only those closest to the Mori bloodline stayed behind, the families who would give birth to some of the prosperous merchants and tradesmen of southern Neldar. The intimacy of the populace had made living here a warm experience, one Vulfram had hoped would never end. He had resisted leaving for many years, staying behind even after his mother moved to Veldaren when he was twenty-seven. Although he had missed her, she'd visited often in the early years, to spend time with her family, and had always been greeted warmly on her return, which had convinced Vulfram it would be the same for him.

It wasn't. After eight years of sporadic visits, and whispers of what had happened in the delta, the same people who had once viewed Vulfram as a member of their extended family now eyed him with dubious expressions as he rode through the township. They seemed friendly enough, offering smiles and salutations, but he could read the fear and uncertainty in their stares. He was no longer Vulfram Mori, son of Soleh and Ibis, no longer the gentle man who loved children and helped build many of the cottages that dotted the township's inner sanctum. Now he was Lord Commander Mori, imposing leader of Karak's Army, come to implement the Divinity's justice. He thought of Darkfall, the giant broadsword sheathed on his back that would carry out that justice if need be, and decided that the people were right to fear him. The thought of what he might have to do to his own girl wracked him with a special kind of anguish, no matter how unlikely it was she'd done something terrible enough to warrant such a punishment. Sometimes he hated so much that King Vaelor had thrust this title upon him.

Ignoring the suspicious looks, he pulled on the reins and nudged his mare faster. More cottages and larger chalets passed him on either side. They were packed so tightly together that elaborate gardens edged by dogwood trees were grown between them to give the residents a semblance of privacy. The sight of so many homes made Vulfram feel decidedly *less* at home. It had only been a few months since his last visit, yet over that short span his childhood village seemed to have grown and changed.

Finally Mori Manor appeared before him. The thick pine logs that formed the outside of the manor were stained a deep shade of reddish brown. The door was painted lavender, a color of which his mother had long been fond. It was the largest structure in the township, stretched out so wide it filled nearly all his peripheral vision. Vegetable and fruit gardens dotted the quad, and the peach tree Vulfram had planted when he was ten years old grew to the left of the front walk, looking decidedly taller than the last time he'd laid eyes on it. His heart warmed despite the dire nature of his visit, for at least some things in Erznia would never change.

The front door creaked open as he tethered his horse to the thick post in front of the walk. He glanced up, and there she stood— Yenge, his wife of nineteen years, resplendent in a simple yellow country dress that clung to a body still supple even after birthing and feeding three children. As Vulfram approached, his gaze moved over the curve of her breasts to the soft nub of her chin, the plumpness of her cheeks, and those blue eyes that seemed to glow against the backdrop of her tanned skin. Her hair was dark and uncontrollably wavy, hanging to the middle of her back. She'd been twenty-five when he'd left to fulfill his duty to Karak, and the only sign that she'd aged a day since then were the tired lines that had sprouted from the corners of her eyes. Vulfram felt his insides tremble, thinking of the last night he'd spent in Erznia—the kisses he and Yenge had shared—and smiled.

Yenge didn't return his smile. Her expression was nervous as she scraped her teeth against her lower lip. He hadn't seen her this way since they'd discovered problems with the health of their youngest child, Caleigh, in the hours after the girl's birth.

His hands found hers as he climbed the steps. There were tears in her eyes. She didn't say a word to him as he gently placed his lips against hers; her response was to kiss him back slowly and then wrap her arms around him.

"I've missed you," Yenge said as the kiss ended.

"As have I you," he whispered. He tipped his shaved head so that it rested in the nape of her neck. She smelled of honey and flour. "Did you receive my letter?"

"I did, yesterday."

"And you told the Magister that I was coming?"

Her eyes dropped. She sniffled but kept her composure. "Yes, Magister Wentner is in the courtyard with the offenders...and others."

He stepped back. "Offenders? Lyana was not alone when she broke Karak's law?"

"No, my love. There is another. Kristof Renson. The boy's father and mother await you as well."

"Kristof? The boy is what—fourteen? What could these two have done to draw the ire of the Magister worthy of a Minister's delegate?"

Yenge sniffled again. "I've been told not to tell you, my love. I'm truly sorry."

"Wentner's instructions?"

Her downcast eyes were answer enough. Vulfram grunted, furious the Magister hadn't thought to contact him personally regarding the matter. He was the girl's *father*, for Karak's sake, as well as Lord Commander and one of the Divinity's most loyal servants. If anyone should have been trusted, it was he.

The interior of the manor looked much like he remembered it, with its open rooms, rustic wood floor, and log walls. Lavish furniture filled the vast spaces, gifts bestowed on his family by the greatest craftsmen in Neldar. The candelabras placed in each crevasse were ornate creations, looping rods of silver and gold that held six candles apiece. But Vulfram forgot them even as he saw them. Nothing could remain on his mind except his daughter.

He stormed through the arched portal cut into the limestone wall of the interior square of the manor, the only part of the dwelling not made of felled trees. The courtyard was vast—two hundred feet in either direction—and surrounded on all by sides by four thick walls. When he was a boy, Vulfram played in this open space with Kayne and Lilah, pretending to fight dragons, giants, and demons from the underworld, thrusting wooden swords at his brother and sister lions while they leapt around him.

Now, all that youthful innocence of the courtyard was gone. In its place were a great many people milling about, all wearing dire expressions. He saw his brother Ulric's wife, Dimona, and her three children. Here also was his other brother, Oris, former servant of the City Watch under Vulfram, his lower jaw and neck rippling with red scar tissue, an injury from when he'd rescued three whores trapped in a burning brothel. Oris's wife, Ebbe, a woman with skin as tan as Yenge's and tightly knotted hair, stood at her husband's side. She was tall and proud, exuding strength and an intensity of faith. Their two children huddled behind her flowing sarong, which was painted with sunflowers. To their right was Broward Renson, young Kristof's grandfather, born on the same day as Vulfram; they had been best friends since they were toddlers playing at being adults, with fake wine to drink and blunted sticks for spears. The man looked much older than Vulfram, carrying the weight of all his sixty-seven years on his broad shoulders. Broward's son, Bracken, stood next to him, along with Bracken's wife, Penelope. Every member of the Renson family looked tense and fidgety, Bracken in particular. The man chewed on his fingernails as if they were kernels of sweet corn.

Beyond the gathered crowd knelt two young people, shackled to a concrete slab. Vulfram's heart dropped when he saw Lyana, his precious little daughter. Just like the town, she seemed to have grown so much since last he saw her. She looked almost an adult, as stunning as her mother, possessing the same blue eyes and untamable hair. But instead of a beautiful, carefree girl, she was presented to him as a broken woman, her lips and cheeks painted like those of a whore. She was dressed in a plain canvas kirtle—prisoner's attire—that was covered with splotches of dirt. Beside her knelt Kristof, his sandy hair as filthy as straw in a horse's pen, his eyes closed and his hands clenched before him as his whole body shivered. His kirtle, nearly identical to Lyana's, was coated with fresh, glistening blood.

Only shock and an iron will forged over decades kept Vulfram from drawing Darkfall and thrusting its blade through the heart of whoever dared insult his daughter in such a way.

"By the order of Karak, all kneel in the presence of the Lord Commander!"

Vulfram turned at the sound of his son's voice, while the rest of those in attendance bowed on a single knee. Alexander Mori, eighteen and looking strong as an ox in his stained riding leathers, escorted his youngest sister, Caleigh, down the steps and into the yard. Behind them walked Magister Wentner, a man looking every bit his eighty years, with a sickly frame, a turkey-like wattle for a neck, and eyes reduced to a haunting gray by age. Alexander stared at his father, jaw unyielding, and it seemed as though his strength were passed along to his sister, for Caleigh kept her expression as hard as the limestone that made up the house's inner walls. As far back as Vulfram could remember, his youngest would startle at the buzz of an insect whizzing by her ear. He couldn't help but feel a queer sort of pride at the strength she now displayed.

The magister in his deep black robes stepped toward him, while his children took their places beside their mother. Wentner offered him a frail bow, the sight of which only enhanced Vulfram's rage. *This is the man who would make my daughter up as a whore, this bastard, years past his prime?*

"What's the meaning of this?" Vulfram said with a growl. "What in Karak's name makes you think yourself justified in humiliating my daughter this way, chaining these children up like common felons?"

The magister didn't flinch at his tone, and when he gazed up at Vulfram his gray eyes dripped with frost.

"The law is direct and strict, Lord Commander," the magister said. "When found guilty, the prisoners will be presented before the bringers of justice with appearances befitting their crimes."

Vulfram's blood boiled. "What crimes have they been found guilty of? And who deemed themselves worthy to determine such guilt?"

"I found them guilty, Lord Commander," said Wentner, the slightest scowl appearing on his withered visage. "I am the Magister of Erznia, and by decree of Highest Crestwell, it is the magister's duty to adjudicate any accused crimes of blasphemy before awaiting a delegate of the Inner Sanctum to serve punishment." He pointed a finger at the two chained youngsters. "These two have been accused of infanticide, the utmost crime against our god and his gift of life."

Lyana and Kristof both began weeping, and the anger broiling inside Vulfram was replaced by a jolt of shock.

"That cannot be," he said, softly. "They are only children."

"They ceased to be children the moment they consummated their attraction," said Wentner. "And they became criminals once they performed the unspeakable."

"It's not true!" shouted Lyana.

One of the magister's gnarled hands shot out, lashing Lyana's painted cheek. Her head snapped to the side, and a string of bloody spittle flew from her lips.

"Silence," the magister said. "The convicted shall speak only when spoken to."

The magister's hand rose again, but this time Vulfram caught it. The two men stared eye to eye, each one challenging the other. Wentner was a representative of their deity, and it would be blasphemy for Vulfram to supersede his granted authority. But Lyana was also Vulfram's child, and Wentner clearly saw the death that awaited him if he pressed Vulfram too far.

After taking a deep breath and releasing Wentner's hand, Vulfram asked for the proof of their crimes. In answer, the magister reached a hand into his robe and withdrew a small burlap sack. From the sack he removed a small wooden vial and an article of clothing. Holding up the vial he said, "Lyana Mori was discovered moaning in pain by her brother Alexander thirteen days ago. Beside her, on her bedpost, was this vial. It was empty, but it still carries the scent of oil of crim."

He handed the vial to Vulfram, who sniffed the opened top. The bitter and unmistakable stench of crim oil, an extract taken from the base stems of crimleaf, assaulted his nostrils. Crim oil was a powerful tonic traditionally used to treat cattle when they fell ill with infection. The oil caused massive internal hemorrhaging while obliterating whatever sickness had struck the bovine. It was rarely used on humans, and never if the victim was pregnant, due to the danger to the growing babe. That fact alone made it a popular—and highly illegal—commodity that was sold only in the darkest of back alleys.

His mind spun as Magister Wentner handed him the article of clothing.

"This was the garment the offender was wearing on the morning she was found. Take a look at it, Lord Commander. Take a good look."

Vulfram held the garment with shaking fingers. It was a satin nightdress, one he had given Yenge many years before as a gift. It was soft and pink, colored using dye made from roses that grew in the Manor's gardens. As it fell open in his hands, he saw the shade grew darker and darker the farther down the garment he looked, until it was a deep red tinted with orange down at the hemline. He crinkled the nightdress in both fists and brought it to his nose. He smelled the blood, along with something that smelled oddly sharp, like vinegar. He dropped the garment to the ground and wiped at his nose.

"What you just smelled," said Wentner, "is all that remains of your grandchild."

Vulfram's stared at his daughter, tears pouring down her cheeks in torrents while she shook her head. It felt as if the entire world stood still, and there was only Vulfram, Lyana, and the vile Wentner.

"Please, Father!" the girl screamed.

Magister Wentner reached back to slap her again, but thought better of it when he caught Vulfram's glare.

"And what of the boy?" Vulfram asked. "What is he accused of?"

"He supplied the oil, Lord Commander," replied Wentner, slowly lowering his hand. "We found four more vials hidden inside his mattress."

"Is that true?"

Kristof didn't answer; he simply dropped his head, closed his eyes, and wept.

Alexander strode forward. "It is true, Lord Commander. I discovered the vials myself when I went to question Bracken Renson on the whereabouts of his son."

"You little *shit!*"

Bracken Renson barreled full steam at Alexander, a club held high to strike. In a single movement, Alexander shielded his sister and mother with one hand and unsheathed his sword with the other. Bracken flung aside Magister Wentner, the muscles in his face tensed to the point of snapping. His club swung, ramming into Alexander's raised sword. The two shoved against one another, the sword buried deep into the thick wood of the club. His shock finally abated, Vulfram grabbed the collar of Bracken's tunic and yanked hard enough to send the father of the convicted boy thudding to the ground. The attached sword and club skittered off to the side. Oris rushed in, a meaty fist drawn back, but Vulfram held his scarred brother at bay with a single glance. Alexander tried to advance on Bracken, but Vulfram stood in the way, feeling like a bull as he breathed heavily through his nose.

"Get Yenge and Caleigh out of here," he told Alexander, who opened his mouth, closed it, and then nodded in respect. As his son led the girls away, Vulfram let out a cry as a sharp heel connected with his shin.

"Enough of this!" he shouted, whirling around and planting a boot on Bracken's chest.

"He's…my…*son!*" shouted Bracken, thrashing beneath the weight.

A gentle hand touched his shoulder. In his wrath Vulfram turned with fist at ready, but when he caught sight of graying hair and sad brown eyes, he let his arm drop. Broward Renson stood there, staring down at his eldest boy.

"I apologize for his actions," the old man said, without once looking in Vulfram's direction. He reached down and grabbed Bracken's hand. Vulfram removed his foot, allowing his old friend to help the man to his feet. Bracken huffed and puffed while the two walked back to their place of waiting.

His blood still racing, Vulfram looked from the magister to the accused children, to Alexander and Yenge, who lingered just inside the doorway, cowering near the shadows as if they didn't want to be seen. Vulfram shook his head and approached Lyana, kneeling before her, taking her chin in one hand and wiping away her tears with the other.

"Tell me, child," he whispered. He fought to keep his hand still, to keep his jaw from trembling. "What they say…is it true?"

It broke his heart the way she looked at him, quivering in fear as if he were a monstrous stranger. Even when he lowered his voice to the levels he had used to tell her stories when she was a young child, her fear never left her. Was he that kind father no longer? Had that man become a distant memory? Was he now just a stranger arriving in their midst to pass judgment?

"Be honest, Lyana," he said. "Karak is merciful to the truthful. You have nothing to fear, not from me. Just tell me the truth. Is the magister right?"

Lyana met his eyes, looked away, and then nodded.

Vulfram's heart broke once more.

"I stopped bleeding," she whispered in a timid voice only he could hear. "I was scared. Mother said I was to marry Boris Corineau, and Kris said his father would kill him if he found out. I'm so sorry, father. No one was to find out. The oil wasn't to leave a trace—that's what he said! Please…."

Vulfram peered to the side, to where Kristof stared at him with wide, terrified eyes.

"And where did you get the crim oil?" Vulfram asked. The boy simply continued staring, his body shaking so hard Vulfram feared his heart would stop. "Speak, son. Where did you get the oil?"

"He got it from me."

Vulfram stood up and faced the voice. It was Broward, his childhood friend, who had spoken. He stood in front of his still fuming son. Broward took a single step, his hands held out in supplication.

"You?" asked Vulfram, wondering if the day could get any worse. "Why?"

"The boy came to me, knowing I had plenty because of my cattle. So I gave him a few vials and told him the decision was his."

"You left poison…and a decision with such dire consequences… to a *child?*"

Broward bobbed his head at Magister Wentner. "As the magister said, they ceased being children the moment his cock entered her."

Vulfram couldn't believe what he was hearing. This was his old friend. They'd played siege the castle together among the tall elm and maple trees of the surrounding forest, shared stories of first kisses. And now, to hear him speak in such a way to him…even worse, he seemed to not care that he'd given Vulfram's daughter—and Broward's own grandson—a potent remedy he knew damn well to be unlawful.

Vulfram didn't know what to do. Wavering in place, he cast his gaze on them all, begging for a sign from his god. *Please, Karak, give me guidance*, he silently pleaded. He looked to his daughter once more, saw her bawling in her whore's garb. Deep inside him, something snapped.

"Get out!" he roared. "All of you, out!"

"But Lord Commander, there must be a verdict," said Magister Wentner. "I must witness Karak's justice as it is passed down."

Vulfram leveled a lethal gaze at the old man and pointed a thick, shaking finger at him. "I couldn't give a shit about what you *must* do, old man. Karak's justice can wait for tomorrow, after I've had time to think. Now everyone. Fuck *off!*"

The people departed, filing out of the interior courtyard with quickened paces. Vulfram breathed heavily, watching them leave with disdain in his eyes. When Magister Wentner started to grab the chains binding the two children, Vulfram stopped him.

"My son will watch over them tonight," he said.

The magister didn't dare argue.

Alexander came over, helping Kristof to his feet, then Lyana. The two were quiet but for their sniffling. Vulfram wanted to embrace them, to tell them everything would be well, but he couldn't. Not now. What he wanted was answers, and not from them. From his son, who looked at his sister as if she were less than human.

"Alexander," he said.

"Yes, Father?"

"Why did you turn your sister in instead of notifying me? Do you want her enslaved or dead?"

"No, Father," he said, coldly. "I wish her truthful and pure, not deceitful. But I suppose I have higher expectations of our blood than you do."

"She is my *daughter*."

"And she is my sister, and I love her no less. Yet she sinned and shamed the family. Not even the offspring of the great Lord Commander are unbound from Karak's law. Or have you forgotten that?"

Without thinking, Vulfram backhanded his son across the face. The boy stumbled back a step, the side of his lip cut, his motions dragging Kristof and Lyana along with him. His hand reached up to touch his cheek, already swelling. When he looked at his father, he appeared genuinely hurt.

"Don't speak to me that way," Vulfram said, his voice ice. "Like you know better. Like you could stand for a moment in these shoes."

Alexander's tone shifted, becoming more contrite. "Forgive me," he said, his head bowed. "I never meant to disrespect you. You always taught me that Karak's will and judgment ruled over all else. That his laws must be obeyed and enforced, no matter what. So I did as you have always taught me. I thought you would be proud."

It was Vulfram's turn to feel ashamed. He gazed at his son, all grown up and taking responsibility just as he had done at that age. Tears formed in the corners of Vulfram's eyes, tears it cost him to hold at bay.

"You're right, son. I've lost my way. I...I'm...."

He thought of Karak and the god's last words to him before he went on his sojourn forty years before. "I have faith in you, Vulfram," he had said. "You will be tested, and tested greatly, but there is no test that you cannot pass." He wished that were true, for he felt lost. More than anything, he wished Karak were there with him now, to offer him guidance, to give him strength.

Vulfram pulled Alexander in close, held the sides of his face as he pressed his own forehead against his son's.

"You were right," he said, his voice nearly pleading. "But don't you dare stop loving her, sin or not. That I could never forgive. Do you understand me?"

Alexander swallowed, and he saw sudden guilt flicker in his eyes, then understanding.

"Good," Vulfram said. "Take the guilty to the magister's hovel. But clean them up beforehand. And tell the magister that he is to treat them with respect, unless he wishes to have a personal meeting with Darkfall. Tomorrow we gather at the common green, in the shade of the statue of the lion, at high noon. I will carry out Karak's justice then, whatever I determine it to be."

"Yes, Father," Alexander said with a bow, and went about escorting the two youngsters out of the courtyard. Vulfram heard Lyana plead for him to stop, to let her stay the night in her own bed, but he closed his ears to the outside world.

Caleigh tried to comfort him as he made his way back to the manor, but it did no good. Even Yenge's words did nothing to improve his mood. He brushed his wife aside, no longer thinking of how he wanted to bed her, but instead telling her he wished to spend the night alone.

It was only half a lie.

He went to Mori Manor's temple, located at the eastern end of the structure. It was a tall room, the ceiling as high as the manor's three floors. In the center of the temple was a life-sized statue of Karak, the first ever sculpted by Vulfram's father. The statue faced the east, twelve feet tall and imperial in stature. Vulfram knelt on the pew before the statue, staring up at the visage of his most beloved god, and prayed.

Late afternoon gave way to twilight, which gave way to night, and still Vulfram moved nary a muscle. He stayed on his knees with his hands clasped before him, uttering words of entreaty. When his stomach rumbled, he did nothing. When darkness moved over the room like the tide over the shore, he did nothing. When the air grew cold, he shivered and did nothing else. Before long he knelt in near complete darkness, gazing up at a vague yet mighty outline of holy strength, as tormented as if he were trapped in the bottommost level of the underworld.

His mind was beginning to falter, his body to give out, when suddenly he heard a soft scraping sound, like linens being rubbed against a grainy surface. He blinked his eyes, bleary with sleep, and watched the god's outline shift before him. It moved as if crouching, until it lay across the expanse of the statue's platform, no longer part of the statue, which remained exactly as it had been when Vulfram entered the temple.

The silhouette of a massive hand reached forward and snapped its fingers. Candles flamed to life all around him, illuminating the temple with vaporous light. Vulfram could have wept with joy. There he was, live and in the flesh—Karak, reclining on the dais as if the hard marble were the most comfortable surface in both kingdoms. His huge yellow eyes gazed at Vulfram with compassion and wisdom.

"My Lord," Vulfram gasped.

"My son," said Karak, his voice loud and booming, seemingly shaking the temple. The statue above, a perfect likeness in white and black marble, trembled. "I heard your prayers. Something troubles you."

Vulfram lowered his head. "I have lost my faith, my Lord," he said, before cowardice could change his mind. When the tears came, he did nothing to stop them. "I'm sorry. I've failed you."

Karak's leisurely posture didn't waver. "You have done no such thing, my son. Why would you think so?"

"My daughter has sinned gravely, yet I do not wish to punish her. More than anything, I wish to take her into my arms and flee this place, running forever if I must. It's a desire I don't think I can overcome."

Karak stared at him with glowing eyes seeming to burn right into his soul, bringing warmth to his quivering bones. "You can overcome anything," said the god. "I have faith in you."

"What if that faith is misplaced?"

The god grabbed his shoulder, engulfing nearly a quarter of his body in his palm. "It is not. I know you will do what is right and that all who deserve judgment shall receive it."

Vulfram nodded. "I have no choice in the matter, do I?"

"There is always a choice, my son. Most often, knowing the correct one is not the hard part. No, what takes courage, what takes *strength*, is making the choice we know is right despite every desire otherwise. Do you love me?"

"Of course. More than anything."

"Then remember that my love supersedes all. If it is torment you fear, remember that the greatest torment would be to exist knowing I am no longer by your side. Do not run, not from me, and not from what you know is right."

The god touched a finger to his forehead, and white light filled his vision....

He awoke on the floor of the temple, his face resting in a small puddle of his own drool. The sunrise cast sparks of shimmering red on the statue above him. Vulfram lifted his head and gazed at the statue. The only sign of Karak's visit was the aching hole in Vulfram's heart. His back sore from sleeping on the hard floor, he limped out of the temple, shutting the door quietly behind him. He heard Ulrich and Oris's children playing in the sitting room and smelled the sweet, narcotic scent of bacon frying over an open fire. Yenge's voice cut through the morning air as she sang the sad song of love and loss she had sung to him on their first night together. His family, those who had not betrayed his trust, was waiting for him. It should have filled him with happiness, but it did not.

His decision was made. He had the hole in his heart to thank for that.

The sky was ominous, but even so, the effigy of the lion cast a long shadow over the damp grass that covered Erznia's center square. Even more townspeople gathered than before, onlookers who congregated on the fringes of the assembly. The whole square was a giant bundle of nervous energy.

Vulfram strode to the center, feeling like a statue carved and come to life. He gazed at Bracken Renson, who stared back at him with fearful eyes. Where was the man who had so brazenly attacked Alexander the day before? In his stead was a frightened, yet hopeful, child. Vulfram wasn't sure what had brought about this change, nor did he care. Bracken realized his son's fate rested in the hands of the Lord Commander. Perhaps that was it.

He stepped up to the executioner's stone, a thigh-high slab of granite positioned in the corner of the lion's shadow. The only other time it had been used was fifteen years ago, when a rapist had been caught stalking the young girls of Erznia. It had been Joseph Crestwell who'd doled out Karak's justice that day, just as it was Vulfram who would carry it out today. The stone still bore the faintest hint of the rapist's blood.

Taking in a deep breath, Vulfram turned to address the crowd.

"We have gathered here today to bear witness to the punishment of Kristof Renson and Lyana Mori. They have been found guilty of infanticide, one of the worst sins against our god and creator, Karak, the Divinity of the East. Our race is in its infancy, and the lives blessed by our god are precious and rare. To end a life before it has even begun is not only a crime against Karak, but against all of us. The cost of this sin has been decreed by the Divinity himself, and that judgment is final. Bring out the guilty!"

A rumble passed through the crowd as Magister Wentner led a hooded Kristof and Lyana through them, flanked by Alexander and Vulfram's scarred brother, Oris. The emotions of the assembly grew tenfold with each passing moment, some sobbing, some shouting in disbelief, a select few jeering. Those jeers cut into Vulfram, but he hardened his heart against them. To think on what he had to do, to dwell on the horror...he couldn't. He just couldn't, so he let it pass over him like water across a stone. Someone shouted *"Karak!"* and threw a rotten potato that exploded against Lyana's pale, cream-colored gown, bathing her in stinking juices. He should have been enraged, but instead it was like a stake driven into the hole in his heart. At least the whore's outfit and makeup had been washed off her. Lyana was about to greet her fate; at least she could do so with some measure of dignity.

The pair was brought before him and their hoods were removed. Lyana's rosebud lips twitched and tears cascaded down her cheeks, but Kristof's expression was wistful, almost dreamlike. His bloodshot eyes gazed up at him, and a half-smile appeared on his lips. Just looking at him, Vulfram felt a new respect for the doomed boy.

Then Kristof stepped forward, fell to one knee, and said, "I have sinned against my god. I accept the penalty without reproach, Lord Commander."

Vulfram's respect heightened even more. He nodded to the magister, who guided the boy back to his feet. Onto the executioner's slab went his head. Oris began to walk away, to rejoin his wife and children at the forefront of the assembly, but Vulfram grabbed his wrist, stopping him.

"Make sure they don't turn away," he whispered into his brother's ear. "Neither your children nor your wife. They must learn a lesson from this. Not even the blood of the First Families supersedes our responsibility to the one who created us. Understand?"

His scarred brother nodded before Vulfram released him. Oris held his wife close and guided his two children in front of him, making sure they had the best view of all.

Vulfram drew Darkfall from its sheath on his back. The steady *hiss* that followed crept along on the breeze, making the crowd shiver. He held the sword aloft with both hands, the blade shimmering beneath the cloudy sky. Kristof offered the tiniest of whimpers from his place on the stone.

"Karak, have mercy on the soul of this sinner, who has so bravely accepted his fate. May he reach Afram safely and in the afterlife find the peace we all seek."

Hands gripped tightly, muscles tensed, Vulfram brought the sword down as hard as he could. The cutting edge sliced through the boy's neck, easily severing the spine. Deep in the crowd, the boy's father screamed. The head fell to the grass and rolled five times before stopping. Kristof's visage stared blankly at the overcast sky, while a few feet away a stream of blood spurted from the stump of his neck. The body shuddered, went taut, and then slumped to the side. The blood flow trickled until it finally stopped, bathing the stone in a fresh coat of red.

Servants came forward to take the body and head, placing both on a flat hay cart supplied by the Renson house, before toting the cart away. Magister Wentner and his young steward then yanked a shrieking Lyana to meet her fate. Vulfram halted them, gesturing instead for Alexander and Oris to approach once more. He heard Karak's words in his head: *All parties who deserve judgment shall receive it.*

"There is another who has been judged," Vulfram shouted to the crowd. "One who betrayed Karak through his irresponsibility and lack of wisdom. It is because of this man that the children have sinned, and his own involvement cannot go without retribution. Broward Renson, it is time for you to answer for your sins."

Broward, who had been consoling his weeping son and daughter-in-law, looked up suddenly, his eyes wide. The crowd gasped. Broward tried to flee, but the gathered bodies formed a barrier behind him, blocking his exit. Bracken collapsed on the ground and his weeping intensified as Oris and Alexander snatched his father by the arms and hauled him backward, kicking and screaming, toward the stone.

"You can't do this Vulfram!" Broward shouted, panic making his voice crack. "We grew up together! We were *friends!*"

"Friendship is not enough," Vulfram said coldly.

Oris and Alexander forced Broward to his knees. The man struggled mightily, but his bones were too old, his muscles too tired to resist the strong hands that held him. His head was pushed against the stone, his cheek slipping against the blood that still glistened on its surface.

"Accept your fate like your grandson did," growled Vulfram as he raised Darkfall for a second time. "With honor."

"This isn't right!" shouted Broward. "This wasn't supposed to happen! I was pro—"

The sword came down, cutting off the protesting man's words. Broward's head rolled away much like Kristof's had, but his body stilled faster. Vulfram glared down at the corpse of the man he had called friend, the same man who had sealed his daughter's fate. Momentarily overwhelmed by his anger, he spit on the headless body before the servants came to take it away.

Vulfram re-sheathed his sword, its blade coated in the blood of the guilty, and turned at last to the remaining sinner. Lyana stared back at him, her eyes wide with shock, her body trembling. His face a mask, hiding his emotions, denying the pounding of his heart, he pointed at her and flicked his finger. Magister Wentner and his steward stripped Lyana of her clothing, leaving her exposed to all of Erznia.

With a crooking of his finger, Vulfram summoned three women from the hushed crowd. The Sisters of the Cloth appeared like phantasms, beings covered from head to foot in gray wrappings and cloaks. Only their eyes peered through slits in their hoods.

Vulfram faced his daughter. "Karak's will is clear; those accused of the most heinous of crimes must be punished, and that punishment is binding. Lyana Mori, daughter of Vulfram and Yenge, you have murdered the child within you, and for that crime, you are henceforth sentenced to twenty-five lashings and a lifetime of servitude to the Sisters of the Cloth. Never again shall your face be seen by eyes other than your suitors', and no longer may you have a will of your own. Any children you birth shall become wards of the kingdom, and you shall give them up willingly. Do you understand your sentence?"

Lyana didn't answer. She simply gaped at her father, shaking, whimpering, pleading.

In many ways, Vulfram felt Kristof was luckier than his daughter. Given the infancy of humanity, it was against Karak's law to execute a woman of childrearing age except in the most extreme circumstances. Women who served with the Sisters were condemned to a life of isolation and servitude to prove their fidelity to their god. They pleased men, served as nursemaids, or worked as enforcers of Karak's law, depending on their talents. They could have no belongings other than the attire of the order, and they could not show any part of their body in public other than their eyes. Lyana might have escaped the blade, but she was now presented with a fate many considered worse than death— she would become less than human, a tool for men and their god, an empty vessel whose personal wants and desires counted for nothing.

The Sisters approached Lyana and dragged her to the stone. Two held down her hands, while the third carried the wrappings and cloak that would become her nearly constant attire. She was left exposed to the crowd, her body glistening with sweat as she struggled against the Sisters' restraints. She cried out into the late afternoon air, her voice filled with anguish.

Magister Wentner handed Vulfram a whip whose five strands were barbed with tiny, sharp stones. Lyana wept and writhed before him as he brought his arm back.

"Karak forgive me," he whispered and lashed out with the whip.

The strands gouged Lyana's flesh, opening ugly gashes that trickled blood down her buttocks and thighs. "Daddy, stop!" she screamed, the cry of a wounded animal, and Vulfram swung again.

As the whip sheared his daughter's back, flecks of bloody skin flying into the air with each crack, he saw her as a child in his lap while he read to her before the fire; saw her at the dinner table, picking through her vegetables with a sour look on her face; saw her in bed at night, listening to his stories of Karak's glory. Tears fell from his eyes, but his arm performed his duty. The air was filled with the crack of the whip and his daughter's wailing. The crowd remained strangely silent. He refused to look at anything but Lyana, didn't want to see his wife's face as he doled out their daughter's punishment. He hoped Alexander and Caleigh were watching. He hoped they learned the bitter cost of their faith. The memories slowly faded away until nothing was left but the sinner and the lashing of the whip.

By the time he had finished and the Sisters had dressed Lyana's battered form in the wrappings that would stay with her for the rest of her natural life, Vulfram felt nothing, nothing at all.

CHAPTER

10

A wolf bayed, raggedly cutting through the midnight silence like a saw through wood. Roland shivered, his eyes flicking from side to side. Just two nights before he'd stumbled on a pack of wolves devouring the corpse of a female deer. The alpha had lifted its head from its meal, observing him with reflective eyes while blood dripped from its huge maw. Roland had stared at it, horrified, and if Azariah hadn't grabbed the reins of his horse and led him away, the entire pack might have fallen on him.

Now, as he sat before their campfire, the flames crackling and licking the night air, surrounded by stunted trees whose branches were becoming lean with the advent of autumn, he couldn't help but imagine that those same wolves might have followed them. Jacob had left a long time ago to find wood for the fire, and in Roland's mind his master had become the doe, his insides spilled over the nettle-covered ground while canine mouths fought over the entrails. For all he knew, the rest of the pack circled the camp, stalking hungrily. More than anything, he wished he could be back in Safeway, with Ashhur a mere jog away. A strange feeling came over him, one he'd never felt before. Everything felt heightened—the light of the fire, the rustling of the bodies around him in their blankets, the sounds of the tethered horses whinnying in the distance, and the snapping of twigs in the surrounding forest.

A cold wind blew, making him shiver. He pulled his woolen blanket tighter around him, wishing he'd thought to bring warmer clothing. Having never ventured out of Safeway and the shadow of the Sanctuary over his twenty years of life, he'd never felt the sting of a northern night. In the south, the first week of autumn was like the last week of summer, with the heat of day persisting late into the evening. Sure, he'd been told of the northern winters, of snow and frost and how it seeped into your bones. And he had always bobbed his head, believing he understood. Now he knew how great a fool he'd been, thinking he could understand such a thing through mere words. Here, camping just off the Gods' Road in the woodlands a few miles north of Mordeina, the moon was like an icy sun casting frigid blue light through the branches of stunted trees.

A silken hand caressed his knee, and Roland glanced to his left. There sat Brienna, her crystalline eyes staring down at him. Her hair was pulled back from her face, bunched in a glossy tress that cascaded over her shoulder, revealing the fine contours of her cheeks and dainty nose. She was quite beautiful in a strong yet youthful way. Roland adored her and thought her far more welcoming than any of the other elves he'd met. He especially appreciated her untamed spirit and bright eyes, so totally unlike her usually calculated brethren. She seemed to be the perfect match for Jacob.

"What's wrong?" Brienna asked. "You're trembling like a woodpecker's jabbing at your soul."

"I don't know," he replied. "I'm worried about my master. He's been gone for too long."

Brienna laughed. "Jacob's fine, Roland. He's a resourceful man."

"But the wolves...."

"The wolves hold nothing over him." She had that sly look about her, a playfulness Roland had often seen. "The creatures of the wood tremble in his presence. He is the most perfect creation in the land. I think he'll be fine."

"And I think you give the man too much credit, Brienna," mumbled Azariah, stirring from his rest. The Warden lifted himself up on his elbow. The light of the fire cast a haunting shade of red on Azariah's normally pale complexion, making Roland shiver once more. "As timeless and perfect as he is, Jacob is only human, and like all of us he can falter."

Brienna eyed him devilishly. Her relationship with Azariah often baffled Roland. Though they obviously enjoyed each other's company, they constantly passed barbs back and forth. Rarely, if ever, did they agree on anything. About the only thing they had in common was their mutual admiration for Jacob.

"You're no more human than I am, Az," Brienna jested. "Actually, I'm not sure you even know what you are."

"I very much know what I am," replied the Warden, sitting up straight and throwing off his blankets. "I am Azariah, brother of Judarius and Laconia, son of Azekiel and Caterina—"

"Yes, but what *world* were you born on, Azariah? Was it here with the rest of mankind? No, I don't think it was. You're a Warden of Ashhur. You're as far from a human as I am."

Azariah glared at her, but he could not keep a straight face. Brienna grinned, and the Warden erupted into a hearty bout of laughter, which the beautiful elf was quick to join. Roland chuckled as well, and he noticed that the chill that had been weighing down his bones seemed to be ebbing.

When the laughter died down, Roland sat there grinning, poking at the fire with a long branch. He was glad Jacob had asked Brienna and Azariah to join them on this mysterious journey into the north, after passing his mentorship of Benjamin Maryll to Judarius. Whatever their flaws, both his travel companions knew how to lighten the atmosphere and set his soul at ease. The only thing he regretted was that the feeling never seemed to last.

Soon his nerves stirred again, just as the crackling of the flames reemerged, along with the chirping of the insects and the rustling of the leaves in the breeze. The coldness came back to him as well, and he inched closer to the blaze, his face scrunched into a grimace.

Azariah and Brienna exchanged a frown.

"And still the boy is ill at ease," said the Warden.

"I'm just cold," said Roland.

"Come here," said the elf. "I'll warm you up."

Brienna inched closer, wrapping an arm around him. He smelled the alluring aroma of her jasmine-scented skin as a strange feeling washed over him from the inside out. It was similar to the one he got when he stood close to Mary Ulmer, a girl of undying faith who never seemed to notice how his mind turned to mush each time they spoke.

"The boy doesn't need warmth," said Azariah. "It's fear he faces, and before it he's clueless as a newborn babe."

Roland squinted at the Warden over the flames, his pride stung.

"I'm not some child," he said. "I'm twenty—old enough to be a man now."

Azariah laughed. "Are you a man? It takes more than age to make a man, boy. What pain have you suffered? What struggles have you overcome? What scars mar your body? Right now, you are a tree stripped of bark. I'd hearken to guess that *none* of the wards of Ashhur's Paradise have grown up yet."

"Shush, Az," said Brienna, shaking her head. "Don't do that to the boy."

Azariah ignored her, leaning in closer, the reflection of the flames dancing off his irises. "Tell me, Roland, what do you feel right now?"

Roland cocked his head and stared back at him, unsure. "I…I don't know. It's like my body won't do what I tell it to. Back home, if it's hot, I tell myself not to feel it, and it gets cooler. When it gets cold in winter, I do the opposite. But here…no matter how hard I tell myself it isn't *that* cold, I shiver and shiver. I keep seeing the wolves ripping apart that carcass, and the shiver becomes a quake."

Azariah stared at him with those penetrating eyes. He'd always understood people, more than any of the other Wardens.

"You see more than just a wolf and a deer, don't you?" he asked. "What is it that flashes before your eyes when you close them? What nightmare won't let you sleep?"

Roland bowed his head. Shame worked its way into his gut, a feeling of weakness that was unrelenting.

"I also see Martin Harrow's body," he said. "I see his mother and father weeping. I see Ashhur standing over them as they buried him in the dirt, telling them their son is in a better place…but when I see their faces, I know they don't believe him. But how? How could they not believe him? Ashhur is their god, and he created us all. Why do they doubt?"

His shame grew, and he blurted the words out before he lost his courage.

"Why do *I* doubt?"

Azariah shifted onto his knees. He was one of the shortest Wardens, and yet his height was still impressive.

"Ashhur speaks the truth. Martin *is* in a better place now, lounging in the golden plains of Afram, the void in which the gods mold an afterlife for their people, drinking wine with his great-great-grandparents. It is natural for you to doubt, and you should feel no shame. But belief in the truth is often thwarted by the great killer of hope, a foe you know so terribly little about."

Brienna sighed.

"What is that?" asked Roland.

"Fear."

Roland sat up straight, even as Brienna tightened her grip on his shoulders.

"You keep saying that," he said. "I'm not a fool. I know what fear is—all of us do. When Master Jacob was visiting the delta, I had many dreams that he would not return, and it frightened me. When I was younger, I used to worry that my parents would scold me when I ignored my chores."

"Such terrible fears," said Azariah. "Have you already forgotten the wolf?"

Roland fought back his shudder.

"That too," he said.

Azariah shook his head, letting out a sigh.

"You'd rather pretend it's not there than face it. None of you in Ashhur's Paradise can face fear; none of you can stand tall and make it your servant instead of your master."

"Az, don't," said Brienna.

"The boy needs to know," the Warden answered. "There might be danger where we are headed." He fixed his eyes on Roland. "Here in the west you have been greatly sheltered," he said. "All of Ashhur's children have been, so do not feel that it's your fault. What is there to do in Paradise but breed and pray to the god who walks among you? A simple life, of oneness with the deity, the land, and your family. But that is not all there is. You know nothing of pain or of loss. Never has anyone in this land died before his or her time…Martin was the first. That is why you know nothing of it, Roland. You're soft. In many ways, it is a beautiful thing, and the people of Paradise cherish one another in a way that exists nowhere else in this world. But we've left that land now. We are in the wild, and nature is a far harsher mistress."

"You act like you know any better," said Roland, a bit harsher than he intended. "You've lived there with us. You've been…been… as coddled as we are! What do *you* know of it?"

The Warden's fire-flickering eyes darkened for a moment, then grew wistful, almost sad.

"I know much. We all do. Ahaesarus, my brother, Icariah, Ezekai, Torian, Uriel…we all experienced a life before Dezrel. Before we came here. Before we lost everything."

Roland immediately regretted his words, almost wished he could take them back. But his curiosity got the better of him.

"I'm sorry," he said. "How did it happen?"

Azariah smiled a gloomy smile.

"I was a carpenter once, working in my corner shop in a small city on a distant world we called Algrahar. I had a wife and children, and I loved my family dearly. And I also loved my god, whom we worshipped each night before the shrine of Rana that sat on the outskirts of the city. Life was full of joy, and much like you, we knew nothing of pain. As with Brienna's people, our god had blessed us with unnaturally long lives. Those I loved remained by my side through the entirety of my existence. It wasn't until one winter day during my sixty-sixth year that I knew even a moment of terror.

"You must understand that in our world, with its two suns burning brightly on either side of the horizon, it was always daylight. Sometimes the world darkened, and we could glimpse the brightest of the stars, but we never had nightfall or true darkness… not until that day. Suddenly the sky split as if a black dagger had sliced through the heavens. From the swirling mists within that darkness emerged a horde of flying beasts. They wore strange armor and bore giant black wings on their backs, and they were legion. We stood dumbfounded, not understanding what was happening until it was too late. The creatures descended upon us, attacking us with swords and spears. Those who fought back were destroyed instantly. The streets of our city ran red with our blood, and the air resounded with our dying screams. My wife was sliced from shoulder to hip before my eyes. My children were lifted by the evil beasts and carried high into the nightmare sky, then dropped down on the streets below.

"It was no coincidence that I lived. The beasts slaughtered the women and children, leaving us, the men who surrendered, to be rounded up and herded into pens. It was there my brother, Judarius, and I awaited the judgment of whatever dark force had brought this misery down upon my people."

Azariah paused, staring into the fire as if he were worlds away. Brienna shifted uncomfortably beside Roland, holding him tighter against her.

"Do you know what the worst of it was?" Azariah suddenly asked. "It seemed as though our god had abandoned us. As hundreds of us sat in that grimy pen, watching our captors soar over the gates, we realized that we were alone. Rana heard our prayers no longer, and his light had been extinguished from the world. That is when we knew fear. That was when we looked into the abyss and saw its darkest face.

"Nothing is as frightening as the thought that only blackness will greet you when you leave this life. Not strange creatures falling from the sky and murdering our families. Not the lack of understanding nor the promise of death every time the gates to our prison opened. No, our despair came from thinking that Rana's teachings were all a lie, and that when we perished we would simply cease to be, never to see our loved ones again in the shimmering forever. *That*, boy, is a fear you've never felt before, a fear that changes you, twists you in its maw."

Roland breathed deep, a rasping breath that filled his shivering lungs. "So it wasn't true?" he asked, both spellbound and horrified. "The words of your god?"

Azariah smiled, and his dark expression lifted.

"No, they were. After the invasion, when the razing of the other cities was completed and we were near starvation, a bright light appeared before us. The light filled our vision, washing out the horror surrounding us. That was when Celestia appeared, shining so brightly we could not look upon her face. Rana had summoned her to protect us. Ashhur was by her side, and the god-made-flesh offered us safety, asking us to join him and his brother in a brand new world. Of course we said yes, and Celestia whisked us away from our now-dead world and into this one. We were made wardens over the lives created by the brother gods. To have Ashhur arrive when he did, presenting my brothers and me with a chance to live out the rest of our lives in peace, rekindled my faith."

"So you're saying you're not one for coincidences, are you, Az?" asked Jacob, leaning against one of the stunted trees at the far edge of the camp. A grin spread on his face as he dumped six large logs beside the fire.

"How long have you been eavesdropping?" asked Azariah.

"Long enough," replied Jacob as he took a seat beside Brienna. She shifted away from Roland, sliding into Jacob's arms and planting a kiss on his face. Roland watched and couldn't help but feel jealous. Still, his master was alive and well, and that overwhelmed any of his more petty feelings.

"What took you so long?" asked Brienna, nudging her lover in the ribs.

"Ran into a couple farmers from the Durham Township," Jacob said, pulling his blanket tighter around him. "They must have thought I was a predator hungry for their sheep, because they came at me with weapons raised. I couldn't help but laugh. What predator do they think their sharpened twigs would repel? Certainly not *me*."

Brienna ran her fingers through Jacob's hair and pulled back his cloak as if searching for a hidden injury. "Did they hurt you?"

Jacob laughed. "Are you even listening? No, when they realized who I was, they fell to their knees and begged for forgiveness. It was rather humorous, really."

Roland noticed something odd about his master. His laugh seemed a bit too hearty, his smile a bit too forced. But he'd been like that a lot lately, and he seemed to be spending more and more time off by himself. While Jacob talked, his hands kept fidgeting with something he'd removed from the pocket of his surcoat, a clear and slender bit of crystal that shimmered in the light of the fire.

"What's that?" asked Roland.

Jacob gave him a strange look, then glanced down at his hands. He chuckled, pinched the object between two fingers, and brought it up so that Roland could see it.

"A good luck charm," Jacob replied, winking at the beautiful elf beside him. "Just a bit of glass Brienna gave me when I bested her brother in a dual."

"It's beautiful," said Roland, mesmerized by his own reflection as it flashed before his eyes.

"Very much so," Jacob said. He flipped the crystal over in his palm and then stuffed it back into his pocket. "Apparently, I am not as brave as our dear Warden here. I've seen much of the world and tasted plenty of fear, but still I find myself unhappy in its presence. It almost makes me wonder why Azariah even bothered to tell such a sorry little tale."

Azariah chuckled, shaking his head.

"The boy wanted to know about fear," he said.

"What boy?" asked Jacob. Brienna giggled and snuggled closer to her man, her head resting against his chest. Jacob glanced over at Roland and winked. "I see before me Roland Norsman of Safeway, my steward and the one *man* I trust more than any other." He winked at Azariah. "Certainly more than any Warden, I can assure you."

"Thank you," said Roland, joy filling his heart.

"It would be wrong for you to think you know more than Roland," Jacob continued. "*Dead* wrong. You know torment, not fear. There is a difference between them that's ten chasms wide."

Azariah chuckled, and there was a sense of familiarity to it that convinced Roland that these two had had such a conversation before.

"So enlighten us," said the Warden. "What do you think true fear is?"

Jacob turned to Roland, fire in his eyes. It was his turn to rule the fireside chat.

"Our tall and graceful friend here has it all wrong. The worst of all fears is not doubt. For one to doubt, one first has to *believe* in something. That belief counts as knowledge. And should we doubt it, as Azariah did, then you have knowledge of a different kind. True fear, the fear that even little children have the moment they are born, is reserved for the unknown. That is the part of Azariah's story that should inspire the most terror. Who were the beasts that invaded his world? What did they want? Why did they slaughter his people? And with each answer he learned, there were thousands more that he did not. The more you learn, the more you realize how much there is you don't know, and *that*, my young steward, is *truly* frightening."

Roland shuffled, trying to imagine it.

"I don't know," he said. "How could anything be scarier than what Azariah said? I'm not sure what I'd do if I found out Ashhur was wrong."

"Your fear isn't because Ashhur is wrong," Jacob said, shaking his head. "It's because suddenly death has become a great unknown. That is what you fear. Let me tell you a story, Roland, one the Neyvar of the Quellan elves told me a long time ago."

"Fantastic," muttered Brienna with a roll of her eyes. "This again." She rested her head in his lap and wrapped her hands around his knees.

"Shush, you," he said, patting her head. "Go to sleep if you don't want to listen. Anyhow, Roland, according to legend, a thousand years ago the elves of Dezrel banded together to fight a wicked yet unknown enemy."

"It's just a story," came Brienna's muffled voice.

"Yes, it's just a story, but one important enough for pictograms to be dedicated to it in the crypts beneath Dezerea. Roland, do you wish to hear the tale?"

"I do," he said, captivated.

"I've not heard of this either," added Azariah, looking interested.

"Then you listen up too, Az. You might learn something."

Azariah laughed. "But if I learn something, won't I realize I didn't learn anything at all? Is that not what you just said?"

"Very funny. As I was about to say, a pox laid waste to this realm a thousand years ago. It was a pestilence from the underworld that came in the form of three demon kings. Their names—Darakken, Velixar, and Sluggoth—are inscribed on the walls of the largest elven crypt, dedicated to Neyvar Kardious, who ruled the Quellan elves for nearly four hundred years before his death at the hands of these demons. They were creatures of immeasurable power, and over the span of three centuries they transformed this world into a wasteland. They were masters of the dead, and their magic made them lords of blood and disease. Darakken was known for his size and strength; Velixar, for his cunning manipulation; and Sluggoth was a bringer of plagues, whose mere presence could kill. They were ancient, and the elves had no defense against them. Worse, they had no knowledge of them, and for a time it appeared that they would raze both the Dezren and the Quellan from the face of Dezrel.

"Although Darakken was the most powerful of the three, commanding a vast army of hell hounds, snake-men, and other lesser demons, it was Velixar who nearly extinguished all elven life. He was a shrewd, manipulative beast, master of the art of blood and the enslavement of the dead. Armies of elven corpses rose from the battlefields, taking up arms against father, mother, brother, and sister. Those too ruined to be resurrected had their remains used as weapons—bones for arrows, blood formed into solid whips, and rotten flesh used as burning ammunition. A few elven tales claim this Velixar once commanded tens of thousands of dead made living, though Ashhur only knows how he obtained the power to control so many."

"You almost sound as if you admire the creature," said Azariah.

"I'd say it's more like I am *intrigued*." He patted the sack propped against his leg. "I've been searching for proof of the demons' existence since the first day I heard this tale. My journal won't be complete until I'm able to inscribe their secrets within...."

"Darling," said Brienna, squirming impatiently in his lap, "you're drifting."

Jacob laughed. "So I am. Where were we? Oh yes, the rise of the undead. With Velixar's desiccated army standing beside those of his brother demons, they pushed the elves far north into Kal'droth, the last vestige of hope in the land, where they fought to a stalemate for fifty years in the mountains. The stalemate worked to the demons' advantage, for the dead require no sustenance. The elves on the other hand...."

"It was Celestia who saved her creations, of course, though why the goddess allowed her children to suffer so, none can say for certain. Some say it was the pride of the elves, who had thought they were above needing Celestia's guidance. Some say the demons were beyond the goddess's power, and even others claim she was slumbering during the attack and was awakened at last by the damage done to her beautiful world."

Jacob's eyes twinkled.

"But no one knows what happened to the demons, or where the goddess sent them. In fact, I dare say they still might be out there, waiting, lurking, hoping to return...."

"What?" gasped Roland. His heart was racing, and suddenly a world he'd believed to be so safe and secure was filled with wolves, winged monsters, and demons of old. "Is that true?"

Azariah rolled his eyes, and Brienna sighed as Jacob nodded.

"I found a scroll that had been hidden deep within the sarcophagus of Neyvar Kardious. Within that scroll was a single prophesy, written in Elvish and with the typical prophetic vagaries. It said that after the deaths of the Mother, the Skeptic, and the False Prophet, the demons will be reborn on the very spot where Celestia had cast them out. A portal will be opened to their prison, and the demon kings will rise again."

Roland gulped. "And where is that? Where will they be reborn?"

The fire created flecks of red that danced across Jacob's features. He leaned closer, looking Roland dead in the eye, and said, "No one knows. The only mention I have found is one that says, *It is in the place of eternal cold, where the rocks on the earth have been sewn shut and not a blade of grass will grow, where the eternal have wandered, and the air is thick with the musk of creation and the darkness of dreams.* That could be anywhere."

Brienna punched her lover in the chest. "Stop it, Jacob. You're scaring the boy with your tall tales."

"I'm *not a boy*," Roland exclaimed, frustrated. "I wished you'd quit saying that."

"So you've said already," laughed Azariah.

The elf sighed. "Fine then. Jacob, tell him where it *really* is."

Jacob nodded. "There are those that think the portal resides in the Tinderlands, some at the Black Spire in Ker, and still others believe it exists anywhere Celestia places her feet when she chooses to descend from the heavens. But *I* know the truth. I discovered it some time ago but kept it secret, not uttering the demons' names lest they hear me and awaken."

Roland's eyes widened. "Where?"

Jacob squinted, reached behind his back.

"Right...*below you!*" he screamed, tossing something long and moving at him.

Roland's heart leapt into his throat. He shrieked as a snake landed in his lap, all glimmering black scales and darting pink tongue. He kicked backward, swiping at it with his off hand, but it tumbled inside his blanket, writhing against him. Roland shot to his feet, letting the blanket fall to the ground, and ran around in a circle, slapping at himself to make sure the slithering creature was gone. The *thump-thump-thump* in his chest raced faster than a hyena chasing after an antelope.

There was laughter all around him. Roland stopped his thrashing and saw Jacob chuckling into his fist, Brienna rolled up in a ball and cackling, and Azariah guffawing at the heavens, his large hands slapping at the ground. In that moment, he felt his neck grow warm as anger worked its way over his shoulders and into his clenched fists.

"You should have seen your face," Azariah said between fits of laughter.

"It was *priceless!*" squealed Brienna.

"Very funny," Roland muttered.

Jacob waved a hand at him. "Oh, Roland, don't be angry. We were just having fun with you."

"You call making a fool of me *fun?*"

"Well, yes. But it also serves a practical purpose."

Roland was still fuming.

"And what might that be?" he asked.

"Are you frightened any longer?"

"Well…no."

Azariah grabbed his wineskin from the stump behind him, lifted it.

"Now that is something I can drink to," he said before bringing the skin to his lips and downing its contents.

Roland walked timidly back to the fire, feeling ashamed and gullible, and sank back town into his previous spot. He wrapped the blanket around him again—making sure it was free of snakes beforehand—and let out a deep sigh.

Jacob's arm wrapped around his shoulders and pulled him in tight. "Listen, my young steward, I meant no offense. However, it is true that there's much you don't know of the world. Despite what I said, Azariah was correct. But you can *defeat* fear if you force your mind not to dwell on what makes you afraid, and act in spite of your terror. It is a skill you are going to have to learn rather quickly, I'm afraid."

"Why?" asked Roland.

"Because if what the merchant told me in the delta is true, if the followers of Karak are massing an army in the Tinderlands, then I have a suspicion your world will never be the same again."

"Oh."

Jacob slapped him on the back before giving Brienna a kiss on her forehead. He tossed a couple of the logs he'd collected onto the fire, and then he and his elf lover reclined on the nettle-coated ground, tugging their blankets up to their necks. Azariah did the same on the other side of the blaze.

"Now get some sleep," Jacob said, his voice sounding far away. "We have a lot of riding to do tomorrow, and you'll need your rest."

Roland tried to do as he was told, but he did nothing but twist and turn for hours. His fear returned in the silence, and the darkness behind his eyelids showed him three horrific creatures with burning red eyes and lashing tentacles, monsters that defied human definitions. They crept about in the interior of his mind, haunting him, stalking him, taunting him. Whenever he dared open his eyes, he saw the moon high above and imagined it splitting open as if it were a painting torn by a knife, an army of winged monsters in red armor spilling out of the crevasse. Before those things, even the tranquility of Safeway felt powerless.

When he finally did fall into a restless slumber, he was shaking.

CHAPTER

11

The creature loomed before the kingling, saliva dripping from its fangs. A thousand limbs stretched out of the darkness, slimy feelers shimmering in the unnatural dreamlight. Eyes burning red emerged from the black, casting a nightmarish glow on a hideous face in perpetual motion, always shifting, becoming people he knew and people he had never met.

Geris screeched and fled the other way, but he seemed to be running too slowly. His heart pounded so hard in his chest that he began to feel faint. And still the monster grew closer, so close he could feel its hot breath on his back, could smell the putrid stench of decay and sulfur rippling off its flesh.

Finally he reached a tunnel, and he dashed inside. It quickly shrank, and he dropped to his hands and knees to scurry along, handfuls of grime coming up in his palms each time he pulled himself forward. The deeper blackness of the void beyond the tunnel entrance seemed to close in around him, threatening to envelop him in nothingness, and once more Geris cried out. He scooped at the dirt faster, sliding his knees along the slick floor of the tunnel as he hauled himself through the dark.

And still the monster closed in.

The tunnel ended, but that didn't stop Geris. He dug into the loam, shoving his body into the wall until he was sucked through. With still no escape in sight, panic overtook him. Mud and dirty water flowed into his mouth and down his throat. He screamed silently, suspended in the dirt, hovering in the empty space between life and un-life. The sickening swish of his pursuer's thousand limbs became muted, far away. He felt his consciousness waning, and for a moment he thought the sensation would last forever.

Be still, child, a calm voice spoke into his mind. *The spirit soars, the body sinks. You know the way.*

Geris recognized that voice. It was Ahaesarus, his mentor, speaking to him from somewhere very far away. He closed his eyes, cleared his thoughts as his teacher had instructed him, and breathed deeply. This time nothing choked him, and the lingering presence of the nightmare creature withered away. He felt his body turn light as a feather, and a second later he was floating. A hundred unseen hands lifted him up and up until his fingers brushed an obstruction above him. Still breathing deliberately, he slid his fingers through the soft ground. They were greeted by a warm gust of air. He felt his body being pulled through the opening his fingers had created, squeezing from one reality and into another like a birth.

When he opened his eyes, he found himself squatting on the edge of two conjoined rivers in a place he had never been before. He was surrounded by rocky terrain and short, stunted trees. The rivers flowed together, their currents picking up at their joining point and rushing away like a herd of rampaging horses. The water shone blue in the pale moonlight. He gazed north, over the rushing water, and looked on a barren landscape whose cracked and lumpy ground appeared to be a topography of disease and ruin. A chill washed over him. The wind whistled past his ears, seeming to speak to him, and he whirled around.

Behind him was a solitary boulder that looked like the ones he had scaled with Martin and Ben when they were given a respite from their studies. The rock shimmered like topaz beneath the moonlight. There was a drawing carved into its surface, a shining star surrounded by a hundred points of light. Geris traced the edges of the etching, feeling the coolness and unnatural smoothness of the stone beneath his fingertips.

Suddenly the stone started to shatter without warning, and he leapt backward. All of Ahaesarus's lessons abandoned him, and he cowered by the moss at the river's edge, looking on in wide-eyed terror as the boulder changed shape. Arms burst from within it, legs lifting its bulk off the ground. A head smashed through the top, rising on a regal neck. Stone eyelids opened, revealing soft, glowing eyes.

Then Ashhur stood before him, a majestic being of granite. The star etching shone on his chest like a sigil. When the god ran his fingers through his beard, shards of rock rained down like dandruff. Geris scuttled back to avoid the falling debris, then rose on a single knee and bowed before his deity. Ashhur knelt down, extending one monstrous, rocky hand to him, a gesture of acceptance and love. Geris smiled and stared back at the stone god, feeling safe once more, secure in the presence of Ashhur's everlasting grace.

I love you, child, the god said, though his stone lips did not move. *The old demons cannot hurt you here.*

Geris touched Ashhur's fingers, which were just as cold and smooth as the boulder had been before the change. The stone god's head tilted to the side, gazing at him with an emotionless countenance, and Geris felt the adoration that had infused his heart begin to waver. This was not the Ashhur he knew, a deity of love and forgiveness whose gaze always conveyed warmth. The expressionless face was a lie; the sturdy stone body a false idol. He withdrew his hand and retreated a step, his foot slipping on the moss-covered riverbank.

From behind the false god came a squishing sound, like worms in wet soil. Black feelers slid out of the darkness, wrapping themselves around the legs of the stone Ashhur. More feelers worked their way across the giant's chest, then its neck, twining down both its arms with tightly flexed, serpentine movements. The stone Ashhur screamed, a noise like a fistful of pebbles ground together, before being forced to its knees.

Geris crouched, frozen in place, as the slithering appendages pulled and pulled, gradually cracking the stone god down the middle, splitting the star ensign in two. The god's head lolled back, uttered another scream, and then for a maddening span of time, all went silent.

From the darkness emerged a face. It rose over the stone god's shoulder, the most hideous thing Geris had ever seen, oily flesh covered with thick boils and with a hole for a nose. Then the face started shifting. First it became a hideous fanged beast with oversized tusks, then a single-eyed blob with snaking ropes of tissue for skin, then Celestia's glowing visage, then Ashhur's, and then Karak's. The image of the eastern god lingered for a moment before it too shifted, the ears rising upward, the snout elongating, whiskers growing from around the nose. The stone Ashhur was pulled lower to the ground despite its protests, and when the change was complete, the dream demon leapt on the false god's chest, a fully formed black lion of rippling muscle and sharp teeth. One of its claws raked against stone Ashhur's breast, creating a smattering of rocks as it grooved the edge of the star ensign.

"The god has forgotten his place," the shadow-lion said in a hissing voice. "The Lord of Justice has fallen in love with another. He cares not about you—only her."

"That's not true," Geris whispered, his heart thrashing wildly in his chest.

"Is it not? Then why send his most trusted servant away? Why allow your friend's death to go unavenged? He spends each evening wrapped in the embrace of the goddess. Look, her sign is upon him now, plain as the day is long."

"That's not Ashhur," said Geris defiantly.

"No? Let us see."

The shadow-lion sank its fangs into the side of Ashhur's neck, yanking and pulling with all its might, loosening the stones and sending them tumbling down the god's boulder of a chest. As the granite chipped away, Geris saw true flesh emerge, pink and smooth as the satin sheets on his bed in the Sanctuary. Geris began to scream as Ashhur's true image emerged, his eyes wide with terror as the shadow-lion mauled him. The stone became a prison around him, leaving him vulnerable. Geris tried to run toward his god, desperate to somehow protect him, but more feelers shot out of the darkness, binding him in place. He struggled against them, his joints stretched to the breaking point.

Ashhur released a final cry of pain before the shadow-lion ripped out his throat. Blood-like stars trickled from its gaping maw, floating vertically through the air, a progressing stream of iridescence. The prison of stone crumbled, and the god's body pitched over, falling face down in the moss. Geris stared at it, wide-eyed, while the shadow-lion sauntered slowly over the unmoving carcass.

"Faith is like a mountain," the beast said. "The foundation is wide and strong, but should that foundation weaken, hollowed out from within, the mountain crumbles, and all who stand upon it will perish."

The shadow-lion leapt at him, claws outstretched, the shimmering blood of Ashhur dripping upward from its snarling lips. Geris tried to move but couldn't, couldn't…until he awoke with a start, covered in sweat and panting, his head pounding as if struck by a twelve-pound hammer. He heard a series of wretched sobs leak from his own throat. His body shivered uncontrollably, still locked in the physical sensation of the nightmare. He closed his eyes and tried counting his breaths, another trick Ahaesarus had taught him, and eventually he felt his heart begin to slow. His fear, however, remained unabated. He didn't want to open his eyes. The demon could be out there, the impersonator who had destroyed his Lord and creator in the recesses of his sleeping mind.

Very slowly he pried open one eye, then the other. He saw a lantern burning softly in the corner of the single-room hut that he and his family called home. His two brothers were asleep beside him, his four sisters in their bed a foot away. Baby Roman, not even a year old, snored quietly in his wicker basinet. Geris rose up on his elbow, taking care not to rouse his siblings, and gazed at his parents' bed beneath the eastern window across from his. They too were sleeping, their bodies twined together. He watched their chests rise and fall, rise and fall. Then, tentatively, he leaned over the side of his straw-filled mattress, gazing from one end of the cabin to the other, seeking out any movement in the darkness. There was none. He lay back down and crossed his arms over his chest, hoping he could get some rest despite his shivering body. The words of the shadow-lion lingered in his mind as sleep finally took him.

He cares not about you—only her.

"Geris, sit down," said Ahaesarus. "We have something to discuss."

Geris bowed his head and stepped into his mentor's large tent. The tent's fabric walls were white and nearly sheer, and the top stood at least thirteen feet high. The Warden himself sat at a rectangular table in the center of the living area, where a simple carpet had been situated atop the grass. Ahaesarus's minimal clothing was stacked atop a wide, flat stone, teetering like a collapsing tree. Geris stopped in front the pile and straightened it; delaying the inevitable with simple chores was a nervous tick he'd developed since joining the lordship.

"Kingling, stop fiddling with the laundry and come to me."

"I'm sorry."

He approached the desk and sat in the chair opposite his mentor. Ahaesarus cut an intimidating figure even while seated, his height accentuated by his broad chest and shoulders. The Warden had a head of long hair that was as gold as the sunrise, smooth tresses that hung straight over his shoulders and came to rest just above his midsection. His eyes were a brilliant green that seemed to shine even come nightfall. With daylight pouring in through the gossamer walls of the tent, they were almost haunting in their brightness.

"What is it, sir?" Geris asked, though he knew perfectly well. His studies had faltered in the week following his nightmare. Concentration had become difficult. In open competition with Ben, he often lost contests he had always won in the past. Just this afternoon he had been handily beaten during the open forum. Many of Safeway's residents had taken a break from their gardening and prayers to pepper the two kinglings with questions about how they would lead the people if they were chosen as king. Geris stammered while Ben answered each question smoothly with confidence. It seemed as though Martin's death had steeled the youth, somehow augmenting his self-assurance.

Ahaesarus leaned back. His chair creaked, the wood bending beneath his substantial weight. He stared at Geris, tapping the fingers of one hand on his chin while he fiddled with the small, curious pouch he wore around his neck with the other. It was a pose to which Geris had grown quite accustomed over the past year or so. The Master Warden was waiting for an answer—an answer Geris was reluctant to give.

"Very well then," Ahaesarus said finally, sighing. "You don't wish to speak. Perhaps slopping out the latrine outside the Sanctuary will make you more talkative."

The Warden reached behind him, bringing forth a shovel and a large wooden bucket.

Geris shook his head. He wanted to be anywhere but here, perhaps out skipping stones in the river with his friends like in the old days. And he didn't like Ahaesarus's tone either. Just hearing it made him miss Jacob all the more. The First Man *never* spoke to him like that.

Jacob is not your mentor, he thought. *Ahaesarus is strict because it's his duty.*

"It's not that," he said, unsure if he should continue but doing so anyway. "I'm just frightened is all."

"Frightened? Of what? Of Ben? Is that why you've allowed that oaf to best you in public competition? He is nothing to be fearful of. He holds not a candle to you. You have always been the best of the kinglings. The presentation of the lordship before the council in Mordeina is but a few weeks away, and you must be at your best once we arrive."

"But what if I don't want this?" muttered Geris with the irritated whininess of the young. "I was chosen; I didn't choose."

Ahaesarus eyed him with uncertainty. "Is that why you are frightened? Because you're not sure if you wish to be king?"

"Um, well, no." Geris struggled with his words, trying to find the right ones. "I'd be honored to be king. It's just that…I don't know…I don't understand…why? Why do we need a king when Ashhur is here, showing us the way? Why do we need a king when our god walks among us? Does he tire of us? Does he wish to pass the duty of leadership along to someone else and disappear, as I heard his brother did? Does he not love us anymore?"

The Warden's gaze softened. He looked almost compassionate, which was an expression Geris had never seen before on his staunch, all-business mentor. Ahaesarus leaned forward, his arms dangling over the front of the desk, and addressed Geris directly.

"I see what this is about, but you are wrong. Ashhur loves all of his children. He always has and always will. In truth, he was opposed to the idea of a ruling class. He sees all his children as equal parts of a united whole. The lordship was my idea, mine and my fellow Wardens'. As the surrogate guardians of your people, we felt it necessary for you to learn to govern yourselves as they have in the east. We told Ashhur that his children deserve the chance to prove that the lessons he has taught them have taken hold in their hearts and minds, by administering their own laws, their own justice. It was not easy to convince him, but he eventually acquiesced." He spread his arms out wide. "Obviously."

Thoughts rushed through Geris's brain. "But why would he listen? Doesn't he know best?"

"Ah," said Ahaesarus, wagging his finger before him. "That is a great truth, but there are layers to every truth that are not so transparent. Even the gods do not know all there is to know. Ashhur is a great and benign deity. He understands his limitations as well as his strengths. He recognizes that there are worthy ideas other than his own. Besides, if you are never given a chance to rule yourselves, then the lessons you learn will go untested, unproven. It is Ashhur's love and trust of his children that has convinced him to agree with our plan."

"Does he *really?*" asked Geris under his breath.

"Does he really what?"

The message of the dream burned in the forefront of his thoughts. "Does he really love us? It's been three weeks since Martin died; yet after the memorial I have seen him only twice. I've heard it said he spends all his time in his solarium, alone with the goddess."

His cheeks burned red.

"What if he loves her more than us?"

Ahaesarus's mouth snapped shut. He glanced about the tent, his jaw tensed, creases lining the faultless skin around his nose. Ultimately, he slapped the table with his palm, creating a loud *thwack* that made Geris jump, and rose from his chair.

"Follow me," he said, the cold authority once more restored to his tone.

The pair exited the tent, which was located on the fringe of Safeway, in full view of the Sanctuary. The Warden led him between plots where cabbage, potatoes, squash, and alfalfa grew, heading toward the towering structure. Ahaesarus didn't speak, and Geris could hear his rigid breathing. His mentor was either angry or in doubt, and he was afraid to guess the consequences of either mood.

The ground floor of the Sanctuary consisted of a huge round chamber with polished wood floors, ringed with various potted plants and other gifts the people had presented to their loving deity. When Geris passed beneath the giant archway and entered within, he was surprised to see that Ben and Judarius were already there, standing in the open space to the right of the altar. Judarius was ranting on about some great offense to the honor of their deity, his black hair whipping about his head. Hearing the sound of the newcomers' footsteps, they both stopped what they were doing and turned around. Ben reacted first, offering Geris a cheerful wave and a goofy smile, looking every bit as young as his fifteen years. Judarius only scowled. The Warden had not acted the same toward him since they'd returned from Haven with Martin's body in tow. He had railed against Jacob for his irresponsibility in bringing the boys to Haven, and since Ashhur's most trusted left just days later, it seemed as though he was now passing that anger on to Geris, which wasn't fair. *Ben* had been Jacob's student. It should have been he that drew the Warden's ire, not Geris. He hated it, but Ahaesarus told him to pay no mind to it, for it would pass in time.

They marched past the duo and down a wide corridor that was virtually hidden by a pair of colossal potted ferns. The immensity of the Sanctuary never ceased to humble Geris. He gazed at the walls they walked past, adorned with a giant, sprawling mural depicting the early days of humanity in the west; Ashhur sat cross-legged in the grass, while children played all around him under the watchful eyes of the kind-hearted Wardens. The beauty of the mural brought tears to Geris's eyes. Finally, the nightmare that had poisoned him began to lose its grip on his soul.

They trod up the wide staircase at the rear of the passage, climbing forty-two steps until they reached the door to Ashhur's solarium.

Geris's heart climbed into his throat. He had never entered the solarium before—his time had always been spent in the Sanctuary's main hall or the many classrooms that populated the other side of the structure. He suddenly felt intimidated, in awe of what he might see.

Ahaesarus rapped lightly on the door. His eyes looked pensive as they stared at the ten-foot-tall entrance. He waited a few moments, until rustling could be heard from the other side. Ahaesarus nodded in response to some directive Geris couldn't hear, and he pushed open the door.

The solarium was huge yet sparsely furnished, making the place seem virtually empty. The walls were a deeply stained mahogany, decorated with only two placards, set on opposite sides of the vast room, upon which the words *LOVE* and *FORGIVE* were printed. There was a lush red carpet underfoot, and its fibers tickled the soles of Geris's bare feet. The only furniture in the room was a single four-poster bed, the largest he had ever seen, its spires rising nearly twenty feet into the air, reaching for the hole cut into the Sanctuary's domed roof.

There were two enormous figures sitting on that bed. Ashhur was on the left, wearing a wrinkled tunic and sandals, his blond locks curiously unkempt. The god stroked his beard and stared at the twosome, a strangely vacant expression in his golden eyes. Beside him was a woman of unmatched beauty whom Geris didn't recognize. She wore a simple but alluring brown dress; her dark hair hung down to her hips; and her eyes were like distant black voids that bore into his soul. It took him a moment to notice that the woman was built on Ashhur's scale, and his jaw fell open when he realized who she must be. Though he had never seen her in anything other than her starlit form, she could be only one person, one being.

Celestia.

Almost at once, both Geris and Ahaesarus dropped to their knees.

"Pardon our interruption, Your Grace," Ahaesarus said. "I meant no disrespect"

"What is the meaning of this?" asked Ashhur. Geris had to fight the urge to cover his ears.

"The kingling has a question for you, Your Grace. I felt he should ask you in person."

"Not here," replied the god, his voice dropping in pitch as if he were sighing. "Not now. Have the boy wait for me in the yard. I shall be there forthwith."

"Yes, Your Grace," said Ahaesarus with reverence, and he guided Geris back out of the solarium, down the staircase, and out of the Sanctuary. Geris was so anxious that he didn't even register the presence of Judarius or Ben this time. His nerves were so electrified it felt as if the tiny hairs covering his body were thousands of needles pricking his flesh.

Ahaesarus had him sit in the courtyard outside the short wall surrounding the Sanctuary.

"He will be with you shortly," the Warden said. "I cannot stand by your side, as your inquiries must be between you and your god in solitude."

Geris nodded, although he didn't like the uncertain tone lingering beneath each word his mentor uttered. It took his every effort to not run off and hide after the Warden took his leave and returned home.

He knew the moment Celestia left the Sanctuary, for the afternoon sky brightened as if invisible clouds had ceased to cover the shining sun. Ashhur appeared almost immediately afterward, ducking beneath the Sanctuary entrance and stepping over the surrounding wall. The deity appeared to be in a much more welcoming mood, and for that Geris breathed a rickety sigh of relief.

"I apologize, young Felhorn, for the way I spoke earlier," Ashhur said. "You caught me unprepared."

Ashhur sat and bade Geris to do the same. Geris gazed up; the deity towered over him like a tree, even though he was sitting.

"How could you not be prepared? You're a god…you *created* us. Don't you know what's going to happen before it does?"

Ashhur smiled a tender, kind smile. "If only that were the truth, my son. There was a time when it was, in an age and place I cannot explain to you. But I am neither omniscient nor infallible. Just like the universe, I am constantly changing, constantly learning, sometimes from mistakes I have made."

"Oh."

"Ahaesarus mentioned you had a question, obviously one of significant importance. Do you wish to share that question with me?"

The way Ashhur spoke, the kindness permeating his voice, resonated through Geris's body, creating a state of calm and casting aside all his doubts. He told Ashhur everything—about the feelers in the dark, the shifting demon, the shadow-lion, the stone Ashhur bearing the sign of Celestia on its chest. He spoke of how he felt, how real the nightmare had seemed, and of the words the demon had spoken, the accusations of love lost and loyalty to another.

Ashhur listened patiently, his radiant eyes gazing at the clouds that gathered over the purple outline of the mountains in the west. When the tale was finished, they both sat in silence. The outside world seemed distant, as if Ashhur had wrapped him in a protective bubble that nothing but the love of the deity could penetrate. The only sounds he could hear were the beating of his own heart and the intake of his breath.

"Dreams can be portentous," Ashhur said after a time. "They are not to be ignored, but considered, for in dreams we can receive warnings of the future or messages from the past. In worlds far from here, dreams have saved lives, stopped wars, and reunited long-lost loves. For when our minds are free from the earthly ties that bind us, we can sometimes see into the distance."

Geris felt Ashhur's finger slide over the back of his palm, and the warmth of his insides heightened.

"And what of my dream?" he asked. "Were the words of the shadow-lion…um…*portentous?*"

"You worry so," laughed Ashhur. "No, my son, they are not portentous. My love for you is as great now as it has ever been. And my love for the goddess is not new. I have loved her from the moment our essences drifted past each other in the milky ether of infinity. I owe her much. She is wise, wiser than I am at times, and I benefit from her counsel. But she could never take your place. You are my children, and my responsibility lies now, and always, with you. Please do not fear my abandonment. It is not in my heart to ever leave you."

"Thank you," said Geris, his gratitude overwhelming him to the point of tears. "I'm sorry I doubted you. I love you so much…more than anything…more than my parents…more than becoming a king…more than my own life. The thought of losing you…I never want to feel that again."

"Hush now," the deity said, pulling the child in close. "There is no shame in fear, and there is no indignity in doubt. Beware your dreams, Geris, for while they can bring wisdom, they can also bring lies and despair. They can be the spreaders of falsehoods, the builders of a life of apprehension. So be still, my son, and hear my words. No harm shall befall you, and I promise, I will never leave your side, whether you become a great king or a simple farmer. You are perfect in my eyes, Geris Felhorn, and always shall be."

Geris allowed the god to embrace him and fell fully into a trance of comfort. So contented was he that he never saw or questioned the touch of concern that darkened Ashhur's features when the god turned his gaze toward the rolling meadows and the lands across the river to the east.

CHAPTER

12

E verything is falling apart.

It wasn't just the palpable miasma of distrust that lingered in the air that made Soleh think this. The eyes of each person she passed on her way through the city skittered from side to side in panic. Shoulders hunched, hands were hidden from view, and footsteps quickened with a furtive sort of speed. The distant screams that cut through the morning air didn't help matters any. People were being hurt, robbed, and murdered, right there in the streets. It was why Soleh now required an armed escort whenever she left the safety of either the Castle of the Lion or the Tower Keep.

Sixteen days. That was how long it had been since Clovis had drafted nearly all of the City Watch into Karak's Army and then sent them south to Omnmount under the direction of two of his own children. Since the Left had served as the proxy Captain of the Watch, those responsibilities now fell to Malcolm Gregorian, the scarred survivor of Kayne and Lilah's loyalty test. Serving as the Captain of both the Watch and the Palace Guard was a daunting task for one man, duties piled upon duties without ceasing. The loyal man was stretched too thin. He couldn't control the commotion in the palace and the turmoil that boiled in the city streets at the same time.

To make matters worse, the new men who had been brought in to replace the guard were nothing more than common thugs. They had an unkempt look about them, with thick guts from years of downing copious amounts of liquor, and there was no pride in the way they wore the purple sashes of the order. Almost all of the new recruits' had a shifty, scheming look to them. Soleh had no idea what King Vaelor, the man responsible for their appointment, had seen in these ruffians other than their apparent aptitude for violence.

"Stay close, Minister," said Pulo, one of the three palace guards who chaperoned her around the city. Pulo was a tall and lean man, but ropy muscles defined his arms. He kept his left hand on Soleh's shoulder while his right crossed over the front of his body, his fingers resting on the pommel of the cutlass that hung from his hip. The burgundy half-cape on his back billowed with each step. His eyes flicked from side to side through the slit in his half helm, and he gritted his teeth. The late-morning crowd was thinner than usual— much thinner—but it seemed more dangerous in every possible way.

"Hold on the left," said another of the Guard, a short, stocky man named Jonn. A bearded drunkard staggered close by, stumbling across the cobbled street and heading right for them. The man's expression was blank and his movements clumsy, but Soleh knew that *clumsy* could present the greatest danger of all.

When the drunkard didn't veer off his course, Jonn stepped away from Soleh and Pulo and, joined by Roddalin, her third chaperone, channeled the swaying man to the side.

"Fuckin' doddling arse," muttered the man, taking a ham-fisted swing at Jonn. The guard ducked it easily and drew the truncheon clasped to the other side of his belt. He swung it hard at the man's knee, striking him in the side of the cap with a sickening *pop*. The drunkard's leg folded under his weight, and Roddalin clobbered him on the side of the head. The man collapsed with all the grace of a falling oak. His eyes rolled back, showing only their whites, just before his head bounced twice on the hard-packed road.

"Move along!" shouted Jonn, waving his truncheon before him. Those ahead gave them a wide berth, going about their business with practiced calm. Soleh noted a small group of older women lingering nearby, keeping an even distance between themselves and the four royal travelers. They looked scared and were likely following the royal troop in the hopes that the Guard would provide them with safe travel as well. Given the attitude that ruled the day, Soleh still eyed them warily.

Pulo ushered her along once more. They passed through sad gray streets of cold stone, avoiding all who looked like trouble. She happened to glance toward the windows of a mercantile building as she passed by and noticed that the shop owner was peering out like a child frightened of his own shadow. She wished she could feel pity for him, but her heart was too heavy. The city was in chaos, and worse, her granddaughter Lyana was far away, soon to be punished for some grave sin, by her own father. Any pity Soleh had, she reserved for herself.

The Castle of the Lion was almost in view when the sounds of a woman pleading for her life reached Soleh's ears from one of the many downtrodden alleyways. There were three members of the Watch standing nearby, but they were lazing against the wall of a bakery, chewing bits of bread while the baker sat, cradling his arm on the front stoop.

She glanced at Pulo, who shook his head. "We mustn't, Mistress," he said. "Too dangerous."

"It is my responsibility to dole out justice, Pulo."

It was Roddalin, the youngest of them, who snapped his heels together first. "Yes, Minister!" he exclaimed and began to cross the road, unfastening the clasp over the handle of his cutlass. Pulo and Jonn exchanged a nervous glance before Jonn followed. Pulo took Soleh by the elbow and guided her through the light traffic, holding up a mailed hand when a horse-drawn cart bore down on them. Once on the other side, they turned to the left and pursued the sound of the now-weeping woman's voice. Soleh glared at the three Watchmen on her way past them. They leered back at her until they noticed the black cloak that hung from her shoulders. Then they covered their faces with whatever shield they could find and scurried off.

They had already sealed their fate, however, for Soleh Mori never forgot a face.

When Pulo ushered her down the alleyway from which the sobs were issuing, Soleh stopped short. Jonn and Roddalin stared at the ground, where a uniform of the City Watch lay in a pile. Beyond them Soleh could make out the backs of four men. Lying nearby in a pool of blood, his neck slit from ear to ear, was a minstrel Soleh had often seen outside the gates of the castle, peddling his songs of praise to Karak for coppers. The sobbing intensified, accompanied by baritone grunts. Soleh took a step forward, shrugging aside Pulo's hand when he tried to stop her.

Between the backs of the standing men she spotted a flash of cream-colored flesh. She took another step forward and heard laughter. A woman's hand slipped between the feet of the onlookers, but the men kicked it away. The woman's screams grew louder, the pain in her voice setting Soleh's blood to boil.

Although Soleh could be timid and prone to outbursts of panic in private, out in the city, where her duty as a mother and wife ended and her duty as Karak's Minister began, she was something else entirely.

"You stand in the shadow of our god!" she roared, her voice launching from her throat like a boulder from a catapult. "Cease at once and face Karak's justice!"

The four onlookers whipped their heads around, staring at her first in surprise, then with dark intentions. Pulo, Jonn, and Roddalin surrounded her, swords drawn in her defense. The men's eyes took note of the burgundy capes and the expertly crafted swords, and they backed away, revealing the horrible scene beyond. The woman's face was so beaten and swollen Soleh couldn't tell how old she was, but the smoothness of her flesh, where it was not gashed and bruised, suggested she was quite young. She was naked and shivering, and when the man slid off her, she drew her legs to her chest, concealing her breasts with her knees.

The man who'd raped her tried to hastily pull up his breeches. His face was flustered and angry, his beard coated in spittle. Soleh noticed that his knuckles were bloody.

"Come, lass," said Soleh, and the girl gazed up at her through one eye, the other swollen shut. She began to pull herself across the ground until a booted foot slammed into her side, stopping her mid-drag.

"What the *fuck?*" the bearded man growled. He focused his gaze on Soleh, murder in his eyes. Even from where she was standing, she could smell the alcohol on his breath. His friends tried to grab at him, but he shrugged them aside.

"Bren, that's the Min—" one began, before the man stopped his tongue with a fist to the face.

"Who do you think you are?" Bren said, grabbing his shortsword off the ground and repetitively sliding it in and out of its scabbard, revealing a few more inches of gleaming, sharp metal with each stroke. "You think your boys with their weapons frighten me?"

Soleh met his stare without flinching.

"Release the girl, or suffer Karak's wrath."

"No."

"Are you of the Watch?"

"Yeah, what of it?"

Soleh held her head high. "Then I am your superior. If I order you to release the girl, you release her. If I order you to fall on your sword, you slide the tip into your belly as quickly as you can. Do you understand?"

"Fuck off." Bren drew his shortsword completely from its sheath and turned to his cohorts. Only one of them came forward to join him, drawing his blade as well. The other three sank further into the darkness of the alley and slipped away.

The rapist threw back his arm and hacked downward with his sword, attempting to drive the point through the chest of his weeping victim. Pulo closed the distance between them in the blink of an eye, and steel clanged against steel. Jonn and Roddalin weren't far behind. Her guards' foes may have been ungainly brutes, but they handled their weapons with skill. Parry after parry, thrust after thrust, they held off her escorts' attacks. The alley was filled with grunts, yelps, and the clanking of steel on steel. Yet for all their skill, the two could only defend. The moment they tried to attack, they found themselves overwhelmed by a coordinated offensive. Bren suffered a gash on his upper arm, his partner a slash on his thigh, and yet Pulo, Jonn, and Roddalin had not even suffered a scratch, and the thin chainmail over their chests and the silver vambraces on their forearms were as shiny as they'd been earlier in the morning. Even so, it was a chaotic ballet, one that allowed the naked, violated girl to crawl across the dirty ground and into Soleh's waiting arms.

When the girl was safe, Roddalin ended the fight, drawing his dagger from his belt. Sliding sideways past a thrust, he dropped to one knee, and his dagger swept through the heel of Bren's ally, severing the crucial tendon there. The man collapsed screaming, clutching at his leg. Jonn silenced him by hacking through his neck, spilling blood over his tunic and his purple sash. The man was dead an instant later.

Bren wasn't so lucky. Pulo struck the man in the forehead with his pommel, and then looped his cutlass around like an oarsman, burying the blade in the man's crotch. He yanked it free with a revolting *plop*, and the rapist backed into the wall, his cries shrill. He grabbed at his severed nether parts, blood spurting between his fingers and darkening his breeches. Soleh watched him suffer, the rage in her breast slowly abating. When she gave a nod, Jonn took off the man's head with a single swipe of his sword.

Holding the shaking girl in her arms, a half-disgusted, half-satisfied grin crossed Soleh's lips. Adeline would have been proud.

They waited as more members of the City Watch arrived, summoned by the commotion. They were members of the old guard this time, men she recognized. They whisked the raped girl to safety, hunted down the three remaining men, and cleaned the bodies out of the alley. Soleh made sure to confiscate the coin purses of the criminals, the living and dead alike. She emptied their contents on the blood-splattered ground of the alleyway. Silvers and coppers bounced and spun on the cobbles. She stared at the contents of each in turn, particularly the crest adorning each coin, and then up at Pulo.

"This is Connington swag," she said. Pulo nodded back at her, his expression dire. She shook her head. It had been the Conningtons who had accused another of hiring a rapist to strike against their family. Now they were lending coin to the kingdom to lure those same types of men into the Watch. She wondered who had suggested these bastards—the brothers, or the king.

When the mess in the alley had been cleared, Soleh handed four of the five sacks of gold to the victim, who thanked her mightily before Roddalin took her away to be treated for her wounds. Soleh then hurried to the castle. The streets were more crowded with curious onlookers now, but all it took was one glance at Soleh's hard expression for them to clear a path. She stormed through the portcullis and into Tower Justice, telling Captain Gregorian she was canceling the day's docket. The poor, overworked man looked less than happy about it, but he bowed and acquiesced, barking orders at the rest of the Palace Guard to stow the prisoners away once more.

Soleh felt for him, but she had more pressing matters to address.

She crossed the courtyard and burst into Tower Honor, still dragging Pulo, Jonn, and Roddalin along with her. She stormed into the King's Court, but the room was empty. Karl Dogon, King Vaelor's personal shield, informed them that the king was ill and would be receiving no visitors. No matter how much Soleh demanded, the man would not cave. "Sickness is sickness," he said with a dismissive wave. Furious, she scoured the rest of the tower, seeking out Cleo or Romeo Connington, or both. One of them was always lingering about the castle somewhere, sidling up to the king or the royal Council, trying—often successfully—to curry favor for his mining and weapons trades or toss more unfounded accusations on Matthew Brennan.

Much to her chagrin, however, neither Connington was to be found. Tower Honor was a ghost town, with only cooks, servants, and whores lingering about. Not even Clovis, who never missed an opportunity to let everyone know how important he was, had shown up yet.

If the esteemed Highest Crestwell wasn't in the palace, there was only one other place he could be.

Soleh left the castle and commandeered a horse and carriage from a jeweler who had been selling his wares in the courtyard. As payment, she tossed him what remained of Connington coins that she'd taken from the purses of the five criminals. Pulo slid in beside her in the front of the carriage; Jonn and Roddalin took the rear; and they set off without delay.

Pulo guided the cart without care for those before them, the horses' hooves pounding away. The wagon bounded along the streets of Veldaren, heading west toward Karak's Temple. She didn't need to look at her escorts to know they were worried, much more worried than they'd been when confronting the gang. Their tension hung in the air like a poisonous mist.

The streets emptied out the farther west they traveled, the buildings and homesteads giving way to wide expanses of dirt where only a few abandoned tents and lean-tos stood. Vulfram had insisted that in time the whole city would become a sprawling paradise of brick and stone, but that had not yet come to fruition. The sight of the bare earth, where all the trees had been felled and grass refused to grow, was actually more depressing than the gray gloominess of the finished sections of the city.

Soleh had embarked on this trek at least a couple times a week since Karak had returned to her, constantly needing to be in his presence. The deity preferred to greet his subjects in the home he had built for himself, located in the far west of the city. The structure slowly appeared before her, rising above the brown ruinous soil like a shimmering diamond in a sea of coal.

It was an overwhelmingly simple construction, square at its base and tall, the thick stones of its walls stained black. The onyx lions guarding the entrance were mirrors of those outside the Castle of the Lion; in fact, they were exact copies carved by Ibis. The entrance to the temple was a huge door marked with three stars set in a triangular pattern—a symbol representing the cooperation between the three gods of the realm.

There was a white mare tied to a post in front of the temple. Soleh recognized it instantly, and her heart started racing. She had Pulo bring the carriage to a stop beside it.

"Stay here," she told her entourage, knowing they wouldn't mind remaining outside. Karak was beloved throughout the realm, but his forty-year disappearance had made him a mysterious figure for most of the populace. *A small dose of fear to keep the people in line*, Lanike Crestwell had told her, and Soleh readily agreed. It was too bad those words hadn't proved true. Perhaps if Karak had made himself more available, the city would not have plummeted into this violence; perhaps it might in fact have retained the short-lived peace and harmony that had emerged just after his reappearance....

She ran her hand along the smooth hairs covering Highest Crestwell's horse on her way by. The mare whinnied and kicked its hind legs slightly. Soleh ignored the irritable beast, so much like its master, and climbed the steps, pulling open the tall temple door.

The inside of the temple was lush, filled with fineries donated from every corner of Neldar and beyond. In the antechamber alone there were stuffed carcasses of pelicans, cranes, and brightly colored kingfishers, pottery from the ruins of Kal'droth, potted plants as tall as grown men, and weapons that predated man by a thousand years, which had been given as gifts by the Quellan elves. The items had built up over Karak's absence, as visiting the temple had become a pilgrimage for many of the deity's children. It struck her as ironic that now that the god had returned, the temple saw far less traffic.

She walked through the antechamber and entered the monastery, where there were no more fineries to distract from the hall's true purpose. Twenty rows of pews lined the floor, leading up to the altar at the rear of the chamber. On his return, the great statue of the deity had been removed. It was the true Karak who now sat on the altar steps, hands dangling between his knees as he listened to the confessions of Clovis Crestwell.

The god glanced up the moment her feet hit the polished stone floor. He didn't move, only acknowledging her with a slight rising of a single eyebrow. Highest Crestwell kept his posture as well, kneeling in the front pew, head bowed, hands folded in prayer, his mouth whispering his wrongdoings so that they could be absolved by Karak. *There must be many*, she thought, but silenced that part of her brain. Soleh clasped her hands in front of her and slowed her pace. No matter what her problems were with the Highest, she needed to show respect to her god, especially in his own house.

By the time she reached the foot of the altar, Clovis had finished his confession. He slid from the pew and kissed Karak's bare foot.

"You may go in peace now, my son," the god said. Clovis bowed his head and shuffled away, nearly running into Soleh. The Highest didn't acknowledge her presence, but she swore she saw a grin spread across his lips.

It wasn't until the sound of the outer door closing echoed through the hall that Karak gestured for Soleh to sit.

"I would prefer to stand, my Lord," she replied.

"As you wish," said Karak, rising to his feet and turning to tend to the candles burning behind him. "Why are you here, my sweet Soleh? It has been many days since you last visited, and I have missed you." Moving back toward her, he looked down at her closely. "Yet there is no peace in your heart as you look upon me. What troubles you?"

"So much more than I can handle, my Lord," she said. "The whole of your kingdom is falling to pieces. You must help us."

Karak faced her, his glowing eyes like portals into the heart of a sun.

"What is wrong with my kingdom, sweet Soleh? And why must I help you?"

She jabbed a thumb over her shoulder. "Clovis is ruining everything. It was difficult enough to keep the peace before, but your Highest ordered most of the good men of the Watch into the army that bears your name, leaving us shorthanded, and replaced them with hired thugs and cutthroats. There is no honor among them and little love for you. The castle dungeons are overflowing, as are the tombs. The merchants are fearful of selling their wares, for the thieves and delinquents the Watch had kept under control are now running unchecked. The new Watchers either can't handle the situation or won't."

Karak sat once more on the edge of the altar and lifted his hands, palms up. "What would you have me do?"

"For one, you can order Clovis to return the men of the Watch to their posts!" she replied, her frustration robbing her of her better sense. She immediately reined herself in. "I apologize, my Lord. I meant no disrespect."

"None is taken."

"My point is this, my Lord…even before the Highest spirited our best guards away, the city was growing difficult to manage. Haven is a tiny community. Barely a thousand live there, of which perhaps half might be capable of mounting a resistance—much less than Clovis now has at his disposal. He has no need of so many soldiers!"

"Would you have me call them back?"

"Perhaps." Soleh swallowed hard and continued hesitantly. She felt like she was tugging on the tail of a lion. "Or, perhaps you could show your face among the people once more. After you came back to me, there were five days of peace. Five days when wrongdoing all but halted. The people saw you, and they rejoiced! There was calm, there was brotherhood, there was harmony. But it seems now as if you have…"

She paused.

"It seems you've given up on your children. I sense the angst when I walk the streets. The people think you no longer care, and if their own god does not care for their lives, why should they?"

Karak stared at her with heart-wrenching intensity, his eyes filled with an emotion she had never before seen on his face: anger. The god-made-flesh stood, and his lips twisted into a frown. When he spoke next, his tone was so cold it chilled her to the bone.

"The responsibility for the current state of affairs lies solely with you, my…sweet…Soleh. Did I not give you life? Did I not give you laws to govern your own land? Did I not provide you with the knowledge of carpentry, farming, metallurgy, and combat? What more would you have me do? Act as nursemaid, sitting you all in a corner when you misbehave? I have seen much, child, and believe me when I tell you that the gifts I have bestowed on you are well beyond any that humanity, in all the worlds it populates, has ever been given so freely. Do you think my brother has allowed this much autonomy to his children, giving them the opportunity to live how they desire, building prosperity that's equal to their efforts? I can assure you, he has not. All *I* have ever required from you is your respect and worship, honoring me by understanding my teachings and bringing order to this world." He laughed then, a frigid sound like ice scraping against brittle steel. "Do you know why my Highest was with me this day giving his confession? He came to beg forgiveness for his failures, for helping to create a city filled with murder, greed, and corruption. He *begged my forgiveness.* And what do you do, sweet Soleh? Do you fall to your knees and beg absolution? No, you dare stand before me and demand further action on my part. You blame me, not yourself. Was the act of creating you not enough? Do you not value this immortal life you have been given?"

The tears came upon her all of a sudden, pouring over her cheeks. Soleh collapsed, her elbows striking the ground as she stooped before her beloved deity. All desire to live abandoned her in that moment.

"I'm sorry," she pleaded. "I was not thinking."

"Stand up, child."

"I deserve no mercy…I deserve no honor…I do not deserve this life you have given me…."

A hand fell on her shoulder, warm and inviting. Soleh lifted her head and Karak was her Divinity again, smiling tenderly as if his tirade had never happened.

"Stand up, Soleh."

She did so mindlessly, and the god took a moment to straighten out her cloak and even tug out a snarl in her hair with his gigantic finger. "I apologize for my tone," he said, "but sometimes one must break a child in order to open their eyes and make them see the folly of their ways. Do you understand?"

Sniveling, Soleh nodded.

Karak rubbed his palms against her shoulders. "Then calm yourself. You have much work to do. You must preach the message, scream it loudly over the rails of every shop and homestead if need be. Show the people the right way, even if that means making an example of some. In a scant ninety-three years our population has risen to nearly eighty thousand. As much as it disappoints me to see the state your city has fallen into, I knew that such growth would bring pains. In Omnmount, across the Ramere, in Thettletown, Brent, and Hailen, things are much better. There it is peaceful, calm...and empty. But a third of our people reside within the borders of this city, and I consider it a notable accomplishment that most are kind, lawful men and women."

"Thank you, my Lord," said Soleh.

"That does not release you from responsibility, my child. That does not absolve your failure. It is still a mess that *you* must fix. When you leave this place, sing my message far and loud. Make sure the people hear you; make sure they understand. And find relief in this: whether Haven repents or we must forcibly burn their temple to the ground, all will see what it means to deface the nobility of their creator. It will be a lesson none will forget."

Soleh curtseyed. "I understand, my Lord."

"Now go from this place, child, and sing my name."

Soleh turned to leave but paused, casting a hopeful glance over her shoulder. She trembled like a schoolgirl, even though she had never once been that young in all her god-crafted life.

"My Lord?" she said.

"What is it, child?"

"Please tell me you love me."

The god laughed sweetly then and strode across the short distance between them. He took her in his arms, lifted her off the monastery floor as if she weighed nothing, and kissed her cheek. Soleh felt the blood rush through her body.

"I love you, sweet Soleh. More than any who have ever come before."

She was crying again when he put her down, but by the time she arrived back at the wagon and rejoined her escort, her cheeks were dry.

There was much work ahead, and she had to be strong. As strong as the title of Minister of Justice deserved.

CHAPTER

13

"I heard that the whippoorwills in the delta have begun tweeting incessantly at night. Morgan told me so. She said they perch outside the windows of the old and dying, singing in tune with the last breaths the people take. It's quite strange, you know? I've never heard *anything* like that."

Patrick rolled his eyes. "Who in the deep, dark underworld is Morgan?"

"Silly," replied Nessa, playfully punching his arm. "We were guests in her home for nearly three weeks. How could you not remember?"

"Forgive me. It's difficult when your head aches like rotten fruit that's been popped. And in my defense, I was asleep for most of those three weeks."

His horse trotted to the side to avoid a depression in the road, jostling Patrick in his saddle. He uttered a pained yelp and grabbed at his knobby forehead. The pain was less than it had been, but its echo still tormented him like the remnants of a bad dream. They had barely stepped foot in Lerder, the easternmost township on the Gods' Road before the delta, when the sickness set in. Patrick's fever rose uncontrollably, coupled with vomiting and a case of the shakes that rattled his teeth. His mind had become so clouded, it was difficult to separate reality from delusion. He remembered Nessa sitting by his bed, holding his hand while she gazed down at him with concern, but also a cloaked man in black who came to him in the night, watching over him from the shadows as he writhed and moaned.

The sickness was made all the worse by the fact that neither the Wardens nor Ashhur's healers seemed able to quell it. Patrick had fallen ill before, but usually all it took to cure him was a healing touch from one of his siblings or the city elders who led the prayers in Mordeina. Whatever had stricken him this time had baffled everyone, and he was left bedridden. Two conclusions entered his mind: either the sickness was so powerful that only time could cure it, or the faith in Ashhur that facilitated the healing touch was waning as he got closer to the Rigon. Neither scenario was pleasant, but the latter frightened him more than anything else.

His fever had finally broken three days ago. He'd awoken, frightened and sweaty, in a stranger's bed. His panicked voice had been so weak, it barely echoed off the bare walls. Nessa didn't come to him until much later, when the sun was painting the horizon with deep reds and purples. She'd seemed distracted and far away while comforting him. But the next day she'd been more attentive and had helped him gather the strength he needed to continue on his journey.

The current state of his aching brain made him wonder if he should have taken more time to rest.

"Patrick, are you all right?"

He turned to his sister and tried to smile. The glare of the sun forced him to avert his eyes, and he caught his reflection in the mirrored crystal adorning Winterbone's handle. Carrying the sword on his back made him unstable in the saddle, so it was strapped to the side of his horse, its scabbard tucked beneath his left knee. Snatching a handkerchief from the pocket of his light coat, he dropped the fabric over the hideous likeness, wanting to banish his reflection. Even on a good day he was a sorry sight, but after a lengthy bout of illness? It was a wonder that passersby didn't lunge for whatever weapons they could find and vow to Ashhur to send this escaped demon of the underworld back to its hole. At least that's the way he felt.

Nessa gave him a queer look and nudged her horse closer. Her hand fell on his leg, the pressure of her touch changing with each bob created by the horses' strides.

"Seriously, are you all right?"

Patrick sighed and gazed into his sister's eyes. There was concern in them, and innocence as well, and he knew that she did not look on his physical deformities the way he did. For the millionth time in his life, he was thankful for that.

"I am, Ness. I'm just hurting."

"Is it bad?"

He waved his hand in front of him. "Manageable."

"Good," she said with a grin. "Because Ashhur's Bridge is coming up soon. I can see it now. Race you there?"

Nessa kicked her horse and took off at a gallop, flying away from him without even waiting for his agreement. His sister's red hair whipped out behind her like a comet's tail. Patrick moaned, the ache in his head persistent, and tried to match her speed. It was no use, for the minute his steed began to pick up its pace, the wind and motion filled his skull with agony. He pulled back on the reins and tried to call out for Nessa to stop, but his throat was dry, and the words died just as they started to emerge.

Defeated, he slumped in his saddle and gazed straight ahead. He watched Nessa and her horse grow smaller and smaller as they approached Ashhur's Bridge over the western spine of the Rigon River. In the distance he could see the misty rise of the Clubfoot Mountains, the small collection of mounts that split the river and formed the delta. There was a strange fog in the air, even though there were no clouds in the sky, but Patrick was in too much agony to think about what that might mean.

Nessa went up and over the bridge, disappearing on the other side. Patrick hoped she wouldn't get too eager and go off exploring on her own. She could be so impatient sometimes—and quick on her feet to boot. The last thing he wanted to do was spend the rest of the day trudging through swamps and wetlands, screaming out her name, while she sat on a rock, splashing her bare feet in the water as tiny fish nibbled at her toes.

Yes, that had happened once before. No, he wasn't bitter about it. *"PATRICK!"*

Her voice came to him like a flash of lightning from on high, full of panic and terror. Patrick bolted upright, the pain in his head swallowed by his sister's distress. He urged his horse onward, slowly picking up speed. He squinted against the glare of the sun, trying to make out what was going on. He saw nothing, only the tall grasses that swayed like water on the other side of the bridge. Closer and closer he rode, each bump horrible, but at last he finally *did* see something—the strange dark fog he had noticed before, except it wasn't fog. It was smoke.

A great fire burned beyond the bridge.

He rode faster.

Moments later he reached Ashhur's Bridge, a wide overpass made from pearly white marble and reinforced with tall, elegant arches, a complex structure that had been created by divine hands before the dawn of humanity. The horse's hooves hit the marble with a series of weighty *thunks*. Patrick could hear the river scuttling below him, rushing out toward the Thulon Ocean.

He became like that water, moving in a steady rhythm with the wind and his horse, steering the mare off the bridge and onto the dirt path that cut between the chest-high grasses. He rode a few feet down the road, and then stopped, making the horse circle in place, gazing out in all directions. All he saw was an endless sea of wavering vegetation. The billowing smoke was actually some distance to the southwest, rising in a triplet of plumes.

"Nessa!" he screamed, listening for a response that never came. At best, he caught what might have been a muffled cry, but the twirling horse kept him from honing in on it. He pulled up hard on the reins, stopping the horse in its tracks. "Nessa!" he yelled again, this time holding his breath afterward and cocking his head to listen.

And then, from behind him, a voice.

"'Ello there."

Taken by surprise, Patrick yanked too hard on the reins, and the horse bucked. He lost his balance in the saddle and teetered until the clasp holding it in place broke, and he slipped off the side. He hit the ground with a thud and immediately covered his head with his arms. His headache had reawakened with a fury, assaulting his eyes with its blinding power. Fighting the pain, he lifted himself up on his elbows.

"Well, what we have here?" the voice said.

Patrick glanced over his shoulder while doing his best to keep nausea from overpowering him. Eight figures stood in the middle of the road. Seven were bandits, with broad chests and fearsome visages, who looked—and smelled—as if they hadn't yet learned the art of bathing. They were all dressed in black and carrying swords and daggers. Patrick could only guess that they'd circled around him in the tall grasses, blocking any retreat across the bridge. The eighth was Nessa, and his sister gasped and screeched as one of the men brought his dagger to her throat. The man held her up by the hair so high that her feet barely touched the ground, and her yellow dress was ripped and dirtied.

One of the men stepped forward. His hair was a long, grease-streaked mess, and Patrick swore he could see fleas leaping about in the man's ratty beard.

"What—you gots no tongue, freak?" he said.

Patrick grunted and shoved off the ground with his knuckles, bringing his short legs beneath him in a single motion. His horse maneuvered close to him again, its panic gone, and he placed a hand on its neck for support.

"Yes, I have a tongue," Patrick replied, trying to keep his gaze locked on the men while searching for his fallen saddle—and Winterbone—at the same time. "But tongues don't do much good for those who don't know how to use them."

The speaker's face scrunched up. "What's that s'posed to mean?"

"It means learn how to speak, you son of a three-tittied whore."

The men behind the speaker laughed, but Patrick noticed that the one holding Nessa tightened his grip, bringing her closer to him.

"Candry," one of them said, wheezing out a guffaw. "The freak... he done said your mama..."

"I heard 'im," said the one named Candry. "The bastard thinks he's a funny one, for sure."

"On no, I don't *think* I'm funny at all," said Patrick. He stepped away from the horse and toward the men, catching a glimpse of something twinkling between the swaying blades of grass. "I *know* I am. Because I understand humor. And soap. And I know it isn't funny when you smell like shit."

More laughter from the men, only this time the one holding Nessa doubled over as she jammed her elbows into his stomach. She fell to the ground and tried to scurry away. Candry planted a foot on her back, keeping her from getting far. Nessa cried out in pain as the man ground his heel into her, which washed away all of Patrick's false bravado. He felt his neck flush.

"Well, now," said Candry. "Looks like the hunchback done got mad. He's turnin' red like a beet!"

The men laughed again. Patrick smiled back, letting his blood boil, his anger giving him newfound courage. Diving to the side, he let the tall grass swallow him and cushion his fall. Swiping his hands from side to side, he searched for what he knew had to be there. When his fingers touched the leather he let out a gasp of relief. It was the saddle, and Winterbone was still secured to it.

"He's gettin' away!" one of the men yelled.

No I'm not, thought Patrick as he grabbed Winterbone's handle, undid the clasp, and slid the blade from its scabbard. The sound it made, the unnatural *hiss* that had fascinated him for so long, seemed to silence the bandits. Rising to his feet, a smile still on his face, he let them see the death in his eyes. His voice filled the sudden quiet, a beastly cry fueled by his pounding heart. He churned his short legs, emerging from the grass like a sea beast leaping from the ocean to nab its prey, the heavy broadsword raised high above his head.

The men were wide-eyed, stunned, but when Patrick swung the blade, Candry raised his own sword. The two met with a loud *clang*. A vibration shot up Patrick's forearms, numbing his fingers, jarring his elbows, and making his shoulders strain. Candry used that opening to shove him away. Patrick stumbled, his uneven legs wobbly on the dirt-strewn road.

"Hunchy's got a big sword," one of the other men said. Candry didn't answer. Nessa watched in quiet horror as the lead brigand narrowed his eyes and brought his sword to bear.

Patrick knew it was hopeless. He had no business taking on seven challengers. Though he'd owned Winterbone for years, he had never swung the sword in battle—not even the practice kind. Who in the west would he have practiced with? The most he had ever done was rehearse his balancing act and occasionally hack at a few dying trees in the garden behind the Homestead as a way of letting off steam. However strong he might be—and Patrick was indeed strong—he was comically overmatched in a swordfight. Hand to hand, sans weapons, he might have stood a chance. But with blades? He didn't have the speed to block and counter, didn't have a feel for the blade like the nasty ruffian before him did.

But none of that would stop him. Hopeless or not, that was Nessa they held captive. He'd often pined for death. At least now he'd have a chance to take it with some measure of dignity.

Candry grunted and rushed forward, holding his sword in one hand. The sword itself, with its pale blade and gnarled wooden pommel, was nothing compared to Winterbone, but its cutting edge was no less dangerous. Candry brought it down in a sideways arc, his feet balanced evenly, his opposite arm serving as a counterbalance. In a surprising feat of strength, Patrick hefted Winterbone with a single sore arm. The blades met, stopping the swipe before it beheaded him. Patrick ground his misshapen teeth and fought through the pain. Candry staggered back from the recoil, staring at his sword, which now had a rather large chip where the two blades had clashed.

A combined roar sounded as the rest of Candry's men rushed Patrick, leaving Nessa where she lay. Patrick panicked, about to be overwhelmed with their killing blades and murderous eyes. His mind spun in confusion. He didn't know what to do, how to defend himself. He acted on pure instinct, whipping Winterbone at the first attacker, then driving his stunted leg at the second. The sound of clashing steel rang through the air as his boot connected with the soft flesh of someone's groin. Two screams filled his ears, screams he echoed when he felt a great white heat invade his body.

Patrick glanced down to see the tip of a sword protruding from the fleshy part of his side. The tip withdrew, and a shower of crimson squirted from the wound. Blood began drenching his tunic, and he heard someone exclaim, "I got 'im!"

Patrick whirled around, gripping Winterbone tightly with both hands, swinging it as he would a heavy sack of meal in with the childhood games he had played with Bardiya. Patrick had always won then, anyway. The tip of the blade clipped the man behind him, sending him backpedaling. Patrick kept up his spin, the long sword creating a wide, lethal circle around him. One of the men got too close, and Winterbone sheared through his belly. Patrick kept right on spinning, thinking maybe this method—crazy though it was—could work. The bandits still continued to rush him, and he heard another cry of pain as one of the men fell to his knees, his intestines spilling across the dusty road. Patrick was so dizzy he could barely register what he was seeing, nevermind understand the man's dying moans.

Suddenly someone slipped beneath the circle of razing steel, taking out Patrick's legs. He continued to twirl even as he fell, and panic took him completely as Winterbone flew from his grasp and disappeared into the grass once more. Patrick hit the ground hard, and he heard what sounded like cracking bone. He teetered on his side, his vision swimming, his legs in agony.

The one who'd tripped him jumped atop him, and before he could react, blows began to land hard on his face, without rest. There was another piercing stab, this time on his massive forearm, and he snapped his arm up and away from the sensation, clobbering his attacker on the side of the head in the process. For a moment he could breath again. Salty liquid dripped over his distended brow, down his cheeks, and into his mouth. He sucked on it while he rolled over and tried to stand.

While braced on one knee, his knuckles plunged into the ground for balance, Patrick's vision finally stopped swirling. Six men were standing now. Many of them were bleeding. The one he'd killed lay atop his bloody heap of insides a few feet away. They were furious now, shouting at one another. Patrick frantically scanned left and right, but found no trace of Nessa.

Thank Ashhur, he thought. *Let her get away from here; let her escape back home. I don't care if I die, as long as she remains safe....*

One man went to charge, but Candry held him back, obviously wanting to finish Patrick off himself. When Candry snarled and reared back with his sword arm, Patrick closed his eyes, prepared for the strike to come, prepared for an end to his never-ending life. It never came. Instead, several people screamed at once, followed by a strange sluicing sound and the ringing of steel on steel.

Patrick opened his eyes to see three human shadows bouncing around the group of bandits, moving so quickly their bodies were mere blurs beneath the afternoon sun. One bandit after another was taken down, their bodies geysers of blood. Candry hopped around in a circle as his men fell around him, thrusting and hacking with his sword, never able to make contact. When all his men were dead, he flung his sword aside and tried to flee. He received two sabers through the chest for his troubles. He collapsed to the road and bled out, a pathetic moan piercing his lips.

Patrick gawked at the scene in wonder, incapable of understanding what was happening.

"All is fine, you can come out now," said an unfamiliar feminine voice. Patrick watched as Nessa emerged from the grass on the other side of the road, dirty and frightened, but very much alive. Her eyes met his, and she gasped. Tears filled his eyes, and he wished he could tell her how happy he was that she was safe.

One of the shadows approached Nessa, wrapping an arm around her and leading her away, while the other two cautiously approached him. They held out their hands as if he were a wild beast they should be wary of, which he found amusing. The throbbing behind his temples, mixed with his body's violent aches and various stab wounds, left him equipped for little more than lying on the ground and bleeding. He couldn't have hurt anyone if he wanted to.

Growing weak and sleepy from loss of blood, Patrick slid down from his knuckles to his shoulders until he finally fell face first into the dirt and rocks. Nessa screamed, and then hands were on him, rolling him over so that the sun shone brightly in his fading vision. One of the shadows bent over him. The figure touched the side of his face with one gloved hand and lifted the hood from its head with the other. A woman gazed down at him, one of the most beautiful women he had ever seen, with bronzed skin and piercing green eyes. Her hair was dark, with two or three pale streaks, wavy almost to the point of curls, and when one of her locks drooped near his nose he smelled a combination of sweat and peppermint. It was a delicious scent.

"I think I'm in love," Patrick whispered, just before losing consciousness.

Patrick awoke on a comfortable bed—by far the most comfortable bed on which he had ever laid—in a lavishly decorated room. Artwork hung from the walls; flower arrangements sprouted from within skillfully crafted vases; and the air was infused with the sweet scent of lilac. A man sat by his bedside. Without a word he handed Patrick a waterskin, which the latter downed in half a heartbeat.

While Patrick wiped water from his chin, everything came back to him. He remembered the attack on Nessa, his defense of her, the loss of Winterbone, and the blessed arrival of the three black-cloaked figures. He patted his stomach and rubbed his forearm, where he had been stabbed, but it seemed as though his wounds had been healed. His body felt free of aches, and it didn't hurt to look into the light. In fact, the headache that had tormented him for days had diminished to a tiny fragment that lingered in the back of his skull like a mischievous mouse. He glanced up at the bearded man beside him, who nodded as if some silent message had passed between them.

"Pardon my rudeness," Patrick said finally, "but who are you?"

The man offered his hand, which Patrick shook.

"Deacon Coldmine," the man said, his smile revealing a set of crooked yet well cared for teeth. "Some here call me the Lord of Haven, but please, just call me Deacon."

Patrick sat up, his jaw dropping open. This was the man he'd been sent to find? Well, find him he had...though it had been more of the other way around.

"I take it that this is your house?" he asked. "I must say, it's wonderful."

"No, no, not mine," replied Deacon, shaking his head and grinning. "My abode is much more...unpretentious than this. This place is a little extravagant for my tastes, not to mention my means."

"Is that so? Then who should I honor for housing me?"

"That would be Lady Gemcroft. She brought you here three days ago."

Patrick whistled, his eyes widening. "Three days?"

"Yes. You were in rough shape when you were discovered—lost a lot of blood. I was called here immediately to assist in your care, but your injuries were beyond my abilities as an herbalist, so...other means were necessary."

"What other means?"

Deacon reached out and rapped three times on the table beside him. The door cracked open, and when Deacon nodded, swung fully inward. Four people entered the room in rapid succession, Nessa in the lead. His sister was beaming, and the moment she spied him she broke into a run, leaping into his lap with every inch of force her tiny frame could muster. Patrick caught her, the air blasting from his lungs, and gave her a tight squeeze.

"Thank Ashhur, you're all right," she whispered into his ear.

"Yes, thank Ashhur indeed," a second woman spoke.

Nessa slid off his lap and fell into place beside him, and Patrick looked up at the sound of that familiar, feminine voice. There she was, the woman he had dreamed of, the one who had saved him. She was as near to perfect as a human could be, every curve of her body faultless, every angle of her face exquisite in its brilliance. She wore a pair of tight, calf-length breeches and a green satin chemise that perfectly matched her green eyes.

Patrick was so focused on her that it took him a moment realize that others were there too—a young woman with silver hair and eyes like azure gemstones, who held the splendid woman's hand in a curiously intimate manner, and an old and frail, dark-skinned man with a thick white beard, who looked strangely familiar.

The splendid woman smiled, curtseyed, and said, "Patrick DuTaureau of Mordeina, my name is Rachida, and I welcome you to my home. This is Moira to my right, and to my left is Antar Hoonen, whom I think you know."

Patrick snapped his fingers. "Antar? Bardiya's friend, Antar? But...you were so *young* when last we met!"

Antar smiled a toothless smile. "Ah, if only we were all bestowed with the blessing of timelessness. I, my friend, am not."

"It's not such a blessing," Patrick muttered out the side of his mouth.

"Anyhow," said Rachida, breezing through the room as if she weighed nothing, "it was Antar here who healed you. He's been acting as the township's healer when it comes to the more...extreme illnesses and has been ever since the masters of House Gorgoros evicted him from their land."

Patrick cocked his head. "Why did they evict you?"

Antar shrugged. "I disagreed with Master Bessus, so I struck him. I was not welcomed after that."

"And yet you can still heal?" asked Patrick, staring at his hands in disbelief.

"I lost no faith in Ashhur, only in Bessus," replied Antar. "My faith has never gone away, and it never will until the day I die."

"Well, thank you, old friend," said Patrick, bowing. He then turned to Rachida. "And thank *you*, my dear, for rescuing us on the road that day. I don't know how you did it, but you and your partners were a wonder to watch. Disregarding all the blood, of course. Who were the others?"

Rachida tapped the head of the lithe, silver-haired girl, who giggled and nuzzled into her touch. "Moira was one of them, and the other was Corton Ender, the man who taught us what we know of fighting."

"Two ladies and an unknown gentleman took down seven bandits? I'm impressed."

"Six men. You took care of one yourself."

"By accident."

Rachida knelt by his bedside. "By accident is a good start. Some of our greatest accomplishments happen when we least expect them to."

"I suppose you're right. I truly never expected to get into a skirmish. The reason I came here was to make sure Deacon took down his temple before the third new moon."

"Wait," said Deacon. "You were *sent* here?"

"Well, yes. Nessa didn't tell you?"

Nessa shook her head. "Wasn't my place."

Patrick sighed. "Well, all right then. I was sent here by Jacob Eveningstar, Ashhur's most trusted servant, with a plea for those in the delta to yield to Karak's will. I wasn't told much, just that Jacob fears the worst will happen to you should you refuse to yield."

Rachida's expression turned from warm and welcoming to hard and blunt.

"So even Jacob is against us now," she said. "I expected better of him." She slapped her knees and stood up, pacing around the room, weaving in and out of those who were standing. "Those men you ran into were sent here by Karak's followers, the same god you would ask us to kneel before. They've burned four holdfasts, slaughtered thirty heads of cattle, and murdered six men. And those seven are just a small number of the many who have 'visited' us here in the delta since Karak's Army loosed their arrows on our temple. Our wills have been made iron. They will *not* best us, even if Karak himself comes here to show us his wrath, as promised."

Patrick swallowed hard. "But…don't you fear being destroyed? Karak created you, all of you…well, except for you, Antar…and trust me, I've spent many hours with Ashhur, and I wouldn't want to get on his bad side either."

Once more Rachida knelt before him. This time she slid a long object out from beneath the bed, grunting as she lifted it and leaned it against the bed. It was Winterbone, retrieved from the marsh grasses, scabbard and all.

"We are tired of being slaves," she said. "Karak preaches freedom and prosperity for all, but the game is fixed. The wealthy are free to amass as much affluence as they wish, so long as their tithes and professions of faith remain plentiful. But they prey on the weak and the unfortunate, and Karak does nothing to stop it. He has abandoned his people. I don't care if he ever returns, though I doubt he will ever step foot in our village. This is a power play by Moira's father. He is trying to prove his might before his followers by scaring us into submission. He hates humanity and is bitter that his family wasn't allowed to rule. He will take us down to prove his point to his beloved god, and trust me, Patrick, he won't stop at the delta—not when your people are so unprepared to defend themselves."

His head swimming, Patrick gawked at the gorgeous woman and asked the only question that popped into his mind. "Moira's father? Who *are* you people?"

Rachida stood and threw back her shoulders. "I am Lady Gemcroft by title only. My husband Peytr bestowed the title upon me to help hide my true heritage. Before, I was Rachida Mori. As for Moira Crestwell…"

Patrick blinked, hardly able to believe it. Mori and Crestwell… two women of the First Families…here in the delta? He looked over at Nessa, whose face was stretched into a huge grin.

"You knew?" he asked, and she nodded exuberantly.

Suddenly, Patrick didn't feel quite so upset that Jacob had sent him there. Things had just gotten far, far more interesting.

CHAPTER

14

T he smell of sweat hung in the air as line after line of the newcomers to Karak's Army practiced their thrusts and parries in an enormous field. The grass was matted, torn down to the rocky soil in spots from the clomping of countless booted feet. The township of Omnmount's lone building was barely visible over the rise of a distant hill. The recruits' swords were cheap and wooden; the genuine articles hadn't arrived yet. According to the bird sent by Romeo Connington, the delay had been caused by Matthew Brennan's attempts to fleece them with high shipping rates, which meant that the Conningtons needed to hire their own people to convey the new weapons all the way from the Thettletown refineries, by horse instead of boat. Crian rolled his eyes on reading the words. He knew for a fact that the Conningtons owned boats of their own. It was an excuse, another way for Romeo and Cleo to curry sympathy in their pathetic turf war with the Brennan family while hiding how far behind they were in production.

But it was all a concern for another day. Real steel would do his inexperienced soldiers little good if they didn't know how to wield

swords properly. The members of the City Watch that he and Avila
had brought with them from Veldaren had spoiled him. They'd
been given leave from their positions—along with a hefty raise of
two silvers a week—to join in the fight against the blasphemers in
the delta. Lord Commander Mori had already trained them well,
training Crian had continued upon taking over as Watch captain.
These new recruits, however, were farmers and peasants plucked
from their homes in Omnmount and the outlying agricultural territories, as far away as Ramere, with the promise that King Vaelor
would make sure there was plenty of gold to feed their families and
pay for their crops.

Crian watched two men in particular as they sparred—a balding
waif named Grant and a fat tub named Harren. Despite Harren's
advantages in both girth and reach, it was always Grant who landed
the winning blows with the tip of his waster. The waif laughed
like a hyena whenever he struck Harren a solid blow, and the fat
man's jowls were growing red with anger. Crian knew a dangerous
situation was building, but he remained silent. Every moment was a
teaching moment, as his father had been wont to say.

Grant sidestepped a clumsy thrust and poked Harren in his
meaty thigh, barely missing his balls. The waif then spun away and
cackled. "Fat man can't move!" he shouted. "Fat man needs another
side of beef!"

When Grant's back was turned, Harren threw down his waster
and, moving much faster than in their training, leapt forward and
wrapped the smaller man in his chunky arms. Grant's eyes bulged
as the breath was squeezed out of him. His slender fingers lost grip
on his waster, which fell harmlessly to the dirt. Harren tossed him
to the ground, where he bounced once, twice, striking a rock hard
enough to make his mouth bleed.

Harren was on the waif a second later, straddling him, and
pressing the whole of his weight down on the smaller man's back.
He grabbed a fistful of his opponent's hair and drove the man's head

into the earth again and again. Grant's screams rose and fell as the fat man pulverized his face to the tune of a series of dull thuds.

All other exercises halted. It was only when the entire group of new recruits had gathered around the scene that Crian stepped in. He used the tip of his saber to wedge his way through the perspiring masses.

"Cease at once!" he bellowed.

Harren acted like he couldn't hear him, continuing to pound poor Grant into the stone-covered earth. Already a wide swath of blood had formed, growing steadily. Crian grabbed the back of Harren's practice armor and yanked him away. The fat man fell off to the side but kept on his knees. In his rage, he twisted and tried to launch a closed fist into Crian's stomach. Crian knocked aside the blow with the base of Integrity's handle, while angling the blade so that its tip lightly pierced the folds beneath Harren's chin. The obese man froze, a thin stream of red trickling down his folds of flesh, disappearing beneath his chipped and filthy practice armor. His lips quivered as he stared up at Crian.

"Are we done now?" Crian asked, keeping his expression serious despite the fat man's preposterous appearance.

"Yes, sir."

"Then help your sparring partner up."

Crian withdrew Integrity and watched as Harren awkwardly got to his feet. The man's fleshy hands groped Grant's prone body. The injured man moaned and began coughing as his small frame was jerked upward from the pool of blood surrounding it. When Grant turned to face the gathered crowd, a series of gasps came from the onlookers. The man's face was dripping with red from pate to chin, his nose flattened, his lips split. He looked wobbly and confused, but at least he was conscious. When he opened his mouth to reveal missing teeth, Crian felt his stomach clench. He pulled his shoulders taut and addressed the pair.

"What happened here?" he asked.

Harren stammered and said, "He been poking fun at me, sir, and I lost control. I'm sorry."

Grant wheezed and tottered.

Crian bent over, picked up Harren's waster, and began swiping at the empty air before him. "I find it strange, Harren Langfeller, that you move so quickly when mauling your opponent from behind, but when handling your sword, you are slower than a slug in salt. Why do you think that is?"

"I don't know, sir. I think—"

Crian lashed out, thumping Harren on the side of the head with the broad edge of the waster. "*That* is your problem. You spend too much time thinking, rather than *learning*. To swing a sword is an art, but it is also a reaction. If you practice your jabs, your thrusts, your defensive positions, and practice them tirelessly, they will become as natural as breathing." He poked the wooden tip into Harren's breastplate. "You, however, look as uncomfortable today as the day you came here. You're slothful and lazy, but at least you have *plenty* of experience lashing out against unsuspecting, lesser men. Am I wrong?"

Harren averted his eyes and muttered, "No."

"I thought not. And you." Crian stepped up to Grant, grabbing both his shoulders to steady the wobbling man. "Grant Tunshackle, what have *you* learned today?"

Grant's eyes rolled into the back of his head, his neck slumped backward, and he collapsed. Crian released the man's shoulders, letting him fall.

He addressed the rest of the men. "Our friend here made light of an opponent. He mocked a strength greater than his because he thought he was faster and more skilled. Remember that. Any adversary can destroy you with a single swipe of a sword or launch of an arrow. *Any* foe we face is to be respected. It is irresponsible—and dangerous—to do otherwise. Fail to show an enemy respect, and all your advantages cease to exist. Your foe will do anything to regain the honor you stripped from him." He whacked the prone Grant on the shin with the waster, eliciting a moan. "Does everyone understand?"

"Yes, sir!" the troupe shouted in near unison.

"Very well. Retake your positions and continue your sparring. You are not dismissed until you hear the dinner bell ringing." He turned to Harren. "And speaking of dinner, you, fat man, bring Tunshackle to the medicinal tent; then find Moorman and assist him in preparing dinner. You will serve your fellow soldiers, but only serve. You can afford to miss a few meals, I believe. When every man has eaten his fill, tend the stables until the witching hour. Do you understand?"

"Yes, sir," Harren muttered before bending over to lift Grant. As the fat man stumbled away, Grant's body bouncing on his shoulders, Crian saw the defeat in his posture. He hoped the lazy, obese ruffian would learn his lesson. If not, it would be *his* face that was pounded into the dirt tomorrow.

The sparring continued until daylight began to wane and the bell began to chime. The exhausted recruits breathed heavy sighs of relief. Dragging their wooden swords behind them, the hundred sweaty, scorched-red men made their way out of the practice field, up the hill, and into the encampment.

Crian walked alongside them, offering slaps on the back and words of encouragement. Though he had been thoroughly disappointed by the ability displayed on this day—for the last eight days, really—he found it best to encourage his charges rather than break them down. From an adjacent field he heard Avila's bone-chilling voice screeching at her own group of future warriors. The sound made Crian's throat tighten. The proper method for training an army was one of the seemingly ten thousand things that he and his sister disagreed about, so they had divided the soldiers among them. Crian hoped his way, of encouragement and discipline through example, would turn out to be more effective.

He cut diagonally across the sloped hill, weaving between his charges, and came to rest on the earthen divider separating his practice space from his sister's. With hands on his hips he watched as man after man collapsed, only to be whacked by Avila's staff while she chastised them. More than half of her men were down for the count, but those who remained standing moved with a precision that could be matched by none of the men in Crian's group. If that was Avila's plan—to cull the herd until she created a handful of perfect soldiers—Crian wished her the best of luck. To accomplish what their father desired, they needed sheer numbers. It was easy for five men to sneak through a barricade and kill an enemy leader, but those five men would be severely overmatched when five *hundred* of that leader's most dedicated came seeking vengeance.

At least that was the theory. But because the human race had never seen true conflict over their short existence in Dezrel, all they really had to go on was theory, plus the wisdom that Karak imparted from time to time. Thankfully, Crian knew none of it would matter. Everything they did—all the preparation and drilling—was unnecessary. Those in Haven would bow to reason. How could they not? He wished his brother were here, for Joseph was far better company than Avila, but he was still in Dezerea and wasn't expected back for several weeks at least.

Crian turned his back on the scene just as Avila launched into another tirade against an exhausted and defeated recruit. He shook his head as he walked, progressing past the mess tent and through a group of his charges. He observed with interest the way his men scarfed down their dinner, but did not join them.

Eventually his feet found the beaten dirt path that led through Omnmount. To call the place a township was a bit misleading; Omnmount consisted of a single stone building, which served as both a temple of Karak and a central market, located at the hub of a sprawling stretch of land dotted with crude huts, tents, burrows,

and low holdfasts. The area the town encompassed was monstrous—
the practice fields they were using were actually located toward the
center. By foot it would take three days to reach the unnamed outlying territories, where the rich soil was farmed for the grains, fruits,
vegetables, and meats that fed virtually all of Neldar. Other than the
thousand soldiers he and Avila had brought with them, the place
was full of transient workers who spent much of their time working
those fertile lands. To Crian, Omnmount was nothing more than
an overwrought labor camp.

Only it *was* something more, for now it was the staging ground
for Karak's Army.

Crian approached his tent, a tall swath of canvas as big as his
room back in Tower Servitude. He wiped his sandaled feet on the
mat before slapping aside the flap and stepping through the threshold. There were already candles burning, lit by his squire, Leonard,
so that the space would be comfortable when he arrived.

Being inside his temporary home brought a bit of relaxation
to his tired bones. All of his amenities from Veldaren had made
the trip with him—his vanity, his wardrobe, his writing desk, and
especially the dragonglass mirror. A thick carpet had been brought
along as well, soft and supple beneath his feet. Grabbing a copper
goblet from his desk, he poured himself three fingers of mulled
wine, took a sip, and began to undress. His sweaty garments came
off with some effort, like shedding a second skin. He hung Integrity
on the corner of his wardrobe, fitted his armor on the frame beside
it, and tossed his breeches and tunic onto a pile for the washwomen
to take away. In the corner of the room was a giant iron bucket,
and he stepped inside it. Above his head was a spigot attached to a
tarred sack filled with water that hung outside the large tent. The tar
kept the burlap sack waterproof while also attracting the sun's rays,
which warmed the water. With a pull of a lever, a gentle stream of
tepid fluid cascaded over him. Crian proceeded to wet his hair and
scrub the day's grime from his body.

By the time he was finished, it was almost dark, and he was exhausted. He slipped his nightshirt over his head and stood before the mirror. Slowly he applied a mixture of watered-down tannins and ground oak bark to the silver streaks in his hair that seemed to multiply daily. That done, he stretched out on his bed, which was made from seven fat blankets stacked atop each other on the ground. Finally alone, all thoughts of training and military theory left him. He allowed his mind to wander to what mattered most: Nessa. He thought of her petite stature and wild red hair, her piercing blue eyes, and the gentle rise of her small breasts. When he closed his eyes, he could smell her rosemary perfume. He hoped the letter he'd sent five days ago had reached her. It had been difficult to find an opportunity to set Atria to flight. The bird had arrived two weeks ago, bearing news of Nessa's journey through the west. With Avila's watchful eyes always around, it had taken unbearable patience to find a safe time to release his message. On several occasions he'd almost been caught by one of his sister's spies. He worried the delay would cause his love to think he had forgotten her.

I could never do that, he thought. And as he drifted off to an easy sleep, he held onto an image of the two of them lying naked by the southern bend of the Rigon, their bodies entwined. Celestia's star shone overhead, and the future before them was one of never-ending joy.

In the dream a hand, cold as ice, caressed his stomach, bringing an uncomfortable sensation creeping up his spine. Crian's sleeping mouth rose into a grin, and he brushed the hand away playfully.

"Stop that," he mumbled.

The hand returned, and his mind began a steady journey back to wakefulness. He felt the fingers tiptoe over the hair on his chest and slide seductively down his sides, tracing his hips and the inside of his thigh until they wrapped around his manhood. He let out a drowsy chuckle.

"I said stop, Ness," he mumbled. "It's cold."

"Who's Ness?" said a familiar yet out of place voice.

Crian's eyes snapped open, his vision greeted by the pale blue light of near darkness. He felt pressure bearing down against his side and held his breath, listening. The light wheeze of inhalation reached his ears as fingers squeezed his upper arm. He uttered a cry of surprise and hastily rolled off his pile of blankets, the frigid midnight air biting at his naked body. The presence on the bed stayed silent. Stumbling, he thumped into the wardrobe and reached out blindly, searching for his tindersticks. He found them on the second try and struck one, touching the flaming tip first to one candle, then another. Soft light filled the tent, creating a dome of brilliance around him. He picked up one of the candles and, very slowly, turned around.

The person on the bed was ghostly white, leaning up on one elbow and staring at him. The eyes reflected the candlelight, refracting back at him like a pair of distant stars. He inched forward, knowing exactly who it was, but refusing to accept it. Only when his ring of light fully revealed the invader did the knowledge register.

"What...why are you here?" he stammered, aghast.

Avila's expression was a mask of intrigue and disappointment. She pushed herself upward on his makeshift bed, her pale flesh and white hair making her look all the more like a phantom. The only color in her was those icy blue eyes and her tongue, which looked red as blood when it snaked out to lick her lips. Like him, she was fully naked, her breasts and sex bared, and yet unlike him, she appeared completely at ease with the night's chill. It was as if the bitter air couldn't penetrate her porcelain skin.

"I was hoping for a release after a difficult day," she replied, her voice emotionless.

He stared at her, confused and horrified at the same time, his mouth unable to form words. Finally he managed to choke out, "A *release?*"

His sister nodded, pulling back her shoulders so that her chest jutted toward him, as if the sight might hypnotize him. "Yes, a release. The decree of our family states that we are the betters of humanity. We are the pure, the holy, the direct offspring of Karak. To sully our bodies by giving them to the impure is forbidden, and yet our bodies still require intimacy. Who better to share that intimacy with than another who is as perfect as we are?"

Crian shook his head defiantly. "No. I am *not* hearing this. You wish…to *mate* with me?"

"No," replied Avila, her chin dropping and her gaze becoming even colder. "I want to *fuck* you, my dear brother, that and only that."

"But you're…you're…."

She shrugged. The gesture was so detached from any sort of feeling, so different from his lingering dream of Nessa, that to Crian's mind she seemed more alien than human.

"And?" she said. "I have shared a bed with Father, Joseph, and Uther. For Karak's sake, Thessaly and I have explored each other as well during our more anxious years."

Crian's horror grew. He felt his jaw hang lower and lower by the second. "That…that's abominable!"

"Father has sheltered you for too long, it seems. He has kept this secret from you out of mother's desire to protect your pure thoughts. I beg to disagree, my sweet brother, but it is not abominable. There is nothing more natural. Like should comfort like in any way they desire. We are different parts of the same whole, Crian. The same blood flows through our veins. I don't see why you would be opposed to us pleasing each other."

He turned away from her and leaned against the wardrobe, holding his throbbing forehead in his hand. "I'm not hearing this.

Please dress and leave my tent at once, and when morning comes, I don't want to hear a word of what happened here."

He stood there in the quiet for a few moments, waiting for Avila to do as he asked, but he heard nothing but her repetitive breathing. His anger grew, and he was about to spin around and scream, when Avila broke the silence first.

"You never answered my question," she said. Whatever sexuality she had tried to exude was gone. "Who is Ness?"

His heart clenched and he found it difficult to draw in air.

"It's no one, just a peasant girl," he replied, but the tremble in his voice exposed his lie. With his family, Crian was always exposed by his emotions.

Avila laughed, and it was such a dispassionate sound that it chilled him to the bone.

"Just a peasant girl? I think not. The men of our house have taken a peasant or two over the years for sport, but they've never whispered their names in passion. Tell me the truth, Crian. Does this Ness have anything to do with the hawk you released?"

Crian spun around and stared at his sister, who gazed back with an expression of cold calculation that showed in the smooth rigidity around her eyes.

"What are you talking about?"

"Oh, did you not wish me to know of that? There are always eyes upon you, Crian, as there are upon the rest of us. At first I thought you were communicating with Father behind my back, but the hawk was not one of ours. Now, though…" Her fingers traced absently through the space between her breasts. "Now you make me wonder."

Crian kept his mouth shut.

Avila laughed. "Your silence is answer enough, brother. There could only be so many women with such a name who are worthy enough to steal your favor. Is it Nessa DuTaureau, youngest daughter of Isabel DuTaureau? A member of Ashhur's First Families? If

so, at least your tastes haven't fallen all the way down to the mud.
I wonder where the child is now...."

"You leave her be," growled Crian. He inched to his right, where
Integrity hung from the corner of his wardrobe. If Avila noticed, it
didn't bother her. If anything, she looked more pleased.

"At last you admit it. I know the girl crossed Ashhur's Bridge
and into the delta. She arrived with her brother, and last I heard,
they were staying at the Gemcroft estates." Her tone became taunting. "Is that why you were sending the bird, sweet brother? Does my
sibling turn down my advances because of forbidden love?"

She paused, her eyes boring into him. Thinking. Plotting.

"I almost didn't believe it," she said. "But it's her, isn't it? The
reason you dye the silver from your hair?"

Her words were like a spear to the gut. His lack of clothing was
nothing compared to the nakedness he felt now.

"You don't control me," he said, doing his best to remain calm.
"I can do as I wish, fall in love with whomever I would like. I have
broken no law, no commandment."

Avila leapt off the bed, her lithe, naked form as agile as that of
a lioness.

"You are Left Hand of the Highest!" she screamed, before regaining her composure. Her voice lowered. "You have a responsibility to
your station and your family, not to mention your *god*. To continue
on with her, you must disown us, your own kin. If you do that, you
will not be welcomed in Neldar any longer. You will be an outcast,
a man without a country. Ashhur's people will not take you, I guarantee you that."

"I'll stay in the delta," Crian said. "We can make a home there,
far to the south, where the people are few. We wouldn't be the only
ones to have left the First Families."

Avila shook her head and sighed. "You have always been naïve,
brother, but this is painful. Why Father chose you as his Left Hand
over me, I will never understand. Haven is doomed no matter what

those heathens do. In five weeks the entire area will be crushed, and the delta will become part of Neldar. Father has ensured that a faction within will resist no matter what the rest might say, and their resistance is all we need. It is on his order, the order of the Highest, that this scenario has been plotted out, and he has Karak on his side."

Crian's blood pumped faster and faster. "What of the innocents? What of the young? What of *our sister?* Moira still resides in Haven! We have not been given word to bring her out."

"We have no sister in Haven, brother. Moira ceased to be a Crestwell the moment she disobeyed our family's edicts. She receives no warning, no special treatment. She is what you will become should you continue your stupid infatuation with this Nessa: banished. And what is this talk of innocents? The delta is populated by miscreants and blasphemers, adults and children alike. There is no innocence to be found. They have all turned their back on their creator, and they deserve every bit of the righteousness they are about to receive."

"You're going to let them all die," he whispered.

"No," replied Avila, folding her arms over her bare chest. "We're going to *kill them.*"

He didn't know what to do, what to say. Crian wanted to tell her she was wrong, deluded, but he knew enough about his father's greed, his cold, unmoving faith in both Karak's and his own perfection, to know that her words were true.

"Come back to us, brother," Avila said, softening her voice. "Lie with me. Don't do anything you might later regret."

What happened next was a blur. Without thinking, Crian snatched an iron candleholder from atop his wardrobe. Avila lunged for a bundle that lay at her feet, possibly containing her hidden sword, but Crian was quicker. Down came the candleholder, striking her in the middle of the forehead. Her head snapped back, a red gash opening up in the middle of her pallid flesh. Again he hit her, and again, spraying dark blood in the candlelight. Avila slumped in his arms, and he shoved her backward, sprawling her across the make-shift bed with her arms and legs splayed. Her face was destroyed, her lovely features warped and speckled with crimson. Her chest rose and then fell, exhaling a bloody fizz that spread over her pale lips.

"What have I done?" he whispered, panic roaring through him, pounding between his ears.

Crian turned away from his sister's still form, tearing through his things. He flung on a smock and leather breeches, and tossed a chainmail vest over his shoulder. Into a sack he dumped a change of clothes, three candles, a dagger, a box of tindersticks, and his wine-skin. As a final keepsake he snatched the dragonglass mirror off the post on which it hung, stuffing it in the sack with everything else. In his haste he didn't bother fastening Integrity to his waist, instead holding the scabbard by its strap and letting it dangle from his hand as he hefted his sack and bolted out of the tent.

The waning moon lit the countryside in an unnatural glow, and to Crian it seemed to stare down at him with a menacing sideways grin. The chill in the air took hold of him, even as the heat generated by his pumping arms and legs grew. His booted feet pounded the grass, shifting between the tents and lean-tos that surrounded him. His senses seemed heightened, his eyes wide, his ears on alert for the slightest shift or call. He ran into the stables, saddled a chestnut mare, fastening his belongings to the saddle, and then mounted her.

"Hey there!" called a voice. Crian spun on instinct, Integrity lashing out. Its sharp steel found flesh. Mouth open, jaw trembling, he watched as Harren crumbled to the ground beside the horse, a wide gash in his throat. Crian stared as the blood pooled beneath the fat man. In his mind's eye, he didn't see the lazy grunt he'd sent to the stables for punishment. Instead he saw Nessa in the ruins of Haven, bloodied and beaten by his father's army.

He fled Omnmount as distant voices began to call out in alarm.

CHAPTER

15

"So is it everything you hoped it would be?" asked Kindren.

Aullienna nodded, her heart skipping a beat as she stared at the massive cavern before her. It was a breathtaking sight, both beautiful and macabre.

Hundreds of jeweled sarcophagi filled the cavern, surrounded by caches of gold, silver, and bronze. Each sarcophagus was covered in images depicting the owner buried within; some of the art was skillfully rendered; some less so. The burial boxes were arranged in groups according to family, and in the center of each assemblage was a giant statue of stone.

"These are so old," Aully said.

"They are," her betrothed answered.

"But why didn't they build the crypts in the old lands? Why here?"

He laughed. "Because the first generation of elves decided that the land above the crypts should be unsettled, that it would be an insult to live right on top of them. So they chose a swath of forest just outside Kal'droth and dug beneath the earth. But when Celestia changed the world, this is where my father decided we would live. Hence, Dezerea."

"You don't seem so upset by that."

"I never saw Kal'droth. I'm *happy* here. There's so much beauty up above, and down here there's so much to learn."

"Like what?"

"Do you see those statues?" Kindren asked her, pointing.

Aullienna nodded. They were frightening—stone faces forever expressionless, their khandars, staffs, and bows looking ready to strike dead anyone who dared enter this sacred place. Somewhere down here would be her own legacy, she knew, her own family heritage. She thought about asking him to take her there, but she decided there would be plenty of time later. Dezerea was her new home. Time for her was a plentiful commodity.

"Those statues represent the founders of each particular family," Kindren said. "They stand vigil over the remains of their children, grandchildren, and so on."

Aullienna was overwhelmed by the sheer number of sarcophagi and statues, and all the more so because according to Kindren, the crypt before her was just one of hundreds beneath Dezerea.

"It would take a thousand trips to see them all," Aullienna murmured as she slowly made her way through the statues, taking in the various names and images.

"Two hundred and seventeen actually," Kindren replied, and he smiled at her when she narrowed her eyes at him. "Trust me. I've seen every single one. And you will too, if you wish."

She gazed up at Kindren with adoration. The last few weeks had been without a doubt the best of her short life, though they hadn't been without their own special sort of irritation. After breakfast with Noni, her nursemaid, her mornings were spent with the Thyne handmaidens, doing everything from trying on clothing and learning the intricacies of court etiquette, to mind-numbing studies that included learning the names and physical attributes of all the elves in the courts of both Dezerea and Quellassar. Why she had to know that a two-hundred-and-twelve-year-old lesser minister named Q'leetho Coresan had a nose bent slightly to the left was beyond her. Yet she suffered through the lessons, dutifully listening as the handmaidens laid open dusty book after dusty book, because she knew lunchtime came next, when she would be awarded with smoked bacon sandwiches and delectable plum pies, washing it all down with the tastiest lemon sour she'd ever drunk.

Of course, lunchtime also meant she was only a single short hour away from spending the rest of her day with her betrothed. Ever since the tournament, the two youths had become inseparable. Aullienna was enthralled by Kindren's sense of humor and chivalry—never was there a puddle he wouldn't carry her across, a time she slipped when he didn't catch her before she fell. Of course, Kindren would always poke fun at her for it afterward, telling her if she watched the ground as carefully as she did him, she'd stumble less. They were always wandering about the streets of Dezerea, exploring the palace grounds and the tree huts of the surrounding forest. They chatted with anyone who was willing to give them the time of day, and it seemed as though much of the city was taken with them.

Some of the Dezren began calling them *The Common Royalty*, a nickname Aullienna, who came from Stonewood, where people were on equal footing regardless of their station, much appreciated.

Aullienna and her parents were staying in the East Garrison, an elegant structure that looked like a miniature version of Palace Thyne. Aully's window overlooked the forest and the hilltops bordering the Rigon River, and on many a morning she sat at that window in rapt attention, watching as the sun slowly rose over the rounded, grassy peaks. The consulate from Quellassar was also staying in the East Garrison, which meant she spent several hours in the same space as Ceredon Sinistel. They often passed each other in the Garrison's jade halls, and over the span of a few days they had taken to conversing lightly. Despite the irritability and general unfriendliness Ceredon had displayed on the day of the tournament, Aully began to see a different side of him. Although he was a bit uptight and full of himself, he seemed to mean well. As they began to warm to each other, she decided that his heart rang nearly as true as Kindren's. Aully excused his previous behavior as that of an uncertain son who felt pressure to live up to his demanding father's reputation. Besides, he was beautiful, his features as flawless as the rest of his family's, which made him agreeable to look upon.

The sound of something rapping on hollow metal wrested her from her daydream. Kindren gazed at her with excitement in his eyes, the tips of his fingers brushing the bare portion of her upper arm, and Aullienna's insides melted.

"Aully, look at this," he said, pointing to a giant, round brass shield that stood as tall as she did. The words *Ambar e Fuin* were engraved on it, *The Fate of Darkness*. Aully felt another of Kindren's stories coming on, and she leaned her elbows on the pedestal nearest her, cradling her chin in her palms. "This shield belonged to Jimel Horlyne," he said, "the honorable warrior who, legend has it, fought the demon kings that laid siege to Kal'droth a thousand years ago. He was the tallest elf ever born, towering over his brothers and sisters by at least a head. That's him right there."

Kindren pointed up and Aully followed his finger, gasping in horror at the behemoth that seemed to be bursting out of the cavern roof. Its enormous head contained a mouth that was opened in an eternal scream, bellowing down at her in pained silence. Unlike the rest of the statuary, this one was just a face and a sword arm. That face was appalling, cheeks lined with creases, nose withered away, teeth chipped and broken. It was beyond her why anyone had decided to embed the partial statue up there, nestled among the stalactites.

As if sensing her question, Kindren said, "According to the tombs, Jimel is the elf who banished Sluggoth the Slithering Famine from this world. During a great battle, he allowed himself to be swallowed by the beast, which stood a hundred feet high. He slowly hacked away at the demons inside with his sword, slicing through its underbelly. He slayed it so that Celestia could banish its poisonous presence from the realm." Kindren's expression appeared reflective, almost sad. "The statue reflects the last any saw of him: Jimel, the great warrior, appearing through a rain of blood and entrails, sword leading, his face shriveled, his body rife with infection. He made the ultimate sacrifice for his people so that many more could live."

"You respect him."

Kindren bowed. "I more than respect him, Aully. Of all the stories, his is the greatest. When I was younger I dreamed of *being* him, of giving my own life to protect my sisters and parents. Then it would be *me* memorialized like Jimel up there—it would be me about whom the stories are told."

"When you were *younger*," Aully snickered. "As if you are *old* now. But why would you want to be him? That's stupid."

Kindren looked over at her suddenly, seemingly shocked by her words. "It is? But why?"

She pointed at the carved figure. "Because he probably had a wife and children, and when he was gone, they were left alone. But you're alive, and you're *mine*. You'd do me no good as a stone statue, Kindren, remembered in fairy tales. I want you by my side, now and forever."

"But the glory...."

"Glory? There hasn't been a war in this land for centuries. All we have are fancy stories, and it's one thing to play pretend, swinging a branch like it's a sword. 'In the mind there are heroes,' my father once told me. 'But in the world there is only life and the struggle to keep it.' Those might be simple words, but they're true. I'm beginning to like you a lot, Kindren. The *last* thing I would want is for you to run off and play champion while I'm at home with young babes. It wouldn't be fair."

She crossed her arms and huffed.

"And if you did, the least you could do is bring me with you," she added.

Kindren laughed.

"What's so funny?" asked Aully, squinting.

"You're only twelve, huh?" he said.

"Yeah. What of it?"

"Only that you speak with more wisdom than those twenty times your age. You truly are an extraordinary girl."

Aully felt her cheeks flush. "Thank you," she replied.

"I mean it. You're wonderful."

She slipped her elbows off the podium and snaked her hand through the crook of his arm. "So are you," she said. "But I'm serious. If something bad happens, we fight together. Understood?"

"Understood," laughed Kindren.

They continued their exploration, wandering through cavern after cavern. Aully marveled at the craftsmanship of the sarcophagi and the untold riches that had been buried with the deceased. In a couple of the chambers torches still burned, remnants of the last mourners to visit their particular ancestral burial nooks, but mostly they had only Kindren's oil-soaked bundle of twig and twine to light the way. Kindren told her the crypts were rarely visited any more. Given the lifespan of elves, he said, many regarded death as the last stopover on the way to returning to Celestia's bosom. With the great length of their lives, the end, by the time it came, was greeted openly by both the dying and those left behind. The only tombs called on with any sort of regularity were those containing the unfortunate who had been taken before their time or those of the great heroes of old.

Aully didn't really understand that line of thinking, as the thought of losing her own parents, who themselves had lived long lives, paralyzed her with fear, but she kept her objections to herself.

As the floor sloped further downward, there came a constant *plink-plink* of dripping water. Though the passageways grew narrower and more claustrophobic, the chambers they opened up into became grander and grander in terms of both size and the amount of treasure they contained. Here they found no lit torches, no signs of visitation.

"The ghosts of the dead murmur here," Kindren whispered softly, yet down here his voice still carried. "These caverns have been here since time immemorial. The deeper we go, the older the crypts. We'll soon come on the most ancient of the burial sites, those of the earliest elves, Celestia's first creations, before the dawn of language. The spirits are restless in these chambers, so far away from the light of their creator, and if you hold your breath and listen, you'll hear them lamenting their loss."

Kindren said that last bit with a sly smile on his face. Aullienna knew he was only trying to scare her, but she felt an ethereal chill that had nothing to do with the moisture or coldness of the deeper tunnels.

They stayed silent after that, the only sounds the sloshing of their footsteps over the damp stone floor, the crackle of the torch, and their own repetitive breathing. Ally gazed up at the stone figures and sarcophagi surrounding her, which were much more crudely constructed than those they had passed earlier. The faces were barely recognizable as elven, and the figures' poses were twisted by the artists' misunderstanding of body structure. Here there were no jewels or gold, no treasure of any sort save for piles of domestic items—cups, bowls, utensils—all primitive and carved from wood. She thought of Noni's words when the nursemaid told her of the age of her people. Elves had existed for a little over two thousand years. Ally did the math in her head. Given their average lifespan and slower rate of reproduction, that meant they were in the fifteenth generation, twentieth at most. All considered, elves weren't all that much older than humans as a species. The thought made her head spin.

"This world is so young," she whispered. "I'm a babe in a land of babes."

"What?" asked Kindren.

"Nothing."

The path continued onward. Kindren had led her in a straight line, bypassing many side chambers. Finally they reached the end of the line, a sparsely filled hollow devoid of any carvings or even caskets. Here the corpses were laid out on the ground side by side, their moldy bones green with fungal growth. The light of Kindren's torch illuminated a hundred lifeless, empty eye sockets staring at the darkened ceiling.

Aully shuddered in the middle of them all. She knelt down and scooped up a stone from the damp ground. It was glossy and black, polished by time and sediment. She flipped it between her fingers, feeling the stone's perfect smoothness. She uttered a silent prayer to Celestia, infusing the stone with her words of love, before placing it down as tribute on the breastbone of a small pile of skeletal remains. Kindren remained silent behind her, but she felt his curious gaze. She closed her eyes and tilted her head back.

And then, just barely over the trickle of distant water, she heard the whispers.

"It's them!" she exclaimed, keeping her voice as low as she could. "They've awoken!"

Kindren's mouth twisted into a half-frown. He stared back at her, one eyebrow raised and his nostrils flaring. Under different circumstances, Aully might have found the expression adorable.

"They?" he asked.

"Listen," said Aully. She stood and placed a hand on his arm, hoping his touch would help keep her calm. "You can hear them."

Kindren closed his eyes and held his breath. His pointed ears twitched ever so slightly as he struggled to hear what she did. Eventually his eyes snapped open, and that funny-looking frown reversed.

"That's not the ghosts," he said, grinning now. He was careful to keep his voice pitched low. "There are others here with us. They've probably been down here the whole time."

"Really?"

"Yes. I recognize that voice."

He grabbed her hand and began to pull her along behind him.

"What are you doing?" Aully protested.

"Come on now," he said, his grin mischievous. "Whoever they are, they scared my betrothed. It only seems fair for us to put a bit of that same fright in them.'

That grin won her over. This was something Brienna would do. And if Brienna would do it, so would she.

They tiptoed through the inner sanctums until they caught sight of a gentle glow emanating from a passage on the right. Kindren led her toward it, snuffing out his torch once they reached the entrance. They passed through the adjacent tunnel cautiously, their footfalls soundless—a remarkable feat given the exhilaration that made Aully's entire body shiver.

When the chamber opened up before them, they found themselves enshrouded by darkness save for the faintly glowing light at the far end of the hollow. Kindren steered a narrow path through the stacks of caskets, moving slowly, not wanting to spoil their surprise by tripping over some unseen artifact or toppling over a burial mound. Aullienna followed, doing everything she could to not give away Kindren's game.

The voices grew louder and the light clearer, until Aullienna could plainly make out four male figures standing around a single, elegantly carved sarcophagus. One held a burning torch that illuminated their faces as they spoke. Two of them she identified right away. One was Joseph Crestwell, the human; the other was Conall Sinistel, Neyvar Ruven's cousin, who had won the fencing competition at the tournament. The other two she vaguely recognized, but judging from how similar to Conall they appeared, with straight hair the color of darkened wheat and slender, haughty facial features, she guessed that they were more relations of the Sinistel family tree.

Aully turned to Kindren and opened her mouth, but her betrothed shushed her with a finger to the lips. "Not yet," he mouthed, his lips moving darkly.

They inched in closer, and finally Aully could make out the words that were being spoken. The tones all four used were hushed and secretive, and she noticed their hardened expressions, their eyes scanning to and fro as if they were suspicious of who might be about. From the fear in her heart, and Kindren's tense posture, she knew they no longer had any intention of scaring these four, and she feared the reason why they crept closer by silent agreement, listening, watching.

"Enough, Aeson," Conall said. "There's no one there."

"I thought I heard something," the elf named Aeson said.

"It's just your mind playing tricks," said the other, whose name she didn't know. "These catacombs have that effect on you."

"I don't know, I thought I heard something too," said Joseph, glancing behind him.

"Ignore it," demanded Conall, looking annoyed.

"Yes," said the unknown elf. "Let us get back to business. I don't like being down here any longer than necessary."

"Of course you don't, Iolas," said Aeson. "Do you have anything to add?"

Iolas jabbed his fists into his hips and glared at the human Crestwell.

"We want assurances," he said. "Our cousin the Neyvar is not one to follow blindly."

"What sort of assurances are you looking for?" asked Crestwell.

"The land we'll receive for our assistance. We want it named now."

Crestwell shook his head. "I am sorry, friend, but that's not possible."

"Why?"

"We don't know which lands will be livable come the end. What happens if we promised you, say, the hill country around Lake Cor, and yet that area is razed of all living things?"

Conall shook his head. "These details don't matter. Who cares for the razing of the land? A simple sacred word and a sprinkling of seed is all that's required to fertilize the soil. We are not slaves to nature as you are."

Joseph Crestwell cocked his head and eyed the elf with skepticism. "It is not nature that worries me. Your old home…if that is all it would take to heal it, why haven't you done so?"

Conall crossed his arms and looked away.

"You know why."

"Exactly. We play in the lands of gods, and nothing can be certain. It was the power of a god, *your* goddess, as a matter of fact, that made your home uninhabitable, and now we risk squabbling between two more gods. Karak is righteous, but his brother is not, and I fear the damage he may bring upon our lands."

"Well," said Iolas, "we would still like a specific land named. If that area is devastated, you can simply name another one later."

Joseph sighed. "You people need to understand that this *is not going to happen*. You are arguing with the word of a god here. If Karak promises that you will be rewarded, you will be rewarded. To think he could lie is blasphemy."

"He is not our god," Aeson said. "And I do not hear these words from his mouth, but a human's."

"I speak for Karak."

"So you say," muttered Conall. "A human's word. A *liar's* word."

Iolas stepped between them, his hands spread in entreaty. "There is no need for fighting," he said. He turned to Joseph. "As the eldest present, I promise you our cooperation."

"I would prefer if the Neyvar were here to confirm this," Joseph said.

"And my cousins of the Triad wish Karak was here to confirm *your* promises," replied Iolas.

"So are we agreed then?" asked Conall, voice tinged with defeat.

The human reached out and shook his hand. "We are."

"Very well," said Iolas. "We will inform the Neyvar that we are moving forward. Shen and the Ekreissar will sail across the river a fortnight from now and guard the Rigon passage from then on. We will use Thyne ships to prevent flight into the west or the delta. Fear not."

"But you haven't answered my greatest concern," said Joseph Crestwell.

"Which was?"

"Will Lord and Lady Thyne agree to this?"

In answer to that question, Conall smiled menacingly, the sight of which sent a shiver up Aully's spine.

"They will," he said. "The Dezren are a languid race, too agreeable for their own good, and they have been since their first creation. They'll agree to the terms we give them, and if they don't, the days ahead will not bode well for their future generations. If there is one thing cousin Ruven is not, it is indecisive. The Thynes know this. They'll obey."

"There is one further condition."

Conall frowned. "What is that?"

"No matter how you plan to execute your plan, I have been told to instruct you that the delegation from Stonewood shall remain untouched. No member of the Meln contingent is to be harmed."

"Consider it done," answered Iolas, cutting off his cousin. "That can be arranged."

"Very well then," said the human, offering a bow. "I must return to Veldaren to inform the Highest that our strategy is in place. My only other concern is the giant Gorgoros and his people. My father says they are the largest threat to our victory. They cannot be allowed to interfere as events unfold."

"Fear not," said Iolas. "We have reached out to the Dezren in Stonewood who are sympathetic to our cause. I am certain they will deal with Bardiya swiftly and brutally."

"Excellent. And if I may speak frankly, let it be said that my respect for your race only grows. It is unfortunate that your goddess destroyed your lands. I understand your decision, but I wish that *you* had been the wardens for our young race rather than the ones we received. If that is any consolation at all."

With that, Joseph reached out, lit a small torch from the larger one, and turned on his heel. He marched out of the chamber, passing within a few short feet of Aully and Kindren. The youths scurried behind a leaning sarcophagus to stay out of sight of the elves, who had much stronger eyesight. Some grumbling between the three elves came next, and then they too exited the chamber, carrying the burning torch with them and leaving the two youngsters trembling in complete darkness.

It took more than a few minutes for Aullienna to gather her courage. She slid across the wet ground and touched Kindren's thigh. He was breathing heavily and lightly sobbing.

"They're gone, I think," she said.

Kindren muttered an unintelligible response. She heard him rummaging about behind him, and then he spoke a few words of magic. A sudden flare of brightness blinded her. She held her hand in front of her face until her vision adjusted to the newfound light, and then peered through her fingers into Kindren's mournful face. He seemed to have aged a hundred years in the short time they had listened to the four conspirators. The heavy bags under his eyes drooped, and the corners of his mouth were set in a frown. He didn't say a word, only stared at her.

"What were they talking about?" Aully asked, nudging him with her knee.

"I don't know," her betrothed replied, his voice shaking. "I've heard Conall poking fun at Father when he visits the palace...and Father just sits and takes it. I never knew why, but now...now...."

"Now what?"

"He has no respect for us," he replied, sounding defeated.

"And he threatened your life," Aully said. "What's going on? I mean, what kind of help are they giving the humans? Why would anyone harm my family? What's going on between the brother gods? Why are the Ekreissar coming *here?*"

"I don't know," whispered Kindren. "I don't know at all."

Seeing the boy she had grown so close to crumbling before her caused Aully's dread to subside. A sort of infantile fury followed in its wake, a sensation she had never felt before. She wished she were a male, wished she were tall and mighty like Jimel Horlyne. Then she could hunt down the Quellans and pound the deceit out of them. For the first time, she began to understand a tiny bit of Kindren's curiosity about heroism, for she felt it too.

Yet she didn't want to do this without her future husband by her side.

"Come," she said, tugging on Kindren's shirt and breaking him from his despondency. "We have to leave—now. We can flee to Stonewood and never come back. We'll be safe there, I promise."

Kindren stood, then shook the fear from his body with a mighty shudder before turning to look at her. The face that gazed back at her was that of young Kindren Thyne again, only a queer sort of despair lurked just behind his eyes that hadn't been there before.

"No, we can't just run away," he said. "I need to go to my parents. They have to know what's happening. They're good, Aully. They would never allow anyone to be hurt, not knowingly."

Aullienna bit her lip. "Can I stay by your side?"

Kindren grabbed her hand and together they weaved their way out of the chamber and back into the main passage, through the Crypts of Dezerea.

"Always, Aullienna," he said. "From life until death, we will be together. This I promise you with all my heart."

Aully clutched his hand tightly as the dreadfulness of what she'd heard in the crypt sunk in. From life until death. She believed him. Every word. She only wished she could know the length of such a life, know it would end with happiness and joy instead of the hints of war whispered about by men in crypts.

CHAPTER

16

B ardiya awoke to the sound of a strange bird cawing. He shifted on his bed of leaves, mindful of the bundles of fur nestled against his sides. One of the bundles exhaled a sleepy breath, and the stink of rotting meat hit Bardiya's nostrils. He cringed and turned his head aside.

He opened his eyes and tilted up his head. The two wolves, a male and female who frequented the fringes of Stonewood, had arrived early that morning to slumber beside him, as they often did. They had taken a shine to him two years earlier, accompanying him when he slept beneath the canopy beside the Corinth River on the southern periphery of the Stonewood Forest. He slipped his hands beneath their bellies and lifted them as he sat up, careful not to injure them by squeezing too hard. Part of the problem with his ever-increasing size, he had found, was that his strength continued to increase proportionately. He had only tested the extent of this newfound strength on a few occasions, but the last time he had, he'd lifted a felled tree blocking his hiking trail and hurled it a good twenty feet. Such strength made tender moments a difficult proposition, for he feared that in a moment of distraction he might crush someone.

It was still somewhat dark as his fists rubbed at the sleep dust rimming his eyes. The morning was overcast, gray clouds billowing through the gradually changing leaves of the canopy above him. He stood to crack his back, causing the still dozing wolves to yelp and rise from their new resting spot. His entire body ached as if he'd been running for hours without end. *I must have grown again*, he thought. *I wonder if it will ever stop.* A touch of fright prickled his insides as he considered the ramifications of that idea. What would happen if he outgrew the world, if he became so big that he towered over not only the trees but the world itself, a solitary being with his feet anchored on solid ground while his hands touched the stars above? The imagery was terrifying.

The strange bird cawed again. It was such an odd, out-of-place sound. Bardiya prided himself on knowing every species of animal he came across, from lizards to antelope, to fish, to birds, but this particular call he'd never heard before. He moved toward the noise, hoping to catch sight of the creature, when a rush of air blew past his ear. A weak smidgeon of pain followed, biting his shoulder like an insect, and a surprised yelp sounded from behind him. Bardiya glanced at his bare shoulder, where he could plainly see a strip of glistening red. He touched the spot, gazing at his fingertips as if it were the first time he'd ever seen blood, and then he realized there was an animal bawling behind him.

Bardiya whirled around. The bawling came from the female wolf, who was nestled up against her mate. The male was on his side, tongue lolling, the shaft of an arrow protruding from his skull. It took Bardiya a moment to realize what was happening. When he finally did, anger cascaded through him, and his ears caught the barely perceptible *thwump* of a bowstring being pulled taut.

His body seemed to react on its own, a survival instinct he had never known he possessed coming into effect. He veered to the side, his movements lumbering but quick, as another arrow pierced the space he'd just occupied. His knees struck the ground, but his body felt weightless. His fingers wrapped around a heavy stone half buried in the soft loam of the riverbank. Yanking it free, he spun on his knees and hurled it as hard as he could at the treetops. The stone was large, as big as a man's head, and the crashing sound it made as it ripped through the branches was like a hundred sparrows panicking and taking flight at once. The stone hit a tree trunk with a *thump*, and someone screamed. From above a solitary figure plummeted down, arms and legs undulating as it fell.

The figure struck the ground in front of him and bounced twice. A series of agonized groans emanated from him or her. The bow his attacker held had snapped on impact. The female wolf, seeing the one who had killed her mate, rose up on her haunches and skulked forward, teeth bared in a snarl.

"Stop," Bardiya said. He held out his hand, ready to use the *seducing whisper* should his friend refuse to obey, but the wolf sat down obediently, gazing up at him with gray, impatient-looking eyes. Bardiya knelt down, caressed the wolf's back, and kissed her on the snout. She snarled a bit in return, but he did not react. He knew her aggression was not aimed at him, but at the rolling, moaning figure that had fallen from the treetops.

He ran his finger between the wolf's eyes, beckoning it to stay put, and approached the wounded attacker. The gloom of the overcast morning made it difficult to see, but as he grew closer, he could plainly tell it was a male elf. He had the pristine, pale skin of the Dezren, the distinctive high cheekbones and slightly upturned nose, and he wore the standard earth-toned clothing. The elf's left leg was bent at a dreadful angle, and one of his ribs had ripped through his chest, shimmering red and deadly at the jagged breaking point. As Bardiya knelt beside him, he realized he knew his attacker, knew him well. This was the elf who had discovered him with the kobo two years ago, the elf whose accusations had started the conflict between their people, poisoning Bardiya's relationship with his father.

Bardiya scooped his oversized hand under the elf's head. The elf's eyelids blinked rapidly, as if he were trying to adjust to the light, and a bubble of blood popped on his lips.

"Davishon, why did you attack me?" he asked.

The elf moaned in reply. Despite all that had just happened, Bardiya's heart broke.

Placing Davishon's head back on the ground, he went to work, shoving the protruding rib back beneath the flesh, forcibly straightening the shattered leg, and tearing open the elf's tunic. Davishon screeched the whole time. When he was done, Bardiya crossed his legs and laid his hands on the elf's chest. What followed was his healing prayer, a song that he imagined lifting into the air and floating across Dezrel, directly into the ears of his god. He felt the burning in his hands that always followed, and suddenly the inside of his eyelids was awash with light. In that instant he felt every trauma that had befallen the elf—the broken bones, the punctured lung, the ruptured kidney, the fractured skull. Those sensations began to lessen the more intensely he prayed, the healing magic flowing from his heart, pouring out his fingertips. The elf below him gasped as if waking from a dream, his body stitching itself back together, piece by piece, with a speed accelerated by Bardiya's faith.

The light subsided and Bardiya fell back, exhausted. He slumped to the ground, striking his elbow on an exposed root. It hurt, but he was too drained to utter a cry of pain. He heard the shuffling of a body hastily retreating and opened his eyes.

Davishon was kicking himself across the ground, backing up until he collided with the base of a tree. When he could move no more, he glanced over himself, as if in disbelief. His eyes flicked up and met Bardiya's, his hands touching the spot on his chest where his rib had pushed through.

"You...you healed me?" he whispered.

Bardiya nodded.

Davishon's eyes darted to his shattered bow, then up into the treetops, where a quiver full of arrows dangled from a branch high above. Once more he turned to the giant who had healed his mortal wounds, and his lips quivered.

"Why?"

"I harmed you with my actions," Bardiya sighed. "I have sworn to *protect* life, not harm it. It was only right to mend the body that I broke."

Davishon stared at him blankly.

The female wolf, still sitting obediently as Bardiya had left her, let out a low, threatening growl. Bardiya gestured toward it.

"I feel you owe someone an apology," he said. "You killed her mate, whom she'd been with since she was just one year old."

The elf glanced from Bardiya to the wolf and then back again, but said nothing.

Bardiya drew in a deep breath, gathering his patience. "Davishon, I know you do not like me—perhaps even hate me. But I ask again…why did you try to kill me?"

Davishon's eyes widened.

Bardiya touched the now-healed slice where the arrow had grazed him. "Please, Davishon. For the respect of this land and its beauty, tell me."

"I'm sorry," said the elf. His expression became one of angst-ridden regret, even as he suddenly jumped to his feet. "If you hurry, there still may be time."

"Time for what?"

Davishon's eyes, glowing as the sun began to melt away the cloud cover, grew wide with despair. "The morning prayers. The mangold grove. Be quick. And again, I'm sorry."

The elf disappeared into the cover of trees. Bardiya heard splashing as Davishon crossed the river at a breakneck pace. He mulled over the elf's words, completely befuddled, until the wolf beside him whimpered. He glanced over and saw that she was once again

244 ■■ DAVID DALGLISH • ROBERT J. DUPERRE

lying against her dead mate. He watched the blood that still flowed around the base of the arrow shaft, dripping over the creature's unblinking eyes and pooling on the ground. Bardiya gasped, a lightning bolt of horror piercing his soul.

There may still be time. The mangold grove.

He leapt to his feet and ran. He ran faster than he ever had before, his long legs covering yards with each stride. In a span of mere moments he was out of the Stonewood borderlands and dashing across open fields that stretched out as far as his eyes could see.

The mangold grove. Morning prayers.

He ran faster.

A few miles outside the village of Ang there lay an isolated grove overflowing with broad-leafed flora whose stems shone red as blood. The mangolds were abundant there, the only place in all of Ashhur's Paradise they could be found. Bessus often talked of how the air was different in the grove, sweeter and more life sustaining. His father also spoke of how the mangolds were red because their roots were connected to the heart of the land. Much like the black spire, it was a wholly unique place, which was why Bardiya's parents and a select few of their people gathered there each morning to bestow their blessings on Ashhur in thanks for the life the god had given them.

If Davishon knew about the grove, and about the prayers conducted there, then so did others of his race....

He shoved his sore, oversized body to its limits. He ran over the hilly ground, grass whipping against him like a million tiny knives, opening slender cuts on his bare shins and knees, while roots, briars, and stray twigs gouged the bottoms of his bare feet. As he ran, the sun slowly climbed higher in the sky, and his body soaked with sweat that evaporated beneath its heat.

It was closing in on late morning by the time he heard the first of the shouts. The bunching of willow and palm trees that contoured the grove came into view. Bardiya pushed himself harder, the echo of those pained, continuous wails piercing his ears like a flaming knife. He roared, moving much too quickly as he came upon the bordering trees and ground cover, his right foot catching a vine and sending him sprawling. Soaring forward, his side struck a thick trunk, which sent him spiraling in the other direction. He put out his hands to brace his fall as he flipped over and over again, his vision a wash of coalescing color. His hip struck the ground first, sending a bolt of pain across his abdomen, and when his back struck something fleshy yet substantive he heard a shout of surprise.

He came to rest on his hands and knees, panting, the ache in his bones cramping his gut and making it difficult to focus. The red and green of the mangolds were beneath him now, but there was something strange about it; the red stems glistened in the soft glow of the late morning sun, appearing much more visceral than they should have.

People bellowed orders. Others howled in misery. A shadow loomed over him, as giant as he, and the sound of displaced air swooshed past his ear. He flinched and was struck with a jolt, something sharp sinking into in his collarbone. Whatever it was didn't strike him deep—Bardiya's bones were thick and strong, and they had never been broken in all his long life.

He snapped to attention, flicking his massive hands out in a warding off motion, sending the figure before him flying. He sat up then, grabbed the object jutting from his flesh, and tore it free. It was a slender blade, a khandar of the sort he had often seen the elves wield in their sparring matches. The steel was soaked red. The air grew thick with an eerie silence. His gaze shifted from the blade to the grove before him, and his heart caught in his throat. The strange color infusing the mangold was blood; the ground was coated with it. There were bodies resting in the tangled plants, unmoving, their forms athletic, their flesh dark. There were eight elves before him, all armed with blood-soaked swords of their own, save the one closest to him. They formed a semicircle around three terrified, huddled forms: Gordo and Tulani Hempsmen, and their young daughter,

246 ■■ DAVID DALGLISH · ROBERT J. DUPERRE

Keisha. Their water-rimmed eyes lifted to meet his, and they huddled even closer together.

The elves made no move against him. They froze as if they knew
not what to do, like a group of deer mesmerized by a predator.
Bardiya shut his mouth and breathed deeply through his nose,
trying to steady himself, trying to quell the pain that squeezed his
bones. Slowly he rose to his feet. He approached the first prone
body and used his foot to roll it over. It was Zulon Logoros, his
father's most ardent spiritual advisor. Zulon's neck had been split
from ear to ear. Blood-bubbled gasps still issued from his mouth,
even though the man's heart no longer beat and breath no longer
blew from his lungs.

There were six bodies beside that one. He knew who two of
them were without turning them over. His ardent desire was to collapse beside his parents' remains, to weep and howl over them and
bathe their faces with his tears. Bessus and Damaspia Gorgoros,
First Family of Ker, embraced even in death, their eyes shut against
the horror of their fate.

Bardiya stood tall, his shoulders back, his vision marred red with
his fury.

"Why?" he bellowed.

There was no answer from the elves, only action. The one in
front, whose khandar had been embedded in Bardiya's neck, clucked
his tongue. The other seven surged past him, swords raised, their
war cries pulsing through the air.

Despite the danger, Bardiya felt unnaturally calm. He still held
the khandar in his hand, his fingers so large that they could have
wrapped around the handle twice. The thing looked pathetically
small in comparison to his great size. He swung the sword sideways
as two elves came near enough to hack at him. So powerful was his
strike that the attackers' blades shattered on impact, as did his own.
Shards of metal rained to the mangold-covered ground with the
sound of tinkling glass.

Bardiya tossed the broken khandar aside and grabbed one of the elves, lifting him as if he were nothing. With a cry, he launched him through the air. The body struck another two assailants, knocking them over like a gale-force wind. Bardiya snatched up a fallen limb from a willow tree, this weapon far more comfortable in his grasp. With an easy swing he cracked the other nearby elf across the face, snapping his head back. A gush of red ejected from his mouth as he fell.

There was sound behind him, soft footsteps and crinkling leaves. Without thinking, Bardiya flipped the tree limb to his side and thrust it backward. It met resistance, followed by the gasp of someone struggling for air. Two more elves came at him from the front, trying to keep their distance, maximizing their reach with elongated lunges. It meant nothing, though; Bardiya's arms gave him a reach far greater than that of the short, lithe elves. His branch crashed through their bodies, smashing bones, pushing aside their blades as if in mockery of their futile attempts at defense.

One of the elves held up his hand, halting the others from advancing. Bardiya looked at him closely, studying his face, and recognized him as one of those who had come to threaten Ang after Bardiya's merciful slaying of the kobo. The elf's name was Ethir, and a hateful sneer twisted his lips.

"Leave," Bardiya said in a low murmur, "and tell Cleotis to never step foot in our land again. Do that, and I will let you live."

"Cleotis is in Stonewood no longer," Ethir replied, puffing his chest out to look bigger, a fool's gesture with Bardiya so close by. "His reign was weak and foolish. I answer only to Detrick Meln, the new Lord of Stonewood. Your threats mean nothing to me."

"They should," Bardiya said.

"And what of them?" the elf asked. He gestured toward the Hempsmen family, still surrounded by the remaining elves. The parents cried as they held their daughter close. Blades rested against all three of their necks.

"Would you let your grief doom them as well?" Ethir asked. Bardiya let his body relax, let his head dip in defeat. Ethir laughed, and the anger that had fueled Bardiya's earlier rampage returned. He leapt from his kneeling position, crossing the distance between them with shocking speed. His hands clamped around Ethir's shoulders, and with a simple twist of his waist he slammed the elf into a nearby tree. Ethir's head crashed against the trunk, and his eyes rolled into the back of his head.

The remaining elves drew their bows and aimed in his direction. Going against his every inner principle, Bardiya screamed over his shoulder, "Which is faster, your arrows or my hands? Put them down, or I'll cave in his skull!"

He sensed their uncertainty, saw the tension of the men who held the family captive. Bardiya prayed Ethir was important enough for them to make such a compromise. It appeared as though he were. Bows dipped, and the elves stepped aside so Gordo and Tulani Hempsmen could shuffle their daughter out of the grove. He hoped they reached safety, that there weren't more elves lying in wait around the grove.

Bardiya turned to his captive, who coughed and wheezed under his grip. Ethir's expression was no longer quite so impudent. The elf looked frightened. Bardiya took a deep breath. Never before had the commandment of forgiveness been so hard.

"I do not know why you hate us so," he said, "nor why you wish us harm. If my parents had lived through this, they would have hunted you down and placed your heads on spikes along the Corinth's western banks. But I am not my parents. I am Bardiya Gorgoros of Ker, the land we have so named. Violence is not in my heart, nor in the hearts of my people. You will never again see us near your forest home, but hear this: should you ever step foot into these plains again with any intention but love and cooperation, I will strike you down. That is a promise, from one man of honor to another. Am I understood?"

Ethir nodded.

"Good."

Bardiya released his grip, allowing the elf to fall. Ethir stood up shakily, brushed himself off, and flexed his arms. He whistled to his fellow elves, and one by one they disappeared from the thicket. Ethir was the last to leave, fixing Bardiya with one final, conflicted stare.

"You will not see us again," the elf said.

"Before you go," said Bardiya. "I must know. Please. Was this my fault, because of our misunderstanding about the birds?"

Ethir shook his head. "Birds? No, giant, there are things much greater than you moving through this world now. I will not weep for the rulers of House Gorgoros, but neither would I have moved against them if not for the gods. Put the blame on them, if you must."

Before Bardiya could ask him what he meant, the elf ducked out of sight. Once he was gone, an emptiness flooded into Bardiya's massive chest. The tree limb, the blood on it still drying, dropped from his limp fingers. Slowly he shuffled over to where his parents lay. He fell to his knees before them, rolling them apart so that he might gaze at their beautiful faces. He placed his hands on their broken, blood-soaked chests, and began uttering his prayers. In the back of his mind he knew it was hopeless, but in that moment he didn't care. His father and mother, the people who had raised him, who had first imparted to him the glory of Ashhur and the virtues of peace and prosperity, were gone. No matter how much healing magic he poured out of his fingers, he could not reverse that.

Death was permanent—forever.

Tears flowed down his cheeks. He felt no hatred for the elves, but he wished he could dive into their minds. He wished he could hunt them down, drag them before the corpses, and plunge into them the sadness and ache he felt. But what could he do? What explanation was there for such madness? He scooped up the corpses, all seven of them, and positioned them in a line beneath the shade of the largest willow in the grove. That done, he knelt beside them and let loose his despair, weeping as he waited for the Hempsmen family to return with more of their people. Then they could begin the procession into the desert, where the bodies would be buried beneath the silhouette of the black spire.

Love and forgiveness, that is the key, he heard Ashhur's voice whisper in his mind. Bardiya clung onto that mantra for all it was worth. The first man solely created by Ashhur, Bessus Gorgoros, was dead. As far as omens went, none could be darker or more ominous.

CHAPTER

17

The liquid burned as it flowed down his throat, but it was better than the pain in his chest. He welcomed the calming numbness that followed, and even the nausea the liquor caused as it worked its way through his veins. In the end, though, it was no real comfort. Nothing was. Vulfram knew that the drunkenness would subside as it always did, and his thoughts would return to Lyana.

He dropped his head into his palms and worked at his eyes as if trying to pry them from his skull. He couldn't sleep, could barely eat. It had been this way ever since that fateful day two weeks ago, when his lashings had stripped the flesh from his daughter's back. On the rare moments he did stumble into unconsciousness, he was plagued with nightmares of Lyana's future life as a Sister of the Cloth, of the abuses she would endure at the hands of the men who purchased her services, especially the young and nubile. More than anything he wanted to seek out the Sisters who had scurried away with her, perhaps even storm into their large vicarage in Felwood and free her. But he wouldn't—couldn't. Lyana's punishment had been Karak's decree, a decree given to him personally the evening before that fateful day. He could never turn his back on the word of his god.

Even if it killed him inside.

It was destroying his relationship with Yenge as well. When he was away, all he did was dream of home, and now that he was here, there was no happiness, no comfort. Yenge blamed him for their daughter's penalty—*him!*—as if he were responsible for her wild behavior. "She was a girl in need of a father," she said, "and you weren't here." Even Alexander and Caleigh grew distant, acting as if they were afraid to speak with him. His children meant everything to him, and seeing their wary glances tore at his heart. Every night he listened as Yenge wailed herself to sleep in the chamber down the hall, and every night he thought to go to her, to comfort her, but he never did. He stayed in his study, using the fireplace to warm his hands on each progressively chillier fall evening, wallowing in self-revulsion.

And it wasn't only Lyana's fate that inflicted him with guilt. Broward Renson was never far from his thoughts; Vulfram was haunted by the image of his oldest friend's head rolling away from the executioner's stone. He often cursed Broward's name, but that was always followed by a moment of doubt. Why would his friend have partaken in an act that hovered between irresponsible and outwardly evil? And why hadn't Vulfram possessed the patience to stop and ask? His friend's cries haunted him. What might Broward have said if he'd stayed Vulfram's blade? But Karak himself had ordered that the judgment be swift, meaning that Vulfram's questions were a sign of doubt and cowardice, a lack of faith in his deity.

It was a destructive cycle of self-hate that saw no end.

He tipped back the jug of brandy and took another hard swallow. This time he choked on the bitter juice while pounding the table with his fist. His lips formed Yenge's name, wanting to call out to her, but his throat remained still. He stumbled to the door of their bedchamber, pressed his ear against it, and heard his wife sobbing again. His fingers brushed the polished ivory door handle but stopped short of lifting it. Instead, he wandered back to his desk and slumped behind it. He pulled out a piece of parchment and then dabbed the tip of his quill into a tub of ink, but in his drunkenness all that came out was an illegible smear when the tip touched the page. He stared at the paper, hardly aware of what he was trying to write or whom he even planned to write to.

It is all my fault.

He tossed the quill across the room, crumpled the parchment, and cried. He only had one more day left before he had to head back to Veldaren and reclaim his position as Lord Commander. More than anything, he wished someone could heal his troubled mind before then.

Perhaps Karak will visit again in the night, he thought. *Perhaps he will tell me what to do.*

It was the lie he told himself every night, the way he calmed himself enough for sleep. Rising from his chair, nearly knocking it over in his tipsiness, he proceeded to the cot in the corner of the room and collapsed on it. He didn't bother to extinguish the candles or close the flue to the hearth. Eyelids half-open, he stared at the flickering light until it sent him off to another drunken and restless sleep.

He was awakened by a foreign scent and something soft touching his face. The shocking revulsion he felt snapped his eyes open with a start. He lashed out with his fist, striking nothing but air.

"Please be calm, Lord Commander," a voice spoke from the darkness. "I mean you no harm, but we must speak."

Vulfram recognized the voice, but distantly. He sat up, rubbing his eyes, the blood pounding in his head a reminder of how much he had drunk. The throbbing across the front of his face was almost as bad. He groaned and leaned over, searching for his waterskin on the ground and not finding it.

"You wish for some water, sir?" the familiar voice asked.

A figure stepped forward in the darkness, and for the first time Vulfram understood that it *was* dark.

"How long have I been sleeping?" he asked, snatching the proffered jug from the stranger and taking a long pull from it.

"I don't know, sir. I just arrived."

"Has the worship bell rung?"

"Um, no sir. That isn't until tomorrow evening."

"Good," he said. He scanned the darkened room, lit only by the still glowing embers within the hearth, but he couldn't find his sword. Instead, he reached beneath his mattress and wrapped his fingers around the handle of his spare dagger.

"Sir, I assure you there is no need for that. I mean you no harm."

A flame was struck in the darkness, momentarily blinding him. Vulfram covered his eyes with his arm, almost cutting himself with his dagger in the process. Silently he cursed his carelessness. His sight adjusted to the new light, that of a lantern. When he lowered his arm, he recognized his visitor as Weston, one of the Renson's elderly family servants. The old man tilted his head and gave Vulfram a queer look.

"Are you all right, sir?"

"I am. Why do you ask?"

A curved, slender finger pointed at him. "You have blood all over your mouth and beard, sir."

Vulfram wiped at the area and sure enough, there was blood there, mostly dried. The ache in his nose…he must have struck it somehow while collapsing onto his cot. He took the jug Weston had given him and splashed water over his face, which served to fully rouse him, and then wiped his face with yesterday's tunic. He felt a cold breeze and looked over to see that the outside door to the study, which opened onto the rear court of Mori Manor, had been left ajar. Rising from the cot, he paced to the door, closed it, and headed back to his desk. The candle there had dribbled wax all over his meager supply of parchment. Sighing, he began peeling the bits of dried wax off, dropping them into an empty cup.

"Weston," he said while he performed his mindless duties, "I'm tired and irritated. Tell me why you snuck into my quarters in the middle of the night. Come to avenge your master's death, perhaps?"

The last part had been said in jest, but the old servant seemed to take it seriously. "Absolutely not, sir. To me, the Lord Commander's decree is as good as Karak's. I would never do such a thing."

"So why are you here?"

"My new master sent me, sir."

"Bracken?"

"Yes."

"Then out with it," Vulfram said. "What does he want?"

"He wishes to speak with you immediately."

Vulfram chuckled. "Two weeks go by, but *now* is when he wants to see me immediately? I supposed he needed time to work up the nerve. I take it *he* will be the one who takes revenge for Broward's death, eh? Better him than a crooked-backed old servant."

Weston didn't laugh; he simply stared at him with a dire expression.

"I apologize," said Vulfram, feeling like an ass. "Please, Weston, what does Master Renson want with me?"

"I do not know, sir. He has been searching the house for days, and this very evening he emerged from the library in hysterics. He told me to find you immediately or he would cut off my head." Weston licked his dry lips. "I hope *you* do not wish me beheaded, sir."

Vulfram shook his head. That a man who had served his friend so faithfully for decades might doubt him filled him with shame.

"Of course not, Weston. I do not punish the innocent, only the guilty. Please, let me put on clothes that do not smell like a brewery. Wait in the front courtyard. I will join you in a few moments."

"Yes, sir," Weston said with a bow and left the room.

Twenty minutes later, under the faint light of a half moon, Vulfram followed Weston down the winding dirt path that led from Mori Manor to the quaint manse that the Renson family called home. The home was solidly built, two stories high, with a garret protruding from the top like a dunce cap. Vulfram remembered the days of his childhood when he and Broward would play in that garret, fooling around with wooden swords in the vast open space. Humanity had only been around for a tad more than thirty years at that time, and the garret had been virtually empty of belongings and knickknacks. He was sure it had filled up now, with four subsequent generations of memories added to the place.

They approached the front entrance to find Bracken standing there. His body was shaking, his eyes frantic. Instinctively, Vulfram reached for Darkfall, which he had strapped to his back. The new housemaster did not seem to notice.

"Good, you brought him," Bracken said, his voice cracking. He didn't look at Vulfram, instead shouting, "Follow me!" and storming back into the manse.

Weston stepped aside so that Vulfram could enter the abode, then turned and began to walk away.

"Where are you going?" asked Vulfram.

"I cannot enter," the old man said. "My master gave strict orders in that regard. All servants have been sent to stay with other households. Even the master's other children have been sent away. You two will be alone. That is what he wanted."

"Why?" Vulfram asked, suspicious.

Weston shrugged. "I do not know, Lord Commander. 'Prying eyes,' was all the master told me."

With that the old man limped away down the dirt path. Vulfram patted his sword's handle for comfort and then walked inside, hoping for the best.

He followed the trail of burning candles, which led him to the library at the far end of the home. Bracken sat behind a table, frantically scanning line after line of whatever document lay before him. The man looked as if his sanity had fled him, and Vulfram took a quick inventory of the room to see whether any weapons were hidden there. He didn't notice any save the great axe that Bracken's grandfather Brutus had used to fell the trees with which he had built this very home.

"It's funny how things work sometimes," said Bracken, still not looking up from the table. "Despite the many vile, lawless men of this world, it is men of good heart who often commit the greatest crimes. Orders, orders, always orders!"

"What madness do you speak of?" asked Vulfram, slowly making his way through the library.

Bracken slammed his fist on the table. "It is *not* madness!" he shouted, looking at the Lord Commander for the first time that evening. Vulfram could see the lunacy shining through in his clenched-lipped gaze. "It is *reality!* We are guided by forces greater than us, forces that *manipulate* us, and we will never understand what it is that they seek!"

"Forget manipulators," said Vulfram. "You don't understand what *you* are saying." He put his hand on Darkfall's hilt. "I think you may have lost your mind."

Bracken cackled, a sound so mad that the very air seemed to vibrate. He shot up and stormed around the table, making Vulfram brace for conflict. But instead of assailing him, Bracken fell to his knees, gazing up at him with crazy, pleading eyes.

"Go ahead," he said. "Kill me like you killed my son and father. Kill me because you were instructed to do so. Because that is why you kill, is it not? Because you are *told to?*"

"Bracken, man, stand up."

"You kill because it is Karak's will. But why would Karak wish the murder of his own creations? He is a god that walks among us! Any faults we possess, *he* gave to us! Can no one else see that? Any criminal, any blasphemer, he could counsel with a snap of his holy fingers. So why, I ask you again, would he order us *dead?*"

"Because we are to make our own way in the world."

"A fool's errand. Would you set your infant alone in the woods with wolves so he could do the same?"

Vulfram backed away a step. "What are you getting at?"

Bracken stumbled to his feet, moving like a drunk himself. Now that Vulfram got a good look at the man, he could tell that he hadn't slept for days. Whatever it was that afflicted him, be it grief or anger or doubt, it was degrading his body along with his mind.

He shuddered, for he felt as though the same thing were happening to him.

"I am saying we are all puppets," said Bracken. "Puppets in a game much larger than any we could ever understand. My father was tricked, as were my son and your daughter. As were *you.*"

Vulfram dropped Darkfall to his side. "These accusations are not to be made lightly, Bracken. Son of my old friend or not, you will not be saved from the executioner's stone should I find you guilty of blasphemy."

Bracken cackled again, his insane grin spreading wider.

"Of course not, *Lord Commander.* I think you proved that when you beheaded the people I love most."

The words sent a knife twisting through Vulfram's heart. He grimaced and nodded for Bracken to continue. Bracken's demeanor shifted when he realized that Vulfram would give him an audience. He took a deep breath, clenching and unclenching his fists. When he spoke again, it seemed as though a measure of control had taken hold.

"I was in abject misery, as you might expect, having lost both Kristof and my father on that dreadful afternoon. Penelope was as well, of course, and she left Erznia to rejoin her parents in Brent. She *left me* because I was a shell of a man. And it did not take long, in my loneliness, for my sadness to turn to hate. Hatred for you,

Vulfram. I wanted you dead. I went so far as to prepare Weston to venture out on the Gods' Road in search of bandits or sellswords who might take what meager coin I have in exchange for your head. It never came to that, of course—Weston would never have done it, and besides, I knew asking any standard thug to cleave your skull was akin to asking him to commit suicide. Instead, I ventured into the garret and sat there for days, shunning food and sleep while I wept. Many of my parents' things are stored there, and I took to combing through their old chests. For the first time I truly missed Mother. She died six years ago, stabbing herself through the heart. It took Father many moons to become anything close to himself again. Did you know that?"

Vulfram shook his head. All the while a new river of guilt overflowed the levees of his soul. He hadn't known, and given the duress he'd been under, it hadn't occurred to him to ask his old friend about Katherine's whereabouts.

Bracken waved his hand. "It doesn't matter. But though old wounds heal, they are always tender, always ready to break anew. My father once said to me, 'It is not her fault. There is always a reason when people act against their nature.' Mother had been suffering with the Wasting, you see. The pain that mounted each day became too much for her to bear, no matter what medicines or herbs or treatments we gave her. The only recourse she could find in the end, the only way to stop the pain, was to take her own life.

"When I thought of that, I knew," Bracken continued, pacing around the library with his head down and brow furrowed in deep concentration. "Something was wrong. Father was a man of responsibility, of dignity and honor. He loved his god more than any other. None of us dared contradict him, and we passed those lessons on to our own. And Father *adored* his grandchildren. He strove for nothing but the best for them. He was as much a teacher of morality and decency as I am, perhaps more so.

"Do you see? I am no fool. I can understand my son surrendering to his urges and bedding your sweet Lyana, but what my father did? I couldn't believe that a man of morality and religious fervor would choose to contradict our god's decrees in such a heinous way. I thought it a lie, a ploy, a falsehood. I tore through the garret in search of clues that might explain why he was foolish enough to offer crim oil to that frightened pair. By Karak, I didn't even know what I was looking for."

Bracken looked up then, and his eyes were utterly sane now. The new Master Renson circled back around and picked up a curling parchment off the desk.

"I nearly gave up. I nearly believed that I didn't know my father as well as I'd thought. But it's when you stop looking that the answers come to you. Three days ago, I started to feel better, more like myself. I gave up any mad thoughts of attempting to end your life and instead decided to used my solitude to read. The first tome I lifted was a collection of poems compiled by Eveningstar. The First Man had traveled here, to Erznia, during one of the first harvest festivals. He wrote down every word of every poem spoken by the townsfolk that night. Do you remember hearing stories of that?"

"I was there. Young, but there."

"That's right," said Bracken with a shrug. "I tend to forget that you are much older than you appear. Well, Father was there too, and Eveningstar handed him the tome when he was finished, as a gift."

"I remember that."

"It was Father's favorite book. He would often sit for hours and pour over every verse of all two hundred and seventy couplets. He loved poetry, even though his own was rather…lackluster." He shook his head. "I'm getting distracted. That night three days ago…I came to the library. I'd begun to hate my father, to believe him a liar and a hypocrite, and that's why I wanted that tome. I wanted to remember who he really was, remember the man who raised me and taught me how to live with decency and honor. But when I opened the cover, I found something strange inside. I found this...."

Bracken extended the parchment, which Vulfram hesitantly took. The paper was thin yet sturdy, the tender of vintage used for royal documents. It was face down, and he could plainly see the waxen seal, split in half, that decorated the top and bottom edges. He folded the parchment over and connected the two halves, revealing the image of a snake wrapped around a lion, the sigil of House Crestwell.

Vulfram's eyes widened. He peered up at Bracken, whose expression managed to convey both horror and victory.

"Read it," he said.

Feeling nervous, Vulfram flipped the parchment over and read. The message was a thank-you note, the final link in a chain of unknown correspondences, the words simple yet menacing in their ambiguity.

It is the mark of the faithful that we accept our roles without question, and yours is perhaps the most important one of all. Now that you have seen the seed planted, it is time to offer a choice. Whatever choice is made, find peace in the knowledge that the Divinity will hold you in his highest regard when he returns and will ensure that no ill befalls you.

The letter was dated three months ago. There was no personal mark on the bottom of the page, but Vulfram didn't need to see one to know who had written the letter. His eyes had scanned many a decree from Clovis Crestwell over the last eight years. There was no mistaking that loose, frantic scrawl.

He let the letter dangle in his hand, dread clamping down on his stomach.

"What does this mean?" he asked.

"You tell me," Bracken replied.

He couldn't. His head began to feel dizzy with the possibilities, and his knees grew weak. Amazingly, it was Bracken Renson, who had just admitted to wanting him dead, who now stopped him from falling. Vulfram accepted his help, leaning on the man as he stumbled across the room. Bracken guided him into the chair behind the library desk and handed him a jug.

"Drink some wine," he said. "You will feel better."

Vulfram tipped back the jug and felt the fruity liquid pour down his throat. It didn't do the trick.

"Stronger," he gasped. "Do you have any rum?"

Bracken shook his head.

Sighing, Vulfram eyed the jug once more, then downed the rest. Liquid seeped out the corners of his mouth and ran down his bare chest, red as blood. When he was finished, he tossed the jug aside, its rounded wooden shape bouncing on the stone floor before rolling beneath a table in the corner.

"Better?" asked Bracken.

"Not in the slightest," he replied.

"Now do you understand my madness?"

"I do, Bracken. I do indeed."

For whatever reason, he had been entrapped by the very people he served. If the letter were to be believed—and he saw no reason why it should not be—Clovis had been in communication with Broward. The vague pieces grouped themselves together in Vulfram's mind. Broward had been instructed to lure Lyana and Kristof into a clandestine relationship, giving them ample opportunity to fornicate. When Lyana was with child, Broward passed along the crim oil, neglecting to mention the side effects, thereby ensuring they would be caught. And all of this had been ordered with the promise that it was the will of Karak himself.

It was nothing but a guess on his part, but it made perfect sense. Why else would his old friend have so fearlessly admitted to his crime? Why else would he have looked on with anything but horror as his own grandson was executed? And why would he have protested so much at the moment of his own death if not because he had thought himself exempt?

This wasn't supposed to happen! I was pro—

Promised was to be that last word. Vulfram clenched his fist, crinkling the parchment as he did so. He almost tossed it into the hearth but thought better of it—instead, he flattened it, folded it neatly, and tucked it into his satchel. By itself the letter proved nothing. The words were carefully crafted and studiously vague, just as Vulfram would have expected from a weasel such as Clovis. But it was something—a weapon to be used. He needed answers, needed to get back to Veldaren as quickly as he could to confront the Highest about his role in this mess, to pry out—by force if necessary—the reason why such torment had been heaped on him. What, in all his life, had Vulfram done to deserve such a punishment?

Broward came over and knelt down beside him.

"Do you see now how you have been used?" he said.

The wine was finally beginning to work its magic, flowing through Vulfram's bloodstream.

"I see betrayal," he growled. "I see innocence lost. And I see blasphemy in the Highest."

Bracken's eyes widened.

"I am heading back to the castle," Vulfram said. "With Karak back in our fold, it will be easy to discern who performed this treachery. However, if this is a trick, *Master Renson*, if this is your way to force me to sign my own death warrant, let me assure you I won't die so easily. And if I find out you are lying, I will storm back here so that you may join your beloved son and father in the afterlife."

Bracken didn't seem at all taken aback by his tone.

"I understand," the man said, and that was all.

"And you're wrong, Renson. Our god is not to blame for this. Our god is perfect in every way. It is *humankind* that is flawed... one man in particular."

Without another word, Vulfram rose from the chair. He swayed on his feet for a moment, but the woozy feeling passed soon enough.

He left the Renson manse a moment later and hurried home. The sky was brightening and the roosters were cawing. He needed to get back to the Manor and must depart quickly if he were to avoid any dangerous questions from his family. There'd be no good-byes, no promises or false hopes. Nothing to delay him further. If there were any way to save Lyana from a life in the Sisters of the Cloth, he would seek it out, even if it killed him.

The least he could do, as a husband and a father, was to try.

CHAPTER

18

Whent they rode into Drake, the northernmost village in all of Ashhur's Paradise, Roland couldn't help but let out a low whistle. The place was so different from anywhere else he'd ever been. The village butted up against the river on one side; a small mountain range bordered its other side, the space between filled with complex structures. Coming from Safeway as he did, he was used to people living in tiny, one-room hovels and tents, or camped out beneath the wide southern sky. Even in Mordeina, the only building of substance was the Manor of House DuTaureau; otherwise, everyone slept in simple shelters of wood, stone, or canvas.

But here…here there were great dwellings of crisscrossing logs and edifices of squared and stacked granite blocks. Complex geometry, beautiful despite the unnatural look of the constructions. Everything appeared solid and enduring, with an aura of grandness that rivaled the Sanctuary itself. Adding to his sense of wonder, at least forty poles lined the road that passed through the village center, each topped with a reflective substance that magnified the sun's rays.

"Yes, it's impressive," said Jacob, nudging him. "Those quartz reflectors atop the poles catch the moonlight at night. If the sky is clear enough, the road is as bright as it is right now. A remarkable feat, really. I'm sure Turock is the one who came up with that idea."

"Who's Turock?" Roland asked.

Jacob chuckled.

"What magic do you know of, Roland?" he asked.

"Same as everyone else," he replied. "How to spur a seed into a plant, how to channel Ashhur's healing magic. Is there a need to know anything more?"

"Well," said Jacob with a laugh, "Turock Escheton is a peculiar man who asked himself that question at a very young age and found the answer to be *yes*. He grew up in Mordeina, but when he was eight, he journeyed east to Dezerea to find the legendary elven mage and teacher Errdroth Plentos. The elf was very old when Turock found him, supposedly close to six hundred. As the story goes, Master Plentos was so intrigued by the boy's idiosyncrasies that he took him on as his last pupil. Turock trained for ten years before the elf passed on, but he learned much during that time and grew to be quite powerful…or as powerful as any human could be in this day of waning magics. Powerful enough to sway the heart of one of Isabel's DuTaureau's children, anyway." He patted his rucksack. "In fact, many of the transcriptions in here were told to me by Turock. He is the only man in the west who has studied the mystical arts—other than myself, of course—which makes him the oddity he desires to be."

Impressive as it was and as much awe as he felt, what made Roland happiest about arriving in Drake was the knowledge that he would be sleeping in a warm bed that night. He hugged himself tight, even though the sun still shone above them. The trip from Durham, a journey that should have lasted a day at most, had ended up taking ten. They'd spent ten long days trying to keep warm with their meager clothing and blankets, the temperature plummeting each time the sun fell. Eight of those days had been spent waiting for Jacob to return from an unexpected distraction. A bird had arrived from Mordeina, beckoning Ashhur's most trusted to a meeting with Isabel DuTaureau. No one in the group knew the nature of the meeting, for Isabel had demanded total secrecy. Roland didn't understand what sort of circumstances could warrant such concealment, but he knew it wasn't his place to question. Jacob was the First Man, and Isabel the matriarch of a First Family. He was but a steward. If there were something they needed to discuss, it would be part of their divine duties to meet and do just that.

The quartet rode their horses onward, and all of a sudden Roland's warm and enticing feelings of expectation began to wane. The streets of Drake were deserted, even though it was midday and the sun was bright in a cloudless sky. There should have been children running about or at least a group of elders commencing their afternoon prayers. But there was none of that. When Azariah called out, it was only his own voice that answered him.

"This is odd," said Brienna, visibly shuddering in her saddle.

"It is," replied Jacob. The First Man glanced left to right, peering into the open windows of every empty domicile they passed. "What do you make of it, steward?"

Roland cleared his throat and thought of the day he had come home to find his parents missing. It had been the Sharing Fair that day, but he'd been busy tending to Jacob's cottage and had forgotten all about it. His terror had been so real, yet afterward, when he'd discovered his parents among the fair goers, he'd laughed it off as nothing.

"Is there a clearing beyond the town border on the other side?" he asked. "Perhaps they're having a festival of some sort."

"A festival?" Jacob tilted his head. "Strange. If that's the case, the festivities must be taking place a long way away from here. I hear nothing but wind and leaves."

"It was just an idea," replied Roland, feeling embarrassed.

"A fine idea," said Azariah. "One I still hope is correct."

"Keep riding," Brienna said, urging her own horse along. "Perhaps we'll find them gathered further into the city, doing something silly and pointless like you humans love to do."

The group voyaged from one end of Drake to the other, where the grand constructions ended and the Gods' Road came to an abrupt halt in front of a field of short, frost-tipped grass, in which grazed a cluster of giant grayhorns. Though his concern was unabated, Roland still gazed on the foraging beasts with wonder. He had never seen a real, live grayhorn before, with its horned nose, enormous tusked snouts, and massive, gray-rippled hide. Each one was the size of his hut back in Safeway; the grayhorns were truly beautiful, yet also frightening.

"So what do we do now?" asked Brienna.

"We push on through," answered Jacob. "There might be some clue up ahead as to what happened."

"But there's no road," Roland said.

"Since when does mankind travel only by roads?"

To Roland's surprise, the grayhorns didn't react at all as their horses trotted by. The beasts kept their noses to the ground, tugging up tufts of grass. Jacob explained that the animals were trying to get as many nutrients from the soil as they could, for when the snows came in a month, food would be scarce, and they would need to survive a long time without eating. It amazed Roland that these massive creatures could go for weeks without nourishment. He was famished if he missed a single meal.

The land started to undulate once they passed the grazing field, becoming more rocky and hazardous. To stay out of the more dangerous terrain, they moved closer to the river. The rushing water hemmed them in on the right; the mountains pushed in closer on their left. Strange sounds—to Roland it sounded like wolves grunting—started to fill the air. Azariah pointed out horse tracks in the soft ground between stone retaining walls, and Jacob found a trench that looked like the impression of something being dragged. They were signs of life, which helped calm Roland's worry, but only a little.

Azariah's horse reared back suddenly, forcing the tall Warden to clamp his hands down on the stag's mane and hold on for dear life.

"Whoa, Thunderclap," he said, his voice unusually shaky. The horse did not calm himself until Brienna steered her mare in front of him and began gently stroking the side of his neck.

"What's wrong with him?" she asked.

"I have no idea," replied Azariah, trying to keep his horse calm.

"Perhaps *that* has something to do with it," Jacob surmised.

Roland noticed that the First Man's eyes were glued to the horizon. He squinted, trying to see what his master was seeing. All he saw up ahead was what looked like a skinny mountain that had been cut in half.

"What is it?" he asked.

"I'm not sure," replied Jacob. Roland found the expression on Jacob's face disturbing. He looked beyond worried, as if there were something about that skinny mountain that could mean the end of them all. Roland began to feel that way too.

Their fear was answered a moment later, when an arrow flew through the air, landing not five feet in front of where they had stopped to gaze at that distant half-mountain. Azariah's horse reared back a second time, throwing him from the saddle. The Warden hit the ground with a thud but rolled quickly to his feet.

Pounding hooves sounded from their left, and six white horses raced into sight from within the canopy of stunted trees on the side of the small mountain, kicking up a massive spray of dirt and stone as they galloped. Jacob quickly steered his horse in front of Roland and Brienna, using the majestic beast as a shield in case anything went wrong. Azariah appeared beside him, a look of grim concentration on his flawless face.

The riders drew closer, close enough for Roland to see that the six men were dressed in heavy furs. They looked like what he imagined the barbarians from the Wardens' stories would look like, and he couldn't help but inch his trusty mare back a few steps, just in case. But when the riders pulled up, stopping within shouting distance, Roland's panic abated. The men might have worn furs and full beards, but they didn't seem to be rough natured. Instead, they seemed just as concerned as his travel companions, with no obvious trace of malice.

"Who rides on these hills?" one of the men shouted, his horse trotting out in front of the others.

For some reason Jacob's smile made Roland more nervous.

"No, I think *I* should be the one who asks who *you* are, considering we are heralds from Safeway, and the village we just passed through is as abandoned as a dried-up well."

One of the other men urged his horse forward. "An envoy from Safeway, eh? What proof do you have?"

"Proof?" laughed Jacob. "What more proof does Ashhur's most trusted servant need than his mere presence?"

"Not one for humility, are you, Jacob?" asked Azariah in an aside.

"Nor you for humor," Jacob scoffed, brushing the Warden aside. "These men pose no threat to us."

The six men across from them huddled together, discussing something in hushed voices. Eventually they broke rank and began to slowly approach. They all had clubs within reach, and two had simple bows slung across their backs.

Jacob urged his horse forward and greeted the men with a half-bow from his saddle. The grin on his face was wide as could be, which obviously made the advancing men slightly uneasy, as the tight formation of their horses faltered.

"By Ashhur, it *is* him!" one of them said.

The man threw his leg over the side of his saddle and jumped to the ground. He virtually ran up to Jacob, casting aside his bow and club as he did so, and then fell to one knee. Despite his beard, he looked very young. "I apologize, Master Eveningstar. We knew not that it was you. Otherwise, we never would have fired a warning arrow."

The others gaped in slack-jawed amazement. Roland found himself envying Jacob for his celebrity within the Paradise. He wondered whether folks reacted to him the same way in the east.

"Stand up, Bartholomew," Jacob said, rustling the man's unkempt hair with his gloved hand.

Bartholomew bounced to his feet, tossing giddy grins at the men behind him.

"You're as silly as a schoolgirl," one of the others said.

"He remembered my name," said Bartholomew.

"Good for you," said yet another.

The man who had first spoken to them dismounted and stepped forward. "You remember the boy's name, but how about mine?" he asked.

Jacob smiled more widely. "Ah, Ephraim. Your boy looks just like you."

Ephraim beamed. "So you *do* remember."

"I never forget a face, my friend. Ever. However nice these pleasantries are, I must ask…why is the village deserted? It was an alarming thing to stumble on, especially for the boy."

"I'm *not* a boy," muttered Roland.

"It's not for me to say, Master Eveningstar," Ephraim said, ignoring him. "Please, follow us. I'm sure Escheton will fill you in on the details."

"So the great Escheton is here, is he?"

"That he is."

Jacob and Brienna exchanged a queer look, but they followed the others just the same. Roland waited until Azariah was able to tame his horse, and then they trailed after the group.

As they neared the strange, skinny mountain, Roland realized it wasn't a mountain at all. No, it had been fabricated by humans—a massive tower that rose up from a wide and round base in a gravelly inlet close to the banks of the Rigon. People were gathered all around it, some raising heavy stones with ropes, while other stones seemed to be floating to the top on their own accord. Others were chiseling the great blocks, and still others were mixing huge vats of a strange gray substance. Hundreds of individuals were busily setting about their tasks—men, women, and children alike. Roland gave a low whistle of awe. Given the sheer number of people present here, it was no wonder the village had looked abandoned.

Even more amazing, however, was what lay in the tower's periphery. It was as if the entire township had picked up and transplanted itself. The rock-strewn field was filled with tents and a few minor stone buildings. Roaring cooking fires peppered the encampment, and Roland could smell the sweet scent of roasting meat. His mouth watered and his stomach grumbled. He hadn't eaten anything more filling than a few lean rabbits over the entirety of the journey north. He sure could go for a home-cooked meal, and soon.

The quartet was guided beyond the tower and past a collection of strangely robed men who chanted around a giant boulder. Their hands began to glow as they chanted, and the boulder started to change shape. It twisted and shifted, splitting into six pieces that became smooth and flat on all sides. It was a mesmerizing process; Roland had seen it a couple of times before, but not on such a grand scale.

"And that's our…special craftsmen division," said Bartholomew, his voice still giddy.

"Turock's training spellcasters now," Roland heard Jacob say to Brienna, which only made him all the more intrigued to meet this odd man.

Four of their guides stayed behind at the work site while Ephraim and Bartholomew led them into the encampment. They tied off their horses, dismounted, and followed the pair through the maze of fabric enclosures. Almost every face Roland saw lit up with a smile, but something wasn't right. There was a certain darkness to the complexions of these northerners, and the heavy bags beneath their eyes told of sleepless nights and constant worry. Roland felt for them and wondered what could cause an entire populace such agony.

They stopped at the largest of the tents, positioned at the center of the encampment. Bartholomew held open the flap, nodding for Ephraim to lead the others inside. Roland allowed his elders and betters to go in before him, entering last and exchanging a strangely cheery farewell with Bartholomew on his way past him.

The interior of the tent was spacious, but that space was being taken up by stack after stack of hand-printed tomes. A man and woman stood in the center of the stacks, arguing so intensely that they didn't seem to notice that others had entered their space. They both had heads of wildly curly red hair, but that's where their similarity ended. The woman was short and very pretty, looking dignified in her blue dress, her upper body covered in a finely made cardigan. The man, on the other hand, was quite tall and wore an outrageous robe made from a greenish-yellow material that was so bright, it seemed to glow. His beard was trimmed to be thin, but it stretched all the way to the top of his stomach, an odd look for someone so young.

Ephraim whispered something into Jacob's ear and then stepped out of the tent. Roland and his travel companions stood in a line, looking on as the argument droned on and on. Finally, Jacob cleared his throat—loudly—and the man and woman rapidly turned toward them.

"What in the name of the three gods are…" said the man. "Wait—*wait!* Jacob?"

Jacob smiled wide. "Hello, Turock, Abigail. Good to see you two again."

The couple's demeanor shifted quickly—in a matter of seconds they went from scowling to cheerily rushing toward Jacob for a hug. They moved on to Brienna and Azariah next, embracing them just as emphatically as they had Jacob. The pair looked absolutely shocked to see the travelers, and both of them kept repeating how surprising it was that Jacob and his band had *made it through*, whatever that meant. The separate parties then turned to Roland, who shifted uncomfortably as his master introduced him.

"Friends, this is Roland Norsman, my humble steward and an upstanding young man. And Roland, standing before you is Abigail Escheton, once Abigail DuTaureau of Ashhur's First Families. The man beside her is her husband, Turock Escheton, student of the mysterious arts and one of the most bewildering men you will ever meet."

"Been called much worse," Turock said with a laugh.

Roland bowed, his heart thumping wildly in his chest as he stared at Abigail. The woman was striking, her small stature accentuating her sprite-like beauty. He'd run across Bessus Gorgoros and his wife many times, and Bardiya, their son, as well, but this was the first time he had met someone from Ashhur's other First Family. The Gorgoroses were of larger stock, and Roland had always felt intimidated by their combined intensity. Abigail, on the other hand, was all charm.

"An honor to meet you, my Lords," Roland said in reverence.

"Oh, stop that shit," said Turock, waving a dismissive hand at him. The grin on his lips was infectious. "We're no gods here. Just men and women of the north, trying to make our way, learning and screwing and doing all sorts of things you could never get away with down in Safeway."

Abigail slapped her husband's shoulder. "Turock, watch your language."

"What? We have six children, Abby." He raised an eyebrow. "Well, to be fair, the fornicating is rather abundant in Safeway as well. Fine. But it's the other stuff that really matters anyway!"

Abigail rolled her eyes.

Jacob placed a hand on Turock's wrist. "Friend, the pleasantries are all well and good, but there are dire matters to speak of, not the least of which is why you've abandoned the village."

Turock's lips twisted into a thin, white line, as did his wife's. For the first time Roland noticed creases of age around both of their mouths and fading streaks in their hair that would soon turn gray. Now that their smiles were gone, their troubled demeanors were as plain as the day was bright. It seemed as though all joy had left the tent.

"Sit, Jacob," said Turock, his voice little more than a whisper. "We have much to discuss."

Abigail handed each of them a finely woven sitting rug, and they all settled down on the gravelly earth as the couple started to tell their tale.

"It's been—what?—a month?" Turock asked, glancing at his wife to confirm the date. "It started with wolves howling. Nothing strange about that, but these howls were territorial; they were vicious. Most nights, it sounded like the wolves were dying. Chilling, let me assure you. Later we found grayhorns slaughtered, their innards torn out and splayed across the grass like someone was playing a sick game. We started setting out patrols, keeping a closer eye on our livestock, but it never seemed to matter. And now...."

Turock let out a sigh and shook his head. Abigail patted his leg, squeezing his knee.

"They started taking children," she said when her husband would not. "Then finally, yesterday, a whole family."

"The Rodderdams," Turock said softly. "We found a trail of blood, and it led from our village to this very spot."

He fell silent, and Roland winced in sudden discomfort. Children taken at night, but by what? It sounded like a bad camp-fire story, one meant to scare him...but there was no glint in their eyes, no smile to betray the amusement of a storyteller. Just exhaustion, frustration, and fear. Roland glanced at his master, wondering what Jacob thought of their tale. To his surprise, he saw a smoldering fury in the First Man's eyes.

"You're both wise beyond your years," Jacob said. "What do you think is happening?"

Turock shrugged.

"Up here in the north, the Gihon's a torrential force. I've seen its waters carry off a man before he knew he was even wet. But everything we've seen indicates that something *is* crossing that river. The blood trail ends at the narrowest passage between our lands and the dead place on the other side. More convincing, we found tracks leading *into* the water."

"Tracks of what?" asked Brienna.

"We don't know," Abigail said. "They're strange—cloven. I've never seen anything like it before in all my life. No one has."

"You have to realize something," Turock added. "The Tinderlands beyond the river are an altered land. Before Celestia reworked Dezrel, they used to be the homeland of the elves—many apologies about that, Brienna. It seems the arrival of humanity was trouble for everybody—for the humans themselves especially. But it seems as though something is living there...and that something has found a way to survive in a wasteland where even crows and vultures stay away. What manner of beast is that? What creature? What monster?"

"Control your mind, Turock," Azariah said, interrupting him. "You speak and speak, and it builds the mystery into something far more horrible than it could ever be. But let's get back to what we know...the children who were taken—were they dead or alive?"

"They must be dead," Turock insisted. "Nothing can live out there."

"But you just said something must be living there," Roland pointed out, and then immediately flushed red when he realized he was interrupting a conversation between people far more intelligent than him. He shrank down as all eyes turned to him. "Sorry," he said. "But you can't say nothing is living there and also say something is living there."

"He's right," Azariah said. "Stop making guesses. Were the children alive or dead?"

The question obviously made Turock uncomfortable, and he shifted on his little mat.

"Sometimes there was so much blood, it seemed nothing could be alive," he said. "But not always. No, it's possible the children were taken alive, and might still be."

"If that is the case, these beings must be hunted down and destroyed all the faster," Jacob said. "But what are we hunting?"

"It doesn't have to be monsters," Brienna offered. "How about mountain dwellers? Or perhaps some of my people who stayed behind?"

Roland gave her a confused look.

Abigail shook her head. "Who would live in the coldness and thin air of those mountains? Why would anyone leave Paradise to scrape together an existence up there? It makes no sense. And as for your people…if any elves went missing a hundred years ago, your leaders would have said something about it. You were few enough as it was."

"True," Brienna said.

"I think Turock is on the right path," Jacob said. "We are fools to think we've managed to tame this world after being here for so few years…we've only touched the surface of its mysteries. Some creature we've yet to encounter is responsible for these disappearances. I'm sure of it."

Roland frowned at Jacob, but this time he dared not interrupt. Someone was crossing the river, yet none of his companions had made mention of the rumored army Jacob had told them of while in the delta. By Ashhur, it was the entire reason they had trekked north in the first place!

"I'm glad you're with me, friend," Turock said.

"So, this great tower—" Azariah said, gesturing toward the exit flap of the tent, "—is it being built to frighten them away?"

"No," replied Turock. "It will be a stationed tower, keeping watch over the comings and goings on the other side of the river.

This is only the first of many that I plan to build. Two of my most trusted men are scouting the river during the day, seeking out narrow points where the wild things might cross next. Assuming our people endure, we'll build towers there as well. I also have a veritable legion of talented spellcasters whom I'm currently training in defense magic. A few spells here, a few incantations there, and anything that crosses with the intent to harm will find itself going *boom* in the night."

Roland shifted again. Unable to keep quiet any longer, he said, "I don't understand. This has gone on for a month? Why has no one been told?"

His three companions exchanged a glance, and Brienna said, "Good question."

The expression on the Eschetons' faces soured even further.

"We've tried," said Abigail. "We've sent out birds, and they never reach their destination. We've sent riders…and have never seen them again. That is why we left the village and came here. The wild things may have infiltrated the forests inside our borders, surrounding us, isolating us. That you made it here safely is stunning."

"That doesn't mean they'll be able to leave," Turock said, eyeing his wife.

"Excuse me?" said Azariah.

"You don't know that," Abigail insisted. She looked to the others. "Our youngest sons are in Mordeina and have been for six months. I fear they will believe we've abandoned them."

"Well, Jacob was in Mordeina just—what?—six days ago?" Brienna said, elbowing her lover in the side.

Abigail and Turock looked to him with pleading eyes, and Jacob sat up straight and cleared his throat. "That's right. I apologize. I *was* there, meeting with your mother. Your sons are fine, and they seem in good spirits. And your mother did seem concerned for your safety, though not terribly so. I think she assumes you've simply forgotten to write. I mean, the two of you *are* a little absentminded."

The married couple shared a look, and it was so private, so hurt, it made Roland uncomfortable. He so wished he could do something to help them out.

"So true," said Turock. "And look how well the world rewards our flights of fancy."

Jacob slid forward on his knees and lifted the man's chin beneath that long red beard. "You're a good man, Turock. Your flights of fancy are what make you special. I'll have no self-hate here. You have endured a terrible situation—and not just that: you have risen to the challenge. Instead of cowering, you have acted. That is what matters. And now that we are here, we may help, at least in deciding what your next course of action should be."

"Thank you, friend," said Turock. "But I'm curious, why *are* you here?"

Jacob paused, leaned back in thought.

"I've heard rumors of strange happenings in the Tinderlands," he said. "Isolated as you feel, it was a merchant in Haven who first mentioned such happenings. So I convinced Ashhur to allow me to venture north to make sure there is no risk to our people."

Roland frowned and opened his mouth to speak, but a sideways glance from his master stopped him.

"Thank Ashhur you have come, my friend," Turock said, and it looked like relief was finally starting to work its way into his face. "Your concern is much appreciated. As for our course of action, what plan do you feel is best?"

"We go in," Jacob replied, as if it were nothing. "We cross the river and discover for ourselves what foul thing troubles your village."

"Are you sure that idea is prudent?" asked Abigail.

"You tell me," Jacob said. "With your people disappearing, and the threat ever present, do you see any other way?"

"But what if you don't come back?" she asked.

Jacob stood, gestured to his party.

"I am the Eveningstar, and with me is a Warden of mankind and an elf of the deep forests. I fear no creature, no monster, no shadow, for what can withstand us? Tomorrow, we go into the dead lands. Tomorrow, we find out the truth of this, and then we will know whether to fight or flee."

He smiled at Abigail.

"Either way, I assure you that we will return."

CHAPTER

19

The courtyard of the Castle of the Lion was already a bustle of activity when Soleh stepped through the portcullis, entering her own secluded world on the other side of the walls. Her regiment of guards was with her, as they had been for the past several weeks. She'd grown quite attached to them, Pulo in particular, whose mane of curly black hair reminded her so much of Adeline's before her daughter had gone gray. But she greatly appreciated all three of her protectors. Given how the mood in Veldaren had taken a sharp downturn over the passing weeks, she could not do without their protection.

She marched up the central walk, passing a pair of arguing merchants whose fingers lingered a little too closely on the handles of their daggers, and climbed the pulpit on the edge of the yard, which had been built on her orders. Behind her was the cobbled footpath that led to the entrances to the three towers. In front of her stretched an undulating sea of grass, carts, and people.

Just as she had done every day since her meeting with Karak, she lifted her arms in the air and let out her cry.

"All who are gathered in the courtyard of the Lion, here in Veldaren, capital city of Neldar, hear my voice! I beg you to pray with me!"

A few turned to face her while the rest went about their business, but she recognized the faces of those who chose to participate. These were the people who visited the courtyard on a regular basis, who had seen her demonstrations and listened. She had done what her god had demanded of her, but she found it amazingly difficult to turn heads. There was so much fear throughout the city—fear of anarchy, fear of starvation, and the sublime fear of *not knowing*. By now, everyone had heard of the attack on Haven, and the rumors were spreading far and wide that the fast-approaching deadline for the delta's surrender would be a bloody affair. Commoners were being drafted into the new army, fathers leaving their families, sons leaving their mothers' bosoms. With Karak's return, it shouldn't have been difficult to draw forth an act of worship from the populace. But from experience, Soleh understood that her fellow humans were a stubborn and doubtful race. They would never believe in their god's wrath until they saw it with their own eyes.

At least she was making progress, however slight it might be.

"Let us pray to Karak, our Lord Almighty, the Divinity of the East who granted to us the lives with which we've been blessed! Bow down before his faithful servant, and prove your dedication. Karak has promised you liberty, the freedom to pursue your life's goals in any way you wish so long as you adhere to his teachings. All he asks for in return is your devotion! Recognize him…kneel in this very grass and sing his name!"

Soleh dropped to her knees. Those who had heeded her call approached the pulpit and lowered themselves down, eyes upturned and hands clasped. Pulo, Jonn, and Roddalin paced back and forth, full of nervous energy, searching among the faithful for any who might have approached the platform with less than honorable intentions. They found none, as Soleh knew they wouldn't. It wasn't the faithful she had to fear, but those who stayed back—watching, doubting, mocking.

"Let your god hear your voice," she told the worshippers. "Let him know just how much love is in your hearts. Sing to him, for the god of order is benign and good, and he requires the adoration of his children."

The people opened their mouths then, rejoicing in different ways. Some chanted their god's name, others hummed a tune from childhood, and still others sang Karak's decrees. Eventually, with Soleh's lead, their voices melded into one, a blend of tones crooning a six-note tune melodically. The voices shifted up and down, rising in volume, and the wordless song uttered by a mere fifteen individuals filled the entire courtyard with its joyful servitude. Pride burned in Soleh's heart, and a smile stretched across her face. She could feel the presence of Karak within her, fueled by the worship of his children, and it brought a certain lightness to her being.

Then something struck the side of her face. She fell over, clutching her cheek, which was covered in crushed tomato pulp. Flicking her fingers, she cast the juicy seeds aside, then faced the crowd. That she'd been heckled did not surprise her; despite her station, the cowardly always found courage when hidden, faceless, in a crowd. But this—this was new. No one had ever before been insane enough to throw something at her.

She spotted the objector in the crowd, a spindly older man wearing a filthy brown robe over his torn clothes. He held a bucket of spoiled fruit in his left hand, and when he opened his mouth to shout a jeer at her, she saw that he was missing half his teeth. The man's skin was dark and rutted, as if he'd spent his whole life tied to a rock in the desert.

"What does Karak care for *me?*" he shouted. "I have lost *everything*—my honor, my land, even my *children*, to the Conningtons! And the courts do nothing. *Karak* does nothing! If he cares so much, let him do something about it! Or does his 'caring' only get me an arrow in the throat?"

Soleh cringed but tried to hide her frustration. This was the type of man who needed to learn to kneel, just as Karak had told her. She had to wake him up to that fact. Her Palace Guard lingered along the interior of the castle wall, watching, honoring her demand that she be allowed to handle whatever happened in the courtyard herself, in whatever way she decided best.

"Karak did not take your lands or your family away," she shouted. "That you even had those lands was because of the freedom he granted you. But if you have lost them, if you have nothing, then that is on *you*. Pick yourself back up and start over. That is the right your god has given you!"

The man spit a wad of reddish-yellow phlegm. "Start over? Start over?! I'm almost seventy years old, woman! Unlike you, my bones actually turn brittle as the years wear on. I didn't get to create my own mate, and I wasn't granted a life in splendor. How can I possibly pick myself up when I can barely lift this bucket of fruit?"

With that he dipped his hand into the bucket and withdrew another tomato.

"One of these, though," he said, "I can lift just fine. You lying, eternal whore!"

The man reared back and hurled the tomato at her. Soleh easily stepped out of the way, but that didn't stop Pulo and Roddalin from rushing forward and grabbing the old man by the arms. He struggled, his teeth clenched, and called out for help from those around him. No one dared come to his aid—not when Jonn walked among them with his sword drawn. Pulo and Roddalin lugged the man before the pulpit. The kneelers, who were watching the proceedings in horror, quickly made room as the guards threw the man face down in the grass.

Soleh stepped off the platform and approached him. Inwardly she shivered, while outwardly she was a wall of iron. This was a test of her wisdom and her ability to convey the hard truths she knew. Eyes were upon her, and whatever they witnessed would spread throughout the city like wildfire. Soleh stood before the elderly man as he raised his head. His jaw swished from side to side, gathering spittle. Pulo stopped him before he could act on his disgrace, planting a booted foot on the man's back.

"You may insult me all you wish," Soleh said, "for I am not perfect. But Karak is divine. Karak is the reason, the Order in a universe of chaos. He is to be praised, not torn down. Will you praise him?"

"Fuck you," the man muttered. "And fuck Karak."

"Very well," said Soleh. She faced the crowd again. Beyond the kneelers she saw that a crowd of nearly a hundred had gathered, watching. Soleh addressed her words to the faithful, but they weren't the ones she was truly addressing. They weren't the ones who needed her message most.

"Karak is mighty, but he is also forgiving. If you have turned your back to him in pride, then kneel. Show your appreciation to your creator."

The distant men and women were watching, and only a small handful stepped forward to join the others in prayer. Soleh sighed, wanting to give up but knowing Karak wouldn't have given her such a task if he had not thought her equal to it. Hard truths, she told herself. They must all learn the hard truths. She turned back to the man her guards held bound.

"You must know that despite Karak's forgiveness, he is merciless before disrespect. If no forgiveness is requested, none shall be received. Turning your back on your creator forever will result in the damnation of your eternal soul. You will be punished for an eternity in the fires in the Abyss below Afram."

The crowd began to murmur, and Soleh knew she had their attention at last.

"However," she cried, "this kind of damnation is a last resort. It is a sad fate that I would not wish on anyone, even this sad, disrespectful mongrel before me. No, it is up to us, the faithful, to spare the weak from the punishing fire. If you do not sacrifice your pride willingly, you will have another sacrifice taken from you by force!"

She nodded to Jonn, who sheathed his sword and withdrew a wicked-looking dagger. Pulo and Roddalin knelt on the dissenter's back, staying him, while Jonn circled around and caught his flailing hand in a firm grip. The old man shrieked as he struggled beneath the guard's weight. Jonn held the dagger's cutting edge over the man's wrist and glanced up at Soleh.

"A hand for your soul," she said, her voice knifing through the stunned crowd. "That is not a lot to ask."

Jonn gritted his teeth and hacked down with the dagger. As the blade pierced flesh, the guard's breastplate was spattered with blood. The old man shrieked even louder as Jonn brought the dagger down again, this time splitting through a few bones—still, the hand remained attached. It took a third swing to finally sever the append-age. Blood poured from the stump, the frayed skin glistening, the jagged bone looking sharp and dangerous. Still the man screamed, now crying out in supplication.

"I'm sorry!" he shouted. "I repent! Give my soul to Karak! He can have it, it's his!"

Soleh gestured for Jonn to switch sides, which he did, grabbing the man's other hand and holding the dagger to his flesh.

Hard truths, she told herself.

"Are you sure?" she asked, her expression hard as granite. "Or do we need to take another sacrifice?"

"No, dammit!" the man squealed. He was sobbing fully now, shock robbing him of his will to do anything but raise his voice. "Praise be to the Divinity! He who created me deserves my love and respect!"

Soleh let the moment linger, let her silence stretch over the crowd. She passed her eyes over them, let them imagine themselves standing before judgment, a knife raised over their own sinful lives.

"I believe you," she said.

She beckoned to the palace servants who had been observing the event and told them to help mend the man's wounds. Then, loudly enough for everyone watching to hear, she spoke: "This man is truly repentant and now stands in Karak's favor. Make sure he is given the best healers at our disposal, and instruct the minister of agriculture to find him a position. Make certain he has a place to rest his head at night and money to keep him fed. That is all."

"Thank you, Minister," the man groveled as the servants led him away, doing their best to staunch the blood still pouring from the stump of his right wrist. "You are merciful, you are great. Praise Karak, praise Karak, praise Karak...."

This continued until the servants brought the man through the entrance to Tower Servitude. Soleh turned around, filled with pride that she had saved the man's soul, and that pride doubled when she saw what awaited her. The rest of those gathered in the courtyard—merchants, commoners, and vagrants alike—were all on bended knee.

A smile, perhaps the largest ever to cross her face, appeared on her lips as she joined them.

"Let us pray."

Court in Tower Justice dragged on and on that day. Thankfully, the docket was empty of the more heinous offenses, but the sheer number of minor crimes Soleh needed to preside over was mind numbing. To make matters worse, for some unknown reason King Vaelor had decided he would sit in on the day's session. The king's bodyguard, Karl Dogon, set up a makeshift throne on the far side of the room, where the king sat through the proceedings, looking bored. It wouldn't have been that much of a bother if not for the way every convict brought before Soleh spent more time staring in his direction than hers. Few commoners seemed to understand that it was Soleh who ruled in the courtroom. When it came to power in Neldar, he was the face, she was the fist, and Karak was the heart.

But finally the day was over. The king returned to his chambers in Tower Honor, and Soleh looked forward to nothing more than getting back home, eating whatever Ibis had prepared for the evening meal, and then falling into a comfortable sleep before she had to do it all over again. Pulo met her in Tower Justice's circular anteroom, helped her remove her cloak, and then held open the door.

"Will you be walking today, Minister?" he asked.

"Not today," she replied. "If you could please find me a carriage, it would be appreciated. My feet are sore."

"Yes, Minister," he said and turned away with a bow.

"Oh, and Pulo—" she called out after him.

He turned around to face her.

"You did well today. All three of you did. I'm proud of you all."

Pulo bowed again and then went along his way, leaving Soleh alone on the pathway outside the tower. She gazed up at the stars on this clear autumn night, lost in thoughts of her home and her god. She felt a stirring in her loins and decided that if she felt up to it, she would throw Ibis down later tonight and remind him why she'd created him.

The sound of beating hooves reached her ears, and Soleh stepped out into the middle of the courtyard to greet her escort. It took her a moment to realize that the hooves were growing too close, striking the ground too quickly, to be a carriage. She took a few hurried steps back, and watched as a brown stallion galloped through the portcullis. The Palace Guard did nothing to stop the horse or its rider, stepping out of the way so as not to be crushed. The bald rider, wearing ratty clothes, yanked up on the reins, bringing the stallion to an uneasy halt. He immediately leapt from the saddle, his hands flexing as he marched toward the doorway to Tower Honor. Soleh's eyes widened.

It was her son.

"Vulfram!" she shouted, just as he grabbed the handle on Tower Honor's great door and gave it a mighty yank. The huge oaken portal flew open as if her son had been granted the strength of ten men. When he stormed inside, he looked angry enough to kill. Soleh swore she could hear him growling.

Picking up the front of her dress, she ran across the pathway as fast as she could, slipping as she took the turn and entered the still open doorway. Thoughts of Lyana overwhelmed her mind. What fate had Vulfram declared for her? She forced her legs to move faster as she raced through the carpeted hall. Up ahead she finally caught sight of her son, who seemed oblivious to her pursuit. He was grabbing the palace's guards, shouting up a storm as he passed, demanding answers to questions she couldn't hear. She got closer, and amid her own panic she heard terrible words. *Treason, Crestwell,* and *murder* came from his mouth. She reached out, close enough to see the sweat soaking through his tunic.

Vulfram wheeled around, fist cocked, ready to strike, only to have that fist snatched by the guard he had just accosted. Soleh saw the gleaming rage in her son's eyes and shrank back. She held her hands beneath her chin, fighting the urge to chew on her knuckles, a nervous tic she'd had since the first day she'd opened her eyes to the world.

"Mother," Vulfram said harshly, tearing his wrist away from the guard. His breath reeked of liquor.

"Vulfram, what are you doing? You're not supposed to be here."

"I could care less where I'm *supposed* to be," he growled. "Fuck the army, fuck Omnmount, and fuck Haven. I have business to attend to."

Soleh was taken aback by his language and the drunken gleam in his eyes.

"What sort of business?" she asked, trying to remain calm.

"None of yours."

He turned away from her, continuing up the hall toward the double doors that led to the royal court. From around the corner appeared Malcolm Gregorian, the Captain of the Guard. He stepped in front of the doors, holding his hands before him, his scar-marked face look drawn and serious. Soleh noticed that the Captain's fingers were twitching over the pommel of his shortsword.

"There is no entrance at the moment, Lord Commander," Gregorian said, calm as could be. "You will have to come back on the morrow."

Vulfram strode up to him, his face inches from Malcolm's. Vulfram was shorter than the Captain, but his girth was greater. He looked like a bull standing before a gazelle.

"You'll get out of my way *now*," Vulfram shouted. "The Highest and I have matters we need to discuss."

"Highest Crestwell is not here."

"I'll see for myself," Vulfram snarled.

When Vulfram moved to pass him, Malcolm drew his sword and pushed the large man back with his other hand. Vulfram tore his own greatsword from its scabbard, holding it unsteadily before him. The tips of their blades were nearly touching, but so far neither of them had made a move. Vulfram breathed heavily, the breath of a desperate man. Malcolm was expressionless, like a living statue.

Soleh was nearly overwhelmed with horror and fury. She stood frozen in place, her hands shaking at her sides.

"Stop!" she screamed. "Vulfram! Captain! Put your swords away, now! Your Minister demands it!"

Malcolm did as he was told without question, slipping his blade back into the scabbard on his belt without pause. Vulfram, however, allowed Darkfall to hover there a few moments longer. Soleh could tell he was unsure—she knew her son better than he knew himself. That he was so upset, so out of control, put a silent terror into her. What must have happened to Lyana for him to be acting this way?

"Please, son," she whispered. Vulfram turned to her, tears streaming down his cheeks, making his beard glisten. She touched his hand, and he released the heavy sword, which bounced twice on the carpeted floor before coming to a rest. Malcolm raised an eyebrow at her, peering over Vulfram's shoulder, and Soleh nodded in response. He nodded back, bent over, lifted Darkfall, and gently slid it into the scabbard that was slung across Vulfram's back. Then the Captain turned, leaving through the same side opening from which he'd appeared.

Soleh took her son by the hand and led him down the hallway, the Palace Guard averting their eyes out of courtesy. She led him out of the tower, to where Pulo waited with the carriage. She lifted a finger to him, telling him to wait a few moments, and guided her strangely silent son back into Tower Justice, where they might find some privacy.

Once the door closed and they were safely locked inside the tower, Vulfram began to pace. He circled the entirety of the round hall, slapping at the doors of the holding cells in turn. Every so often he would run his hand across his shaved head, whipping his fingers out afterward as if he were trying to rid himself of some taint that wouldn't go away. Soleh stood in the middle of the anteroom and watched him in silence. He would come to her when he was ready.

That time came after three more laps around the interior. Vulfram strode before her, his eyes still red but his expression more composed. The flush was gone from his face. He knelt before her and took her hand.

"I apologize, Minister. I spoke out of place."

"Vulfram, forget the titles. We're alone, and I'm your mother. What is wrong?"

He nodded, still reluctant to meet her gaze. He was ashamed of his earlier outburst, she knew. An urge to gather him to her bosom washed over her, but she resisted it as best she could. Too often she had shown weakness. It was time for her to display the strength Karak had assured her she possessed.

"Talk to me, son," she said. "Tell me what vexes you so."

His hands shook, this large beast of a man who now looked fragile as an eggshell.

"I kept it together for so long," he said. "Nearly the entire journey here I was fine. My exhaustion caught up with me, I think. I shouldn't have snapped at you so."

"All is forgiven, my precious boy. Now tell me, what was the matter with Lyana?"

Vulfram swallowed, looking away again.

"One of the local boys, named Kristof, got her pregnant. They panicked, went to Broward Renson, the boy's own grandfather, for help." Vulfram sighed. "He gave them crim oil, Karak help us. My son discovered the evidence, and put on trial, Lyana confirmed it."

The story hit Soleh like a blow to the face. Suddenly, remaining strong in front of Vulfram felt impossible. She pleaded with Karak to give her his aid.

"What was your ruling?" she asked, her voice hoarse.

"Broward and Kristof were executed," he said. His head hung lower. "I swung the sword, both times."

"And Lyana?"

At last he met her eye.

"Forced into the Sisters of the Cloth."

Soleh couldn't contain her muted cry. Her fingers pressed against her mouth. The thought of her precious Lyana imprisoned in that secretive organization filled her with horror. Worse, she knew of the initiation rites they endured. Lyana would have been stripped naked and then whipped. Whipped by….

She saw the same horror in Vulfram's gaze, the lingering guilt and doubt. Soleh suddenly felt so proud of him for containing himself so well. It was astounding that he had made it through such a public spectacle without cracking.

"My dear Vulfram," she said, wrapping her arms around his neck and pressing her forehead against his broad chest. "I know you think yourself a monster, but you mustn't. You acted according to your god's law."

"You're right," he replied, tapping on the pouch attached to his belt. "The punishments were just for the crimes committed. If that were all, I think I would be fine in time, once given chance to grieve. But this…this…I fear all may not be as it appears."

"What do you mean?"

"Although Karak's judgment is true, I fear the crimes were not."

Soleh frowned, confused.

"You said that Lyana confessed?" she asked.

Vulfram reached into his pouch, removing a folded bit of parchment. He handed it to her and she stared at it, unsure of what to do.

"Read it, Mother," her son said.

"Very well."

She wandered closer to one of the torches fastened to the wall and unfolded the letter. Her eyes scanned every indistinct word and phrase. It was a note of gratitude sent to Broward Renson, written in a familiar script whose author nevertheless eluded her, but other than that it told her nothing.

"I don't understand," she said, holding out the paper. "What is this?"

"Master Bracken Renson found that in his father's library," Vulfram said. "A conspiracy is at work in Neldar, and I am the target."

She looked at the letter again. "What makes you think so?"

"Read the words!" he said with a hint of frustration. "This letter spells it out, albeit in a devious way. The writer wished to disgrace my family, to cause my faith in Karak to waver and plunge me into madness."

"It seems to have worked," she said, unable to hold her tongue.

"It has, most brilliantly. By soiling Lyana, then forcing me to punish her…I was broken, Mother. Fully broken. He wants to take it all away…my family, my position, possibly even my life."

Soleh tugged at her hair. "Vulfram, you are making no sense. *Who* wants this, and why?"

"How is it not obvious?" her son asked. "Don't you recognize that handwriting? It's the Highest himself. He wants my position as Lord Commander; he has since the day the king bestowed that honor upon me. I never knew he would sink to such lows…."

"Vulfram, listen to what you are saying. Clovis is the Highest of Karak and the king's advisor. Surely he must have had a part in Vaelor's decision to appoint you?"

Vulfram's eyes widened, and she could almost see sparks of frenetic energy burst forth from them. He shook his head.

"One would think, but I've heard many times that Vaelor chose me to *spite* the Highest, that Clovis demanded leadership only to be denied."

"Where have you heard this?"

"Men talk, Mother. Fighting men especially."

Soleh rubbed her cheek. "And men lie. It makes no sense. Why go through with this…conspiracy?" she asked. "Why not simply put a blade in your back and be done with it?"

"Would that it were so easy!" Vulfram said with a laugh. "Should the Lord Commander end up dead in his bed, questions would be asked, especially now that Karak has returned to us. And if questions were asked, then many eyes would turn toward our beloved Highest and his recent dealings."

"What dealings would those be?"

"Haven."

"And why would he not wish for any to look deeper?"

"What if his plans for the delta aren't Karak's true wishes?"

Soleh shook her head. "You're being delusional. Karak wishes to teach the deserters a lesson, a lesson that will ring out to all of Neldar. He has told me as much."

Soleh felt helpless as her son squirmed before her. He was convinced of this conspiracy, she realized, so convinced that her words were nothing but an annoyance for him to brush aside.

"But look at the handwriting! That letter was written by the Highest; I would wager my very soul on it."

She glanced again at the words on the paper, and now she understood that nagging sense of familiarity she'd felt earlier. The penmanship *did* look very much like Clovis's, but something was different about it. The letters were too sloped, the *t*'s crossed too elegantly.

"This is *not* Clovis's handwriting," she said. "Similar, but penned by a different hand."

"How can you say that?" Vulfram exclaimed. He snatched the letter from her grasp, crumpling it in his massive fingers. "Look at it! *Look at it!* I've read decree after decree written by this man, and the writing is the same!"

Hoping her son wasn't beyond reasoning just yet, Soleh walked toward the Station of the Guard, the desk used by Captain Gregorian to notate the daily court dockets. Bending to reach the cabinet beneath, she rifled through a stack of documents, pulled out a particular piece of parchment, and placed it atop the desk.

"Come, look," she said.

Vulfram stepped up to the desk and placed his note directly beside it.

"What am I looking at?" he asked.

"This is one of Clovis's decrees, written around the same time as your letter. Look at the handwriting, son. Look at it closely."

Vulfram leaned in, his eyes squinting. Soleh grabbed a torch from the wall and lowered it closer to the desk. She watched as her son's appearance shifted, at first rock-jawed and stubborn; then his lips creased in confusion, and finally his shoulders slumped.

"It's not the same," he whispered.

"No, it is not," Soleh replied. "It is comparable, but Clovis had no hand in its making. The author of this note has much more of a flair for style; he or she was a storyteller rather than a simple compiler. But I fear you are right, my son. You *were* being deceived… and it was by yourself."

Vulfram's knees gave out. His head struck the edge of the desk. He fell back on his rump, holding the now bleeding spot on his scalp and moaning. Soleh knelt down beside him, taking him in her arms as she had been longing to, rocking him and humming.

"She's lost," her son moaned. "I'll never get her back."

"Hush now, sweet boy," she whispered. "All will be all right. Trust in Karak, he will see to that."

Vulfram didn't answer. He simply grabbed her arm and sobbed into its crook, soaking her with his warm tears.

It took quite awhile for him to calm down, and when he did, Soleh bid him to return to his room in the Tower Keep. He declined, saying he wished to take a walk to clear his thoughts. A frown on her face, she watched as he stumbled across the anteroom, threw open the tower door, and disappeared from sight. She debated for a moment whether she should go with him but decided against it. His display of weakness notwithstanding, her son was a man, and a man made his own way. Instead, she gave him time to make headway before she exited Tower Justice, climbing into the waiting carriage beside a sleeping Pulo. She didn't wake him; instead, she used the stillness and silence to think.

As she stared into the night sky and saw Celestia's star winking down on her, her confidence wavered. What if Clovis *had* penned the letter, altering his writing ever so slightly in case someone recognized it?

"Pulo," Soleh said, deciding silence was actually the last thing she needed right now. "Take me home."

The guard stirred in his seat, his eyes fluttering open.

"Of course, Minister," he said groggily.

On their way to the keep, Soleh decided to tell Vulfram that he was not going to Omnmount to rejoin the army under his command. No, she wanted him here, with her, because she was determined to find out exactly who had written that letter. Whoever it was would be punished, no matter if it were some lowly merchant or the Highest himself.

Come morning, she looked, but Clovis Crestwell was nowhere to be found.

Neither was her god.

CHAPTER

20

The old man with the gray beard circled Patrick, one eye opened larger than the other, studying him as they practiced atop the grassy hill overlooking the fields where the others sparred. The grass was damp, and the air was filled with the sloshing sound of skittering feet. The Temple of the Flesh lurked in the distance like a sleeping giant.

"No, brace yourself. Weight on the back leg. Now turn at the waist. The *waist*. You know what your waist is, right? Keep your shoulders locked, but give yourself room for quick motions. Better. Now relax your wrists ever so slightly. You're gripping with two hands, you can afford some slack. Lift it over your head, then hold it straight out. Good. Let go with your off hand. No, not your *dominant* hand, the other one. Excellent. Now hold that stance. Steady now. Amazing."

The graybeard was Corton Ender, a tall man who was long in years but spry of spirit. He seemed genuinely impressed, and Patrick felt honored by his attention. Corton had taken leave of training from Deacon Coldmine's militia just to oversee his progress. Ender had been an accomplished swordsman in his younger days, back when he had served as a mercenary for a rich man named Matthew Brennan, though this information meant very little to Patrick. He knew nothing of the east or of the doings of mercenaries. It sounded like an unsavory way to live, although he couldn't deny that a certain part of him was indeed drawn to the notion, and even excited by it.

"Tilt that majestic thing to the side," said Corton. "Flex your arm. Now *that* is impressive."

The wizened old bastard had been truly awed upon his first sight of Winterbone, and he'd wondered openly how Patrick could carry such a large weapon with relative ease given his "condition." Rather than being offended by the accusation, Patrick had appreciated the old coot's bluntness. His family always treated him with caution. It felt liberating to be around someone who was honest with him for a change.

Corton pointed at a log that was propped up on a pair of stumps a few feet away.

"If you would, shift the weapon down slowly and place your off hand on its handle, beneath your other hand. Now swing from the legs up. Gather the strength in your calves, and send it up through your thighs. Let it flow through your trunk and expel out your arms, just like you would with a good punch. Bring the weapon down in a wide, sweeping motion, and split that log."

Patrick followed the instructions, planting his right foot behind him, breathing deliberately in his effort to maintain the balance between his mismatched legs. He arched his back as far as he could. In a single, fluid motion, he cocked his elbows until Winterbone's pommel was beside his ear, then reversed his momentum, stepping back with his left foot while bringing the sword up over his head in a long, winding arc. When the tip reached its apex, he felt himself lose control of the weapon. Still, it careened downward in a straight line, striking the center of the log. The steel drove through the wood, pulping it, splitting the log in two. Patrick didn't feel any resistance when it happened; in fact, the only sensation he *did* feel was a frightening teetering as his body was yanked forward by the weight of the sword. Winterbone's tip pierced the ground, halting his fall, jarring his wrists. He squinted and gritted his teeth, forearms shaking.

"Well, I'll be," said Corton, his eyes wide and cheeks flushed red. "You still have worlds to learn about control, but that'll come with practice. The strength you have, however…it is truly amazing. That log was oak, almost two feet thick. Normally, it'd take five swings of an axe to halve it."

"So I did well?"

"Well?" the old man laughed. "I don't think that word gives justice to what you just did. I've never seen anything like it. It was damn near freakish."

Patrick's elation dipped. He kicked a foot, pulled Winterbone back from the split log.

"Freakish?" he asked.

Corton stopped staring and shook his head vehemently.

"No, no, I apologize. Not freakish in that way, Mr. DuTaureau. Yes, your body might be…unique…but it seems to have been built for one distinct purpose—to swing that sword. The shortness and unevenness of your legs plays perfectly for the sideways stance that's required to handle a weapon of that size. Your humped back prevents you from bending too far backward—the bane of the backswing, where a man is at his most vulnerable. And those arms…I've never seen a more powerful pair in all my years. You may look odd, son, but when it comes to that sword, you are unfailingly perfect."

The old man looked downright whimsical. Patrick lifted Winterbone and held it in one hand, beaming. For once, his body was not a subject of ridicule or pity, but of awe and even envy. He tossed the sword from one hand to the other, feeling the weight, the blade's downward momentum threatening to snap his wrist. But he succeeded in keeping it straight, virtually parallel to the ground, stretching his tendons near the breaking point. He smiled through clenched teeth.

Corton smiled, shaking his head. "Now you're just showing off."

Patrick grinned, ear to ear.

The old man set up another log, and Patrick split that one as well. Corton put up a third, this one larger than the first two, and this time Patrick took several swings to punch through.

"I think we're done for the day," Corton said after that last one, and Patrick sheathed the sword. "You're getting tired and hurrying through what I've shown you. Even with all that power, you must have patience and control. Never forget that."

The old man offered him some wine and a towel, items Patrick accepted without hesitation. As Patrick nursed the wineskin, flexing his sore hands, he watched a pair of young militiamen spar at the base of the hill. They were like leaping rabbits as they poked and prodded each other with their thin steel blades. It was a thing of beauty to see, a coordinated dance of skill and grace, and it made Patrick feel clumsy and slow by comparison.

The old sellsword caught him watching the duelists and chuckled.

"There are many different ways to swing a sword," he said. "All of them works of art. View them as dances, if you will. There is the water dance, the air dance, the dance of cloaks, the moonrise dance, and many others known to the elves that they will not share. No one way is greater than the other, and each has its advantages. But one must learn the style meant for his or her body, and you, Patrick, were meant to be a bull dancer. Your dance is one of power, of always moving forward and never turning back."

He pointed to the duelists.

"Those men have more skill than you, but they've also had more practice. And they're more graceful, something no amount of practice will fix for you. But do you know what matters most? With not much improvement on your part, you'd annihilate them.

A single swing of your sword would shatter theirs and spill their guts across the dirt."

"A lovely image," whispered Patrick, remembering how he had done much the same thing to one of the bandits when he and Nessa had first stepped foot on the delta's moist soil. Ever since that moment he'd been able to relive the memory with painful clarity. He remembered the blood, the odd smell of copper, the look of disbelief and fear shining in the eyes of the dying man. It should have been horrible, but something about it intrigued Patrick. Even as he thought of the blood, he remembered the exhilaration.

The words of Ashhur popped into his head, his god preaching about the sin of violence and the virtue of forgiveness: *If a man strikes you on one cheek, offer him the other.* Patrick hung his head.

"You should go now," he told Corton. "You have other students to tend to."

"Of course," replied the old man. "Will you be heading back to the manse?"

"No, I think I'll stay here for a while. Watch a little. Perhaps learn a little too."

"Very well."

Corton left to care for the rest of his charges, and a stillness overcame Patrick in his absence. He removed his sweat-soaked top, ringing it out, and then rolled his shoulders. *It will be wonderful to get back to Deacon's and relax in the bath*, he thought. He'd been staying at the Lord of Haven's manse while he trained, just outside the township itself, which was hidden by the thin section of forest a few hundred yards behind him. Slogging all the way to the Gemcroft estate, where Nessa was staying with Moira, was just too long a journey for his body to suffer through after the hours of training.

He heard a *pop* when he stretched his neck to the side, and that old familiar pain shot up his spine. Cringing and feeling a bit dizzy, he lowered himself to the ground and lounged in the grass, staring at the billowing clouds that floated across the sun-drenched afternoon sky. The heat was intense and the air humid, as it had been every day since he'd arrived—so different from Mordeina, with its four distinct seasons and often-dreary skies. From what he'd heard, the weather in Haven was measured by degrees of brutality: it was oppressive in the winter and like the burning fires of the underworld in the summer.

It made Patrick very happy it was autumn.

He rolled onto his side and his neck popped again, sending yet another shooting pain across his back. He lay there, watching the two duelists continue their endless dance, the *clang* and *clink* of their meeting swords sounding so far away they could have been on a different continent. For a moment he thought he saw a dark blur dash across his vision, down by a distant line of trees, but he excused it as an apparition brought about by the heat. His mind once more drifted to his memory of killing that man. The fact that Corton, who now acted as his mentor, had been one of his saviors that day only added to the unreal quality of his recollections. He thought of the violence, the life lost, and wondered if he could force himself to forget it all. Would the experience disappear from his mind like his injuries had disappeared from his body? With that contemplation came a pang of regret. Though he was glad Antar had healed him of all his wounds, in a way he wished the old Kerrian had left a tiny bit of nagging hurt. It would have done him well, would have made the fright he felt and the blood he spilled seem more real. To walk away unscathed seemed disrespectful, not only to the soul of the dead man but to the souls of all who had suffered a tragic end.

"Stop it, Patrick," he muttered. "Think of better things."

He did. He thought of his first few days in the delta, which had been spent at the Gemcroft estate; of mead, warm meals, and hot baths drawn by the house servants. Servants…now wasn't *that* a noble idea! People there to serve you, bring you whatever you wanted, cater to your every whim as if it were the most important moment of their day. The closest comparison in Paradise was the stewards who cared for the needs of the elders and religious leaders, but that was an act of servitude and kindness, not a result of affluence.

Life was easy on the estate, and Patrick was glad to see Nessa smiling like never before. Despite the threatened attack from the east, which cast a pall over the manor, a strange calmness surrounded the estate grounds, which Patrick found wholly satisfying. He credited it to the ladies of the house, as Rachida and Moira seemed to be constantly wrapped in a bubble of lightness and joy. And they truly were happy with each other, however strange it was for him to comprehend their relationship. He had never seen that kind of adoration between women before. A part of him found it unnatural, while a wholly different part thought it beautiful.

Truth be told, he was more than a little jealous of Moira, she who was on the receiving end of Rachida's gentle pecks and adoring embraces, she who disappeared into Rachida's bedroom each evening. He wondered what they did in there, and if Peytr Gemcroft, the absent man of the house, knew that his wife was taking a woman to bed while he was away. Patrick was so focused on Rachida that he had resumed searching for gray hairs with renewed vigor. If *he'd* been lucky enough to marry such a precious creature, he would never let her lie in bed with another, no matter how innocent it might be.

He felt so captivated by her face, it seemed as though he could hear her voice while he stared at the crystal-blue sky.

"Patrick?" she said, the memory of her voice filling his head like rum sweetened with orange slices. "Patrick, are you deaf?"

He started and turned quickly from where he lay in the grass, wrenching his neck in the process. He rubbed the sore spot and stared with wide eyes at the vision that approached him in a flowing yellow dress. Rachida's dark, curly hair bounced with each step she took, and Patrick noticed a few peculiar strands of silver woven within. Her green eyes, deep as the ocean depths, stared intently at him. A moment of panic hit him when he realized he'd taken off his sweaty tunic when he finished sparring, and he reached for it so that he might hide his wretched body.

"I was told I could find you here," Rachida said, not batting an eye at his modesty, or his abnormality. "Antar had a…gift of sorts prepared for me by my request. I expected you back at Deacon's manse sooner."

"Er…sorry?" he replied, uncertain.

"What's the matter? Why do you cover yourself so?"

"I'm, uh…cold."

Rachida cast those dazzling green eyes of her skyward. "Cold? It's sweltering outside. This shift is thin as parchment, but still it feels too heavy."

Rachida reached down and yanked the discarded tunic out of his hands. She didn't seem to mind that it was damp and probably stank horribly. She held it up, looked at the grass stains dappling the beige material, and frowned.

"This is no good," she said. "Do you have another?"

Patrick froze, trying to get his mind to start working again. He pointed to the rucksack that sat beside Winterbone.

"I have a change of clothes in there," he said.

"Good," replied Rachida. "You need to get changed now."

"Why?"

"Because you're coming with me. I have something wonderful to show you."

"We're going here?" Patrick asked, staring at the huge wall of granite before him. It was the only safe place he could look, for he found it quite difficult to tear his eyes away from the scantily clad women who were exiting the gates of the Temple of the Flesh, breasts swaying, faces flushed, skin shining, gaits wobbly.

Rachida laughed beside him.

"You're not afraid, are you?" she asked, nudging him.

Patrick grinned at her, and just like every time before, he found himself lost in the beautiful woman's eyes, as if she were the only person alive in the universe. The rumors of Rachida Mori's beauty had been legendary even in Ashhur's Paradise, thanks to Jacob's stories. To see that the woman not only matched the legend but exceeded it filled him with wonder.

"I must say, your change is quite an improvement," she said. "You look...well, dashing."

Patrick felt heat rush into his face. He didn't think he looked all that special. He had on another plain, cream-colored tunic, leather breeches, and the boots his mother had specially made for him to accommodate his disproportionate legs. Yet what he thought right then was irrelevant. Hearing such a compliment from Rachida made his heart skip beats.

"Oh, it's nothing special," he said. "Just rags I've owned for years."

Rachida tilted her head forward to whisper.

"It is not your clothing, Patrick, but your poise. You are carrying yourself like a man of honor, a man of strength. Like I said—dashing."

"Oh. Well, thank you."

"You're very welcome. However, you best not shrink from praise next time, or I will clobber you."

Patrick chortled loudly. "Yes, *Mother*."

Rachida laughed as well, and grabbed hold of his arm.

"You make me laugh. I like that. An important quality for a man to have...and a rare one."

"Well, I'm a rare specimen."

"That you are, indeed."

They drew nearer to the temple, and now Patrick could see that there were armored men standing just inside the open gates,

carefully checking over any who entered. They wore a combination
of chainmail and platemail, all of which seemed finely crafted—
though in reality that was nothing but a guess, for Patrick had only
seen a suit of armor a very few times in his life. He recalled Corton
Ender telling him how all the weapons and armor in Haven had
come from raiding shipments that had been sent down the Rigon,
headed for someplace called Omnmount. Again Patrick felt that
same lingering sense of unease, as the need for such protective
measures was completely alien to him. That these peoples' lives
were at stake because of the structure they were now approaching made it all even harder to understand. But even if he couldn't
understand, the danger was certainly real. The bridge that crossed
into the eastern realm of Neldar was within sight of the place
where he stood.

"So this is what all the fuss is about, eh?" he asked, trying to
sound nonchalant.

"It is," Rachida replied.

They entered the gates, and a pair of women walked toward
them. Their gazes turned to Patrick, and their expressions momentarily soured. One whispered in the other's ear, and they both
steered wide of him, giggling and pointing. The lightness Patrick
felt at being by Rachida's side quickly vanished.

"Pay no attention to them," Rachida whispered. "They aren't
important."

The guards at the gate, thankfully, were all business, patting Patrick down in search of weapons they wouldn't find. The only weapon
he had was Winterbone, and he'd left the greatsword with Corton at
the practice fields. When the search was over, Rachida took him by
the arm and led him through the circular path inside the wall. The
path was wide, almost fifty feet, and it circled the center structure
of the temple, a tower of red brick that rose like an erection but
was hidden by the high walls. The temple inside was an imposing
monument, with many doors lining its curved stone foundation.

On multiple occasions Patrick saw a door open and a couple skulk out, looking sweaty and relaxed, eyes half-lidded. The place was teeming with people from all walks of life—young and old, men and women, unattractive and striking. Unlike in the village surrounding the Gemcroft estate, however, there was no apprehension in the air, no fear of a god's wrath. In fact, the air tingled with a current of excited energy racing across time and space, connecting one person to another and locking them together even if their bodies never touched.

"What *is* this place?" asked Patrick, feeling anxious and awed.

"It is a place of worship and intimacy. It is here that we celebrate the forms we have been given."

"And this was Deacon's idea?"

"It was."

"What was his inspiration?"

She shrugged. "I'm not entirely sure, actually. You will have to ask him."

"I'll do that."

The temple was much larger than he'd expected, and it took them almost fifteen minutes to walk halfway across the spherical path. There Patrick saw the entrance to the temple proper, a tall rectangle bordered by thick stone and topped with the image of a dove flying into a waiting pair of hands.

"We only find peace with each other," Rachida said. "That is the meaning of the symbol."

"Interesting," said Patrick.

She stopped him just outside the entryway, pulling him aside so that others could go through unimpeded. She looked at him gravely, those luminous green eyes so seductively framed by her dark hair. She seemed like a legendary creature who wished to lure him into harm's way. Patrick grinned at the thought, knowing that no matter where she led him, he would follow willingly.

"What's wrong?" he asked.

"This is a holy place to us, but sometimes people lose control. The prayer service is…stimulating, you could say. I want to make sure you are ready for it."

"I'll be fine," he replied, wishing he were as confident as he sounded. "Trust me."

Rachida nodded. "Very well."

Her fingers slid down his arm until they found his hand, which she took in hers. She stepped through the portal and led him down a long, cramped passage that opened up into a tall, circular room. That was when Patrick noticed that the temple had no ceiling, only a hole above that allowed the light of the heavens to shine down on those inside. Given that it was past noon and the sun had taken root lower on the horizon, the torches on the walls were blazing.

In the center of the room was a round stone rostrum, the sole furnishing. There were no seats at all, simply cushions stacked by the door, a couple of which Rachida snatched up, handing him one. The place was packed, and Rachida led the way as they wedged through the cramped maze of worshippers until she found an open space a few short feet from the base of the rostrum. Claiming it, she threw down her cushion. Patrick followed her lead. When they sat, Rachida leaned into him, her satin-covered breast pressing into the side of his arm. He thought his head might explode from the contact.

It took quite awhile for the crowd inside the temple to situate themselves. There was a living buzz in the air, a palpable charge that made all the tiny hairs on Patrick's arms stand on end. Rachida leaned in, propping her chin on his shoulder.

"Just remember," she told him, "feel the energy. Feed off it, but do not act. Priestess Aprodia directs the service and provides the inspiration, but she is not to be touched, no matter how close she comes to you."

Feeling lost, Patrick said, "As you wish."

The deafening layer of murmurs ceased, and all fell quiet. Patrick watched as a set of double doors swung inward. Out slunk a nude woman, her flesh bronzed, her hair straight and black, her eyes as pale as spent coals. She had the body of an earth goddess, with wide hips and abundant breasts, between which was a strangely alluring tattoo of a bird with wings spread. The woman—Priestess Aprodia, he assumed—was indeed a splendid creation, and were it not for the woman sitting beside him, he might have thought her the most exquisite in all the land.

The priestess climbed atop the rostrum and stood there, motionless, for what felt like an incredibly long time. Her head then suddenly snapped to the side, lashing her hair about, and her body began moving in wild gyrations. Sweat slicked her flesh, making it shine, as she whipped this way and that, reaching her arms to the sky and then drawing them in like she was holding all of creation against her abdomen, sliding her legs apart until they formed a straight line, rocking back and forth, cupping her breasts with her hands, lifting them, separating them, lolling her head around in circles, panting, moaning, yelping like a wolf in heat.

Aprodia leaned forward, pulling herself across the floor, then slid her legs out from beneath her. She rolled onto her back and lifted her legs high in the air; then, with her hands gripping her ankles, she spread them wide. Patrick, sitting eye level with the platform, stared directly into her womanhood, eyes bulging in disbelief. It was certainly the strangest form of worship he'd ever seen. He had no notion how to react.

The priestess spun around, allowing those on the other side of the room to see her as well. Patrick felt the energy in the room multiply, doubling and then doubling again, and when he finally tore his eyes off the dancing beauty before him, he saw that he and Rachida were among the few who were still watching the display. The rest were locked in private passions all their own, lips pressed together, tongues probing, hands exploring. He glanced at Rachida and saw that she was staring at Aprodia as intently as Patrick had.

The soundless dance kicked up in tempo, the priestess thrashing about as if she were caught in a cyclone that would surely rip her from the ground and send her shooting into the heavens. She leapt from the stage, amazingly not landing on any of the spectators, and continued to gyrate as she made her way around the room. Her hands caressed her body, moving over her nipples, her stomach, her hips, her sex. She stopped a few feet from where Patrick and Rachida sat, thrashing her head around so violently that her hair became a blur, and then reached down and slipped a finger inside herself. Patrick's jaw dropped open. The priestess began to shudder, working her hand up and down, round and round, yelps and hisses escaping her tightly clenched teeth.

Patrick discomfort grew, yet Rachida's eyes were still locked on the scene playing out a few mere feet from them. He noticed her hand was inching closer and closer to *down there*. He hesitated before leaning toward her and whispering, "Um, Rachida, we should go."

Rachida was snapped from her trance.

"Now?" she said, sounding disappointed. "The service isn't over."

"I'm sorry. It's just…I don't…this isn't for me, I think."

Rachida's face froze, then spread into a smile. Patrick was beyond relieved.

"Very well," she said. "I understand."

By then Aprodia had moved on to the other side of the room, continuing with her unabashed, animalistic cries and shrieks. Patrick helped Rachida to her feet, and together they maneuvered through the maze of grinding and copulating couples.

It wasn't until they'd exited the cramped passageway that Patrick realized that the inside of the temple reeked of sweat and unwashed bodies. He looked at Rachida, who bore an odd expression on her face. He wanted to ask her what was wrong, but before he could, she grabbed him by the elbow and yanked him along the circular path. She seemed hurried now, frantic. She banged on a succession of wooden doors as they passed them by, hearing the surprised yelps of those within.

"What are you *doing?*" Patrick asked, winded from both the odd sexual show he'd just witnessed and the effort it took his short legs to keep up with her much longer ones.

Instead of answering, Rachida continued with her frenzied running and pounding on doors. Then she suddenly stopped short, and it took Patrick a second to grasp the reason—the last door had given no answer. She grabbed the handle, yanked the door open, and then pulled Patrick inside.

The room was small and stank like the inside of the temple had, offset somewhat by a stick of incense burning on the table in the corner. The only other furniture was a slender cot. Rachida stood before him, trembling, her fingers nervously tapping just below her breasts. The tentative yet restless look in her eyes worried him.

"What's wrong?" he asked.

"I like you," she replied, the words spurting out. "I need to be with you. Now. Right here."

Patrick was speechless.

"Please, Patrick. This is important."

"Well...I...um...what about your husband?" he finally managed.

Rachida waved her hand dismissively, though her gaze still danced with edginess.

"Peytr is my husband in name only. It is a matter of convenience and no more. His interests lie elsewhere...as do mine."

Tentatively, Patrick reached out and touched her. She closed her eyes, still shaking, and let him. Part of him wasn't entirely sure whether he should be doing this, but his bewildered mind berated that part of himself into submission. His thick fingers lifted the straps of her satin dress and slid them off her shoulders. The dress dropped, stealing down her body, exposing her bareness underneath. Patrick gasped when he looked at her. She was perfect in every way.

He gently touched her nipples. She cringed at first, but then seemed to relax. Slowly he steered her to the bed and sat her down. She began to quake so violently, he feared her nervousness and tried hard not to think about why. As she lay down, he gently began to kiss her all over. She kept her arms by her sides, not touching him. He found it odd but was willing to accept it.

His hand slipped down from her breasts to her belly, to the tuft of hair below that, then between her legs. Her thighs tensed, trapping him there. Her eyes shot open and she stared at him.

"I'm sorry," she whispered, looking away from him.

"What's wrong?" he asked.

She was crying, and the small tears running down the sides of her face were like knives cutting into his chest.

"I'm sorry," he said, turning away. "I should have known better."

"No," she said, grabbing him. "It's not you. It's not…what you think."

"Then what?" he said, whirling on her.

Rachida slid away from him, her head drooping, her eyes downcast.

"I have never been with a man," she said. "I have never even *liked* a man. Moira is the love of my life and has been ever since we were children."

"So…you don't like me?"

"No, I like you, Patrick, just not…in that way."

Patrick couldn't contain his exasperation.

"Then why are we here?"

She sucked on her upper lip, looking absolutely radiant despite her obvious sadness. "I wish to be with child. I wish to be with *your* child."

Patrick groaned. *Not this again. Not now.* Why didn't she ask him for a ride to the moon or for him to shit gold into a chamber pot? There were plenty of other impossible things she could try to barter out of him for sex.

"I see," he said, sighing. "I thank you for telling me so, but I'm sorry to say, you're going to be greatly disappointed."

"Why?"

"I can have no children."

That caused a sad grin to stretch across Rachida's exquisite countenance.

"I know of your...problem," she said. "Your sister told me. I have taken precautions in that regard."

"You what? How?"

"A little bit of research. A little bit of magic. Antar helped greatly in that regard. And Peytr's library is extensive."

"And that's all it takes? I won't have to lick a toad or eat a bunch of mushrooms? Because I've tried both, at my sisters' behest, and I assure you, neither had the promised effect."

"No toads, no mushrooms."

"Oh." Patrick leaned back on the bed. He looked to Rachida again and narrowed his eyes. "But why *me?*"

"You are from one of Ashhur's First Families," she said, running a hand through that exotic curly hair of hers. "It *had* to be you. Haven was built for the solidarity of all peoples. All who want to live within our borders can do so. I have always wanted a child, and I want that child to reflect the values that we've instilled in this land. What better symbol than a child born of the offspring of the First Families of both gods?"

Patrick really didn't think such a child would be all that special or amazing, but then again, it wouldn't take much convincing for him to give her what she wanted. The word *please* was really all that was necessary, and even that was debatable.

"You are *certain* your spells and whatnot will work?" he asked.

She bit her lip.

"As certain as I can be," she said.

316 ■ ■ David Dalglish · Robert J. Duperre

He reached out and fanned his fingers over her eyes, closing them.

"Despite my appearance, I do know my way around a bedroom. If you've never been with a man, then let me guide you. Don't look if you don't want to. Think of Moira or your hope for a baby—whatever you need to do. Just let me know if I hurt you."

"You're still willing to do this?" asked Rachida in a faraway voice, keeping her eyes closed. "You do not find this an insult to your honor?"

Despite the bizarreness of the past hour, Patrick let out a heartfelt laugh.

"Trust me, Rachida, I've been insulted in far, far worse ways than this."

CHAPTER

21

A sentry patrolled the bridge in the deep of night, blocking any chance Crian had at crossing, as usual. He lingered at the edge of the Ghostwood, peering around the trunk of a giant spruce tree, waiting, hoping he might get his chance soon. The sentinel disappeared around the bend, offering him a brief opening, but a replacement soon appeared. He fell back into the safety of the woods, cursing to himself.

There was smoke in the distance, appearing over the sepia-colored grasses like a bulbous black snake. A cookfire, he assumed, lit by the unit that had been sent to capture him. He snuck back through the trees to the small camp he'd made untold days before. It was a rustic setup, nothing but a pile of clothes for a bed and a torn-apart nightshirt tied to a tree for shelter. He'd lost his candles while in flight, dropping them in the middle of the dark and confusing woods. Not that he minded too badly. These woods, and the lengthy river that ran through them, were all that had saved him from capture. All throughout Neldar, the Ghostwood was considered a haunted and evil place. Superstitions and legends abounded of how the ghosts of the dead resided there alongside the lingering specters of the creatures that Celestia had supposedly spirited from Dezrel to pave the way for humankind.

But Crian knew better. Of all his family, he was the only one whose relationship with Jacob Eveningstar had been amicable, and when he was younger—before the First Man had left the east to take up permanent residence in Ashhur's Paradise—Jacob had taken pains to teach him the topography of all of Dezrel, disclosing what was legend and what was not, describing the many natural oddities that existed throughout the land's four corners. Jacob had laughed off the legends of Ghostwood, which was known for its haunting murmurs.

At the center of the forest lies a bubbling hot spring. The heat creates gas that must escape, which it does through tiny gaps in the ground. When those gaps breathe, it sounds like moaning, or a steady, sinister whisper. But that is all there is. There is no such thing as ghosts, child, and if they once existed, they are as gone as the dragons are.

Crian slumped down cross-legged beneath his shoddily con-structed lean-to and, reaching into his sack, removed the mirror he'd brought with him when fleeing Omnmount. He placed it in his lap and took a swig of stream water, which stung his throat with its odd, sulfurous tang. He stared at his reflection in the vibrant moonlight. Gently he touched at the silver strands of his hair, which were poking through more and more now that he lacked the means to hide them.

So be it, he thought. *I'm never going back to Veldaren, and I will never sit at my father's left hand again. When I take Nessa and Moira away from here, we'll flee deep into the Paradise. I can grow old there.*

He didn't know if his plan would work, but he had heard that Ashhur was a loving and forgiving god, with an undying affection for the pathetic and downtrodden, and none were more pathetic and downtrodden than he. All he *did* know was that he could never return home again. Avila's words were proof of that. If all of Haven were to be massacred, including his own excommunicated sister, there was no mercy to be found in Karak's lands. Crian's own hand had signed his death warrant with a flourish of blood the moment he brutalized Avila. It was an act he regretted. He truly did love his sister, even though their relationship was contentious. But for her to do what she did, to come on to him like that and then taunt him with promises of Moira's and Nessa's deaths....

That was in the past, a different problem for a different day. If he wanted to survive, he had to focus on the present, and right now his greatest dilemma was finding a way to cross Karak's Bridge and escape into the delta. Hardly an easy task. The soldiers chasing him were his own, men he'd trained, men he'd considered his brothers. They knew he lurked in the forest, and constant patrols hemmed him inside. Always their bows were at the ready. Crian couldn't even risk wandering deeper into the woods so that he could jump into the river and bypass the bridge entirely. Should they hear him or spot him swimming along, he'd have no safety from their arrows. His only saving grace was time—and their superstitions.

"It's a shame you're not with me, Nessa," Crian said, sighing at his exhausted reflection. "We'd have all the privacy in the world in here."

A high-pitched whistle suddenly bit at his eardrums and made him wince. He glanced all around him, but there was nothing there. The whistle sounded again, again coming from nowhere. Something tickled at the back of his mind, and as if by instinct he glanced down at the mirror that lay in his lap. His lips quivered, and his eyes nearly bulged from his head.

The mirror no longer showed his own reflection; instead, a vaporous apparition fogged over the reflective glass. He could make out the shape of a face, or perhaps a skull of some sort, along with a deep red outline that shimmered when the smoke inside the mirror billowed. He wiped at it with his sleeve despite his fright and the pain of the constant whistle in his ears. Nothing. No change, just the phantom leering out at him. A paralyzing tremor froze his limbs and set the nerves behind his eyes to throbbing, as if invisible lightning had coursed through him.

Go.

The word entered his head much like the tip of an arrow, piercing the front of his brain and making him cry out in surprise. He collapsed to his side, the mirror sliding off his lap, now clear of smoke and haunting images. He rolled on the ground, over leaves and jutting roots, pain shooting through his entire being. Pressure built in his head, threatening to explode his skull, gradually becoming more and more awful until he let out a primal scream of terror. The pain began to dissolve, but that word kept repeating in his head, louder than before. This time he listened.

GO!

More screams, these not from his own mouth. He jerked his head up and looked around, but the forest was empty save for the chattering birds in the canopy overhead. He scurried to his feet, snatching his sword from its dry place beneath the lean-to, and stumbled down the path he had created. Branches tore at him, scratching at his face as he ran in the darkness. He made it to the path's end, where he used to sit for hours, day and night, watching the soldiers safeguard the bridge. The screaming multiplied the closer to the forest's edge he ran, and in his waking nightmare he imagined a parade of hideous monsters slipping out of the shadowed gaps of the world, lopping off heads and devouring entrails, turning the southern banks of the Rigon into a bloody form of the fiery underworld.

And then he reached the carnage at the edge of the forest. Soldiers, those still alive anyway, fled in all directions. Chasing them, almost lazily, was a formless mass of smoke that shimmered black and silver in the moonlight. It surrounded the men, gray tendrils whipping from its swirling center, knocking them aside as they shrieked in unimaginable terror, and then disappeared into the tall grass in a spray of red. The smoke was gradually moving away from him, progressing toward the opposite side of the Gods' Road. Crian watched, his feet made of lead, his mind locking tight. What he saw—it just couldn't be. Jacob couldn't have been this wrong about the forest.

Again that voice, this time softer, more serene, yet oddly more urgent than ever.

Go.

The spirits of the Ghostwood were real. They had watched over him, lurking in his thoughts, stealing into his dreams. Had they felt his love for Nessa? Did they sense his frustration and anger toward the soldiers who chased him? This shapeless creation before him— was that its normal form, or could it shift and change, perhaps even becoming human?

He didn't know. He wasn't sure he even *wanted* to know. Before him was an opening, and he would not dare refuse the spirits' command. Crian burst from the line of trees, running at a full sprint through the open space. All that separated him from the bridge was a couple hundred feet of green grass. He didn't dare take his eyes off his goal, didn't want to even acknowledge the misty cloud that slowly receded away, leaving trails of body parts strewn about the grass. As he ran through its lingering presence, a chill seeped into the very depths of his bones. He held his breath, waiting for it to take him, to crush him like any other mortal, mocking his hopes.

It never did. His feet churned up bits of grass and chunks of dirt and rock, and his ears still rang with the echoes of the soldiers' piercing screams. By the time his boots fell hard on the steel-reinforced granite surface of Karak's Bridge, he felt like sobbing.

It took much less time to cross the bridge, and once he was on the other side, he spied a large structure of some sort in the near distance, situated at the base of the mountain that rose behind it—the Temple of the Flesh, he assumed—and then he was flying alongside the river, keeping up a constant speed, no matter how dicey the footing became. Integrity swung useless in his hand. A part of him wanted to stop, to rest his burning chest, but he didn't dare. His footfalls would not slow until the Ghostwood was banished from his sight. Besides, there was still the chance he was lost in a delusion or a dream, that Avila's men, *his* men would come storming into the delta. These lands were considered neutral no longer. It was enemy territory now, and according to his sister, it was full of enemies to be crushed.

The terrain became marshy and damp, and finally Crian's mind returned to him. He collapsed to his knees, gasping in air. He couldn't run further. He just couldn't. A glance behind him showed Karak's Bridge in the distance, and beyond that....

He looked away. The Ghostwood terrified him, and a deep part of him wanted to never, ever think about it again. When his breathing grew more controlled, Crian rose back to his feet. He had to be careful now. With things as they were, there was no guarantee he would be treated as a guest rather than a threat. Sticking to the cover of the twisting wetland mothertrees and swampy vegetation, he struggled through the quagmire, his boots constantly getting sucked beneath the mud or ensnared in vines. He heard recognizable animal sounds: the repetitive bleats of the whippoorwills, the throaty exclamations of whooping cranes, and the ominous *splash* of large, hidden bodies dropping into the bog. He kept his wits about him, remembering the lessons Moira had taught him about staying alive when trapped in the delta swamp. *Head down, keep moving, don't turn around for anything.* This wasn't his first venture into the wilds, after all. Hopefully it wouldn't be his last.

It was morning by the time he found the landmark he was seeking—a vast garden of blood roses and orchids that exploded in red and white brilliance from the drab greens and browns of the swamp. The sound of the ocean rumbled in his ears, not very far away. He immediately climbed the bank, yelping as he narrowly avoiding the snapping fangs of a frightened bogsnake. Keeping close to the spiky vines of the roses, he worked his way through a tightly woven copse of trees. When he emerged on the other side, he breathed a sigh of relief, almost falling to his knees and crying his thanks to the sky. A small, brown-rooted courtyard led to the rear of a simple log cottage with a hay-lined roof. Moira's cottage. He was here at last.

Throwing caution to the wind, he went straight for the front door. He didn't care who saw him now—he had no secrets left to hide. He rapped lightly on the wood, a grin stretching across his face, and tapped his foot impatiently as he waited for Moira to answer.

She never did.

Gently he leaned his weight into the door. It rotated inward, unbarred. He stepped inside, hesitating just before he crossed the threshold. The windows were unshuttered, letting in the light of the rising sun as well as buzzing insects that circled the bowl of fruit sitting on Moira's simple kitchen table. It was the same table they sat around whenever he visited, chatting about loved ones, the taste of the many luscious and exotic soups Moira would set to boil in her inglenook, the beauty of the sunrise over the vast eastern waterways—anything but the life of enforcement and violence he lived outside this peaceful delta.

Moira's simple three-room cabin, filled lovingly with a lifetime's worth of trinkets and curiosities, was his own sort of haven. For the first time in his thirty-eight years of life he appreciated the significance of the place's name. Haven: a place of safety and shelter, a refuge for the unwanted, the outcasts…but this place would be none of those things once his father had his way.

Swatting at a large horsefly that was hovering in front of his face, Crian pivoted on his heels and left the cabin. If his sister wasn't here, there was only one other place she could be. He strolled out the door, making sure to close it behind him, and veered left down the dirt cart path that passed in front of the property. He walked casually, as if he hadn't a care in the world. This far south, the delta was sparsely populated. Not twenty years ago it had been a disorganized harbor for miscreants and starving thieves who dwelled in the swamps and survived by assaulting passing wagons en route to the meager docks that bordered the Thulon Ocean. Deacon Coldmine had led the drive to clean the place up, aided by Rachida and Peytr Gemcroft. The scum had scattered in all directions. It was in the delta that Crian's carriage had been attacked that fateful day he met Nessa and her malformed brother. Crian had given up his sword in thanks for their aid. The thought of the blade put a smile on his face. Winterbone, a beast of a thing he'd had difficulty carrying. Father had been none too pleased to learn he had "lost" it, but of course his reaction would have been far worse if he'd learned the arduous thing had been given to an offspring of Ashhur. Crian knew the mutant DuTaureau still had it, and that thought brought his mind back to Nessa.

Fifteen minutes later, the Gemcroft Estate loomed before him, rising above the surrounding mothertrees and apple blossoms like a mythical stone monster. What had started out as a simple log cottage had, over time, grown into a building whose immensity was only dwarfed by the amount of ardor that had gone into its construction. The stones making up its walls had been extracted from the Pebble Islands and were inlaid with traces of precious gems. The roof was made from the halved logs that had formed Peytr's original cottage, painted with exotic dyes produced from the ink of a hundred thousand miniature squids farmed off the delta's shores.

When he rapped on the door, a young servant girl named Una, whom he had met many times, answered it almost immediately. He asked to see the lady of the house, smiling as Una cast a disapproving glance at his muddy, unkempt appearance. She escorted him inside, passing through the vestibule that overlooked the pathway and down a long hall that opened up into the solarium.

There were several people in the room, but Crian saw only one—his beloved Nessa. She lit up with joy the moment he stepped inside, casting aside her knitting so that she could lunge at him. Crian dropped Integrity on the table beside him and wrapped his arms around her, accepting her kisses across his dirty face, letting the tiny pecks wash away all the lingering horror of the Ghostwood.

"You came!" she cried out between kisses. "Atria just arrived two days ago. I wasn't expecting you for another week!"

"I'm early," replied Crian, easily supporting her tiny frame.

"What happened to you?" she asked, pulling away. "You're all a mess."

"I had to…let me just say I walked here."

"Are you all right?"

He nodded, not wanting to answer her fully, for he *was* all right now.

It was Moira's turn to embrace him. Her blue eyes watered at the edges as she took in the sight of him, and she played nervously with her silver-white hair. Crian was able to pry Nessa off for a warm embrace, although his love still managed to attach herself to his side like a human barnacle.

"It's good you came," Moira said. Despite how similar she appeared to Avila, she had none of their sister's mannerisms. Moira exuded kindness, simplicity, and passion, while Avila had done any-thing *but*. When Crian looked into those blue eyes, he saw a woman at peace, a woman who had everything she needed and was more than willing to give it all away for those she loved. It hurt him terribly, knowing the reason he had come, the ill tidings he brought with him.

"Not as good as I would like," he said, lowering his gaze to the floor.

Nessa circled around in front of him, her curly red hair frizzing up about her head like a crimson halo, hands clasped, eyes wide with sudden concern.

"What's wrong, my love?" she asked.

Crian cast his gaze aside. "I was discovered, Ness. *We* were discovered."

"So?" uttered Nessa, incredulous.

"It's about time," Moira interrupted. "If Father has thrown you out, you can come down here and live with me. I have been trying for years to convince you to do so, anyway."

"It's not just that," he said, glancing between them. "Haven is no longer safe."

Moira took a step back as Nessa began to chew on her knuckles, a nervous habit that he had always found adorable until now.

"Why?" Moira asked.

"It's Father. In a month he is coming here, with an army at his back."

"Which only makes him a man of his word," said a gruff male voice. Crian glanced up at the speaker, who was rising from a reclined position on the divan. He was solidly built and was wearing a thin white robe covered with a long maroon jerkin. His hair was close cropped yet shaggy, his beard thick but well maintained. Wisps of gray suggested he was an older man, but he carried himself with the strength and confidence of youth. His eyes were a deep brown, and they seemed to convey a sort of veiled intelligence that reminded Crian of his father.

"Who are you?" Crian asked.

The man stepped past Moira and extended his hand. "Deacon Coldmine, Lord of Haven."

"*You're* Deacon?"

"The last I heard."

"Wait, isn't your brother—"

"On the king's council, yes."

"Funny, he never mentioned you."

"He had no reason to."

"Oh," Crian replied, shaking the man's hand.

He stepped back after the greeting. "Listen, all of you," he said, glancing in turn at each of the three people standing around him. "Yes, you know my father, the Highest—*our* father, Morry—is coming here. But his proclamation was dishonest. He doesn't care whether or not you fall down before Karak and beg forgiveness. To be honest, I'm not sure Karak does, either. This city, your temple—they're going to make an example of it for the rest of Dezrel. You've been pronounced enemies of Neldar, and Clovis will wipe out every man, woman, and child. There is no turning back now, no safety to be found in Haven. We must all flee, *all* of us."

The joy that had filled Nessa's eyes only moments ago slowly faded.

"Is this true?" she asked.

"It is. We haven't much time. We must go, and soon."

"And where will we go?" asked Deacon. His arms were crossed over his chest, and Crian could tell there was only one person he had to convince, and then the whole delta would follow.

"To Ashhur's lands," Crian said, meeting the hard man's gaze. "We'll find shelter there."

Deacon frowned.

"And what of the four thousand other good people who live deeper in the delta?"

"They can come with us, of course. Why wouldn't they?"

Deacon let out a laugh so devoid of humor that it reminded Crian once more of his father. A chill ran up his back, making him shiver.

"Is that so?" the man asked. "How easy then, how simple. You have the wisdom of a child—perhaps worse than a child's. Do you think Ashhur would be brave enough to accept us with open arms?"

"He would!" shouted Nessa. "Ashhur loves and respects all life!"

"Perhaps he does," the bearded man said, rustling Nessa's hair. "But Ashhur also knows his place. If the God of Order wishes death upon us, do you really think Ashhur will grant us sovereignty? That would invite open conflict between the two brothers, something they've both taken great pains to avoid. By the Abyss, Celestia even split the land with the Rigon to help separate their creations. No, Ashhur will not protect us. He will not risk open warfare for a few of his brother's miserable failures. He will say he's sorry and see us back to our fates."

"That's not true!" cried Nessa.

"Sometimes I find it hard to believe you're thirty years old," Deacon said with a roll of his eyes. He fixed Crian with a hard yet sympathetic stare. "I appreciate the warning, boy, but these contingencies have already been measured. And considering we never had any intention of bowing down, we have been preparing for war."

Crian opened his mouth, then closed it.

"Did you think us cowards?" Deacon asked. "Haven is my creation. I brought the first settlers into this unclaimed land twenty years ago. I oversaw the taming of the ruffians who called the delta home. Most importantly, I taught the people what it meant to be *free*. *I* had the temple built so that they could exercise that freedom to its fullest potential. Never once, not even when your bastard father rained down arrows upon my people, did I consider tearing that temple down."

Crian threw up his hands. "This is madness!" he exclaimed. "You cannot win. The force my father commands outnumbers your citizens two to one! And you're fighting more than just a king here; you're fighting your own god!"

"One man defending his home is worth ten invading soldiers, boy," Deacon said, his face hardening even more. "Do we sign our own death warrant? Perhaps. But I would rather die a free man than live as a slave to a theocracy, beneath a puppet king who has less faith than I do. Have I made myself clear?"

The air went out of Crian's lungs. His shoulders sagged and he glanced at Moira, who stood beside the Lord of Haven.

"Morry," he said, turning to her. "Sister, please say you do not agree with him."

Moira tilted her head and gently parted her lips.

"I'm sorry, but I do. Father disowned me long ago for the indignity of following my heart. The people of Haven are my people now. I cannot abandon them. I *will not* abandon them."

"But—"

"But nothing, Crian. The decision is made, and it is ironclad."

He felt close to tears. "If you were to perish, I couldn't…."

She approached him and cupped his face in her hands.

"Don't worry about me," she said. "There is more of Avila in me than you realize. I know how to defend myself. I will be fine…and even if I am not, you can go on knowing that I went out the way *I* chose."

He opened his mouth to protest but snapped it shut when he saw the determined look on his sister's face. Her mind was made up. There was nothing he could say to make her feel otherwise.

"I'll go with you," Nessa said, piercing the sudden silence. She pressed herself against him, this time far more subdued. "I'll never leave your side. Never again."

"I know," he said, running his fingers through her hair. "And I won't leave yours either."

Deacon slapped him on the shoulder, jarring his tired body.

"You know," he said, "we're always on the lookout for another good swordsman. As it is, our one lone warrior is a bit…overmatched…given the number of citizens he is saddled with training. You were the Left Hand of the Highest, the instructor of countless troops of Karak's Army. Your knowledge and skills could aid us in so many ways."

Crian clutched Nessa tighter.

"I can't," he insisted. "My devotion is to Nessa, and she holds precedence over all else. I must get her out as soon as possible and enter Paradise before it's too late. Her place is not in this battle, and I couldn't bear to lose her."

"You needn't say more," said Deacon, nodding. "I understand your dilemma, and I'm sure Moira does as well."

"I do," said Moira.

"Thank you both for your understanding," whispered Crian.

He gave Nessa a last, loving embrace and then sent her off to gather her things. He lingered in the solarium with Moira and Lord Coldmine after she left, and an uncomfortable silence spread over them. The bright southern sun shone through the gaps in the solarium dome, gaps that were cutouts of human bodies standing hand in hand, with a hole in the center shaped like a shining star. Sunlight glowed off the sparkling, gem-encrusted edges of the cutouts. Crian clutched his hands behind his back and stared through each opening, admiring the blue autumn sky and wondering how the interior of the room could ever remain dry during the rainy summer months. He shivered, feeling a sudden chill wash over him.

Deacon cleared his throat, looking to him with uncertainty.

"I was wondering," said Deacon, "how do you intend to reach the western bridge? Does your horse require new shoes? And are you low on food?"

"I have no horse," Crian replied. "I left him behind when I fled the Ghostwood. As for food…in that I am severely lacking."

"Do you have any coin? There are a few markets between here and there that offer reasonable options."

Crian shook his head, eliciting a dry laugh from Deacon.

"No money, no horse, no nourishment—nothing at all but a sword and a will. How very rugged of you."

"We'll manage," Crian muttered.

Deacon rolled his eyes. "Come now, boy. Your clothes are filthy and soaked; you're shivering like a whore standing before a vanguard of angry wives; and there are bags the size of feed sacks beneath your eyes. You are exhausted."

Crian breathed deeply. "I am."

"Then stop acting like a fool, rushing into things you're not prepared for. That's what put you in this situation in the first place, I'd wager. I have supplies aplenty back at the homestead, including a stable filled with fine young geldings. Come with me, have dinner with my family, and rest your weary bones. I'll give you a horse and all the provisions you require for your trek through the desert. My home may be more humble than this one, but it is a home nonetheless."

"Could we not just stay here?"

Deacon shrugged. "You could, I suppose. But if you wish to flee quickly, it would be best for you to stay with me. The Gods' Road is a few hours' ride from here, but my home is half that distance. You could leave the stables at first light and cross the bridge before it's time for breakfast."

"Take him up on his offer, Crian," said Moira, placing a warm hand on his cheek. "Do it for Nessa's sake, if not your own. She's a sensitive girl, strong in some ways but fragile in many others. Besides…she means a lot to Patrick, who is staying with Deacon. He should get a chance to say good-bye."

"Very well," said Crian. The notion of a warm place to rest his head was indeed inviting given his makeshift accommodations the past few nights. He offered Deacon an appreciative bow. "Thank you for your hospitality, Lord Coldmine. It is very much appreciated."

Nessa came running into the room then, lugging a rucksack stuffed to overflowing with clothes. She dropped the bag and embraced Moira, the rose color of her flushed cheeks making her look much younger than her thirty years.

"Thank you. I love you, Miss Moira," she said, her voice childlike.

Crian slung a heavy arm over Nessa's shoulder. "Come now, my love. The kind lord here has invited us to his estate this evening for food and a warm bed."

"He has?" Her face lit up with a smile, and he was surprised by how relieved she seemed to be. "Good. I wanted to say good-bye to Patrick—I really did. And there's a few more dresses I can pack in here if I fold them tightly."

She looked him over, poked him.

"And I have every intention of running you ragged tonight," she said. "So thank Ashhur you'll get to take a bath beforehand."

Despite everything, Crian let out a laugh.

"My beloved Nessa," he said, grinning. "How will you ever survive the journey west?"

"With you," she said, kissing his nose.

The road to the Coldmine homestead was an arduous one, snaking through perilous swampland, rushing waterways, and knee-deep mud. Crian and Nessa rode on Moira's horse. Despite the size and apparent amenities of the Gemcroft estate, their stables were extremely lacking. The only saddle they had on hand was fitted to his sister's measurements, meaning he had to go bareback on the large mare. His tailbone ached and the pressure on his back, where Nessa was resting her head, threatened to warp his spine. The terrain was so treacherous for the horse that on more than one occasion he wished they were simply hiking instead.

Then again, even on horseback it took more than an hour to reach the Coldmine homestead, and the last thing he had wanted was to try to navigate his delicate Nessa through a potentially hazardous bog under the cover of night. They'd wasted enough time chatting with his sister, repacking Nessa's things for the journey, and getting him cleaned up.

By the time they arrived, the whippoorwills were frantically chanting, filling the dusk with their macabre song. The homestead was indeed more humble than the grand Gemcroft estate, but only to a degree. The home itself was a practical, square construction made of tall logs and carefully placed stone pillars, two stories high and with numerous casements dotting the walls, giving it the look of a garrison. The setting sun silhouetted the dwelling, made it appear like a menacing obelisk rising up between tall, lavish gardens of roses and yellow daylilies.

They left their horses in Deacon's stables, which were certainly as well stocked as the man had claimed they were, with at least twenty horses stowed away inside. Crian picked out two strong-looking steeds, one of which was very similar to his father's favorite white mount.

"Good choices," Deacon said. "They're all yours."

The stable boy gave his master a queer look and then quickly turned his head and went about his chores, brushing the horses down and filling their feed bags. Crian chuckled, figuring the boy was confused about why his master would bestow such a handsome gift upon a stranger. Crian figured he should get used to this sort of anonymity. Perhaps he could change his name, lie about his heritage....

Nessa held his hand as they paraded up the front walk and through the main entrance to the ample home. The inside was brightly lit, with candles placed on every available flat surface. Numerous servants bustled about, dusting the simple country furnishings and scrubbing the floors. They were a quiet lot, and they kept their eyes downcast, politely nodding if they were ever addressed. It reminded Crian of his time among the wealthy in Veldaren. So it seemed as though pieces of the two kingdoms had slowly made their way into the delta.

The scent of food reached his nose, succulent meats and exotic spices cooked over open flames, and Crian's mouth began to water.

"Dinner will be ready shortly," Deacon announced almost offhandedly, not bothering to turn around as he continued his way through his vast home. "I should have an open room upstairs where you can spend the night. It isn't much, but it will suit you fine, I think, given the circumstances."

They entered a long hallway lined with expertly painted portraits of Deacon and his family. Lady Coldmine was a beauty, Crian thought, pulling his own lady love closer to him. In the paintings, all the children seemed so happy and carefree. Crian hoped he might meet a few of them before he left, perhaps at dinner.

The hallway ended at a large set of double doors. Deacon stopped before them, placing a palm on each and bowing his head as if in prayer. Crian waited patiently behind him while Nessa fidgeted. Finally, the bearded lord of Haven turned around. The strange expression on his face, with narrowed eyes and twitching mouth, revealed a sudden conflict.

"I hope you don't mind," he said, "but I've invited company."

Deacon swung the doors wide.

The dining room was modest, and because it was located in the center of the abode, it was also windowless. Candles lined the center of a long table that was surrounded by chairs. Sitting opposite each other, looking almost bored, waited Clovis and Avila Crestwell.

Nessa yelped beside him, while at the same time something sharp pointed into his back. Crian peered over his shoulder; two servants were behind him, holding a dagger apiece against him and Nessa. A hand reached down and snatched Integrity from his grasp, slipping the sword from its sheath as silently as if it were covered with oil. Nessa looked frightened enough to faint, and though he tried to impart comfort through their clasped hands, she began to cry all the same.

"Please, come in," said Deacon, standing against the side wall of the dining hall, his once firm voice suddenly unsure.

Crian urged Nessa into the dining hall, trying to remain outwardly calm despite the fact that his entire body was numb with apprehension. The double doors closed behind them, sealing them in the room with Lord Coldmine, Avila, and their father, the Highest.

His father sat back in his chair, eyeing them with the faintest spark of interest. Avila leaned forward, scowling at him, her forehead and the left side of her face an ugly mishmash of pulped flesh and yellowing bruises from where he'd struck her with the candlestick. A person of lesser strength would not have survived. She flexed her fingers, mere inches away from the pommel of her sword, which was lying on the table, the tip facing him. They were both wearing their traditional black riding leathers, the insignia of the Crestwell house outlined in red on their chests. Crian slowly moved Nessa behind him, as if by some miracle he might defend her.

Crian looked at Deacon, torn between pity and fury.

"Why?" he asked, barely able to squeeze the sound from his throat.

The lord of Haven swallowed.

"Some things are more important than others," he said. "And nothing is more important than the orders of my god, whether or not I understand them. I'm sorry, Crian. The faithful rarely walk an easy path."

The older lord turned to Crian's father and bowed.

"If you are done with me, my Highest, I will take my leave."

His father wagged two fingers toward the door, still silent. Deacon backed away gradually, one tiny step at a time, bent at the waist. Keeping Nessa behind him, Crian slid out of the way so that Coldmine could exit. He had a thought to charge the doors when they opened, but that idea was quashed the moment he saw the servants—no, not servants, he realized, but his own men from Omnmount in disguise—holding their rapiers at the ready. Instead, Crian let the doors shut, sealing him in with his executioners.

"Sit...*down*," his father hissed, and Crian immediately pulled out a chair and complied. Nessa lingered behind him, so white she looked ready to fade away completely. Avila slapped her gloved hand on the table, ordering Nessa to sit as well. She obeyed at once, slipping in beside Crian, tears streaming down her cheeks as her tiny chest rose and fell with wheezing sobs.

The Highest placed a curved dagger on the table and started to twirl it, his eyes fixed on the spinning blade.

"I am very, very disappointed in you, son," he said. His tone was the one he usually reserved for those under his command. He had never used it with Crian before, and right then Crian knew he was going to die.

He hung his head and said nothing.

"Imagine how distressing it was for me, coming to the Omnmount staging grounds to find a recruit dead and my precious daughter beaten beyond recognition. Her beautiful face was smashed, and her hair ran red with blood. We are lucky she is a strong girl, for a mortal woman would have died from the injuries you bestowed on her."

His finger traced the ugly bruising, the line of cracked and bleeding flesh that ran from the center of his daughter's formerly pristine forehead, looped around her left eye, and then bulged along her cheek to her ear, which was swollen to twice its normal size.

"She is stronger than you, Crian," he said. "So much stronger. I now know my mistake. I should have made Avila my Left Hand, not you."

A defiant streak rose in Crian, and against his better judgment he spat, "Perhaps you should have. After all, you do enjoy fucking her. If she were on your left, you would be able to do it more often."

"There is no need for such crudeness," his father replied, his tone not rising in the slightest. "You are in the wrong here. You have gone against my decree and, by proxy, that of your god."

"So you speak for Karak now?"

"I always have. If not, why would he have arrived in Omnmount along with me?"

Crian froze.

"Yes, that's right. The god you turned your back on now stands beside your brother, watching over his army as they prepare for the day they will raze this land into the Abyss. Had you stayed your upheaval, you would have seen it for yourself."

"I never lost faith in my god," Crian whispered, his head bowed. "Only in you and your rules."

Clovis laughed, the sound filling the room and making Nessa cry all the harder.

"Shut her up," growled Avila, finally gripping her sword and leveling it at him, without budging from her seat. "Or I will shut her up for you."

Crian placed a hand on Nessa's chest, silencing her. He knew his sister wasn't one to make idle threats.

"How did you find us?" he asked, rocking his love in an attempt to ease her fear. "How did you know where I was?"

Clovis regarded him evenly.

"My Whisperer sees much. He said you fled across the bridge, and once I knew that, I knew precisely where to find you."

"How did he see me cross?" Crian asked, thinking of that horrible night. "Was he one of the soldiers?"

His father shook his head, laughing once more. "Not at all, you impudent whelp. My Whisperer *paved the way for you*. He was the one who chased the soldiers away, allowing you to cross unmolested. An unfortunate loss of life for those who perished, yes, but you are worth a hundred of them, my dear son. I had to know. I had to be certain."

Crian's jaw dropped open. He remembered how fortunate he had felt when the giant beast of smoke had lashed out at the soldiers. But still, the terror that had accompanied it, the bloody spectacle....

With newfound horror, Crian stared at his father, wondering what manner of monster Clovis called ally.

"So you know," Clovis said, reaching underneath the table, "I went into the Ghostwood myself to gather your things." Up came Crian's dragonglass mirror. He slid it across the flat surface, and Crian stopped it with hands that seemed to move on their own. His father's gaze seemed to linger on the mirror, and the faintest trace of sadness flashed across his face.

"We only had to wait for you to come to us," Clovis said, the corner of his lip upturned. "I never imagined you would arrive so quickly."

"But why?" Nessa murmured so quietly that Crian could barely hear her. But his father did, and to Crian's shock the man's expression softened.

"Oh, sweet child," he said, "if I had caught my son fleeing into the delta by himself, he could have accused his sister of lying and given me any excuse rather than admitting to his sins. I needed to catch him in the act—catch him with *you*, my sweet—in order to prove how much he has betrayed me."

His father grinned then, an expression so malicious that Crian flew up from his chair, knocking it back against the double doors, and grabbed Nessa around the shoulders, moving her behind him. Avila lifted her sword and began to rise, but the Highest grabbed the sleeve of her shirt and yanked her back down. Her ruined face sneered at him.

"None of this is Nessa's doing!" Crian screamed. "You will let her go, and you will let her go *now*. Take me if you want—execute me—but let her live, or so help me, I will end you both right here and now."

His father sighed and closed his eyes. He pulled the silver-white hair back from his forehead, a gesture he always used when frustrated.

"I am not going to hurt her," he said. "And although I would so enjoy hurting *you*, I will refrain from doing that either. Though you turned your back on your deity, you did so without fully realizing it, which makes you a far different case from your renegade sister."

Crian's jaw dropped open. This was a most unexpected answer to receive. The tiniest hint of hope rose in his belly as he listened to his father speak.

"However, you have broken the laws of our family, and that carries a price. Your title of Left Hand is at once rescinded, an honor I now place on Avila's shoulders."

"Thank you, Father," said Avila.

"Silence." He turned back to Crian. "Also, you will accompany us back to Veldaren and be stripped of the Crestwell name. You are no longer welcome at the family compound on the other side of the Queln. You will no longer regard me as father, and should you ever see your mother again, you shall not look her in the eye. Your room in Tower Servitude is hereby revoked. You will serve as a member of the Watch, living in the Tower Keep alongside the other mongrels who chose to give in to weakness, until you earn enough coin to find a dwelling of your own."

Crian was shocked. He stepped back, a hand over his heart. *I am to live?* His blood pumped faster and he glanced behind him at Nessa, who was shaking, her hands clenched in front of her mouth.

"And what of my love?" he asked.

"Her?" said his father. "She's Ashhur's concern. What the girl does is up to her. She is free to go home if she chooses, or she can join you in Veldaren. I hold no ill will against her, naïve and stupid as she is. I expected better from you, Crian, not her."

Nessa abruptly ceased her crying. Her wide, pleading blue eyes gazed up from beneath the snarled tangle of red hair.

"I am free to choose?" she asked.

The Highest pushed his chair back, stood up, and rounded the table. He knelt down until their faces were level.

"It is your choice," he said. "Do you love this traitor enough to relinquish your god and fall into the arms of Karak? Do you love him enough to give up your life of ease and simplicity and spend the rest of your days washing clothes, raising babes, and cooking meals for a man who will never earn enough coin for you to live comfortably?"

Nessa gazed up at Crian, and for a moment he thought for sure she would flee from him, flee from the hardships that such a life would entail. Instead she rose from the floor, walked up to him with a confidence he had never seen before in her, rose up on her tiptoes, and planted a kiss on his cheek.

"Always and forever, I choose you," she said, biting her lower lip. "No matter what hardships we face, comfort will always come if you are by my side."

"So be it," said his father.

"You would do this for me?" Crian said to Nessa. "For us? Give up your life, your god?"

"What is a god to someone like me?" she replied. "All the prayer in the world would mean nothing if I never saw you again."

"The choice is made," declared the Highest. "You leave with us tonight, and your sentence begins the moment we arrive back on Veldaren soil. And do not even *think* of trying to rescue Moira. Your sister has made her choice, and she will die with the rest of the blasphemers in this godforsaken swampland."

His father nodded to Avila, who scowled as she worked her way around the table, giving them both a wide berth. She yanked open one of the double doors and stormed out of the room. The Highest stood and approached him. He leaned in and whispered into Crian's ear, just loud enough for his son to hear.

"Be glad forces other than myself wish you alive, boy. You tread dangerous ground here. You will be watched."

With those foreboding words, Clovis left the room, his white hair trailing behind him like the tail of a sea serpent.

Once he and Nessa were alone, Crian tried to put his father's anger out of his mind. He turned to his love and kissed her lips, softly, slowly. It felt as if she stole the breath from his lungs.

"Are we making the right choice?" he asked. "Deacon is no ally of theirs. Can we really leave them here under his control? He's the one preparing the defense of Haven, a defense which I'm sure will capitulate the moment the battle begins."

"What other choice do we have?" Nessa asked.

"I don't know," Crian said. "We can still try to flee—maybe run in opposite directions. Something, Nessa, something! They'll die otherwise."

"We are the only people we can hope to save," Nessa whispered, but she didn't sound confident. She opened her mouth again, but nothing came out. She simply latched onto his arm and didn't let go.

"We will send a letter to the others once we get to Veldaren," he said. "They can't watch us forever."

She nodded. "That we can do."

The decision made, Crian let out a sigh and accepted it. He scooped up his mirror from the table, tucked it beneath his elbow, and offered Nessa his arm. Together they walked out of the dining hall, virtually running toward the open door at the end of the corridor, where his father and Avila waited with the horses to bring them to their new lives as hard-working, nameless commoners.

CHAPTER

22

Neither of their parents listened. Or if they did listen, they didn't believe.

After sharing all they had heard in the crypts below Dezerea, earning nothing but confused, disbelieving stares, Aully and Kindren had sworn never to speak a word of what had happened again, either to each other or anyone else.

It proved an easy promise to keep, given what came next.

Orden Thyne arrived at the East Garrison not a full day after the two children had spilled their hearts out to their families. The Sovereign of Dezerea expressed concern to Cleotis and Audrianna over the dangerous imaginations of their respective children. "Accusations such as these are irresponsible," he said, "if not utterly perilous to the survival of our people. And you— staying in the same dwelling as they!" Aully sat in the corner, hands between her knees and head down, listening as the father of her beloved prattled on about how the Quellan would react if they found out that the heirs to the two noble family lines were spreading vicious rumors about them. "Neyvar Ruven would accuse us of being traitorous. We have tried for centuries to improve the relations between our nations; we mustn't risk a return to discord."

It was decided that the two youths needed a break from each other. That had been twelve days ago, and Aully had neither seen nor heard from Kindren since. Her heart felt like it was breaking, and while she stood alone in her quarters in the East Garrison, gazing out the window at the nighttime fires that burned among the trees throughout the forest city of Dezerea, she considered leaping from the ledge and plummeting to her death.

Strangely enough, it was Ceredon who rescued her from herself. The beautiful, bronze-skinned Quellan knocked on her door that night, asking if she would like to talk. She did, and as they sat across from each other on her bed, tossing innocuous chatter back and forth, she felt an odd sensation of safety overwhelm her. The impetuous egotist she had met at the tournament was gone now, replaced by a man of dignity and respect who treated her like a beloved younger sister.

There were thankfully no romantic notions between them, certainly not on Ceredon's part. Eighty-three years her senior, he acted a perfect gentleman at all times, just as he had during the entirety of her stay in the East Garrison. As their visits continued, she began to act flirtatious in her own immature way, compelled by his attractiveness and confidence. She'd nudge closer to him during his nightly visits, hold his stare longer than necessary, and when she felt particularly daring, she'd try to touch the skin of his hands or face, just to see how it felt. She felt guilty each time it happened, and without fail she would kneel and pray to Celestia for forgiveness when he left her room. Then she'd sit by her window, gazing at the emerald splendor of Palace Thyne, glowing beneath the light of the rapidly waxing moon.

On more than one occasion she would catch sight of a figure gazing out of a tiny porthole on the sixth story of the palace, the humanoid outline no bigger than that of the smallest ant. She felt a connection pass through the great distance between them, a wave of delicate energy that massaged her heart and made her sigh.

It was Kindren. She didn't need the proof of seeing his face to know it was true.

It was dawn when they arrived from the northeast, where the low mountain chain separated Dezerea from the Gihon River.

Aully was awakened by footfalls and a series of rhythmic shouts, almost like singing, and she rolled from her bed, padding sleepily to her window. The blinding rays of the morning sun reflected off the East Garrison's sparkling crystal walls, forcing her to shield her eyes with her hands. A cold wind blew in the window from the north, catching her unprepared, and goose pimples rose on her flesh beneath the thin nightdress she wore. Jetting streams of gray clouds passed over the low-hanging sun, granting her eyes a temporary reprieve. She took that opportunity to scan the expanse of ancient trees for the source of the noise.

They emerged from the forest, moving into the shadow of the East Garrison with dreadful speed. A seemingly endless parade of elves, Quellan all, marching in unison, bows slung over their shoulders and sheathed khandars hanging from their belts. An immensely large elf marched at their lead, his broad chest as wide as that of any two in his regiment combined. As he passed beneath her window, Aully saw his face, which was as large as the rest of him, his eyes too far apart, his lips constantly locked in a sneer. Unlike the rest of the elves, who were dressed in the traditional green tunic and brown breeches, he wore a glistening black top that looked like solid oil. It left his shoulders exposed, revealing the great musculature of his arms. He also differed from the others in that he carried no bow or khandar; instead, two long, thick swords were strapped to his back, so black they seemed to blend into whatever material made up his clothes. She only knew they were swords by the two handles that bounced on either side of his too large head.

She remembered the elder Iolas's words when the four secret keepers had gathered in the crypts—*Shen and the Ekreissarian will sail across the river a fortnight from now*—and an instant later she was out the door, sprinting down the hall without getting dressed, shouting her parents' names.

A few moments later, the family stood gathered together, first in Aullienna's room and then in the abutting space where her nurse-maid Noni slept, trying to get a better view of the force that was snaking its way down the packed-dirt lane toward Palace Thyne. Aully's father snatched one of her hands and held it tightly, and her mother did the same with the other. All were silent—even Noni, whose tongue had a comment ready for any situation. It was only when the tail of the snake emerged in the form of the last few soldiers in the line, holding high pikes topped with a series of pointed barbs, that any dared to speak.

Lucius, a relatively young elf of seventy-two, who served as Cleotis's bodyguard alongside his wife, Kara, came running up the stairs and careened around the corner, almost slamming into the wall of Noni's room.

"Cleotis!" he shouted. "Do you see?"

Her father nodded, releasing his daughter's hand after giving it a final, gentle squeeze.

"We have," he replied, gesturing at the open window to his right.

"They're Quellan," said Lucius. "Are they the Ekreissar?"

"Possibly. But why are the rangers here? Have you any word from the Neyvar?"

Lucius shook his head violently. When he spoke, his words were rasping, hurried.

"They're gone. All of them. No one is in the Neyvar's quarters— not his advisors or his son—no one. The entire level that was housing the delegate from Quellassar has been abandoned."

Aully glanced up, and her father's eyes met hers. His lips quivered as if he wished to say something to her, but he abruptly turned to face Lucius again instead.

"I need you to wake Kara," he said.

"No need, my Lord. She's already awake."

Cleotis nodded. "Good. The two of you head over to the palace, and find out the meaning of all of this. But be cautious. The Quellan may be our friends"—he paused for another quick glance at Aully—"but these are strange times. Be prepared for anything."

"Yes, my Lord," Lucius said, darting out of the room.

"Cleotis, what's happening?" Audrianna asked. Aullienna hated the fear she heard in her mother's voice.

"We'll find out soon," her father replied.

Hours went by, and still there was no word from Lucius or Kara. Aully feared for them. They had been a constant presence in her family's home for as long as she could remember. Losing them would be tantamount to losing her sister, Brienna.

Slender fingers brushed her cheek, and Aully gazed up into Noni's milky, aged eyes. Noni was indeed old—according to her father she was the oldest elf who'd ever lived, at almost seven hundred years—but her pale hair and craggy flesh had done nothing to diminish the strength of her spirit. Noni was as active as an elf a third her age, and on more than a few occasions she'd held her own when confronting belligerent drunkards who attempted to harass Aully during the nighttime walks she was fond of taking.

A folded turquoise dress hung from Noni's other hand. She pressed the garment lightly into Aully's chest.

"Your father told you to pack just in case we need to leave, and yet you stand by the window?"

"I'm sorry," replied Aully, dropping her eyes. She grabbed the dress and walked over to the bed, stuffing it into a large, plain sack.

"You don't want to leave, do you?"

Aully shook her head without looking up.

Noni sighed. "You love him, don't you?"

"In a way, I suppose. I've known Lucius all my life."

"No, child, I mean the Thyne boy."

Of course that's what she meant, and they both knew it. Aully let her shoulders slump.

"I do," she whispered.

The ancient elf knelt down in front of her and took her by the shoulders. The opaque sheen that always covered her eyes seemed to fade away, leaving a pair of blue-green gems that shone with the strength and knowledge of one who'd lived for a very, very long time.

"Love is a whimsical thing, sweet dear," she said. "Completely unnecessary in the grand scheme of existence. When Celestia created us, her intention was to form a race of beings whose entire purpose would be to perfect themselves over time. So she made two separate groups—us, the Dezren, and the Quellans—to see which would achieve perfection first. Since the beginning, the Quellan have attempted to shed love from their relationships. All marriages are arranged, just as yours was, and copulation—you will know of it when the time comes—is, by rule, partaken in for breeding, not pleasure. Perfection is expected of all children, and every single day of their long lives is spent attempting to reach a state of absolute grace. These practices have made them a powerful race, much more so than us in our...current condition. To them we are weaklings, slaves to our feelings and personal imperfections. The Quellan say that had it not been for their fighting strength, we all would have perished when the demon kings ravaged our land."

Aully scrunched up her face, disturbed by her nursemaid's words.

"That can't be true," she said. "We're just as strong as they are. The stories say we fought by their side in the great war. And there *is* strength in love, strength that cannot be understood by those who don't own it."

Noni smiled. "Ah, from the mouths of babes," she whispered. "In many ways that is correct, my dear. But always remember that there are different paths to the same goals, and it is best to study those who are not like you, as well as to identify your own short-comings. Have I not tried to teach you this?"

"You have."

"Good. And you must also remember that any great strength is, at the same time, a great weakness. It creates pride. It blinds you to alternatives. No matter what happens, keep your eyes open and be ready. Do you understand?"

"I do," said Aullienna. "Thank you, Miss Noni."

The nursemaid stroked her fine, golden locks.

"I've lived many years," she said, her eyes softening again. "But you are something special, Aullienna. Never forget that, and never let them break you."

There was shouting in the hall outside her door, and Aully's heart leapt into her throat. Noni turned to the entryway, hold-ing her breath. Knuckles pounded on the wood, and Aully's father announced himself. When Noni unlocked the door, Cleotis stepped inside, his pale complexion an angry red along his cheeks.

"You both must come," he said, huffing, and turned in a whirl, the cloak he wore over his supertunic flapping like a banner in a strong wind. Aully and Noni both rose and hurried out behind him, joining the line of elves from Stonewood who were filing out of their rooms and progressing down the stairwell.

At the bottom, they were greeted by the smiling faces of Kindren's parents and a handful of their most devoted sentries. Kindren was nowhere to be seen, however, and something about the expressions on the Thynes' faces—especially that of Phyrra, Kindren's mother—seemed off. Their smiles were too wide, as if their flesh were a mask hiding something awful.

"Where is Lucius?" Cleotis asked them the moment he neared. "Where's Kara?"

"Why are the Ekreissar here?" shouted another of the Dezren elves, and many took up his cry.

"Are we at war?"

"Send the Ekreissar away! We are not prisoners!"

The din became so loud, it felt like Aully's brain would dribble out her ears. Lord Orden held out his hands, trying to calm the crowd, and Lady Phyrra shouted at the top of her lungs.

"Please quiet down, and we will explain everything to you!" After a few moments of mayhem, Aully's father joined Lord Orden's side, and his people listened. The roar shrank to a dull murmur.

Lord Orden stepped forward.

"I understand your confusion," he said, his voice cracking in a way that Aully didn't trust. To her youthful ears it sounded a lot like it did when he told her the forest was out of sweetbread just because he wanted her to stop asking for more. "I have been meeting with Neyvar Ruven all morning, as the arrival of his general, Aerland Shen, caught us off guard as well. However, I can assure you that the elite are here for a good reason. They've brought disturbing news with them from beyond the forest."

Lady Phyrra nodded gravely, backing her husband's words.

"When were we to be informed of this?" asked Aully's father. "And where are the people I sent to you?"

Lord Orden cleared his throat. Aully noticed a line of sweat trickling down his neck. He began to tug at his collar, and he and his wife shared a strange, offhanded glance.

"Please, come with us," he said. "The Neyvar wishes to explain everything himself."

Aully slipped out of Noni's grasp and pushed to the front of the assembly.

"Will Kindren be there?" she asked, louder than she'd intended. "Will I get to see him?"

Neither the lord nor lady answered her; they turned around and hurried out of the room through doors that were held open by their sentries. The crowd followed them, exiting into the open air beneath an ominous gray sky.

The trip to the gates of Palace Thyne was one Aully had taken nearly every day since arriving in Dezerea, but this morning her feet ached and her back throbbed, and it seemed to take twice, perhaps three times, as long. The Thynes led the Stonewood elves past the monument to Celestia, which stood off to the right of the path. The statue of the benign goddess was naked and standing on tiptoes, one arm crossed over her breasts and the other lifted skyward. On the evening of the New Year, her finger pointed directly to the goddess's star, burning brightly in the darkened heavens.

Once the monument was behind them, the front quad of the palace opened up. The countless Quellan Ekreissar loomed before them, maintaining formation on the very grounds that had hosted the Tournament of Betrothal not so long ago. Aully shivered as she glanced at them, each standing rigid, as stone-like as Celestia's statue, their eyes empty of any emotion. They crowded both sides of the path, forcing the procession to narrow. Aully found herself squeezed into the middle, too short to see where she was going, too slight of build to keep from being jostled by the crowd.

"Halt," she heard a voice shout, and she knew immediately that it was the Neyvar's.

Her mother's soft fingers gently wrapped around her forearm, the elegant Lady of Stonewood guiding her through the maze of elves until she stood front and center with her family. Aullienna was frightened by those who were facing them—Orden and Phyrra Thyne, flanked by the massive Aerland Shen with his black, fitted armor, and Neyvar Ruven, surrounded by the conspirators Conall, Aeson, and Iolas. Aully forced herself not to shiver, channeling Brienna's impudent strength, and she searched for Kindren amidst the throng. She didn't see him, but her gaze did find Ceredon. The prince of Quellassar stood off to the side, a queer expression overtaking his formerly beautiful features.

Aully's father turned and hushed the crowd before addressing the Neyvar.

"What is the meaning of this?" he asked. "Where are my people?"

"You mean those you sent to spy on us?" the Neyvar replied. He gestured with his left hand, and one of the sentries hauled out Lucius and Kara. Their hands were bound behind their backs, and a fresh bruise covered the right side of Kara's face, but otherwise they appeared unharmed.

The sentry shoved them forward, and the two lost their balance, falling into the empty space between Aully's family and the Neyvar. They started to rise, cursing under their breaths, but Aerland Shen planted a boot into each of their backs in turn, shoving them face first into the grass.

"It is disrespectful to play underhanded games with me," said Neyvar Ruven. "You only had to come to us and ask, and we would have informed you of the nature of my people's visit."

"And it is disrespectful to bring an armed force into this municipality during a time of peace," snapped Cleotis. His eyes fixed on Orden Thyne, fiery enough to burn holes into the lord's soul if that were possible. "*Especially* without informing your guests."

Aully watched as the Lord of Dezerea's posture slumped. She then looked over at the Neyvar, who began shaking his head in an odd way, as if he were about to admonish a child.

"You cannot blame the Thynes for their silence, Cleotis. They did not come to you because I did not allow it."

Cleotis seethed. "You aim to instruct a lord on how to act in his own territory?"

"I would do no such thing," said the Neyvar. "But Orden and Phyrra are Lords of Dezerea no longer."

He threw back his shoulders and addressed the congregation at large.

"The Quellan have hereby lifted the burden of leadership from the family Thyne, heaping that responsibility on our own capable backs. This is no longer Dezren land, but ours. The lord and lady have agreed to this of their own accord."

"Is this true?" Audrianna gasped.

Like her husband, Phyrra Thyne looked away.

"Why?" asked Cleotis.

Iolis, the elder of the Neyvar's cousins, opened his mouth to speak, but Neyvar Ruven shushed him.

"There are trying times ahead," he said, his tone confident and full of pride. "The humans march toward war, man on man, brother on brother. I fear even the gods will war, and all the world will suffer for it. And here stands Dezerea, directly in the middle of whatever will come."

A collective murmur spread through the swarm of Aully's people. Her father shook his head as if clearing water from his ears.

"So you're saying you brought your forces here...to *protect* us?"

Ruven smiled down at Cleotis as if he were terribly naïve.

"Protect?" the Neyvar said. "No, we will do more than protect. We have come to take sides. If hostilities do break out, the followers of Karak will hold the advantage, and we must be there to ensure a swift victory for them to minimize the damage done to Dezrel, as well as to our own people."

Aully's mother gasped. "You cannot be serious! The goddess herself instructed us not to meddle in the affairs of men. She handed the brother gods land to do with as they please. To throw ourselves into the fray is tantamount to blasphemy!"

The massive Shen growled, and Neyvar Ruven flipped his fingers toward the sky.

"Yes, the great Celestia demanded our neutrality—after asking us to ward the humans, which we denied of her! She split the land in two regardless, destroyed our homeland, and *left us destitute! This* is the goddess whose demands you wish to follow? Where is she?" The Quellan ruler lifted his angry gaze to the dark clouds overhead. "Celestia!" he shouted. "Do you hear me, goddess? Are we taking the wrong path? If so, strike me down now, or wrestle yourself from your beloved Ashhur's arms and instruct us on the right way! Can you do this? Can you? *Will* you?"

Aully watched the sky, hoping the clouds would part and the blinding light of her goddess would shine down, but nothing of the sort happened. The clouds continued to churn overhead, the same as they had been all morning.

"Do you see?" the Neyvar said. "Celestia does not care what we do. We are writers of our own destiny."

Aully's father suddenly turned to face her, dropping to one knee so he could look her in the eye. His fingers reached out and twined through her hair. A tear fell from one of his olive-shaped eyes, trailing over his nose and around the curve of his lips.

"I'm sorry I didn't believe you," he whispered.

Aully nodded, frightened and confused, her mother's hand pressed firmly on her shoulders from behind. She didn't like the look on her father's face.

Lord Cleotis slowly stood upright and raised his fists above his head. She'd never seen him more afraid—or braver.

"People of Stonewood!" he cried. "My brothers and sisters in faith, we cannot allow this blasphemy to go unanswered! If the Thynes wish to take part in this abomination, let them! But let us return home and remain as Celestia wished us to be—neutral."

The Neyvar grabbed his arm, whirling Cleotis around.

"You will not," Ruven Sinistel growled. He looked panicked, though his voice hid it well. "You no longer have a place in Stonewood. Our sympathizers have already overtaken the forest. Detrick Meln is lord there now."

Aully's father planted his fist in the Neyvar's chest, and the Quellan leader stumbled backward, clutching at his breast and gasping for air. Those gathered around him looked on with wide eyes, as if they were shocked that anyone would dare to raise a hand against their sovereign ruler.

"Liar!" Cleotis shouted. "Detrick is my brother, and faithful to his goddess. He would never betray my trust." He faced his people again. "We must depart! There is nothing more for us he—"

His words ceased abruptly as a black blur flashed across Aully's vision. Her mother screamed. A ring of red formed around her father's neck, and his head began to tilt forward, eyes bulging. Aully stared up at him, frozen. Cleotis's eyes looked into hers, but there was no recognition there, and his head kept slanting downward until it detached from his neck with a sickening *plop* and rolled down his chest. A geyser of blood erupted from the stump of his neck. Aully shrieked, caught in the shower of her father's life essence, holding her hands in front of her face as crimson droplets fell on her. Audrianna's hand left hers, her body falling limp as she collapsed in shock.

Everything became a blur. The intimidating Aerland Shen stood before her, blood dripping from one of his black blades. The Neyvar was shouting something about broken promises to the huge elf, but then one of the cousins—Conall—grabbed the Quellan ruler by the collar, screaming, "We are not slaves to the word of humans!" Aullienna saw Lucius and Kara stand up and try to fight, then watched helplessly as khandars burst from their chests, spilling even more blood on the grassy courtyard of Palace Thyne. She felt the Thyne sentries closing in from the front, the Ekreissar from the sides and back. She didn't see Ceredon, and somewhere deep in the anguished recesses of her mind she wished she could rip his disloyal throat out before she too was slaughtered. Then there were hands upon her, violently yanking her to her feet, dragging her across the blood-drenched lawn, while all around her people—her friends, family, and countrymen—screamed and screamed.

She was heaved through a door on the side of the palace and down a steep flight of stairs. Her head thumped with each footfall of the man who carried her. Once they reached the bottom of the stairwell, which led to a corridor lined with crude, barred cages, she was unceremoniously dumped into one of them, striking her head on the stone-littered, hay-strewn floor.

Her unconscious mother was dumped beside her, the stunning Audrianna of Stonewood looking like a corpse, her face and formerly exquisite clothes covered with dirt and her husband's blood. An angry voice shouted the vilest of insults her way, and then the cage door was slammed shut with such force that the vibration wracked her already frazzled nerves. She broke down right then and there, cradling her unconscious mother's hand, knowing that she would never see Brienna or Kindren again.

All the while, the screams and pleas of her dying people assaulted her ears.

She retreated inward, trying to hold onto the last shreds of her fleeing sanity, and above the din of torment that surrounded her, she imagined she heard the voice of her betrothed, howling for her in agony, trapped and alone, beyond her reach.

CHAPTER

23

S oleh had examined the handwriting of the Connington brothers, the king, Karl Dogon, and each member of the Council of Twelve, but it had led nowhere. She sent Pulo, Jonn, and Roddalin out to whisper among the merchants, including Matthew Brennan, trying to discover who might have a motive to sabotage her family. Still nothing. The only person she had yet to confront was the Highest himself, and that was only because he had yet to return.

If only Karak were here, she muttered to herself one cold morning. *I'm tired of secrecy and games. Surely he would be able to tell with a glance who wrote it.*

Once more she climbed her podium to preach Karak's word. The crowd before her was in stark contrast to those who had gathered when she'd first begun her sermons. Now they echoed her every word and listened to her on bent knees. Just as she was finishing up, a convoy of horses trotted through the portcullis, Clovis's white mare in the lead. Sure enough, the Highest sat in the saddle, his expression a mixture of irritation and bland resignation, the heavy shawl draped over his shoulders flapping as a cold wind blew

357

through the courtyard. There were another fourteen horses behind him, ridden by his daughter Avila, his son Crian, and other high-ranking officials from Karak's Army. All bore the red sigil of the lion over their chainmail.

She immediately thought of Vulfram—Vulfram, who now lingered in the Tower Keep, a shell of the man he'd once been. Often he cowered in his father's studio, watching Ibis sculpt whatever masterpiece he was currently working on. Other times he stumbled aimlessly through the empty halls, drink in hand.

He had not been sober since the day he rode through the castle gates with mind bent on murder, and his outward appearance was starting to suffer for it. His formerly bald pate began to grow stubbly, and his posture, slumped and defeated. At all times his eyes were bloodshot from drink and lack of sleep. He was like a man wasting away, and Soleh feared for both his health and his sanity. The fear that she kept silent—the one she was reluctant to whisper even to herself—was that he might end up like Adeline, ranting and raving like a loon. It pained her that all she could offer him was a loving shoulder to cry on each night as he bemoaned the fate of his daughter and the treachery that had brought about that fate.

Staring across the palace courtyard at the arriving envoy, she wondered if the Highest might indeed be responsible for it all. Clovis was many things—rude, pompous, at times irrationally violent, and impatient to the needs and qualms of the common populace—but he was not a deceiver.

"Worship is done for today," she announced, her eyes still fixed on Clovis, and she descended the podium amidst the confused mutterings of her parishioners. The convoy trod a wide path around the quad, heading for the rear stables. It was then, as she drew closer to them, that she finally peeled her eyes from Clovis and noticed the long red hair that was flopping over his son's shoulder. She stopped in her tracks, jaw agape, as her flock slowly drifted toward the gates.

Red hair was an extremely rare trait east of the Rigon, so rare she could not remember ever setting eyes on it. In Neldar, those who originated in the north were typically fair skinned, with the characteristic silver, blond, or chestnut hair color, whereas those from the south, such as Soleh's entire family, were generally darker of flesh, with curly tresses that ran the gamut from deep brown to black. Over the last ninety-some-odd years much interbreeding had occurred, causing some of the physical attributes to blend, but still…Soleh had never seen anything like that shock of red before in the east.

The red-haired girl riding behind Crian Crestwell leaned back, and Soleh caught a clear glimpse of her. She was small and looked very much like a child. Her cheeks were flecked with numerous tiny blemishes that seemed even brighter beneath the light of the deepest pair of blue eyes she had ever encountered. Unlike the northern Neldar blue, which seemed almost as clear as ice, this girl's irises were solid, like the azure hue found on the chests of hummingbirds or in the sky when the clouds cleared after a summer rainstorm.

This girl—whose wary expression conveyed an agedness that belied her youthful appearance—was from the western Paradise. In fact, she looked very much like Isabel DuTaureau, the matriarch of the second of Ashhur's First Families, whom Soleh had last seen forty years earlier, just after Karak had left his children on their own and she had relocated to this drab, chaotic city. She picked up her pace, lifting her dress so she wouldn't trip on the hem. Why was one of Ashhur's children here, and why was she riding so close to Clovis's youngest, her arms wrapped around his waist?

Soleh neared the entrance to Tower Justice, hoping to reach the procession before it moved out of sight, when the door to the tower flew open. Captain Gregorian stepped out, chest huffing, his skin red beneath his collar. She stopped short, staring up at him, as his one good eye found her two.

"Minister," he said, respectfully bowing. "Your presence is requested in the Arena."

"By whom?" she asked, trying to peer around the broad Captain. She caught one final glimpse of those scarlet locks before they disappeared around the edge of the tower.

"I cannot say," the Captain replied. "I only know that you must come. *Now.*"

His insistence captured her attention. Captain Gregorian was a man prone to neither over-excited utterances nor secrecy. His every word was measured and had been ever since he first stood before her, seeking judgment for his crimes. When he spoke with urgency, it was best to listen.

He nodded to her, silently communicating that she must go alone, and she brushed past him, dashing across the antechamber and down the stairs to the main dungeon. She shoved open the door to the Arena, running into the chamber so quickly that slamming into the sandstone balustrade was all that stopped her from toppling over the edge of the raised platform.

Soleh was surrounded by the flickering light of hundreds of torches, which revealed that the gates to the Judges' cages were open. Kayne and Lilah lay in the center of the arena, their heads resting in Karak's lap as he kneaded the furry flesh beneath their jowls. Her god's eyes were fixed on the massive beasts, a loving smile on his face, while purrs of ecstasy vibrated from the lions' throats.

"Sweet Soleh, come down here," Karak said without glancing up at her.

She descended the staircase mechanically, joy spreading through her body, though not enough to quash the uncertainty of everything that had happened over the past few days. Walking into the arena, she kept her head bowed low in reverence to the one who created her, the only entity she had ever truly loved.

"You have been busy," Karak said, continuing to knead the lions' necks. "I am proud of what you've done. When I entered the city on this morn, I felt respect from all I came across. Mothers presented their babes for me to bless, and men fell to their knees to pledge their thanks for the lives they have been given. The city appears to be much more at ease, much more…ordered…than before."

"I have only done as you asked, my Lord," she whispered, reverence dripping from her every word. "All is not perfect, however. I still have much work to do."

"You do," replied the god with a bob of his divine head. "But I am proud of you nonetheless. You never cease to prove that you are my most precious of creations. However, that is not why I called you here this day. We have other matters to discuss."

"What is it, my Lord?"

Karak lifted his right hand from Lilah's fur and held it up to her, palm raised. "You are carrying a deep concern in your mind as well as in the pouch on your belt. I wish to see the letter."

"You…you know?"

Karak's eyes met hers, and in them she saw the benevolence he had always displayed to her, but those golden orbs seemed different somehow, duller.

"I know many things, sweet Soleh. I am your creator, and your heart in particular sings to me from miles away."

She removed the folded parchment and placed it in the god's huge hand without hesitation. Karak leaned back and opened it. The letter looked so small in his godly clutches, like a useless scrap and nothing more.

"Vulfram brought this to me," she said. "It was given to him by the father of a boy he judged in Erznia. My son thinks it was written by the hand of the Highest, that there is a scheme to dishonor him and—"

"There is no scheme, sweet Soleh," Karak said, shifting his head to stare at her. He pinched the note between two fingers and held it up in the air. It caught fire before her eyes, burning from one corner to the other until it was nothing but a tiny, glowing cinder that dissipated in the arena's moist air. "This letter was not written by my Clovis."

"Then by whom, my Lord?"

"I have no way of knowing for certain. However, I can tell you with the utmost certainty that none of my most precious children had a hand in it."

"Could Broward Renson have written it?"

Karak shrugged. "Perhaps. It could be that the doomed man wished for the commander of my army to doubt his calling and hence spare him. But your son is a strong man, one of the strongest of my children, and I know that doubt does not come easily to him."

Soleh dropped her gaze. Part of her was relieved to hear that no conspiracy was afoot, but relief quickly turned to dread when she thought of telling her god the next part of the sorry tale. She didn't want to open her mouth but knew she had no choice.

"But you are wrong, my Lord," she said softly. "Vulfram *has* doubted. His faculties seem to have left him, and he has turned to drink. Each day he spends wallowing in the Tower Keep, muttering to himself of murder, treachery, and conspiracies. I fear that if Lyana is not returned, he will never become the man he once was." She knelt before her god, causing Kayne and Lilah to stir when she did so, and clasped her hands before her. "Please, my Lord, is there a chance of bringing Lyana back into the fold?"

Karak sighed, and Kayne and Lilah both lifted their heads from his lap, staring at her with shimmering golden eyes that seemed to convey more intelligence than ever.

"Sweet Soleh," Karak said, "the choices your granddaughter made were hers and hers alone. Though deceived by Renson, she could have declined to spread her legs or murder her unborn child. These are the laws I have decreed, and the penalties are binding. You know this. Lyana will forever be a Sister until the day she leaves the mortal coil behind. I am sorry, but that is the way it must be. Vulfram's wounds will heal. Humans are a resilient breed, and I have faith in him."

Soleh dropped her hands into her lap.

"I understand," she said. "And I hope you are right."

"I know you do, my child, and I am," said Karak. The god patted the lions on their heads and then shooed them away. They sauntered back into their open cages without hesitation, and Soleh couldn't help but feel shock when she saw them standing at their full height. They seemed even bigger than ever.

"There is something else I must discuss with you," the god then said. "I have returned from visiting the troops that have massed in Omnmount. The day of reckoning in Haven is fast approaching, and I require my most faithful to be completely dedicated to the task at hand. Did you catch sight of the convoy returning this morning? They must have arrived no more than a few minutes ago."

"I did," replied Soleh.

"And did you see something strange, something out of place in our land?"

"I did. The western girl."

Karak nodded. "Crian Crestwell has been engaged in a long-standing courtship with Nessa DuTaureau, the youngest daughter of Isabel DuTaureau, of my brother's First Families. In so doing, he broke the Crestwell family law and will therefore be stripped of his duties as Left Hand of the Highest. That duty is to be passed on to Avila Crestwell. Crian will be repositioned at the lowest rung of the City Watch, with his new residence in the Tower Keep."

"A dishonored Crestwell is to stay in our home?" gasped Soleh. "But why?"

"The Tower Keep is not your home, sweet Soleh, no more than Tower Honor is the home of the Crestwells. It is simply a lodging, far enough away from the castle that father and son need not see each other. I consider Crian to be an honorable boy, and his betrayal was one of the heart and loins, not the mind. He will be an asset to this kingdom, no matter what his function. He never renounced my name, as his sister Moira did. He may be a dishonored *Crestwell*, but I still look on him with love and affection."

"And what of the DuTaureau girl?" asked Soleh. "Is she to stay, as well?"

"She is, on the condition of conversion. In three days' time she will be baptized in my name, or she will be sent back to the land from which she came." The god laughed, and Soleh's ears rang with the hollowness of it. "I do not expect that the latter will come to pass, however."

Soleh swallowed hard. "And what of Vulfram, my Lord? What if I cannot break him from his stupor? What if he is not 'completely dedicated to the task at hand'?"

The god's eyes stared through her, chilling her very soul with their coldness.

"Then you had best make sure he comes around. If by the day of young Nessa's baptism he is still meandering in sorrow and distrust, the Highest will have no choice but to replace him as Lord Commander. I am sure you do not want that to come to pass, do you, Soleh?"

She shook her head.

"Make sure his soul has healed by then," the god said. Karak rose to his feet and walked past her, saying nothing else. The torches burning on the wall behind her were suddenly extinguished, pitching half of the underground chamber into darkness. Wind rushed past her ears, followed by a *whoosh* that rocked her on her knees, and when she glanced over her shoulder, Karak was gone.

"I will try," she said, and then departed, leaving the shadows behind.

His vision swam, his stomach cramped, and yet still Vulfram tilted back the skin, pouring more stinging liquor down his throat. He stumbled down the corridor, bumping into walls, toppling end tables, almost starting a fire at one point when he knocked over a candle. He extinguished the flames with one of the many tapestries hanging from the walls, ruining the finely crafted embroidery in the process.

He didn't care.

Using Darkfall as a crutch, the sword's tip striking the stone floor of the Tower Keep with a hollow *clunk* with each wavering step, he continued mindlessly on his way. Images of Yenge, whom he had left behind without so much as a good-bye, and Lyana, who was even now performing whatever unholy servitude was demanded of her by the Sisters of the Cloth, wouldn't leave his mind. He heard Adeline's mad cackling echo from somewhere within the keep's cavernous walls, and the sound made him tremble and cackle along with her.

You and I are the same, sister, he thought, laughing to himself. *We will meet on the other side of sanity, and only then will we find peace.*

He grinned, gripping Darkfall's hilt with sweaty palms. His fanatical laughter turned to sobs as he thought once more of his daughter, of her childlike face staring back at him in torment and disbelief as he whipped the flesh from her back.

It was Karak's will, he told himself. *She only received what she deserved.*

And yet he couldn't make himself believe that. Lyana was *his daughter*, blood of his blood, a precious creature who should have been nurtured, not sent off to live a life of perverse servitude. Anger churned in his gut, turned his heart into an iron fist that slammed into his ribcage with nearly enough force to break the delicate bones there. All excuses washed away, leaving behind a single, simple declaration that repeated over and over again in the foreground of his thoughts, one he had never believed, for all the life of him, that he would ever utter.

Fuck Karak.

His angry sobs grew in intensity, and he took a final swig from his skin. When it was empty, he tossed it aside with so much force that he smashed a vase filled with colorful wild irises. He continued on his aimless journey, wanting nothing more than for the liquor to do its magic and send him into the oblivion he had so frequently sought since that fateful day.

Before long he found himself on the first floor of the keep, staring across the open hall at the bottom of the steep staircase. His shaky vision shifted to the entrance to his father's studio. None of the usual sounds emerged—no clanking, no grinding, no grunts of exertion as the man whose seed had created him fashioned yet another stone monument to the god in whose image he had been molded. *Father must be asleep already*, he thought, which seemed odd. Vulfram hadn't seen him all day—though in fairness, his thoughts had been locked in such a drunken stupor, he rarely knew when one day ended and the next began.

He stepped into the darkened studio, all the perfect renderings of Karak staring back at him in disappointment and accusation beneath the thirty-foot ceiling. Their features shifted in and out of focus, bathed in yellow from the flickering candlelight that filtered in from the hall. The same sort of gut-wrenching vertigo he always felt when inside this room followed, dropping him to his knees as bile rose in the back of his throat. Darkfall slipped from his grip and clattered to the hard ground. He crawled across the floor and rested his head against the raised threshold of the arched doorway, waiting for the feeling to pass.

He was breathing deeply, trying to quell the coming sickness, when suddenly the sound of rushing wind filled his ears. The door to the keep opened and closed, and then voices echoed off the walls, speaking in a hushed conversation that was peppered with uneasy laughter.

Curiosity momentarily curing him of his ills, Vulfram straightened up and peered around the edge of the doorway, his eyes catching sight of four people who were standing in the middle of the hall, locked in quiet conversation.

His mother was there, looking elegant in her purple dress, her shoulders covered with a heavy shawl. His father stood beside her, hands on his hips, not speaking, and Vulfram shuddered at the sight of him. When the other two figures came into focus, Vulfram furrowed his brow in confusion, for before his parents stood the Left Hand of the Highest, Crian Crestwell, Clovis's youngest child. A broad smile stretched across the young man's face, one that belied the cautious expressions of Vulfram's mother and father. Even stranger, however, was the small wisp of a girl whose hand was locked in Crian's. She was absolutely beaming, a perfect illustration of youthful innocence, with a shock of bright red hair and a lithe frame. She was gazing up at Crian with the same sort of naïve wonder with which his wife had once looked at him. It was a look that spoke of the clarity of dreams, the purity of love. Tears formed in Vulfram's eyes once more, and he had to hold his breath in order to stay his faltering composure.

"This will be your home for the foreseeable future," his mother said to the young couple. "There is a room for you upstairs, but mind you, the one next to our daughter Adeline's. Her raving may prove an unwanted antidote for sleep. If it becomes a problem, please let me know, and I can prepare a chamber higher up in the tower."

"I'm sure it will be fine," replied Crian, gazing lovingly at the girl on his arm. "As long as Nessa is by my side, there is nothing we cannot overcome."

"How quaint," said Vulfram's father.

The group made their way toward the stairwell. Vulfram caught a glimpse of his mother's face, hardened yet striving for compassion, a look he had seen often of late as the pressures of her duty as Minister of Justice bore down on her soul.

She said, "I hope you realize how fortunate you two are. You assaulted your sister and deserted your post. And you, Nessa...you have blasphemed against your own creator. That is unprecedented in this land, and I imagine in yours as well. I have had men executed for lesser offenses. Crian, I do not know why your father has chosen to spare you both. What you did to your sister alone deserves harsh punishment. Though your lives will be difficult from here on out, you should look at this turn of events as a blessing. Your heads could very well be set on spikes right now."

"I know, Minister," said Crian, but the way he smiled broadly and held the young girl showed he didn't truly understand the threatening words that came from her mouth. He was oblivious, as was this strange Nessa, the two of them trapped in a bubble of infatuation.

Vulfram and Yenge had been like that once. A long, long time ago.

That was when Vulfram noticed a strange rectangular object wedged beneath Crian's arm. It was a mirror, framed with elegantly polished ivory. He had seen a similar one hanging from the wall in the Renson library. The sight of it set his blood to boiling, and his thoughts started spinning wildly.

The group started up the stairs, continuing their conversation, and when they were out of sight, Vulfram eased his way quietly out of the studio. He crept to the bottom of the stairwell, trying to decipher what was being said.

It was his mother's voice he heard next.

"...as your father the Highest knows, the position is a difficult one. It is a lot of responsibility for one person, especially considering the duties he already holds. But should he take up the mantle for himself, I am sure he will make a fine Lord Commander...."

The voices became muffled after that, as the four climbed higher up the tower. Vulfram felt faint and collapsed against the wall. The words he'd heard replayed in his mind, creating dark scenarios that threatened to undo the very fabric of his being.

His mother had betrayed him. His kingdom had betrayed him. His *god* had betrayed him. And though it didn't come without its own form of heavy-handed guilt, given the way he had profaned against Karak this very evening, anger rose within him. He twirled around, making his way uneasily back to his father's studio and snatching Darkfall from the ground. The sword had come to rest at the feet of a white marble sculpture of Karak, standing ten feet tall. He reared back and lopped the head from the statue with a mighty swipe. It clanked to the floor, cracking in two upon impact. The two halves rocked in place, both eyes seeming to stare up at him accusingly.

Vulfram slumped down, letting the sword trail out before him. In his inebriated mind, the conspiracy deepened. The mirror was further proof. They were all against him; they wished to devastate his family, take his mantle of leadership, and leave him a ranting lunatic like his sister. And then there was Crian. The man had broken his oaths, attacked his sister, and been caught red-handed with his red-headed tart. Yet Crian had been allowed a stay of punishment, given the opportunity to live his life in whatever way he saw fit, all the while holding onto the western deserter he loved.

But Lyana, whose only sin had been naïveté and fright, was being forced to perform heinous acts as a form of sadistic punishment.

The world spun out of control, and Vulfram collapsed, holding his head in his hands, wailing to the empty hall that he wanted a second chance, that he deserved it. He'd been loyal over the many years of his life, loyal as he bore down the whip and scarred the flesh of his beloved. He wailed and wailed over the fact that everything that had happened was, at its core, not fair in the slightest.

CHAPTER

24

They set up camp in a rock-strewn valley. Jacob was unusually silent while striking his flint, the sparks he created bringing his body in and out of focus like a phantom. Roland wanted to offer to take up the camp-making duties, as doing so might take his mind off the air's numbing iciness, but he refrained. The First Man was frustration personified at the moment. Seven days of searching, of winding deeper into the Tinderlands and then back toward the river, and nothing had crossed their path—no stray humans, no wild beasts, not even a pack of wolves. Traversing the barren terrain was akin to hiking across an endless, dead steppe. Even during the cloudless days, when the sun shone down on the land with all the intensity it had in the south, there was an ever-present chill in the air. The small spattering of grass that covered the stony earth was brown and dead, brittle as hay, and there were wide swaths of ice that seemed to appear from out of nowhere.

Roland sighed. The trip across the Tinderlands had been a monotonous undertaking for the most part. The only excitement the group had experienced occurred on the first day, after he, Jacob, Brienna, and Azariah crossed the narrow strip of rapids opposite the defensive tower the Drake villagers were constructing. They had been greeted by a mudslide on the other side of a hill they crested. Roland had plummeted down the slope, flipping and slipping and whacking his head on dried roots and hard stones. When his descent finally came to an abrupt stop, he found himself surrounded by craggy rock faces on all sides, standing tall and dead like monuments to long-forgotten gods. He emerged covered with sticky sludge, his brain pounding in his skull, his entire body sore. When he called out to the other members of his party, he discovered them spread out along this odd desert of crude, naturally formed shrines. All but Jacob, that is. They searched the maze for hours, not discovering him until well past dusk, sprawled out on his back, moaning. Brienna had needed to slap him across the face to wake him.

Now the seventh day of searching came to a close, the sun dipping behind the mountains, allowing the blackness to swallow them whole. The mudslide and maze seemed so long ago. The monotony of each passing day bore down on him, causing his feet to twitch impatiently. He wanted to leave this place now, wanted to go home before something bad happened to them in this dead land.

Azariah warmed his long, elegant hands before the fire, his words breaking the lengthy silence.

"I think one of the villagers might have gone insane," he said, the firelight reflecting in his eyes.

"Why would you say that?" asked Brienna.

The Warden raised his hands and gestured all around him. "Take a look. There is nothing about. This place is completely, irrevocably dead."

Brienna muttered something incomprehensible in response.

"There *is* something out here," said Jacob. Roland glanced at his master, watching him toy with his knife while he sat there with crossed legs.

"I think you are mistaken," said Azariah.

"I think not," Jacob snapped back. "I *know* there is something out here. We're close. I can feel it."

Azariah laughed. "You're becoming as delusional as the villagers then, my friend. Perhaps it is *you* who has lost his senses. Should I be sleeping with one eye open from now on?"

"Perhaps you should."

"Boys," said Brienna, her tone weary. "Can we please stop this? My head aches. I need sleep."

"Very well," said Azariah.

Brienna turned to her lover. "Jacob, please come here. I need comfort tonight."

Jacob jammed his knife into the ground and stood up. He sauntered around the fire, an odd look of frustration painted across his features, and slipped beneath the blankets with which Brienna had covered herself. The elf wrapped herself around him, and he around her, pulling the blankets up over their heads. Roland expected to hear the muffled giggles that usually came next, and to see the pile of blankets bulge and shift as the couple wrestled playfully, but it remained still but for the steady rise and fall of their breathing.

There would be no games tonight, it seemed. Brienna's mood had soured along with Jacob's. This awful place had once been her homeland, lush and alive and teeming with game. Now it was cold, desolate, and uninhabitable. All this she had told him one night while they shivered together in front of the fire, Brienna pining for the beauty of Kal'droth, her every word followed by harsh and biting profanities.

Roland took a swig from his waterskin, then uncorked the small vial of apple brandy Ephraim Wendover had given him and downed a gulp of that as well. The liquor warmed him ever so slightly, taking the most abrasive edge off the cold, but the feeling didn't last long. To Roland, the cold was the absolute worst part of this entire, ill-fated journey. He thought he'd had it rough on the way to Drake, but the town had seemed downright balmy compared to where he was now. In the Tinderlands, he found, the cold was a living thing, a demon that circled him at all times, crystallizing the moisture in the air, filling his lungs with its frigid evil, making every breath laborious. No matter how many layers he piled atop himself—and Turock Escheton had been more than generous in supplying them with the necessities for their journey—his body was locked in a near-constant shiver. Even pushing himself physically didn't seem to help, as exertion only made him sweat, and that sweat soon cooled, occasionally freezing on his flesh and making him colder than ever. He thought to ask Azariah for a swig from the large wooden carafe he carried with him, but the Warden was fast asleep, bundled to the neck, and snoring heavily.

Roland was all alone—the last conscious being in a land of the dead.

He lay awake for a long time, coverlets stacked atop him. Halfway through the night, as always, the cold invaded even those. The combination of the chill and the uncomfortable hardness of the uneven ground beneath him told him to give up on sleep. He sat up, poked a twig into the bed of glimmering coals, and tossed another couple of dried-out logs onto them. They caught fire almost immediately, crackling as the flames grew higher. If there was one good thing about the Tinderlands, it was the fact that there was plenty of undisturbed and well-seasoned firewood about.

He sat there for some time, poking at the fire, adding more sticks while his mind drifted to home. He was thinking of Mary Ulmer and the way her perky little breasts heaved whenever she scrubbed the family laundry in a thin, sheer blouse two sizes too small for her, when a strange sound echoed through the valley. The stirring in his abdomen retreated. For days he had heard nothing but the hiss and pop of the fire come evening, along with Azariah's snores, but this was different—this was foreign. He froze in place, afraid to move, when he heard it again. It was an odd sound, like waves crashing against living rocks, making them all sigh at once.

The third time it happened, a very human-sounding scream followed, and Roland tore off his blankets and shot to his feet. He frantically lit the end of a dried stick and thrust it all about, searching for whatever beast was stalking them. The sound came a fourth time, and he retreated a step, tripping over the lump of Jacob and Brienna in the process. He careened backward, the dark vertigo playing tricks on him, and smacked his elbow when he landed.

"Ouch!" he exclaimed.

"What in the name of Ashhur?" Jacob's voice called out.

Roland flipped onto his stomach and lifted his head. The light from his quaint fire was enough to illuminate Jacob and Brienna's sleepy, stunned gazes. He opened his mouth to tell his master about what he had heard, but the effort was unnecessary. The sound rang out through the valley again, louder than before, this time not fading away, but seeming to linger, like fizz bubbling at the top of a mug of mead. It was droning and deep, yet its tone was oddly inconsistent.

"What was that?" asked Brienna.

Roland shrugged.

"How long has it been happening?" asked Jacob.

"Not long. A few minutes, maybe."

Roland watched Jacob cock his head. When the sound came again, still increasing in volume, the First Man grinned.

"I knew it," he whispered.

A short while later—it had taken a bit of effort to rouse Azariah, who was a deep sleeper—the quartet was wandering through the darkness, a single torch lighting their way. They progressed in a single line: Jacob in the lead, Brienna behind him, Roland third, and Azariah taking up the rear, each holding the shirt of the one in front so as not to fall out of line. The strange sound increased in frequency and consistency the farther north they tread, until it became as ever present as the insects that rubbed out their nightly song back in Safeway's numerous gardens. Roland's heart started to race. He knew he should be frightened, but Jacob diffused that fear with his unyielding excitement and curiosity. The fact that his master wasn't scared meant he shouldn't be either.

The noise led them up a steep incline, the loose rocks underfoot making each step treacherous, and then along a narrow ridge, the right edge of which fell into a steep drop. Jacob kept his eyes focused on the landscape before him, calling out urgent whispers to those following him whenever he came across a potential hazard. Somehow, despite the array of dips and cracks and sharp stones that littered their path, all four of them made it across the precipice without losing their footing.

And still the sound rose in volume.

Jacob steered them downward, through a narrow passage cut into the rock that reminded Roland very much of the Cavern of Solitude back home, complete with the sharp edges jutting from either side. With Jacob's torch as their only light, Roland found himself flailing in the darkness. Once he veered too close to the wall, and a pointed stone slashed through his heavy woolen tunic, leaving a shallow gash on his arm. Roland bit down his cry. The last thing he wanted to do was to appear a burden to the others.

The cavern emptied out behind a row of boulders twice his size. A strange glow lit the top of the boulders, flushing the surface red and yellow. Once they emerged, the strange sound could be recognized for what it was—voices chanting. It was almost like prayer, an everyday occurrence for anyone who had been born and raised in Paradise. Jacob stopped, extinguished his torch, and pressed them all against the rocks, raising a finger to his lips. He was still grinning.

"I think this is another valley," he whispered. "Proceed with caution. We do not know who lies beyond this wall."

They all nodded in silent agreement and followed him.

The wall of stone progressed in a curve, the narrow duct they found themselves in gradually expanding until they had room to walk abreast of one another. The height of the wall lowered, allow-ing in more light from the other side. Roland tugged at his collar, sweat building up at the base of his neck, and it took him a few moments to realize he was no longer cold. In fact, he felt hotter than he had on the most sun-drenched summer day while slather-ing fresh tar on Jacob's roof. Though it was a surreal feeling, he was silently thankful that his bones were no longer rattling.

A few hundred yards farther along the crevasse, they came upon a gap in the wall. Jacob halted them there, gazing around the uneven stone portal, his entire body bathed in red light. Roland saw his eyes widen, his jaw drop open, and his hands fall to his sides.

"What is it?" asked Brienna.

Jacob turned toward her slowly and then moved so that the rest of them could get a look at whatever strange ritual was taking place on the other side. It seemed to take forever for the line to progress, and impatience tickled the back of Roland's throat and tingled in his legs.

When he finally arrived at the gap, squeezing in next to the beautiful elf while Azariah wedged his head in on the other side, he understood Jacob's shocked reaction.

It wasn't a valley below them, but a ravine, a bowl-shaped gorge of blackened rock and glistening crystal. A large group of cloaked individuals had gathered, hundreds of them, all arranged in five tightly packed groups. They were on their knees, folded over at the waist as if in appeal to a god, their outstretched arms pointing toward a gigantic bonfire so bright it was as if the sun itself had dropped from the sky and settled there. They chanted in a language Roland didn't recognize. It sounded nothing like Elvish, and was as far removed from human dialect as the chirping of insects.

Hands grabbed either side of his head and moved it, shifting his field of vision. "Look at that," Jacob whispered into his ear. "I knew it."

Jacob had brought his attention to at a single man who was standing on the outskirts of the gathered worshippers. From a distance, Roland couldn't make out his facial features, but he could tell that the man was bald and wore a long black robe. His arms were lifted up toward the star-dappled sky. This was the man who was leading the chanting, and each time words exited his mouth, the rest of the congregation answered.

"Who is it?" Roland whispered.

"Uther Crestwell," Brienna answered. She gave Roland a grave look, then Azariah, and finally turned about to fix Jacob with an intense, knowing stare. "The mad priest. You were right."

"Unfortunately," Jacob replied.

"Is that Karak's Army?" asked Roland, not understanding what they were talking about.

Jacob swallowed hard, gesturing for Roland to keep watching what was going on below. "Part of it, I assume," he said in a soft voice. "But it's worse than I thought."

"Why?"

"Uther Crestwell, better known as the mad priest, is a zealot. Before I left Neldar for good, he and I argued about the practicality of having a land divided by three deities. He was an outcast of his own family, yet so dedicated to Karak that no one dared deny him his birthright, as they did his sister Moira. He believed Karak and only Karak should rule Dezrel, and even went so far as to suggest genocide for not just those created by the other gods, but the other gods themselves. Hence his more common name, for those brave enough to use it. Twenty years ago he retreated to the Crestwell stronghold in the north, at the base of Mount Hailen. Then, from what I've heard, he began researching the magics of blood and darkness, which were expelled from this realm long before the dawn of humanity."

"The same sort of magics that were used by those demons you told me about?" asked Roland.

Jacob smiled. "Yes, Roland. It is good to know you listened."

"What does he mean to do?"

At that, Jacob frowned. His lips compressed a thin white line and he shrugged.

"I guess we need to find out," he said, turning his attention back to the happenings below.

A change had come over the assembly during their short conversation. The worshippers were standing now, and the man in charge—Uther, the mad priest—had moved into the throng and was standing directly in front of the raging, unnaturally bright bonfire. He motioned with one outstretched hand, and six more cloaked figures appeared from the other side of the ravine. Roland felt his blood rush through his veins as he watched them drag three individuals—a man, a woman, and a young girl—dressed in torn and filthy rags across the blackened, uneven floor of the culvert. They were handled roughly, without any care for their well-being, treated like they were less than animals. Roland remembered what Turock had said about the family that had been taken—*the Rodderdams, that was it*—and his breath caught in his throat.

The prisoners screamed and pleaded, and Roland watched the woman pound her fists into the hard-packed ground. Her keeper, faceless behind his black hood, violently yanked her arm until she stopped.

"We must do something," he heard Azariah say, a frightened sort of rage rising in his voice.

"And what is that?" Jacob asked. "The four of us against hundreds? We watch and learn, so others may learn as well. That is the best we can do here."

The Warden had no reply to that, and Brienna began to silently sob.

Back in the gully, the prisoners were forced to their knees, facing the blaze. Uther took his place before them, hands clasped in front of him, head down so that the fire reflected off his bald pate. Then he reached into the sleeve of his cloak and withdrew a dagger. The mother and daughter shrieked and began to struggle once more, this time so fiercely that it took eight men from the congregation to hold them in place.

Uther lifted his gaze skyward, and Roland thought he could make out the whites of the mad priest's eyes in spite of the distance. Then he shouted a series of nonsensical phrases into the air, barking like a dog, twirling his hands in circles, firelight dancing off the dagger's blade. Jacob gasped, and Roland felt the First Man's hand wrap around his arm, squeezing so tightly that his fingers began to numb.

"No, no, no," repeated Jacob.

"What?" asked Brienna, sniffling.

Jacob pointed to the far wall of the ravine, where a strange symbol, three diagonal lines intersected and overshadowed by a large circle, had been carved.

"I know why the villagers were taken. I know that symbol. I know *this place*. According to legend, back when Kal'droth still existed and this ravine was filled with rushing water, it was here that the war with the demon kings ended. It was here that Celestia banished the monsters from Dezrel, sending them to an unknown point in the universe."

"So that means what, exactly?" Azariah asked.

A red shadow crossed Jacob's face.

"Uther is trying to resurrect them."

"And will it work?" Azariah asked, the blood seeming to drain from his face.

Jacob shook his head.

"But how can you be sure?" asked Roland.

"Because they're in the wrong place," Jacob said, adamant.

A scream split the night, and Roland glanced through the rocky portal to see Uther standing above the woman. He clutched her hair in one hand, yanking back her head, while the other lifted the dagger. The zealot plunged the blade into her neck, and even from high above Roland could see blood gushing from the wound, soaking the front of Uther's robe. Brienna threw her hands over her mouth and backed away from the portal, eyes squeezed shut.

Shrieks reverberated from down below. Uther moved to the man next, performing the same duty with his sharp blade, and then finished off the young, sobbing girl. In moments, the Rodderdams were no more than three bodies bleeding out on the ground. Uther then went about tearing open their tattered clothes, using the dagger that had taken their lives to carve dreadful runes on their backs.

Roland felt like he was going to be sick. It was the first time he had ever watched anyone die, let alone in such a violent manner. Life with Jacob was steadily becoming a never-ending string of unwanted firsts.

When the mutilation of the corpses was complete, those who had dragged the prisoners before the congregation returned. One by one they tossed the bodies into the bonfire, the flames rising higher as each corpse was fed to it. Uther turned to face the blaze, dropped to his knees, raised his hands, and began chanting once more.

Bolts of black and purple lightning danced from Uther's fingertips, growing both deeper and brighter in the same instant. Jacob and Azariah gasped, while Roland simply watched, spellbound and horrified. The raging of the bonfire diminished, darkening the air, and an inky pool of blackness appeared above the flames. It started out the size of an apple but grew with each passing second, until it looked large enough to swallow a man whole. The sphere of blackness undulated and writhed, as if alive, the meniscus stretching into ungodly shapes.

For the first time, Roland heard the sadistic man's true voice as he shrieked up at the writhing orb.

"Come, beasts of the underworld, lords of death, emissaries of the darkness, reveal yourselves now and bow before the glory of Karak!"

The floating sphere rippled, looking like a school of tiny fish were pecking at it madly just beneath the surface. The bonfire's flames flared once more, licking the bottom of the orb. Uther shouted in disbelief, and the orb seemed to collapse in on itself, folding over and over again, a shriek emanating from within that was so shrill, Roland thought it might burst his eardrums. He covered his ears, the pain so intense it whitewashed his thoughts, and he screamed along with the orb, his voice completely drowned out.

And then he *could* hear his own voice, as well as Brienna's and Azariah's. He felt hands on his back, shoving him, pulling him, shaking him. He opened his eyes to find his three companions staring back at him, each of their faces a mask of panic.

"Run," Jacob said, but he could barely hear the words through the echo inside his skull. He stood still, frozen by his lack of understanding, even as Brienna and Azariah scampered away, disappearing around the bend of the narrow causeway. Roland turned toward the portal, saw a multitude of eyes staring up at him. Their screams had lasted longer than that of the sphere, alerting the murderous bastards to their presence. Some of the men began to dart out of sight, disappearing below the wall.

Jacob grabbed his shoulders and shook him, hard.

"Come on, Roland!" he shouted. "Snap out of it!"

He did, albeit sluggishly. Jacob took his hand and yanked him around the bend, heading back the way they had come. Only this time they didn't break off where they had originally entered the chasm, instead continuing to follow it in a wide circle, even as the sound of shouted orders and the clank of metal on rock sounded all around them.

"We missed the opening!" said Roland.

Jacob pulled him harder.

"I know a different way."

It was a different way indeed. Just as the cloaked men appeared ahead of them, brandishing swords and daggers, Jacob leapt on top of the passage's low-standing wall. The First Man still had a grip on Roland's wrist, so he had little choice but to follow his lead. They dashed across the thin ridge until Roland noticed that his rapid footfalls were now splashing instead of thumping. Jacob then leapt off the other side, dragging Roland along with him. They hit a slope, ice-cold water cascading all around them, propelling them downward. The freezing water made every nick and scrape Roland had amassed on the way down hurt far more.

They hit solid ground without warning, because the moon was shielded from them by what Roland now realized was a hollowed-out mountain. He scampered to his feet, no longer attached to Jacob, and tried to follow the sound of his master's voice as he scurried across the hard, slate-like ground.

"It's only a few more feet!" Jacob shouted. "Stay with me!"

The sound of rushing water reached his ears, and suddenly Roland was grabbed from behind. His feet flew out from under him and he dangled in the air, as if flying, until his legs swung back down and his heels collided with the earth.

"Shit," he heard Jacob mutter.

"What now?" asked Brienna's voice, and Roland was thrilled to realize that the elf was with them.

"Look at them all," said Azariah, revealing his presence as well.

Roland's eyes began adjusting to the dark, and he glanced down and saw that his feet were positioned perilously close to the rocky riverbank. Only Jacob's arm, firmly wrapped around his waist, had spared him from a terrible fall. The river was wide and moving swiftly, numerous white caps appearing and disappearing, seeming to glow in the faint light. There were a great many rafts floating there, bobbing up and down, stretching the ropes that tethered them to shore.

The rumble of countless running feet seemed to be closing in from behind them. Jacob pulled Roland away from the river's edge, depositing him a few feet away, and then shouted, "You two—get in a raft!"

Roland heard swishing and clunking as Brienna and Azariah climbed aboard one of the rickety boats.

"I'll meet you in Drake," Jacob said, and Roland saw the reflection of light off steel as Jacob whipped out his knife and slashed through the rope. The raft began to drift away quickly, as if it were being pulled by an invisible string on the other side.

Still the robed men came closer.

"Are we next?" asked Roland, bracing himself on the edge of the bank and testing the solidity of the next raft.

"No water for us, son. We're sticking with dry land."

Before he could protest, Jacob leapt to action, working his way down the line, cutting the tethers that held the rafts in place. When he was done, he rushed back to Roland and grabbed him again. The mob of angry Karak worshippers sounded like it was right on top of them.

"Sorry, but I had to do that," panted Jacob as he dragged him quickly along. "Couldn't let the bastards chase after the others. If they go on foot, they'll have a much harder time catching them."

"And what...about...us...?" Roland was able to wheeze. His lungs felt like they were on fire as his exhausted, frozen limbs struggled to keep up.

"You and I, we hit the high ground. Lose them in the cliffs."

As the land beneath his feet began to rise sharply upward and the burn in his muscles became so intense, it felt as though he'd been dipped into a vat of magma, Roland couldn't help but wish his master had let them climb onto the last raft before cutting the rope.

CHAPTER

25

B ardiya felt his god's presence long before he arrived. It was an itch that spread inward from his extremities, settling in his chest, making his heart thrum quickly with anticipation. His knees began to quake as he sat cross-legged on the hot desert sand. He opened his eyes, which had been closed for untold hours while he honored the memory of his dearly departed parents, and stared at the black monument before him.

The Black Spire was a magnificent natural creation, a twenty-foot-high slab of sparkling onyx, granite, and clay that had broken through the thin earthen crust when the world was first created, rising into the desert sky like the giant finger of a deity pointing the way toward salvation. The Dezren elves called it *Ker-dia*, which meant "the light of night" in their peculiar native tongue. Bardiya's father had told him the Black Spire was the first landmark they'd come across after Ashhur gave life to his First Families, when Ezekai and his fellow Wardens led Bessus, Damaspia, and the litany of wailing babes to the land that would become their home. Bessus thought the Spire, a beacon that swallowed moonlight and cast it out tenfold, was a gift from Ashhur, a lighthouse in the middle of a tranquil yet hazardous sea of sand, and he'd dubbed this land Ker in its honor.

The endless stretch of rolling dunes around the Black Spire, miles from the nearest vegetation or water source, became a secluded holy place. It was also the final resting site for all Kerrians; their bodies were buried beneath the shifting sands, and the light emanating from the Spire guided their souls to the gateway of the golden afterlife.

An ache of sadness overcame Bardiya as he thought once more of the corpses buried here. It did not escape him that Bessus and Damaspia Gorgoros, along with the rest of their brethren who had been slaughtered by Stonewood elves, were the first individuals in all of Ashhur's Paradise to expire before their time. Never before had anyone lost their lives due to a fit of rage or perished from sickness or an animal attack—though Lamarto Dusoros, one of Bardiya's childhood friends, had come close once, when a hunt went badly and he found himself on the wrong end of a hyena's claws. Bardiya remembered the blood spilled that day, the screams as Lamarto lay writhing in the tall grasses of western Ker, crying out for his god, his mother begging the healers to come quickly.

And yet the healers *had* arrived, and after Warden Ezekai channeled Ashhur's power, it was as if Lamarto had never fallen beneath the beast's attack. But no Wardens or healers had been there when Ethir brought his elves to destroy Bardiya's parents.

Bardiya placed his hands on the sand before him, sifting it, feeling its tiny granules as they rubbed against his flesh. They were under there, two supposed immortals whose bodies were now rotting, becoming one with the land that had created them. Yet he could feel no sorrier for them than any of the others who had died that day—Zulon, Tunitta, Hermano, Cruckus, and Drieson, good men and women, all so young, so full of life. They would never breathe the air again, nor run with the horses across the plains, nor hunt, nor splash in the river, nor help raise the side of a cabin—and that fact hurt Bardiya more than anything.

He touched his shoulder, where Ethir's sword had tried to halve him, and felt the soreness beneath his fingers. The wound was stitched and scabbed over, hidden beneath a thick layer of healing mud. He had refused the healers' magic, insisting that the gash should heal on its own. Had it been wiped from his body, he feared he might one day forget it had ever been there, and if he forgot that, then what of the rest of his memories? Forgetting was something he could not do, *would not* do, and he allowed that horrible day to linger in his mind even as the shimmering loveliness of his god's looming presence washed over him.

Heavy footsteps pounded the sand. Bardiya glanced to the east and saw Ashhur's towering figure span a dune's crest, though somehow he looked shorter than usual. The god was dressed simply, in a plain white robe and a pair of sandals. The last time Bardiya had seen him, his hair had been long, almost down to the middle of his back, but now both his hair and his beard were trimmed and neat. His stride was purposeful, each step seeming almost rigid or angry, making Ashhur appear much unlike the whimsical and peace-loving deity he had known all his life.

Bardiya's heart clenched with fear.

Ashhur didn't once look at him directly, even when the god stopped before the Spire, his chin tilting back so that he could gaze on its gleaming apex. A hand did fall to his shoulder, however—his injured one, at that—and Bardiya breathed a sigh of relief. He felt Ashhur's calming energy flow through him, just as constant and reassuring as it had ever been. Ashhur began whispering to the spire. Bardiya bowed his head and prayed along with him.

"Where are they buried?" Ashhur asked softly, breaking a long silence.

"Right beneath me," Bardiya answered without raising his head.

"And where are your brothers and sisters?"

"I sent them away yesterday. I wished to be alone. With my parents, I mean."

He felt Ashhur nod. "I understand. I felt the pain of his loss the moment his heart ceased to beat...just as I feel the loss of all my children when they depart this realm. There was a piece of me in each of them, and when that piece is ripped away, it aches."

"I know, Your Grace. So you have told me."

Ashhur removed his hand from Bardiya's shoulder.

"Stand up, my child," he said. "Please, I wish to know what transpired on that day."

Bardiya glanced at his god, bemused.

"You do not already know?" he asked.

Ashhur lowered his eyes. "I do not."

Grunting and pushing off the sand with his knuckles, Bardiya stood. He faced his god, the reason for his existence, and noticed again that Ashhur's once awe-inspiring size seemed to have lessened. Now Bardiya was less than a foot shorter than he, a realization that caused that familiar panic to establish itself again in the recesses of his brain. In time, if he kept growing the way he always had, he would dwarf the deity.

"I assumed you knew about everything that happened in our Paradise, Your Grace," he said.

Ashhur shook his head. "I feel much, but the specifics of any situation are lost to me. It is part of the price we paid to descend, to walk the land, and to create with our hands instead of our thoughts." He placed his hand over Bardiya's bare chest. "Now my power lies within each of you. It was a sacrifice we chose to make."

"I see. I did not know."

Ashhur sighed. "Please, my child, I must know what transpired."

Bardiya told him of Davishon's unsuccessful attempt on his life in the forest and Ethir's successful assassination in the mangold grove. The god gave him his rapt attention the entire time, nodding whenever Bardiya's ramblings wandered into contemplation, and then waving his divine hand to get him back on track.

Ashhur was quiet for a while after he finished his story, fist gripping his chin in concentration.

"They lie," he finally said, mouth drawn inward, making his lips pucker.

"They lie about what, Your Grace?" asked Bardiya.

"The gods had no part in this attack. Celestia would never allow it. She has instructed her children to stay out of the affairs of Humankind."

Bardiya grunted, noticing the far-off look in his god's eyes when he mentioned the goddess.

"Yes, but what of your brother?" he asked. "I ran across Patrick more than two months ago, while he was on his way to the delta. He spoke of Karak's people threatening harm to the populace of Haven and that he had been sent there by Jacob Eveningstar to warn them to submit. Could the murder of my parents be part of a larger plot against our Paradise? In the absence of the eastern deity, could the people of Neldar be going against the wishes of their god and his pact with you?"

Ashhur shook his head.

"It is not possible. Karak has returned to them, I have felt it. Whatever happens in the delta, it has nothing to do with us. Jacob is a good man, honest and strong. Yet he is also empathetic, and you must remember that my brother and I created him together. He sent Patrick east because he is concerned about the well-being of the people there."

"And where is the First Man now? Why did he not head to the delta himself if he was so worried?"

"Jacob had...other matters to attend to in the north."

"Such as?"

"It does not concern you at the moment."

"Your Grace, it is entirely my concern. My parents are dead. The first children of Paradise have perished before their time."

Ashhur shook his head. "Not the first."

Bardiya's mouth snapped shut.

"Martin Harrow, the kingling," Ashhur continued without any prodding. "*He* was the first to perish. In Haven, at that accursed temple they constructed."

Bowing his head, Bardiya said, "I apologize, Your Grace. I did not know."

A great sigh escaped the god's lips, like an agitated breeze gusting across the desert sand, rousing it. His golden eyes stared at the bright and cloudless sky above.

"There is much you do not know, my child," he said. "Just as there is much *I* do not know. I do not know why the elves slaughtered my children."

He paused, and the silence was frightening.

"And I do not know what my brother is thinking at this moment."

He sounded so defeated when he said this that Bardiya's panic overrode his god's calming influence.

"What are we to do?" he asked, noting the quiver in his own voice.

"We move on," replied Ashhur. "And we make preparations in the event that something *is* amiss. Jacob has long suggested that I send the remaining two kinglings to Mordeina, saying that we must finally choose a king....Finally, I have listened."

"Why?"

"Although I have created a paradise west of the Rigon, I fear that we will be woefully unprepared should another unexpected hardship come our way. If the elves truly wish us harm, for example. Like all children, my children require a leader, and there are some who feel I have been neglectful for waiting so long to give you one."

"Do you mean the Wardens?"

"Yes."

Bardiya shook his head. "Yet we *have* a ruler, Your Grace. We have you."

Ashhur ran a hand through his hair, and his booming voice cracked.

"At one time I would have agreed with you. After all that has transpired since late summer, however, I am no longer certain."

The doubt shown by an entity Bardiya had always believed infallible shook him to the core. He stumbled backward, his knees almost giving out. When another of his constant aches wracked his body, he leaned against the Black Spire to keep from falling. The surface, cool—almost cold—despite the day's heat, fed his feelings of disorientation and disbelief.

"You are perfect," he whispered.

Ashhur chuckled, and he sounded tired, so very tired.

"That, my child, I truly am not."

Bardiya collapsed to his knees.

"Uncertainty is the way of the universe, Bardiya," said Ashhur, concern showing in his eyes. "Nothing is forever, and none—not even I—can control the passage of time. Gods rise and fall, stars are born and die, life is given and taken away. Perfection is a concept, an ideal to be strived for that may never be achieved. That is what I have been trying to teach you, what I have been guiding you toward, so that when you reach Afram's golden afterlife, you will be prepared for what lies beyond."

Bardiya looked at first his god, then the Spire, and finally the desert sand into which his knees were sinking, beneath which his parents were now buried. He breathed in deeply, silencing the voice of his inner doubt, and willed his heart to slow its beat. He shut his senses off from the outside world and retreated inward, thinking of all the lessons he had been taught and hence taught to others, of the oneness he felt with the land, with his god, with nature itself. In that moment he understood that Ashhur was correct, that nothing was perfect. At least nothing *physical* was.

"But ideals," he said, smiling, his panic receding. "In ideals we can find righteousness."

"Yes, my child," said Ashhur. "You are correct."

Bardiya rose up, his knees cracking as he gradually stood.

"The ethics you have taught us—do you believe them?" he asked.

"Of course."

"Then all I ask of you is this, Your Grace: No matter what transpires, no matter what hardships may or may not befall Paradise, promise me that those ideals *will not change*. Promise me that violence will never permeate our hearts and minds, that love and forgiveness will always reign above all else, even if adherence to those ideals might be the end of all you've created."

Ashhur grabbed his hand, and he noticed it was only slightly larger than his own. "I cannot promise that."

Bardiya pulled away. "Why is that?"

"As I said, circumstances change. Should it come to a choice between watching my children die or fighting to save them, I will fight."

"And will you do the same for those in Haven?"

"No. They are not my children."

"But you would fight to save me? Or Patrick? Or Isabel?"

"Yes."

"*All life is sacred.* You told me that once."

"And so it is."

Bardiya felt his confidence grow. "You may believe things will change, but I never will, Your Grace. Your teachings are law to me and my people. Peace and harmony will never be ripped from the hearts and minds in this land, even if our blood is spilled across the prairie and desert both. If it comes to a choice between fighting and dying, we will choose dying."

Ashhur smiled a sad smile and shook his head.

"Let us hope it does not come to that."

"Let us hope. Also, I recognize no authority but yours. We will bow to no king."

"Even if I decree it?"

"Be that as it may...no."

Without another word, Ashhur bent down, kissed his fingertips, and touched the sand beneath which Bessus was buried. The ground seemed to moan under his feet. The god offered Bardiya a final look—*Was it disapproval or calculation?*—before he turned and walked away, disappearing over the same dune from which he had appeared. The sunlight seemed to capture his image, leaving a blackened blur on the precipice long after the deity had departed.

Bardiya stood there, his only companions the Black Spire and the spirits of the dead, and stared toward the east, toward Safeway, toward Haven. He knew in his heart that all he'd told his god was true, but it didn't matter. He had just stood before his deity and dared to pretend he knew more about his god's teachings than the god himself did. He felt fear crawl up his spine, and he fought it down. This was a test, he told himself. A test of his faith. A test of his understanding. Ashhur's apparent disappointment was only a way of forcing Bardiya to prove his faithfulness.

Because the other possibility, of fulfilling his vow and disobeying one of his god's orders, was even more terrifying.

CHAPTER

26

Night had fallen, which filled Geris with fear. Chilled to the bone, he slumped in the back of the carriage as it lumbered up the rough-hewn Gods' Road. Ben Maryll lay beside him, peacefully snoring away. Geris both envied and hated him for it. The caravan had left Safeway more than two weeks ago, after Ashhur—with ample input from Ahaesarus and Judarius, surely—had decided that the lordship would be brought to a close and a king would be named. Ben had been excited by the news, and Geris felt he should be too, but his original nightmare had begun to return each night, and it just wouldn't let him be.

The carriage hit a bump, vaulting him off the rough wooden slats. On landing, he jarred his elbow and let out a pained cry. The curtain at the front of the carriage was swept aside, and Ahaesarus poked his head through.

"What's going on, boy?" the Warden asked. His blond hair looked like the tendrils of a phantasm in the eerie moonlight that seeped through the carriage's thin canvas covering. "Why did you yelp?"

Geris rubbed his sore arm. "It's nothing," he replied. "Just hurt myself when the cart jostled."

"Very well," said Ahaesarus. "You shouldn't be awake. Close your eyes and get some sleep. You won't have that chance tomorrow, once we arrive in Mordeina."

"Yes, sir."

Ahaesarus disappeared back into the front of the carriage, taking his ghost-like halo of hair with him. Geris wrapped himself in his blanket once more, shivered against the cold, and closed his eyes. He wished he were in the carriage with his parents. They were traveling in a separate carriage along with his brothers and sisters. Mother always had a way of comforting him when he felt restless or frightened. She would gather him to her ample bosom, sing a sweet lullaby to him, and gently rock him until he drifted off. She smelled so lovely, like rosemary and sage with a dash of mint. He longed to be in her lap right then.

It was with her in mind that he finally fell asleep.

That sleep was far from peaceful, however. The nightmare returned, the demon chasing him through the shadows once again. He bolted through an empty forest, plunged into a freezing river, climbed a rocky slope, but still he could not lose the beast. His terror reached its apex. The backdrop of the dream rushed all around him, flashes of red and black, green and brown, mixing and twirling, spiraling all around him. He knelt down and screamed and screamed until his lungs burned, his head filled with nothing but his own wailing. That was when a heavy hand fell on his shoulder.

Geris leapt up, the scream dying in his throat. The world had stopped spinning, and he found himself standing atop a weather-beaten crest, staring down at the twinkling fires that dotted the town below. The giant stone Ashhur stood before him, benevolent in gray, the moon dancing off his smooth, granite flesh. The stone god smiled, and the gravel that made up his cheeks grinded as it shifted. He noticed that the star carved into his chest, the symbol of Celestia, had been rubbed away so that it was barely visible. This made him smile.

The demon hissed behind him, then roared like a lion underwater. Geris jumped forward, wrapping his arms around the legs of the stone god. A stiff, cold hand brushed through his hair.

"Fear not, my child," stone Ashhur said. "He does not wish to harm you."

"He doesn't?"

"No."

Geris watched the demon stalk up the side of the cliff, like blackness within blackness, ringlets of shadow pluming from its thickly rendered form. It sat down across from him, gathering solidity with each passing moment. Before long the blackness had faded away like the shed skin of a snake, disappearing into the atmosphere with a barely detectable *whoosh*. Revealed beneath was a lion with yellow fur whose eyes shone with familiar, golden intensity.

"Sit," stone Ashhur said, and Geris did. The stone god took a seat beside him.

"Why are you here?" Geris asked the demon. The lion dipped its head forward, staring at him intently. It seemed to blink in and out of reality, fading into a smoky apparition one instant, then returning to solidity the next. Thin wisps of shadow still thrashed around behind it.

"You are in grave danger," the lion said.

Geris looked at stone Ashhur. "Is that true?"

The god's granite visage nodded.

"What kind of danger?" he asked, turning back to the lion.

"The darkness follows you, for all is not as it seems. The family collapses from within. Witchcraft spoils the will of mere mortals, leaving dust in its wake."

Geris shook his head. "You're not making sense."

"My messenger speaks the truth," said stone Ashhur's gritty voice. "He always has."

"He does?" asked Geris, confused. "Then why is he always chasing me?"

"I chase you because you run," the lion answered. "If you had stopped to listen, you would have known the truth sooner."

It was all too much for him to take.

"Please," he whispered. "Leave me alone. I just want to sleep."

"There is no sleep for the Chosen One," said the lion.

"Chosen one? Me?"

"Yes, you. The future king of humanity, the champion of its people."

"But...I'm not special. It was Martin who was special. I'm just...me."

"But you *are* special," said stone Ashhur. "Those who aren't special do not receive portentous visions."

"Yours is the most important role to play," said the lion. "The fate of Paradise lies in your hands."

The lion inched forward and sprawled out in front of him, its body shifting this way and that, becoming transparent, solidifying again. Geris stared at it, unable to form words.

"The family collapses from within," the lion said once more.

"I don't understand," said Geris, frustration bringing an edge to his dream voice.

The lion sighed. "The lordship is not what it seems to be. There are two enemies in your midst, a witch and an imposter, unleashed upon this land by the lord of darkness who tries to control me. The witch is a whisperer of falsehoods. She thinks me her pet, a thing set upon this land to do her bidding, but I lurk in the shadows, the thing on the doorstep that is heard but never seen. I bow to none but my creator."

"But you're bowing now."

And then it hit him. Geris stared up at stone Ashhur, who inclined his head in his boulder-crunching nod. Geris thought of his conversation with Ashhur—the *real* Ashhur—back in Safeway. The god hadn't seemed surprised by his story of the shadow-lion, or by the accusations leveled against him. That could only mean that Ashhur himself had a hand in the visions.

"I understand."

"Now think," said the lion. "Think of the imposter. Is there any among you who is different now from before? Is there any who has become a new person altogether?"

Geris mulled it over, and realization struck him like a reed to the backside. He thought of a timid boy, a tubby weakling who had once been afraid of his own shadow. A boy who had emerged as a bastion of strength and cunning since Martin's death. Although Geris had always bested him in the past, the rapidly improving Benjamin Maryll now won more than half the time, in everything from arithmetic to footraces, to reciting the names of the landmarks and towns. Geris glanced at the lion, the images in his mind projecting through his eyes and into the dreamscape, and the lion nodded.

"Ben."

It made perfect sense. In his exhaustion, his weary mind could not fully explain why Ben had been constantly outdoing him of late. He almost kicked himself for not realizing it sooner.

"The boy that was once Benjamin Maryll is no more," said the lion. "The imposter has taken his place."

"But why?"

"The Lord of Shadows is a cunning, vile beast. It hates the beauty my creator has forged in this land. It wants to raze Paradise, to cast all of Dezrel into the darkness in which it thrives. The witch will use all her power to realize this depraved vision, whether or not the imposter succeeds in becoming ruler of the west."

"Wait," Geris said, trying to think through the murky swamp that was his dreaming mind. "What do you mean? It doesn't matter which of us is named king?"

"It will not matter whether you or the imposter is named king. With the assistance of the witch, the imposter will sow seeds of discontent in the people. Panic will race across the land, bringing about the death of the deity who created all that is good and holy. The only way to stop it is to kill them both. This is why you are the

Chosen One, Geris Felhorn. You are the only one who knows the truth. You are the only one who can stop the destruction of everything you know and love."

He shivered at the thought of killing anyone, nevermind a boy like Ben. Yes, Ben had changed, but was he truly possessed? His mind returned to the Temple of the Flesh, to the blood pouring over Martin's hands as he clutched the arrow embedded in his chest. His dream-self shivered, yet even as a large part of him rejected the notion of murder, another smaller part—a part for which the act seemed natural, as if he had been born to do it—pressed further.

"Who's the witch?" he asked.

The lion seemed to grin, something powerful sparkling in its eyes. Geris retreated, only to be stilled by stone Ashhur's giant hand on his back.

"She is the mother of a nation, a would-be murderer of her own children. Her eyes reflect the glimmer of the western sea, her cheeks are spotted with the stars above, and around her head is a ring of fire."

"Where is she?"

"She is where you are headed, at the center of the place called Mordeina."

Geris exhaled deeply and gazed up at the granite likeness of his creator. "Is it all true, my Lord?"

Grimly, stone Ashhur nodded.

The lion rose on its legs and skulked toward him, its yellow eyes burning with ethereal fire, its image wavering like a lie on the tongue of an unsure child.

"If it is proof you desire, then I shall give it to you."

Without thinking, Geris extended his hand. The lion placed a monstrous paw in his palm, the claws digging into his wrist, burning him. Then the creature lost solidity and the darkness returned, swirling about him like a million black flies. Visions assaulted Geris's mind, boiling his eyes, piercing the fabric of his thoughts. He saw fields running red with blood, strange men with the heads of wolves, hyenas, vultures, and lizards. He watched as Ashhur was devoured by a huge creature with blazing red eyes, whose face shifted from one moment to the next, never the same, never constant, always horrific. And then the god bled, and the heavens wept, and stars burst from his sternum to fill the sky with flames that rained sulfur to the ground, melting flesh, scorching the grass, smoldering the gardens of Haven, Safeway, Ker, Mordeina, and everywhere else in the land.

Lastly he saw his family, his parents and siblings, hanging by their wrists from the gallows, slit from chest to belly, their insides piled beneath them like mounds of raw sausage. Their eyes had been plucked out, and their empty sockets stared outward in agony, their faces forever frozen in the terror and pain they'd felt as they died. Behind them, lurking in the shadows, was Ben the Imposter and the nameless, faceless witch, laughing, laughing, laughing....

Geris awoke screaming, thrashing about on the floor of the carriage, lashing out blindly as the vision continued to torment him. He saw only the images, heard only the laughter. As if from another world he sensed Ahaesarus trying to calm him, felt the touch of his mother. But her fingers were rotted, her throat slit. The night passed, his throat raw from his cries, but still he thrashed and howled.

When the convoy entered Mordeina a few hours later, he was still screaming.

His eyes felt crusty when he opened them, and his head pounded.

"Nice of you to join us," he heard Ahaesarus say.

Geris lifted himself up and looked around. He was on a bed in a round room of some sort, the curved walls of pale clay brick pressing in on him. It was unlike anything he had seen—beautiful paintings hung from the walls, the candelabras that lit the space were heavy with gold and silver, and the bed itself was the softest he had ever rested his body upon. He swallowed hard to still his nerves, and when he slid his legs over the side of the bed, he was amazed to feel the plushness of the carpet beneath his feet.

Ahaesarus was in the room with him. The Warden's back was turned as he sat at a desk a few feet to his right—a desk that was far too small for him. His long, angular body was contorted at odd angles as he scratched his quill across a piece of parchment. Geris began to say something but kept his mouth shut. His thoughts were muddy, and he couldn't remember how he'd gotten to be where he was. For all he knew, he was in trouble, and when it came to his mentor, if he were in trouble, the best thing to do was sit and await punishment.

Ahaesarus finished his scrawling and swiveled in his much too tiny seat. The Warden's long hair was pulled back from his face, fastened in a knot at the top of his head, forming a golden tail that draped over one shoulder. He wore a tailored cerulean smock—Ahaesarus's favorite color—the breast embroidered with silken thread in a looping, regal floral pattern. The being who sat before him now seemed to be entirely different from the one who had mentored him for years. The itch of memory made Geris's eye flutter, but whatever the sensation was trying to tell him, he didn't know. All he *did* know was that his entire body felt like it had been stuffed with the fluffy white seedpods that floated through the plains during spring, looking like a billion whimsical fairies.

The Warden leaned forward, resting a slender hand on Geris's knee. His eyes brimmed with compassion and understanding, two sentiments that Ahaesarus usually had in rather short supply.

"How do you feel?" he asked.

Geris swallowed, feeling a lump in his throat once more.

"Thirsty."

Ahaesarus nodded. "That can occur with nightwing root," he replied, grabbing a waterskin from beneath the desk and handing it over. Geris snatched the skin and guzzled down its contents, his thirst overriding the fact he had never heard of this *nightwing root* before.

When he finished drinking, he wiped spittle from his chin, and dropped the waterskin beside him on the bed. He reeled back, his head suddenly wobbly. Ahaesarus was up in a flash, holding him steady so he wouldn't topple headfirst off the bed.

"Easy, young lordling," the Warden said. "Mustn't drink so quickly."

The strange sensation of vertigo caused a cyclone of fear to emerge from the dark corners of his mind. He thought again of how he had no memory of arriving in this strange and window-less round room. The last thing he remembered was riding with Ben in the carriage, bouncing along in the night while unable to sleep. The darkness of his memories frightened him, and the more he tried to restore them, the more a strange anxiety filled the pit of his stomach. Ahaesarus held him closer and gently rubbed his back.

"It will be fine, boy. Calm yourself. Shush now."

Eventually, the trembling fit ended. Geris leaned back and stared up into his mentor's twinkling green eyes. Ahaesarus bent over and—in an act that shocked young Geris to his core—placed a tender kiss on the boy's forehead.

"What was that for?" Geris whispered.

"You deserve it," replied the Warden.

"For what?"

"For being strong."

Geris, still locked in his mentor's caring embrace, felt his jaw drop. Ahaesarus, whose favorite words seemed to be *lazy, inept, spoiled, indignant,* and *foolhardy,* had told him he was strong. He would have been overjoyed if he weren't so stunned. He tilted his head to the side, felt a crick in the back of his neck, and once more a wave of dizziness washed over him.

"Warden," he murmured, bringing his hands up to cover his eyes, "what's happening to me? How did I get here?"

Ahaesarus's fingers began playing a staccato beat along his spine, easing the pressure in his head. "You do not remember?"

Geris shook his head slowly, so as to not incur more pain in his head.

"You suffered a fit of madness three days ago. You began screaming and crying in the middle of the night, and there was nothing we could do to stop it. Even your mother could not calm you down. We tried every healing spell we knew, all for naught. When we entered Mordeina and were greeted by our hosts, you finally fell into a black sleep. You were slick with fever, your breath shallow. Thankfully, Lady DuTaureau saw to your care and brought you to Daniel Nefram, one of her sons-in-law. He found a lump at the base of your skull"—the Warden reached out and tapped the sore spot on the back of Geris's neck—"and immediately began to pray."

"What was it?" Geris asked. The tale intrigued him, though he felt detached, as if it were the story of someone else's life.

"You were stricken with the Wasting. Very much so, actually. You were blessed that Daniel is such a powerful healer, for had it been anyone else caring for you, you would have died within the day. But Daniel's faith eradicated the poisonous growth." Ahaesarus removed from beneath his shirt the pouch that always hung from a string around his neck. "I fed you a pinch of nightwing root—a powerful herb from my world that thins the blood and increases circulation—and then waited."

"Thank you," said Geris. He felt truly honored.

Ahaesarus's voice shifted tone, becoming even softer, yet somehow more serious. His eyes never left Geris's.

"I also owe you an apology, boy. I have been rather rough on you of late. I took you for a miscreant; you seemed at times to be a frightened weakling, and at others, a cocky fool so confident of victory that he stopped trying. However, given the size of the growth, the Wasting has been with you for quite some time. That explains many things—your lethargy, your forgetfulness, the force-fulness of your nightmares...."

"You know of them?" Geris asked, shocked.

"Do not look so surprised," the Warden said, chuckling. "My tent is beside yours when we train. Many a night I felt like slap-ping you awake, both to spare you the dreams and allow me some rest."

Geris smiled weakly. "Thank you for not doing so."

"I am very glad I did not. It would have been a...most regret-table action, given what I know now."

Geris leaned into his mentor, wrapping his spindly, thirteen-year-old arms around him. He wanted no more words, only for this newfound comfort and compassion to continue.

"Why don't we bring your family in?" Ahaesarus said after a time. "I am sure they are desperate to know you've awoken. And then, if you feel up to it, later this evening we can all meet our hosts for dinner. Is that agreeable to you?"

So shocked was Geris at Ahaesarus's words—his mentor was actually *asking permission* and treating him *like an equal*, which was a very Jacob Eveningstar way of behaving—that he could only nod dumbly in response.

The gathering was long, filled with desperate embraces and a multitude of frantic kisses from his mother. Even his father, who usually carried himself with an air of disinterest in regards to his kingling son, seemed touched. There were tears in the man's eyes, and his lower lip quivered when he told Geris he was glad he'd made it through the ordeal unscathed.

With each passing moment, Geris felt better and better. His sluggishness dissipated, his thoughts became less muddled, and he no longer became dizzy each time he turned his head. The smile he wore almost never left his face; it was so persistent that the muscles in his cheeks began to feel sore. The nightmares that had plagued him for weeks seemed like distant childhood memories. By the end of it all he was refreshed and reinvigorated, feeling better than he had since the day Martin had been killed.

That thought of the nightmares caused a bit of the darkness to resurface in him, but he shrugged the feeling aside, especially because Ahaesarus was so intent on spending nearly every moment by his pupil's side. He wanted nothing more than to bask in the Warden's approval.

I will be a good king, he thought, and his smile grew all the wider.

When it was time for dinner, Ahaesarus left the room, leaving Geris's mother and two of his sisters to assist in cleaning and dressing him. They fitted him with a delicately crafted red undertunic, a black doublet, and a tight-fitting pair of tan, spun-cotton breeches. The clothes were uncomfortable—much more constricting than the loose rags and animal hides he was used to wearing—yet he did not once complain. *A king needs to look stately*, he thought, remembering the regal lords and ladies in the swashbuckling tales that Ahaesarus, Judarius, Azariah, and the other Wardens often told. So instead of whining, he stood up straight, flexed himself to loosen his clothing, and allowed his sister Margo to brush the kinks from his overly long golden locks. All the while his mother looked on, smiling.

A rapping sounded at the door, followed by a gruff voice announcing that dinner was about to be served. A powerful-looking young man dressed in a draping pallium entered. His hair was close-cropped and black, a highly unusual color in the light-haired north. The beard on his face was neatly trimmed, with a zigzag pattern along his sideburns. Around his waist was a belt, fastened to which was the second blade Geris had ever laid eyes on in his life, the first being the sharp knife Jacob always carried with him. It was half a foot long, with a simple ivory handle. The steel, visible through gaps in the scabbard that contained the blade, shimmered in the candlelight. The man introduced himself as Howard Phillip Baedan, master steward and counselor of Lady DuTaureau. Ahaesarus noticed him eyeing the blade and pulled him aside. Baedan had once been a steward in Lerder, he told him, and the blade had been a gift from a merchant from Neldar who used the riverside town as a way station on his journeys to the north and south of his kingdom. "It is a rarity that Howard thinks heightens his image," the Warden whispered, before guiding Geris back into place.

"As the Lady's most trusted servant, I will advise the new king, whomever that may be," Baedan said. "But for now, my duty is simply to escort you to the hall."

With Howard Baedan leading, Geris and his mother and sisters made their way through the wide, lavish, and strangely empty hallways of Manse DuTaureau. This was about as different from the Sanctuary as possible; even Ashhur's home and cathedral did not hold a candle to the elegance of this residence. Geris closed his eyes as he walked, remembering the Wardens' stories once more, and imagined a sprawling city outside the walls of this giant stone structure. The image excited him.

That excitement was somewhat tempered when they passed through a windowed corridor. Outside the slender portholes he saw a familiar scene—tents and crude huts, in front of which people and Wardens huddled, rubbing their hands over blazing firepits. Only the setting differed from Safeway; instead of tall, swaying grass, they were surrounded by gently rolling hills dotted with pine trees.

He noticed that the people seemed to be highly agitated, however. They gathered close to the manse, their eyes flicking toward the monstrous building as if they expected Ashhur himself to appear at any moment. A palpable sort of nervous exhilaration clung to their every move.

"They are awaiting the presentation of the kinglings," Sir Baedan said, as if reading his mind. "They have been waiting for days to see you and young Maryll, and after dinner tonight they will get what they have been seeking."

"I see," said Geris. He stuffed his hands in the pockets of his doublet, suddenly uncomfortable at the thought of being paraded before such a large throng.

"Will the First Man be in attendance?" he asked, thinking it would do wonders for his nervousness just to see Jacob's face in the crowd.

Sir Baedan shook his head.

"Not to my knowledge. Eveningstar has not graced the north with his presence in near a full year, and I do not expect that to end this night."

"I see," replied Geris, disappointed.

Their journey ended at the entrance to the dining hall. Sir Baedan pulled open the double doors, standing aside to let his charge enter first.

"Stand straight," Geris's mother whispered, and he did. She then offered him her hand, which he took. He gazed up into her warm blue eyes and then at her flowing hair, which was a darker shade of blond than his own. She appeared nervous but strong, and Geris tossed aside any of the misgivings he'd felt on hearing the rumble of voices echoing from inside the foyer. Instead of waiting for her to lead him, he took the first step, entering the huge dining hall.

"I present Kingling Geris Felhorn!" shouted Sir Baedan, and a sudden hush overtook the crowd. All eyes turned to the entrance.

Geris stepped confidently, even though his stomach rumbled from the combination of nerves and the palatable scents of roasting meat. There were simply dressed people and tall Wardens everywhere. He made sure to look each person in the eye, offering him or her a slight bow as he passed. Almost everyone returned his bows. He and his mother strolled down the center aisle, surrounded on all sides by gawking people, heading for the large table at the back of the room and the throng of regal-looking people that stood before it.

As Geris gazed at them and their features registered in his mind, his confidence shattered into a million pieces.

The final dream struck him like a deadly poison that had waited patiently before bursting forth and infecting every part of him at once. The gathered diners gasped as he stumbled backward. His hand slipped from his mother's as he fell, breathing heavily and staring at those who awaited his company. There was Ahaesarus on one side, his proud expression quickly replaced with concern. With him was Judarius, dressed in an ensemble similar to Ahaesarus's, his dark hair flowing down his wide shoulders, his mouth locked into a scowl that never seemed to leave his face.

But it was the pair who stood between them that had caused the dream to roar back into memory. They were a man and woman, similar to the point of being nearly identical. The man appeared disinterested with the whole affair, never taking his gaze off the woman beside him, but the woman stared intently at Geris with narrowed eyes and a furrowed brow. It seemed as though the light that suffused the dining hall refused to shine on her fully.

Her eyes reflect the glimmer of the western sea, her cheeks are spotted with the stars above, and around her head is a ring of fire, the lion had said, and before him stood a woman with blazing green eyes, skin dotted with ruby freckles, and the reddest hair Geris had ever seen. Even her clothing seemed wrong—much too tightly fit, displaying her womanly form in a way more appropriate to the Temple of the Flesh.

Ahaesarus turned to face the woman. "I am sorry, Lady DuTaureau," he said frantically. He seemed to be afraid of her, even though he stood more than a full head taller. "I fear we have pressed Kingling Felhorn too much given his recent illness."

Shock filled Geris, making his elbows quaver. One of Ashhur's first creations was the witch of whom the dream-lion spoke? It didn't seem possible, not until he gazed back into her hardened expression, which had not changed even after Ahaesarus's plea for understanding. She looked at him not as a person to be cared for, but as a thing to be tolerated, perhaps even loathed. It reminded him of the way his father looked at the rake beside the door to their hut when it came time to clean out the firepit. Geris began to mutter to himself, strange words even he didn't understand, unintelligible sounds like those of a wild beast. And still his heart beat out of control. Not even his mother, who knelt beside him, anxiously swiping the hair from his forehead, could do anything to stop it.

"What's wrong with him?" another voice asked, and then Ben Maryll appeared, strolling past Geris with Sir Baedan by his side. The crowd remained hushed, looking on with curious dread. Geris glanced at his friend and fellow kingling, taking in his coldly inquiring expression. It was then Geris noticed how slender his old friend had become: where once Ben Maryll had tended toward plumpness, now he possessed the lean body of an athlete. The well-developed muscles in his neck flexed when he bent his head downward.

All that change in two months? It didn't seem possible. The lion was right. Ben wasn't Ben. He was the imposter.

The visions of death and destruction that had been imparted to him filled his mind, and Geris screamed. He scrambled to his feet, tossing aside the restraining grasp of his mother, and ran full bore into Sir Baedan's hip. His sudden actions caught the head steward off guard, knocking him backward. Senses overridden by terror and desperation, Geris gripped the ivory handle of Sir Baedan's dagger and ripped it from its sheath. A shriek tore out from the crowd, followed by another, but everyone was too shocked to actually *do* anything. Somewhere in the back of his mind, Geris knew that violence was not expected. This was Ashhur's land, the land of healers and Wardens and forgiveness. No one would know how to react, which would give him the time he needed to do what he had been chosen to do—save Paradise from the witch and her deceiving bastard child.

Ben was closest to him, his eyes wide with shock, and Geris charged. He held Sir Baedan's blade out wide, the handle fitting snugly in his grip, as if he had always been destined to hold it. Ben backed away, exhibiting some of his newfound athleticism, until he clumsily bumped into a chair and nearly fell over. Geris was there to break his fall, grabbing his false friend by the hair and pulling him upright.

His blade pressed against a now sobbing Ben Maryll's throat, drawing a sliver of blood that trickled down the boy's neck and saturated the front of his white tunic.

"He's an imposter!" Geris yelled, his voice cracking. He wanted them to see this, *needed* everyone gathered in the hall to bear witness as he exposed the charlatan for what he—or it—truly was. He bore down harder, sliding the dagger across flesh, opening a tiny mouth that yawned when Ben thrust his head back, trying to escape Geris's grip. But Geris was fueled by something different now, something *meaningful.* He was fueled by destiny, by duty, by the need to be the savior.

Strong hands gripped him from behind. They yanked him off the screeching boy and lifted him into the air. The dagger clanked on the dining hall floor, covered with slick, red wetness. Ben collapsed to his knees, covering his neck with both hands as blood spilled between his fingers. Others—including Sir Baedan, the witch, and her look-alike lover—rushed to the imposter's aid. Geris grinded his teeth, growled, and tried to free himself from his captor's grasp, but their hands were too strong.

"Are you mad!" he heard Ahaesarus shout. "What have you *done?*"

His body was thrown to the floor and then spun around. He faced the two Wardens, the normally pallid flesh of their cheeks flushed red. Ahaesarus reared back and backhanded him across the face, causing one of his teeth to puncture his tongue, drawing blood. All the while his mother sobbed in the background, comforting his sisters while she watched Ben's parents join those who were trying to save their son's life. The white linens they pressed against the imposter's neck quickly turned a deep crimson.

"Someone get Daniel!" the witch shouted, frantic now that her imposter was dying. "Get him quickly!"

"There is no time!" shouted Ahaesarus. "I will do it. Judarius, handle this...this boy."

Ahaesarus flung him into Judarius's arms, then rushed to the Ben's side. Judarius dragged him out the door by the throat. Geris protested, trying to warn them of what the dreams had told him, to convince them to let him finish the job he had started, but Judarius's grip was too strong. He could not form words of any kind, he could only thrash and wail and scream.

CHAPTER

27

As he strolled into the solarium of the Gemcroft Mansion, the first thing Patrick thought when his eyes came to rest on Peytr Gemcroft was that he was a beautiful man. He hadn't seen the merchant since Peytr's arrival in the delta four days earlier, but now that he did, he could see that he and Rachida were well matched. The man's hair was close-cropped and black with a few flecks of white, his skin the lightest shade of peach, his eyes a deep, soulful brown, his features delicate but strong. Just beautiful, through and through. And strong of voice as well.

"I do not agree," said the merchant. "It is folly."

"Says the man who has spent perhaps five days in Haven over the past year," snapped Deacon.

There were three of them sitting around the table—Peytr, Lord Coldmine, and Moira. None of them lifted their eyes to him as he approached the table. It was clear that their argument was all that mattered to them.

"You don't understand, Peytr," said Moira. "Must we turn our back on our ideals, on our way of life? And for what?"

414 ■■ David Dalglish • Robert J. Duperre

"It seems to me it is pride you speak of, not ideals," replied the merchant.

Deacon growled. "What do you know of pride? We are protecting our freedom, nothing more."

"Yet you do not wish to protect your lives," said Peytr.

"No, obviously our lives are important." Moira placed her hand on his arm. "But if we give up our homes and our beliefs, we go back to being slaves. What are our lives worth then? Did we not leave Neldar for that very purpose? Why give it all back now?"

"Because the fight is hopeless. You all know this. You need to either tear down the temple or flee. There is no other choice."

"There is *always* a choice!" shouted Deacon.

Sighing, Patrick closed his eyes and began tapping his foot on the marble floor. Still no one looked at him. It was as though he were invisible again.

Impatience grew in his belly, a tight knot slowly unwinding, fraying his nerves. He was getting too used to feeling this way. Ever since Nessa had left Haven eleven days ago, it had become his natural state of being. He had spent his days penning letter after letter. He wrote to his mother, the Warden Pontius, Master Clegman, and anyone else he knew in the west who might assure him of his sister's safe arrival. He had received no answer to his queries. Of course, eleven days was hardly enough time for a letter to return to him, but that did nothing to quell his anxiety.

He knew he was being foolish. Nessa was with Crian, the very man who had handed him Winterbone so many years before. Crian was a good man with a good heart who loved Nessa entirely, at least according to Moira. So long as they made it out of the delta, Patrick knew no harm would come to them. It was irrational to be as worried as he was, but he was worried nonetheless. No one had gone with them when they left Lord Coldmine's estate, and no one had escorted them to Ashhur's Bridge. Anything might have happened between here and there.

That isn't all, and you know it, he thought, feeling pathetic.

What bothered him more than anything was how much of Nessa's life had been hidden from him. She and Crian had been carrying on a secret love affair for more than a decade, according to Moira. She told him how Crian had courted her, taking leave of his duties to both god and kingdom to spend a few fleeting moments with her in the soggy bog of the delta. It made for a beautiful, tragic story, but it also made Patrick jealous. No matter how loyal and dedicated Crian was, no matter how much the eastern deserter loved his sister, the one person Patrick loved almost as much as his god had been stolen away…and he hadn't even had the chance to say good-bye. His darker half insisted that all of Nessa's sweet talk about how important he was to her had been lies. It was silly and childish, but Patrick had to find out for certain that she was all right. He needed *confirmation*.

The argument between the three seated at the table grew louder. Patrick placed Winterbone on the floor, pulled out a chair, and sat down. Still nary an eye turned to him. He drummed his fingers on the table, but still they did not address him.

"Then what of the young?" shouted Peytr. "An honorable man would at the least protect the innocent."

That statement brought a pause to the conversation, and Patrick leaned forward, sensing an opening for his voice to be heard, but then Deacon thumped his fist against the table.

"Honor," Deacon grumbled. "Will honor fill our bellies? Will honor slay the army that threatens us, that will chase us wherever we flee? What of preserving what is right?"

Frustrated, Patrick slumped, his hunched spine pressing against the hard back of his chair. Moira joined in, making the same argument as Deacon. Peytr rolled his eyes as their voices assaulted him, but he didn't back down. His posture remained rigid, his gaze strong.

Finally, Patrick had had enough. He reached down and picked Winterbone up off the floor. Without removing the heavy sword from its scabbard, he slammed the iron-plated tip against the solarium's marble tiles. The ensuing *clang* stopped the argument midcomplaint, all eyes turning to him.

"Aaaah, silence," he muttered, and returned the sword to its resting position.

Peytr eyed him queerly, the attractive man's expression impossible to interpret. Moira's gaze dropped while she picked up her wooden mug in shaking hands and took a sip. Deacon fumed silently, his shoulders rising and falling, his cheeks red with frustration. He stared at Patrick as if he'd just levied a vile insult against his mother.

"*What?*" Deacon growled.

"So you're finally acknowledging my presence," Patrick said. "Good to know that I'm not fucking invisible."

Peytr cocked his head to the side, a hint of a smile playing at the corners of his plump lips.

"Patrick DuTaureau, I presume?" he said. "Your reputation—and your language—precedes you."

Patrick nodded and offered his hand, which Peytr accepted.

"State your business, man," said Deacon, impatience burning in his eyes. "Can you not see that we have much to discuss?"

"I see no discussion," Patrick replied. "I see three people screaming at each other."

Deacon leaned forward, his face beet red, his knuckles white as he gripped the table. He looked as though he were ready to leap over the top and crash into him head on. It was Moira who calmed him, placing her slender, waifish fingers on the older man's back. She leaned over and whispered into Deacon's ear, and he grunted and sat back.

Patrick hadn't moved during Deacon's outburst and was still slouched in his chair, his heavy arms dangling by his sides. Of the many things Corton Ender had taught him during their daily training sessions—sessions that had been on hold since Nessa's departure—the one that had stuck with him most was that his oddly powerful upper body gave him a marked advantage in hand-to-hand combat. Deacon was strong and athletic despite his age, but Patrick was stronger.

Peytr turned to fully face him. Patrick took in the man's expression, which was remarkably similar to the one he and Bardiya would have as they studied odd-looking insects during their formative years.

"Please," Peytr said, "there is no need for sarcasm or accusations. We might not agree with each other, but I assure you that every man at this table—I apologize for the designation, Moira, dear—holds the utmost respect for the others. Many apologies if it seemed otherwise to you."

Patrick grunted.

Deacon shook his head and exhaled loudly. Moira shot him a look, and he straightened his posture.

"Yes, yes, that is true," he said, his voice calmer now. "I'm sorry for not greeting you sooner. Please, tell me why you've come."

"My sister," said Patrick. Peytr developed a confused expression, but Moira offered him a sympathetic nod. Deacon, meanwhile, shuffled his feet beneath the table, blinking rapidly.

"And?" the older man said, strangely nervous.

Patrick hesitated, taken aback by the sudden change in Deacon's attitude.

"I…well, I think it is time for me to leave," he finally said. "I wish to head west to look for her. I fear for her safety."

Deacon let out a long sigh.

"You are being rash, young DuTaureau. Crian is a capable young man. They love each other. Nessa will be safe with him. Whatever in Ashhur's Paradise could harm them?"

"Even so, I would like to see her one last time. I was never given the chance, due to…well…other activities."

Other activities being his glorious night with Rachida, which he didn't dare mention with her husband, Peytr, in the room. He felt his neck flush; it hurt him to know that his little rendezvous had cost him the chance to bid farewell to his beloved little sister.

"So be it, then," Deacon said. "You don't need my permission to run off to find her. You aren't a prisoner here. You can leave any time you wish."

Patrick shrugged. "That is true, I suppose. However, my horse is locked in your stables, Deacon, and she is the only mare accustomed to my condition." He stood up and leaned forward, bowing in respect. "I just wish to have her returned to me, and your new stable hand refused me when I asked. Odd of him to do so, considering I have been a guest in your home for some time."

Deacon nodded.

"I apologize, that was my fault. The old stable hand decided to run off to Corton and be a soldier. Johan just came into my employ yesterday, and he knows you not. The mare is all yours again if you wish to retrieve her. I will make sure of that once I return home. You can depart this evening if you wish, tomorrow at the latest."

"Thank you," Patrick replied.

Moira leapt up from her chair, knocking it backward with a sudden clatter that made Patrick flinch. Her pale cheeks were flushed when she said, "But you cannot leave, Patrick. We need you here."

"Let the man go," said Deacon dismissively, tugging on her sleeve.

"I will *not*," she replied, and pulled away from the older man's grip. She faced Patrick once more. "Why would you choose to leave now, Patrick? It's less than a month away from the next full moon, when Karak's Army promised to return. Corton has said you are his best pupil, the most natural with a sword he has ever seen. We *need you*. And besides, were you not instructed to come here? Is this not where your god wishes you to be?"

Patrick shrugged. "To be honest, Moira, I'm not sure *why* I am here. I haven't spoken with Ashhur in years. It was Eveningstar who sent me here, under instructions to convince you all to tear down that temple, though I've struggled with that task since I arrived. It seems as though I've joined you instead. The temple still stands, and none of you have any intention of tearing it down anytime soon. I've clearly failed at what I was sent here to do." He glanced at Peytr, who now held a glum expression. "I apologize, but in all honesty, I have no horse in this fight. I am no soldier, and though Corton may say I am good at it, I have no desire for violence. All I wish to do, beyond making sure that my sister and Crian made it home safely, is to return to Paradise. What I do *not* desire is to lose my life protecting a temple dedicated to *fucking*."

Patrick bent over, picked up Winterbone, and offered Peytr a cursory nod before turning on his heels and strolling awkwardly out of the room. He heard footsteps follow after him as he walked down the hallway. He anticipated that it would be Moira, pleading with him to stay, but when he turned, ready to offer his best dismissive words, Peytr was the one standing there. Patrick expected him to be angry, but he seemed appreciative instead.

"Yes?" Patrick asked.

Peytr's hand came up, soft, powdered fingers stroking the knotted flesh on the side of Patrick's face. His touch was as delicate as a lover's, which made Patrick feel somewhat uncomfortable. As if sensing this, Peytr pulled his hand away.

"I understand your decision," the merchant said. "And I do not wish to change your mind. In fact, I wish you *had* convinced my people to tear down that monstrosity. I do not know why it was constructed in the first place. At times it seems as though Deacon is trying to test Karak's patience."

"He obviously succeeded."

"That he did," said Peytr with a nod. "And I will not be here to reap what he has sown. I will be gathering my wife and some… others who are important to me…and heading to the Pebble Islands. I have another estate there, and the ocean will keep us safe for a time."

"Why are you telling me this?" Patrick asked hesitantly.

Peytr shrugged. "I suppose I just wish to thank you. I understand that Rachida holds the utmost respect for you, and you are very special to her. It means a great deal to me that you have been a companion for her. I know how lonely it can be for a wife when her husband is gone for months at a time."

Peytr smiled then, and it was sincere. Patrick breathed a sigh of relief.

"Not a problem," he said. "Not in the slightest."

"I thought not," replied Peytr with a wink. "She *is* a beautiful woman, the most beautiful in all the land. Even someone like me can admit that."

After saying his piece, the merchant turned to leave.

"And by the way, Master DuTaureau," he called out over his shoulder before disappearing into one of the adjacent hallways. "I know you think yourself ugly, but you are not. You are simply different. Remember that."

And then he was gone. Patrick shook his head, looked to make sure no one else was coming to stall him, and exited through the mansion's back door. The early afternoon air kissed his flesh, pricking his neck. It was a cool day, the humidity bearable for once. *It will get much colder soon*, he thought, and the memory of Mordeina's frigid winter nights made him wrap his oversized arms around himself.

He strolled through the rear courtyard until he found Rachida sitting on a wooden bench, tossing bits of bread into the stream that lolled along lazily behind the Gemcroft mansion. Gulls, geese, and whippoorwills—the latter of which were thankfully silent, as their incessant nightly tweeting had brought him close to insanity on many an evening—swooped down, snatching the bits of bread from the water, swallowing each in a single gulp.

Rachida was, of course, a vision of splendor. On this day she wore a simple white dress that flowed around her body like the water in the stream below, hinting ever so slightly at the exquisite shape hidden beneath. Her dark hair draped lazily over her shoulders, and a stray sunray pierced the canopy above, shining only on her shoulder, turning the wisp of hair that rested there a brilliant gold.

She didn't look up as he approached, keeping her focus on feeding the birds. Patrick dropped his sword onto the grass, slid onto the bench beside her, and sat back. It was amazing that he still felt comfortable around her after their excursion to the temple, but it was true. Every other woman he had lain with had treated him differently afterward, whereas Rachida acted as if nothing had changed. He appreciated that, but sometimes he wondered if it were truly better. It was as if their time together was so unmemorable that it had been wiped from her memory altogether. And seeing the way she acted with Moira, the way the two women brushed up against each other, their gazes lingering far too long, made her lack of interest in him all the more painful.

Some things are for the best, he thought.

Patrick shivered and leaned forward, waiting for her to make the first move. She did, slowly turning her head toward him, gazing on him as if she were busy contemplating one of life's grand mysteries.

"What did they say?" she asked.

"Deacon told me to meet him later," he replied. "I will fetch the mare this evening and be on my way."

"That's too bad," she said. "I will miss you."

"All my ladies claim that," Patrick said with a chuckle. "I never believe them."

Rachida paused for a moment and began rubbing her stomach.

"You do understand that we will likely never see each other again?" she said, her alluring eyes staring blankly ahead. "You will go and live your life in Paradise, and I will die here, defending my home from whatever may come."

"That's…that's nonsense," Patrick said, a lump rising in his throat. "You aren't staying here. You aren't fighting. Your husband is bringing you to his estate in the Pebble Islands. He told me as much only a few minutes ago."

She laughed, though it was a humorless sound.

"Yes, Peytr tries to play the nobleman. He will demand I come, but when I decline, he will go off with his lover, Bryce, leaving me behind with only a token argument."

Patrick shook his head. "But *why* are you staying?" he asked, incredulous. "And why were you in such a rush to get pregnant if you were planning to simply throw it all away a month later?"

She shrugged. "I am an idealist. I never thought it would come to this."

"But what will you gain from your obstinacy? You owe these people nothing!"

"Oh, but I do. I owe Moira my love, and I refuse to leave her to die." She glanced down at her hand, which still rubbed the satiny fabric over her belly. "And I refuse to run from my home, and the home of my child. Should I die protecting Haven, at least he will die with me without having to exist in a world where men and women are slaves to the ones that created them."

Patrick froze.

"Your child?"

She looked at him then, and her eyes blazed with compassion. "Yes, my child, Patrick. The one you gave to me."

"You mean…it actually worked?"

Grabbing his hand, she guided it until it rested atop her stomach. His fingers slid over the fabric, feeling the hint of flesh underneath.

"Yes, Patrick. The spell worked. Your seed found purchase, and now a life is growing inside me. Here, let me show you."

She reached up with her free hand and gently touched him on his right temple. She closed her eyes and began breathing heavily, muttering words he didn't understand.

"Close your eyes," she whispered as bright light assaulted Patrick's vision. "And see."

He did, and he saw what was inside of her, a tiny, beating heart within a clump of matter the shape of a bean. The bean rested within a nest of fluid, surrounded by a clear wall that contained an interconnected web of pulsing red lines. The image overwhelmed him. Never before had he seen life in the way he was seeing it now, and his heart filled with joy.

A child, he thought. *A son. I have been granted a son.*

Rachida pulled her fingers away from him, and the image shattered. He was once more in the rear of the courtyard, sitting on the bench before the stream. Tears trickled down his cheeks as he looked blindly at the splendor all around them. He reached out for her, but she backed away. His hand fell from her stomach, whacking against the wooden bench with a *thud*.

"The child is yours, but it is not," Rachida said, and he sensed she was trying to remain firm for some reason.

"What does that mean?" he asked.

She glanced down and began to rub her stomach again.

"This child, this miracle, is to be the only one of his kind, the offspring of two opposite yet equally perfect bloodlines. He will be a great leader of men, and he will carry Peytr's name. Should we prevail when Karak comes for us, should we win our freedom, my son will be the one who leads humankind to greatness. It will be his destiny." She looked at him then, and her front teeth bit into her plump lower lip. "I mean no disrespect, Patrick. You must understand. Peytr knows of our tryst, and he knows of my pregnancy, and he is at peace with it. Given his desires, he never wished to put a child in me, but he is more than happy to have an heir. However, only the three of us—you, my husband, and myself—know what actually transpired, and it must stay that way, for the good of the people our son will one day lead. Do you understand?"

Patrick shook his head. In truth, he didn't. It tore him up inside. The impossible had happened, and he'd sired a child. Two of the different First Families had intermixed to create a life. Yet now, when he could finally have a son of his own, he was being told he must not have anything to do with it? Was this his lot in life, to remain a timeless freak who would forever be alone? Not even his child would know him. And if Rachida insisted on following the path she had chosen, the boy would never reach the light of day. He looked at her, saw the determination in her eyes, and knew he could never deny her what she wished. If it was to be his destiny to be immortal and lonesome, then so be it.

Unless…

"I don't care what you say," he said. "You're leaving."

"What?"

"The only thing that matters is that this child lives. You will leave with Peytr, you will find safety on the islands, and you will only return if and when it is safe to do so."

She squinted at him. "Is that so? And what of you?"

He thought of his sister, who had ridden off to Paradise with the man she loved. He had been foolish to worry, selfish for her company. She had left because she could, because it was her *choice*, just as it was his choice to do what he wanted. His actions had saved Crian's life and allowed their love to blossom. Maybe, just maybe, he could help foster something that good again by saving his son.

"I will stay here," he said, "and fight in your place, should it come to that."

"You will?" she asked, her eyes widening.

Patrick nodded.

"But who will keep Moira safe?" she asked.

Patrick laughed.

"You really think Moira needs someone to keep her safe? She's a better fighter than I am, but if it comforts you, I promise to protect her life with my own."

"I…" Rachida looked flattered, and somewhat satisfied, by his offer. Yet still she protested.

"No," she said. "No, I can't leave Moira. I won't. I love her too much."

Grunting, Patrick tried one last gamble to get her to listen.

"Is that so?" he asked. "You say you love Moira too much to leave her…but what does she say? Does she wish you to stay or go?"

Rachida tossed another scrap of bread into the stream.

"She wants me to leave," she said. "She wants me to be safe."

Patrick put an arm around her shoulders and pulled her against him. His head leaned against hers, and he enjoyed the gentle embrace, which lacked any sexual tension.

"If you love her, then perhaps you should listen to her," he said. "Go, and feel no guilt. We live in a world where the gods walk among us. Perhaps we can forge ourselves a miracle. And if we fall, well…" He looked into her eyes. "You said your son will be a great leader. Perhaps he'll be the one to make Karak regret his decision to ever come here."

Rachida leaned into him, kissing his cheek.

"Thank you," she said with a sly smile. "I think you're manipulating me and just trying to spare me unhappiness…but at least you're good at it."

Patrick laughed.

"Now go pack your things," he said. "I have a sneaking suspicion your phony husband is going to want to leave soon, and you will not be left behind."

"You are one of the most wonderful creations in this world, or any," she said, offering him one last kiss on the lips. "I will never forget this. Never."

"I know," he replied a second later, watching her as she walked away. He leaned back and threw his hands over the back of the wide bench.

"So," he said to himself. "You've just volunteered to give your life fighting for a land you've barely lived in for a month, to protect a temple you would rather see torn to the ground, all because of your love for a woman who only used you for your seed. Patrick, you devil, I fear you're getting dumber by the hour."

He then thought of her words about manipulation and realized that *he* had most likely been the one who had been manipulated. Dumber indeed.

The funny thing was, he really didn't mind all that much.

CHAPTER

28

A s if the cold weren't bad enough, dampness now soaked into Roland's bones as he pressed against the jagged stone wall, knees to his chest, shivering. His lungs burned with each struggling breath and his heart raced. He felt like he was about to die, so intense was the pain that filled him. He had never experienced anything this horrible in all his life. He began to moan, the sound of his chattering teeth bouncing off the cave walls.

"Please stop," Jacob's voice said. "If you're cold, put this on."

Something heavy flew through the air, landing beside him with a wet *plop*. He drew his head out from between his knees and saw Jacob's cloak lying in a heap next to him. He grabbed it, and though the outside was sodden, the inside was dry. He hurriedly draped it over his body, and after a momentary rush of even more coldness, his body began to warm ever so slightly. He stopped shivering, and even though his lungs still hurt, at least the rattle he'd felt earlier had dissipated.

"Better?"

Roland slid his back up the jagged wall until he could see over his knees. Candlelight flickered all around him, illuminating the rock formations that hung from the cave's ceiling. Jacob was sitting cross-legged a few feet away, wearing nothing but his thin tunic. Somehow, he seemed oblivious to the cold. His dark hair hung in front of his face as he leaned over his journal, his blue eyes darting back and forth, absorbing the words he had just written therein. He'd held the same pose ever since they'd ducked into this cave in the mountainside after fleeing Uther Crestwell and Karak's hidden army. Jacob had instantly yanked the journal and writing utensils from his rucksack and started scribbling away with his quill, dipping it into the inkwell as if possessed. When it came to his journal, the man was practically inhuman.

Every now and then they heard the shouts of their pursuers outside the cave walls, and more than once Roland had to plead with Jacob to extinguish his candle.

"Don't worry, they will not find us," his master said dismissively each time, and in the end the First Man had been right. No one had entered the cave, and the ruckus outside had died down to nothing.

It seemed like hours had passed, and yet Jacob still wrote as if his life depended on it. Every so often he lifted his head and rested the feather of his quill against his chin in thought, the light from the candle illuminating only his cheeks, making his eyes black voids of nothingness. Roland had asked him several times what was so important that he had to write it down right there and then, but Jacob simply brushed aside his questions and bent back over his journal. He wished his master would talk to him, if for no other reason than to distract him from the horrible images running through his mind, the memories of the ravine that just wouldn't leave him alone.

The warmth gradually returned to his bones, thanks to his master's cloak, and Roland stood up. He stretched his numb legs, cracked his sore spine, and wrapped the cloak more tightly around him. The roof of the cave was low, so he had to stoop a bit as he crossed the short expanse separating him and Jacob. The First Man didn't look up from his work, not even when Roland's hand fell on his shoulder.

"What is it?" Jacob asked, still jotting down letters in his tight scrawl.

"Please, master, just tell me what you're doing."

For a moment Jacob said nothing while his hand continued to craft words on the parchment, but finally he placed the quill on the damp stone beside his skinning knife and looked up at him.

"Done," he said. There was a wide smile on his face.

"So...."

Jacob shook his head, as if he'd momentarily forgotten where he was, and then said, "I apologize, Roland. I needed to document what we just witnessed while it was still fresh in my mind. The words the mad priest spoke, the gestures he made, the symbols they used, all of it."

"But why?"

"Roland, you've known me your whole life," Jacob replied. "When have I *not* written down the things I've learned?"

"But did you have to do it while we're hiding from those who wish to kill us?"

"Come now, Roland," said Jacob, shaking his head. "What *should* I have done? Huddled in the corner, afraid and unwilling to do anything about it? Ashhur forbid I find a way to pass the time instead of worrying about my beloved Brienna."

Roland stepped back, his heart sinking in his chest. He felt his face drain of color, and his throat hitched. Jacob noticed this and shot to his feet, whacking his head against the ceiling of the cave in the process. He cursed and rubbed his wound.

"I'm so sorry, Roland," he said afterward, wrapping his arms around him. "That was foolish of me. I need to remember that you have been sheltered...all of you have. You may be a man now, but inside you're still a child, as are your mother, your father, and your siblings. None of you have seen the things

I have, nor experienced your life nearing its end. I should be more understanding."

"It's all right," Roland whispered into his master's shoulder.

"No, it's not. I was thoughtless and cruel. Now here, sit down and let me show you what I've written."

"Shouldn't we be leaving?" asked Roland. "We need to find out if Azariah and Brienna made it back all right. And someone needs to find out about that army!"

"Not now," replied Jacob. "I'm sure Az and Brienna are fine. They're more than capable, and the river's current is strong, besides being a much more direct route than by foot. They've probably already told Turock about what we saw. Uther's men may still be out there searching for us—in fact, I'm sure of it. I say we wait for daylight so that nothing can leap out at us from the darkness. Now sit down."

Roland did, and for the next hour he listened to Jacob prattle on about his theories on ancient rituals, thin points in time, and bridges between worlds. The First Man tried to show him some of what he had documented, explaining his assumptions and conclusions about what they'd seen, but it was so far above Roland's head that all he heard was gibberish. Jacob seemed agitated, however, and so Roland sat back, listened, and pretended he understood. He did not want to risk his master's ire if he were made to repeat himself.

"But the best part," Jacob said, "is that I think I have finally discovered the missing piece. For years I have searched for the missing words, the magical syllables and phrases that would allow for passage between one world and the next. It is obvious that Uther discovered such rites, for how else can we explain what happened tonight, that floating, fleshy portal above the ravine? It's astounding, really."

Roland shivered at the memory.

"It was disgusting," he protested. "Disgusting and immoral and, well, *evil*." He surprised himself then, as he had never used that word—*evil*—before in his life. Until tonight, it had been an abstract concept that existed only in the Wardens' stories.

Jacob looked at him for a long moment and then shook his head and smiled.

"Yes, of course. The death of innocents is *always* disheartening."

"Then why do you speak of it as if you don't care?"

"It's not that I don't care," Jacob said with a shrug. "It is only that, in the universe at large, death is a natural occurrence. You don't see a mother deer decrying the unfairness of it all when her child is eaten by a wolf or wildcat. You do not see a school of fish protest when one of their numbers is caught in a fisher's nets. And you certainly don't hear one word of complaint from the hyenas when one pack comes in and overthrows another. The cycle of life is all about survival, of moving from one point in time to the next without losing your neck. You have been protected in Paradise, and you haven't been shown the truth of existence outside your perfect little bubble. I have. I was here long before any other human stepped foot on this land, and therefore I can be a bit more...objective about the matter."

"The way you speak," said Roland. "It's like you disagree with everything Ashhur has taught us."

"You misunderstand me," Jacob replied. "Come now, boy. I have resided in the west for nearly twenty years. I have stayed because I *chose* to stay, because I believe in the purity of the ideals Ashhur teaches. Just because I may be critical of your lack of knowledge does not mean I am critical of the way of life. I just wish that sometimes things were more...balanced, I suppose. No matter how hard Ashhur tries, this world will never be perfect or absolutely safe. I fear for how Paradise will handle hardships, even those that are temporary."

Roland scratched at the week's worth of stubble covering his chin.

"I see," he said. "But Ashhur has said that to reach the golden eternity, we must be pure of heart. Can we be pure of heart if we're taught these things?"

Jacob set down his plume.

"Who was your family's Warden?" he asked.

"Um, Loen. Why?"

"Ah, Loen. He of the tall tales. Did he ever tell you the one about the witch who lured two small children to her home, wishing to fatten them up and eat them, only to be stopped by the brave knight who comes to rescue them?"

"Yes. The story of Penelope and Rutgard. Why?"

"Think about it, Roland. It is a story of a *witch*…who wants to eat *children*…until she is *slain* by a *knight*."

The reasoning snapped together in Roland's head.

"Oh," he said.

"Exactly," said Jacob. "Knowledge is never evil. What Uther did may be vile, but the knowledge of it is still fascinating to me, and might serve some greater purpose in my hands in the decades to come. The same goes for you. Although you have learned of violence, you, Roland Norsman, still have one of the purest hearts I have ever encountered."

Roland's face reddened.

"Thank you," he said.

"You're welcome. Now go away for a while," the First Man said with a wave of his hand.

They laughed together, but after a few moments Roland realized that Jacob was serious. His master sat there, straddling his journal while the candle flickered away, staring at him. Finally, Roland said, "You really want me to go?"

Jacob nodded.

"But where?" Roland replied, aghast.

"There's a ledge beside the cave entrance. Why don't you head out there for a bit, sit and watch the sunrise, perhaps?"

"But…why? And what if there are men out there waiting for me?"

"There aren't any men out there," replied Jacob with a sigh. He pointed to the ground before him, where a pair of glass beads shimmered. "See these? I tossed a few of them out over the ledge after we scurried up the side of the mountain. Should anyone pass within the scope of their magic, these beads—the twins of the ones I threw—will shine, alerting me. You will be safe out there, believe me, and with my cloak, which was charmed by the great elf Anton Ludden of Dezerea, you will not be affected by the cold. As for what I'm doing…let's just say that I wish to try a few experiments."

"You're going to try to reach across the void, aren't you?"

"Something like that."

Roland suddenly felt faint.

"Easy now, boy," said Jacob, his eyes widening as he rose off the ground to try to calm him. "I do not wish to release any demons or any such nonsense. I've been altering some of Uther's words, and I think I have found a way to commune—to *commune*, you hear?— with beings from a different plane of existence. I only wish to talk, to learn. Nothing more. Please, there is nothing to worry about."

"Then why are you sending me off?"

Jacob let out a sigh.

"Because no matter how certain I am, I'm also not arrogant enough to think it's impossible for me to be wrong. If there is danger, you'll be safe out there…and you won't be in my way if I need to handle a tricky situation. For all I know, we might get a glimpse of the beast of a thousand faces, and I'd rather spare you that. The sight might cost you your sanity."

"And you don't fear for yourself?"

The First Man grinned and pulled the crystal Brienna had given him from his pocket.

"I do not, my dear steward, for love is my safeguard. And besides, it won't happen. This is a precaution, nothing more."

Roland nodded. He didn't like the idea in the slightest, but in the end he trusted Jacob Eveningstar more than anyone in the world. If Jacob said everything would be fine, then everything would be fine.

"Very well," he said with a nod. "Come find me when you're finished."

"Oh, and Roland," said Jacob, reaching down to grab his wineskin off the floor. "Take this with you. The cloak may keep you warm, but if you *really* wish to keep the shivers away, take a few sips of what's inside."

Roland stared at the skin, jiggled it, and heard liquid *swish*.

"I will," he replied. "But please, take care of yourself."

"I will. You have nothing to worry about."

Roland picked up his candle, turned away from his master, and squat-walked his way back through the cave's narrow passageway. The channel seemed thinner than it had before, his uncertain nerves playing games with his sense of perspective. He took a deep breath and, telling himself that Jacob knew best, tried to clear his mind of unease.

He walked out into the cold air of night, a biting wind assaulting his face the instant he stepped outside. He flipped the hood of Jacob's cloak over his head and immediately felt its blessed warmth. He then positioned himself against the side of the mountain, a few feet from the opening to the cave, and slid down to his rump, tucking his legs up under the cloak after he was seated. He listened for signs of life around him, but all he could hear was the rush of flowing water somewhere off to his right. For the moment, at least, he seemed to be alone. Tilting back the wineskin, he took a few swigs of the bitter fluid, feeling the alternating burn and comfort as it slid down his throat. Then he stared at the sky, noticing that a few streamers of deep purple were beginning to crawl their way across the horizon. That meant sunrise was only an hour away, two at most. Although he was sitting on the wrong side of the mountain to actually *see* the sunrise, as Jacob had suggested, that was fine by Roland. He was much more interested in the way the rising sun changed the colors in the sky, the way it shoved aside the darkness like Ashhur vanquished pain and sin from the hearts of his children.

His head began to grow dizzy, and Roland leaned back against a hard stone. For a second he thought he heard multiple voices whispering from somewhere deep within the cave, but the dizziness increased, and soon all he heard was the rush of blood between his ears. He didn't fight against the sensation, and a few moments later, he was fast asleep.

When he opened his eyes again, the day was bright as could be. The sky was no longer overcast, the way it seemed to have been during their entire stay in the Tinderlands. Roland found himself lying face down in the dirt. He rolled onto his back, stretched his arms high above his head, and yawned.

When he sat up, a strange wave of vertigo came over him. He teetered there for a moment, his stomach feeling as if it would empty itself of its meager contents. The only other time he'd felt this way was when he'd stolen a few swigs of ceremonial wine when he was fourteen years old. He'd become extremely ill, and his head had ached for days afterward. He pulled the hood of Jacob's cloak down low, shielding his eyes from the day's brightness, and looked around.

He was still on the ledge outside the cave, and by the position of the sun, which was still hidden behind the peak of the mountain behind him, he assumed it was early morning. That meant he'd been sleeping for perhaps two or three hours. Still feeling queasy, he lifted the wineskin, which lay empty beside him, and stared at it.

That has to be the most potent wine I have ever tasted, he thought. He had only imbibed of a drop or two. That was when he realized how long Jacob had left him out here. Panic surged through him. In his mind's eye he saw his master lying in a pool of blood, his body mutilated by whatever strange creature he had been trying to commune with, dismembered like the poor folks whom Karak's followers had butchered the previous night.

A strange sound reached his ears, like the screeching of a distant hawk, and Roland's panic multiplied. He staggered to his feet, ignoring the dizzy spell that ensued, and stared across the wide space of dead, sloping earth. He was high up on the side of the mountain, which offered him a clear view of the land for miles. To his left were numerous mountains and hills, all brown limestone and craggy granite. In the center was a valley filled with patches of yellowing grass, at the end of which was another slight rise that emptied out into a huge, circular depression—most likely the same depression where the horrible ritual had taken place. Nothing was alive anywhere he looked. In fact, it wasn't until he glanced to his right, where the waters of the Gihon flowed, that he saw any movement at all.

The hawk's screech came once more, and he squinted against the bright light and the headache that spiked behind his eyes, trying to make out something far off in the distance. A thin black cloud sprouted from a tiny monument somewhere on the far side of the river, seemingly miles away. The distant black cloud rose higher and higher, its smoky tendrils wafting this way and that. When it mixed with the puffy white cumulus that hung low on the horizon, the different colors of vapor combined, and Roland swore he saw the visage of a roaring lion.

That was when he realized that the tiny monument producing the smoke was the half-constructed tower by the Drake Township. Panic swelled inside him. He imagined Uther Crestwell and his minions performing the same rituals they had enacted the night before on all the poor, tormented people of Drake.

"Ja-*COB!*" he screamed, falling back against the side of the mountain, his fingers digging into the rock and dirt. He scrabbled across the ledge, lingering in front of the cave's mouth. A moment later Jacob emerged into the light of day, his dark hair disheveled, his tunic ripped and torn, his face smeared with a crusty sort of dirt.

"What happened?" he asked, looking and acting as dazed as Roland felt.

Roland's fear overwhelmed any relief he might have felt for the fact that his master was alive and well. Unable to form words, he pointed toward the smoke, which now rose in twin columns. Jacob followed his finger, and the First Man's eyes opened wide.

"Wait here!" he shouted and then disappeared back into the cave. When he reemerged, he was carrying his hastily packed ruck-sack. He took Roland by the arm and began leading him down the steep side of the mountain at a fast clip. Both of their feet slipped and slid on loose rocks, and Roland feared he might fall the rest of the way on his face. It didn't escape him how miraculous it was that they'd scaled this peak in near-complete darkness only a few hours before, but that thought was soon swallowed by the terror that steadily rose up his throat.

For now there weren't two columns of smoke, but four. Jacob pulled him along all the faster, steering him toward the river.

He never once asked Jacob what had happened with his experiment. At that point, the only thing that mattered was reaching the camp before it was too late—which it probably already was.

CHAPTER

29

Crian opened the door to the Tower Keep and carried Nessa inside. His love lounged in his arms, her head thrown back, a broad smile plastered on her face. The sheer baptismal gown she wore was soaked, as was her stunning red hair, which dangled below his forearm like ocean weeds. The thin material of her gown had gone transparent, and he could see the outline of her nipples, the depression of her belly button, the gentle slope of her thighs, and the hair between her legs, which shone as brightly as that atop her head. His manhood rose, and he suddenly found it difficult to hold her, despite her diminutive size.

"Are you all right, love?" she asked, her eyes still closed, the smile never leaving her face.

"I'm...fine," he grunted in reply, feeling his cheeks flush in embarrassment.

"I think I know what's wrong," she said and, leaning back in his arms, grabbed the back of his neck and stared into his eyes. Her other hand crept over his elbow, moving down until her fingers brushed against the crotch of his thick breeches. He let out a moan and stumbled. Nessa laughed, Crian cursed, and he eventually set her down while he leaned against the wall, shaking his head.

"You're insufferable," he said.

She bit her lip seductively and leaned against the wall too, using it to brace herself as she walked forward, swaying her slender hips in the process. He couldn't help but smile.

"I'm not insufferable," Nessa said. "I'm simply in love. You're my everything, Crian Crestwell, and I want to *give* you everything." She grinned wickedly, an expression that made her seem like a clever seductress rather than the little girl she often appeared to be. "We are free now, my love, free to do whatever we wish. I need to have you beside me, atop me, *in* me again. It's been far too long already. Now that our love is no longer forbidden…and I'm to be your wife…."

Crian needed no more urging. He kicked himself off the wall and crashed into her, his plain, itchy wool clothing—the staple of his existence now that he'd been exiled from his family—crumpling as he lifted her into the air. Their lips met, their tongues probed, and he pressed her into the wall, holding her up with one arm while he caressed her with the other. Her lips tasted sweet, like strawberries, and he was filled with the desire to rediscover what the rest of her tasted like.

…and I'm to be your wife…

Amazingly enough, it was true. Nessa DuTaureau, daughter of the first of Ashhur's children, was to be his bride. They had just come from the city quad, where Nessa had been baptized. He had been so proud of her, watching from a distance as his love stood in the center of the great fountain at the center of the four interconnecting streets that formed the quad, surrounded by onlookers. Soleh Mori had been there, along with every member of the Council of Twelve. All had come to see the very first convert of Ashhur. Karak had been there as well, and though Crian kept his distance—he had never met the god in the flesh before, and he was instantly afraid that the deity would strike him down for disobeying his laws—he was somewhat eased by the pious kindness in the god's eyes. He had also been taken aback by the sheer *size* of him, standing twice the height of even the tallest man present, his fingers large enough to crush a head in a single hand.

Yet Nessa had not been afraid, even as Karak stepped into the fountain with her and demanded she kneel before him. She did so willingly, eagerly, raising her hands up to the deity without hesitation. When the priest poured the cold water of creation over her head, she did not even flinch. And when Karak spoke his decrees, she affirmed each one, her innocent voice suddenly full of strength and conviction. It had not escaped Crian's attention the way Karak had looked at her afterward, with all the affection of a father welcoming a long-lost child back into his arms, nor did he fail to notice the way the god then looked at him, those shining, golden eyes piercing straight into his soul.

You had best appreciate this creature, were the words he heard, though no lips moved to speak them.

And appreciate her he did. After the ceremony, once Nessa was officially dubbed a free child of Karak, they were informed that they could now marry. He knew they would in time. All he had to do was collect the proper coin to pay a priest to preside over the ceremony, for unlike baptisms, which were offered free of charge, marriages cost money. *To ensure that those dedicating their lives to each other are in the position to care for themselves*, had been standard reason given by his father, and since Crian had always agreed with that philosophy in the past, it would be hypocritical to decry it now.

Yet the collection of the necessary funds continued to be a problem. As a low-ranking member of the City Watch, he earned a pitiable weekly salary. It would take him months to save up enough for the ceremony, even more if they decided to find lodging outside the Tower Keep. He could not even afford to pay the rookery to send the letter Nessa had written to her brother yet. Depressing, sure, but at the moment the only thing that *really* mattered was that he and Nessa were free to live their lives as they chose. In truth, that was

all he had desired since the day he first met her in the delta swamp-
lands, and he would gladly give up all of his titles, responsibilities,
and influence if it meant he could spend the rest of his life with her.

"I will be your husband," he whispered into her ear after finally
pulling his lips away from hers. "And I will protect you always."

He felt her body shudder against his, and he could take it no
longer. He glanced around, making sure they were alone, and then,
slipping his hands underneath her, lifted her, and after she wrapped
her legs around his waist, he carried her up the stairwell, down the
hall, and into their room. He barely had time to shut the door and
light a candle before Nessa pulled him down on the bed, tugging at
his clothes and kissing him all over. He slipped the sodden baptismal
gown over her head and tossed it aside. Once they were both naked,
her body still damp from the ceremony, they fell on one another, each
devouring the other's essence, enjoying the feeling of their connection,
the taste of sweat on flesh, the smell of desire that permeated the room.

Crian let out a cry of animal passion that he hoped would never
end. Despite everything that had happened, he'd never been happier
in all his life.

Vulfram heard the cries of ardor as they echoed through the halls
of the Tower Keep. He was in father's studio again, drink in hand,
propped up against one of the countless statues of Karak. Since
Crian had arrived with the DuTaureau girl, this had been the only
place he could find solace, despite its odd effect on his faculties. He
slept in here, took his meals in here; in fact, the only time he left was
when his father wished to work, which, given his son's sour mood
and brooding attitude, didn't seem to happen very much at all.

His deceitful mother had, of course, begun acting strange
around him. Whenever she came home and tiptoed into the studio
to see him, she acted hesitant, as if he were a wild animal that could

strike out at any moment. This from the woman who had raised Kayne and Lilah. And her attempts at communication were laughably inconsistent. At times she would coddle him, ushering in freshly baked goods and urging him to eat. Other times she would chastise him for his behavior, for his lack of resiliency, telling him how his position as Lord Commander was hanging by a delicate thread. Although that was typical behavior for her—Vulfram had experienced it since he was a child, the private vulnerability turning into hardheadedness in the public eye—there was a sort of desperation behind it now that was unbecoming. But that didn't matter. *Nothing* mattered anymore. His little girl was gone, his mother was secretly plotting against him, and he was a broken man.

Tonight his god would visit him, and when Karak saw what a miserable wretch he was, he would be demoted, just like Crian had been.

The thing was, Vulfram just…didn't…care. About any of it, not even Yenge, Alexander, and Caleigh, sitting back in the safety of Erznia, unaware of the hardships he was enduring.

But he *did* care about Lyana still, and now he had to be tortured by listening to the Crestwell whelp and his turncoat whore fucking upstairs. The sounds of their passion brought forth images of his daughter's future, of her trapped with some sadistic bastard like Romeo Connington, forced to obey his every command. Whenever a man purchased her services, would she be forced to scream out the way that DuTaureau girl was screaming?

He covered his ears with his hands and screamed himself, trying to drown them out. When his heart raced out of control and his throat went dry, he stopped. Other than his own voice echoing in his ears and the faint sizzle of the candles that burned all around him, everything was silent. He offered a quiet *thank you* to the unseen heavens, lifted his jug of home-brewed rum, and swallowed a large gulp. Then he stood and stumbled across his father's workshop, his vision swimming.

He walked past statue after statue, not wanting to raise his eyes to meet the accusing glares they leveled at him. He lazily held Darkfall's handle with the hand that was not clutching his jug, dragging the unsheathed sword behind him, its tip scraping against stone with a metallic *hiss*. He didn't know where he was going, didn't care. He brought the jug up to his lips once more, the liquor sloshing inside its ceramic bubble, and downed yet another gulp. Then he heard more noises from the floor above, more moans coupled with the grating of wooden bedposts sliding along the stone floor. Forward, back, forward, back, forward, back. Vulfram began to get dizzy from the repetitiveness of it.

"Just finish already," he groaned.

At last he could take no more. He cocked back his arm and hurled the jug across the studio, where it smashed against the chest of one of his father's statues. Rum splashed everywhere. Normally Vulfram would have chastised himself for wasting good liquor, but he was too consumed with rage to care.

He hated them all. He hated his mother for her betrayal and false sense of concern, hated Karak for taking his daughter away. He hated Broward for his role in the whole mess and Clovis for being such an insufferable prick. But most of all he hated those two bastards upstairs, who taunted him with their zeal, their love, their *youth*— none of which Lyana would ever get to experience. Not anymore.

In a fit of rage, he rushed the statue against which his jug had shattered. Time and again he pummeled it with his fists. He heard bones break, but his entire body stayed numb. Blood streaked the chest of the statue where his fists met it, forming interlocking lines. And still the face of Karak mocked him.

"Not good enough?" he shouted at it. "Still want to judge me, do you?"

He rammed his forehead into his god's visage, hoping to strike it hard enough to knock the head from the body. But the statue was solid stone, and a hollow *clang* rang inside his own head in the aftermath.

He stumbled backward, his vision spinning, his knees feeling suddenly weak. He collapsed, falling on his side, jarring his elbow. He blamed even the pain that shot through him on the couple upstairs.

The world slowly faded to blackness. Swirling in the shadows was the image of the bodies of Crian Crestwell and Nessa DuTaureau, mutilated beyond all recognition. It taunted him with its simplicity, its blessed relief.

"I could only wish," Vulfram muttered as he felt his consciousness slip away.

Crian rolled off his love, gasping for breath. Slowly his mind returned from the isolation of his passion, and he took in the world around him once more. He heard the creaking in the walls, felt the subtle bite of cool air inside the room. Nessa lounged on the bed, her naked body covered with sweat and sparkling in the candlelight. He touched her belly, which elicited a moan from her puffy lips.

"Really?" he said, exhausted. "You're not satisfied *yet?*"

Nessa gazed at him, her blue eyes twinkling, and shook her head.

"What? Isn't that what you want?" she asked, grinning.

He shrugged. "Perhaps. But it's been twice already. I'm sore."

"Sore?" she said, slapping his arm. "You best make yourself *not* sore."

"Isn't that your job?"

She slapped at him again, and he laughed as he blocked her playful swipes.

"Fine," he said with a sigh. "But let me piss first."

He stood up and walked to the bucket that rested in the corner of the room.

"Please don't do that in here," she said. "It's...unsavory. Isn't there a washroom down the hall?"

He turned toward her, still naked as the day he was born.

"Really?" he asked.

She sat up, hugging her knees close to her chest, looking once more like a little girl he had to protect rather than the woman he had just ravaged.

"Please?" she said.

"All right," he said, strolling out of the room without bothering to put on his clothes.

Halfway down the candlelit corridor he had second thoughts about prancing naked around the tower. Though Soleh, Ulric, and Adeline weren't present—the three Moris had been called to the Temple of Karak for a meeting—it was possible that Lord Commander Vulfram, or the specter the once proud man had become, could be lurking about. The thought of him made Crian shake his head. Vulfram had been his hero for years. Only once had he seen him since taking up residence in the tower. The state the man was in saddened him—Vulfram's normally shaved head was covered with thick stubble, his eyes bloodshot, and his breath reeking of liquor. He hated seeing a good man broken down like that. Hurrying toward the washroom, Crian hoped he wouldn't have to see Vulfram like that again while also naked himself.

He stepped into the washroom, lit a candle, and tried to put thoughts of Vulfram Mori out of his mind. He hummed while he pissed in the bucket and then turned to leave. He was cautious this time, peering both ways down the hallway to make sure no one was looking. The coast was clear, and he started back to his room. He thought of Nessa waiting for him, her exposed body bent and ready, and he surprised himself by getting excited all over again.

"Three times," he muttered. "Why not? Going to hurt like the abyss tomorrow, though…."

When he turned the corner into their shared room, that excitement was ripped away in an instant.

All around him, splattered on the walls and ceiling, dripping down the nightstand, even coating his precious dragonglass mirror, was a sea of red. The candlelight refracted off its watery surface, making the entire room appear to be on fire. Crian's knees buckled and he stared at the bed he'd left just moments before. On it lay Nessa, face soaked with the same red that covered everything else, her unblinking, glassy eyes staring at the ceiling. Her arms and legs were splayed out wide and her chest was split open from the center of her neck all the way to her pelvis. The skin had been peeled back like flaps, and it dangled over her sides, exposing her ribcage and the glossy, pulpy mess of her spilled innards.

Crian gagged on his own bile.

This is not real, this is not real, his mind repeated over and over, a mantra that failed to change the horror in front of him. Falling on his knees, he began to weep, his arms dropping limply beside him. He tried again to convince himself it was all a nightmare, but a second glance at his dead and mutilated lover was enough to destroy that idea, as well as break the last vestiges of sanity in his mind.

"It really is a shame," said a slurred voice behind him.

Crian recognized that voice. He slowly climbed to his feet, trying to stay upright despite the anguish that cramped his insides and turned his knees to jelly. Vision blurry through tear-soaked eyes, he turned around to face the intruder, a huffing man bathed in shadow. Crian's mind emptied, his body numb long before he saw the flash of silver that danced before him. The knife bit into his flesh and he felt the strange, wet sensation of liquid spilling over his chest. The room tilted on its side and began to spin. Then after a sudden flash of light, Crian saw no more.

The headache hit him the second he tried to open his eyes. Vulfram ground his fists into them, wincing at the gritty sensation behind his eyelids. His chest felt constricted, as if there were a great weight resting atop him, and when he rubbed his fingers together, he realized they were strangely wet.

"My gods, Vulfram!"

The voice came from somewhere above him, to the left, and Vulfram lifted his head toward it. His vision was blurred, and he could only make out a vague figure. The figure then lifted a torch, revealing a gruff face marred by four wicked-looking scars.

"Malcolm," Vulfram said to Captain Gregorian, his speech slurred.

The Captain of the Palace Guard stared down at him, his features twisted with horror. To complete the bizarre image, he held a vase full of flowers in his hands.

"What did you *do*, you bastard!" he yelled.

Vulfram winced at the volume of Gregorian's voice and brought his hands up to cover his ears. His left reached its destination, but he held something in his right that first bounced off his cheek and then brought a quick, needle-like pain to his temple. He opened his fingers reflexively, and something clanked on the floor beside him. When he looked at his hand, he saw that it was stained red.

"What the…." he began, confusion overwhelming him. Glancing down at the floor, he saw an elegantly crafted knife, its blade curved and sharp, the grip rounded with finger notches. He couldn't tell what material the handle was made of, however, for the entire weapon was soaked with blood.

The Captain took a few steps into the room from the doorway where he'd been standing. His eyes kept flicking in Vulfram's direction, bulging in disbelief. A few moments later, the man dropped the vase. It shattered, spilling water everywhere and scattering the assorted lilies, orchids, and hyacinths that had filled it. Vulfram's gaze followed the path of the flowing water, watching it twist around the strange red blotches that covered the smooth stone floor, until it reached the legs of a bed. He then glanced up, and from his vantage point on the floor all he could see were four feet hanging off the edge of the mattress above him, blood dripping from the toes.

"Shit!" he yelped, kicking out his legs, suddenly not feeling so groggy any longer. He tried to stand, but his feet slipped and he fell back down. It was only then that he realized there was blood *everywhere*—on the floor, the walls, the ceiling, and even all over himself.

In a panic he looked up at Captain Gregorian, whose attention was focused on the bed. More slowly this time, Vulfram rose to his feet. His survival instinct told him to flee, to knock the Captain out and run from this room, from this tower, from this city, from this *kingdom*, never to return again. That instinct was cut off the moment he saw what Gregorian was staring at.

The feet belonged to Crian Crestwell and Nessa DuTaureau. Crian's throat was slit, whereas Nessa had been sliced open from breast to belly. They lay beside one another, and to complete the macabre picture, their fingers were entwined, as if they'd held hands throughout the entire horrific ordeal.

The stench hit him suddenly, the scent of ammonia and rot. He doubled over and hacked and hacked, his insides emptying, his fluids covering the blood that was smeared over everything, making him sick anew.

Hands grabbed him from behind, yanking him out of the room and into the hallway. His world turned dizzy again, and for a split second he wondered how he'd gotten to the third floor of the tower. He cried out as he was thrown against the wall. His head struck with a loud *thud*, smacking off the stone, and a loud buzzing flooding his ears. He collapsed, momentarily losing control of his bodily functions and shitting himself right then and there.

He gathered enough strength to turn his head, watched as Gregorian disappeared inside the room again. When he emerged, he was carrying two weapons—the bloody knife and Darkfall, which he slid into its scabbard. The Captain whistled loudly, and Vulfram heard multiple booted footsteps echo through the foyer on the first floor far below them. That done, Gregorian knelt before him, staring at him with a mixture of disgust and anger. Blood was smeared on his forehead, and the four scars that had come from Vulfram's childhood pets seemed to expand and contract like the gills of a fish as he breathed.

"Vulfram Mori, I hereby detain you for the murder of Crian Crestwell and Nessa DuTaureau, beloved children of Karak," the Captain growled.

Vulfram tried to deny it, but an armored fist slammed into his face, ending his protest before he could utter it.

CHAPTER

30

I t was dark but for a single peephole. Light shone through the narrow opening, creating a lance-like beam that pierced the darkness, illuminating a single spot on the slatted wood floor. Geris sat there, slumped on his knees, staring at the beam, watching flecks of dust dance within it. He tried to focus on them in an attempt to shut out the jovial sounds from outside, for in no way did he wish to witness the wicked ceremony that was even now taking place.

Eventually his curiosity got the best of him. He stood up, made his way to the side of his makeshift prison, and peered through the hole.

The cart he was stowed in was one they'd brought with them on the journey from Safeway. Ahaesarus and Judarius had removed the canvas and nailed excess wooden slats to the outside and above his head. He would never forget the look of revulsion and disappointment on his mentor's face, nor the fury that had seeped from Judarius's green-gold eyes. He tried to explain to them why he'd done what he had done, but they would hear none of it. If only they'd believe him! The strongest Wardens were blessed by Ashhur to know with absolute certainty when a factual truth was spoken, yet they *still* didn't understand. They had both told him more than once that he'd lost his mind and shamed them both in the process.

"Just listen," Geris moaned as he pressed his fingers against the wagon. "Why won't you just listen?"

Now Geris was imprisoned in a place faraway from home, and the rest of his family had been sent away in disgrace. The wagon had been parked on the very edge of a vast courtyard, and he was left to watch helplessly through that tiny slat in his prison as the people of Mordeina gathered around Manse DuTaureau to observe the crowning of the first ever King of Paradise, the imposter Benjamin Maryll. *"A punishment,"* Judarius had said, and oh what a punishment it was.

It was a joyous scene, and laughter and singing filled the night. Great bonfires were lit, fires that burned so strongly that the normally chilly northern fall air was hot as summertime. Even Geris, many yards away, was sweating because of it. People danced around the bonfires, arms locked. There were children everywhere, hundreds of them under the watchful eyes of the Wardens, and the expressions on their faces spoke of blissful joy. He wished he could feel that joy, but instead his insides twisted and his cheeks flushed with anger. *You're blind!* he wanted to shout. *Can you not see the truth?* But what good would it do? The people of Paradise were ignorant fools, as the shadow-lion had said, happy just to make babies, grow vegetables, and pray to Ashhur. A simple life was what they had, and they thought themselves lucky for it.

That simple life was going to be the end of them.

The party raged on, as if the events of the previous evening had never happened. It was yet another example of their ignorance, yet another example of why the witch would win. At that point the singing toned down a bit, and as if on cue, the witch scaled the platform that had been raised in front of the manse's back gate in between two bonfires. The creature was elegant, that much Geris

could admit, what with her silken clothing and the crystal diadem
that shone atop her fiery red hair. The witch hushed the crowd with
a wave of her hand, and she smiled at them—a smile that only faltered when her eyes darted toward Geris's prison. Within moments
it returned. Geris was taken aback by how she glowed, how beautiful she was—Ashhur's mark was all over her.

When the crowd quieted, the witch signaled for others to join
her on the platform. First it was the witch's male look-alike, then
Ahaesarus, who never once glanced in his ward's direction. Howard
Baedan followed, the witch's master steward. Finally, Judarius
scaled the steps, his chest puffed out with pride, his dark hair neatly
trimmed, the light of the twin bonfires reflecting in his intense eyes.
The two Wardens flanked the witch and her steward, towering over
them, looking like the otherworldly creatures they were.

"Citizens of Mordeina," the witch said, addressing the crowd,
both human and Warden, with her hands clasped together in a
show of humility that was much too convincing for so vile a creature. "Citizens of the Paradise created by Ashhur, our creator most
divine, this is truly a special evening. On this night we cast aside the
restraints of our childhood. Our species is no longer in its infancy,
and like birds, we are finally ready to step out from the nest that
has sheltered us so long and spread our wings. For we children of
Ashhur, self-governing is our first glorious moment of flight."

The crowd cheered at that, but there seemed something off
about their applause. Even to Geris's young ears, it sounded like
they weren't really sure what they were cheering *for*.

"We gather here tonight to crown our first sovereign king. The
process has been a long one, and not without error, but at last a suitable ruler has been chosen. Citizens of Mordeina, I would like to
introduce you to the King of Paradise, Benjamin Kartalan Maryll!"

The crowd roared, this time much louder than before, as Ben
appeared from behind the platform. He didn't climb up, but
just…rose, as if he need not obey the laws of nature. Geris stared,

slack-jawed and amazed, until he saw the witch standing aside, her eyes closed and her neck tensed, her mouth uttering silent words as her fingers pointed at Ben. When he had floated up over the platform, she gently lowered him. Once he was firmly on his feet, the witch gasped, falling backward a bit, only to be caught by Judarius's massive paws.

"Witch's magic," Geris muttered, disgusted. A pathetic display to enhance Ben's image in the people's minds.

Ben stood before the host of hundreds and bowed. He wore purple clothing that shimmered in the firelight, much like the witch, and a cloak of fur was wrapped around his shoulders. His long, dark hair was tied back, leaving only a couple of strands, one at each of his temples, that curled down like corkscrews. A black scarf was wrapped around his neck, no doubt to hide the wound Geris had given him the night before. Geris grunted in disgust. Martin would have looked better up there, with his deep ginger hair and broad shoulders.

But then again, Ben wasn't Ben. This Ben was an imposter. He had to remember that.

Geris ducked away from his tiny portal just as Ben knelt before Ahaesarus to receive his crown. It lacked any jewels or precious metals, and was instead made of simple polished wood. "A crown fashioned by a carpenter, to instill humility in the new king," his mentor had told him. Geris couldn't watch any more of the sham ceremony. All he wanted to do now was sit alone in his dark prison, drink stale water from the ceramic bowl they'd given him, and think of ways to escape so he might take down the witch and her imposter.

"You've done well," said a voice in the darkness.

Geris started, his head whipping back and forth, trying to find the source of the voice. There was a deeper blackness on the other side of the wagon, a dark, misty cloud that swirled around the shaft of light created by the peephole. He *knew* that voice. It was the one from his dreams, the voice of the shadow-lion. *Have I fallen asleep?*

he wondered. He slapped his own cheek to make sure. The sound echoed through the interior of his prison, and the side of his jaw throbbed.

The deep shadow drew in on itself, solidifying, becoming even blacker. In the darkness Geris could make out the outline of the smoky lion. It drew nearer to him, so near that he could smell the rankness of its breath—damp soil mixed with sulfur. The thing leaned forward then, getting closer to the shaft of light, and he could see its features clearly.

The lion grinned at him, black fangs poking over an even blacker maw. By comparison, its eyes were like fire. They stared at him, pits as deep as the underworld, and despite the heat from the bonfires outside, Geris began to shiver.

"Don't mock me," he said, lowering his head in shame. "You know I failed."

"You did not fail me," the shadow-lion said. "All is how it was meant to be."

"But the imposter still lives," Geris sniveled. "He is king now, and the witch is by his side."

"There is no imposter, boy," said the shadow-lion with a laugh. "There is no witch."

Geris's head shot up, his eyes widened.

"What?"

"Benjamin Maryll is who he has always been—a weak child. This new strength he shows is born of cowardice and a desire to please. It will not last, no more than snow beneath a summer sun. Ashhur's Paradise deserves such a king, a nation of rot hiding behind an image of strength and perfection."

"But...you told me...."

"Aye, I did. And your parents said dreams could be misleading, as did your own god...."

"You're not from him," he whispered, fear forming a layer of ice around his heart. By Ashhur, what had he done?

"No. I am of something better. Something wiser. You are the puppet, and I am the one holding the strings. What a shame it is that no one will ever believe you, Geris. No one will ever listen to your mad ramblings, your screams of witches and imposters. Try if you wish, of course, but you know they won't. Only a fool would believe such a laughable story. Only a stupid, arrogant boy grasping for a reason as to why he's losing his only chance for glory—beyond his own slothfulness and pride."

Geris began to sob, thick tears rolling down his cheeks.

"Do not cry," the shadow-lion said, its voice cruelly shifting into Ahaesarus's. "You played the only part you were ever meant to play. But if it will ease your burden, know that you would have been a fine king. A strong king. A better king than Benjamin Maryll...."

Collapsing to the floor of his prison, Geris wailed into the night, his cries drowned out by the din of the coronation taking place only a few hundred feet away. The shadow-lion roared one last time and then disappeared, leaving him alone in the darkness. He slammed his fists into the floor of his prison again and again, bloodying his hand, breaking one of his fingers. The whole time he screamed.

"I'm sorry, I'm sorry!"

He pleaded for Ashhur's forgiveness, but it seemed as though his god weren't listening any longer. There was no one out there to hear him. There was no one to care, no one ready to believe a scared, sick, confused young boy.

CHAPTER

31

Roland's feet were sore as he pounded them into the uneven ground, running as fast as he could. His lungs burned, and sweat poured down his face despite the coolness of the day. He didn't know how much longer he could keep this up.

They had been on the move for hours, following the eastern bank of the Gihon, constantly keeping one eye on the smoldering tower in the distance, which didn't seem to get any closer, no matter how long or far they ran. It was hard to keep up with Jacob; the First Man was seemingly tireless as he sprinted and leapt across the rocky banks, a frightening sort of desperation shining in his eyes. Roland had tried to stop him twice, just so he could rest for a moment, but Jacob just shot him a dirty look and kept on going.

Eventually Jacob did tire, however, lying down beside the river and scooping water into his mouth with his palms. Roland followed suit, dropping to his belly a hundred feet or so behind him, not wanting to wait until he caught up for fear that Jacob might be sprinting away again by the time he reached him. The water was icy cold, and it burned his parched throat going down. He kept on drinking anyway. Thankfully, the cramp that had started to take over his left leg began to wane. He put his head on the slick rocks of the bank and closed his eyes. Despite their need to get to the camp, despite the dread that filled him with each passing second, it was difficult to hold off the urge to lie down and sleep.

"Roland," Jacob said, stirring him from a slumber he hadn't realized he'd fallen into. The First Man's hand was on his shoulder, shaking him. "Roland, get up. We are not far now."

Roland's heart sank at the thought of more running, but he pushed to his feet anyway. The mere seconds of sleep had left him disoriented, and he kept his gaze on Jacob as they started a slow jog that gradually picked up speed as they eased back into the effort. In no time they were both at it again, running to beat the demon, arms pumping, hearts thumping, minds racing.

By the time they reached the camp, the sun was low on the horizon, casting purple and crimson rays over the sparse cloud cover. The camp lay on the other side of the river, and a spasm of fear attacked Roland when he looked across, staring at the burnt grass and mangled tents that surrounded the half-built tower. The clouds of smoke that had risen earlier were long gone, having disappeared into the atmosphere. In a moment of blind optimism, Roland took that as a good sign—at least any fires that had been lit were now extinguished. Maybe, just maybe, that meant everyone was safe....

Jacob didn't hesitate; he leapt into the water and started paddling with one hand while holding his rucksack high in the air with the other. Roland followed him in, after discarding the cloak, gasping as the freezing water assaulted him, tightening his muscles and making it difficult to move. The current tried to carry him along, and it took all his remaining effort to fight it and stay afloat in his waterlogged clothes. A distant part of his mind stood in awe of his master, who seemed to have no trouble traversing the flowing river with only one hand to help him along.

At last Roland emerged on the other side, shivering and numb. He panted as he climbed the rocks, their sharp edges piercing his wet clothing as he dragged himself out of the water. He stayed there on the bank, coughing out the water he'd gulped down, while Jacob ran on ahead, past the tower and smashed tents, over the hill, and into the main encampment. Roland tried to put himself in motion, tried to run after his master, but he couldn't make his body move. His ears rang, and the rushing river behind him was all he could hear. Then a shrill scream pierced the air, infusing him with adrenaline, and he forced himself into action.

Once he crested the hill, it took him a long moment to understand what he was looking at. There were smoldering tents everywhere, some still erect, with long, sharpened wooden poles sticking out of them, and others that had been trampled flat. People milled all around, worn and bloodied folks who stared aimlessly at the ground, wearing glassy-eyed expressions. A few of them were in the middle of the encampment, tossing broken tent posts and furniture into a large, hastily assembled firepit.

It was the mound positioned in front of the pit that gave Roland pause and made the scene so surreal. It was a pile of bodies, stacked four high and stretching at least thirty feet in either direction. He started to descend the hill, staring at the ghastly sight in horror and disgust. He spotted the plain clothing of farmers in the pile, as well as black cloaks and chainmail armor. There were children in the pile as well, their bent and broken limbs intermingling with those of their attackers, their empty gazes staring out into nothingness. A massive river of blood streamed from beneath the pile, spouting tributaries that flowed in every direction, macabre crimson rivers that cut through the brittle grass.

"Jacob?" Roland murmured, wanting his master to comfort him, to reassure him about the nature of death and its part in the cycle of nature. Because what he saw felt utterly unnatural. He fell to his knees, emptying his stomach of what little wine remained.

He hacked, his throat burning along with the rest of him, until that bloodcurdling scream sounded again, much closer this time. Any hope of comfort left him. That voice, that agonized voice, was Jacob's. Lifting his head beneath the rapidly darkening sky, he caught sight of the Eschetons' large pavilion, half standing, half flattened, surrounded by a group of townsfolk and fifteen lanterns on stakes. It was where the scream was coming from.

"I'm on my way, Jacob," he said, struggling to his feet. He felt feverish from the water, numb from the run. He made his way forward with a lurching, uneven trot, his eyes never leaving the pavilion. Suddenly he saw Turock Escheton emerge from the throng. The crimson-haired oddity meandered away from the tent, his head shaking. His bright orange robe was soiled, whether with dirt or blood, Roland couldn't tell. He held his pointed hat in his hands, staring at it as if tearing his eyes from it would mean the end of his life.

Roland was almost there, his legs picking up speed, when Azariah's tall form emerged from inside the pavilion. The Warden's eyes were watering and his shoulders were shaking. Without warning he collapsed into the grass, hiding his face with his hands as his body was thrown into a massive quake. Roland had never seen the Warden show this amount of emotion before—he had never seen *any* Warden show so much emotion. Roland's heart thumped even harder. The scream came once more, softer now, more defeated, as he went dashing for the tent.

Azariah lifted his head when Roland was only a few feet away.

"Roland, wait...*NO!*" he shouted, just as Roland passed him by. Roland felt fingers reach for—and miss—his drenched clothing, but he did not stop. He did not even pause. The tortured wailing of the First Man issued from within the tent. Even though he didn't want to admit it, Roland knew what it meant. His heart steeped in terror and sorrow, he bulled his way through the crowd until he emerged on the other side.

He wished he hadn't.

Abigail Escheton lingered at the rear of the pavilion, near where structure had collapsed, surrounded by overturned chairs, smashed crates, and torn articles of clothing. She was sobbing, silently but uncontrollably, while staring down at Jacob Eveningstar. The First Man was hunched over on the ground, his head down, his dark hair hanging over Brienna's unmoving body. It was the beautiful elf's face Roland saw most clearly in that frozen moment, her perfect features twisted into a mask of pain, her wheat-colored hair matted with blood. Jacob shuddered, and tears dripped from his chin, soaking the front of Brienna's blouse. There was a thick, black scorch mark at the center of her stomach. It had charred the fabric of her shirt, and on the bare flesh beneath he could see thick, blue-black veins that stretched away from the wound, disappearing beneath what was left of her garments.

Overwhelmed, Roland's knees went out and he crumpled to the ground. He couldn't avert his gaze from the dead elf's face, this exquisite woman who had made his master so happy, whose joy had been infectious, her spirit one of a kind. Dark liquid began to ooze from her open mouth.

"Brienna?" he whispered, but her eyes never moved.

"She's gone," moaned Jacob without looking at him. "Gone."

Roland crawled forward and grabbed her wrist, which lay limp on the grass, and lifted her hand. It dropped with a *thud* after he released it and fell still. Never again would those long, slender fingers play with his hair, never again would that hand gently squeeze his shoulder, never again would those arms wrap him in a welcoming hug. He broke down, crying into the sleeve of his already wet tunic. His prayers meant nothing any more, nor the words of his god. Even if he could count on Ashhur's promise of the Golden After-life, Brienna was one of *Celestia's* children. He would never see her again, even after he'd drawn his last breath. As Jacob said, she was just…gone.

For the first time, Roland Norsman understood what death truly meant.

Jacob's head shot up then, his manic, bloodshot eyes staring first at Roland, then at the crowd beyond. Abigail went over to him, trying to offer him comfort, but he shrugged her aside. He leapt to his feet, letting Brienna's body fall to the earth, and violently hauled Roland up by the collar as he passed him. Roland struggled to stand as he was towed along. The crowd parted before them, and Turock was there to greet them once they reached the other side.

"Where is he?" Jacob shouted into Turock's face.

Turock simply pointed to the west in reply.

Jacob released Roland's collar and stormed off, heading for points unknown. Roland thought to follow him but decided otherwise when he saw that Azariah was approaching him. His clothes were torn and bloodied and his pristine skin covered with wicked-looking gashes, including one that ran from the tip of his scalp to just below his ear. The Warden stopped in front of him, looking down at him with sorrowful eyes.

Despite the numbness that pervaded his every fiber, Roland finally managed to ask what had happened.

"They followed us," Azariah said, shaking his head. "The bastards followed us. The moment our feet reached solid ground they were on us, hurling spears, firing arrows. They hovered their way across the river and came at us with swords. They *hovered*. The mad priest even threw fire with his hands. We didn't have time to warn Turock or Abigail or Ephraim or Bartholomew. They were here so quickly...."

Roland swallowed, trying to keep his composure.

"Ephraim and Bartholomew, where are they now? Did they live?"

"They did," whispered Turock. "They were positioned at the far end of the camp. The butchers never reached them."

"So violent," Azariah said, as if he hadn't heard Turock speak. "We tried to fight them, but it was no use." He stared at his hands. "These are so useless. We had no weapons, nothing but the sticks and stones that were strewn along the ground. I couldn't...couldn't... and Brienna, she...by the time I reached her, it was too late to heal her...she was already gone...."

Azariah lost his composure then, standing in place and sobbing. Roland pulled the Warden close and did his best, even in his deadened state, to comfort him. His face only came up to Azariah's chest, and he felt heavy tears fall atop his head.

"It was my fault," said Turock, who appeared to have regained some of his equanimity. He still spoke as if in a dream, but at least he was looking at Roland now, however mournfully. "One of my men complained of sickness, and instead of replacing him, I let one less man watch the river. If only I had been there...."

"What could you have done?" asked Roland. He was completely besieged now, playing a role he didn't know how to play.

"I could have *stopped them!*" Turock screamed suddenly. He swept his arm out wide, gesturing to the pile of bodies. "There were only thirty of them, and they ended the lives of sixty of my people." His expression kept shifting, first a terrible grin, then a scrunched-up look of anguish. "When I arrived with my spellcasters, we crushed them, all but one. Our magic was greater. If I had just assigned another watcher, if I had taken up the duty *myself*, then—"

Roland grabbed his shoulders and shook him. Despite all the horror, sorrow, and pain he had just experienced, frustration was the emotion he felt most keenly.

"Who lived?" he asked, staring into Turock's wide, shocked eyes. "You said you ended all but one. Who was it?"

Turock tilted his head as if Roland shaking him had broken him out of his stupor, and pointed in the direction where Jacob had run off. Roland whirled around and put one foot in front of the other, hit by a sudden surge of panic that momentarily cured his tired and worn-out body. He sprinted around the crowd, around the tent and into the open space behind it, chasing after his master. Two pairs of heavy feet followed hard behind him.

He spotted the First Man the minute he rounded the collapsed end of the tent. Jacob stood over a man who had been strapped to a pole in front of a small fire. Roland skidded to a stop a few feet away, recognizing the man's shaved head, black robe, and piercing, ocean-blue eyes.

It was the one Jacob had called Uther Crestwell, the mad priest.

Azariah and Turock almost collided with him from behind, and they all stood and watched as Jacob leaned forward and whispered something into the mad priest's ear. Uther's eyes widened, and he began screaming, struggling against his restraints, trying desperately to free himself. Jacob reached for his belt, the spot where he normally kept his skinning knife, but he ended up patting his side, looking confused. The knife wasn't there. Roland's breath caught in his throat, and he began moving slowly forward, as if caught in a dream. Helpless, he looked on as his master bent down and lifted a burning log from the fire. Uther's cries cut through the night as the First Man brought the log down on his head, the sound of snapping bone echoing between them with a resounding *crack*.

"No! Stop!" Turock yelled.

Roland forced his feet to move, but it was too late. Jacob brought the log down again and again, blackening Uther's face, sending streamers of blood flying. Even when the monster had fallen still, Jacob continued to beat his motionless body, caving in his face, snapping his neck so that his head hung at an unnatural angle. By the time Roland reached him, and Azariah grabbed Jacob's arm, halting him mid-swing, all life had left Uther Crestwell's body.

Jacob whirled around, yanking his arm free of Azariah's grasp, swinging the log as if he were ready to attack. Both Azariah and

Roland backtracked and stumbled, but Turock stepped forward, holding his hands out wide.

"It's all right, Jacob, we're not going to hurt you."

Jacob stared at them each in turn, his eyes looking crazed as his wild gaze passed over their faces. Then he threw down the log and ran past them.

Roland turned, watching helplessly as Jacob bellowed at the small crowd that had gathered to watch what was happening. Then he disappeared into the Eschetons' tent and, after a few moments of cursing and loud rustling, he emerged with Brienna's lifeless body slung over his shoulder. The First Man made a beeline for the edge of the camp, where their horses were tethered.

"Azariah! Roland!" he shouted. "Come now or stay—I do not care!"

Roland glanced up at the Warden, and then they both followed. They reached the horses just as the sky turned completely dark and the nearly full moon began its ascent. Jacob tied Brienna's corpse to his horse and then hurried back to the unmoving body of the mad priest. After lugging it behind him like a sack of flour, he flung it over the steed Brienna had ridden north, unceremoniously binding the corpse's hands around the beast's neck. The horse bucked and snorted, as if uncomfortable with its forced proximity to a vile predator. Jacob untied both horses from the posts. His gait was one of a man on the verge of insanity.

The First Man then glared at Turock, who had followed them and was watching Jacob's preparations in silent confusion.

"Escheton!" Jacob shouted. "You call yourself a caster, so make me a portal!"

Turock stepped closer to him, his lips askew. "A what?" the spellcaster asked.

"A gate! A portal! A dimensional passage to elsewhere—do these words mean anything to you?"

"Um...to where?" Turock replied, sounding completely bewildered.

Jacob took a few menacing steps forward, looking as if he was ready to strike his friend, but his head swiveled and his gaze settled on Brienna's body. Roland watched his master's demeanor shift once more. When he turned back around, his jaw was slack, defeated, and when he spoke his words were deliberate but tinged with melancholy.

"I must return to Safeway—and quickly," he said, gesturing behind him. "All of us."

Turock grimaced, seeming uncertain.

"I can't get you that far," he said softly. "In theory, the farthest I can send you is to the outskirts of the Gorgoroses's land, but I have never sent anyone that great of a distance."

"How far *have* you sent someone?"

"Safely, only a few hundred feet," said Turock, coughing and refusing to meet Jacob's eye. "I know the spell, and I can gather the power, but I fear you might not be in one piece when you arrive."

Jacob bowed his head. "I will take the risk," he replied, and he sounded more than appreciative when he said it.

"But—"

"Just do it!"

With that, the First Man grabbed his horse's mane and swung up into the saddle. He pulled Brienna's lifeless body into his lap, before taking the reins of the steed that carried the corpse of Uther Crestwell. Azariah stayed by his side there in the middle of the field, seemingly willing to let Jacob try whatever he had planned.

Roland heard whispered words of magic, and he looked on as Turock closed his eyes and rubbed his wrists together. The air seemed to shimmer around the red-haired spellcaster, and his features shifted in and out of focus beneath the moon's ghostly glow. A glowing blue orb formed in front of the four horses, hovering above the ground. Its swirling beauty stole Roland's breath away. It grew rapidly outward, becoming the size of a fist, a man, a horse, then so large Ashhur himself could have walked through it. Roland stood in awe, watching shapes alter within the vaporous, resplendent mist. Jacob nodded and thanked Turock.

"Don't thank me yet," said the spellcaster. "Save your thanks for when you all get there safely, with all the proper limbs and digits."

Jacob nodded.

"Very well, then," he said.

"What will you do if you survive?" Turock asked, shouting over the steadily growing roar of wind that was pulsing from the portal. Jacob urged his frightened horse forward, and when he answered the question, there was a chilling flatness in the First Man's voice.

"I will demand a miracle from a deity."

Jacob kicked his horse, imploring it and the steed carrying Uther into a gallop. They disappeared into the swirling blue portal as if they'd never been there at all. Azariah shrugged and followed after, vanishing in the same way. Roland stood paralyzed, watching the colors swirl, afraid of getting lost in whatever had been opened before him.

"Better make it quick, son," Turock told him, the strain of what he was doing clearly evident on his grimacing face. "I can't hold this thing open forever."

Roland took a deep breath, then jostled the reins. His horse leapt forward, heading for the potentially deadly gateway. It was only because of his faith in the man he called master that he didn't soil himself as he passed through it.

CHAPTER

32

Her name was Aubrienna Meln of Stonewood, Brienna to those closest to her, and she was a ball of raging fire in the deep blackness of the approaching dawn. Brutes in armor and vile men in heavy black robes chased after her. They leapt across the river, seeming to float through the air, after she and her tall companion left their raft. The attackers' arrival had been unexpected, and in no time she and her friend were separated. She faced a cadre of foes armed with swords and spears, with nothing but the cloak on her back and her bare hands to combat them.

It would be enough.

Power leapt from her fingers as she drew from a well of energy that she had not fully accessed in decades. She lifted one arm, and a wall of ice formed in front of her enemies. Another arm lifted, and the earth beneath their feet folded upward, crushing them in a tomb of dirt and stone. Brienna stepped back, gritting her teeth. She was frightened, but a part of her savored the force she was controlling. The ice wall shattered, and more men rushed forward with swords, their expressions showing no fear, only anger. Her hands worked their magic, twisting into the necessary formations, mimicking the secret runes born into the earth itself when the goddess formed Dezrel. Lances of ice and fire flew at her enemies, cutting them down one by one, the ice smashing their armor and the fire ravaging the flesh locked within.

Brienna desperately searched for her companion as the space around her grew more cluttered and chaotic in the aftermath of her attacks. Off in the distance, she could see the tents surrounding the half-completed tower. There would be people within, frightened and huddled together. The elf screamed with all her might as she saw more attackers hurrying toward the meager haven. Electricity danced off her fingertips, cutting them down as they glided over the violently rushing river.

That was when a sharp pain slammed into her, tensing muscles that had reached their peak ability after a century of training. She dropped to the ground. Her ears rang, and she found it hard to concentrate on anything. She sensed men rushing past her as if from afar, and the terrified, distant screams of the villagers became a terrible song.

With blurred eyes she looked up to see a man standing before her. He was bald, with crystal blue eyes that glimmered each time light flashed in her field of vision. He wore a dark cloak, and his grin showed the glee he took in torment. The man raised his hands above his head, bringing a rumble of thunder to the sky and a brightness so intense that it washed out all else that followed. Lightning pierced her flesh, sending agony throughout her body, making her quake uncontrollably. She was horribly aware of her muscles seizing, of her organs ceasing to function. With her last remaining breath she called out to her sister, a young elf she adored more than the world itself, to say good-bye before the darkness took her, before that blinding white faded into....

Aully awoke shivering, her cheeks covered in tears, in the grimy hay on the floor of the cell that was now her home. Her eyes flew open, and she stared at the drab, gray wall, too horrified to move, too horrified to utter a word. What she'd seen, what she'd felt, had been far too vivid for a nightmare. Far too real. She didn't know who the bald man and his lackeys were, but she knew in the deepest fibers of her being that they were somehow connected to the enemies who had turned her life into a never-ending string of horrors. She curled her knees to her chest and cried silent tears, wishing she could join her sister in whatever lay beyond death.

First her father, now Bree. All she had left was her mother and a brother whom she had never met and probably never would. Would the anguish never end?

Comforting hands caressed her back. Aully rolled over and saw Noni hovering above her, face lit solemnly by the torch that burned in the corridor outside their cell. The old elf gently wiped her tears away before leaning over and placing a kiss on her forehead.

"Don't fear your nightmares," she whispered. "They mean nothing."

"This one did."

Aully pushed away the old elf's hand and sat up. She brushed her dirty hair from her face and glanced to her right, where her mother lay sleeping. From the looks of it, the Lady of Stonewood hadn't received the same vision she had, and for that Aully was glad. Her mother had retreated within herself during the endless days of their imprisonment. She feared more bad news might be the end of her.

"Brienna's gone," she whispered. Aully looked up at her nursemaid, needing something without being sure what it was. Sympathy? Understanding? Someone to believe her?

"In what way, child?" Noni asked.

"Gone," Aully insisted. "Forever. She's dead."

"How do you know this?"

"She said good-bye to me while I slept."

Aully thought her nursemaid might doubt her, but she nodded instead.

"The connection between sisters is strong," the old elf said. "Even those separated by so many years."

Her words made the corners of Aully's eyes twitch, tears readying themselves to be spilled anew. She sighed and closed them, only to be struck with the sensation of the lightning coursing through Brienna's body and the image of her father's head falling from his neck. The twin horrors should have broken her, but this time she felt a potent rage building inside her. She held her hands in front of her face and rubbed her fingers together, feeling the magic flow through her. She wished she were as strong as Brienna, wished she had studied the arts with the deceased Errdroth Plentos for fifty years, as her sister had. Brienna's connection to the weave had been natural, as it had been for their father. Aully knew she should be stronger than she was. As her rage twisted inside her, she wished she were the strongest caster in all of Stonewood. She wished she had the power to turn the stone walls to rubble, to protect her people as they fled the horror that was now their lives.

A soft, whining *creak* split the pre-dawn darkness, and Aully shifted her gaze to her nursemaid. Noni stared back at her, shoulders slumped, resigned to what was to come. Each morning in the seemingly endless days since she and her thirty-one fellow elves from Stonewood had been thrown into this dungeon, a single jailer—always a member of the Quellan Ekreissar, not one of the regular Thyne sentries—would descend the stairs into the dungeon, placing food in front of the six cells that held them. When he left, he always brought a prisoner with him. First it had been Aully's cousin Meretta, then Fressen, her father's personal tailor. The worst had been when they'd taken Zoe, a young girl half Aully's age who had been tapped to act as Presenter of Celestia when Aully and Kindren were married in four years' time. She would have stood on the dais beside the Master of Ceremonies, flowers in her hair, and sung a song to the goddess above.

That day she sang no songs to Celestia—only screamed.

No one who had been taken was ever returned.

After Zoe, Aully had started closing her eyes whenever the jailer came, not wanting to know who would be ripped from her next. This time, though, she stood defiant, glaring through the iron bars and into the passage beyond, even as Noni gasped and tried to retreat deeper into the cell. She would not be frightened. She would not accept *this* as her fate, not even if it meant she would be the next to greet the executioner's ax.

Bree would have fought back, Aully decided as the flickering light descended into the dungeon. And so would she.

Aully leaned against the bars of her cell, watching the light grow brighter as the footfalls became louder. She breathed in deep, concentrated pulls of air, trying to gather as much energy as she could into her body. She might not be able to command lightning and fire like Brienna or her father could, but she promised herself she would bring as much pain as she could to whoever came to torture them.

A sleek form emerged from the dungeon entrance and turned, and the power flowing through Aully's veins dissipated in shock. She knew that lovely face, that delicately sloped nose, those intense, widely set eyes, that dark hair infused with strands of gold that flowed elegantly over the interloper's shoulders. A sense of betrayal broke her fighting spirit as she watched Ceredon step forward, his free hand hovering over his khandar's grip. It was the first time she had laid eyes on him since her world had come unhinged. The Quellan prince shoved the torch he carried into a brass loop embedded in the wall, removed a ring of keys from his belt, and approached the gate to Aully's cell. She moved back, her hands dropping to her sides, tears already pricking behind her eyelids again.

"Not you," she said softly. "It can't be you."

Ceredon jammed a key into the iron lock and twisted until the catch disengaged. Then he swung the gate open and stepped inside. Aully squeezed her hands into fists and closed her eyes, ready for him to grab her and rip her from the cell. Only no hands touched her. Instead Ceredon knelt before her and held a finger to his lips.

"Wake Lady Audrianna," he whispered. "Come—we must hurry!"

Aully stood, shocked, as Noni slid next to her mother and shook her awake. The Lady of Stonewood, despite her grogginess and misery, seemed to understand what was happening the moment she laid eyes on Ceredon.

Everything grew more surreal with each passing moment. Aully's mother rose from her resting place, trying to appear strong despite her dishevelment, and helped Ceredon as he opened each of the remaining cells. Door after door was unlocked, and the prisoners within awakened. Soon all that was left of the delegation from Stonewood stood shoulder to shoulder in the dungeon's narrow passageway, expressions of confusion, fear, and relief stretched across their faces. Aully stood in front of them, next to her mother, and gazed at the Quellan prince with trepidation. For a moment she wondered if it were all a terrible trick, if Ceredon had been sent to instill her people with false hope before sending them all to their deaths.

No, she decided. After all her talks with Ceredon, the one thing she knew for certain was that the elf would rather die than play a part in such a horrific act of cruelty.

Ceredon gestured to the stairs, signaling for Aully and her people to follow him out. They formed a winding snake of shuffling footfalls as they climbed the constricted channel. The walls closed in on Aully, making her feel like a lamb being led to slaughter. She gazed at the heavy oak door up ahead, and in her mind she saw a row of archers awaiting them outside, ready to put arrows in their hearts the moment they emerged.

Only there weren't archers awaiting them—or anyone living at all. Instead, the dimness of the dungeon was exchanged with the relative brightness of the moon-dappled early morning. Revealed in its light was a field of death.

First was the body of the Quellan elf guard sprawled out on the ground outside the dungeon entrance, his throat slit. But that sight paled in comparison to what came next, for the many who died the day their forest city had been taken were strung up on poles, as were those who had been stolen away each morning by the jailer. Each one faced away from Palace Thyne's gilded emerald walls, a macabre warning to any who might think to turn against the new rule of Neyvar Ruven and his Ekreissar enforcers. Aully froze, staring in horror at the bodies of Demarti, Kara, Lucius, Meretta, and Fressen. Little Zoe was there too, dangling from a post by her wrists, the grass below her dark with a stain that glowed purple beneath the light of the moon. And farthest out, at the head of the trail of terror, was her father. Cleotis Meln, the former Lord of Stonewood. His head was shoved atop a pike, mouth hanging open, and beside it, nailed to a tall wooden plank, was the rest of his body.

Aully doubled over, gagging. She would have collapsed if not for Ceredon, who wrapped his arms around her, buried her face in the crook of his elbow, and ushered her forward. All sound was muffled with her ears blocked, and she was grateful that she did not have the chance to witness her mother's reaction to seeing her husband presented in such a ghastly and degrading way.

She walked for what felt like hours, and Ceredon only released her when they were far beyond the city. Dawn was approaching, the sky swirling with deep purples and crimsons, when they reached the very edge of the forest of Dezerea. On one side was the massive expanse of Lake Cor, the lowland mountains on the other. Finally their liberator stopped and swiveled around. Aully turned too and saw that her people had gathered together.

"I apologize," Ceredon said, addressing the congregation with a still-hushed voice. He'd seemed reluctant to talk during their escape, and no one had pressed him during their march. "For everything. I know it's not much, not anything, really, but…."

His voice trailed off. He looked as lost as everyone else there at the forest's edge.

"Why?" Lady Audrianna asked, her anger boiling over into her voice. "Why has this happened? Why did you kill my husband and imprison us?"

"I did no such thing," replied Ceredon, lowering his head and placing a hand on his chest. "I was not informed of my father's plans, I swear. What happened was as much a shock to me as it was to you."

"Do you think we would accept the apology of a Sinistel?" came Noni's weak voice. "You cannot know the pain...."

Ceredon winced but kept his head held high.

"I apologize for myself," he said. "For my inaction. For my cowardice in waiting as long as I did to free you. I will not speak for my father, nor for my people. But I have lost much in all of this as well, do you not understand?"

Aully nodded. She could see it and almost understand it. He'd lost faith in his family, his beliefs, in the very morality of his people. She took a tentative step forward, gazing up at the beautiful prince, and when he looked back at her, she saw eyes full of conflict.

"Why?" she asked. "They'll order your death for this."

"Not mine," Ceredon said. His cheeks flushed, and he suddenly looked embarrassed.

A call sounded from behind them. At first Aully felt panic, certain they'd been discovered, but when she turned she saw their rescuer, saw the elf who would be blamed for everything.

Kindren.

The elder Thynes approached them tentatively, but Kindren held his head high, refusing to hide his face. Lady Phyrra gave an awkward curtsey and Lord Orden bowed low, staying down longer than usual, as if he were fighting the need to look into the eyes of the people whose lives he had assisted in ruining.

"Your freedom has been granted," Ceredon said. "Not by me, but by them."

Lord Orden opened his mouth to say something but closed it quickly.

Kindren pushed past his parents and approached Ceredon. The Quellan prince offered his arm, and Kindren took it, an acknowledgment of mutual respect passing between them. Their hands released, and Kindren turned around, facing Aully. Their eyes met, and then all his attempts at remaining solemn and proud broke down, and he was once again the young elf Aully had fallen in love with. He dashed toward her, all pretenses gone, letting out a heart-wrenching sob as he wrapped his arms around her. Aully dug her fingers into the clothing on his back, never wanting to let him go. She melted into him, sobbing, letting his gentle kiss on her cheek wash away, if only for the briefest of moments, her painful memories. She heard gasps from those gathered behind her, and then Kindren released her, stepping back to face them.

"I will be held responsible for your release," he said, struggling to sound strong, like the lord he would one day have been had the world's sanity not collapsed around him. "Ceredon used my blade to slice the guard's throat, and clues pointing toward my culpability have been placed around the palace. I will bear the sole blame; I'm sure of it."

Lady Thyne stifled a sob, and then her husband came forward, standing beside his son.

"Please, all of you," he said, sounding timid and afraid. "I need you to understand we had no choice. The Neyvar is strong, and the might of his nation would have obliterated us. We had no choice but to obey, lest we lose our own lives."

On hearing his words, Aully's mother advanced on the Lord of Dezerea. No one dared stop her, not even when she slapped Orden across the face, and then grabbed the lapel of his overcoat and pulled him close to her.

"No choice?" she said. "You allowed my husband to be murdered; you allowed men, women, and children to be strung up like animals, and you now ask for our *understanding?*" Audrianna spat in his face, a shimmering glob that struck him above the eye and dripped down over his nose. "In your position, we would have given our lives to protect you, even if the Neyvar had shown up with an entire legion. But I see now that honor ends at Stonewood's borders and exists nowhere else in this forsaken world of humankind. Even our fellow Dezren have cast it aside."

Behind them, Lady Thyne began to cry.

"There is no forgiveness for you," said Aully's mother, first to Orden, then Phyrra. "Not now, not ever."

With that, she released the Lord of Dezerea and backed away. Orden, for his part, shuffled nervously from foot to foot, his head hanging in shame. Part of Aully felt sorry for him; but another part, the one that had watched her father beheaded and seen the mutilated bodies of her people on display, wished him a horrible, drawn-out death.

"And what of you two?" said her mother, facing Kindren and Ceredon.

"I will return to Dezerea and take my place by my father's side," said Ceredon, a darkness falling over his complexion. "Know that I do not condone his actions, nor do I understand them. All I know is that some sort of pact has been made with the god of the east, a pact that goes against our goddess's decree. So I will stay, and learn what I can. I must find out all that I can to save my people from themselves, before they fall out of favor with Celestia forever. Know that in the court of Quellassar you have at least one ally."

Lady Audrianna seemed touched, and she dipped her head in respect.

"And you?" she asked, turning to Kindren.

In response, Kindren dropped to one knee, took her hand, and kissed the back of it. A look of surprise came over the face of the Lady of Stonewood.

"The sins of my family have forever indebted me to you, Lady Audrianna," he said, gazing up into her eyes. "Please, let me join you in exile from this place. I do not fear the death that will come for me if I stay, only that I would die without ever seeing my beloved Aullienna again."

His gaze flicked over to Aully, and she stood breathless, unable to move. Her mother's expression remained stoic as she stared at the young elf kneeling before her, giving no answer. She looked to Aully, then back at Kindren.

"Time is short," Ceredon dared say. "They will discover your escape within the hour, if they have not already. It will not take them long to find our trail."

"Of course you can join us," Lady Audrianna whispered. Her hardness suddenly broke, and she was once more the frail woman who had huddled silently in the dungeon cell. "Though we may not have a home to return to…not if the betrayal the Neyvar spoke of is true."

"Where we stay does not matter," Kindren replied. "All that matters is that we stay alive and we stay together."

He reached out for Aully then, and she went to him, accepting his arm around her waist as the rest of her people turned away from the shimmering lake. The sky brightened overhead, and the sun was close to poking over the eastern horizon. Lord and Lady Thyne left silently, and Aully bid them a soundless *good riddance*. Ceredon stood before the group for a moment longer, brushed his dark hair off his shoulders, and offered them a salute, his elbow locked and his fist clenched. Aully shrugged out of Kindren's grasp and ran to him, throwing her arms around his waist and pressing her head against his chest.

"Thank you," she said, gazing up into his soulful brown eyes. There were tears in them. Aully had never seen the prince of the Quellan cry. Oddly, the sensitivity suited him.

"What I do, I do for us all," he said, and then he kissed two fingers of his right hand and pressed them against her temple. "But I also do it for you. Always."

Those were his last words. He turned and ran into the surrounding trees with nary a sound. Aully watched him disappear, her heart going out to him. She worried for his safety. Should his father find out what he'd done….

Don't think like that, she thought. She rejoined Kindren and the rest of her people. They began the journey southeast, deciding to stay in the shelter of the low mountains until it was time to return home. They could not return to Stonewood, not if Detrick had truly taken over. Aully leaned into Kindren and imagined life going forward, wherever that might happen. *Going forward.* It was all they could expect from then on out, for it was a brave new world.

Beneath the burgeoning light of morning, the haggard group of elves disappeared over a mountain ridge, heading bravely for points unknown, with only their mutual love and the clothes on their backs to protect them. Aully prayed it would be enough. She knew it would have been for Brienna.

CHAPTER

33

She had been sitting at the feet of her god, listening to his sermon alongside her husband, Ibis, and their children, when the rider came barging into the temple. Soleh leapt up at the sight of the soldier—his skin was pale, his hair disheveled, and his armor hastily donned. She exchanged a look with Ulric, who shrugged his shoulders in reply. Adeline smiled at the newcomer, giggling madly to herself, as she had done for the majority of Karak's homily. Soleh looked over at her husband, who had just grabbed her hand, and then at her god, whom she had crafted Ibis after, resplendent in his black platemail, his golden eyes peering at the man at the door.

"Why do you interrupt us?" Karak demanded, his voice excessively loud.

The soldier dropped to his knees in an instant, the *clank* of his platemail echoing through the hall of worship.

"Many apologies, my Lord," he stammered. "It is not my purpose to intrude. I was sent by the Highest to inform our lady the Minister that her presence is required at the castle."

Karak looked at Soleh, his eyes boring into her soul, and she shivered as she faced the soldier.

"Why would Highest Crestwell require me now? It is barely dawn."

"He did not tell me, Minister. He said only that I must come fetch you and that it was a matter most dire." The soldier gulped and turned to the god. "And…h-he said you would want to be there as well, my Lord."

"Is that so?" Karak asked. The tone in his voice had not changed at all, but the sheer volume with which he spoke made it all the more imposing. The soldier bent his head even closer to the ground, his affirmation whispered so quietly that Soleh could only guess at his words.

"Very well," said the god. "Take your leave of us."

"Sh-shall I tell the Highest you will be arriving shortly?"

Karak smiled. "There will be no need of that."

The soldier stood, bowed, and then clanked out the door as noisily as he'd arrived. Soleh glanced at her god, her beloved Karak, and held her hands together beneath her chin, awaiting his command.

"Ibis, take your children home to the Tower Keep. Stay there until I tell you your presence is required."

Ibis bowed, so handsome with his twinkling eyes and dimpled chin, a near perfect replication of the god who was now addressing him. Then she glanced at Ulric, who had inherited many of those same traits. Soleh felt a shimmer of pride just looking at them, so long as she ignored Adeline, who continued her mad cackle, albeit under her breath now.

"I will, my Lord," said Ibis. He grabbed Adeline by the wrist and dragged her out of the temple, where Soleh's bodyguards awaited with a carriage. Ulric followed close behind.

"And what of me?" asked Soleh. "We arrived in a single wagon. Should I depart with them?"

"No, sweet Soleh," Karak said, his voice lowered. "You require neither horse nor carriage—not when your creator is by your side."

The deity held his hand out to her, which she took. He scooped her up, as though she were a small child, and carried her toward the inner sanctum of the temple, where darkness loomed. Soleh couldn't stop staring at him as she rode along, drinking in his scent, fussing over every smooth line and crease in his perfectly chiseled face. So lost was she in her obsession that she never once thought of the words the soldier had spoken, nor of the aura of portent they carried.

Karak stepped behind his altar, around a vast collection of potted ferns that grew as tall as he, and entered the shadows. Soleh's head grew dizzy, her vision swelling and then fading until all she saw was blackness. She felt herself reduced to the smallest of particles, soaring along the cosmos at a speed her human mind could not comprehend. She knew she should be alarmed, but the presence of her god surrounded her, infused her, soothed her, and Soleh Mori knew no fear.

When the light returned to her eyes, she could see a dimly lit sky in the distance. They were sheathed in darkness, beneath the stables on the far side of the Castle of the Lion. Soleh gasped in wonder. She knew Karak could ride shadows to wherever he wished, but she had never experienced it for herself. That she had been given the opportunity made her feel very blessed indeed.

Karak placed her two feet on the ground and gestured for her to lead the way. She did, feeling light as air, almost floating along the cobbled walk as she pulled open the door to Tower Justice. Karak did not enter, instead signaling for her to go on without him.

"Remember, sweet Soleh," he said. "To maintain order, sacrifice is sometimes necessary."

With that he turned away from her. She sighed, stepped into the tower, and closed the door behind her with a heavy *thud*.

Once inside, any lightness she'd felt instantly disappeared.

Standing in the rounded antechamber was Highest Crestwell. With him were Thessaly, Captain Gregorian, King Vaelor, two Sisters of the Cloth, and half of the Council of Twelve. They had been deep in discussion when she entered, a conversation that ceased so quickly, it was as if a thousand stones had been dropped on them all at once. Every eye turned her way, the group's panic and anger shining through at her. Captain Gregorian seemed particularly fearsome; his face was so taut it seemed as though his flesh would split along the fissures in it. He wore common breeches and a tunic rather than armor, but his swordbelt was fastened around his waist. It was then she noticed his clothes were soaked with blood.

"What happened?" she asked, panic beginning to gallop up her spine. "Why have I been summoned?"

The Highest grimaced, giving King Vaelor a disapproving look. He then said, "You are the Minister of Justice, Soleh, and it is time to do your job."

The king and the council members nodded in agreement, and then ushered their way out of the tower, without giving Soleh the courtesy of an acknowledgment. She felt more than insulted, though her anger could do nothing to override the fear of the unknown that was building up inside her.

"I demand to know what this is about," she said, trying to sound forceful.

"You will," mumbled the Captain.

The Sisters remained silent, as was their wont.

"Tell me, both of you. *Now!*"

"No!" the Highest snapped. Soleh was taken aback by both his tone and the better-than-thou look that crossed his face. "You will *not* make demands of me. I am still your superior, *Minister*. I expect you to treat me as such."

Soleh forced her head to bow. "You have my apologies, Highest. Please, show me where I must be, so I can dispense Karak's justice."

Strangely, Clovis motioned to the two Sisters and allowed them to lead the way as he walked toward the staircase at the far end of the circular room. Captain Gregorian scaled the steps after him, with Soleh on his heels. She had to get up there. She had to see what was important enough to rip her from the arms of her beloved creator. Thessaly took up the rear, a guarded look on her face as she climbed the steps one at a time. She refused to look Soleh in the eye.

When they reached the courtroom's antechamber on the second story of the tower, the Sisters walked straight through it, not stopping to wash their hands or to genuflect before the placard professing Karak's commandments. Neither did Clovis. Soleh would not allow herself such insolence, though she seemed to be the only one who felt that way, as Captain Gregorian mimicked the Highest and Thessaly; normally just as much a stickler for court tradition as she was, he passed her by. Shivering, Soleh hastily wetted her hands with lukewarm water from the carafe, whispered a few quick words of praise to her god, and followed the rest into the main courtroom, where she promptly began to feel weak in the knees.

The scent hit her first, nearly knocking her off her feet. It was a pungent, coppery scent, smelling strongly of ammonia and human waste. The sight hit her second, and that finished the job the smell had started. She collapsed to one knee, holding a hand over her mouth, gagging.

Laid out in the middle of the courtroom, on a pair of wooden slabs, were two bloodied bodies that were so debased she couldn't tell whether they were male or female. There was blood everywhere; it covered the corpses, the slabs. Drips even speckled the courtroom floor. Soleh noted, though not consciously, that one of the cadavers was unnaturally bloated, whereas the other was not. That accounted for the horrible smell.

"What...*is* this?" she gasped.

"Get off the dais," said the Captain. "See who they are for yourself."

She didn't want to. In the name of all that was holy, she *truly* didn't. Yet she saw in the faces all around her, save for those of the Sisters, which were expressionless as always, that this emergency call of justice would not commence until she had. She covered her nose with her hands, took a deep breath, and steeled herself for what lay ahead. She took each step deliberately, just as she had done every day for many, many years. The appalling odors became all the more dreadful the closer she came, but she dared not stop. She realized that the bodies belonged to a man and a woman. The woman was in a horrific state, completely disemboweled, while the man's throat had been slit and his member mutilated. She grew pale.

Soleh looked at their faces closely, the only parts of either body that had been scrubbed clean of blood. Both were badly bruised and distended from the gases of death, but she almost immediately found something familiar about them. Then she noticed their hair—the woman's was red and curly, the man's brown with a few streaks of gray. Their identity hit her all at once, and she backpedaled, almost tripping over her own feet in the process.

It was Crian Crestwell and the western deserter, Nessa DuTaureau.

Her eyes shot up, seeking out Clovis.

"I am so sorry," she said, her voice echoing throughout the chamber.

The Highest scowled at her. "Save your apologies for when your duties are complete," he said harshly.

Soleh wanted to retort but held her tongue. *His outrage is understood*, she thought. *I cannot imagine how I would feel if I lost a child in this way.* She thought of the time that had almost happened, when Oris had been badly burned, trapped in a raging fire while stupidly trying to rescue the three whores trapped inside. He had been unconscious for nearly a month, and during that time Soleh had been nearly inconsolable. There were moments when she'd wished she could take her son's place. It was only when Oris finally opened his eyes—scarred for life, but alive—that she allowed herself to *live* once more. She then thought of Vulfram, residing in the same tower as the two of them, and immediately feared for his safety. He wasn't there, not standing with the others, not dead on a slab. That could mean….

She shook with fright even as she nodded to those who formed a bracketed line around the two corpses. She then made her way uneasily across the remainder of the courtroom floor, climbed the stairs on the other side, and took her place in the Seat of the Minister. Thessaly did not join her, instead remaining by her father's side. The woman who had sat at Soleh's right hand while she interpreted Karak's justice for the guilty still refused to look at her. Soleh drummed her fingers on the armrest of the throne, a lump in her throat, and waited.

Captain Gregorian took two steps forward. He swallowed hard and snapped his feet together. Unlike the way he had been down in the antechamber, he was now completely composed and businesslike. It was a transformation that gave an illusion of normalcy to this strange and disturbing call to duty.

"Court is in session," stated the Captain. He genuflected on one knee before the Seat of the Minister, then stood to his full height once more, following protocol.

"Bring out the accused," Soleh said, fearful anticipation causing the knot in her stomach to tighten. *Please let it not be him.*

Gregorian bowed his head and made his way not to the main vestibule, which was where the criminals were normally ushered in from, but to the side passageway, built into the tower as an alternate route of escape in case of fire. The Captain yanked open the door and dipped inside. When he returned, he dragged behind him a stumbling man whose arms and legs were chained together. The man was bare chested, with a messy stubble of hair on the top of his head. His face was bruised and bloodied, and he walked with the lurch of one who'd either taken in far too much liquor or had been beaten senseless.

Soleh's heart sank despite the shock of his condition.

She wheeled on the Highest. "Why is my son in this state? Why has he been beaten?"

"*SILENCE!*" screamed Clovis, his voice echoing so loudly, she could imagine it reaching the top of the spire. "Your responsibility on that throne is to pass judgment on the accused, not question the bearers of the law."

She sat back down, flabbergasted and afraid.

Gregorian hauled Vulfram through the courtroom, past the onlookers, past the two mutilated corpses, and threw him down before her. Her son's back flexed with each breath he took. He stayed where we was, on his shackled hands and knees, head down. The Captain walked in front of him and addressed the court.

"Before the Seat of the Minister I present Vulfram Jorah Mori, son of Ibis and Soleh, a man whose current position is that of Lord Commander of the Army of Karak. He stands accused of the murder of Crian Crestwell and Nessa DuTaureau, children of Karak, the Divinity of the East."

Soleh swallowed hard, trying her best to keep calm. "And who witnessed these crimes?"

"I have, Minister," the Captain said, glaring down at Vulfram as he said it.

At those words, Vulfram vaulted up. His irons caught, limiting his movement, but he strained his neck, looking like he was trying to force his skeleton from his body. He stared up at Soleh, eyes so wide it seemed as though they might explode out of their sockets.

"It is not true!" he yelled. "I swear on all that is holy, it isn't. You must believe me!"

Gregorian planted a boot in his back, knocking him to the floor, where he bashed his chin against the bottom step of the dais.

"He lies," the Captain said. He reached behind him, pulled a knife from the bag that hung on the side of his belt opposite his sword. "I found him in the deceased's room in the Tower Keep, passed out on the floor. The Lord Commander was completely unharmed, though he reeked of liquor and was covered with their blood. He held this blade in his hand—the very same blade responsible for the mutilation of the victims. I swear upon my life that this is true."

Soleh believed him. Malcolm Gregorian was not a man predisposed to lying. He certainly believed Vulfram was the murderer and had found her son in a very compromising position. But was he mistaken? Had Vulfram been attacked by an unseen assailant and framed for the crime?

She shook her head and tugged at her hair, trying to ready herself for what might come next.

"Accused," she said, as coldly as she could, "what say you?"

"It's not true! I didn't...I couldn't...." He sighed and dropped his head. "I have never seen that blade before in my life. Look at me, Minister. Mother! Do you think me capable of such atrocities?"

"What I think matters not," replied Soleh, her heart breaking even more. "Only the facts do."

The Captain stepped on the dais, handed Soleh the knife, and then beckoned Thessaly forward. Thessaly lifted a sack from beside the two bodies and emptied the contents. At least a dozen empty bottles and half as many wineskins fell to the floor.

"I discovered these strewn about the keep," Gregorian said, looking beyond disgusted now. "Many are freshly emptied. With the amount of liquor consumed, I fear the accused would not be capable of remember his name, let alone his actions."

"Is this true?"

Vulfram slid up on his knees, blood dribbling from his newly split lip. His bloodshot eyes drooped downward, and he nodded shamefully.

Soleh's heart nearly dissolved in her chest, and she let out a long, agonized moan. The proof against her son—and his acknowledgment that he had been too intoxicated to remember anything—was staggering. He had been found in the room, covered in their blood, with the killing blade in his hand. She had sentenced men to death based on much less. A cry began to build in her throat, but she held it down. She remembered Karak's last words to her before she entered Tower Justice: *To maintain order, sacrifice is sometimes necessary.*

He had known. All along, Karak had known, and in his love for her, he had allowed her to face this trial on her own, giving her the chance to prove herself worthy of him. That was when she realized that Vulfram would receive that same chance.

With renewed confidence, she looked down on her son and stated the required words.

"By the power of this court, handed down by Karak, the Divinity of the East and father to us all, I find you guilty of all charges and hereby sentence you to death by beheading. Do you accept this judgment with an open heart, knowing that Afram awaits if you are repentant, or do you wish to prove your faithfulness before the Final Judges?"

The Captain went to grab Vulfram, but her son shoved him away. He defiantly rose to his full height, threw his shoulders back, and said, "I will do it. I will prove my faithfulness."

Inwardly, Soleh smiled. Standing up, she ordered her son taken to the Arena. She then glanced down at the knife, the murder weapon, and hefted it in one hand. It looked strangely familiar, but she could not recall why. She lifted it, staring at the finger notches, and ran her finger down the blade. Her memory betrayed her. She flipped it over and carried it with her as she descended the dais, hoping that the answer would come to her if she had longer to study it.

The truth was, she had other pressing things to worry over at the moment, for she knew in her heart that Vulfram was innocent, no matter what the evidence stated. She only hoped that Kayne and Lilah felt the same way.

The Captain of the Palace Guard shoved Vulfram down the cold, damp stairwell leading to the Arena, jostling him from side to side.

His mother followed behind with a veritable posse, which oddly consisted of two members of the Sisters of the Cloth. They had arrived at Tower Justice perhaps an hour after Gregorian threw him into the courtroom's barred emergency cell as he kicked and screamed, proclaiming his innocence all the while. He kept giving the Sisters sidelong glances. His loathing for them grew with each passing second, these beasts who had stolen his daughter away. He wanted nothing more than to toss Gregorian aside, break his shackles, and slice their throats.

Stop it, he admonished himself, wishing his chains allowed him enough freedom to reach up and slap his own face. *They are not the enemy. Their lot has been forced on them, just as it was for Lyana.*

Suitably shamed by his own common sense, he bit his tongue and concentrated on walking. Perhaps if he kept his mind on putting one foot before the other, Gregorian wouldn't have to shove him around so maliciously.

Once he reached the bottom of the stairwell, the door was opened for him, and Gregorian guided him around the viewing platform to a second staircase, this one leading to the entrance to the Arena. Vulfram couldn't help but feel a bit awed at the sight of this place. The ceiling was high, perhaps as tall as the top three floors of the Tower Keep combined. The area was lighted by what looked to be thousands of torches, lining the walls of the platform that overlooked the arena. The Arena itself was a huge circle ringed with massive boulders that seemed as smooth as marble. The entrance to the ring was an iron gate at least three times as tall as a man. There was an aura of hopelessness about the place, which, combined with the cold and damp air, made him feel almost despondent. He had never seen the place where Kayne and Lilah, his childhood companions, passed final judgment on the guilty, and he finally understood why any who *had* seen it called it *the atrium of the abyss*, the place where all hope goes to die.

Gregorian removed his shackles, unlocked the gate, swung it wide, and tossed him inside. The gate slammed shut a moment later, a certain finality to the sound. Vulfram lay sprawled out on the dirt of the arena floor, his entire body feeling like one gigantic bruise. Over the past few hours the Captain had physically accosted him, and for the last month, perhaps two, he had been spiritually battered by his own conscience. He closed his eyes, gritted his teeth, and in a silent proclamation told himself he was through with the pain. This would be the end of it, of that he was certain. Kayne and Lilah would prove his faithfulness, and he would demand, right then and there, that his daughter be released.

A faint whisper met his ears. Vulfram lifted his head. It had sounded like his name. He squinted through the bars of the gate and into the blackness behind the staircase. There he saw a pair of eyes staring back at him, burning yellow like twin suns. He felt a gentle vibration in the air, the same whole-body tremor he experienced each time Karak came to visit him, and he clumsily scrambled to his feet. He was about to offer his respects to his god, but he paused. No one else on the platform above him, including his mother, seemed to have noticed that Karak was in attendance. He ran a hand over the stubble atop his head and turned away from the gate. If Karak wished to be noticed, he would have made himself visible. It was not Vulfram's duty to honor his wishes.

Instead he faced the gathered onlookers and held his arms out wide.

"I wish to be judged!" he decreed. He tried to sound confident, but his voice cracked nonetheless. Knowing that Karak was watching made him nervous, made him doubt the certainty of his innocence.

His mother waved her hand at Gregorian, who had reappeared on the platform and was standing next to the two Sisters. The Captain leaned over and pulled a massive lever. Pulleys spun and whined, and to his left a pair of iron gates, each larger than the one leading to the Arena, slowly grinded upward.

He turned to face the cages, two giant black holes like the eyes of eternity cut into the wall of rock. A low growl shook the very floor of the Arena, making loose particles of dirt bounce as if locked in a macabre dance. He took a few steps toward the grottos, slowly at first, then more quickly, more confidently, until finally one of the lions emerged from the darkness. It was Lilah who showed herself first, as tall on four legs as he was on two, her fur glowing surreally in the glittering light. Then Kayne appeared, stalking out of his cage, his mane grand and stately. Both lions' eyes glowed yellow with flecks of green and blue mixed in, looking so very much like the eyes of Karak.

They approached him gradually, their giant heads swinging to glance at each other before turning back to him. Kayne's mouth yawned open, his blood-red tongue licking at his massive incisors, and Lilah rose up on her haunches, her fur standing on end, as if preparing for an attack. Vulfram was speechless. It had been so long since he had seen the two lions, so long since they'd played together in his family's inner sanctum in Erznia. They were bigger now—more frightening. Their eyes shone with an intelligence he hadn't seen there before. They had always been smart creatures, but now their stares seemed almost human. Human or perhaps even godlike.

But as human as their eyes were, he saw no compassion in them.

Lilah burst into motion. She bolted around Kayne, who still skulked deliberately, and pulled up short a few feet in front of Vulfram. A threatening rumble reverberated from her throat—a throat so large that if Vulfram were to throw both his arms around her neck, he doubted his hands would touch on the other side. The lioness leaned in close, sniffed his feet, then his hands, then his face. She let loose with a grunt, showering his face with breath that reeked of meat and putrefaction. He wondered if he smelled the same way to her, as he was covered with blood.

Kayne slunk past Lilah, and then behind Vulfram's back. Vulfram closed his eyes, mouthing, *Please, Karak, I am sorry. Karak, I love you—Karak*, while the male lion sniffed at him the same way Lilah had. Kayne let out a sharp, bark-like sound, soaking Vulfram's shoulders with hot saliva. Vulfram tensed, clenching his fists, defiant to the last.

Wetness suddenly assaulted his face and he was nudged heavily from behind. He fell to one knee, his back pressing against a mountain of fur while the battering continued. He opened his eyes to see Lilah's giant tongue lash out, slapping him across the cheek, slathering his face with spittle.

"Whoa, girl," he said, almost laughing at the absurdity of it.

He leaned to the side to avoid another attack of Lilah's persistent tongue, which smacked against his chest instead, and he ended up face to face with Kayne. He was reclined against the male lion's side, and Kayne gazed deep into his eyes, as if studying him. Kayne then lolled his neck, his cheek sweeping against Vulfram's. Both lions began purring—throaty, shuddering hums that sounded almost sexual in nature.

Vulfram placed a hand atop each creature's head, pulling them in closer, these beasts he had known all his life, and began to laugh. That laughter soon turned to sadness and then finally evolved into a righteous conviction that flowed from his pores like steam from a hot mountain spring.

Kayne and Lilah swiftly backed away from him, and he stood, casting a quick glance toward the gate, where Karak's eyes still glowed, before whirling around to confront those on the platform. Each of them looked down at him with their own unique expression—his mother's joyful, Clovis's deeply irritated, Gregorian's wide-eyed and disbelieving, and Thessaly's almost sad. The Sisters, of course, showed no emotion at all, as their faces were covered.

"I...have...been...*JUDGED!*" Vulfram shouted at them. This was it, he knew—the moment Karak had been waiting for, the reason the deity had lingered in the darkness instead of exposing himself to the rest. Because what Vulfram did now, he had to do on his own.

"You have, Lord Commander," said his mother, her smile all teeth. "Under law, this court grants you a full pardon. Your station shall be restored, and you will be released immediately."

Clovis mumbled something under his breath, and the Captain shot him a quick look.

"That is right," Vulfram said, making sure to pronounce every word clearly. "I *have* been found faithful, and I *will* be released with a full pardon." He gestured behind him. "The Final Judges have decreed my faith to be true, and in so doing, they have validated every thought that led me to standing right here, right now."

"What are you talking about?" asked Thessaly.

"My daughter!" he screamed. "My daughter was manipulated by devious forces that wished to wrong my family through *her inno-cence*. My entire purpose for returning to Veldaren was to clear her name, to free her from a fate worse than death, and now that I have been found worthy of life, I decree that she has been, as well!"

"Well, I...." Soleh began.

She was cut off when Clovis began to laugh, a deeply resound-ing, almost maniacal cackle that echoed throughout the cavernous chamber.

"Her innocence is not yours to decree," he said, venom seeping out with every word he spoke. "Karak's law is true, his law is final, and you yourself carried out the verdict against her. Your god is infallible, *Lord Commander*. Are you claiming otherwise?"

"No!" shouted Vulfram defiantly. "I am saying that *men* inter-pret the laws of our divine deity, and men *are* fallible! My daughter is but a child." The words were like knives as they left his mouth. He wished he could scale the smooth stone and strangle Clovis where he stood.

Clovis shook his head. "So foolish, Vulfram. So vain and foolish." He then stepped around Thessaly and approached the two Sisters.

The one closest bowed and backed away, and he placed his hands on the second one, moving her to an open area of the platform not blocked by the sandstone balustrade. His fingers laced around a piece of wrapping that dangled from the side of the Sister's face, and slowly Clovis began to unwind it. The wrappings peeled off like petals from a rose, gradually revealing the face hidden beneath.

Vulfram gasped. His heart leapt into his throat.

It was Lyana up there, her eyes wide and glassy, the hair shaved from her head. Her face was expressionless, her jaw rigid, even as Clovis removed the cloak from her shoulders, even as he unwound the coverings from her chest, her midsection, her hips. It all fell to the ground like the molting skin of a snake, until his daughter stood naked before him, her youthful body firm but scarred at the sides—the marks of the whipping Vulfram had given her on that fateful day. She did not move. She did not speak. For all he could tell, she did not breathe. She simply stood there as if in a trance, staring out into space, gazing over and beyond him.

"No," Vulfram moaned. "Oh, Lyana, no."

Somewhere in the back of his mind, he heard his mother shriek.

"This is the child you so seek to reclaim," Clovis said, taunting him by peeking over her shoulder and leering downward at her supple breasts. "This child who sinned knowingly against her god, who broke the most sacred of laws, all to keep her name from being sullied."

Vulfram shook his head in defiance.

"Oh, but it is true," said Clovis. "The girl admits it herself."

"She does not!"

Clovis waved a hand in front of Lyana's face. Her eyes did not even blink.

"Go ahead, Sister," he said to her, his voice just loud enough for Vulfram to hear. "Tell us why you have entered the order."

"I have sinned against my god," she said, and Vulfram's whole body quaked. Her voice didn't sound like her own any longer, as if some strange, emotionless being had crawled into her skin and taken over. "It is my life's regret, one that I will spend the remainder of my days attempting to absolve. The child that was inside me deserved life, and I denied it that life. This is a fate I accept willingly, and as such I have given up my name forever. I am only Sister now, and Sister is all I will ever be."

"NO!" wailed Vulfram, falling to his knees in the dirt.

"You see, it is done," Clovis said as he removed his cloak and covered Lyana—or the impassive being Lyana had become. "There is no innocence for you to prove, for the Sister has freely admitted to her wrongdoing. Her life is what it is now, one that belongs to her god and whoever wishes to purchase her services." Before he wrapped the cloak around her entirely, he reached over and pinched one of Lyana's nipples between his thumb and forefinger. Lyana winced slightly, but remained otherwise motionless. "And to be honest, after seeing what she has to offer, I might be the first to do just that. Gold may not be able to buy happiness, but it can buy a few hours of contentment."

"You bastard!" Vulfram heard his mother proclaim, but he didn't look at her. His eyes were locked on the show that was playing out for him, to taunt him, to *toy* with him.

And in that moment, he knew it had been Clovis all along.

"Fuck you!" Vulfram screamed. His trance broke and he charged the wall of stone, beat his fists into it. He broke a bone in his right wrist as it slammed against the rock-hard surface, one to match the broken bone in his left hand, but his rage was so complete, pumping through his veins so strongly, that he hardly noticed.

Glancing up, his eyes met Captain Gregorian's. The man's expression was queerly conflicted but hard, which made Vulfram all the angrier. None of them would listen to him. Not that bastard Clovis, not Gregorian, not his mother, who was leaning against the balustrade weeping, while his supposed murder weapon dangled from her fingers, and certainly not his brainwashed daughter and her handler. Not even his god would hear him out, it seemed. His god. His god....

He backed away from the wall, kicking it for good measure, and ran toward the gate.

"Karak!" he bellowed, desperately seeking out those glowing eyes in the darkness. "Karak, why have you done this?" He slammed into the bars. When he saw the figure of the deity lurking in the back, he reached his ruined hands through the gap. His fury turned to sorrow, and he began weeping. "Why have you forsaken me, my Lord?" he cried. "Why...have you...*FORSAKEN ME?*"

He spit through the bars, and those glowing eyes flickered. From behind him came the roar of a lion, followed by another, then the sound of thudding paws. That was when the cacophony of pain began. Teeth bore into Vulfram's sides, his neck, his thighs. He was ripped backward, his elbow catching on the bars on its way through, shattering his forearm. Lilah threw him to the ground with a thud, her jaws clenched tightly around his midsection. One of her massive paws raked down his shoulder, the claws shredding his flesh, and try as he might to beat her off with his flopping, useless arm, it was no use. Kayne leapt in front of him, swiping at him so powerfully that he severed the broken arm that Vulfram held up to defend himself. Blood erupted in a geyser from the stump, splashing the ground, the lions, his face, everything. In the distance, his mother's screams were unending.

Vulfram felt a moment of agony, then nothing, as he watched himself being devoured by two beasts that he had called brother and sister. It was as if the part of his mind that allowed him to feel pain had been shut off, replaced with a hollow sensation that was almost blissful in its emptiness. When Lilah lifted her head, a tangle of his dripping intestines dangling from her maw, he felt not fear or loathing, but an all-encompassing love. He tried to tell her that, to whisper how much he adored everyone in that room, even Clovis and Gregorian. But Kayne's jaws clamped down around his neck, tearing out his throat, ending his words a second before they came out, and his life a moment later.

Soleh watched in horror as her son was devoured by the Final Judges. Her gullet was in agony from shrieking, and her pulse throbbed in her temples. She felt like she might die herself at any moment. She didn't want to keep watching as Kayne and Lilah tore into Vulfram's midsection, lapping up his blood as if he were just some common blasphemer and not a man who had been raised alongside them, but she could not tear her gaze away. Her shock locked her in place, and she watched helplessly as Karak appeared, stepping through the Arena's gate, shooing the lions away. The Judges skulked off, licking blood from their chops, while Karak knelt over her son's unmoving body. For a moment she thought she was imagining his presence, for he looked distraught, disbelieving, and she had never seen him this way before.

She caught movement from the corner of her eye and looked up. It was Clovis, guiding the two Sisters—one of whom was Soleh's *granddaughter*—toward the stairs leading out of the Arena. The sight of the man, and the memory of how he had taunted Vulfram into his eventual death, destroyed the last shreds of her sanity. She glanced at her hand, which still held the strangely familiar, blood-soaked blade that had been used to murder the young lovers. She gripped the handle tight, felt its killing weight. *Vulfram will never hold his daughter again*, she thought. *He will never see his wife. He will never again stand proud by my side.* These thoughts darted through her mind, swirling the cocktail of sorrow and rage that was quickly building up inside her.

A savage roar left Soleh's throat, and she brought up the knife and ran. The Highest turned at the last moment, his eyes bulging in surprise at the sight of her. She saw her reflection in them for the briefest of moments; she looked like a demon from the Abyss, her mouth hanging open, her hair like writhing snakes, her flesh stretched and pale. Clovis brought his hand up, trying to push her away, but she had surprise on her side. She barreled into him with her shoulder, driving him backward while the two sisters scampered out of sight.

"You did this!" she shrieked. "You killed him!"

Voices shouted at her, from beside her and from below, but she ignored them. She thrust the knife at Clovis, the first time she had done any such thing in all her life. The Highest was much stronger than her, and he was able to knock her strike off target. But the weapon found purchase in his flesh nevertheless, the ultra-sharp blade sliding through his black leathers and piercing his side. Clovis let out a scream of pain and thrashed, knocking her away. He pulled the knife free of his side, which spurted blood.

The Highest collapsed, frantically kicking himself across the floor while staring at the blood that covered his hand. He tried to draw his own dagger, but its hilt caught in his belt. Soleh, her mind white-hot with fury, charged once more, knife raised above her head with both hands, ready to plunge it directly into the murdering bastard's heart.

Hands grabbed her from behind, spinning her around. She reacted on instinct, swiping out with the blade, bent on death. Her attacker slid to the side, the faintest glimpse of four diagonal scars flashing before her vision. That was when Soleh felt a great pressure in her midsection, a tugging sensation that gradually worked its way beneath her ribcage. A sound like tearing parchment reached her ears and she grew dizzy. She glanced down to see Captain Gregorian crouched below her, arm stretched out, his shortsword deep inside her lower torso. The man was clearly dismayed. Her dizziness grew and she stumbled forward, driving the sword even deeper beneath her ribs, ever closer to her heart.

The last thing she heard before she collapsed, and her eyes closed forever, was the sound of her god screaming.

The sound was loud enough to shatter the fabric of reality. Clovis held his head, trying to block it out while attempting to stem the flow of blood that leaked from his side. He watched as Soleh slid down on Captain Gregorian's sword until its tip exited her back with a plop. The bloody knife fell from her hand, clattering to the floor. The screaming from below abruptly stopped.

Captain Gregorian hefted to the side, removing Soleh from his blade. Her body flopped to the ground, her head teetering for a moment before falling still. The Captain stood over her, his agonized expression making Clovis quite nervous. Not wanting to think too much about what it might mean, Clovis forced himself to sit up and then stole a glance toward the balustrade, trying to catch the eye of his god. He saw nothing through the sandstone slats, only the bumpy rise of the Judges' cages of rock and steel.

"Captain, bring her to me," he heard Karak say. The god's voice hitched, suffused with sorrow.

"Yes, my Lord," replied Malcolm. Then the Captain closed Soleh's sightless eyes, gently kissed her forehead, and lifted her dead weight over his shoulder. He did so with great ease, as if the Minister of Justice were but a child. He left the platform with thudding footsteps.

Thessaly, tears streaming from her eyes, knelt before him.

"Father," she said, reaching for his leaking wound. "You are hurt."

He batted her hand away. "It is nothing," he grumbled.

"She could have killed you."

Clovis offered a contemptuous laugh. "She could have, yes," he replied. "But alas, I live, while she does not."

She nodded. "It is a tragedy."

"A tragedy?" He reached out quickly, ignoring the pain in his side, and grabbed the front of her shirt, pulling her close. "A tragedy that she perished while I did not? Do you wish that it had been otherwise, daughter of mine?" He reached with his free hand for the dagger on his hip. "Should I allow you to join your minister in death?"

Thessaly shook her head and began to tremble, which made Clovis seethe.

"Leave me!" he shouted, shoving her away. His daughter ran past him and up the stairs. *She is so weak, that one*, he thought. *Just like Crian was. So focused on the moment instead of the bigger picture. So much more like her mother. If she stays on that path*, he continued, *I do not think I could bear the consequences.* Despite his show of coldness, he loved his family dearly and regretted threatening Thessaly so. It had even hurt him to banish Moira, though he would never let anyone outside of Lanike know that.

Clovis struggled to rise, weakened by blood loss. The bitch had cut him. *Cut him.* He stumbled across the platform and collapsed against the balustrade, rage burning inside him. Leaning against the rail, he peered into the Arena below. He saw the two lions sitting before their cages, heads bowed in respect. Captain Gregorian was there as well, his hands gripping the iron gate. His back was turned to the body of Soleh, which had been positioned respectfully on the blood-and-dust-covered ground. Karak knelt at the dead woman's side, her tiny hand held in his massive one. The god's great body shuddered as he caressed her arm, her neck, brushed wisps of hair from her pasty white brow.

"Sweet Soleh," Karak whispered. "Oh, sweet Soleh, what have you done?"

Despite the torment of his still-leaking wound, despite the agony of his god, Clovis smiled, shielding the expression with one hand. His every desire had come to fruition. Vulfram's blasphemy had sealed the Lord Commander's fate, removing a rather potent obstacle from Clovis's path. The soldier's conscience and his doubts about Clovis could have proved disastrous. Clovis had played him brilliantly, and the man had reacted just as Clovis's Whisperer had said he would. And now, with Soleh's unexpected demise, the Mori line was truncated, leaving himself as Karak's only true child.

It was all coming together, just as the Whisperer had promised. Clovis pressed against his wound, gritted his teeth, and offered a silent *thank you* to his unseen guide, the voice in the dark that was helping to bring about Clovis's vision—a united people worshipping one single god. The attack on Haven, the rise of a weakling king in Ashhur's lordship, the elves' standoff with the Gorgoros clan, and now the fall of the Mori family, had all been a part of his unknown accomplice's design. The end game was in sight, apparent even in the events the Whisperer had *not* brought about.

The lone fly in the ointment was Jacob Eveningstar. The First Man was knowledgeable and an immortal, like himself, and his understanding of magic and the inner workings of their world was unmatched by any but the gods themselves. *Jacob could have muddied the waters of the coming conflict*, he mused.

Clovis thought of the message he had received that morning and shuddered with anticipation. Unbeknownst to anyone, including his Whisperer and Karak, he had sent his mad son Uther into the Tinderlands, giving him the task of releasing the legendary demon kings from their prison to assist in their decimation of the west. Clovis knew that Ashhur had Celestia on his side, which left Karak at a distinct disadvantage should the final solution he envisioned play itself out. The demon kings would even those scales. Although his son's efforts had been unsuccessful thus far, his trials had recently brought about an unanticipated advantage: Eveningstar was now trapped in the northern lands, hunted by Uther's dedicated soldiers. He would be dead soon, Clovis just knew it, clearing the path for the toppling of Ashhur's Paradise, paving the way for Crestwell to prove to his god, once and for all, that he and his family were the only ones truly fit to rule. And if that were the case, perhaps he could at last convince the deity not to stop there....

Karak's sobbing abruptly stopped, and the god lifted his shimmering golden eyes to the platform above. Clovis forced the smile from his face and lowered his head, attempting to appear somber.

"This day has been most distressing indeed," he said.

The god glowered at him. He looked as though he were ready to climb the platform and throw Clovis to his death, but he did no such thing. Instead, he ran a hand through his close-cropped hair and asked, "Are the armaments in place?" His tone was flat, detached.

Clovis nodded. "Avila has been sent back to Omnmount. Joseph is already there, readying the troops to march."

Captain Gregorian turned from the gate, stepped forward, and knelt before the deity.

"If you are intent on moving toward Haven, my Lord, would you like me to fetch King Vaelor? With all due respect, a new Lord Commander is needed, for your army requires leadership...."

Karak waved him away.

"I have no need of advice from that man, nor any man at all," the god said. "I am through with this sport of kings and subjects. I am the god of the land, the creator of you all. I will pass the mantle on to whomever I see fit." His eyes once more lifted to Clovis. "I am dismayed, my child. Two of my greatest creations are gone. You are the last, my final hope for order. You are Lord Commander now. See to your wound, then ready my troops. We march on Haven come dawn."

A well of gratification built up in Clovis's heart upon hearing those words, even though they were spoken so dully. The only title that would have made him happier was King of Dezrel. He could not wait to see the expression on Vaelor's face when he shoved a blade into the puppet ruler's belly. *That* would be a memory he would cherish forever, possibly even more than the sight of Soleh's head lolling off her neck.

Karak lifted his eyes to the ceiling, as if he were looking through the layers of stone and earth and into the sky above.

"Come," he said. "The third full moon is nearly upon us. I wish to teach my children a lesson."

The god left the arena, standing tall at the base of the staircase. Clovis limped to the side of the platform, which the Captain had scaled. He draped his arm over Malcolm's shoulder and allowed the man to help him up the stairs. His blood left a trail of tiny droplets behind him.

Omnmount awaited on the other side, as did his destiny. It could not come soon enough.

CHAPTER

34

Roland emerged from the portal at full gallop, his body still intact, stomach churning, head spinning. One moment he was on the outskirts of Drake, the next he was barreling over the grassy hills on the other side of the Corinth River. The sensation was indescribable, as though his mind had been pulled from the rest of his body and was rushing after it to catch up. He felt sick, and he collapsed into his horse's neck, squeezed his eyes shut, and tried not to lose consciousness.

The feeling eventually passed, and he repositioned himself in his saddle. His mouth was dry, and he realized he had no water with him. He looked ahead and saw his companions' horses in the distance, growing farther away by the second. The pace Jacob kept was breathtaking, and given Azariah's immense size, he feared the Warden's stallion might collapse from exhaustion and perish right then and there. Roland ground his heels into his own horse's side, urging it to go faster. They rode on through the night and into the morning, retaining their breakneck pace. The sun slowly moved higher in the sky as they hurtled across the land, the welcome heat and constant breeze gradually drying the clothes on Roland's back.

He was thankful to be free of the cold, but the steady warmth held none of the relief he had hoped it would.

"Our horses cannot withstand much more," Azariah said as they paused for a brief break at a stream so their mounts might drink. "What is it we race against, Jacob?"

"No more questions," Jacob said, drinking a bit of the water himself. "I'm tired of them. It is Ashhur's turn to answer."

They prodded him, but he said nothing else. After a break that was not nearly long enough, they resumed riding. The pain in Roland's back made him want to cry, and the dead look in Jacob's eyes somehow made everything worse.

It was just past midday when they crossed the dusty Gods' Road. They saw few people as they rode—only some Kerrian farmers in the distance and one hunting party, lying in wait in the tall flatland grasses. Even the wildlife seemed to stay away, with nary a deer, antelope, or wolf crossing their path. When they passed through the sliver of desert sand that marked the border of Safeway, the sun had already begun its descent. More and more people came into sight, tending the fields or milling about aimlessly. Roland couldn't tell if they were surprised by the sudden appearance of four wildly galloping horses, for they were nothing but blurs as he rushed past them.

By the time they reached the Cavern of Solitude, it was nightfall. The moon appeared in the north, the thinnest shard away from being full. Roland heard a loud crack, and he glanced behind him. Azariah's horse had finally collapsed, shuddering. Azariah tumbled from the saddle, rolling away, his long body a whirl of arms and legs.

Jacob didn't stop for him, so neither did Roland. They kept riding hard until they were within sight of the Sanctuary.

A crowd was gathered in the vast open space before the short stone wall surrounding the edifice. The people were on their knees as they took in the words of their god. Ashhur sat on the wall, his great size making it look like a child's construction. His hands gesticulated wildly as his mouth moved, no doubt offering his children another parable of kindness, forgiveness, and love. Under the light of the newly risen moon and the dozens of torches that burned around the assembly, the white robe he wore shimmered as if it were made of diamonds.

Jacob halted his horse on the edge of the gathering. The mare shook her head and snorted loudly, her legs trembling. The one beside him, carrying Uther Crestwell's corpse, fell to its knees, then toppled over onto its side. Not wanting to suffer the same fate as Azariah, Roland quickly dismounted. He pressed his hand against his horse's side, feeling its heart race beneath its ribcage. Its eyes rolled into the back of its head, and its legs folded as it crumpled into the grass. Roland looked around, hoping to see some water and food to give the poor animal. Given how severely it had been pressed, Roland feared it wouldn't live through the night.

Jacob showed no such concern. He lifted his eyes from Brienna's fallen horse, stared over the heads of the kneeling congregation, and met Ashhur's gaze. The sermon had stopped upon their arrival, and every man, woman, and child in attendance turned to face him. Ashhur remained still, one arm resting on his monstrous knee while his other hand stroked his trimmed beard.

"I am glad that you have returned, Jacob. A message came today. Your former pupil was named king, though Isabel was short on details in her letter, so I do not know how the contest was won. I am sure you are most proud nonetheless."

"You and I must talk," Jacob said, ignoring the god's greeting. "Send these people away."

Ashhur tilted his head back. "I am in the middle of a lesson, Jacob," the deity replied. He spread his arms out wide, gesturing to the congregation. "Or do you find yourself more important than the rest of these people? I will hear whatever you learned in the north when I am finished."

Roland watched as Jacob's expression shifted from desperate to enraged in the span of a second. The First Man's cheeks flushed and his throat tensed. Brienna's corpse was still draped over his lap, and he grabbed her hair, pulling up her head so that her vacant eyes stared at his god. Ashhur's mouth twisted into a frown, and a collective gasp emanated from the gathering. Jacob held his pose, presenting his macabre message to his god even as his horse shuddered beneath him.

"Is this important enough?" the First Man seethed.

"Children," said Ashhur, his eyes fixed on Brienna's dead stare. "I ask that you return to your homes. Prayers are done for the evening. We will reconvene tomorrow morning."

They did just that, fifty or more people shuffling away from the wall, casting curious and mystified glances behind them. As Roland scanned the crowd, he realized that none of them had a clue as to what had happened, what was to come. Not long ago, he had been like them: ignorant of loss, of fear, of premature death. He was that naïve child no longer, although deep down he longed to be.

Ashhur's head steward, Clegman Treadwell, stayed behind for a moment, gazing at Jacob with uncertainty. Ashhur nodded to the man, but then he left through the narrow gap in the wall, heading up the gravel-strewn walk, and disappearing inside the Sanctuary. The great door seemed to sigh in relief when it closed.

They were alone now—Roland, Jacob, Ashhur, three horses, and two corpses. Jacob swung down from his steed, which lowered its head and began nibbling the grass, Brienna's lifeless body still draped over it. Roland looked behind him, seeking out Azariah, but the Warden was nowhere in sight.

Ashhur stood from the wall. He loped across the grass, touching each horse in turn, ending with Roland's. He stroked the beast's snout with one hand, and its shuddering ceased. From inside his robe he produced a skin filled with water and handed it to Roland, which he guzzled down. Then Ashhur lifted Brienna's corpse off the newly revitalized horse's back, carried it to the center of the small clearing, and placed it on the ground. Kneeling over her, he gently straightened her limbs, brushed her hair, and closed her eyes. When he was done, she looked like she was simply sleeping.

"May you live eternally in the shadow of your goddess," Ashhur said. The compassion in his booming voice was genuine, and he seemed hurt. His eyes lifted to the heavens, to Celestia's shining star above. "Please accept your child with love and gentleness," he said, "and let her live on forever in your bosom."

Jacob knelt beside Ashhur, all of the anger completely washed from his face. The deity looked over at him, the kindness in his eyes enough to melt a mountain of ice.

"I am sorry for your loss," he said.

A tear rolled down the First Man's cheek.

"It should not have been this way," he said, a hitch in his words.

Ashhur nodded to him.

"The merchant was right, my Lord," Jacob continued, stunning Roland with his ability to maintain his composure given his evident shock and sorrow. "Your brother's people had a small army massed in the northern deadlands. They'd been tormenting the people of Drake, kidnapping the townspeople only to murder them in sacrificial rituals. We searched the Tinderlands, and stumbled on Karak's forces as they were attempting to raise creatures from a different world. We were spotted and chased. Roland and I hid in a cave while…while Bree and Azariah went to warn the townspeople. They were followed, and…and…and Bree was killed when the camp was attacked."

Jacob was clearly descending into a pit of sorrow, but he soldiered on nonetheless.

"Turock Escheton has begun teaching others in the ways of magic, did you know that? A whole group of spellcasters, all up there in the north." He laughed, but it was a humorless sound, and his tears flowed freely now. "They crushed the army, but it was too late to save Bree. She's…gone…."

Jacob leaned forward, crying into his palms. Ashhur placed a massive, consoling hand on his back.

"Again, I am sorry, my son," he said. "Such a horrible turn of events. If there's anything I could do…."

Jacob's head snapped up with a start, and he stared in desperation at his deity.

"But there is," he said, the words sputtering from his lips. "You can give her back to me."

Ashhur frowned. "That I cannot do."

"You are a god, my Lord. You hold the power of life in the palm of your hand."

"I do not, my child. You are mistaken."

"No!" Jacob screamed, his hands balled into fists. "I watched you create a thousand young men and women from jars of clay! I watched them form from the earth, life coming where there had been none before. How is this any more impossible? Grant Brienna the life she was *supposed* to have, the life she was already *living* before it was ripped from her!"

Ashhur glanced at Jacob for a long moment, then sighed. He placed two fingers on Brienna's cold forehead before rising to his feet. The god backed up, looking down on his most trusted servant. He seemed beyond sad at that point. In fact, Roland thought he appeared ready to break down himself.

"I cannot do what it is you ask," Ashhur said. "You must understand, Jacob, I do this because I love you. If I granted your request, you would hate me. What I can give you would be a shell and nothing more. You would never forgive me for it."

"If you deny me," Jacob said, his words halted, broken, "*that* is what I will never forgive. Bring her back. Now."

Ashhur let out a sigh that seemed to come from the very deepest part of him.

"Because I love you," he said. "Remember that when you see what you have demanded of your god."

He snapped his fingers, and the air shimmered. Roland watched in awe and horror, as Brienna's chest rose and fell. She sat up sharply, as if pulled by a string, and her eyes opened, staring straight ahead. For a moment, Roland felt overjoyed, but that joy ended when he saw black, rotting gunk trickle from her slightly parted lips, when he noticed that her eyes were still glossed over and milky from death.

It seemed as though Jacob didn't, however. His expression was one of mad glee, and tears of joy poured down his cheeks as he wrapped his arms around Brienna's body, holding her close, sobbing into her neck. Brienna didn't respond, not even when he whispered how much he loved her into her ear. She simply stared straight ahead, unmoving, and Roland's heart broke.

Ashhur frowned at the display.

"When my brother and I created life," he said, "we did so at great cost. A piece of our immortality went into each and every one of you, just as a piece of Celestia went into each of her creations. The power it required to accomplish such a feat was enormous, and when we finished, we found ourselves to be much lesser than what we'd been when we soared through the heavens. It is strength that we will one day regain, but that is a slow process, one that will not reach its fruition for millennia. Such is the price of creation, but both Karak and I paid that price willingly. Neither of us can give you what you want."

"You gave her back to me," Jacob sobbed, as if he hadn't heard a word the god had said. "You gave her back."

"I did not, my child," said Ashhur. "Brienna is not alive. I have animated the shell, but what was contained within that shell has moved on. You hold a puppet, nothing more. Her essence has returned to the goddess and is once more a part of Celestia's heavenly host."

Jacob kissed Brienna's cheek, then looked at Ashhur.

"Then summon it back," he said. "Pull her soul down, or ask Celestia if you must."

"I cannot," the god said, his lips forming a tight line of despair. "And even if I could, I still would not. Jacob, this life, this world, is only a beginning. And since it is a beginning, it must also have an end. How many times have you yourself lectured on this? Life is a cycle, a wheel, a gift. You act as if the reversal of death were no greater than the creation of life. But look at what my children do with their own imperfect, frail bodies, with lives as long as the flame of a candle. They create life together, yet can any one of them face death and make it tremble? The time for eternity is coming, but it is not here. It is not now. I will not break the greatest of laws, not even to ease your sorrow. Is this not what you have told me the people of my Paradise must learn to accept? Is this not what you have insisted my children are unprepared to face? No, Jacob. You are the First Man. You are the greatest. And you of all should know the limits of life and death."

"But you are immortal," Jacob whispered. "You made *me* immortal. Does our very nature not contradict your *limits?*"

"No," Ashhur replied with a shake of his head. "In my present form, even I can perish. The only eternity that exists will not be found in this mortal realm. We are all beings with a beginning," he snapped his fingers once more, and Brienna's body went limp in Jacob's arms, "and an end."

"No!" Jacob shouted, hysterically trying to keep her corpse upright. "You bastard! Bring her back! *Bring her back!"*

In a movement much too quick for a being his size, Ashhur grabbed Jacob, pulled him away from the corpse, and then touched Brienna's forehead again. He muttered a few words, and her body lit aflame, the fire devouring her remains in mere seconds, until all that remained was a clump of ash lying in the grass, holding her form for a short second before Ashhur blew on the pile, scattering the ashes to the wind.

"NO!" Jacob screamed once more, reaching for the billowing ash, trying to pluck it from the air.

Roland collapsed to his knees and then let out another sob. The finality of it all struck him dumb, left him feeling like he'd been stabbed in the gut. And, oh, how much worse Jacob appeared.

"Your love for her and her memory must never end," Ashhur said. "But I will not watch you debase yourself as you cling to a rotting corpse. The flesh is dead. The soul lives on."

Roland knew by the look of dismay on the god's face that it was perhaps the most difficult thing he had ever done.

Jacob's expression slowly changed. It was like watching a broken thing gradually rebuild itself, only with jagged edges and everything not quite in its proper place. His eyes, which had shimmered with life and knowledge, now glared at his deity with a dark rage that left Roland terrified.

"The soul may live on," Jacob said. "But the men responsible live as well. You must act."

"What do you mean?"

He went to the horse that had collapsed, the one holding the mad priest's corpse. He violently grabbed Uther's head and lifted it, showing the distorted, burned, and broken face to Ashhur.

"Do you know who this is?" he asked, his voice dripping with disdain. "Uther Crestwell. Placed in charge of the men who have been tormenting the children of Drake—*your children*—for months." He threw the dead man to the ground and lifted his hands in a helpless gesture. "We watched their citizens butchered by the son of Karak's Highest. Will you sit back and deny your brother's hand in this?"

"Uther shamed his family. He left Neldar on his own. Whatever force he commanded up north, he did so independent of my brother's knowledge."

"Do you really believe that?" Jacob asked, aghast.

"I do."

"Why? How? Look above you, my Lord. The moon will be full in two days. When your brother marches into the delta, do you think he is going to do so innocently? Do you think the people there will grovel at his feet and beg for mercy? His army already killed more than forty of them three months ago. Are you willing to let even more perish?"

"Such is the way my brother has chosen to discipline his children," Ashhur said softly. "It is not my responsibility to stop him, as I have told you."

Pulling at his hair, Jacob kicked Uther's corpse and began to pace. Roland felt ill at ease. His master seemed unstable, ready to snap—sorrowful one moment, raging the next. He had never seen Jacob act in such a way. It scared him almost more than the ritual performed by Uther.

Finally, it seemed Jacob could stay silent no longer.

"They are *people*," he said. "They aren't toys! They aren't playthings for you and Karak to divvy up like children. You act as if you care for my sorrow. You tell me to love the one lost. What of the delta? What of those people? Their families will wail. Their children will scream. You will sit idly by and watch death befall hundreds, if not thousands, and for what? In order to not interfere? To prove that your way is better in this sick little game you two brothers play? What will it take, Ashhur? What will it take to convince you that Karak will not stop until your people are crushed, and the nation of Neldar spans all the way from the east to the west?"

Coming to the end of his rant, Jacob stood there, arms shaking, body trembling, as his god stared into his eyes in silence. If Jacob was afraid, he did not show it. At last, Ashhur looked away, his gaze turning skyward. Jacob noticed the gesture, and his face reddened.

"Do not look to her for answers, my Lord."

"I must," the deity whispered. His head lowered, and he looked so uncertain that Roland thought the world itself might begin to crumble. "I bid you good evening, Jacob Eveningstar. You have given me much to think over. I will tell you of my decision come morning."

Without another word, Ashhur strode up to Jacob, held him at arm's length for a moment, and then bent down and touched Uther Crestwell's corpse. It caught flame just as Brienna's had, burning away into the night, leaving behind little sign that the man ever existed. After that was finished, he turned and silently loped back to the Sanctuary, stepping over the wall in the process. When he disappeared through the great door, it closed behind him. An unnatural silence fell over the land. It was so complete that even the insects seemed to have ceased their nightly song.

"Master," Roland said, his voice shaking, "what's going to happen?"

"He'll come around," Jacob replied, not turning to look at him. "No matter what he says, he will not stand idly by watching the slaughter of innocents."

"And…and if he doesn't?" asked Roland.

Jacob glared at him.

"He will," said the First Man. "The future of this land depends on it."

Jacob offered one last glance to the spot where Brienna's body had been, and he began to walk away. Roland called after him, but Jacob did not respond.

When he was gone, Roland stood alone, shivering despite the warmth of the evening. His mind was a jumble of contradictions, as everything he had witnessed over the last few months came to a head in his thoughts. When the torches began to burn out, one by one, he heard footsteps behind him. He turned, expecting to see Jacob but finding Azariah instead. The Warden seemed exhausted, and his eyes were deep wells of concern. He handed forth a jug, which Roland took and sipped from. His stomach began to cramp as the wine reached his belly, but he ignored it. When he finished, he handed the jug back, feeling very, very tired.

"What happened, Roland?" Azariah asked. "Where is Jacob? Is he well?"

Roland opened his mouth, closed it. He thought of the look on Jacob's face as he stared down Ashhur, unafraid, unrelenting. He shook his head, looked to Celestia's star, which seemed to have dimmed in the nighttime sky.

"I don't know."

CHAPTER

35

There were people everywhere, a bustle of activity that rivaled the chaos Patrick had witnessed the one and only time he'd visited the Temple of the Flesh with Rachida. Ah, Rachida. He hadn't seen her since she'd departed with her husband for the southern islands. He would do anything to spend just one more moment with her, alone, naked, ravenous....

"Patrick!" Deacon shouted. "Patrick, stop daydreaming! We need to get these people to safety."

He sighed and tried to straighten his deformed spine so he could see over the gaggle of people—the very old, the women, and the children—standing in front of him. He caught a fleeting glance of Deacon, who was manning the other side of the temple threshold beneath the sweltering late afternoon sun, his cheeks flushed as he handed out pillows, blankets, and sacks of food to those who were heading inside.

"I'm not daydreaming," he shouted back.

"Well, your line is growing. I don't want people to skip your line for mine. Our supplies are divided equally. So hurry up!"

Patrick grunted, forced himself to look presentable, and handed a bundle of goods to a young woman wearing a drab gray dress. She looked haggard, with two small children clinging to her sides, and when Patrick smiled his hideous, uneven smile, he could tell she was trying her best not to appear revolted.

"Name?" he asked.

"Matilda Brownstone," she replied.

He jotted her name on the massive roll of parchment that sat on the desk beside him and ushered her along.

"Thank you, kind sir," she said, and then curtseyed and walked through the temple gates. Another woman with another group of children stepped up in line, and Patrick repeated the process again.

It was going to be a long day, made all the longer because the plan he was helping facilitate was so shockingly stupid.

When Deacon had suggested stowing those who could not defend themselves in the temple and reinforcing the gates to keep them safe, Patrick had freely expressed his opinion that it was a stupid strategy. Send them all farther south, he'd said, where there were several other small settlements. Or better yet, have them wait out whatever was to happen at the Gemcroft's island estate—a scheme that Peytr himself had proposed. But Deacon would have none of it. He promised them all that the temple was the most secure structure for the women, children, and indigent, and that they would be hunted down and executed if they hid anywhere else. At least in there, he reasoned, the thick walls would give them a chance at escape through the sally port and into the Clubfoot Mountains should their defenders fall.

I refuse to be intimidated, Coldmine had said. *If we send our loved ones away, we are admitting our fear that we might lose.*

All of which completely ignored the fact that defeat was a probability, not a possibility. Every single man, woman, and child in the delta knew they clung to only the tiniest sliver of hope. Given how

Deacon's own wife had taken their children and fled to the shores of Pebble Island with Peytr and Rachida, Coldmine's statement seemed rather hypocritical.

Patrick sighed. The longer he stayed in Haven, the more he realized how stubborn and pig-headed Deacon could be; he was a man who always thought he was right and wouldn't listen to reason. Unfortunately, he was considered a hero in Haven, and his words were taken as gold. Even Moira, as strong and independent-minded a woman as he'd ever met, bent to Coldmine's whims. Only Rachida and Corton Ender seemed to be able to think for themselves, but Rachida was gone and the old man had been raised a warrior. To him, talk was cheap. He did his talking with the pointy end of his sword, as he was fond of saying, and it was not his place to question those whose station in life was higher than his own.

To Patrick, that fact alone confirmed what Rachida had said about the uneven nature of life in the east. How could the people of Haven claim their freedom when they had been raised not to question their superiors? How could there be equality if the term *superiors* existed at all?

He shrugged those thoughts aside, focusing instead on the faces of all the women who passed through his station, making a mental note of their differing levels of attractiveness, and allowing his mind to wander when one or two of them accidentally brushed his hand with their own. Might any of them be the one to end the ever-loving torture of immortality from which he suffered? He laughed at himself. Here he was, a man from Paradise, ushering women and children into a temple designed for worshipping sexuality, all so they might wait for that night's full moon, and the attack that had been threatened to follow thereafter. It didn't seem real.

Finally, the last stragglers—an old woman and man who walked arm in arm, their hunched, uneven strides nearly matching—were escorted through the gates. Patrick looked over his list of names.

Two hundred sixteen adults and two hundred eighty-seven children, and he still had nine sacks of foodstuffs sitting in the cart. He whistled, amazed at the amount of preparation that had been put into this endeavor. Given that each sack contained enough food to last a family of five for three days, Deacon had cultivated or purchased virtually three full years' worth of food. It seemed an amazingly generous amount, especially considering that farming in swampland didn't necessarily yield the most favorable crops. Although a great number of those who resided in the other townships around haven had came to them in search of safety, it was a good thing the many who resided in the far south of the delta had not decided to join in the fight. It would have been nice to have more men to fight by his side, but Ashhur only knew how Deacon would come up with the provisions to feed those who needed protection.

Two men gathered up his cart and Deacon's and pushed them into the temple, most likely to be stored for emergency rations. The gates swung shut and a low *thud* could be heard as the people inside dropped the heavy wooden crossbar into place. Deacon strolled over to him, smiling broadly, though his good cheer seemed to be forced. He chuckled, as artificial a sound as Patrick had ever heard, and ran his fingers through his beard. They began walking back toward the forest's edge, where their makeshift army awaited. Deacon threw an arm over his shoulder.

"Have I told you how glad I am you decided to stay?" he asked.

Patrick sighed. "Relentlessly."

"And have I told you how sorry I was for the way I treated you that day at the estate?"

"Again, more often than you should."

Deacon swallowed hard and glanced at him sideways, as if uncertain.

"It's just that I am impressed with your resolve," he said hesitantly. "Giving yourself so freely to others is truly a gift. You are a god among men, Patrick DuTaureau, no matter what your father thinks."

Patrick stopped in his tracks, allowing Deacon's arm to slip off him.

"What does *that* mean?" he asked.

"If you don't know," said Deacon, "then I'd much rather act as though I'd said nothing."

Patrick stood baffled. Deacon appeared to regret his words, but at the same time, he'd been the one to clumsily bring up the subject in the first place. His father? What did the Lord of Haven know about his father?

"Just speak, man," he said, grunting in frustration. "You can't say something like that and then fall silent."

Deacon opened his mouth, shut it, shifted his weight from one foot to the other, and then grimaced. Patrick rolled his head back.

"Forget it," he said. "I'm getting some wine."

"Wait."

Patrick stopped and tapped his foot, gesturing for the man to get on with it.

"It's just…I have heard stories. The Paradise has long been intriguing to those of us who grew up in Neldar. The song, the dance, the simplicity of existence. We hear of your freedom to do whatever you wish, whenever you wish it, living free of sickness and early death… none of us had any of that growing up. When Antar Hoonen arrived, he fed us all the tales we so desired. You must understand, we fled our land because we were either destitute or criminals. We downtrodden lived under constant fear of hanging or the executioner's ax. So to hear him say how Ashhur forgave all sins so long as the sinner was truly repentant…how could I not be intrigued?"

Patrick shook his head. "Do they often execute those who swipe an apple from a farmer's field? Because to be honest, that's about the most major sin I witnessed while growing up. Antar is telling tales, alright, and tall ones at that."

"According to Antar, there was at least one man in Paradise guilty of more than petty theft," said Deacon, lowering his voice. "He told me the story of your parents."

That got Patrick's attention. "Go on," he said, his lips curling inward.

"According to the story, your mother was so vain that when Ashhur granted his First Children the ability to craft a mate, she chose to make one who was nearly her twin, simply so she could look on her own image at nearly all times..."

He paused, and Patrick motioned for him to continue.

"Because of the vanity Isabel put into the vat of creation, the being she created—your father—emerged just as vain and conceited as she was. He wanted your mother for himself, to be with her night and day, and for no other man to come between them. When your sister Abigail was born, she looked just like your mother, and your father was pleased. But when Isabel became pregnant a second time, she was convinced she was to have a son. Rumors abound of your father's anger and of how he supposedly took it out on those around him. Antar is convinced he feared you would come between him and his lover, no matter how mad, how nonsensical it was for him to feel that way. He didn't want you to be born, and he told your mother so. Your mother refused.

"It was in her seventh month of pregnancy, when the stars said the child would be born soon, that your father dropped a vial of crim oil into her milk. How he got his hands on the drug, Antar didn't know. All he *did* know was that your mother was ill for days afterward. She suffered from high fevers and night bleeds, and cried often for fear of losing the baby. Neither the Wardens nor those with Ashhur's gift of healing could mend her. They didn't know what was wrong. But Ashhur did. He traveled north on hearing the news of your mother's illness, placed his hands on her stomach, and removed the poison from her system, saving you. But it was too late. The poison had altered your form, and you ended up being born…the way you are now."

Patrick crossed his arms, refusing to look at Deacon as he let the story settle into his mind. When he stayed silent, Deacon continued.

"Ashhur confronted your father, told him he knew what had been done. Your father fell to his knees, groveling before the deity, begging for his life. Now, in Neldar perhaps the greatest sin one could commit is to murder—or *attempt* to murder—an unborn child. Yet Ashhur decreed that your father was truthful in his contrition and absolved him of all sins."

Patrick lowered his head, looking at Deacon from beneath his distended brow.

"Is that it?"

Deacon shrugged, looking uncomfortable. "Yes."

"Interesting story."

"Are you sorry I told you? Do you wish I had stayed silent?"

"No. And no."

He sighed. "It is but a story, however horrible it may be. I would understand if you wished to depart now and confront your parents."

"Why would I do that?"

"Well," said Deacon, his cheeks growing redder by the second, his fingers nervously playing with the hem of his doublet. "I figured you might want to be…certain?"

At that, Patrick laughed. Hearty, *true* laughter that rattled his crooked spine.

"Are you trying to be rid of me?" he asked. "To be honest with you, Deacon, it wouldn't surprise me in the slightest if it *were* true. To be even more honest, I couldn't give two shits and a piss. None of that matters. What was done was done a long, long time ago, in a place where I never felt true belonging. Nessa has gone to live her fabulous life with her little renegade. She was my last remaining tie to Paradise other than my god. I belong *here* now, among these people, and I feel that truly. Besides, I've never liked my father much." He winked. "I guess now I know why. Perhaps I still carry a few old, old memories from floating around in the womb, eh?"

He slapped Deacon on the back hard enough that the man began coughing, which brought on another fit of laughter.

"Come on, man, it was only a tap!" he exclaimed, and away he ambled across the wide, soggy field, heading for Corton and the soldiers who were waiting by the forest's edge.

He had been honest in his reaction to the story and honest in the words he'd spoken to Deacon afterward. Strange as it seemed to his waking mind, he really didn't care, no matter how disturbing the tale was or how true it rang. Richard DuTaureau could shove a goose egg up his own ass, and Isabel too. Patrick had come on people who viewed him as more than his deformities or his lineage. Here he had friends, even if his relationships with a few of them might be awkward, to say the least. What mattered was that his last name had no bearing on the impressions he made here. Something just seemed *right* in Haven, even with that atrocious temple rearing over everything. As far as Patrick could tell, living a life free of sickness, fear, and disagreement was not the best way to go. He offered a silent apology to Ashhur for thinking thus, but he'd never been happier than he was here. Perhaps humanity had been meant to *battle through*, to learn to live in harmony through strife, through hardship. It was the people of Haven who had taught him this, people he would die for if need be—which he had to admit wouldn't be such a bad thing. After all, how many times had he moaned and groaned like a spoiled little child about his desire for a mortal life?

He joined Corton's side and spent the next several hours laughing and drinking with the many men and few women who were around. Later, when the liquor was all but gone, Moira joined them, and she and two other men—Opal and Mertz, if he remembered their names correctly—assisted him in donning the mishmash of armor Corton had set aside for him. It was an arduous task given his strangely shaped body, but eventually the plates were fastened, the chainmail draped over his chest, the vambraces clasped to his forearms. He stood there, holding a half helm in his arm (his misshapen head made it impossible to wear a great helm; the bottom was loose because his cheeks and jaw were so thin compared to his bulbous cranium), and addressed the crowd that had gathered.

"How do I look?"

They cheered and whooped in response.

Sunset came before he knew it, and a man named Varimor arrived from the deserted township, lugging a cart full of cider for everyone to drink. The conversation went on and on, peppered with irreverent and nasty jokes, until finally a rider came galloping across the distant field, coming from the direction of Karak's Bridge.

"They're here!" he shouted. "The soldiers—they're actually here!"

"They damn well better be," Patrick shouted before nervousness grabbed hold of those around him. "I didn't spend half an hour getting dressed for nothing!"

The men smiled through clenched teeth, laughed amid grunts and frightened looks. Cups were carelessly tossed aside, replaced by the swords, daggers, axes, mauls, and shields Peytr Gemcroft had supplied them with as his parting gift. The moon rose full in the night sky, and the air was filled with the sounds of clanking metal and animalistic grunts as the ragtag defenders of Haven formed their first line of defense under Corton's instruction.

Patrick hefted Winterbone, the massive sword feeling natural in his grip, and took his place at the front of the vanguard. Adrenaline rushed through him, making his heart race and his toes twitch, but he did not feel scared. If anything, he felt expectant, as if this were the natural next step in his life's path. The thud of marching footsteps hit his ears, followed by the repetitious shouts of what sounded like thousands of voices, and on the horizon, coming across Karak's Bridge, there was a flurry of movement. Row after row of men stormed over the bridge, marching in rhythm, twelve bannermen leading the way. In their hands waved the sigil of the Lion, the flags held high enough for all to see. A single voice called out above the rest, ordering the approaching army to stop. Patrick looked at them, then at his comrades, and for a moment he felt paralyzing fear. They were horribly outnumbered. Whereas the approaching army had what looked to be two thousand men, if not more, they were but three hundred. They would be overrun in seconds. Deacon must have realized this as well, for Patrick caught sight of the man slowly inching away from the line of defense, heading for the trees. "Figures," Patrick whispered, and returned his attention to his impending doom.

The next call came, and he watched as a row of archers stepped away from the rest. They raised their bows to the sky, waiting, and Patrick realized that there would be no discussion; there would be no demands to drop their weapons and surrender to the eastern god. The temple still stood, and that meant annihilation. Still, he wondered, given the vigor with which the army marched into the delta, if there would have been mercy even if they *had* torn it down. He squinted and stared, past the army, past the bridge, and into the lands beyond.

Barely visible in the intense moonlight, surrounded by three other riders, was a being larger than life, standing with its hands on its hips. Even though his companions were mounted on horses, this great man towered over them. And Patrick caught sight of the man's eyes, which looked like swirling stars of fire and brimstone.

Karak was here. There would be no mercy.

Another shout from the opposing force, and the archers drew back their strings. Patrick braced himself, holding Winterbone out to the side with both hands as Corton had taught him, his fear dwindling down to nothing.

"Steady!" he heard Corton scream. "Don't do a fucking thing before my orders!"

Two more riders came galloping over the bridge.

"Release! Release!" the riders shouted back to the gathered force, and all at once, a hundred arrows climbed high into the blackened sky.

The assault on Haven had begun.

Clovis sat atop his horse beside his god, on the eastern side of the bridge, watching his army spread out beneath the solemn near-daylight of the full moon. The pain in his side from the wound Soleh had given him lingered like an impure thought. Far off to his right loomed the Temple of the Flesh, the monstrosity that had been necessary to set these events in motion.

Deacon was a good choice, he thought. His pride wavered, however, when he saw how well the people of Haven had armed themselves. Bringing his looking glass to his eye, he gazed across the expanse and saw two hundred, perhaps three hundred men, clad in polished armor and brandishing weapons. They presented no flags, bowed before no monuments, and showed no loyalty to any but one another. A short but hulking figure stood at their center, holding aloft a giant sword Clovis recognized. The man looked like a demon, with his hunched gait and warped body. It was Patrick DuTaureau, Clovis was sure of it. He knew Deacon had done what he'd asked, for the man was nothing if not reliable, but Isabel's boy was still there, ready to fight, which could be a problem. DuTaureau was an unknown, and Deacon had told him that the man inspired confidence in the forces of Haven. He'd thought to murder the man in his bed, yet the Whisperer had advised against it. His unknown accomplice had never steered him wrong yet, so he'd let the matter drop. Lowering the looking glass, Clovis reached inside his shirt, wincing as his rough stitches pulled taut, and lifted out his pendant. It shone purple under the light of the moon, but there were no swirls of deep shadow to be seen within the crystal, no sign whatsoever that his Whisperer was ready to give him more guidance.

Two horses circled in front of him. Mounted upon them were Avila and Joseph, the children he was proudest of, ready to carry out any order he decreed.

"What is your command, Highest, our Lord Commander?" Avila asked, bowing low in her saddle, her silver hair like satin in the moonlight.

Clovis paused, then looked up at Karak. The deity stood motionless, his shimmering golden eyes fixed on the temple and the small number of men ready to die for it.

"They are not afraid," Karak said, his voice like thunder that rumbled along the countryside.

"Then we shall give them reason to be," said Clovis, trying to sound confident.

Karak gave him a nod.

Clovis turned to Joseph and Avila.

"Let loose the arrows," he said.

On hearing his words, his two most precious children kicked their steeds into motion. They rumbled over the wide bridge toward the rows of soldiers. Clovis heard Joseph's voice ring out, unnaturally loud.

"Release! Release!"

Arrows flew into the air. Karak remained motionless while Clovis allowed himself a nervous smile, hoping beyond hope that his Whisperer would reveal the next part of the plan to him when the time was right.

"Hold!" shouted Corton as the arrows rose high in the air, passing beneath the moon and casting a litany of ominous shadows on the ground. "Hold, I said!"

Patrick did as he was told, his body rigid, his arms growing sore from Winterbone's weight. He glanced to his left and saw that Moira was beside him, decked out in her boiled leather and light chainmail, holding aloft a slender cutlass. Her hair cascaded from the back of her helmet like a silver waterfall. She winked at him, and he chuckled.

"Ready for this?" she asked, having to shout to be heard over the din.

"Ready," he shouted back.

"Shields up!" came Corton's voice, and the clamor and clang of steel was deafening. Patrick knelt down. Moira and the two shield-bearers on either side of him lifted their enormous curved buffers, forming a dome of protection over them. A second later the arrows struck, clanking off metal, thudding into wood. A few shrieks of pain came as arrows found purchase in human flesh, but thankfully there seemed to be few injuries. The barrage lasted only a few seconds, and then Corton was back at it.

"Up, now!" he screamed. "Up, and charge until they fire again!"

A battle cry rose up from all those around him, three hundred bellowing as one, and Patrick joined in. He shouted until his throat ran dry, shambling to his feet, running as fast as he could while weighted down by the fifty pounds of armor on his back and the forty pounds of sharpened steel in his hands. But he soldiered on nonetheless, guided forward by Moira, who was shoving her shoulder into him. He gazed ahead with narrowed eyes, watching the column of enemy soldiers draw ever closer.

"Stay in formation!" shouted Corton from behind, his voice sounding small beneath the clanging of armor.

Patrick watched as the archers lifted their bows once more, aiming lower this time, and another volley released. He kept pushing his feet to move, his legs sore, his back barking in agony, until he heard the command to hunker down yet again. He skidded to a stop, falling on his side in the process. The shieldmen were slower this time around, clumsy in the handling of their much too large shields. They failed to get close enough together, and as the arrows rained down, Patrick heard Moira shriek. He shifted abruptly to the left, found her lying there, and covered her body with his own. Again the arrows pummeled the shields, bringing still more screams from those gathered around him. Two arrows passed through the gap between the shields, one clanging off his right pauldron, the other skimming past his side, where there was no protection. He felt an instant of burning pain, but then it was gone—though now there was a warm sort of wetness dribbling onto his stomach.

"You're all right?" he asked Moira.

She nodded in reply.

The shields were lifted and the charge began anew. This time Patrick didn't struggle; his legs moved with a mind of their own, and his arms swung forward and back, easily holding Winterbone aloft. It was as if the bolt that had pierced his side had severed his ability to feel pain.

He didn't need Corton's next bellowed command to know that this was it. No more volleys would come their way, as they had gotten too close for a rain of arrows to be practical. Instead the archers spread out, making way for the men with pikes who stood behind them. The pikemen stepped forward and knelt down, holding their spears out at an upward angle, waiting for the charging force to collide with their sharpened tips. Meanwhile, the archers began picking off the approaching force, one by one, using measured shots.

One man fell. Then another. The shield bearer who had stood to Patrick's right collapsed, grabbing his abdomen and screaming in pain. From his peripheral vision he saw one of his sparring partners—Big Chuck, they called him—take a shaft in the face. The man collapsed right then and there, falling backward, hands at his sides.

As Patrick worked his way toward the awaiting pikemen, arrows missing him by mere inches, he could only hope his end would be that quick.

He drew ever closer to the awaiting army, so close that he could begin to make out their features. Some appeared angry, barking back at the loud, quickly approaching mass, but they were in the minority. Others appeared exhausted, as if the act of holding their weapons aloft took more energy than they could afford to expel. But mostly he saw wide eyes and clenched teeth, shaking hands gripping swords they weren't prepared to handle, archers who winced at every yelp and shout, sending their arrows flying wildly, looking like they wanted to be anywhere but right there, right then.

They were frightened. Terrified. Patrick grinned and forced his uneven legs to move faster. For the first time, despite the opponent's much greater numbers, he truly believed the haggard residents of Haven could win.

He crashed into the first line, twisting to the side and avoiding the outstretched pikes. His armored shoulder struck a man in the jaw, shattering it, splashing blood and spittle across his back. Patrick braced his legs, swung Winterbone up in an upward-arcing circle, and then brought it down diagonally the way Corton had taught him. The two soldiers in front of him held up their swords to parry the blow, but it was too fast, too powerful. Both their blades shattered on contact, and Winterbone continued on its sloping trek, severing one man's head from his spine and cutting through the thin leather armor worn by a second man. Winterbone took off the man's arm before getting lodged midway through his midsection. Blood erupted in a thick sheet, drenching Patrick's face and shoulders. He planted a boot in the dead man's abdomen and kicked, freeing his blade.

The rest of his team followed his lead, barreling into the line of defenders, hacking and slicing, jabbing and thrusting. The pikemen fell, as did a good number of the archers, and those standing behind them moved forward. Patrick pushed on, his people killing and dying alongside him. He felt something strike his back and turned ever so slightly. Moira was leaning against him, using his bulk for balance as she whipped about, her sword in one hand and a dagger in the other. Men fell at her feet like flies, throats slit, all with a simple flick of her wrist. He marveled at her speed even as he fought through the danger before him. For every one swing he completed, she achieved five or more. She was like a dervish of ruin, dodging every strike that came her way.

Patrick batted aside a thrust from a tall soldier with hair so black it shone blue in the moonlight, then rammed Winterbone's pommel into his nose. Cartilage snapped, gushing blood down the soldier's face, and Patrick took that opportunity to lope back, and then plunge forward, piercing the man's heart with the tip of his sword. That man fell away, replaced by another and another. Patrick cut each of them down, though not without cost to himself. His armor was dented, his chainmail torn away, and his arms were starting to tire. Everywhere he hurt, numerous gashes covering the unarmored portions of his body. The blood of the enemy mixed with his own, turning his entire body into a glistening red monstrosity. His vision began to waver and he stumbled, which caused Moira to cry out in surprise from behind him.

But still he would not stop, could not stop.

After ending the life of yet another soul, he saw a breach in the defenses. He threw back his arms, looked at the sky, and bellowed so loud, he was sure even Celestia could hear him from her secluded, heavenly star. His compatriots had thinned substantially on either side of him—perhaps half now lay on the ground, bleeding into the damp, swampy grass—but the rest continued to fight, every shred of their will hurled into their efforts. He spotted even Corton among them, the old man taking on two soldiers at the same time, his gray hair whipping around his helmless head. Seeing his bravery and prowess gave Patrick new strength.

"Behind me!" he shouted to his people, and they complied, disengaging from their opponents and falling in line as he charged like the bull Corton told him he was, deep into the third line of

resistance. The enemy soldiers fell back, looking like they wanted
no part in what was to come. Patrick held Winterbone out before
him like a lance and drove into them, impaling two men at once,
hurtling ever deeper into the line while his cohorts fanned out wide,
striking out at those who attempted to overwhelm him. Man after
man fell to the ground beneath their fury.

The sound of thundering hooves reached his ears, and Patrick
glanced up to see a pair on horseback charging into the melee,
weapons drawn. One was a man with a sword that looked like
Winterbone's smaller twin, the other a woman with an evil-looking
mace. They shared a similar appearance, each with silvery-white
hair and a porcelain face. They galloped in, looking like phantoms,
and when Moira flashed beside him, bending to one knee to fend
off a wild swing with her dagger while gutting another opponent
with her sword, Patrick knew *exactly* who the riders were. Twenty
more riders appeared behind them, surging over the bridge in an
equestrian tide.

"Horses!" he heard Corton shout. "Horses! Everyone get—"

The command ended there, mid-word. Patrick dared a glance.
Corton was kneeling on the ground out in the open, hands hanging
limp, half his face a bloody pulp, his left eye hanging by a slender
tendon down to the middle of his blood-washed cheek. Patrick
screamed as the male rider galloped by, swinging low with his great
sword, severing the old man's head in an instant. Corton's body
collapsed, his life's fluid spurting into the air as he fell.

The sight of Corton's death broke something inside Patrick.
He turned away from the main battle and ran headlong at the soldiers on horseback. One struck him in the back with an ax, which
stunned him but did not pierce his platemail. He hacked at the legs
of one of the passing horses, and the beast tumbled down, sending its rider careening through the air. He shoved his shoulder into
another horse, his strength immense in his rage, and the thing fell
over, crushing the rider beneath its weight.

At last Patrick found him, Moira's brother, Joseph, with his short-chopped white hair. He was facing away from Patrick, hacking at someone on the other side of his horse. Patrick took the opening, and leapt into the air, hoping to tackle the man and wrest him from his saddle. But even with his battle-fueled strength, his short legs couldn't lift him high enough, and he crashed face first into the side of the horse, which bucked on contact. Patrick jarred his neck, sending a spasm of numbness through his spine, and he clutched madly for something, anything, to break his fall. He ended up snagging the top of the man's greave. The metal dug into his fingers, but he held on tightly. A cry of pain followed. Patrick tumbled to the ground, yanking Moira's brother down with him. He landed hard on his back.

While he lay there, the wind knocked out of him, everything grew muddled. The sounds of crashing swords and dying humans were like the honking of migrating geese in autumn. His vision blurred, shapes merging with one another until all he saw were brief flashes of light against a bluish-grey backdrop. His stomach hitched and he rolled to the side, trying in vain to keep his wits about him.

Hands grabbed his shoulders, pulling him back, and everything started to come back into focus.

"Patrick, get up!" a woman's voice said, so close that her wet breath slapped his ear. "Come on, man, *stand!*"

He glanced over his shoulder, but his vision was partially obscured by his crooked helm. He tore it off and looked up at Moira, whose expression was one of pure, unadulterated terror as she gazed behind him.

Turning, he saw Joseph rise from the ground, holding his side, where blood trickled from beneath his armor. Grime streaked his silver, spiky hair. The man glanced at his hand, saw the blood on it, and then fixed his eyes on Patrick. If a look were capable of killing a man, this one would have done it.

"Stay back!" Moira shouted at him. Her voice was shaky, and as she pointed her sword at him, her arm began to tremble. She was terrified of him. Patrick struggled to his feet, saw Winterbone lying in the grass a few feet away, and made a dive for it. Joseph simultaneously leapt into action, and before Patrick could lay a hand on the hilt, a fist connected with the top of his head. The blow brought stars to his vision, but Patrick's head was harder than most. He heard bones snap, and he watched as Joseph pulled back his hand and stared at his mangled fingers, a look of shock and agony painted across his elegant features.

Patrick swung a backhand, catching Joseph flat in the mouth. The chainmail glove he wore shattered the man's front teeth, sending him flying backward at an awkward angle. Then Patrick reached down, grabbed Winterbone—the sword was so heavy that he could barely lift it in his exhaustion—and swung wildly. The tip caught Joseph in the midsection as it flashed by, in the gap just below his breastplate. His stomach opened like the maw of some hideous ocean fish, spilling forth his innards. Joseph's eyes bulged from their sockets. He reached down, grabbing at his intestines as if he could stuff them back into his belly. Consciousness fleeing him, he fell with a *thud*, his broken face landing hard against the ground.

Patrick dropped Winterbone to his side and panted, the strength sapped out of him.

"*NO!*"

Patrick turned at the sound of the shrieking voice and saw a woman galloping toward him. Moira still stood there, sword outstretched, eyes locked on her dead brother. She never saw the approaching rider, and the mace connected with the back of her helm with a *thunk*. Moira collapsed as if she'd been hit by a charging boar, smashing down face first. The horse ran on by, missing him by mere feet. From Patrick's fleeting glance, the woman could have been Moira's twin if not for the right half of her face, which was a twisted mess. It looked as if she had been tenderized by a meat hammer, an image that would have made him chuckle if he had been any less terrified.

The woman steered her horse around, her silver hair flying out behind her like the hem of the goddess's dress. Her face was twisted in rage, her mouth opened in a constant, primal cry. She kicked the horse and it charged, heading right for him. Patrick tried to stand one last time but couldn't. He couldn't even get Winterbone off the ground. He fell back on his ass, and then closed his eyes. He'd accept his fate with dignity and begged Ashhur that it wouldn't be painful or long.

It never happened.

He heard a *clunk*, and opened his eyes. The woman's mace was no longer in her hand, and she sat atop her horse, spinning in all directions, searching for something. A dark object flashed seemingly out of nowhere, colliding with her and knocking her from her steed. The woman hit the ground and rolled to avoid further injury. The shadow, meanwhile, landed a few feet away. Patrick looked upon his savior—a slender female figure dressed in tight black leather, her body bent in such a way that the twin blades held in her hands were pointed directly at her opponent. Patrick gulped down a breath, looking on in shock as Rachida flashed her eyes in his direction.

"Are you hurt?" she shouted, keeping most of her focus on the white-haired woman with the mangled face, who had risen to her feet and drawn her sword.

"More than I'd prefer," Patrick said.

"Doesn't matter. Get up. Sound the retreat. I'll handle this one."

Without waiting for his response or explaining her sudden presence, Rachida charged. Her twin shortswords crashed with the woman's saber, and the two women began a dance that would have been quite beautiful if life hadn't been on the line. Parry and thrust, hop and dodge, swing and retreat. Patrick was mesmerized.

"Go!" Rachida shouted, sensing his delay.

Patrick followed her command, pushing his feet beneath him and rising shakily from the ground. He looked out at the battle that raged around him and was amazed to see just how far it had spread in all directions. He began to run at a limping trot, dragging Winterbone behind him because he didn't even have the energy to sheathe it on his back.

"Retreat!" he yelled, his voice hoarse and weak. "Come on now, re—"

He stopped short, standing alone in the middle of the grass. There…in the sky…

Patrick fell to his knees, his eyes wide with horror while his mouth shrieked, *"No, no, no, no, NO!"*

The battle was going quite well. Better than Clovis had expected as a matter of fact. He chuckled at his own foolishness for thinking that the DuTaureau boy might spur the enemy on to greatness. No matter how charismatic a leader might be, numbers always mattered more, and Karak's two thousand trained soldiers would crush three hundred ruffians every time.

Peering through his looking glass, he could see that perhaps fifty or sixty of the Haven traitors were left, and though they battled diligently, killing hundreds, they would soon be finished. He leaned back in his saddle, another wave of pain knifing his side. Then he glanced at Karak, who seemed disinterested in the events down below, and smiled. Perhaps he didn't need the help of his Whisperer after all.

As if in answer to that thought, he felt a gentle vibration against his chest. He leaned forward with a start, grimacing with pain, and stared at the pendant. There it was, swirling with mist blacker than night. He clutched it tight in his palm, closed his eyes, and listened.

And the Whisperer spoke.

Clovis's eyes snapped open. He felt a moment of intense guilt, thinking of the instructions he'd given Deacon, but he stubbornly shoved his weakness aside.

"My Divinity," he said, "it is time to end this."

Karak stirred like a statue coming to life.

"It is," his god said. "They will soon be crushed. When they are, we will move inland and set the town ablaze. No one who resides in the crook of the rivers shall live."

"Yes, we will crush their bodies, but do you not think it best to crush their spirits as well?"

Karak's glowing eyes turned to him.

Clovis pointed to his right. "The temple. It is the source of their mutiny, the insult they spit in your face. Let us send a message to any who might survive or flee to Ashhur's Paradise. This blasphemy will never be allowed ever again."

Karak inhaled deeply, then let the breath out.

"You are right," he said. "A message must be given."

"However, you must know—"

"Do not think me a fool, Lord Commander. I see more than you do."

The deity raised a single hand, pointing two fingers at the heavens. His mouth began to utter words of magic, strange and powerful phrases Clovis had never heard before. Karak's voice grew louder, more insistent, and then, with a final, demanding bellow, he clenched his giant fist and sent it crashing down onto his opposite palm.

Clovis's eyes lifted, and he stared up in disbelief as a giant ball of flaming rock lit up the night sky, screaming in toward the township of Haven as if from the very heavens.

CHAPTER

36

The sounds of battle could be heard from a mile away. The clanking steel, the bloodcurdling screams, the thudding of horse's hooves—all of it. It was the first time Roland had ever heard such a thing, and it chilled him to the bone. He wanted to turn around, to flee in the direction he'd come from. And when he reached Paradise, he'd snatch Mary Ulmer from her tent and tell her how much he thought of her, how beautiful she was to him—everything he feared he would never have the chance to say again, for no matter how strong the impulse, he would not turn around. He would not abandon Jacob.

They had crossed Ashhur's Bridge not two hours before and had been following the edge of the Clubfoot Mountains ever since. The moon shone brightly overhead, casting a ghostly pallor on everything around him. The path ahead was like a milky river they might sink into, the forest to their right a dead place filled with monsters. Roland shivered and closed his eyes, squeezing his legs tight around his horse's body, trying to force away the images that haunted him. It did no good, for he kept seeing Brienna's reanimated face, staring blankly ahead and dripping blackened rot from her lips.

He wished Ashhur had not agreed to come. He wished Ashhur had not listened to Jacob. He wished that after thinking it over, the god had simply declined to abide by the First Man's dire words. But mostly, he wished he could be anywhere but *here*.

There were twenty in their party—himself; Jacob; Azariah; Master Steward Clegman along with two more Wardens, Loen and Shonorah; and sixteen other capable men and women, including Stoke and Tori Harrow, who wished to finally set sight upon the structure for which their son had needlessly perished. When Roland had asked why they wanted to do such a thing, Ashhur had told him they required closure. Roland did not know what *closure* meant, but he thought the idea itself sounded stupid.

Ashhur walked alongside the group, his long, tireless strides easily keeping pace with the horses. His white robe billowed whenever a cool breeze gusted, revealing the powerful form of the god-made-flesh beneath. He had stayed silent for the entirety of their two-day journey, and everyone in their group seemed to know instinctively that silence was what the god wanted. None asked him questions, none asked for blessings. Roland wasn't sure if they knew what they were in for when they reached Haven. He knew he surely didn't, and that, after all the unexpected horrors that had befallen him over the last couple months, was what frightened him the most.

They rounded a bend in the path, the rocky base of the mountain jutting out, forcing them closer to the forest. A sudden, intense cavalcade of sound emerged from the trees, a chorus of mad tweeting and chirping that put his hair on end.

Azariah guided his horse—the largest steed Safeway had at its disposal—over to him.

"That is the song of the whippoorwills," he said. "They are but birds, despite how sinister they sound."

"They sound sad," Roland said, his body wracked with shivers.

"They often do," Azariah replied.

Roland looked past the Warden to his master. Just like Ashhur, Jacob had kept silent for most of their journey. At times he seemed outwardly angry, and at times contemplative and sad. But mostly he looked detached, his gaze empty, as if there weren't a thought in his head that wasn't well guarded. The few times Roland tried to speak with him, the First Man shooed him away. That might have been the most difficult part of all of this. During a time of inner turmoil, when the horrors he'd witnessed haunted him and his innocent view of the world had been shattered, the man he respected more than his own father wasn't there to pull him back to safety.

Now, as they drew ever closer to the battle at Haven, Jacob looked like a man simmering in conflict. His lips were puckered, his head tilted forward, his eyes narrowed, and his forehead creased. Roland glanced back at Azariah, and the Warden placed a large, comforting hand on his knee.

"He will come around," Azariah said, sensing his concern.

The words didn't help.

Their path narrowed, steering them up a slight incline, and the convoy soldiered on. The horrific sounds of combat grew ever louder, drowning out the somber cries of the whippoorwills. When they crested the hill, the land flattened out and the path ended. A dense thatch of trees stood before them. They spread out in a line and wandered in. The forest was thin, only a hundred feet deep at most, and soon they reached its end. One by one they dismounted their horses and peered through the foliage at the vast clearing on the other side, each gasping when their eyes alighted on the horrible scene that awaited them. When it was Roland's turn, his jaw fell open.

There were bodies everywhere, far more than had been stacked beside the fire in the camp outside Drake. They littered the ground like nettles, dark shapes bulging from the grass, unmoving. In the near distance there was a large mass of people locked in battle. It all took place in the shadow of a monstrous construction of stone that hovered over everything less than a mile away. The combatants looked like a pulsating group of flesh and steel, the particulars of the fight indiscernible to him. Even so, he could see a steady mist hovering above the mass, a pinkish fog that grew sometimes thicker, sometimes thinner, but never completely dissipated. He thought of the way the blood had spurted when the mad priest slit the throats of those poor innocent souls in the ravine and was overcome by the urge to flee.

Something brushed past him, and Roland shifted to see that Jacob was close by, his eyes suddenly more alert as he took in the awful scene. His lips moved as if on their own accord, forming words Roland couldn't hear, and his hands were shoved into the front pouch of his dirty tunic. Roland felt for him. His master looked completely horrified.

Ashhur stepped forward as well, standing alongside Roland. His face a mask of disbelief and resignation, the god shook his head.

"Such madness," he said. "Such unnecessary bloodshed."

"We are too far away," Jacob said. "Do you see Karak?"

Roland was shocked by his master's voice, which didn't match his expression; it sounded more curious than sad.

"I do," the deity replied. "I sense that he is here, but hidden."

"How about Patrick?"

"I see him on the battlefield. He is injured, but still alive."

"Do we go retrieve him?" asked Loen the Warden.

"No," said Ashhur. "It was his choice to join this conflict."

"What of the people?" asked Jacob. "The children, the elderly? Did they flee?"

Ashhur closed his eyes and tilted his head back. He rocked back and forth as if listening to a song only he could hear. When he opened them again, his lips stretched into a smile that looked heavy with relief.

"They did not," he said. "I sense them in the temple. They are afraid, but they are safe."

Jacob squeezed his eyes shut and nodded. His unseen hands clutched at the fabric of his tunic.

"Should we get closer?" he heard Azariah ask.

"I think not," Ashhur replied. "We will watch from here. I trust my brother. Those in the temple will be allowed another chance to kneel, to turn their hearts back to the deity who loves them with all his—"

The sky suddenly lit up, a supernova of blinding yellows and reds that burned through the canopy, illuminating the forest like the brightest day. All but Ashhur shielded their eyes from the intensity; the god's gaze was lifted upward, watching the white-hot column of fire blaze overhead. Roland could hear nothing but the roar of flames and an insufferably loud yawning sound, but he could see his god's mouth open and close, screaming unheard admonitions at the heavens.

The center of the fireball was black like obsidian, and the tail trailing behind it shimmered as if it were cooking the air itself. Then it picked up speed, fell straight downward, and struck the earth.

Right into the center of the temple, that strange edifice that had stood so proud behind its wall.

The explosion was so loud, it was as if no other sound had ever existed. The ground quaked with such ferocity, it knocked Roland to his knees. An extreme flash of light turned the world temporarily translucent, and then came the wind. It was a stiff, hot breeze that carried with it the scent of sulfur and scorched meat, pummeling Roland's face with such force that he covered it in his hands lest his eyeballs roast in their sockets. He was momentarily deaf, dumb, and blind; the only thing that existed in his awareness was overwhelming, sweeping, paralyzing fear.

When it was over, a muddy silence followed, as if the delta had been plunged into the depths of the ocean. Roland risked a glance over his elbow, and through the starbursts in his vision he saw the rubble that remained of the distant temple. Stones were pulverized,

scattered across the battlefield, some large enough to crush a man—
and many of them had. A thick column of smoke rose from the
ruins, the moonlight making it look like a billowing manifestation
of all the nightmares that had ever disturbed Roland's sleep. An
inferno blazed around that column, burning bright as the sun. It
was all too horrible to be real, and in a daze Roland stumbled from
their hidden spot in the forest, emerging onto the far end of the
clearing. He glanced over the sprawling meadow, where warriors
from both sides of the conflict were standing around, staring at the
blaze. They all seemed as horrified and dumbstruck as he was.

That was when he learned that sound did still exist, for a thun-
derous *crack* reverberated from behind him. A tree came crashing to the ground. Ashhur was the one who had felled it, and the
deity leapt over the fallen trunk, landing so hard on his feet that he
formed a shallow crater in the grass. The expression on his godly
face was one of pure rage.

"*KARAK!*" he bellowed. His golden eyes burned just as bright as
the temple inferno, his jaw stretched wider than Roland had ever
seen it as he roared. The veins in his neck bulged so prominently
that for a moment it seemed as though his head would extend away
from the rest of him, devouring everything in his path.

It wasn't far from the truth.

Ashhur began to run. As his legs and arms pumped, his body
shimmered, and his fine white robe began to transform itself—
hardening and melding to his body until he was wearing a full array
of shining silver plate. His every footfall was like a sledge striking the
soil. Roland stepped forward, still disbelieving, wondering who had
taken the place of his calm, forgiving Ashhur. He felt himself close
to blacking out when a pair of hands grabbed him on either side.

"Come!" shouted Azariah in one ear.

"Yes, move your feet, boy!" Jacob screamed into the other.

He had no choice but to obey, as the First Man and the Warden
seemed intent on dragging him with them. They were far behind

the god now, but still he dominated their field of vision. Roland looked on as Ashhur approached a group of Karak's soldiers. They cowered before him, some fleeing, others tossing aside their weapons and falling to their knees. Ashhur pulled his arm back. From his fist came a great iridescent light that grew outward and upward, forming a thick shaft that ended in a point. When he swung downward, the glowing object, now fully recognizable as a sword, hacked the soldiers to pieces. With a single blow, seven men died in an instant. Their bodies caught fire as they fell to the ground, burning bright blue, consumed by the flames of Ashhur's wrath.

Jacob urged the group to stop once they reached the site of the first massacre. There they stood, not more than two hundred feet away from the carnage, with little to do but watch Ashhur work his way from unit to unit. The god was a hulking figure that towered over every man he killed, his sword—massive, radiant, and blue—making quick work of them all. Roland thought it the most horrible thing he had ever seen: his creator, who had preached always of *love* and *forgiveness*, was now taking the lives of dozens in what appeared to be a thoughtless rage. One glance at Azariah showed Roland that the Warden felt the same way, but when he looked at Jacob, a chill came over him. His master appeared fascinated. A hint of a smile played on the corners of the First Man's lips.

"What's *wrong* with you?" Roland gasped.

Jacob glanced his way, jutting his chin toward the battlefield.

"Poetry in motion," he replied, then fell silent.

Looking to his right, Roland caught a glimpse of a lone fighter kneeling in the grass, staring out at the temple, his face streaked with tears. His skull was malformed, his arms were too large for his body, and his hunched back and blood-matted red hair completed the wretched picture. He seemed to be the only one who was not intent on watching Ashhur's irreconcilable outburst of violence.

"BROTHER!"

The cry rocked over them all, and Roland turned to see Ashhur had ceased his butchery. The god stood in the center of the killing field, chest rapidly rising and falling, his glowing sword held low. Ashhur's eyes narrowed, staring off into the distance. Roland did the same, and he saw a figure emerge from the darkness on the other end of the clearing, entering the light of the inferno.

It was a man, incredibly tall, dressed in black plate armor, the breastplate bearing the glowing red symbol of a roaring lion. The man's hair was dark and wavy, his face chiseled and smooth, and his eyes glowed golden, just like Ashhur's.

This time Roland did fall to his knees, yanking Azariah down with him.

"Karak," the Warden whispered, as if in awe.

The two gods faced each other, Ashhur shaking with rage, Karak firm and calm. All else seemed to halt at their meeting, as if the entire world were focused on the reunion of the two brother gods in the center of a battlefield strewn with blood and death. Even the flames erupting from the temple's ruins seemed to die away.

It was Karak who spoke first.

"Has justice been served, brother?"

"Do you know what you did?" Ashhur spat through clenched teeth.

"You slaughtered my children," said Karak, ignoring his question.

Ashhur pointed toward the temple. "You butchered the helpless. *Hundreds* of them. Is this not what we came to this world to prevent?"

Karak tilted his head forward. His eyes glowed brighter.

"I will punish my creations as I see fit. That is the deal we made; that is the deal I have stood by."

"They were children!" Ashhur screamed. "Innocents! We did not come to this world to slaughter those who do not agree with us."

Karak shrugged.

"I gave them their chance. It is out of their own vanity and defiance that they hid in the very object I had ordered them to destroy."

"And the children, given no choice? The young, the helpless?"

"Do not chastise me on this, brother. You would have done the same."

Ashhur's teeth ground together, the sound like two boulders colliding.

"Never," he said.

"Of course, the pacifist, Ashhur," laughed Karak. "My gentle brother, who bribes his children with flowers and fornication and loathes violence." The god gestured to the bodies lying all around him. "It is a poor god who cannot practice what he preaches."

"Enough," growled Ashhur.

"Yes, enough. This land is *mine*, brother, as are its people. I will do with them as I choose."

"This land was given to neither of us."

Karak shook his head.

"You are an ignorant, idealistic fool, brother. We fled here for a reason, seizing the chance to make amends. We would wash away our failure, give life to a far greater kingdom than the one we saw destroyed. Yet it seems that as long as you are here with me, there will always be at least one failure hanging over our perfect world."

Ashhur lunged, his colossal blade aimed for Karak's head. The Eastern Divinity raised his hand, and a blade of purple-tinged blackness, the mirror of Ashhur's, appeared where before there had been none. The swords met, and an explosion of light flashed across the meadow. Sparks rained down all around the gods, and as their blades slid against each other, the sound was like a thunderclap. Energy sizzled overhead as the gods danced. Ashhur swung, Karak blocked. Karak jabbed, Ashhur parried it aside. And that same rumble and flash came each time their blades collided. The ground beneath them cracked from the power of their movements, and the air became supercharged. Roland could fe it penetrating his flesh, setting his insides abuzz, making goose pimples rise on his flesh.

Karak landed a blow on Ashhur's left breast, charring his brother's polished silver armor. Ashhur fell to a knee, holding his sword up with one hand, his body jolting each time his brother battered it with his own. Roland feared the his god was done for, that Karak would sever Ashhur's head from his spine right there and then, but Ashhur was far from beaten. He dropped his sword arm, providing a tantalizing opening. Karak immediately lunged for it, and when he did, Ashhur rolled to the side. Karak stumbled past him, and Ashhur spun in a circle, chopping slantwise at his brother. The blade found purchase in the bare flesh below Karak's coal-colored vambrace. Its cutting edge sank deep into the eastern god's forearm, almost to the elbow. Streams of liquid shadow flowed from the wound, snaking around Ashhur's blade, dulling its brightness.

Ashhur pulled his weapon free, and Karak's wound closed almost instantly. It was his turn this time, and he slashed out with his sword of shadow. Ashhur tried to lean back but was not quick enough. The blade passed through his neck without the slightest resistance. Ashhur's throat bled out smoldering magma, dripping down his chest and coating his breastplate. Roland screamed in horror, thinking that he was witnessing the death of his god, but then that wound closed too.

The two gods met each other once more, slamming their ethereal swords together in mid air. Clouds rolled in, blocking out the moon, and a light rain began to fall, forks of lightening flashing down from above. Roland looked up at the pitch-black sky that sizzled with electricity and wondered with strange detachment if this were Celestia's way of closing her eyes.

Karak leapt into the air, holding his blade above him like an executioner's ax, and landed hard. Ashhur's sword came up, and the two weapons locked together, sliding downward until their pommels touched. The blades wound together, their light and darkness swirling together into a single beam of gray. The brother gods began to thrash wildly, trying to free their swords, but both slipped from their grasp at the same time. The weapons disappeared, vanishing into the night before they ever reached the ground, the magic that formed them dissolving as soon as they left the gods' hands.

The loss of their swords didn't mean an end to the gods' battle. Now weaponless, they rained fists down on each other. Heads snapped back and bodies doubled over as blow after blow landed. Ashhur flipped backward, barely avoiding a swinging punch from his brother, but then Karak leapt high into the air and knocked Ashhur flat by planting both feet firmly on his chest. Karak slid down, pinning down his brother's shoulders as he mercilessly clouted his face, time and again, until Roland's beloved god was covered in a litany of bulging, magma-leaking wounds.

"Stop, please!" Roland shouted, running forward. Azariah snatched him by the collar and pulled him back before he could get too close, but his sudden outburst seemed to have distracted Karak, for Ashhur managed to slide a hand out from beneath his brother's knee. His usually powerful voice was weak and rasping as he whispered something Roland couldn't hear. His free hand touched Karak's chest, then a loud *thwump* followed, like a hammer striking a sack of flour, and the eastern god was sent airborne. He landed on his back twenty feet away, a smoldering hole burned into his chestplate, revealing the charred flesh beneath.

Karak and Ashhur each struggled to rise, and they knelt across from each other, gasping, their eyes locked together. It was Karak who got to his feet first. Ashhur looked tired and defeated, as if his attempt to save himself had drained the last of his power. Karak fared no better; he clutched at the hole in his armor as his entire body rose and fell with his breaths.

"Why?" asked Ashhur. Even in his weakened state, his voice still boomed. He reached beneath his armor and pulled out his pendant, the bas-relief of the lion standing atop the mountain. With a single sharp motion he snapped the chain and tossed the pendant across the span between them. "Does this mean nothing to you now?"

Karak scowled at him, picking up the pendant. "It does, but its meaning has changed. Do you remember why we came here? Why we came to Dezrel, why we created humanity on this planet?"

"We were to find a better way—one that would not destroy each another. Violence is not the better way."

"*Life* is destruction, dear brother, it always has been. You should know that better than anyone." Karak smiled then, perhaps the most hideous and malignant smile Roland had ever seen. "But you are right; we wanted to find a better way. A way for humanity to fully realize its potential, without the destruction and war that has always befallen it. And I *have*, brother. I spent many years in the mountains, contemplating this very subject, and do you know what I realized? In every world we have visited where humans existed, they were locked in a never-ending chain of unnecessary death. What did all of these places have in common? In each world, every single one, the humans fought over the dominance of one god over another. Do you not realize what that means, brother? *We* are the cause of this violence! We will never be able to leave them. Never be able to step aside and watch our creations flourish to their greatest heights. No matter how long our pact remained strong, one day our people would clash, and they would clash over *us*." Karak's expression became passionate. "Look how little time it took for a blasphemous temple to be built. Look at the soldiers who clashed in this place, even as you preached against violence and I remained distant in the mountains. There is a better way. Let there be *one* truth, *one* god, *one* faith. Imagine it, brother—all of humanity, united! An end to violence, an end to warfare, an end to chaos. What would follow would be a rise of order! Would that not be wonderful? All I need… is for you to step aside."

Ashhur stared at him, wide eyed and appalled.

"*This* has been your plan? You are mad," he said.

Karak offered him a sad shake of his head.

"Not mad, brother, nor did I plan this. I stood back and watched as the events unfolded. Despite our teachings, our wisdom, our First Families, humankind sank to the same conflicts as always. This cycle must be stopped, and I will put a stop to it, no matter what the cost. My way is the *only* way, and I promise you now that if you stand aside, if you relinquish your Paradise to me, it will remain unscathed."

"And if I do not?"

"I will march west and burn all that you have created. Either way, there will only be one truth. *My* truth."

Ashhur stared him down, then placed his hand on the ground and used it as leverage, shoving his body upright until he stood at his full height. He looked his brother dead in the eye and gave his answer.

"No."

Karak sighed.

"Very well. Then let it be war." His next words were spoken louder; he was clearly addressing all who remained in the flickering light of the burning, corpse-riddled temple. "Consider this a warning to you all. The men who came here in my name are but a fraction of the warriors Neldar will soon have at its disposal. We will march again, with far greater numbers, and all who stand before us shall either pledge obedience or perish. Citizens of Haven, consider this my gift to you. If any wish to join me now, you may do so. All sins will be forgiven. This is your chance to serve a true deity."

Roland felt the sensation of falling backward. No, that wasn't it; he wasn't moving *back*, it was Jacob who was moving *forward*. It was a nightmare coming true, a sight that Roland could not comprehend. The First Man took great, prideful strides, crossing the empty space that separated him from the eastern deity. Roland ran after his master, frantic, but then realized that it might look as if he too were betraying his beloved god. Horrified, he fell to his knees, close enough to hear Jacob's stunning words.

"Karak, my Lord, my Creator, I am your humble servant," he said.

Roland's heart almost stopped beating.

Ashhur's eyes shimmered and his lips parted ever so slightly.

"Jacob," he asked. "What are you doing?"

"I am a child of two gods, not one," Jacob said. "I have always chosen whom to serve, and I have come to realize that I believe in Karak's vision."

Ashhur shook his head in disbelief. He showed more pain than he had from any of the blows his brother god had unleashed on him. "I do not understand. You said you loved me. You said you believed in my teachings…and I sensed no lie…."

"That's because I never lied, your Grace. You are my father, one of two. I do love you and always will. And I truly do believe that your teachings are righteous and well intentioned…but unfortunately, I believe in Karak's more. You would never lead humankind to true greatness. You would only coddle us like children, denying us wisdom, denying us knowledge, until some greater threat came along and destroyed everything we held dear."

Having said his piece, Jacob took his place by the eastern god's side. He looked at Roland, eyes full of hope, and beckoned him to follow. Roland almost did. His master was all he had ever known, his hero since the first day he could remember, his cool breeze on a warm day, his burning light in the darkest night. If it had not been for Azariah, who clamped down on his shoulder and locked him in place, he might have run across that field and embraced Jacob once more, allowed him to drag him down into the underworld by his side.

"Don't," said Azariah, tears cascading down his cheeks. "You know what is right."

He did. He cast his eyes to the floor, sensing his master's frown without having to see it. Only Jacob wasn't his master anymore. Betrayal, Roland thought, felt. Nothing but betrayal.

Karak turned away, Jacob alongside him, heading for the other side of the field, where a white-haired man on horseback awaited them. With a wave of the deity's hand, the soldiers who still drew breath, were rounded up by the horsemen, forming lines and marching wearily back toward Karak's Bridge. They disappeared into Neldar, the sound of their clanking armor a ghostly echo. The few remaining defenders of Haven—those who had not fled to join the invading force, as a few had done—stood there silently, staring at Ashhur, who seemed frozen in place. The light in his eyes had nearly extinguished, and the aura of kindness and invincibility he normally displayed had all but been shattered. His silver armor receded, becoming a simple robe once more, the torn and burnt sections slowly fading away. He looked not like a divine being, but like a simple farmer after a day spent tending his fields: exhausted, beleaguered, vulnerable. At that moment, Roland realized that all innocence was lost, for everyone, everywhere, and it would never return.

And the Temple of the Flesh, along with the bodies of more than a thousand old men and women, mothers and children, continued to burn.

CHAPTER

37

The First Man, Jacob Eveningstar, was a betrayer against his own god. It was a sin that made Patrick's jaw hang ajar. He never would have expected such an outcome, not given how much effort Jacob had expended over the years in Ashhur's name. It was like a son attempting to debase his father, which, judging from Jacob's parting words, had been the exact point. Patrick wanted to hate him for it, but he still felt a reluctant appreciation for the man. If Jacob had not sent him to Haven, he would never have found his purpose or a sense of belonging; he would never have fathered a child. It was surreal.

In fact, the whole damn *outcome* was surreal. Here he was: Patrick DuTaureau, the unwanted only son of one of Ashhur's first creations, kneeling in a field, covered with blood, both his own and that of the countless men he'd killed, watching as Karak's Army retreated over the eastern bridge. He had gone into this endeavor expecting death—perhaps even *wishing* for it—and yet he'd lived. It didn't seem quite fair, not when countless innocents, both young and old, had perished. Why had he been spared when so many others had not? What right did *he* have to keep breathing whe babes who should have been suckling at their mothers' breasts were now blackened and charred, lost beneath the rubble of a toppled monument to unbridled human desire?

The clouds overhead parted, allowing the light of the full moon to once again bathe the landscape in eerie blue light. Patrick laughed. It felt as though Celestia were pulling back the curtain to inspect the damage. All around him the men who had fought picked up the pieces. There were so few left, and they moved as if their arms were too heavy for them to hold up. A few cried over the bodies that were strewn across the battlefield, but most of the wetted and sorrowful eyes were reserved for the blazing temple. He squinted across the expanse and caught sight of Deacon Coldmine, who was crouched on his knees, much too close to the crumpled walls and the flames that spewed forth from them. He seemed to be tearing at his hair and shrieking in anguish.

"They should never have been in there," Patrick said, unable to hold back his anger. "It was a *stupid* plan."

He heard the muffled grunts of someone struggling and glanced behind him. It was Rachida, her black leather shimmering with sweat. She was hoisting up Moira, who had somehow managed to survive her sister's attack, although her white hair was so saturated with blood from the wound on the back of her head that it had turned as red as his own. He looked around but did not see the body of the sister.

"Did you kill the other one?" he called out to her.

Rachida's attention never left her lover when she answered.

"No. She rejoined her bastard father."

"Oh."

Those were the only words she offered him.

Alone in the midst of a thousand corpses, Patrick turned his attention to Ashhur, who slumped on the ground a few hundred feet away from him. He had watched with a lump in his throat as his god rmed the battlefield, slaughtering dozens with his ethereal sword.

All of it, including the mighty clash between the brother gods, he had witnessed from where he knelt, feeling as if he were trapped in a dream. Now that it was over, he managed to spur his body into some semblance of motion. He stood on his uneven legs, his extremities tingling from the lack of movement. After snagging Winterbone by the handle, he took a few lurching steps forward, dragging the blade behind him.

There were a great many people surrounding the god now, both survivors of the battle and a group of new arrivals he had never seen before. In fact, the only one he recognized was one of the three Wardens present—Azariah, if he remembered the name correctly. As he drew closer, he saw that everyone except for Azariah and a youth whom Patrick had never seen before seemed to be giving the kneeling god a wide berth. The stranger was a stout, strapping man with long and wavy brown hair, who looked like he had only recently passed his teens. The pair hovered in front of Ashhur, their expressions heavy with concern, yet still no one dared speak a word.

Patrick would change that.

Lumbering up to them, he released his sword and let it fall, then proceeded to fall on his knees before the god to whom he owed his existence. His mismatched armor jangled and clanked, drawing Ashhur's attention. The deity glanced over at him, still sitting on his giant legs. His eyes were dim, his lips sunken. In the background, the only sounds were the crackle of flames and Deacon Coldmine's grief-stricken wails.

"Not a very good night, was it, my Grace?" Patrick asked, feeling the impulsive need to lighten the mood.

Ashhur frowned at what might have been the greatest understatement in the history of Dezrel.

"No," said Ashhur, "it is not."

The young man with brown hair stepped forward. "I think it would be best for him to be left alone," he said.

"That is for Ashhur to decide," Patrick snapped. He turned back to the deity, shuffled forward on his knees, and then removed hi glove and placed his bare hand on his god's. "My Grace, you saved many lives coming here this night. The people of Haven will thank you." He pointed to the south, to the thin line of trees that separated the vast temple grounds from the township that lay beyond. "Many more live past those trees, deeper in the swampland. Without your intervention, the entire delta would have been crushed by morning. You heard his words. Karak would have spared no one."

Ashhur's faded eyes stayed fixed on the simmering remains of the temple.

"It is not enough. The delta will fall, as will Paradise. Karak will return. His people hold every advantage. I have been a fool, too blind to see the betrayal of my brother and my most trusted servant. Because of that blindness, thousands upon thousands will suffer."

"Oh, come on now," said Patrick, shaking his head. "I know you've preached pacifism, but I didn't think you were a coward."

"I am no coward," replied the god, his nostrils flaring, his brow furrowing.

"Then don't act like one," Patrick said, slamming his fist into his own dented breastplate. "Look at me, my Grace. Not three months ago I was but an ugly, deformed, craven being, with no skill save using my station as a child of Isabel DuTaureau to bed the occasional maiden. But these pathetic legs carried me into battle; these arms hefted a sword against this delta's enemies; and this back, warped and aching as it is, carried these people's burden. I am proof of what even the lowliest and ugliest of men can do when given something to fight for. You, my Grace, the deity who created us, who led us through ninety-plus years of peace and harmony, can light the way. Please. You have given this world too much beauty to allow it to be destroyed without a fight."

Ashhur looked him over, his head tilting to the side, his eyes regaining some of their luster. Suddenly, he rose from the blood-drenched grass, ascending to his full height. Patrick remained on his knees, feeling insignificant beneath the god's stare, and then he leaned over, bowing with his arms outstretched.

"My life for you, Ashhur. Always, my life for you."

A giant finger touched the nape of his neck, and a wonderful, all-encompassing warmth washed over him. It infused his muscles with life, sealed the gashes that sliced his flesh, even snatched away the pounding headache that burned behind his eyes. It was like when Antar had healed him after he and Nessa had been attacked, only a thousand times more intense. He tingled all over, and when the god withdrew his hand, he felt *alive*.

"Patrick DuTaureau, rise."

He did as he was told, standing before his god with pride, straightening his back as much as he could while people looked on all around him.

"You are a good man, Patrick," he said. "But I must ask you a question."

"What is it?"

"Do you still believe in me?"

Patrick chuckled. "It is difficult to question belief in a deity when that deity stands before you."

"That is not the question. Do you believe in my wisdom? How can a human hold faith in love and forgiveness, and still kill?"

"We fight to survive," Patrick said. "We fight to protect those we love."

"He's right," said a voice from behind him. Patrick peered over his lumpy shoulder to see that the brown-haired young man had stepped forward. Azariah had as well.

"Indeed he is," said the Warden.

"All of you," Ashhur said, addressing the entire crowd now, sixty men deep. "Do you wish to fight should it come to that? All of your lives may be lost, but if I surrender, you will be spared."

"You mean if he kills you," Patrick said. He met Ashhur's ey and saw the truth in them. The god nodded. It was answer enou for them all. They had seen the mercy of Karak. They had seen the torment of Ashhur when the temple came crashing down.

Armor clanked, weapons rose into the air, and the surviving warriors of Haven chanted. It was a communal cry, as if they possessed a single, commanding voice. It took no time at all for the newcomers to join in the chant, and soon the entire pasture was awash with the fury and certainty of their cries.

"Ashhur!" they cried. "For Ashhur!"

When it ended, Ashhur turned away from his congregation, tears in his eyes.

"We have a long road ahead," he said, his voice once more resounding across the countryside. The god glanced momentarily at the sky, toward Celestia's burning star, and said, "We will face many trials ahead, and we are already at a disadvantage. There is not a moment to waste. Come now, my children. All of Paradise must be warned of what will come, and I fear we will face this test alone."

Patrick didn't need it spelled out for him. He knew exactly what Ashhur meant.

"She won't help you, will she?" he asked, sidling up to the god.

"No," Ashhur replied. "For as long as Karak and I are at odds, she will remain far away from here."

"But you were lovers, were you not?"

The deity smiled sadly. "Above all things, Celestia is devoted to Balance. To choose sides…."

He shook his head.

When the sun finally began to rise, those from Haven who had lived through the night moved back through the trees, intent on spreading word of the tragedy that took place here, warning the survivors in the delta of what was to come. Meanwhile, the party that had accompanied Ashhur on his journey headed back the way they had come. Patrick joined them, taking Jacob's place at Ashhur's side. He mouthed a silent prayer for those who were not with him. He wished to see Rachida one more time, if only to glimpse the gentle slope of her belly as the child within her—*his* child—grew. He also prayed for those whose lives had been lost, trying to remember as many faces as he could, hoping beyond hope that they had reached the golden Paradise safely. Deep in his heart, he needed to believe they would be waiting for him when his life ended…if it ever did.

Leaving Haven behind, Patrick glanced back only once, to see Deacon Coldmine impaled on his own sword before the ruin of the temple.

CHAPTER

38

Veldaren was sleeping when Jacob returned to it. He had not seen the city in seventeen years and was amazed to see how much it had grown in his absence. Though the outskirts were still underdeveloped, the central area, miles wide and crisscrossed with cobbled streets, was a veritable jungle of gray stone and stained wood. Merchant buildings rose up all around him, and candles burned in the windows of the various homes, their dancing flames doing their best to chase away the nightmares of those who slept inside.

The journey back from the delta had taken more than two weeks, for Jacob had convinced Karak that it would be best to accompany the remaining army instead of opening a portal and taking the easier route—though in truth he questioned whether the god was strong enough to ride the shadows even if he desired it. *To keep spirits high*, had been his reasoning. *To show them their god is by their side through thick and thin.* Jacob had walked for most of the voyage, his preferred method of travel, spending time mingling with the fighting men, both healthy and injured, listening to their stories, their fears, their sorrows over the loss of their fellow soldiers. H did his best to further the idea that the attack on the delta had been justified, promising that their selfless service to their god would be rewarded in both this world and the next. Most of the soldiers had never laid eyes on him before, but most had heard stories of the fabled First Man, the only human crafted by the hands of the two gods combined, and after witnessing the esteem with which Karak treated him, they accepted his words as if they had been uttered by the deity himself.

For long stretches he walked alone, mulling over events now past. Twenty years of preparation had come screaming together over the past three months. The speed of it had nearly overwhelmed even him, and in spite of all his care, not everything had gone according to plan. Even with his excellent mind, he could barely remember the first time he had contacted Clovis Crestwell under the shadowy guise of the Whisperer, filling his mind with visions of a united Dezrel with Clovis its king. Jacob's first failure had been letting Martin die in the initial attack, a simple oversight that had rattled his plans. Martin Harrow and Geris Felhorn were to have been his clandestine spies in the west after he rejoined his true Lord, strong boys malleable enough to bend to his subconscious urgings, who would eventually step down to allow the pathetic Benjamin Maryll to take the mantle of King of Paradise. But Jacob was hardly slave to a plan, and Geris's mind had been easily broken once he'd discovered the right method of attack. Although it frustrated him to lose Geris as a spy, at least the weakest of the three kinglings had assumed the throne, for the weak were predictable and easily manipulated. Just as frustrating was his inability to dispose of Patrick DuTaureau, even though he had poisoned the freak day after day 'n Lerder. He had misjudged the hunchback's strength, both then ¹d when he'd altered his scheme once more to try to lessen the ⸗rale of those who wished to oppose the true god of the land. ⸗would not do so again.

Despite those catastrophes, he forced himself to smile, to take pride in all that had gone right. The downfall of the Lord Commander had been inspired, set into motion by a promise he had made to Broward Renson that the old man would earn a place of high esteem by Karak's side if he facilitated the ruin of Vulfram's daughter. He was also able to rid Neldar of its greatest threat: Crian Crestwell. The boy had strayed too far from his father's ideals and might have one day overthrown all that Jacob had set into motion. His love for the DuTaureau girl was a dangerous, flawed example that the two gods could coexist peacefully. It was Jacob's hand that had performed the murders; he had stepped through the dragon-glass mirror while Roland slept outside the cave. The worst had been hauling the drunken, unconscious Vulfram up the stairs. The man weighed a ton. But at least one of the First Families had been broken. They were irrelevant now, unnecessary remnants of the early period of man, no different from the Wardens of the east, who had been cast aside long ago. Jacob had a far better plan for how to instill order in the populace.

The First Families....

"Damn you, Clovis," Jacob whispered as he walked through the streets of Veldaren. The man had acted beyond his orders, sending his mad son into the Tinderlands to stir up trouble in a doomed grab for power. Jacob never should have been there, but he'd gone anyway, needing to ensure that nothing disturbed his carefully set plans. And because of that, because of their involvement....

Jacob fingered the crystal in his pocket, the gift from his dead love. He'd been so close to giving it all up. Everything he'd done, every measured step to bring about the great future human-kind deserved; he would have tossed it all away if it would have brought Brienna back to him. Ashhur had called him a hypocrite, and he'd been right. He had been overwhelmed by sorrow, and if the god had managed to bring life back from death, Jacob ha been prepared to forsake everything he'd been working towa

But no. No life. Instead, Ashhur had caved to his demands and brought him back a corpse. And then, as if to mock him, Ashhur had scattered her body as ashes, denying him the chance to say good-bye, the chance to bury her with his own hands and place a stone above her final resting place. Her remains floated on the wind, and with them floated every last doubt Jacob had in betraying Ashhur.

Everything else had come together so perfectly: the death of Bessus Gorgoros, and the elves' isolation of Ker; the coercing of Deacon Coldmine, through Clovis, to place the innocents in the temple, leading to the temple's destruction and Ashhur's fit of rage; the brother gods coming to blows, which had proven that they could not defeat each other in single combat. Despite his losses, Jacob had still won.

And no matter what the cost, there were still secrets to learn, a hidden power over death that he was certain Ashhur had knowingly denied him. Time and space could still bend to his will, for he walked at the side of a god. Perhaps, just perhaps, Brienna might return to his arms....

They came on the hub at the southern end of the city, and Jacob, Karak, and Clovis separated from the rest of their convoy, curling northeast around the fountain upon which stood a giant statue of the deity. Jacob could tell by the look on Clovis's face that the man did not understand why they were heading away from the Castle of the Lion, but he kept his protests silent. Instead he stared at Jacob as if he were a strange creature from a different dimension. The revelation that the First Man had been his secret Whisperer had changed him, and his usual arrogance was slowly ebbing away, leaving behind a desperate sycophant. The constant adoring looks and unrelenting questions were beginning to wear on Jacob, and he longed for a return to the quiet and tranquility he had been awarded during their walk. He realized right then why he had secretly given the man the dragonglass pendant in the first place, why he had spoken to him in dreams and whispers rather than approaching him outright.

The Tower Keep came into view, its abominable, fist-like apex catching the light of the stars above in its many windows. Jacob felt a surge of pride; this edifice, despite its ugliness, had been his design. He had chosen its structure and location with exactitude. It was a shame that Karak had decided the ruling class of Neldar required a more lavish assembly, ceasing construction on the Tower Keep after only the residential tower and throne room had been completed. That had been enough, however, for the throne room was the only room of importance in any building in all of Veldaren. It was also where the next step of Jacob's plan would take place.

Captain Malcolm Gregorian met them outside the front entrance of the Keep. Jacob had never laid eyes on the man before, though his survival of the Final Judges had made him a legendary figure. He certainly looked the part, what with the ugly scar that marred his face and his stalwart posture. He looked like a man who would do anything, *could* do anything, in the name of his god—the type of man who would prove quite useful in the times ahead.

Gregorian held open the massive door and then kneeled to Karak, his head bowed low.

"My Lord," he said. "I humbly welcome you home."

Karak said not a word but ducked through the entryway and disappeared inside. The Captain looked up, nodding at Clovis as the Highest limped on by. His gaze settled on Jacob, and the man's eyes widened as he slowly rose to his feet.

"Jacob Eveningstar," he said, extending his hand. "It is an honor. I have heard much of you."

"And I, you," Jacob replied. "Is everything in order?"

Gregorian nodded. "I received your letter two days past. T' was much clutter, and I had to clear it away to make the roc you requested."

"Excellent. You're a good man, Malcolm. I'm sure Karak will reward you greatly for the duty you provide."

"He has rewarded me enough already," he replied, his eyes hard, his head dipped low. "I require nothing else but the glory of his blessing."

"That, you will receive, my brother in faith. That, you will receive."

Jacob walked through the doors and entered the wide antechamber. Gregorian moved past him, heading for the stairs that led to the tower's upper levels. Jacob gave his arm a gentle squeeze and then strolled across the empty space, heading for the room at the far end of the structure.

There Karak and Clovis awaited him. The space was rectangular and enormous, stretching two hundred feet in either direction beneath a ceiling that stood four stories high. Various statues of Karak had been shoved along the walls, some finished, some not. Jacob marveled at the sight of them all: life-sized, exact likenesses of the eastern deity, carved out of sandstone, onyx, topaz, ivory, and marble, pounded out of great metal sheets, pressed out of clay. The attention to detail was astounding, and if he were not so angry that this sacred room had been reduced to an artist's studio, he would have called Ibis Mori down right then and there to congratulate him on his accomplishments.

Jacob walked through the center of the room, past the haunted, leering eyes of Karak's many lifeless copies, and came to a stop before the slightly raised platform upon which the king's throne should have sat. He stared at the massive portrait on the wall, which depicted Ashhur, Karak, and Celestia together, and then walked up and removed it. He placed it far away, where it would not be damaged by the coming events, and then turned to face his god.

"We are ready," he said.

"Are you certain you are adequately prepared?" asked Karak.

"I am. This is a delicate procedure, however, one that requires elements that I am currently lacking. My steward Roland was to act as my apprentice in this regard, but I misjudged his strength. Now I require a new one, unfortunately."

He glared at Clovis. The silver-haired man, Highest of Karak, fell back, a hand on his chest.

"What is it?" he asked, his usually patronizing tone starting to crack.

Jacob stepped up to him, grabbing him by the collar of his black tunic. He pulled Clovis close to him, under the gaze of their god, loving the way the Highest's eyes bulged from their sockets.

"You stupid, arrogant whelp," Jacob growled. "Your ego got the better of you. Does Karak even know that you sent your insane son to try to raise the demons himself? I thought not. Do you know what your actions wrought?"

Clovis shook his head, his body quavering. Jacob turned, addressing his god.

"Uther kidnapped commoners from Drake to use in the ritual of resurrection. He caused a panic in the town, and do you know what they have now? A whole legion of spellcasters who are learning the craft to *defend themselves*, and from a powerful caster at that." He turned back to Clovis. "Do you know the problems that has caused our Lord? Do you know the potential hazards your forces will face, now that your enemies are learning to hurtle fire, earth, and ice with their bare hands? You've killed thousands with your eagerness, Clovis, for these people will not to be easily conquered. Your son, you miserable wretch—your son killed my love and trapped me in the mountains. That you live at all is only out of Karak's mercy."

"But…but…I did not know you were the Whisperer!" shouted Clovis in reply.

"So much you didn't know," Jacob said, releasing the man and letting him stumble backward. "Yet that never once stopped you. Because of your actions, you have sealed your fate. You are to assist me in the ritual. *You* are to take Roland's place."

"You will," Karak echoed.

Clovis dropped to a knee. "Anything, Jacob. Anything, my Lord. My body and mind are yours."

"Of course," Jacob said. He shouted, "Captain, bring in the blasphemers!" and turned his attention to the wall where the painting had sat.

A deep murmur echoed through the vast room as Gregorian entered, dragging Ibis, Adeline, and Ulric Mori behind him. The three were bound and wore tattered rags, their bodies worked over and displaying many bruises and cuts. Thessaly Crestwell was also present, the last member of the court who was not dead or dishonored.

Ibis and Ulric glared at Jacob, while Adeline cackled through the rag stuffed in her mouth. Captain Gregorian had informed Karak in a letter that father and son had stormed into the castle after learning of Soleh's and Vulfram's deaths, shouting curses against king, god, and realm. Ulric had even put his sword through a palace guard in his anger, before being restrained and thrown in the dungeon. Adeline was dragged there with them, having followed her family into the castle, cackling and throwing rotten eggs as she went. Jacob took this as welcome news; he had planned to use a few of the many men who had been wasting away in the dungeon for tributes. Having the three Moris instead was an unexpected bonus.

Ulric struggled against his restraints, then spit a wad of phlegm in the direction of his god. Karak glared back at him, his glowing eyes growing in brightness.

Jacob began pacing along the raised platform as the Captain dragged the captives toward him. Ignoring Adeline's ranting, he removed his journal from his rucksack, set it atop a temporary podium that had been erected on the dais, and addressed Clovis once more.

"Despite everything, *Highest*, I must say that Uther's missteps ere not without benefit. I don't know how he found out what he , but he learned ancient words and phrases I had never heard of before, and I believe they may be the key to unlocking the demon kings from their prison."

"The demons," Karak said, a bit of life returning to his eyes. The whole journey back to Veldaren he'd appeared distracted, but it finally felt as if he was standing in the same room as them. "Are you certain I need their aid?"

"I watched your battle," Jacob said. "There is a reason you left before either of you found victory: because you knew there would never *be* a victor. You are too evenly matched. We will need armies, magic, and power beyond measure if we are to tip the balance in your favor. And most important of all…Celestia has not made her presence known." Jacob met his god's eyes, saw the smoldering anger in them. "You know she loves Ashhur far more than you. We must have power, power so great that even the goddess will be forced to tremble."

"And they will obey you?"

Jacob smiled, his confidence overflowing.

"They will have no choice in the matter."

Karak nodded, and Jacob cleared his throat. He stared at the pages before him, line after line written in his own hand, chronicling the history of the world and the magic of the unknown. He looked up at Clovis.

"Your son attempted to raise these demons," said Jacob. "But his errors were twofold. His first mistake was the location. The inscriptions on Neyvar Kardious's tomb were written in the first Elven tongue. The loose translation was 'the very spot where Celestia cast the demons out.' However, I have come to learn that the old language contains many words that have developed double meaning over the centuries. *Mu'tarch* does indeed mean demon, though in different context it can also mean 'god.' The most common translation for *tragnar* is 'to cast out,' though I have found that in early texts it often means 'to bring forth.' That changes the phrase to 'the very spot where Celestia brought the god

That coincides with the words written on the Neyvar's tomb: 'In the place of eternal cold, where the rocks on the earth have been sewn shut and not a blade of grass will grow, where the eternal have wandered, where the air is thick with the musk of creation and dreams of darkness prevail.'"

Clovis gasped. Karak narrowed his eyes.

"That's right. The place where Karak and Ashhur stepped into Dezrel is the area where the wall between the realities is thinnest. And where did that occur?"

He looked at Karak. The god dipped his head.

"Right beneath your feet," he said.

"Indeed," said Jacob. "Uther's second mistake was one of ignorance. For him to think he held even a scrap of the power required to enslave one of the demons is laughable. No matter how many corpses he sacrificed, no matter how much blood he splattered, he was doomed to fail from the start."

Pulling out a scrap of chalk, Jacob drew a triangle on the floor just behind the throne, inscribing runes he'd found in the darkest corners of the elven caves. When finished, he returned to the podium, grabbed his journal, and then offered his hand to Karak.

"I will need your power," he said. "Are you willing to give it?"

Karak met his eye, pausing, deciding. "How can you be sure the demon will follow your bidding?" he asked.

"I am the greatest of your creations, my Lord. I have lived ten years longer than any human in Dezrel, and have learned much. You aided by instilling in me the knowledge of ages when I was created. I know what I must do; I know how to control the beast. You must believe that."

"I do, as much as I believe my brother will never surrender to and his resistance will devastate this land. You may have what sk for."

god's hand engulfed his own.

Jacob took in a deep breath, feeling his nervousness and excitement start to overwhelm him. Fingers caressing his journal, he began to speak, uttering words foreign to him, whose pronunciations he had no way of knowing. Nonetheless they rolled off his tongue so fluently, it was as if someone else were controlling his functions. He felt the deity's power roar through him, the fabric of creation contained within a malleable physical shell. It filled his mind with a swirl of brilliant light and the deepest darkness. He threw his head back, now virtually screaming out the words, and then it happened.

From the runes shone columns of light that swirled with every color imaginable, both named and not. The shafts of light rose to the ceiling, then slowly shifted, coming together in the center. There they mixed and eddied, creating a pulsing sphere so very much like the one Uther had brought forth in the ravine. The spinning colors expanded, the sphere growing larger, until a black circle formed at its center. The blackness grew, and within it Jacob could see luminous balls of gas, the stars from distant worlds. He stepped away from his podium, released Karak's hand, and approached the churning sphere, continuing his chanting despite not having his journal to guide him. He felt the heat coming off the thing, felt the pull of divine gravity the closer he drew to it, until it seemed his every particle would be ripped apart, every piece of him disassembled.

The scream grew deep in his breast, a command infused with the power of a god that would not be denied.

"COME FORTH, VELIXAR, BEAST OF A THOUSAND FACES!"

From within the portal stepped a formless mass. It swelled and retracted, belching out a green-yellow mist. The mass was translucent, there but not quite, and it began to take shape. Wh emerged was the form of a man made of clay, with burning eyes. Tentacles writhed all around its body, as transparent as the rest of it, and Jacob saw that though the beast had a face, the rest of it was skeletal, as if it had been ravaged in a fire. Atop its head, a giant brain pulsed.

Jacob faced the thing that was there, but not. Its burning red eyes, the only aspect of it that had any substance, glared at him in hatred. Its face shifted with each passing second, becoming various nightmarish images of elves and humans and a hundred things Jacob had never once laid his eyes upon.

"We are the one and the many," the beast said, sounding like a dozen voices speaking at once. "Who disturbs us?"

Jacob did not cower before its anger, did not wilt before its furious eyes.

"So long," he whispered as mad winds swirled about the room and Clovis sobbed in terror. "I have waited so very long for this moment."

Jacob stepped into the void of the beast's incorporeal from. Its essence swirled about him, engulfed him.

"*What is this?*" the beast cried, pulsing, constricting, trying to squeeze every bit of life from Jacob's body.

Words of magic came forth from his mouth, and Jacob breathed in deep. He felt the core of the beast fill him, and though it struggled, the power he had received from his god was enough to overcome the ancient demon's strength. The creature's energy infused him, and long-forgotten spells flooded into his memory. In an instant he lived forever, witnessing the birthplace of the stars, the spawning of gods, the formation of the very fabric of existence itself.

And then he saw something else, something wonderful that made him laugh and laugh…and the beast shrieked, its sentience dangling by a thin umbilical thread. Jacob clenched it tightly in his otherworldly st, severing the thread, and the Beast of a Thousand Faces drifted off o the blackness of space, its screams fading as it descended to join ong-deceased brother Sluggoth in the timeless void.

Jacob snapped back into his body and collapsed. The energy he had swallowed, the same energy that had opened up avenues to forgotten magics, impelled him to stand. The portal still throbbed before him, its blackened center opening all the wider as it awaited the coming of another traveler. In the background, the captive Moris screamed in protest.

Jacob turned, pointed at Clovis, and beckoned him over with one finger. Karak shoved the man, who was as pale as the snow atop a mountain, and the Highest landed hard at Jacob's feet. He glanced up, and the look he gave Jacob was one of pure horror. Had he not just drank his fill, had the wonders of eternity not been filling him in that moment, Jacob might have wondered why.

Instead he reached down, grasped Clovis by the shoulders, and lifted him to his feet. He felt so strong, as though he could crush mountains in the palm of his hand. He thrust the screaming Highest toward the portal, just as another, much larger mass of billowing matter leaked out of the gateway. This being was just as transparent as the previous one, but it took shape much more quickly. It grew up, up, until it stood nearly thirty feet high. Huge, rounded shoulders formed, giving birth to scaly arms the size of the oldest trees in the Ghostwood, with paws that ended in curved, razor-sharp claws. Its body was massive, thick and wide on top with narrow hips, and short, stocky legs that were balanced out by a taloned tail. Its head was the last to appear, looking almost like that of a horse, only with a pair of giant tusks that ejected from the back corners of its jowls, curling forward around the front of its maw. The eyes were red and burning, just like those of the Beast of a Thousand Faces, and when it roared, making the air pulse with the pain of rebirth, a mad cackle filled Jacob's throat.

It was the most beautiful thing he had ever seen.

The image of the beast began to waver as its mass was pul back toward the swirling vortex. Jacob chanted louder, clutc Clovis's arm so that he could not escape. Then he thrust the front and center before the flickering beast, forcibly tilting his head back with one hand and prying his mouth open with the other.

"Accept this vessel!" he shouted. "Your physical form may be no more, but I offer another to you!"

He recited primeval verses he hadn't known until moments before.

The monstrous, ghostly beast suddenly lost all structure, becoming a swirling tube of shadow that first crashed against the ceiling of the room, then careened downward. Lightning and gale-force winds rocked the interior of the room, making all inside hold on for dear life lest they be flung against the walls; only Jacob and Karak withstood its rage. The murky, twisting shaft plummeted into Clovis's mouth, and his face throbbed as the force invaded his body in a revolting frenzy. Finally the last bit of shadow disappeared; the air grew still; the lightning ceased to flash; and the thunder rolled no more.

At long last, Jacob's chants ceased. He collapsed to his hands and knees as the portal vanished, dissipating in a flash of white light that momentarily washed out all color. He remained as he had fallen, panting, still feeling the lingering effects of the power and acumen he had ripped from the demon before he crushed its conscience beneath his superior will.

"I am the child of two gods," he gasped. "I am the oldest. I… am…victorious."

Slowly, he once more became aware of the sights and sounds around him. The captives were screaming, struggling against the might of their lone jailor. Karak stood off to the side, leaning on a bronze statue of himself, looking mildly curious. Clovis lay motionless, half on and half off the raised platform, his head resting in the center of the triangle, the chalk lines burned into the floor as if drawn with molten rock.

Jacob swiveled his head and caught his reflection in a mirror the of a divan that had been stowed against the far wall. He looked just as he ever did—all but for his eyes. The blue of his irises had been charred away, replaced by a deep crimson that shone as if a fire burned in the recesses of his skull.

Clovis moaned, rolling over onto his back. He sat up slowly, clutching at his stomach. The skin on his face rippled—as did his body beneath the tight black leathers he wore. The silver hair atop his head began to fall out in clumps. He started to screech, his jaw protruding outward as if something inside him were trying to escape.

Jacob faced Captain Gregorian, who was gawking at the scene with his jaw hanging open.

"Captain!" he shouted. "Now! The feast!"

It took a moment, but finally Gregorian got the message. He reached down and grabbed Ulrich and Ibis, dragging them behind him as they kicked and protested. Jacob rushed over, gathering up a laughing Adeline and searching for Thessaly to assist him. He didn't have to look far. Unexpectedly, Clovis's third-born had rushed to her father's side; she was kneeling before him, putting her hands on each spot of his body that swelled with bone and muscle. There were tears in her eyes and in her father's.

"You have been chosen," Jacob said to her. "It is an honor."

She glanced over at him as he yanked Adeline by her hair, and Thessaly sadly shook her head. She was about to say something, but she never got the chance, for suddenly her father was upon her, his mouth opening wider than humanly possible. His teeth had become daggers, and they tore into Thessaly's face, ripping the flesh from her skull. Her only form of protest was a bloody gurgle. Her father opened his maw wider, taking her head, her shoulders, her entire upper body into him. His neck bulged as his daughter was pulled down his throat, and the rhythmic cadence of a thousand snapping bones filled the air. Ibis and Ulric shrieked and struggled, while Adeline guffawed, until Jacob gave the orde

Captain Gregorian silenced all three with his sword, and their slit throats bled out onto the polished floor of the Tower Keep's great hall.

Thessaly's feet disappeared down her father's gullet, and after a few more seconds of snapping bones and jaws, the thing that had been Clovis Crestwell pivoted around. His flesh still rippled, but it seemed more under control now, as if the beast within had been satiated.

"Who dares awaken the Darakken?" it hissed. A pair of eyes that burned the same shade of red as Jacob's looked at each of the hall's occupants, not stopping until they fell upon Karak. Those eyes opened wide then, and he fell to his knees, bowing before the deity.

"Master Kaurthulos," said the beast in reverence. "I recognize you and will serve your will, so great is my gratitude for my freedom."

"Not Kaurthulos," the god responded. "Though I do remember you, as if from a dream. We are splintered now, Order and Justice, War and Love. I am Karak, and though you are right to serve, I am not the one you should thank. It is he, over there, who set you free."

The beast lifted its head, gazing at Jacob from across the expanse.

"Fellow child of the mighty Kaurthulos, I thank you for releasing me," Darakken said, bowing low. "Please, tell me your name, so I may call it out in reverence when I shear the flesh of our enemies."

"His name is Jacob Eveningstar, First Man of Dezrel," said Karak.

Jacob shook his head as the power of the beast he had devoured surged through him. He was no longer who he was. No, he was something greater. His mind exploded with knowledge that made his journal a pale mockery of wisdom. Everything he used to be was gone. He cast aside the last vestiges of his weakness, swearing to never again whisper the name Brienna. Standing to his full height, shadows and light playing off his fingers as if he could command the universe itself, he stared into the beast Darakken and let it know he was its master. A child of two gods, commander of demons, the first man of a fledgling world. The pathetic human name no longer fit him…it would no longer suffice. So he took another.

"Jacob Eveningstar no longer exists," he said through clenched teeth. "Let me bear a name far more worthy."

And as Darakken fed on the corpses before him, Velixar laughed and laughed.

EPILOGUE

A
ng was a quaint little fishing village, a rocky land filled with nothing but crude wooden huts and tents. It was unlike anything Aully had seen before, for even the homes built within the trees of Stonewood had been elaborate constructions, many with separate living areas, bedrooms, and even solariums. Living in a single, cramped space? That compared favorably only to the cells in the dungeon below Palace Thyne. She cursed at her own selfishness for the unworthy thought.

Beggars cannot be choosers.

Kindren came up beside her. They were hiding out in a thatch of trees just outside what looked to be the village's common area. There were people everywhere, humans whose flesh were differing shades of brown, chatting among themselves, wandering the narrow, dusty path that led through the center of the clearing. She recognized a few of them from her days at her father's court, when there had been disputes over borders, as Ang was positioned very close to Stonewood's southern boundary. She remembered Bessus Gorgoros and his wife, two of the loudest, most intense, and intimidating people she had ever met. Of course that had been before she came to understand *true* intimidation so she guessed that it was possible she was building the pair up in her mind.

"I don't see a palace," said Kindren, whispering. "Or a fortress of any kind. Where do the leaders reside?"

Aully shrugged. "I don't know."

A sharp pain flared inside her knee, and she winced and flopped down on her rump. She rubbed the sore spot vigorously, gritting her teeth. *I should be used to this by now*, she thought, and shook her head. Cramps had become an unwelcomed friend over the last month, as she and the rest of her people who had escaped from Dezerea traipsed from place to place, first to the river, then south along its banks, until finally they reached the coast, which they followed to what Aully was convinced would be friendly territory. When they weren't walking or trying to avoid hunting parties sent out by Neyvar Ruven, they were scavenging for food, trying to rest their weary bones and blistered feet, or hiding from those who traveled across the Gods' Road. They never knew who might be friend or foe, and that weighed the most on Aullienna's heart—even more than the constant worry over whether she should inform her mother of Brienna's death.

It had been the most discouraging part of her short life, and Aully just wanted it to end.

The people of Ker had not been friends to her people. Bessus and Damaspia held a long-standing loathing for her father, and her mother and her advisors constantly brought up this fact as Aully insisted on the trip. She refused to listen. Instead, she was placing her entire hope on one man and one man alone, the giant named Bardiya.

She had met the son of Gorgoros only once in person, though she had spied on him often. He had been the sole human in all of Ker who talked sensibly with her people, who seemed to care about the sanctity of their forest as much as they did. When news had come of him needlessly butchering a flock of kobo, she'd refused to believe it. Not long after that unfortunate event she'd run into him in the forest. He had been sitting there calmly with a pair of wolves, his tree trunk legs crossed and his eyes closed. When he spoke to her then, his voice had been soft and delicate. It was only because of her father's warnings that she'd remained wary.

I believe in the sanctity of all life, the giant had said. Now, it was time to put that statement to a test. If she could simply talk to Bessus, convince him to hold court with his son, then perhaps….

Her mother came from behind her, speaking in hushed tones.

"What are you doing, Aullienna?" she asked. "Will we remain here or ask for help?"

Aully rolled her eyes. Her mother was filthy beyond compare—they all were—and she looked desperate. Aully wanted to tell her to do it herself. But that wasn't fair. Traveling to Ang had been her idea, which made it her responsibility to make contact. She took a deep breath, blew a kiss to the ancient Noni, and then grabbed Kindren's hand.

"My love?" she said.

He nodded.

Together they stood and left the cover of the copse where they'd been lurking, walking hand-in-hand into the center of the clearing. At first they were paid no mind, and Aully imagined that with the dirt and grime covering them, they must have blended in with their surroundings. Finally someone spotted them and voices were raised in alarm. Fingers pointed, and a woman quickly shooed a group of small children away. *"Elf!"* became the rallying cry, and the word was spoken with disdain, as if they were wild beasts set on devouring the village young. Men carrying spears with tips o sharpened stone rushed up to them, and those spears were poin their way.

"There are others!" Aully shouted in the common to "Hiding in the woods. We mean you no harm. Please…we ju to speak with the master of House Gorgoros."

That statement drew confused glances from their captors, but that confusion was replaced by determination as the men lunged into the forest, where Aully had pointed, and rounded up the rest of their group.

None of them were harmed, but they were kept at arm's length as they were ushered down a dusty path and led to the coast, where a rocky beach jutted out into the crystal blue waters of the southern Thulon Ocean. On a large, flat rock sat a mountain of a man, his skin black as coal and beaded with sweat. Aully and Kindren were escorted away from the others, and they approached the giant Bardiya. He opened his eyes and surprised her by greeting her with the first smile she'd seen that day.

"Ah, young Aullienna. What brings you to our fine paradise by the sea?"

Aully curtseyed. *He remembered my name*, she thought.

It was Kindren who spoke. "We come seeking asylum, Prince of Ker." He dropped to a knee before the giant. "Please, our group is hungry and afraid, and we seek shelter within your…" his darted from side to side, "…walls, as it were."

Bardiya chuckled. "I am no prince, young elfling. There are no titles in this land."

"What should I call you then?"

"Bardiya is fine. It is my name, after all."

The giant laughed at that, looking off in the distance as if remembering a long-lost friend.

Aully finally found her voice, and she asked, "Where is Bessus? I asked to see him but was brought to you instead."

The giant's grin faded away.

"Unfortunately, my parents are no more. They were murdered a ▪th or more ago." He tilted his head. "By elves from Stonewood, ▪atter of fact."

▪ly frowned. That explained the chilly reception, at least.

"I apologize," she said, bowing her head. "There has been an… uprising. My father was murdered as well, before my very eyes." She felt the tears begin to well. "We were imprisoned…executed one by one…by the Neyvar of the Quellan…and…and…."

She never finished the thought. The giant Bardiya grabbed her around the waist and pulled her into his ample lap, wrapping his arms around her, holding her close, rocking her. Beneath her sobs she heard her mother shriek, as if she were afraid the man meant her harm. But Bardiya had no such thing in mind. His embrace was warm and comforting. She felt like she had when she was a tiny little thing and her father had used to hold her in *his* lap while she drifted off to sleep. The memory made her all the sadder, and her tears turned the giant's knitted tunic into a wet, salty mess.

"Calm, child," his soothing voice said. "You are safe now."

"Does that mean…." began Kindren.

The giant let go of Aully and set her back to standing. He nodded at Kindren and then rose, turning to face the remaining Stonewood elves, who gathered on the ridge above, surrounded by the spear-bearing men who had brought them there.

"These are our friends," Bardiya announced, his voice carrying on the wind, loud as a thunderclap. "The child of Cleotis Meln has begged sanctuary, and we shall grant it. Ki-Nan, get them food and water. Maliya, have your sons gather lumber so we can assist them in building shelters. Hear me now. All life is precious, and it is our duty as inhabitants of this world to protect those in danger. The restless and the weary are ours to protect. Stonewood elves, welcome to Ang. It is with joy in my heart that I tell you this is your home now for as long as you wish to stay."

The expressions softened on the faces of the armed men. They still seemed slightly apprehensive, but they lowered their weapo and departed, leaving her people alone on the ridge. Still cryi

Aully grabbed the giant's hand, placing a kiss on fingers that were nearly as wide as her arm.

"Thank you," she whispered. "Thank you."

"Yes," said Kindren. "It is very honorable what you did."

Bardiya shrugged. "Who am I to turn you away?" he asked.

"So we are safe?" Aully said, her voice pleading. "Are we really, truly safe?"

The giant's eyes gazed to the east, where it looked as if roiling thunderclouds had formed in the distance. He looked back down at her, and though his eyes were kind, there was a dark uncertainty there that sent chills running down her spine.

"You are for now," he said. "But I fear this world is breaking, and I know not how long that safety shall last."

Aully followed his gaze, staring up at those gathering storm clouds along with him. Despite the warmth of the day, despite the reassuring presence of the giant beside her, she shivered.

- E N D -

AFTERWORD

David

I've said it repeatedly, but I'm going to say it again: This project, this book you've just read, would not have happened without Rob's amazing effort. For a few years now I've gotten occasional requests for me to write up the earliest history of my world of Dezrel, particularly the Gods' War that sunders everything and shapes much of the future conflict. I had a vague idea of how that war went, several of the major battles, but I never could summon up much enthusiasm for the story. A large reason why was because it felt like it would be nothing but warfare, with no real interesting characters other than Velixar, Ashhur, and Karak. And of those, I'd done all of them pretty much to death, particularly Velixar.

Now, I'd discussed this with Rob before. Rob was my sounding board for ideas, a good friend I respected who had read all my work and could help me out whenever I hit a stumbling block in a current project. So on a whim, I half-heartedly pitched an idea of coauthoring the Gods' War together. He'd just finished his four-part set of horror novels, The Rift, and was looking at stepping into fantasy. I thought, well, maybe this could at least get the project the ground—plus, I could help him out a little.

Help *him*. Hah.

Rob's response? "I've been hoping you'd ask that." The very next day he sent me a detailed outline, full of characters, events, and the absolutely brilliant idea of having Velixar (a major recurring villain of mine) not be known as Velixar, but be hidden among the initial cast of characters. I was floored. The bloodlines, the betrayals, things like the Wardens and the First Families, all were outta his brain. The best way I can describe what he brought to this story is through a simple example. The battle you witnessed between Karak and Ashhur amid the smoldering ruins of Haven? That was going to be the *prologue* to my version of the first book.

All the drama, all the human elements, the mystery and sacrifice—everything I didn't picture in my own head, he found. He added. From that point on, I was just basically a tour guide, keeping characters consistent, keeping the world consistent, and making sure my own brand of humor and combat stayed intact. The result is a book we're both incredibly proud of, a blend of us both. Everything I feel weak at, particularly world building, is something in which Rob excels. And well, I'd like to think I have a way with characters and combat, and you should still see a few glimpses of that as well.

To all you long-time readers, I hope this is everything you were waiting for. There are dozens of characters and callbacks to my other books, and hopefully you caught them all. And in case you were wondering, it was Rob's idea to introduce Kayne and Lilah. He kept it as a surprise, purposefully telling me nothing of their particular chapter until he'd written it and then sent it my way, demanding read it at once. Needless to say, I was thoroughly amused, and now eems those two creatures from The Paladins might have a few moments to shine. And eat.

aid it in the dedication, but I'll say it again: Thank you, Sam s, for putting up with our long phone calls and Facebook ve figured out where to take this story, or how to fix it when we went a bit off the rails. Thank you, Michael, for nabbing us a deal we never thought would happen when we first started this project. Thank you everyone at 47North for working with us, dancing around our bizarre schedules, and for having the confidence that we might deliver to you something special. Thank you, Rob, for giving me the absolute privilege of working with you on a novel and for adding depth to my world far beyond what I could have dreamed. Last of all, thank you, dear readers. When it all boils down, we're still doing this for you, hoping that our silly stories of lions and gods might steal you away from your world and into ours. May your stay, however long it lasts, always be entertaining.

Robert

There really isn't much that I have to add to Dave's note above, other than to say that nothing has brought me as much pleasure (in regards to writing) as working on this project. As someone who hadn't read fantasy in ages before dabbling in Dave's world of Dezrel, I can say it was an absolute blast to dive into this strange place and expand on it as best I could. Never before have I enjoyed the art of writing as immensely as I did working on this book, even though the shift from the modern stories I'm used to creating to a place where none of my precious pop culture references would mean anything was challenging at times. That, my friends, is saying something.

A little bit on the creation of the story in general: I did in fact have tons of notes stored up for this project, stuff I jotted down while reading Dave's books. I even went so far as to draw maps of the major cities (*because I in my laziness never bothered to do so myself, much to his annoyance—-David*). Long story short, all of this pre work, done without ever thinking that I'd be asked to write a bo with Dave, gave me one hell of a head start when I did indeed be the writing process. I consider myself lucky in that way, beca I'd been any less anal in my reading habits, this project migh been difficult to get off the ground. That patience and attention to detail is something that really helps with world building, which in some ways is the prime reason I was brought in to work on this. I guess you could say that if Dave didn't suck at remembering the specifics of his own world, *Dawn of Swords* would never have been written!

I'll reiterate Dave's note about our wives. We're both quirky individuals, so the fact they put up with us is nothing short of miraculous. I also need to thank our agent Michael for taking me on even though he'd never heard of me before this. And I need to thank my parents for always loving me and instilling in me the drive to seek out what I want in life; my in-laws Alan and Sharon for being just awesome people; Jesse, Pat, Greg, and Steve, my best friends for life; and all my extended family and friends. I also would be remiss if I didn't offer a great big "yee-hah!" to Angela Polidoro, who put forth tons of effort on the story edits for this book and caught *tons* of stuff neither Dave nor I had thought of before. You're the greatest, Ang!

And of course there's Dave Dalglish himself, without whom this book—or its coming sequels—would never have been written. I owe you tons, brotherman.

Hope you enjoyed, and we'll see you all in book 2!

David Dalglish & Robert Duperre
April 2, 2013

ABOUT THE AUTHORS

David Dalglish currently lives in rural Missouri with his wife, Samantha, and daughters Morgan and Katherine. He graduated from Missouri Southern State University in 2006 with a degree in Mathematics and currently spends his free time playing not nearly enough Warhammer 40K.

Born on Cape Cod and raised in northern Connecticut, Robert Duperre is a writer whose main ambition is to create works that defy genre. He lives with his wife, the artist Jessica Torrant, his three wonderful children, and Leonardo, the super one-eyed Labrador.

Gregory Duffey